Frank Edward Smedley

Frank Fairlegh

Scenes from the Life of a Private Pupil

Frank Edward Smedley

Frank Fairlegh
Scenes from the Life of a Private Pupil

ISBN/EAN: 9783337416744

Printed in Europe, USA, Canada, Australia, Japan

Cover: Foto ©Raphael Reischuk / pixelio.de

More available books at **www.hansebooks.com**

Frank Fairlegh

OR

SCENES FROM THE LIFE OF A PRIVATE PUPIL

BY

FRANK E. SMEDLEY

AUTHOR OF "LEWIS ARUNDEL," "HARRY COVERDALE'S COURTSHIP," ETC.

"How now! good lack! What present have we here?
A Book that stood in peril of the press;
But now it's past those pikes, and doth appear
To keep the lookers-on from heaviness.
What stuff contains it?"—

DAVIES *of Hereford.*

*WITH THIRTY ILLUSTRATIONS BY GEORGE CRUIKSHANK
FROM THE ORIGINAL STEEL PLATES*

DOWNEY & CO., LIMITED
12 YORK STREET, COVENT GARDEN, LONDON
1899

Dedication

To M. U. S. and M. B. S.

My dear Cousins,—As it is mainly owing to your joint advice and encouragement that this tale has been either written, or laid before the public, there can be none to whom I may with greater propriety dedicate it.

When I add that my satisfaction in making this slight acknowledgment of the countless acts of affectionate kindness I have received at your hands, is one among the many agreeable results of the advice which has eventually led me to adopt a literary career, you will not refuse to accept this assurance, that you have contributed to the happiness of one whose sphere, both of duties and pleasures, Providence has seen fit to limit.

That our friendship may continue uninterrupted through Time, is the hope, and through Eternity, is the prayer, of your affectionate friend and cousin,

THE AUTHOR.

PREFACE

HAVING, from causes of a physical nature, much leisure time upon my hands, I amused myself by working into a story my recollections of certain boyish escapades at a private tutor's. My reason for selecting such a theme was twofold. In the first place, it struck me, that while volume after volume had been devoted to "Schoolboy Days" and "College Life," the mysteries of that paradise of public-school-fearing mammas—a "Private Tutor's"—yet continued unrevealed; and I resolved to enlighten these tender parents as to the precise nature of the rosebed into which they were so anxious to transplant their darlings. In the second place, I wished to prove to the young Hopefuls themselves, that a lad, hitherto shielded from evil by the hallowing influences of home, may successfully resist the new trials and temptations to which, on this his first essay in life, he may be subjected; that the difficulties which surround him will yield to a little firmness and decision; and that such a course, steadily persisted in, will alike gain him the esteem of his companions, and lay the foundation of the character which it should be his aim to support through life—viz. that of a Christian and a gentleman. With such views, the earlier "Scenes from the Life of a Private Pupil" were written, and appeared originally in the pages of SHARPE'S MAGAZINE. The tale proved popular, and was continued, at the request of the then editor, till it attained its present limits.

In the delineation of character, my desire has been to paint men as they are, rather than as they should be; and the moral (if moral there be) is to be derived quite as much from their faults as from their virtues. To this design must also be traced all inconsistencies of character,—as, for example, when Frank Fairlegh, possessing sufficient religious principle to enable him to look upon duelling as a crime which no combination of circumstances can justify, yet becomes involved in such an affair himself. These shortcomings doubtless evince a lamentable contrast to the perfection of the stereotyped novel hero; but as it has never been my good fortune to meet with that faultless monster, a perfectly consistent man, or woman, I prefer describing character as I find it.

Should this, my first work, fall into the hands of my former Tutor, let me take this opportunity of thanking him for the trouble he bestowed upon a graceless boy, who even then possessed sufficient sense to perceive and appreciate his many high and endearing qualities. If any of my fellow-pupils peruse these pages, and, recognizing certain incidents of their boyish days, seek to fit my ideal sketches to living prototypes, let me beg them to bear in mind that the character of Richard Cumberland is purely fictitious, and introduced, like that of Wilford, to satisfy the requirements of a tale-writer, and enable me to work out the details of my story. In regard to the other 'dramatis personæ,' although I have occasionally taken a hint from living models, and although certain incidents (e.g. the bell-ringing scene) are founded on fact, I never have copied, and never will copy, so closely as to flatter or wound the feelings of any person; and those who imagine that, in their sagacity, they have discovered Lawless was intended for Mr. A., or Mrs. Coleman for Mrs. B., deceive themselves, and attribute a degree of skill in portrait-painting, of which he is equally unconscious and undeserving, to

THE AUTHOR.

CONTENTS

LIST OF ILLUSTRATIONS

FRANK FAIRLEGH

OR

Scenes from the Life of a Private Pupil

———◆———

CHAPTER I.

ALL RIGHT! OFF WE GO!

" Yet here . . . you are stayed for
. . . There my blessing with you,
And these few precepts in thy memory
See thou character——"
" Home-keeping youth, have ever homely wits.
. . . .
I rather would entreat thy company
To see the wonders of the world abroad,
Than living dully, sluggardis'd at home,
Wear out thy youth with shapeless idleness."
" Where unbruised youth, with unstuffed brain,
Doth couch his limbs, there golden sleep doth reign."
Shakespeare.

"NEVER forget, under any circumstances, to think and act like a gentleman, and don't exceed your allowance," said my father.

" Mind you read your Bible, and remember what I told you about wearing flannel waistcoats," cried my mother.

And with their united, " God bless you, my boy !" still ringing in my ears, I found myself inside the stage-coach, on my way to London.

Now, I am well aware that the correct thing for a boy in my situation (i.e. leaving home for the first time) would be to fall back on his seat, and into a reverie, during which, utterly lost to all external impressions, he should entertain the thoughts and feelings of a well-informed man of thirty ; the same thoughts and feelings being clothed in the semi-poetic prose of a fashionable novel writer. Deeply grieved, therefore, am I at being forced both to set at naught so laudable an established precedent, and to expose my own degeneracy. But the truth must be told at all hazards. The only feeling I experienced, beyond a vague sense of loneliness and desolation, was one of great personal discomfort. It rained hard, so that a small stream of water, which descended from the roof of the coach as

I entered it, had insinuated itself between one of the flannel waistcoats, which formed so important an item in the maternal valediction,
and my skin, whence, endeavouring to carry out what a logician
would call the "law of its being," by finding its own level, it placed
me in the undesirable position of an involuntary disciple of the cold-
water cure taking a "sitz-bad." As to my thoughts, the reader shall
have the full benefit of them, in the exact order in which they flitted
through my brain.

First came a vague desire to render my position more comfortable,
ending in a forlorn hope that intense and continued sitting might,
by some undefined process of evaporation, cure the evil. This
suggested a speculation, half pleasing and half painful, as to what
would be my mother's feelings, could she be aware of the state of
things; the pleasure being the result of that mysterious preternatural
delight which a boy always takes in everything at all likely to injure
his health, or endanger his existence, and the pain arising from the
knowledge that there was now no one near me to care whether I was
comfortable or not. Again, these speculations merged into a sort of
dreamy wonder, as to why a queer little old gentleman opposite (my
sole fellow-traveller) was grunting like a pig, at intervals of about
a minute, though he was wide awake the whole time; and whether
a small tuft of hair on a mole at the tip of his nose could have
anything to do with it. At this point, my meditations were interrupted by the old gentleman himself, who, after a louder grunt than
usual, gave vent to his feelings in the following speech, which was
partly addressed to me, and partly a soliloquy:

"Umph! going to school, my boy, eh?" then in a lower tone,
"Wonder why I called him my boy, when he's no such thing: just
like me, umph!"

I replied by informing him that I was not exactly going to school
—(I was nearly fifteen, and the word "school" sounded derogatory
to my dignity)—but that, having been up to the present time educated
at home by my father, I was now on my way to complete my studies
under the care of a private tutor, who only received six pupils, a very
different thing from a school, as I took the liberty of insinuating.

"Umph! different thing? You will cost more, learn less, and
fancy yourself a man when you are a boy; that's the only difference
I can see;" then came the aside—"Snubbing the poor child when
he's a peg too low already, just like me: umph!"

After which he relapsed into a silence which continued uninterrupted until we reached London, save once, while we were changing
horses, when he produced a flask with a silver top, and, taking a sip
himself, asked me if I drank brandy. On my shaking my head, with
a smile caused by what appeared to me the utter wildness and
desperation of the notion, he muttered,—

"Umph! of course he doesn't; how should he?—just like me."

In due course of time we reached the Old Bell Inn, Holborn,
where the coach stopped, and where my trunk and myself were to be

handed over to the tender mercies of the coachman of the " Rocket,"
a fast coach (I speak of the slow old days when railroads were unknown), which then ran to Helmstone, the watering-place where my
future tutor, the Rev. Dr. Mildman, resided. My first impressions
of London are scarcely worth recording, for the simple reason that
they consisted solely of intense and unmitigated surprise at everything and everybody I saw and heard; which may be more readily
believed when I add the fact that my preconceived notion of the
metropolis had led me to imagine it perhaps might be twice the size
of the town nearest to my father's house; in short, almost as large
as Grosvenor Square.

Here, then, I parted company with my fellow-traveller, who took
leave of me thus,—

" Umph! well, good-bye; be a good boy—good man, you'd like me
to say, I suppose; man indeed! umph! don't forget what your
parents told you;" then adding, " Of course he will, what's the use
of telling him not? just like me;"—he dived into the recesses of a
hackney coach, and disappeared.

Nothing worthy of note occurred during my journey to Helmstone,
where we arrived at about half-past four in the afternoon. My
feelings of surprise and admiration were destined once more to be
excited on this (to me) memorable day, as on my way from the coach
office to Langdale Terrace, where Dr. Mildman resided, I beheld, for
the first time, that most stupendous work of God, the mighty ocean;
which, alike in its wild resistless freedom, and its miraculous
obedience to the command, " Thus far shalt thou come, and no
further," bears at once the plainest print of its Almighty Creator's
hand, while it affords a strong and convincing proof of His
omnipotence.

On knocking at the door of Dr. Mildman's house (if the truth
must be told, it was with a trembling hand I did so), it was opened
by a man-servant, whose singularly plain features were characterized
by an expression alternating between extreme civility and an intense
appreciation of the ludicrous.

On mentioning my name, and asking if Dr. Mildman was at home,
he replied,—

" Yes, sir, master's in, sir; so you're Mr. Fairlegh, sir, our new
young gent, sir?" (here the ludicrous expression predominated);
"hope you'll be comfortable, sir" (here he nearly burst into a laugh);
" show you into master's study, sir, directly" (here he became pre-
ternaturally grave again); and opening the study door, ushered me
into the presence of the dreaded tutor.

On my entrance, Dr. Mildman (for such I presumed a middle-aged
gentleman, the sole tenant of the apartment, to be) rose from a
library table, at which he had been seated, and, shaking me kindly by
the hand, inquired after the health of my father and mother, what
sort of journey I had had, and sundry other particulars of the like
nature, evidently with the good-humoured design of putting me a

little more at my ease, as I have no doubt the trepidation I was well
aware of feeling inwardly, at finding myself 'tete-a-tete' with a real
live tutor, was written in very legible characters on my countenance.
Dr. Mildman, whose appearance I studied with an anxious eye, was
a gentlemanly man of five-and-forty, or thereabouts, with a high
bald forehead and good features, the prevailing expression of which,
naturally mild and benevolent, was at times chequered by that look
which all schoolmasters sooner or later acquire—a look which seems
to say, "Now, sir, do you intend to mind me or do you not?" Had
it not been for this, and for an appearance of irresolution about the
mouth, he would have been a decidedly fine-looking man. While I
was making these observations, he informed me that I had arrived
just in time for dinner, and that the servant should show me to my
sleeping-apartment, whence, when I had sacrificed to the Graces
(as he was pleased to call dressing), I was to descend to the drawing-
room, and be introduced to Mrs. Mildman and my future companions.

My sleeping-room, which was rather a small garret than otherwise,
was furnished, as it appeared to me, with more regard to economy
than to the comfort of its inmate. At one end stood a small four-
post bedstead, which, owing to some mysterious cause, chose to hold
its near fore-leg up in the air, and slightly advanced, thereby impress-
ing the beholder with the idea that it was about to trot into the
middle of the room. On an unpainted deal table stood a looking-
glass, which from a habit it had of altering and embellishing the
face of anyone who consulted it, must evidently have possessed a
strong natural taste for the ludicrous: an ancient washing-stand,
supporting a basin and towel, and a dissipated-looking chair, completed the catalogue.

And here, while preparing for the alarming ordeal I was so soon to
undergo, let me present to the reader a slight sketch of myself,
mental and bodily; and, as mind ought to take precedence of matter,
I will attempt, as far as I am able after the lapse of time, to paint
my character in true colours, "naught extenuating, nor setting down
aught in malice." I was, then, as the phrase goes, "a very well-
behaved young gentleman;" that is, I had a great respect for all
properly-constituted authorities, and an extreme regard for the
proprieties of life; was very particular about my shoes being clean,
and my hat nicely brushed; always said, "Thank you," when a
servant handed me a plate, and "May I trouble you?" when I
asked for a bit of bread. In short, I bade fair in time to become a
thorough old bachelor; one of those unhappy mortals whose lives
are a burden alike to themselves and others; men who, by magnify-
ing the minor household miseries into events of importance, are
uneasy and suspicious about the things from the wash having been
properly aired, and become low and anxious as the dreadful time
approaches when clean sheets are inevitable! My ideas of a private
tutor, derived chiefly from "Sandford and Merton," and "Evenings

at Home," were rather wide of the mark, leading me to expect that Dr. Mildman would impart instruction to us during long rambles over green fields, and in the form of moral allegories, to which we should listen with respectful attention, and affectionate esteem. With regard to my outward man, or rather boy, I should have been obliged to confine myself to such particulars as I could remember, namely, that I was tall for my age, but slightly built, and so thin as often to provoke the application of such epithets as "hop pole," "thread-paper," etc., had it not been that, in turning over some papers a few days since, I stumbled on a water-colour sketch of myself, which I well remembered being taken by a young artist in the neighbourhood, just before I left home, in the hope of consoling my mother for my departure. It represented a lad about fifteen, in a picturesque attitude, feeding a pony out of a very elegant little basket, with what appeared to be white currants, though I have every reason to believe they were meant for oats. The aforesaid youth rejoiced in an open shirt-collar and black ribbon à la Byron, curling hair of a dark chestnut colour, regular features, a high forehead, complexion like a girl's, very pink and white, and a pair of large blue eyes, engaged in regarding the white currant oats with intense surprise, as well indeed they might. Whether this young gentleman bore more resemblance to me than the currants did to oats, I am, of course, unable to judge; but, as the portrait represented a very handsome boy, I hope none [of my readers will be rude enough to doubt that it was a striking likeness.

I now proceeded to render myself thoroughly wretched by attempting to extricate the articles necessary for a change of dress from the very bottom of my trunk, where, according to the nature of such things, they had hidden themselves; grammars, lexicons, and other like " Amenities of Literature," being the things that came to hand most readily. Scarcely had I contrived to discover a wearable suit, when I was informed that dinner was on the table; so, hastily tumbling into my clothes, and giving a final peep at the facetious looking-glass, the result of which was to twist the bow of my Byron tie under my left ear, in the belief that I was thereby putting it straight, I rushed downstairs, just in time to see the back of the hindmost pupil disappear through the dining-room door.

" Better late than never, Fairlegh. Mrs. Mildman, this is Fairlegh; he can sit by you, Coleman—' For what we are going to receive,' etc. —Thomas, the carving-knife."

Such was the address with which my tutor greeted my entrance, and during its progress I popped into a seat indicated by a sort of half-wink from Thomas, resisting by a powerful act of self-control a sudden impulse which seized me to bolt out of the room, and do something rash but indefinite, between going to sea and taking prussic acid; not quite either, but partaking of the nature of both.

" Take soup, Fairlegh ? " said Dr. Mildman.

"Thank you, sir, if you please."

"A pleasant journey, had you?" inquired Mrs. Mildman.

"Not any. I am much obliged to you," I replied, thinking of the fish.

This produced a total silence, during which the pupils exchanged glances, and Thomas concealed an illicit smile behind the bread-basket.

"Does your father," began Dr. Mildman in a very grave and deliberate manner, "does your father shoot?—boiled mutton, my dear?"

I replied that he had given it up of late years, as the fatigue was too much for him.

"Oh! I was very fond of carrying a gun—pepper—when I was—a spoon—at Oxford; I could hit a—mashed potato—bird as well as most men; yes, I was very sorry to give up my double barrel—ale, Thomas."

"You came inside, I believe?" questioned Mrs. Mildman, a lady possessing a shadowy outline, indistinct features faintly characterized by an indefinite expression, long ringlets of an almost impossible shade of whity-brown, and a complexion and general appearance only to be described by the term "washed out."

"Yes, all the way, ma'am."

"Did you not dislike it very much? it creases one's gown so, unless it is a merino or mousseline de laine; but one can't always wear them, you know."

Not being in the least prepared with a suitable answer, I merely made what I intended to be an affirmative ahem, in doing which a crumb of bread chose to go the wrong way, producing a violent fit of coughing, in the agonies of which I seized and drank off Dr. Mildman's tumbler of ale, mistaking it for my own small beer. The effect of this, my crowning 'gaucherie,' was to call forth a languid smile on the countenance of the senior pupil, a tall young man, with dark hair, and a rather forbidding expression of face, which struggled only too successfully with an attempt to look exceedingly amiable, which smile was repeated with variations by all the others.

"I am afraid you do not distinctly perceive the difference between those important pronouns, 'meum' and 'tuum,' Fairlegh? Thomas, a clean glass!" said Dr. Mildman, with a forced attempt at drollery; but Thomas had evaporated suddenly, leaving no clue to his where-abouts, unless sundry faint sounds of suppressed laughter outside the door, indicating, as I fancied, his extreme appreciation of my unfortunate mistake, proceeded from him.

It is, I believe, a generally received axiom that all mortal affairs must sooner or later come to an end; at all events, the dinner I have been describing did not form an exception to the rule. In due time Mrs. Mildman disappeared, after which Dr. Mildman addressed a remark or two about Greek tragedy to the tall pupil, which led to a dissertation on the merits of a gentleman named Prometheus, who, it seemed, was bound in some peculiar way, but whether this referred to his apprenticeship to any trade, or to the cover of the book containing his history, did not appear. This conversation lasted about ten minutes, at the expiration of which the senior pupil "grinned horribly a ghastly smile" at the others, who instantly rose and conveyed themselves out of the room with such rapidity that I, being quite unprepared for such a proceeding, sat for a moment in silent amazement, and then, becoming suddenly alive to a sense of my situation, rushed frantically after them. My speed was checked somewhat abruptly by a door at the end of the passage being violently slammed in my face, for which polite attention I was indebted to the philanthropy of the hindmost pupil, who thereby imposed upon me the agreeable task of feeling in the dark for a door handle in an unknown locality. After fumbling for some time, in a state of the greatest bewilderment, I at length opened the door, and beheld the interior of the "pupils' room," which, for the benefit of such of my readers as may never have seen the like, I will now endeavour shortly to describe.

The parlour devoted to the pupils' use was of a good size, nearly square, and, like the cabin of a certain "ould Irish gentleman," appeared to be fitted up with "nothing at all for show." In three of the corners stood small tables covered with books and writing materials, for the use of Dr. Mildman and the two senior pupils; in the fourth was a book-case. The centre of the room was occupied by a large square table, the common property of the other pupils; while a carpet "a little the worse for wear," and sundry veteran chairs, rather crazy from the treatment to which many generations of pupils had subjected them (a chair being the favourite projectile in the event of a shindy), completed the catalogue. Mr. Richard Cumberland, the senior pupil, was lounging in an easy attitude on one side of the fireplace; on the other stood, bolt upright, a lad rather older than myself, with a long unmeaning face, and a set of arms and legs which appeared not to belong to one another. This worthy, as I soon learned, responded to the name of Nathaniel Mullins, and usually served as the butt of the party, in the absence of newer or worthier game. Exactly in front of the fire, with his coat tails under his arms, and his legs extended like a pair of compasses, was stationed Mr. George Lawless, who, having been expelled from one of the upper forms at Eton, for some heroic exploit, which the head-master could not be persuaded to view in its proper light, was sent to vegetate for a year or two at Dr. Mildman's ere he proceeded to one of the universities. This gentleman was of rather a short, thick-set figure, with a large head, and an expression of countenance resembling that of a bull when the animal "means mischief," and was supposed by his friends to be more "thoroughly awake" than anyone of his years in the three kingdoms. The quartette was completed by Mr. Frederick Coleman, a small lad, with a round, merry face, who was perched on the back of a chair, with his feet resting on the hob, and his person so disposed as effectually to screen every ray of fire from Nathaniel Mullins.

"You are not cold, Fairlegh? Don't let me keep the fire from you," said Lawless, without, however, showing the slightest intention of moving.

"Not very, thank you."

"Eh! quite right—glad to hear it. It's Mildman's wish that, during the first half, no pupil should come on the hearthrug. I made a point of conscience of it myself when I first came. The Spartans, you know, never allowed their little boys to do so, and even the Athenians, a much more luxurious people, always had their pinafores made of asbestos, or some such fireproof stuff. You are well read in Walker's History of Greece, I hope?"

I replied that I was afraid I was not.

"Never read 'Hookeyus Magnus'? Your father ought to be ashamed of himself for neglecting you so. You are aware, I suppose, that the Greeks had a different sort of fire to what we burn nowadays? You've heard of Greek fire?"

I answered that I had, but did not exactly understand what it meant.

"Not know that, either? Disgraceful! Well, it was a kind of way they had of flaring up in those times, a sort of 'light of other days,' which enabled them to give their friends a warm reception; so much so, indeed, that their friends found it too warm sometimes, and latterly they usually reserved it for their enemies. Mind you remember all this, for it is one of the first things old Sam will be sure to ask you."

Did my ears deceive me? Could he have called the tutor, the dreaded tutor, "old Sam"? I trembled as I stood—plain, unhonoured "Sam," as though he had spoken of a footman! The room turned round with me. Alas, for Sandford and Merton, and affectionate and respectful esteem!

"But how's this?" continued Lawless, "we have forgotten to introduce you in form to your companions, and to enter your name in the books of the establishment; why, Cumberland, what were you thinking of?"

"Beg pardon," rejoined Cumberland; "I really was so buried in thought, trying to solve that problem about bisecting the Siamese twins—you know it, Lawless? However, it is not too late, is it? Allow me to introduce you, Mr. Fairplay—"

"Legh, sir." interrupted I.

"Ah, exactly; well, then, Mr. Fairlegh, let me introduce this gentleman, Mr. George Lawless, who has, if I mistake not, been already trying, with his usual benevolence, to supply a few of your deficiencies; he is, if he will allow me to say so, one of the most rising young men of his generation, one of the firmest props of the glorious edifice of our rights and privileges."

" A regular brick," interposed Coleman.

" Hold your tongue, Freddy: little boys should be seen and not heard, as Tacitus tells us," said Lawless, reprovingly.

The only reply to this, if reply it could be called, was something which sounded to me like a muttered reference to the Greek historian Walker, whom Lawless had so lately mentioned, and Cumberland continued,—

" You will pay great attention to everything Lawless tells you, and endeavour to improve by following his example, at a respectful distance—ahem! The gentleman on your right hand. Mr. Mullins, who is chiefly remarkable for looking" ("Like a fool," put in Coleman, sotto voce) "before he leaps, so long, that in general he postpones leaping altogether, and is in the habit of making" ("An ass of himself," suggested Coleman)—"really, Freddy, I am surprised at you—of making two bites at a cherry—you will be better able to appreciate when you know more of him. As to my young friend Freddy here, his naturally good abilities and amiable temper" ("Draw it mild, old fellow!" interrupted the young gentleman in question) "have interested us so much in his favour that we cannot but view with regret a habit he has of late fallen into, of turning everything into ridicule" (" What a pity!" from the same individual), "together with a lamentable addiction to the use of slang terms. Let me hope his association with such a polished young gentleman as Mr. Fairlegh may improve him in these particulars."

" Who drank Mildman's ale at dinner?" asked Coleman; "if that's a specimen of his polished manners, I think mine take the shine out of them, rather."

"I assure you," interrupted I, eagerly, " I never was more distressed in my life; it was quite a mistake."

" Pretty good mistake—Hodgson's pale ale for Muddytub's swipes —eh, Mull?" rejoined Coleman.

"I believe you," replied Mullins.

" Well, now for entering your name; that's important, you know," said Lawless; "you had better ring the bell, and tell Thomas to bring the books."

I obeyed, and when Thomas made his appearance, informed him of my desire to enter my name in the books of the establishment, which I begged he would bring for that purpose. A look of bewilderment that came over his face on hearing my request, changed to an expression of intelligence, as, after receiving some masonic sign from Lawless, he replied,—

" The books, sir; yes, sir; bring 'em directly, sir."

After a few minutes he returned with two small, not overclean, books, ruled with blue lines. One of these Lawless took from him, opened with much ceremony, and covering the upper part of the page with a bit of blotting paper, pointed to a line, and desired me to write my name and age, as well as the date of my arrival, upon it. The same ceremony was repeated with the second.

"That's all right: now let's see how it reads," said he, and, removing the blotting paper, read as follows: "'Pair of Wellingtons, £1 15s.; satin stock, 25s.; cap ribbon for Sally Duster, 2s. 6d.; box of cigars, £1 16s. (mem. shocking bad lot)—Nov. 5th, Francis Fairlegh, aged 15.'—So much for that; now, let's see the next: 'Five shirts, four pair of stockings, six pocket-handkerchiefs, two pair of white ducks—Nov. 5th, Francis Fairlegh, aged 15.'"

Here his voice was drowned in a roar of laughter from the whole party assembled, Thomas included, during which the true state of the case dawned upon me, viz.—that I had, with much pomp and ceremony, entered my name, age, and the date of my arrival, in Mr. George Lawless's private account and washing books.

My thoughts, as I laid my aching head upon my pillow that night, were not of the most enviable nature. Leaving for the first time the home where I had lived from childhood, and in which I had met with affection and kindness from all around me, had been a trial under which my fortitude would most assuredly have given way, but for the brilliant picture my imagination had very obligingly sketched of the "happy family," of which I was about to become a member; in the foreground of which stood a group of fellow-pupils, a united brotherhood of congenial souls, containing three bosom friends at the very least, anxiously awaiting my arrival with outstretched arms of welcome. Now, however, this last hope had failed me; for, innocent (or as Coleman would have termed it, green) as I then was, I could not but perceive that the tone of mock politeness assumed towards me by Cumberland and Lawless was merely a convenient cloak for impertinence, which could be thrown aside at any moment when a more open display of their powers of tormenting should seem advisable. In fact (though I was little aware of the pleasures in store for me), I had already seen enough to prove that the life of a private pupil was not exactly "all my fancy painted it;" and, as the misery of leaving those I loved proved in its "sad reality" a much more serious affair than I had imagined, the result of my cogitations was, that I was a very unhappy boy (I did not feel the smallest inclination to boast myself man at that moment), and that, if something very much to my advantage did not turn up in the course of the next twenty-four hours, my friends would have the melancholy satisfaction of depositing a broken heart (which, on the principle of the Kilkenny cats, was all I expected would remain of me by that time) in an early grave. Hereabouts, my feelings becoming too many for me at the thought of my own funeral, I fairly gave up the struggle, and, bursting into a flood of tears, cried myself to sleep, like a child.

CHAPTER II.

LOSS AND GAIN.

"And youthful still, in your doublet and hose, this raw rheumatic day ! "
"His thefts weré too open ; his filching was like an unskilful singer, he kept not time. . . . . Convey, the wise call it. Steal! foh! a fico for the phrase !"—*Shakespeare.*
"From *Greenland's* icy mountains."—*Heber.*

AMONGST the minor phenomena which are hourly occurring in the details of every-day life, although we are seldom sufficiently close observers to perceive them, there is none more remarkable than the change wrought in our feelings and ideas by a good night's rest ; and never was this change more strikingly exemplified than on the present occasion. I had fallen asleep in the act of performing the character of chief mourner at my own funeral, and I awoke in the highest possible health and spirits, with a strong determination never to "say die" under any conceivable aspect affairs might assume. "What in the world," said I to myself, as I sprang out of bed, and began to dress ; "what in the world was there for me to make myself so miserable about last night ? Suppose Cumberland and Lawless should laugh at, and tease me a little at first, what does it signify ? I must take it in good part as long as I can, and if that does not do, I must speak seriously to them—tell them they really annoy me and make me uncomfortable, and then, of course, they will leave off. As to Coleman, I am certain—— Well, it's very odd "—this last remark was elicited by the fact that a search I had been making for some minutes, in every place possible and impossible, for that indispensable article of male attire, my trousers, had proved wholly ineffectual, although I had a distinct recollection of having placed them carefully on a chair by my bedside the previous night. There, however, they certainly were not now, nor, as far as I could discover, anywhere else in the room. Under these circumstances, ringing the bell for Thomas seemed advisable, as it occurred to me that he had probably abstracted the missing garment for the purpose of brushing. In a few moments he answered the summons, and, with a face bright from the combined effects of a light heart and a severe application of yellow soap, inquired, "if I had rung for my shaving water ? "

"Why, no—I do not—that is, it was not—I seldom shave of a morning ; for the fact is, I have no beard to shave as yet."

"Oh, sir, that's no reason ; there's Mr. Coleman's not got the leastest westige of a hair upon his chin, and he's been mowing away with the greatest of persewerance for the last six months, and sends his rashier to be ground every three weeks, regular, in order to get a. beard—but what can I do for you, sir ? "

" Why," replied I, trying to look grave, " it's very odd, but I have lost—that is, I can't find my trousers anywhere. I put them on this chair last night, I know."

" Umph! that's sing'lar, too; I was just a coming upstairs to brush 'em for you; you did not hear anybody come into your room after you went to bed, did you, sir?"

" No; but then I was so tired—I slept as sound as a top."

" Ah! I shouldn't much wonder if Mr. Coleman knew something about 'em: perhaps you had better put on another pair, and if I can find 'em, I'll bring 'em back after breakfast."

This was very good advice, and, therefore, of course, impossible to follow; for, on examining my trunk, lo and behold! dress pantaloons, white ducks, " et hoc genus omne," had totally disappeared, and I seemed to stand a very good chance of making my first appearance at my tutor's breakfast-table in an extemporary " kilt," improvised for the occasion, out of two towels and a checked neckcloth. In this extremity, Thomas, as a last resource, knocked at Coleman's door, informing him that I should be glad to speak to him—a proceeding speedily followed by the appearance of that gentleman ' in propria persona.'

" Good morning, Fairlegh, hope you slept well. You are looking cold; had not you better get some clothes on? Mildman will be down in a minute, and there will be a pretty row if we are not all there; he's precious particular, I can tell you."

" That is exactly what I want to do," replied I; " but the fact is, somebody has taken away all my trousers in the night."

" Bless me; you don't say so? Another case of pilfering! this is getting serious; I will call Lawless—I say, Lawless!"

" Well, what's the row?" was the reply. " Have the French landed, or is the kitchen chimney on fire, eh? What do I behold? Fairlegh, lightly and elegantly attired in nothing but his shirt, and Thomas standing like Niobe, the picture of woe! Here's a sight for a father!"

" Why, it's a bad job," said Coleman; " do you know, here's another case of pilfering; Fairlegh has had all his trousers stolen in the night."

" You don't say so!" rejoined Lawless: " what is to be done? It must be stopped somehow: we had better tell him all we know about it. Thomas, leave the room."

Thomas obeyed, giving me a look of great intelligence, the meaning of which, however, I was totally at a loss to conceive, as he went; and Lawless continued,—

" I am afraid you will hardly believe us—it is really a most unheard-of thing—but we have lately missed a great many of our clothes, and we have every reason to suspect (I declare I can scarcely bear to mention it) that Mildman takes them himself, fancying, of course, that, placed by his position so entirely above suspicion, he may do it with impunity. We have suspected this for some time

and lately one or two circumstances—old clothesmen having been
observed leaving his study, a pawn-ticket falling out of his waistcoat
pocket one day as he went out of our parlour, etc.—have put the
matter beyond a doubt; but he has never gone to such an extent as
this before. Mind you don't mention a word of this to Thomas, for,
bad as Mildman is, one would not wish to show him up before his
own servant."

"Good gracious!" cried I, "but you are joking; it never can be
really true!" Reading, however, in the solemn, not to say distressed,
expression of their faces, indisputable evidence of the reality of the
accusation, I continued: " I had no idea such things ever could take
place, and he a clergyman, too!—dreadful! but what in the world
am I to do? I have not got a pair of trousers to put on. Oh! if he
would but have taken anything else, even my watch instead, I should
not have minded—what shall I do?"

" Why, really," replied Coleman, " it is not so easy to advise: you
can't go down as you are, that's certain. Suppose you were to wrap
yourself up in a blanket, and go and tell him you have found him
out, and that you will call a policeman if he does not give you your
clothes instantly; have it out with him fairly, and check the thing
effectually once for all—eh?"

" No, that won't do," said Lawless. "I should say, sit down
quietly (how cold you must be!) and write him a civil note, saying
that you had reason to believe he had borrowed your trousers (that's
the way I should put it), and that you would be very much gratified
by his lending you a pair to wear to-day, and then you can stick in
something about your having been always accustomed to live with
people who were very particular in regard to dress, and that you are
sorry you are obliged to trouble him for such a trifle; in fact, do
a bit of the respectful, and then pull up short with 'obedient
pupil,' etc."

" Ay, that's the way to do it," said Coleman, " in the shopfellow's
style, you know—much obliged for past favours, and hope for a
continuance of the same—more than you do, though. Fairlegh, I
should fancy; but there goes the bell—I am off," and away he
scudded, followed by Lawless humming :—

> " Brian O'Lynn had no breeches to wear,
> So he took an old catskin, and made him a pair."

Here was a pretty state of things : the breakfast bell had rung,
and I, who considered being too late a crime of the first magnitude,
was unable even to begin dressing, from the melancholy fact that
every pair of trousers I possessed in the world had disappeared;
while, to complete my misery, I was led to believe the delinquent who
had abstracted them was no less a person than the tutor, whom I had
come fully prepared to regard with feelings of the utmost respect,
and veneration.

However, in such a situation, thinking over my miseries was

worse than useless; something must be done at once—but what?
Write the note as Lawless had advised? No, it was useless to think
of that; I felt I could not do it. Ah! a bright idea!—I'll try it.
So, suiting the action to the word, I rang the bell, and then jumping
into bed, muffled myself up in the bedclothes.

" Well, sir, have you found them ? " asked Thomas, entering.

" No, Thomas," replied I, dolefully, " nor ever shall, I fear; but
will you go up to Dr. Mildman, and tell him, with my respects, that I
cannot get up to breakfast this morning, and, if he asks what is the
matter with me, say that I am prevented from coming down by
severe cold. I am sure that is true enough," added I, shivering.

" Well, sir, I will, if you wish it; but I don't exactly see the good
of it; you must get up some time or other."

"I don't know," replied I, gloomily, " we shall see; only do you
take my message."

And he accordingly left the room, muttering as he did so, " Well,
I calls this a great deal too bad, and I'll tell master of it myself, if
nobody else won't."

" Tell master of it himself!"—he also suspected him, then. This
crushed my last faint hope that, after all, it might turn out to be
only a trick of the pupils; and overpowered by the utter vileness
and depravity of him who was set in authority over me, I buried my
face in the pillow, feeling a strong inclination to renew the lamentations of the preceding night. Not many minutes had elapsed, when
the sound of a heavy footstep slowly ascending the stairs attracted
my attention. I raised my head, and beheld the benevolent countenance (for even then it certainly did wear a benevolent expression) of
my wicked tutor, regarding me with a mingled look of scrutiny and
pity.

" Why, Fairlegh, what's all this?—Thomas tells me you are not
able to come down to breakfast; you are not ill, I hope ? "

" No, sir," replied I, " I don't think I am very ill; but I can't come
down to breakfast."

" Not ill, and yet you can't come down to breakfast! pray, what in
the world prevents you ? "

" Perhaps," said I (for I was becoming angry at what I considered
his unparalleled effrontery, and thought I would give him a hint
that he could not deceive me so easily as he seemed to expect),
" perhaps you can tell that better than I can."

" I, my boy!—I'm afraid not; my pretensions to the title of doctor
are based on divinity, not physic:—however, put out your tongue—
that's right enough; let me feel your hand—a little cold or so, but
nothing to signify; did this kind of seizure ever happen to you at
home ? "

Well, this was adding insult to injury with a vengeance; not
content with stealing my clothes himself, but actually asking me
whether such things did not happen at home! The wretch! thought
I; does he suppose that everybody is as wicked as himself?

"No," I answered, my voice trembling with the anger I was scarcely able to repress; "no, sir, such a thing never could happen in my dear father's house."

"There, don't agitate yourself; you seem excited: perhaps you had better lie in bed a little longer; I will send you up something warm, and after that you may feel more inclined to get up," said he, kindly, adding to himself, as he left the room, " Very strange boy—I can't make him out at all."

The door closed, and I was once more alone. "Is he guilty or not guilty?" thought I; "if he really has taken the clothes, he is the most accomplished hypocrite I ever heard of; yet he must have done so, everything combines to prove it—Thomas's speech—nay, even his own offer of sending me 'something warm'; something warm, indeed! what do I want with anything warm, except my trousers?" No! the fact was beyond dispute; they were gone, and he had stolen them, whilst I, unhappy youth, was entirely in his power, and had not therefore a chance of redress. "But I will not bear it," cried I; "I'll write to my father—I'll run away—I'll—"

"Hurrah!" shouted Thomas, rushing into the room with his arm full of clothes, "here they are, sir; I have found the whole kit of them at last."

"Where?" exclaimed I, eagerly.

"Where? why, in such a queer place!" replied he, "stuffed up the chimbley in master's study; but I have given them a good brushing, and they are none the worse for it, except them blessed white ducks; they are a'most black ducks now, though they will wash, so that don't signify none."

"Up the chimney, in master's study!" Here was at last proof positive; my clothes had been actually found in his possession—oh, the wickedness of this world!

"But how did you ever find them?" asked I.

"Why! I happened to go in to fetch something, and I see'd a little bit of the leg of one of them hanging down the chimbley, so I guessed how it all was, directly. I think I know how they got there, too; they did not walk there by themselves, I should say."

"I wish they had," muttered I.

"I thought somebody was up too early this morning to be about any good," continued he; "he is never out of bed till the last moment, without there's some mischief in the wind."

This was pretty plain speaking, however. Thomas was clearly as well aware of his master's nefarious practices as the pupils themselves, and Lawless's amiable desire to conceal Dr. Mildman's sins from his servant's knowledge was no longer of any avail. I hastened, therefore (the only reason for silence being thus removed), to relieve my mind from the burden of just indignation which was oppressing it.

"And can you, Thomas," exclaimed I, with flashing eyes, "remain the servant of a man who dares thus to outrage every law, human

and divine? one who, having taken upon himself the sacred office of
a clergyman of the Church of England, and so made it his especial
duty to set a good example to all around him, can take advantage of
the situation in which he is placed in regard to his pupils, and
actually demean himself by purloining the clothes of the young
men" (I felt five-and-twenty at the very least at that moment)
"committed to his charge?—why, my father—"

What I imagined my father would have said or done under these
circumstances, was fated to remain a mystery, as my eloquence was
brought to a sudden conclusion by my consternation, when a series
of remarkable phenomena, which had been developing themselves
during my harangue in the countenance of Thomas, terminated
abruptly in what appeared to me a fit of most unmitigated insanity.
A look of extreme astonishment, which he had assumed at the
beginning of my speech, had given place to an expression of mingled
surprise and anger as I continued; which again in its turn had
yielded to a grin of intense amusement, growing every moment
broader and broader, accompanied by a spasmodic twitching of his
whole person; and, as I mentioned his master's purloining my
trousers, he suddenly sprang up from the floor nearly a yard high,
and commenced an extempore 'pas seul' of a Jim Crow character,
which he continued with unabated vigour during several minutes.
This 'Mazourka d'extase,' or whatever a ballet-master would have
called it, having at length, to my great joy, concluded, the performer
of it sank exhausted into a chair, and regarding me with a face still
somewhat the worse for his late violent exertions, favoured me with
the following geographical remark,—

"Well, I never did believe in the existence of sich a place as
Greenland before, but there's nowhere else as you can have come
from, sir, I am certain."

"Eh! why! what's the matter with you? have I done anything
particularly 'green,' as you call it? what are you talking about?"
said I, not feeling exactly pleased at the reception my virtuous
indignation had met with.

"Oh! don't be angry, sir; I am sure I did not mean to offend you;
but really I could not help it, when I heard you say about master's
having stole your things. Oh, lor!" he added, holding his sides with
both hands, "how my precious sides do ache, sure-ly!"

"Do you consider that any laughing matter?" said I, still in the
dark.

"Oh! don't, sir, don't say it again, or you will be the death of me,"
replied Thomas, struggling against a relapse; "why, bless your
innocence, what could ever make you think master would take your
clothes?"

"Make me think? why, Lawless told me so," answered I, "and he
also said it was not the first time such a thing had occurred, either."

"You'll have enough to do, sir, if you believe all our young gents
tell you; why, master would as soon think of flying as of stealing

anything. It was Mr. Coleman as put them up the chimbley; he's always a-playing some trick or another for everlasting."

A pause ensued, during which the whole affair in its true bearings became for the first time clear to my mind's eye; the result of my cogitations may be gathered from the following remark, which escaped me as it were involuntarily—" What a confounded ass I have made of myself, to be sure!"

Should any of my readers be rude enough to agree with me in this particular, let them reflect for a moment on the peculiar position in which I was placed. Having lived from childhood in a quiet country parsonage, with my father and mother, and a sister younger than myself, as my sole companions, " mystification "—that is, telling deliberate falsehoods by way of a joke—was a perfectly novel idea to me; and when that joke involved the possibility of such serious consequences as offending the tutor under whose care we were placed, I (wholly ignorant of the impudence and recklessness of public school boys) considered such a solution of the mystery inconceivable. Moreover, everything around me was so strange, and so entirely different to the habits of life in which I had been hitherto brought up, that for the time my mind was completely bewildered. I appeared to have lost my powers of judgment, and to have relapsed. as far as intellect was concerned, into childhood again. My readers must excuse this digression, but it appeared to me necessary to explain how it was possible for a lad of fifteen to have been made the victim of such a palpably absurd deception, without its involving the necessity of his not being " so sharp as he should be."

The promised " something warm " made its appearance ere long. in the shape of tea and toast, which, despite my alarming seizure, I demolished with great gusto in bed (for I did not dare to get up), feeling, from the fact of my having obtained it under false pretences. very like a culprit all the while. Having finished my breakfast and allowed sufficient time to elapse for my recovery, I got up, and selecting a pair of trousers which appeared to have suffered less from their sojourn in the chimney than the others, dressed myself. and soon after eleven o'clock made my appearance in the pupils' room, where I found Dr. Mildman seated at his desk, and the pupils apparently very hard at work.

" How do you find yourself now you are up, Fairlegh ? " inquired my tutor, kindly.

" Quite well, sir, thank you," I replied, feeling like an impostor.

" Quite recovered ? " continued he.

" Everything—entirely, I mean," stammered I, thinking of my trousers.

" That's well, and now let us see what kind of a Latin and Greek lining you have got to your head."

So saying, without appearing to notice the tittering of the pupils. he pointed to a seat by his side, and commenced what I considered a

c

very formidable examination, with the view of eliciting the extent of
my acquaintance with the writers of antiquity, which proved to be
extremely select. When he had thoroughly satisfied (or dissatisfied)
himself upon this point, he recommended Horace and Xenophon to
my particular notice, adding that Coleman was also directing his
attention to the sayings and doings of the same honourable and
learned gentlemen—and that, therefore, we were to work together.
He then explained to me certain rules and regulations of his
establishment, to which he added a few moral remarks, conveying
the information that, if I always did exactly what he considered right,
and scrupulously avoided everything he deemed wrong, I might
relieve my mind from all fears of his displeasure, which was, to say
the least, satisfactory, if not particularly original.

Exactly as the clock struck one, Dr. Mildman left the room (the
morning's " study," as it was called, ending at that hour), leaving us
our own masters till five, at which time we dined. Lest any kind
reader should fancy we were starved, let me add that at half-past one
a substantial luncheon was provided, of which we might partake or
not, as we pleased. As well as I remember, we generally did
graciously incline towards the demolition of the viands. unless
" metal more attractive " awaited us elsewhere—but I am digressing.

CHAPTER III.

COLD-WATER CURE FOR THE HEARTACHE.

> " Oh! grief for words too deep,
> From all his loved ones parted,
> He could not choose but weep,
> He was so lonely-hearted."
> *Shortfellow.*
>
> " How does the water come down at Lodore?
>
> Dashing and flashing, and splashing and clashing,
> All at once and all o'er, with a mighty uproar,
> And this way the water comes down at Lodore."
> *Southey.*

"Pray, Fairlegh, what did you mean by not coming down till
eleven o'clock ? " asked Cumberland, in an angry tone.

" Did its mamma say it was always to have its breakfast in bed, a
dear ? " sneered Lawless.

" When she fastened that pretty square collar round its neck,"
chimed in Coleman.

" Just like a great gal," added Mullins.

"Mildman was exceedingly angry about it, I can tell you," continued Cumberland, "and desired me to speak seriously to you on the subject; such abominable idleness is not to be tolerated."

"It was not idleness," answered I, warmly; "you all know very well why I could not come down, and I don't think it was at all right or kind of you to play me such a trick."

"Eh—now don't say that—you will hurt my feelings; I declare it is quite affecting," said Coleman, wiping his eyes with Mullins' handkerchief, of which he had just picked his pocket.

"I'd have given five pounds to have seen old Sam's phiz, when he was trying to make out what ailed young stupid here, whether he was really ill or only shamming," said Lawless; "depend upon it, he thinks it was all pretence, and he can't bear anything of that sort; that was why he began spinning him that long yarn about 'meriting his approbation by upright and straightforward conduct,' this morning. I saw what the old boy was aiming at in a minute: there's nothing puts him out so much as being deceived."

"Won't he set him all the hard lines to construe, that's all!" said Mullins.

"It will be 'hard lines' upon him if he does," observed Coleman.

"Hold your tongue, Freddy! your puns are enough to make one ill," said Cumberland.

"Well, I don't know whether you are going to stand here all day biting your pinafore, Cumberland," interrupted Lawless; "I'm not, for I've got a horse waiting for me down at Snaffles's, and I am going to ride over to Hookley; there's a pigeon match coming off to-day between Clayton of the Lancers—he was just above me at Eton, you know—and Tom Horton, who won the great match at Finchley, and I have backed Clayton pretty heavily—shall you come?"

"No," replied Cumberland, "no, I am going down to F—— Street."

"As usual, the board of green cloth, eh? you will go there once too often, if you don't mind, old fellow."

"That's my look-out," replied Cumberland.

And away they went to their different pursuits, each, as he left the room, making me a very low obeisance; Coleman taking the trouble to open the door again after he had gone out, to beg "that if I were going to write to my mother, I would tell her, with his love, that she need not make herself in the least uneasy, as he had' quite got over his last little attack." In a few minutes they had all quitted the house, and I remained the sole tenant of the pupils' room.

Many a long year has passed over my head since the day I am now describing, and each (though my life has been on the whole as free from care as that of most of the sons of Adam) has brought with it some portion of sorrow or suffering, to temper the happiness I have enjoyed, and teach me the much required lesson, "that here we have no abiding place." I have lived to see bright hopes fade—high and

noble aspirations fall to the ground, checked by the sordid policy of
worldly men—and the proud hearts which gave them birth become
gradually debased to the level of those around them, or break in the
unequal struggle—and these things have pained me. I have beheld
those dear to me stretched upon the bed of sickness, and taken from
me by the icy hand of death; and have deemed, as the grave closed
over them, that my happiness, as far as this world was concerned,
was buried with them. I have known (and this was grief indeed)
those loved with all the warm and trustful confidence of youth, prove
false and unworthy of such deep affection; and have wished in the
bitterness of my soul, that the pit had shut her mouth upon me also,
so I had but died with my faith in them unshaken. Still, although
such sorrows as these may have produced a more deep and lasting
effect, I do not remember ever to have felt more thoroughly desolate
than upon the present occasion. The last scene, though trifling in
itself, had made a great impression upon me, from the fact that it
proved, as I considered, the animus of the pupils towards me.
'Every man's hand was against me." Even the oaf Mullins might
insult me with impunity, secure that, in so doing, if in nothing else, he
would be supported by the rest. Then I had offended my tutor, all
my predilections in whose favour had returned with double force,
since I had satisfied myself that he was not addicted to the commission of petty larceny; offended him by allowing him to suppose that
I had practised a mean deception upon him. Moreover, it was impossible to explain my conduct to him without showing up Coleman,
an extreme measure for which I was by no means prepared. Besides,
everyone would think, if I were to do so, that I was actuated by a
paltry spirit of malice, and that would have been worse to bear than
anything. No—turn my gaze to whichever side I would, the horizon
seemed alike clouded; there was no comfort for me anywhere. I
looked at my watch—two o'clock! Three long hours to dinner-time.
in which I might do what I liked. What I liked! there was mockery
in the very sound. What was there for me to do? go out and see
more new faces looking coldly on me. and wander up and down in
strange places alone. amidst a crowd? No! I had not the heart to
do that. Sit down, and write home, and by telling them how
miserable I was, render them unhappy too?—that was the worst of
all. At length I found a book, and began reading as it were
mechanically, but so little was I able to fix my attention, that, had I
been questioned at the end of the time as to the subject of the work
I had been perusing, I should have been utterly at a loss for an
answer. I had fairly given it up as hopeless, and closed the book,
when I heard footsteps in the passage, followed by the sudden
apparition of the ever-smiling Mr. Frederick Coleman, who, closing
the door after him, accosted me as follows:—

" What, Fairlegh, all in the downs, old fellow?—' never say die!'—
come, be jolly—look at me."

As he said this, I involuntarily raised my eyes to his features, and certainly if ever there were a face formed for banishing blue devils by a glance, it was his. It was a round face, not remarkable for beauty of outline, inasmuch as it bore a strong resemblance to that of the gentleman on the blue China plates, in two pigtails and a petticoat, who appears to pass a mild ornithological and botanical existence in studying intently certain fishy-looking birds, and a cannon-ball tree, which form the leading features of the landscape in his vicinity. With regard to expression, however, Coleman had a decided advantage over the Chinese horticulturist, for whereas the countenance of the latter gentleman expresses (if indeed it can be said to express anything) only meek astonishment, Coleman's small black eyes danced and sparkled with such a spirit of mischief and devilry, while such a fund of merriment, and, as it now for the first time struck me, of good nature also, lurked about the corners of his mouth, that it seemed impossible to look at him without feeling that there was something contagious in his hilarity.

"Why," said I, "everything here is so new to me, so entirely different from all I have been accustomed to before, and the unkind —that is, the odd way in which Lawless and the rest of you seem to behave to me, treating me as if you thought I was either a fool or a baby—it all seems so strange, that I confess I am not over-happy."

"Precious odd if you were, I think," replied Coleman; "and it was a horrid shame of me to hide your trousers as I did this morning Oh! how delightfully miserable you did look, as you stood shivering up in the cold! I'm sorry for it now, but I'm such a chap for a bit of fun, that if a trick like that comes into my head, do it I must. Oh! I get into no end of scrapes that way! Why, it was but the other day I put a piece of cobbler's wax on the seat of Mildman's chair, and ruined his best Sunday-going sit-upons; he knew, too, who did it, I'm sure, for the next day he gave me a double dose of Euclid, to take the nonsense out of me, I suppose. He had better mind what he's at, though! I have got another dodge ready for him if he does not take care! But I did not mean to annoy you: you behaved like a brick, too, in not saying anything about it—I am really very sorry."

"Never mind," said I; "it's all right again now; I like a joke as well as anybody when I know it's only fun; the thing I am afraid of now is, that Dr. Mildman may think I wanted to deceive him, by pretending to be ill, when I was not."

"I dare say he has got a pretty good notion how it is," said Coleman; "but we'll get Thomas to tell him what I was up to, and that will set it all straight again."

"That will be very kind indeed," replied I; "but will not Dr. Mildman be angry with you about it?"

"Not he," said Coleman, "he never finds fault unless there's real necessity for it; he's as good a fellow as ever lived, is old Sam, only he's so precious slow."

"I am glad you like him, he seems so very kind and good-natured,"

said I, " just the sort of person one should wish one's tutor to be.
But about Cumberland and Lawless; what kind of fellows are they
when you come to know them ? "

" Oh, you will like Lawless well enough when he gets tired of
bullying you," replied Coleman; "though you need not stand so much
of that as I was obliged to bear; you are a good head taller than I
am—let's look at your arm; it would be all the better for a little more
muscle, but that will soon improve. I'll put on the gloves with you
for an hour or so every day."

" Put on the gloves! " repeated I; " how do you mean?—what has
that to do with Lawless ? "

" Oh, you muff! don't you understand?—of course, I mean the
boxing-gloves; and when you know how to use your fists, if Lawless
comes it too strong, slip into him."

" He must bully a good deal before I am driven to that," replied I;
" I never struck a blow in anger in my life."

" You will see before long," rejoined Coleman; "but at all events,
there is no harm in learning to use your fists; a man should always be
able to defend himself if he is attacked."

" Yes, that's very true," observed I; " but you have not told me
anything of Cumberland. Shall I ever like him, do you think ? "

" Not if you are the sort of fellow I take you to be," replied he;
" there is something about Cumberland not altogether right, I fancy;
I'm not very straitlaced myself, particularly if there's any fun in a
thing, not so much so as I should be, I suspect; but Cumberland is too
bad even for me; besides, there is no fun in what he does, and then
he's such a humbug—not straightforward and honest, you know.
Lawless would not be half such a bully either, if Cumberland did not
set him on. But don't you say a word about this to anyone; Cumberland would be ready to murder me, or to get somebody else to do
it for him—that's more in his way."

" Do not fear my repeating anything told me in confidence," replied
I; " but what do you mean when you say there's something wrong
about Cumberland ? "

" Do you know what Lawless meant by the 'board of green cloth,'
this morning ? "

" No—it puzzled me."

" I will tell you then," replied Coleman, sinking his voice almost to
a whisper—" the billiard-table ! "

After telling me this, Coleman, evidently fearing to commit himself further with one of whom he knew so little, turned the conversation, and finding it still wanted more than an hour to dinner,
proposed that we should take a stroll along the shore together. In
the course of our walk, I acquired the additional information that
another pupil was expected in a few days—the only son of Sir John
Oaklands, a baronet of large fortune in Hertfordshire; and that an
acquaintance of Coleman's, who knew him, said he was a capital
fellow, but very odd—though in what the oddity consisted did not

appear. Moreover, Coleman confirmed me in my preconceived idea, that Mullins's genius lay at present chiefly in the eating, drinking, and sleeping line—adding that, in his opinion, he bore a striking resemblance to those somewhat dissimilar articles, a muff and a spoon. In converse such as this, the time slipped away, till we suddenly discovered that we had only a quarter of an hour left in which to walk back to Langdale Terrace, and prepare for dinner; whereupon a race began, in which my longer legs gave me so decided an advantage over Coleman, that he declared he would deliver me up to the tender mercies of the "Society for the Prevention of Cruelty to Animals," for what he was pleased to call "an aggravated case of over-driving a private pupil."

We had not more than five minutes left when we arrived at Dr. Mildman's door, Coleman affording a practical illustration of the truth of the aphorism, that "it is the pace that kills"; so that Thomas's injunction, "Look sharp, gentlemen," was scarcely necessary to induce us to rush upstairs two steps at a time. In the same hurry I entered my bedroom, without observing that the door was standing ajar rather suspiciously, for which piece of inattention I was rewarded by a deluge of water, which wetted me from head to foot, and a violent blow on the shoulder, which stretched me on the ground in the midst of a puddle. That I may not keep the reader in suspense, I will at once inform him that I was indebted for this agreeable surprise to the kindness and skill of Lawless, who, having returned from his pigeon-match half an hour sooner than was necessary, had devoted it to the construction of what he called a "booby trap," which ingenious piece of mechanism was arranged in the following manner: The victim's room-door was placed ajar, and upon the top thereof a Greek Lexicon, or any other equally ponderous volume, was carefully balanced, and upon this was set in its turn a jug of water. If all these were properly adjusted, the catastrophe above described was certain to ensue when the door was opened.

" Fairly caught, by Jove! " cried Lawless, who had been on the watch.

" By Jupiter Pluvius, you should have said," joined in Coleman, helping me up again; for so sudden and unexpected had been the shock, that I had remained for a moment just as I had fallen, with a kind of vague expectation that the roof of the house would come down upon me.

" I suppose I have to thank you for that," said I, turning to Lawless.

" Pray don't mention it, Pinafore," was the answer; " what little trouble I had in making the arrangement, I can assure you, was quite repaid by its success."

" I'll certainly put on the gloves to-morrow," whispered I to Coleman—to which he replied by a sympathetic wink, adding,—

" And now I think you had better get ready, more particularly as you will have to find out 'how to dress jugged hair,' as the cookery-books say."

By dint of almost superhuman exertions, I did just contrive to get down in time for dinner, though my unfortunate "jugged hair," which was anything but dry, must have presented rather a singular appearance. In the course of dinner, Dr. Mildman told us that we should have the whole of the next day to ourselves, as he was obliged to go to London on business, and should not return till the middle of the day following—an announcement which seemed to afford great satisfaction to his hearers, despite an attempt made by Cumberland to keep up appearances, by putting on a look of mournful resignation, which being imitated by Coleman, who, as might be expected, rather overdid the thing, failed most signally.

CHAPTER IV.

WHEREIN IS COMMENCED THE ADVENTURE OF THE MACINTOSH AND OTHER MATTERS.

> " How oft the sight of means to do ill deeds,
> Makes ill deeds done."
> " Come, tailor, let us see't ;
> Oh ! mercy . . . What masking stuff is here ?
> What's this ? a sleeve ? "
> " Disguise, I see ; thou art a wickedness
> Wherein the pregnant enemy does much."
> " A horse ! a horse ! my kingdom for a horse."
>   *Shakespeare.*

On returning to the pupils' room, Lawless commenced (to my great delight, as I thereby enjoyed a complete immunity from his some-what troublesome attentions) a full, true, and particular account of the pigeon-match, in which his friend Clayton had, with unrivalled skill, slain a sufficient number of victims to furnish forth pies for the supply of the whole mess during the ensuing fortnight. At length, however, all was said that could be said, even upon this interesting subject, and the narrator, casting his eyes around in search of where-withal to amuse himself, chanced to espy my new writing-desk, a parting gift from my little sister Fanny, who, with the self-denial of true affection, had saved up her pocket-money during many previous months, in order to provide funds for this munificent present.

" Pinafore, is that desk yours ? " demanded Lawless.

Not much admiring the sobriquet by which he chose to address me, I did not feel myself called upon to reply.

"Are you deaf, stupid? don't you hear me speaking to you?—where did you get that writing-desk?"

Still I did not answer.

"Sulky, eh? I shall have to lick him before long. I see. Here you, what's your name? Fairlegh, did your grandmother give you that writing-desk?"

"No," replied I, "my sister Fanny gave it to me the day before I left home."

"Oh, you have got a sister Fanny, have you? how old is she, and what is she like?"

"She is just thirteen, and she has got the dearest little face in the world," answered I, earnestly, as the recollection of her bright blue eyes and sunny smile came across me.

"How interesting!" sighed Coleman; "it quite makes my heart beat: you could not send for her, could you?"

"And she gave you that desk, did she?—how very kind of her!" resumed Lawless, putting the poker in the fire.

"Yes, was it not?" said I eagerly. "I would not have any harm happen to it for more than I can tell."

"So I suppose," replied Lawless, still devoting himself to the poker, which was rapidly becoming red-hot. "Have you ever," continued he, "seen this new way they have of ornamenting things? encaustic work, I think they call it:—it's done by the application of heat, you know."

"I never even heard of it," said I.

"Ah! I thought not," rejoined Lawless. "Well, as I happen to understand the process, I'll condescend to enlighten your ignorance. Mullins, give me that desk."

"Don't touch it," cried I, bounding forward to the rescue; "I won't have anything done to it."

My design was, however, frustrated by Cumberland and Lawless, who, both throwing themselves upon me at the same moment, succeeded, despite my struggles, in forcing me into a chair, where they held me, while Mullins, by their direction, with the aid of sundry neckcloths, braces, etc., tied me hand and foot; Coleman, who attempted to interfere in my behalf, receiving a push which sent him reeling across the room, and a hint that if he did not mind his own business he would be served in the same manner.

Having thus effectually placed me 'hors de combat,' Lawless took possession of my poor writing-desk, and commenced tracing on the top thereof with the red-hot poker, what he was pleased to term a "design from the antique," which consisted of a spirited outline of that riddle-loving female the Sphinx, as she appeared when dressed in top-boots and a wide-awake, and regaling herself with a choice cigar! He was giving the finishing touch to a large pair of moustaches, with which he had embellished her countenance, and which he declared was the only thing wanting to complete the likeness to an old aunt of Dr. Mildman's, whom the pupils usually designated by the endearing appellation of "Growler," when the door opened, and Thomas announced that "Smithson" was waiting to see Mr. Lawless.

"Oh yes, to be sure, let him come in; no, wait a minute. Here, you, Coleman and Mullins, untie Fairlegh; be quick!—confound that desk, how it smells of burning, and I have made my hands all black too. Well, Smithson, have you brought the things?"

The person to whom this query was addressed was a young man attired in the extreme of the fashion, who lounged into the room with a "quite at home" kind of air, and nodding familiarly all around, arranged his curls with a ring-adorned hand, as he replied in a drawling tone,—

"Ya'as, Mr. Lawless, we're all right—punctual to a moment—always ready 'to come to time,' as we say in the ring."

"Who is he?" whispered I to Coleman.

"Who is he?" replied Coleman; "why, the best fellow in the world, to be sure. Not know Smithson, the prince of tailors, the tailor 'par excellence'! I suppose you never heard of the Duke of Wellington, have you?"

I replied humbly that I believed I had heard the name of that illustrious individual mentioned in connection with Waterloo and the Peninsula—and that I was accustomed to regard him as the first man of the age.

"Ay, well then, Smithson is the second; though I really don't know whether he is not quite as great in his way as Wellington, upon my honour. The last pair of trousers he made for Lawless were something sublime, too good for this wicked world, a great deal."

During this brief conversation, Smithson had been engaged in extricating a somewhat voluminous garment from the interior of a blue bag, which a boy, who accompanied him, had just placed inside the study-door.

"There, this is the new invention I told you about; a man named Macintosh hit upon it. Now, with this coat on, you might stand under a waterfall without getting even damp. Try it on, Mr. Lawless; just the thing, eh, gents?"

Our curiosity being roused by this panegyric, we gathered round Lawless to examine the garment which had called it forth. Such of my readers as recollect the first introduction of macintoshes, will doubtless remember that the earlier specimens of the race differed very materially in form from those which are in use at the present day. The one we were now inspecting was of a whity-brown colour, and, though it had sleeves like a coat, hung in straight folds from the waist to the ankles, somewhat after the fashion of a carter's frock, having huge pockets at the side, and fastening round the neck with a hook and eye.

"How does it do?" asked Lawless, screwing himself round in an insane effort to look at the small of his own back, a thing a man is

certain to attempt when trying on a coat. " It does not make a fellow look like a guy, does it ? "

" No, I rather admire that sort of thing," said Cumberland.

" A jolly dodge for a shower of rain, and no mistake," put in Coleman.

" It is deucedly fashionable, really," said Smithson—" this one of yours, and one we made for Augustus Flareaway, Lord Fitzscamper's son, the man in the Guards, you know, are the only two out yet."

" I have just got it at the right time, then," said Lawless; " I knew old Sam was going to town, so I settled to drive Clayton over to Woodend, in the tandem, to-morrow. The harriers meet there at eleven, and this will be the very thing to hide the leathers, and tops, and the green cut-away. I saw you at the match, by-the-bye, Smithey, this morning."

" Ya'as, I was there : did you see the thing I was on ? "

" A bright bay, with a star on the forehead ! a spicy-looking nag enough—whose is it ? "

" Why, young Robarts, who came into a lot of tin the other day, has just bought it ; Snaffles charged him ninety guineas for it."

" And what is it worth ? " asked Lawless.

" Oh! he would not do a dirty thing by any gent I introduced," replied Smithson. " I took young Robarts there : he merely made his fair profit out of it ; he gave forty pounds for it himself to the man who bred it, only the week before, to my certain knowledge : it's a very sweet thing, and would carry him well, but he's afraid to ride it ; that's how I was on it to-day. I'm getting it steady for him."

" A thing it will take you some time to accomplish, eh ? A mount like that is not to be had for nothing, every day, is it ? "

" Ya'as, you're about right there, Mr. Lawless ; you're down to every move, I see, as usual. Any orders to-day, gents ? your two vests will be home to-morrow, Mr. Coleman."

" Here, Smithson, wait a moment," said Cumberland, drawing him on one side ; " I was deucedly unlucky with the balls this morning," continued he, in a lower tone, " can you let me have five-and-twenty pounds ? "

" What you please, sir," replied Smithson, bowing.

" On the old terms, I suppose ? " observed Cumberland.

" All right," answered Smithson ; " stay, I can leave it with you now," added he, drawing out a leather case ; " oblige me by writing your name here—thank you."

So saying, he handed some bank-notes to Cumberland, carefully replaced the paper he had received from him in his pocket-book, and withdrew.

" Smithey was in great force to-night," observed Lawless, as the door closed behind him—" nicely they are bleeding that young ass Robarts among them—he has got into good hands to help him to get rid of his money, at all events. I don't believe Snaffles gave forty pounds for that bay horse ; he has got a decided curb on the off

hock, if I ever saw one, and I fancy's he's a little touched in the
wind, too; and there's another thing I should say—"

What other failing might be attributed to Mr. Robarts' bay steed,
we were, however, not destined to learn, as tea was at this moment
announced. In due time followed evening prayers, after which we
retired for the night. Being very sleepy I threw off my clothes, and
jumped hastily into bed, by which act I became painfully aware of
the presence of what a surgeon would term "certain foreign bodies"
—i.e. not, as might be imagined, sundry French, German, and Italian
corpses, but various hard substances, totally opposed to one's pre-
conceived ideas of the component parts of a feather-bed. Sleep being
out of the question on a couch so constituted, I immediately commenced an active search, in the course of which I succeeded in
bringing to light two clothes-brushes, a boot-jack, a pair of spurs,
Lempriére's Classical Dictionary, and a brick-bat. Having freed
myself from these undesirable bedfellows, I soon fell asleep, and
passed (as it seemed to me) the whole night in dreaming that I was
a pigeon, or thereabouts, and that Smithson, mounted on the top-
booted Sphinx, was inciting Lawless to shoot at me with a red-hot
poker.

As Coleman and I were standing at the window of the pupils'
room, about ten o'clock on the following morning, watching the
vehicle destined to convey Dr. Mildman to the coach-office, Lawless
made his appearance, prepared for his expedition, with his hunting-
costume effectually concealed under the new macintosh.

"Isn't Mildman gone yet? Deuce take it, what a time he is! I
ought to be off—I'm too late already!"

"They have not even put his carpet-bag in yet," said I.

"Well, I shall make a bolt, and chance it about his seeing me,"
exclaimed Lawless; "he'll only think I'm going out for a walk
rather earlier than usual, if he does catch a glimpse of me, so here's
off."

Thus saying, he placed his hat upon his head, with the air of a man
determined to do or die, and vanished.

Fortune is currently reported to favour the brave, and so, to do
her justice, she generally does; still, at the best of times, she is but
a fickle jade—at all events, she appeared determined to prove herself
so in the present instance; for scarcely had Lawless got a dozen
paces from the house, before Dr. Mildman appeared at the front
door with his great-coat and hat on, followed by Thomas bearing a
carpet-bag and umbrella, and his attention being attracted by footsteps, he turned his head and beheld Lawless. As soon as he
perceived him he gave a start of surprise, and pulling out his eyeglass
(he was rather short-sighted), gazed long and fixedly after the retreating figure. At length, having apparently satisfied himself as to the
identity of the person he was examining, he replaced his glass, stood
for a moment as if confounded by what he had seen, and then turning
abruptly, re-entered the house, and shut his study-door behind him

with a bang, leaving Thomas and the fly-driver mute with astonishment. In about five minutes he re-appeared, and saying to Thomas, in a stern tone, "Let that note be given to Mr. Lawless the moment he returns," got into the fly and drove off.

"There's a precious go," observed Coleman; "I wonder what's in the wind now. I have not seen old Sam get up the steam like that since I have been here. He was not so angry when I put Thomas's hat on the peg where he hangs his own, and he, never noticing the difference, put it on, and walked to church in it, gold band and all."

"I wouldn't be Lawless for something," observed I; "I wonder what the note's about?"

"That's just what puzzles me," said Coleman. "I should have thought he had seen the sporting togs, but that's impossible; he must have a penetrating glance, indeed, if he could see through that macintosh."

"Lawless was too impatient," said Cumberland; "he should have waited a few minutes longer, and then Mildman would have gone off without knowing anything about him. Depend upon it, the grand rule of life is to take things coolly, and wait for an opportunity; you have the game in your own hands then, and can take advantage of the follies and passions of others, instead of allowing them to avail themselves of yours."

"In plain English, cheat instead of being cheated," put in Coleman.

"You're not far wrong there, Freddy; the world is made up of knaves and fools—those who cheat, and those who are cheated—and I, for one, have no taste for being a fool," said Cumberland.

"Nor I," said Mullins; "I should not like to be a fool at all; I had rather be—"

"A butterfly," interrupted Coleman, thereby astonishing Mullins to such a degree that he remained silent for some moments, with his mouth wide open as if in the act of speaking.

"You cannot mean what you say; you surely would not wish to cheat people," said I to Cumberland; "if it were really true that one must be either a knave or a fool, I'd rather be a fool by far—I'm sure you could never be happy if you cheated anyone," continued I. "What does the Bible say about doing to others as you would have others do to you?"

"There, don't preach to me, you canting young prig!" said Cumberland, angrily, and immediately left the room.

"You hit him pretty hard then," whispered Coleman; "a very bad piece of business happened just before I came, about his winning a lot of tin from a young fellow here, at billiards, and they do say that Cumberland did not play fairly. It was rather unlucky your saying it; he will be your enemy from henceforth, depend upon it. He never forgets nor forgives a thing of that sort."

"I meant no harm by the remark," replied I; "I knew nothing of

his having cheated anyone ; however, I do not care ; I don't like him,
and I'm just as well pleased he should not like me. But now, as my
foreign relations seem to be rapidly assuming a warlike character
(as the newspapers have it), what do you say to giving me a lesson
in sparring, as you proposed, by way of preparation ? "

" With all my heart," replied Coleman.

And accordingly the gloves were produced, and my initiatory
lesson in the pugilistic art commenced by Coleman's first placing
me in an exceedingly uncomfortable attitude, and then very considerately knocking me out of it again, thereby depositing me with
much skill and science flat upon the hearthrug. This manœuvre he
repeated with great success during some half-hour or so, at the end
of which time I began to discover the knack with which it was done,
and proceeded to demonstrate the proficiency I was making, by a
well-directed blow, which being delivered with much greater force
than I had intended, sent Coleman flying across the room. Chancing
to encounter Mullins in the course of his transit, he overturned that
worthy against the table in the centre of the apartment, which,
yielding to their combined weight, fell over with a grand crash,
dragging them down with it, in the midst of an avalanche of books,
papers, and inkstands.

This ' grand coup' brought, as might be expected, our lesson to a
close for the day, Coleman declaring that such another hit would
inevitably knock him into the middle of next week, if not farther,
and that he really should not feel justified in allowing such a serious
interruption to his studies to take place.

" And now, what are we going to do with ourselves ? " asked I ;
" as this is a holiday, we ought to do something."

" Are you fond of riding ? " inquired Coleman.

" Nothing I like better," replied I ; " I have been used to it all my
life ; I have had a pony ever since I was four years old."

" I wish I was used to it," said Coleman. " My governor living in
London, I never crossed a horse till I came here, and I'm a regular
muff at it ; but I want to learn. What do you say to a ride this
afternoon ? "

" Just the thing," said I, " if it is not too expensive for my pocket."

" Oh no," replied Coleman ; " Snaffles lets horses at us cheap a rate
as anyone, and good uns to go, too : does not he, Cumberland ? "

" Eh, what are you talking about ? " said Cumberland, who had just
entered the room ; " Snaffles ? Oh yes, he's the man for horse-flesh.
Are you going to amuse yourself by tumbling off that fat little cob of
his again, Fred ? "

" I was thinking of having another try," replied Coleman ; " what
do you say, Fairlegh ? Never mind the tin ; I dare say you have got
plenty, and can get more when that's gone."

" I have got a ten-pound note," answered I ; " but that must last
me all this quarter : however, we'll have our ride to-day."

" I'll walk down with you," said Cumberland ; " I'm going that way; besides, it's worth a walk any day to see Coleman mount; it took him ten minutes the last time I saw him, and then he threw the wrong leg over, so that he turned his face to the tail."

"Scandalum magnatum! not a true bill," replied Coleman. "Now, come along, Fairlegh; let's get ready, and be off."

During our walk down to Snaffles' stables, Cumberland (who seemed entirely to have forgotten my 'mal à propos' remark) talked to me in a much more amiable manner than he had yet done, and the conversation naturally turning upon horses and riding, a theme always interesting to me, I was induced to enter into sundry details of my own exploits in that line. We reached the livery stables just as I had concluded a somewhat egotistical relation concerning a horse which a gentleman in our neighbourhood had bought for his invalid son, but which proving at first too spirited, I had undertaken to ride every day for a month, in order to get him quiet; a feat I was rather proud of having satisfactorily accomplished.

" Good-morning, Mr. Snaffles; is Punch at home ? " asked Coleman of a stout red-faced man, attired in a bright green Newmarket coat and top-boots.

" Yes, sir. Mr. Lawless told me your governor was gone to town, so I kept him in, thinking perhaps you would want him."

"That's all right," said Coleman; "and here's my friend, Mr. Fairlegh, will want a nag too."

"Proud to serve any gent as is a friend of yours, Mr. Coleman," replied Snaffles, with a bob of his head towards me, intended as a bow. "What stamp of horse do you like, sir? Most of my cattle are out with the harriers to-day."

" Snaffles—a word with you," interrupted Cumberland.

" One moment, sir," said Snaffles to me, as he crossed over to where Cumberland was standing.

" Come and look at Punch; and let's hear what you think of him," said Coleman, drawing me towards the stable.

" What does Cumberland want with that man ? " asked I.

" What, Snaffles ? I fancy he owes a bill here, and I daresay it is something about that."

" Oh, is that all ? " rejoined I.

" Why, what did you think it was ? " inquired Coleman.

" Never mind," I replied; "let's look at Punch."

And accordingly I was introduced to a little fat, round, jolly-looking cob, about fourteen hands high, who appeared to me an equine counterpart of Coleman himself. After having duly praised and patted him, I turned to leave the stable, just as Cumberland and Snaffles were passing the door, and I caught the following words from the latter, who appeared rather excited:—

" Well, if any harm comes of it, Mr. Cumberland, you'll remember it's your doing, not mine."

Cumberland's reply was inaudible, and Snaffles turned to me, saying,—

" I've only one horse at home likely to suit you, sir ; you'll find her rather high-couraged, but Mr. Cumberland tells me you won't mind that."

" I have been mentioning what a good rider you say you are," said Cumberland, laying a slight emphasis on the " say."

" Oh, I dare say she will do very well," replied I. " I suppose she has no vice about her."

" Oh dear no," said Snaffles, " nothing of the sort.—James," added he, calling to a helper, " saddle the chestnut mare, and bring her out directly."

The man whom he addressed, and who was a fellow with a good-humoured, honest face, became suddenly grave, as he replied in a deprecatory tone,—

" The chestnut mare ?   Mad Bess, sir ? "

" Don't repeat my words, but do as you are told," was the answer ; and the man went away looking surly.

After the interval of a few minutes, a stable door opposite was thrown open, and Mad Bess made her appearance, led by two grooms. She was a bright chestnut, with flowing mane and tail, about fifteen and a half hands high, nearly thorough-bred, and as handsome as a picture ; but the restless motion of her eye disclosing the white, the ears laid back at the slightest sound, and a half-frightened, half-wild air, when anyone went up to her, told a tale as to her temper, about which no one in the least accustomed to horses could doubt for an instant.

" That mare is vicious," said I, as soon as I had looked at her.

" Oh dear no, sir, quiet as a lamb, I can assure you. Soh, girl ! soh ! " said Snaffles, in a coaxing tone of voice, attempting to pat her ; but Bess did not choose to " soh," if by " sohing " is meant, as I presume, standing still and behaving prettily ; for on her master's approach, she snorted, attempted to rear, and ran back, giving the men at her head as much as they could do to hold her.

" She's a little fresh to-day ; she was not out yesterday ; but it's all play, pretty creature ! nothing but play," continued Snaffles.

" If you are afraid, Fairlegh, don't ride her," said Cumberland ; " but I fancied from your conversation you were a bold rider, and did not mind a little spirit in a horse : you had better take her in again, Snaffles."

" Leave her alone," cried I, quickly (for I was becoming irritated by Cumberland's sneers, in spite of my attempt at self-control), " I'll ride her. I'm no more afraid than other people ; nor do I mind a spirited horse, Cumberland ; but that mare is more than spirited, she's ill-tempered—look at her eye ! "

" Well, you had better not ride her, then," said Cumberland.

" Yes, I will," answered I, for I was now thoroughly roused, and determined to go through with the affair, at all hazards. I was always, even as a boy, of a determined, or, as ill-natured people would

call it, obstinate disposition, and I doubt whether I am entirely cured
of the fault at the present time."

" Please yourself; only mind, I have warned you not to ride her if
you are afraid," said Cumberland.

" A nice warning," replied I, turning away—" who'll lend me a pair
of spurs ? "

" I've got a pair here, sir ; if you'll step this way I'll put them on
for you," said the man whom I had heard addressed as James—
adding, in a lower tone, as he buckled them on, "for Heaven's
sake, young gentleman, don't mount that mare, unless you're a first-
rate rider."

" Why, what's the matter with her ? does she kick ? " inquired I.

" She'll try and pitch you off, if possible, and if she can't do that,
she'll bolt with you, and then the Lord have mercy upon you ! "

This was encouraging, certainly !

" You are an honest fellow, James," replied I ; "and I am much
obliged to you. Ride her I must, my honour is at stake ; but I'll be
as careful as I can, and if I come back safe you shall have half-a-
crown."

" Thank you, sir," was the reply ; "I shall be glad enough to see
you come back in any other way than on a shutter, without the
money."

" Of a truth, the race of Job's comforters is not yet extinct,"
thought I, as I turned to look for Coleman, who had been up to this
moment employed in superintending the operation of saddling
Punch, and now made his appearance, leading that renowned steed
by the bridle.

" Why, Fairlegh, you are not going to ride that vicious brute, to
be sure ; even Lawless won't mount her, and he does not care what
he rides in general."

" Never mind about Lawless," said I, assuming an air of confidence
I was very far from feeling ; " she won't eat me, I dare say."

" I don't know that," rejoined Coleman, regarding Mad Bess with
a look of horror; " Cumberland, don't let him mount her."

" Nay, I can't prevent it ; Fairlegh is his own master, and must do
as he likes," was the answer.

" Come, we can't keep the men standing here the whole day," said
I to Coleman ; " mount Punch, and get out of my way as fast as you
can, if you are going to do so at all "—a request with which, seeing I
was quite determined, he at length unwillingly complied, and having,
after one or two failures, succeeded in throwing his leg over the cob's
broad back, rode slowly out of the yard, and took up his station outside, in order to witness my proceedings.

" Now, then," said I, " keep her as steady as you can for a minute,
and as soon as I am fairly mounted give her her head—stand clear
there ! "

I then took a short run, and placing one hand on the saddle, while
I seized a lock of the mane with the other, I sprang from the ground

D

and vaulted at once upon her back, without the aid of the stirrup, a feat I had learned from a groom who once lived with us, and which stood me in good stead on the present occasion, as I thereby avoided a kick with which Mad Bess greeted my approach. I next took up the reins as gently as I could, the men let go her head, and after a little plunging and capering, though much less than I had expected, her ladyship gave up hostilities for the present, and allowed me to ride her quietly up and down the yard. I then wished Cumberland (who looked, as I thought, somewhat mortified), a good afternoon, turned a deaf ear to the eulogies of Mr. Snaffles and his satellites, and proceeded to join Coleman. As I left the yard my friend James joined me under the pretence of arranging my stirrup leather, when he took the opportunity of saying.—

"She'll go pretty well now you're once mounted, sir, as long as you can hold her with the snaffle, but if you are obliged to use the curb— look out for squalls ! ! !"

CHAPTER V.

MAD BESS.

" Away, away, my steed and I,
Upon the pinions of the wind ;
All human dwellings left behind,
We sped like meteors through the sky.

With glossy skin and dripping mane,
And reeling limbs, and reeking flank,
The wild steed's sinewy nerves still strain
Up the repelling bank.
We gained the top ; a boundless plain
Spreads onward.

My heart turned sick, my brain grew sore
And throbbed awhile, then beat no more ;
The sky spun like a mighty wheel ;

And a slight flash sprang o'er my eyes,
Which saw no farther."
Mazeppa.

OUT of consideration for the excitable disposition of Mad Bess, we took our way along the least bustling streets we could select ; directing our course towards the outskirts of the town, behind which extended for some miles a portion of the range of hills known as the South Downs, over the smooth green turf of which we promised ourselves a canter. As we rode along, Coleman questioned me as to what could have passed while he was seeing Punch saddled, to make me determine to ride the chestnut mare, whose vicious disposition was, he informed me, so well known, that not only would no one ride her who could help it, but that Snaffles, who was most anxious to get rid of her, had not as yet been able to find a purchaser. In reply to this I gave him a short account of what had occurred, adding my more than suspicion that the whole matter had been arranged by Cumberland, in which notion he entirely agreed with me.

" I was afraid of something of this sort, when I said I was sorry you had made that remark about cheating to him this morning—you see, he would no doubt suppose you had heard the particulars of his gambling affair, and meant to insult him by what you said, and he has done this out of revenge. Oh, how I wish we were safely at home again ; shall we turn back now ? "

" Not for the world," said I—" you will find, when you know me better, that when I have undertaken a thing, I will go through with it—difficulties only make me more determined."

" Ah ! " said Coleman, " you should get somebody to write a book about you; that is the kind of disposition they always give to the heroes of novels, the sort of character that will go and run his head against a brick wall to prove that it is the harder and thicker of the two—they knock out their brains, though, sometimes in doing it, when they happen to have any—it is very pretty to read about, splendid in theory, but I much doubt its acting so well if you come to put it in practice."

" You may laugh at me if you please," replied I ; " but depend upon it, a man of energy and determination will undertake great deeds, ay, and perform them too, which your prudent, cautious character would have considered impossibilities."

" Perhaps it may be so," was the reply ; " I know I am not the sort of stuff they cut heroes out of—woa, Punch ! steady, old boy ; holloa, what ails him ? this is getting serious."

During this conversation, we had been gradually leaving the town behind us, and approaching the downs, and had arrived at a point where the road became a mere cart-track, and the open country lay spread for miles before us. Our two steeds, which had up to the present time conducted themselves with the greatest propriety, now began to show signs of excitement, and as the fresh air from the downs blew against their nostrils, they tossed their heads, snorted, and exchanged the quiet jog-trot pace at which we had been proceeding, for a dancing, sidelong motion, which somewhat disturbed Coleman's equanimity, and elicited from him the expressions above recorded. The road at the same time becoming uneven and full of ruts, we agreed to turn our horses' heads, and quit it for the more tempting pathway afforded by the greensward. No sooner, however, did Punch feel the change from the hard road to the soft elastic footing of the turf, than he proceeded to demonstrate his happiness by slightly elevating his heels, and popping his head down between his forelegs, thereby jerking the rein loose in Coleman's hand ; and, perceiving that his rider (who was fully employed in grasping the pommel of his saddle in order to preserve his seat) made no effort to check his vivacity, he indulged his high spirits still further by setting off at a brisk canter.

" Pull him in," cried I, " you'll have him run away with you; pull at him."

Whether my advice was acted upon or not I was unable to observe, as my whole attention was demanded by Mad Bess, who appeared at length resolved to justify the propriety of her appellation. Holding her in by means of the snaffle alone had been quite as much as I had been able to accomplish during the last ten minutes, and this escapade on the part of Punch brought the matter to a crisis. I must either allow her to follow him, i.e. to run away, or use the curb to prevent it. Seating myself, therefore, as firmly as I could, and gripping the saddle tightly with my knees, I took up the curb rein, which till now had been hanging loosely on the mare's neck, and gradually tightened it. This did not, for a moment, seem to produce any effect, but as soon as I drew the rein sufficiently tight to check her speed, she stopped short, and shook her head angrily. I attempted gently to urge her on—not a step except backwards would she stir—at length, in despair I touched her slightly with the spur, and then "the fiend within her woke," and proceeded to make up for lost time with a vengeance. The moment the mare felt the spur, she reared until she stood perfectly erect, and fought the air with her forelegs. Upon this I slackened the rein, and striking her over the ears with my riding-whip, brought her down again;—no sooner, however, had her forefeet touched the ground than she gave two or three violent plunges which nearly succeeded in unseating me, jerked down her head so suddenly as to loosen the reins from my grasp, kicked viciously several times, and seizing the cheek of the bit between her teeth so as to render it utterly useless (evidently an old trick of hers), sprang forward at a wild gallop. The pace at which we were going soon brought us alongside of Punch, who having thoroughly mastered his rider, considered it highly improper that any steed should imagine itself able to pass him, and therefore proceeded to emulate the pace of Mad Bess. Thereupon a short but very spirited race ensued, the cob's pluck enabling him to keep neck and neck for a few yards; but the mare was going at racing speed, and the length of her stride soon began to tell; Punch, too, showed signs of having nearly had enough of it. I therefore shouted to Coleman, as we were leaving them: " Keep his head up-hill, and you'll be able to pull him in directly." His answer was inaudible, but when I turned my head two or three minutes afterwards I was glad to see that he had followed my advice with complete success—Punch was standing still, about half a mile off, while his rider was apparently watching my course with looks of horror.

All anxiety on his account being thus at an end, I proceeded to take as calm a view of my own situation as circumstances would allow, in order to decide on the best means of extricating myself therefrom.

We had reached the top of the first range of hills I have described. and were now tearing at a fearful rate down the descent on the opposite side. It was clear that the mare could not keep up the pace at which she was going for any length of time: still she was in first-rate racing condition, not an ounce of superfluous flesh about her, and, though she must have gone more than two miles already, she appeared as fresh as when we started. I therefore cast my eyes around in search of some obstacle which might check her speed. The slope down which we were proceeding extended for about a mile before us, after which the ground again began to rise. In the valley between the two hills was a small piece of cultivated land, enclosed (as is usual in the district I am describing) within a low wall, built of flint-stones from the beach. Towards this I determined to guide the mare as well as I was able, in the hope that she would refuse the leap, in which case I imagined I might pull her in. The pace at which we were going soon brought us near the spot, when I was glad to perceive that the wall was a more formidable obstacle than I had at first imagined, being fully six feet high with a ditch in front of it. I therefore selected a place where the ditch seemed widest, got her head up by sawing her mouth with the snaffle, and put her fairly at it. No sooner did she perceive the obstacles before her, than, slightly moderating her pace, she appeared to collect herself, gathered her legs well under her, and rushing forward, cleared wall, ditch, and at least seven feet of ground beyond, with a leap like a deer, alighting safely with me on her back on the opposite side, where she continued her course with unabated vigour.

We had crossed the field (a wheat stubble) ere I had recovered from my astonishment at finding myself safe, after such a leap as I had most assuredly never dreamt of taking. Fortunately there was a low gate on the farther side, towards which I guided the mare, for though I could not check, I was in some measure able to direct her course. This time, however, she either did not see the impediment in her way, or despised it, as, without abating her speed, she literally rushed through the gate, snapping into shivers with her chest the upper bar, which was luckily rotten, and clearing the lower ones in her stride. The blow, and the splintered wood flying about her ears, appeared to frighten her afresh, and she tore up the opposite ascent, which was longer and steeper than the last, like a mad creature. I was glad to perceive, however, that the pace at which she had come, and the distance (which must have been several miles), were beginning to tell—her glossy coat was stained with sweat and dust, while her breath, drawn with short and laboured sobs, her heaving flanks, and the tremulous motion of her limbs, afforded convincing proofs that the struggle could not be protracted much longer. Still she continued to hold the bit between her teeth as firmly as though it were in a vice, rendering any attempt to pull her in utterly futile. We had now reached the crest of the hill, when I was not best pleased to perceive that the descent on the other side was much more precipitous than any I had yet met with. I endeavoured, therefore, to pull her head round, thinking it would be best to try and retrace our steps, but I soon found that it was useless to attempt it. The mare had now become wholly unmanageable; I could not guide her in the slightest degree; and, though she was evidently getting more and more exhausted, she still continued to gallop madly forwards, as though some demon had taken possession of her, and was urging her on to our common destruction. As we proceeded down the hill, our speed increased from the force of gravitation, till we actually seemed to fly—the wind appeared to shriek as it rushed past my ears, while from the rapidity with which we were moving, the ground seemed to glide from under us, till my head reeled so giddily that I was afraid I should fall from the saddle.

We had proceeded about half-way down the descent, when, on passing one or two stunted bushes which had concealed the ground beyond, I saw, oh, horror of horrors! what appeared to be the mouth of an old chalk-pit, stretching dark and unfathomable right across our path, about 300 yards before us. The mare perceives it when too late, attempts to stop, but from the impetus with which she is going, is unable to do so. Another moment and we shall be over the brink! With the energy of despair, I lifted her with the rein with both hands, and drove the spurs madly into her flanks;—she rose to the leap, there was a bound! a sensation of flying through the air! a crash! and I found myself stretched in safety on the turf beyond, and Mad Bess lying, panting, but uninjured, beside me.

To spring upon my feet, and seize the bridle of the mare, who had also by this time recovered her footing, was the work of a moment. I then proceeded to look around, in order to gain a more clear idea of the situation in which I was placed, in the hope of discovering the easiest method of extricating myself from it. Close behind me lay the chalk-pit, and as I gazed down its rugged sides, overgrown with brambles and rank weeds, I shuddered to think of the probable fate from which I had been so almost miraculously preserved, and turned away with a heartfelt expression of thanksgiving to Him who had mercifully decreed that the thread of my young life should not be snapped in so sudden and fearful a manner. Straight before me the descent became almost suddenly precipitous, but a little to the right I perceived a sort of sheep-track, winding downwards round the side of the hill. It was a self-evident fact that this must lead somewhere, and as all places were alike to me, so that they contained any human beings who were able and willing to direct me towards Helmstone, I determined to follow it. After walking about half a mile, Mad Bess (with her ears drooping, and her nose nearly touching the ground) following me as quietly as a dog, I was rejoiced by the sight of curling smoke, and on turning a corner, I came suddenly upon a little village green, around which some half-dozen cottages were scattered at irregular distances. I directed my steps towards one of these, before which a crazy sign, rendered by age and exposure to the weather as

delightfully vague and unintelligible as though it had come fresh from the brush of Turner himself, hung picturesquely from the branch of an old oak.

The sound of horse's feet attracted the attention of an elderly man, who appeared to combine in his single person the offices of ostler, waiter, and boots, and who, as soon as he became aware of my necessities, proceeded to fulfil the duties of these various situations with the greatest alacrity. First (as of the most importance in his eyes) he rubbed down Mad Bess, and administered some refreshment to her in the shape of hay and water; then he brought me a glass of ale, declaring it would do me good (in which, by the way, he was not far from right). He then brushed from my coat certain stains, which I had contracted in my fall, and finally told me my way to Helmstone. I now remounted Mad Bess, who, though much refreshed by the hay and water, still continued perfectly quiet and tractable; and setting off at a moderate trot, reached the town, after riding about eight miles, without any further adventure, in rather less than an hour.

As I entered the street in which Snaffles' stables were situated, I perceived Coleman and Lawless standing at the entrance of the yard, evidently awaiting my arrival. When I got near them, Coleman sprang eagerly forward to meet me, saying,—

" How jolly glad I am to see you safe again, old fellow ! I was so frightened about you. How did you manage to stop her ? "

" Why, Fairlegh, I had no idea you were such a rider," exclaimed Lawless; " I made up my mind you would break your neck, and old Sam be minus a pupil, when I heard you had gone out on that mare. You have taken the devil out of her somehow, and no mistake ; she's as quiet as a lamb," added he, patting her.

" You were very near being right," replied I ; " she did her best to break my neck and her own too, I can assure you."

I then proceeded to relate my adventures, to which both Lawless and Coleman listened with great attention; the former interrupting me every now and then with various expressions of commendation, and when I had ended, he shook me warmly by the hand, saying,—

" I give you great credit; you behaved in a very plucky manner all through ; I didn't think you had it in you; 'pon my word I didn't. I shall just tell Cumberland and Snaffles a bit of my mind, too. Here, Snaffles, you confounded old humbug, where are you ? "

" Oh, don't say anything to him," said I ; " it's never worth while being angry with people of that kind ; besides, Cumberland made him do it."

" That does not signify ; he knew the danger to which he was exposing you, perhaps better than Cumberland did. He had no business to do it, and I'll make him beg your pardon before we leave this yard. Here, you ostler fellow, where's your master ? " shouted Lawless, as he turned into the yard, where I soon heard the loud tones of his voice engaged in angry colloquy with Snaffles, whose replies were inaudible.

In a short time, the latter approached the spot where I was standing, and began a very long and humble apology, saying that he should never have thought of giving me the mare, if he had not seen at a glance that I was a first-rate rider, and much more to the same purpose, when Lawless interrupted him with,—

" There, cut it short ; Mr. Fairlegh does not want any more of your blarney ; and mind, if anything of the sort occurs again, I shall hire my horses somewhere else, and take care to let all my friends know why I do so. Now, let's be off ; it's getting near dinner-time."

So saying, he turned to leave the yard, a movement which, as soon as I had found my friend James, returned his spurs, and given him the promised half-crown, I proceeded to imitate ; and that ended the episode of Mad Bess.

CHAPTER VI.

LAWLESS GETS THOROUGHLY PUT OUT.

> . . " What 'tis
> To have a stranger come—
> It seems you know him not.
> No, sir ! not I."　　　　　　*Southey.*

> " Either forbear . . . or resolve you
> For more amazement ; if you can behold it,
> I'll make the statue move indeed."　　　*Winter's Tale.*

> " Since the youth will not be entreated, his own peril on his forwardness . . .
> You shall try but one fall.—*As You Like It.*

On reaching home, the door was opened by Thomas, who accosted us with,—

" Here's such a bit of fun, gentlemen ! The new pupil's arrived, and ain't he a rum un, jest ? Oh, I never ! "

" Why, how do you mean ? what's he like, then ? " asked Lawless.

" Oh, he's very well to look at, only he's as tall as a life-guardsman ; but he's sich a free and easy chap, and ain't he got a pretty good notion of making himself comfortable, too !—that's all. But come in, gents, you'll soon see what I mean. He chucked the flyman who brought him here half-a-guinea, and when I asked him if he did not want the change, for the fare was only half-a-crown, he merely said ' Pooh ! ' and told me not to talk, for it tired him."

With our feelings of curiosity somewhat excited by this account, we hastened into the pupil's room, anxious to behold the individual who had so greatly astonished Thomas.

Seated in Dr. Mildman's arm-chair, and with his legs resting upon two other chairs, so arranged as to form a temporary sofa, reclined a young man, apparently about eighteen, though his length of limb, and the almost herculean proportions of his chest and shoulders, seemed rather to belong to a more advanced age. He raised his head as we entered, disclosing a set of features which, in spite of an expression of languor and indifference, must have been pronounced unusually handsome. His complexion was a rich nut-brown; the high fore-head, white as snow, contrasting well with the dark hue of his hair, which, in short, clustering curls, harmonized well with the classical outline of his head, reminding one involuntarily of the young Antinous. The short curling upper-lip, and well-chiselled nostril, told a tale of pride and resolution, strongly at variance with the mild sleepy appearance of the large dark hazel eyes, to which the long silken lashes that shaded them imparted an almost feminine expres-sion. He did not attempt to alter his position as we approached, but, merely turning his head, gazed at us steadfastly for a moment, and then observed in a slow half-absent manner,—

"Oh, the other pupils, I suppose—how do you do, all of you?"

Lawless, who was foremost, was so much surprised, and so little pleased at this nonchalant style of address, that he made no reply, but turning on his heel, proceeded to leave the room, in order to divest himself of his hunting costume, muttering as he went. "Cool enough that, by Jove, eh!"

The duty of doing the polite having thus devolved upon Coleman, he winked at me by way of preliminary, and, making a low bow in the true dancing-master style, replied as follows :—

"Your penetration has not erred, Mr. Oaklands; we are the other pupils; and in answer to your obliging inquiries, I have much pleasure in informing you that we are all in perfect health and very tolerable spirits; and now, sir, in return for your kind condescension, allow me, in the absence of my superiors, to express a hope that you are feeling pretty comfortable—ahem!"

Having thus delivered himself, Coleman drew up his figure to its utmost height, and folding his arms with an air of pompous dignity, awaited an answer.

"Oh, yes, I'm comfortable enough," was the reply; "I always am; only I'm so done up, tired as a dog—the least thing fatigues me; I'm weak as a rat! Don't they give you sofas here, Mr. What's-your-name?"

"My name is Norval—I mean Coleman; my father divides his time between feeding his flocks on the Grampian Hills, and fleecing his clients in Lincoln's Inn; though I must confess that ever since I can remember, he has dropped the shepherd, and stuck to the solicitor, finding it pays best, I suppose. Regarding the sofa, we have not one at present, but Dr. Mildman went to town this morning; I did not till this moment know why. But now I see it all—he was doubtless aware you would arrive to-day, and finding he could not get a sufficiently comfortable sofa for you in Helmstone, he is gone to London on purpose to procure one. There is still time to write by the post, if there is any particular way in which you would like to have the stuffing arranged."

This speech made Oaklands raise his head, and look Coleman so fixedly in the face, with such a clear, earnest, penetrating gaze, that it appeared as if he would read his very soul. Having apparently satisfied himself, he smiled slightly, resumed his former attitude, and observed in the same half-sleepy tone,--

"No, I'll leave all that to him; I am not particular. What time do you dine here?"

I replied (for the look I have described seemed to have had the wonderful effect of silencing Coleman), "At five o'clock."

"Very good; and I believe there's a Mrs. Mildman, or some such person, is there not? I suppose one must dress? Will you be so kind as to tell the servant to bring some hot water, and to look out my things for me at a quarter before five. I hate to be obliged to hurry, it tires one so."

Having said this, he took up a book which was lying by his side, and murmuring something about "talking being so fatiguing," soon became buried in its contents.

Whilst I was dressing for dinner, Lawless came into my room, and told me that he had been speaking to Cumberland with regard to the way in which he had behaved to me about the mare, and that Cumberland professed himself exceedingly sorry that the affair had so nearly turned out a serious one, declaring he meant it quite as a joke, never expecting that when I saw the mare, I should venture to mount her.

"So you see," continued Lawless, "he merely wanted to have a good laugh at you—nothing more. It was a thoughtless thing to do, but not so bad as you had fancied it, by any means."

"Well," replied I, "as he says so, I am bound to believe him; but his manner certainly gave me the impression that he intended me to ride her. He went the right way to make me do so, at all events, by hinting that I was afraid."

"Ah! he could not know that by intuition, you see," said Lawless; "he thought, I dare say, as I did, that you were a mere molly-coddle, brought up at your mother's apron-string, and had not pluck enough in you to do anything sporting."

"It's not worth saying anything more about," replied I; "it will never happen again; I am very much obliged to you, though."

"Oh, that's nothing," said Lawless; "if Cumberland had really meant to break your neck, I should have fallen out with him; that would have been too much of a good thing : however, as it is it's all right."

And so the conversation ended, though I felt far from satisfied in my own mind as to the innocence of Cumberland's intentions.

On reaching the drawing-room, I found the whole party assembled with the exception of Mr. Henry Oaklands, who had not yet made his appearance. At the moment of my entrance, Mrs. Mildman, who had not seen the new arrival, and who, like the rest of her sex, was somewhat curious, was examining Coleman (who stood bolt upright before her, with his hands behind him, looking like a boy saying his lesson), as to his manners and appearance.

" Very tall, and dark hair and large eyes," continued Mrs. Mildman ; " why, he must be very handsome."

" He seems as if he were half asleep," observed I.

" Not always," said Coleman; " did you see the look he gave me ? he seemed wide awake enough then ; I thought he was going to eat me."

" Dear me ! why, he must be quite a cannibal ! besides, I don't think you would be at all nice to eat, Mr. Coleman," said Mrs. Mildman, with a smile.

" Horrid, nasty, I'm sure," muttered Mullins, who was seated on the very edge of his chair, and looked thoroughly uncomfortable, as was his wont in anything like civilized society.

At this moment the door opened, and Oaklands entered. If one had doubted about his height before, when lying on the chairs, the question was set at rest the instant he was seen standing : he must have measured at least six feet two inches, though the extreme breadth of his chest and shoulders, and the graceful setting-on of his finely-formed head, together with the perfect symmetry and proportion of his limbs, prevented his appearing too tall. He went through the ceremony of introduction with the greatest ease and self-possession ; and though he infused rather more courtesy into his manner towards Mrs. Mildman than he had taken the trouble to bestow on us, his behaviour was still characterized by the same indolence and listlessness I had previously noticed, and which indeed seemed part and parcel of himself. Having bowed slightly to Cumberland and Lawless, he seated himself very leisurely on the sofa by Mrs. Mildman's side, altering one of the pillows so as to make himself thoroughly comfortable as he did so. Having settled it to his satisfaction, he addressed Mrs. Mildman with,—

" What a very fatiguing day this has been ; haven't you found it so ? "

" No, I can't say I have," was the reply ; " I dare say it was warm travelling : I'm afraid, in that case, Dr. Mildman will not have a very pleasant journey—he's gone to town to-day."

" Ah, so that short, stout, young gentleman " (the first two adjectives he pronounced very slowly and distinctly) " told me."

" Mr. Coleman," insinuated Mrs. Mildman.

" Pleasant that," whispered Coleman to me.

" Take care," replied I, " he will hear you."

" I'm afraid," continued Oaklands, " the old gentleman will be quite knocked up. I wonder he does not make two days' journey of it."

" Dr. Mildman is not so very old," observed Mrs. Mildman, in rather an annoyed tone of voice.

"I really beg pardon, I scarcely know why I said it," replied Oaklands, "only I somehow fancied all tutors were between sixty and seventy—very absurd of me! My father sent all kind of civil messages to the o— to Dr. Mildman, only it is so much trouble to remember that sort of thing."

At this point the conversation was interrupted by the announcement of dinner. Oaklands (from whom I could not withdraw my eyes, so unlike anything I had ever met with before was he) was evidently preparing to hand Mrs. Mildman down to dinner, as soon as he could summon sufficient energy to move, but perceiving Cumberland approach her for that purpose, he appeared to recollect himself, smiled slightly, as if at what he had been about to do, and taking me by the arm, said,—

"Come, Master Curlylocks, you shall be my lady, and a very pretty girl you would make, too, if you were properly be-muslined;" adding, as we went downstairs together, "You and I shall be great friends, I'm sure; I like your face particularly. What a lot of stairs there are in this house! they'll tire me to death."

When we returned to the pupils' room after dinner, Lawless found, lying on the table, the note Dr. Mildman had written in such a mysterious manner before he left home in the morning, and proceeded to open it forthwith. Scarcely had he glanced his eye over it, when he was seized with so violent a fit of laughter, that I expected every moment to see him fall out of his chair. As soon as he had in some measure recovered the power of speaking, he exclaimed,—

"Here, listen to this! and tell me if it is not the very best thing you ever heard in your lives."

He then read as follows :—

"It is not without much pain that I bring myself to write this note; but I feel that I should not be doing my duty towards your excellent father, if I were to allow such extreme misconduct on the part of his son to pass unreproved. I know not towards what scene of vulgar dissipation you might be directing your steps, but the simple fact (to which I was myself witness) of your leaving my house in the low disguise of a carter's smock-frock affords in itself sufficient proof that your associates must belong to a class of persons utterly unfitted for the companionship of a gentleman. Let me hope this hint may be enough, and that conduct so thoroughly disgraceful in one brought up as you have been, may not occur again. I presume I need scarcely say that, in the event of your disregarding my wishes upon this point, the only course left open to me would be to expel you, a measure to which it would deeply grieve me to be obliged to resort."

His voice was here drowned by a chorus of laughter from all present who were aware of the true state of the case, which lasted without interruption for several minutes. At length Lawless observed,—

" I'll tell you what, it will be a death-blow to Smithson ; a macintosh made by him to be taken for a smock-frock! he'll never recover it."

" Mildman might well look like a thunder-cloud," said Coleman, " if that was the notion he had got in his head ; what a jolly lark, to be sure ! "

" How do you mean to undeceive him ? " inquired Cumberland.

" Oh, trust me for finding a way to do that," replied Lawless ; " ' the low disguise of a carter's smock-frock,' indeed ! What fun it would be if he were to meet my governor in town to-day, and tell him of my evil courses ! why, the old boy would go into fits ! 1 wonder what he means by his ' scenes of vulgar dissipation ' ? I dare say he fancies me playing all-fours with a beery coal-heaver, and kissing his sooty-faced wife ; or drinking alternate goes of gin-and-water with a dustman, for the purpose of insinuating myself into the affections of Miss Cinderella Smut, his interesting sister. By Jove ! it's as good as a play ! "

More laughter followed Lawless's illustration of Dr. Mildman's note. The subject was discussed for some time, and a plan arranged for enlightening the Doctor as to the true character of the mysterious garment.

At length there was a pause, when I heard Coleman whisper to Lawless,—

" Thomas was pretty right in saying that new fellow knows how to make himself comfortable, at all events."

" He's a precious deal too free and easy to please me," muttered Lawless, in an undertone ; " I shall take the liberty of seeing whether his self-possession cannot be disturbed a little. I have no notion of such airs. Here, Mullins ! "

And laying hold of Mullins by the arm, he pulled him into a chair by his side and proceeded to give him some instructions in a whisper. The subject of their remarks, Harry Oaklands, who had, on re-entering the room, taken possession of the three chairs near the window, was still reclining, book in hand, in the same indolent position, apparently enjoying the beauty of the autumnal sunset, without concerning himself in the slightest degree about anything which might be going on inside the room.

Lawless, whose proceedings I was watching with an anxious eye, having evidently succeeded, by a judicious mixture of bullying and cajolery, in persuading Mullins to assist him in whatever he was about to attempt, now drew a chair to the other side of the window, and seated himself exactly opposite to Oaklands.

" How tired riding makes a fellow ! I declare I'm regularly baked, used completely up," he observed, and then continued, glancing at Oaklands, " Not such a bad idea, that. Mullins, give us a chair ; I don't see why elevating the extremities should not pay in my case, as well as in other people's."

He then placed his legs across the chair which Mullins brought him. and folding his arms so as exactly to imitate the attitude of his opposite neighbour, sat for some minutes gazing out of the window with a countenance of mock solemnity. Finding this did not produce any effect on Oaklands, who having slightly raised his eyes when Lawless first seated himself, immediately cast them upon the book again, Lawless stretched himself, yawned, and once more addressed Mullins.

"Shocking bad sunset as ever I saw—it's no go staring at that. I must have a book—give me the Byron."

To this Mullins replied "that he believed Mr. Oaklands was reading it."

"Indeed! the book belongs to you, does it not?"

Mullins replied in the affirmative.

"Have you any objection to lend it to me?"

Mullins would be most happy to do so.

"Then ask the gentleman to give it to you—you have a right to do what you please with your own property, I imagine?"

It was very evident that this suggestion was not exactly agreeable to Mullins; and although his habitual fear of Lawless was so strong as completely to overpower any dread of what might be the possible consequences of his act, it was not without much hesitation that he approached Oaklands and asked him for the book, "as he wished to lend it to Lawless."

On hearing this, Oaklands leisurely turned to the fly-leaf, and having apparently satisfied himself, by the perusal of the name written thereon, that it really belonged to Mullins, handed it to him without a word. I fancied, however, from the stern expression of his mouth, and a slight contraction of the brow, that he was not as insensible to their impertinence as he wished to appear.

Lawless, who had been sitting during this little scene with his eyes closed, as if asleep, now roused himself, and saying. "Oh, you have got it at last, have you?" began turning over the pages, reading aloud a line or two here and there, while he kept up a running commentary on the text as he did so,—

"Hum! ha! now let's see, here we are—the 'G-I-A-O-U-R,'—that's a nice word to talk about. What does G-I-A-O-U-R spell, Mullins? You don't know? what an ass you are, to be sure!—

> 'Fair clime, whose every season smiles
> Benignant o'er those blessed isles '—

blessed isles, indeed; what stuff!—

> ''Tis Greece, but living Greece no more '—

that would do for a motto for the barbers to stick on their pots of bears' grease!—

> 'Clime of the unforgotten brave;'

unforgotten! yes, I should think so; how the deuce should they be forgotten, when one is bored with them morning, noon, and night, for everlasting, by old Sam, and all the other pastors and masters in the kingdom ? Hang me, if I can read this trash ; the only poetry that ever was written worth reading is ' Don Juan.' "

He then flung the book down, adding,—

" It's confoundedly cold, I think. Mullins, shut that window."

This order involved more difficulties in its execution than might a first be imagined. Oaklands, after giving up the book, had slightly altered his position by drawing nearer the window and leaning his elbow on the sill, so that it was impossible to shut it without obliging him to move. Mullins saw this, and seemed for a moment inclined not to obey, but a look and a threatening gesture from Lawless again decided him ; and with slow unwilling steps he approached the window, and laid his hand on it, for the purpose of shutting it. As he did so, Oaklands raised his head, and regarded him for a moment with a glance like lightning, his large eyes glaring in the twilight like those of some wild animal, while the red flush of anger rose to his brow, and we all expected to see him strike Mullins to the ground. Conquering himself, however, by a powerful effort of self-control, he folded his arms, and turning from the window, suffered Mullins to close it without interruption. Still I could perceive, from the distended nostril and quivering lip, that his forbearance was almost exhausted.

" Ah, that's an improvement," said Lawless ; " I was getting uncommonly chilly. By the way, what an interesting virtue patience is ! it is a curious fact in Natural History that some of the lower animals share it with us ; for instance, there's nothing so patient as a jack-ass—"

" Except a pig," put in Mullins ; "they're uncommon—"

" Obstinate," suggested Coleman.

" Oh, ah ; it's obstinate I mean," replied Mullins. " Well, you know donkeys are obstinate, like a pig ; that's what I meant."

" Don't be a fool !" said Lawless. " Deuce take these chairs ; I cannot make myself comfortable anyhow—the fact is, I must have three, that's the proper number—give me another, Mullins."

" I can't find one," was the answer ; "they are all in use."

" Can't find one ! nonsense," said Lawless ; " here, take one of these ; the gentleman is asleep, and won't object, I dare say."

When Mullins was shutting the window, his head had been so turned as to prevent his observing the symptoms of anger in Oaklands, which had convinced me that he would not bear trifling with much longer. Presuming therefore, from the success of his former attacks, that the new pupil was a person who might be insulted with impunity, and actuated by that general desire of retaliation, which is the certain effect bullying produces upon a mean disposition, Mullins proceeded, con amore, to fulfil Lawless's injunction. With a sudden snatch, he withdrew the centre chair, on which Oaklands' legs mainly rested, so violently as nearly to throw them to the ground, a catastrophe which was finally consummated by Lawless giving the other chair a push with his foot, so that it was only by great exertion and quickness that Oaklands was able to save himself from falling.

This was the climax ; forbearance merely human could endure no longer : Lawless had obtained his object of disturbing Harry Oaklands' self-possession, and was now to learn the consequences of his success. With a bound like that of an infuriated tiger, Oaklands leaped upon his feet, and dashing Mullins into a corner with such force that he remained lying exactly where he fell, he sprang upon Lawless, seized him by the collar of his coat, and after a short but severe struggle, dragged him to the window, which was about eight feet from the ground, threw it open, and taking him in his arms with as much ease as if he had been a child, flung him out. He then returned to the corner in which, paralyzed with fear, Mullins was still crouching, drew him to the spot from whence he had removed the chair, placed him there upon his hands and knees, and saying in a stern voice, " If you dare to move till I tell you, I'll throw you out of the window too," quietly resumed his former position, with his legs resting upon Mullins' back instead of a chair.

As soon as Coleman and I had in some degree recovered from our surprise and consternation (for the anger of Oaklands, once roused, was a fearful thing to behold), we ran to the other window, just in time to see Lawless, who had alighted among some stunted shrubs, turn round and shake his fists at Oaklands (who merely smiled), ere he regained his feet, and rang the bell in order to gain admittance. A minute afterwards we heard him stride upstairs, enter his bedroom, and close the door with a most sonorous bang. Affairs remained in this position nearly a quarter of a hour, no one feeling inclined to be the first to speak. At length the silence was broken by Oaklands, who, addressing himself to Cumberland, said,—

" I am afraid this absurd piece of business has completely marred the harmony of the evening. Get up, Mr. Mullins," he continued, removing his legs, and assisting him to rise ; " I hope I did not hurt you just now."

In reply to this, Mullins grumbled out something intended as a negative, and shambling across the room, placed himself in a corner, as far as possible from Oaklands, where he sat rubbing his knees, the very image of sulkiness and terror. Cumberland, who appeared during the whole course of the affair absorbed in a book, though, in fact, not a single word or look had escaped him, now came forward and apologized, in a quiet, gentlemanly manner (which, when he was inclined, no one could assume with greater success), for Lawless's impertinence, which had only, he said, met with its proper reward.

" You must excuse me, Mr. Cumberland, if I cannot agree with you," replied Oaklands ; " since I have had time to cool a little, I see the matter in quite a different light. Mr. Lawless was perfectly right ; the carelessness of my manner must naturally have seemed as if I were purposely giving myself airs, but I can assure you such was not the case."

He paused for a moment, and then continued, with a half-embarrassed smile,—

"The fact is, I am afraid that I have been spoiled at home; my mother died when I was a little child, and my dear father, having nobody else to care about, thought, I believe, that there was no one in the world equal to me, and that nothing was too good for me. Of course, all our servants and people have taken their tone from him, so that I have never had anyone to say to me, 'Nay,' and am therefore not at all used to the sort of thing. I hope I do not often lose my temper as I have done this evening; but really Mr. Lawless appears quite an adept in the art of ingeniously tormenting."

"I am afraid you must have found so much exertion very fatiguing," observed Coleman, politely.

"A fair hit, Mr. Coleman," replied Oaklands, laughing. "No! those are not the things that tire me, somehow; but in general I am very easily knocked up—I am indeed—most things are so much trouble, and I hate trouble; I suppose it is that I am not strong."

"Wretchedly weak, I should say," rejoined Coleman; "it struck me that you were so just now, when you chucked Lawless out of the window like a cat."

"Be quiet, Freddy," said Cumberland, reprovingly.

"Nay, don't stop him," said Oaklands; "I delight in a joke beyond measure, when I have not the trouble of making it myself. But about this Mr. Lawless, I am exceedingly sorry that I handled him so roughly; would you mind going to tell him so, Mr. Cumberland, and explaining that I did not mean anything offensive by my manner?"

"Exactly, I'll make him understand the whole affair, and bring him down with me in five minutes," said Cumberland, leaving the room as he spoke.

"What makes Cumberland so good-natured and amiable to-night?" whispered I to Coleman.

"Can't you tell?" was the reply. "Don't you see that Oaklands is a regular top-sawyer, a fish worth catching; and that by doing this Cumberland places him under an obligation at first starting? Not a bad move to begin with, eh? Besides, if a regular quarrel between Lawless and Oaklands were to ensue, Cumberland would have to take one side or the other; and it would not exactly suit him to break with Lawless, he knows too much about him; besides," added he, sinking his voice, "he owes him money, more than I should like to owe anybody a precious deal, I can tell you. Now do you twig?"

"Yes," said I, "I comprehend the matter more clearly, if that is what you mean by twigging; but how shocking it all is! why, Cumberland is quite a swindler—gambling, borrowing money he can't pay, and—"

"Hush!" interrupted Coleman, "here they come."

Coleman was not mistaken: Cumberland had been successful in his embassy, and now entered the room, accompanied by Lawless

E

who looked rather crestfallen, somewhat angry, and particularly
embarrassed and uncomfortable, which, as Coleman whispered to me,
was not to be wondered at, considering how thoroughly he had been
put out just before. Oaklands, however, appeared to see nothing of
all this; but, rising from his seat as they entered, he approached
Lawless, saying,—

"This has been a foolish piece of business, Mr. Lawless; I freely
own that I am thoroughly ashamed of the part I have taken in it,
and I can only apologize for the intemperate manner in which I
behaved."

The frank courtesy with which he said this was so irresistible that
Lawless was completely overcome, and, probably for the first time in
his life, felt himself thoroughly in the wrong. Seizing Oaklands'
hand, therefore, and shaking it heartily, he replied,—

"I'll tell you what it is, Oaklands we don't 'Mr.' each other here
—you are a right good fellow—a regular brick, and no mistake; and
as to your shoving me out of the window, you served me quite right
for my abominable impertinence. I only wonder you did not do it
ten minutes sooner, that's all; but you really ought to be careful
what you do with those arms of yours; I was like a child in your
grasp; you are as strong as a steam-engine."

"I can assure you I am not," replied Oaklands; "they never let me
do anything at home, for fear I should knock myself up."

"You are more likely to knock other people down, I should say,"
rejoined Lawless; "and, by the way, that reminds me - Mullins!
come here, stupid, and beg Mr. Oaklands' pardon, and thank him for
knocking you down."

A sulky, half-muttered "Shan't" was the only reply.

"Nay, I don't want anything of that kind; I don't, indeed,
Lawless; pray leave him alone," cried Oaklands, eagerly.

But Lawless was not so easily quieted, and Oaklands, unwilling to
risk the harmony so newly established between them, did not choose
to interfere further; so Mullins was dragged across the room by the
ears, and was forced by Lawless, who stood over him with the poker
(which, he informed him, he was destined to eat red-hot if he became
restive), to make Oaklands a long and formal apology, with a short
form of thanksgiving appended, for the kindness and condescension
he had evinced in knocking him down so nicely, of which oration he
delivered himself with a very bad grace indeed.

"And all went merry as a marriage-bell," until we were summoned
to the drawing-room, where we were regaled with weak tea, thin
bread and butter, and small conversation till ten o'clock, when Mrs.
Mildman proceeded to read prayers, which, being a duty she was
little accustomed to, and which consequently rendered her extremely
nervous, she did not accomplish without having twice called King
William, George, and suppressed our gracious Queen Adelaide
altogether.

CHAPTER VII.

THE BOARD OF GREEN CLOTH.

" What have we here—a man or a fish ? "
                                The Tempest.

" The devil he baited a trap,
  With billiard balls and a cue ;
  And he chose as marker,
  An imp much darker
Than all the rest in hue.
And he put on his Sunday clothes,
And he played with saint and with sinner,
  For he'd found out a way
  To make the thing pay.
And when losing, he *still was the winner !* "
                                Old Legend.

THE moment Dr. Mildman arrived at home the next day, Lawless watched him into his study, and, as soon as he was safely lodged therein, proceeded, by the aid of sundry nails and loops previously placed there for the purpose, to hang his macintosh right across the passage, so that no one could leave the study without running against it. He then ambushed himself near the open door of the pupils' room, where, unseen himself, he could observe the effect of his arrangements. Coleman and I, also taking a lively interest in the event, ensconced ourselves in a favourable position for seeing and hearing. After waiting till our stock of patience was nearly exhausted, we were rewarded by hearing the study door slowly open, followed by the tread of a well-known footstep in the passage. The next sound that reached our ears was a quick shuffling of feet upon the oil-cloth, as if the person advancing had " shyed " at some unexpected object ; then came the muttered exclamation, " Bless my heart, what's this ? " And immediately afterwards Dr. Mildman's face, wearing an expression of the most thorough perplexity and bewilderment, appeared cautiously peeping from behind the macin-tosh. Having apparently satisfied himself that no enemy was concealed there, and he had nothing further to fear, but that the whole plot was centred as it were in the mysterious garment before him, he set himself seriously to work to examine it. First he pulled out his eyeglass and, stepping back a pace or two, took a general survey of the whole ; he then approached it again, and taking hold of it in different places with his hand, examined it in detail so closely that it seemed as if he were trying to count the number of threads. Being apparently unwilling in so difficult an investigation to trust to the evidence of any one sense, he replaced his eyeglass in his waist-coat pocket, and began rubbing a portion of the skirt' between his hands ; the sense of touch failing, however, to throw any new light upon the subject, as a sort of forlorn hope, he applied his nose to it.

The result of this was an indescribable exclamation, expressive of intense disgust, followed immediately by a violent sneeze; then came a long pause, as though he were considering of what possible use such a garment could be. At length a ray of light seemed to break in upon the darkness, and once more laying hands on the macintosh, he proceeded, after unhooking it from the nails on which it hung, slowly and deliberately to put it on, with the back part foremost, somewhat after the fashion of a child's pinafore. Having at length accomplished this difficult operation, he walked, or rather shuffled (for his petticoats interfered greatly with the free use of his limbs), up and down the hall with a grave, not to say solemn, expression of countenance. Appearing perfectly satisfied after one or two turns that he had at last solved the enigma, he divested himself of the perplexing garment, hung it on a peg appropriated to great-coats, and approached the door of the pupils' room.

By the time he entered, Lawless was seated at his desk studying Herodotus, while Coleman and I were deeply immersed in our respective Euclids.

After shaking hands with Oaklands, and addressing some good-natured remarks to each of us in turn, he went up to Lawless, and, laying his hand kindly on his shoulder, said, with a half-smile.—

" I am afraid I have made rather an absurd mistake about that strange garment of yours, Lawless ; I suppose it is some new kind of great-coat, is it not ? "

" Yes, sir, it is a sort of waterproof cloth, made with Indian rubber."

" Indian rubber, is it ? Well, I fancied so; it has not the nicest smell in the world. I certainly thought it was a smock-frock, though, when I saw you go out in it. Is not it rather awkward to walk in ? I found it so when I tried it on just now, and buttoning behind does not seem to me at all a good plan."

" No sir, but it is meant to button in front; perhaps you put it on the back part foremost."

" Hem ! " said Dr. Mildman, trying to look as if he thought such a thing impossible, and failing—" it is a very singular article of dress altogether, but I am glad it was not a smock-frock you went out in. I hope," continued he, turning to Oaklands, with an evident wish to change the conversation—" I hope they took good care of you when you arrived last night ? "

This was turning the tables with a vengeance ! Lawless became suddenly immersed in Herodotus again.

" Oh, the greatest," was the reply ; " I had so much attention paid me that I was almost upset by it. I was not quite overcome, though," he continued, with a sly glance towards Lawless, " and Mrs. Mildman gave us some very nice tea, which soon restored me."

" Well, I'm glad they managed to make you comfortable among them," observed Dr. Mildman, turning over his papers and books preparatory to beginning the morning's study.

" Hadn't you better ask him when he expects the sofa will be down ? " suggested Coleman to Oaklands, in a whisper.

" No, you jackanapes," was the reply ; " and don't you make me laugh when that old gentleman is in the room, for there's nothing more fatiguing than the attempt to smother a laugh."

Coleman's only answer to this, if answer it could be called, was a grimace, which had the desired effect of throwing Oaklands into a fit of laughter, which he found it very hard labour indeed to stifle ; nor had his countenance quite recovered from the effects of his exertions, when he was summoned to the Doctor's table to undergo an examination similar to that which had appeared so formidable to me a few days before ; and thus terminated the notable adventure of the carter's frock, though I observed that after a week or two had elapsed, the macintosh was handed over to Thomas, and Smithson was called upon to tax his inventive powers to furnish Lawless with a less questionably-shaped garment of the same material.

A few days after this, as I was walking with Coleman, he suddenly exclaimed,—

" Well, of all the antediluvian affairs I ever beheld, the old fellow now coming towards us is the queerest ; he looks like a fossil edition of Methuselah, dug up and modernized some hundred years ago at the very least. Holloa ! he's going mad, I believe ; I hope he does not bite."

The subject of these somewhat uncomplimentary remarks was a little old gentleman in a broad-brimmed white hat, turned up with green, and a black cloth spencer (an article much like a boy's jacket exaggerated), from beneath which protruded the very broad tails of a blue coat, with rather more than their proper complement of bright brass buttons, while drab gaiters and shorts completed the costume.

The moment, however, I beheld the countenance of the individual in question, I recognized the never-to-be-mistaken mole at the tip of the nose of my late coach companion to London. The recognition seemed mutual, for no sooner did he perceive me than he stopped short, and pointed straight at me with a stout silver-mounted bamboo which he held in his hand, uttering a sonorous " Umph ! " as he did so ; to which somewhat unusual mode of salutation may be attributed Coleman's doubts as to his sanity.

" Who'd ever have thought of meeting you at Helmstone, I should like to know ? " exclaimed he in a tone of astonishment.

" I was going to say the same thing to you, sir," replied I : " I came down here the very day on which we travelled together."

" Umph ! I came the next ; well, and what are you doing now you are here ? Schoolmaster lives here, I suppose—tutor, you call him, though, don't you ? "

I informed him of my tutor's name and residence, when he continued,—

" Umph ! I know him ; very good man, too good to be plagued by

a set of tiresome boys—men, though, you call yourselves, don't you?
Umph! Is he a man too?" he inquired, pointing to Coleman

" I've been a man these seventeen years, sir," replied Coleman.

"Umph, a man seventeen years ago! a baby, more likely: what
does he mean? what does he mean?"

I explained that he probably intended a pun upon his name, which
was Coleman.

"A pun, umph! He makes puns, does he? funny boy, funny boy,
I dare say. How does the doctor like that, though? Make puns to
him, he'd punish you, umph? Stupid things, puns—made one
myself then, though—just like me! Well, give the doctor my compliments—Mr. Frampton's I live at No. 10, Castle Street—he knows
me; and ask him to let you come and dine with me next week; bring
funny boy too, if he likes to come; " and away he posted, muttering,
"Umph! plaguing myself about a pack of boys, when I might be
quiet—just like me!"

We did not fail to deliver Mr. Frampton's message to Dr. Mildman on our return home, who willingly gave us the required
permission, saying that he knew but little of the old gentleman
personally, though he had resided for several years at Helmstone,
but that he was universally respected, in spite of his eccentricities,
and was reported to have spent great part of his life abroad. The
next time I met my new friend, he repeated his invitation to
Coleman and myself, and, on the day appointed, gave us an excellent
dinner, with quite as much wine as we knew what to do with;
amused and interested us with sundry well-told anecdotes of
adventures he had met with during his residence in foreign lands,
and dismissed us at nine o'clock with a tip of a guinea each,
and an injunction to come and see him again whenever we
pleased.

For many succeeding weeks nothing of any particular moment
occurred to interrupt the even tenor of the new course of life I had
entered upon. The liking which Oaklands seemed to have taken to
me at first sight soon ripened into a warm friendship, which
continued daily to increase on my part, as the many noble and
lovable qualities of his disposition appeared, one by one, from behind
the veil of indolence which, till one knew him well, effectually
concealed them. Coleman, though too volatile to make a real friend
of, was a very agreeable companion, and, if it were ever possible to
get him to be serious for a minute, showed that beneath the frivolity
of his manner lay a basis of clear good sense and right feeling, which
only required calling forth to render him a much higher character
than he appeared at present. For the rest, I was alternately bullied
and patronized by Lawless (though he never ventured on the former
line of conduct when Oaklands was present), while Cumberland, out-
wardly professing great regard for me, never let slip an opportunity
of showing me an ill-natured turn, when he could contrive to do so
without committing himself openly.

A more intimate acquaintance with Mullins only served to place beyond a doubt the fact of his being a most unmitigated, and not over-amiable, fool. The word is a strong one, but I fear that, if I were to use a milder term, it would be at the expense of truth.

For my tutor I soon began to conceive the warmest feelings of regard and esteem ; in fact, it was impossible to know him well, and not to love him. Simple as a child in everything relating to worldly matters, he united the deepest learning to the most elevated piety, while the thoroughly practical character of his religion, carried, as it was, into all the minor details of everyday life, imparted a gentleness and benignity to his manner which seemed to elevate him above the level of ordinary mortals. If he had a fault (I suppose, merely for the sake of proving him human, I must allow him one), it was a want of moral courage, which made it so disagreeable to him to find fault with any of us, that he would now and then allow evils to exist which a little more firmness and decision might have prevented ; but had it not been for this, he would have been quite perfect, and perfection is a thing not to be met with in this life.

Cumberland, after the eventful evening on which he acted as peacemaker between Lawless and Oaklands, had persevered steadily in his endeavour to ingratiate himself with the latter; and, by taking advantage of his weak point, his indolence and dislike of trouble, had at length succeeded in making Oaklands believe him essential to his comfort. Thus, though there was not the smallest sympathy between them, a sort of alliance was established, which gave Cumberland exactly the opportunities he required for putting into execution certain schemes which he had formed. Of what these schemes consisted, and how far they succeeded, will appear in the course of this veracious history.

The winter months, after favouring us with rather more than our due allowance of frost and snow, had at length passed away, and March, having come in like a lion, appeared determined, after the fashion of Bottom the weaver, " to roar that it would do any man's heart good to hear him," and to kick up a thorough dust ere he would condescend to go out like a lamb, albeit, in the latter state, he might have made a shilling per pound of himself at any market, had he felt suicidally inclined.

" This will never do," said Oaklands to me, as, for the third time, we were obliged to turn round and cover our eyes, to avoid being blinded by the cloud of dust which a strong east wind was driving directly in our faces ; " there is nothing in the world tires one like walking against a high wind. A quarter to three," added he, taking out his watch. " I have an appointment at three o'clock. Will you walk with me? I must turn up here."

I assented ; and, turning a corner, we proceeded up a narrow street, where the houses, in a great measure, protected us from the wind. After walking some little distance in silence, Oaklands again addressed me,—

" Frank, did you ever play at billiards ? "

I replied in the negative.

" It's a game I've rather a liking for," continued he ; " we have a table at Heathfield, and my father and I often played when the weather was too bad to get out. I used to beat the old gentleman easily though at last, till I found out one day he did not half like it, so then I was obliged to make shocking mistakes, every now and then, to give him a chance of winning ; anybody else would have found me out in a minute, for I am the worst hand in the world at playing the hypocrite, but my father is the most unsuspicious creature breathing. Oh, he is such a dear old man ! You must come and stay with us, Frank, and learn to know him and love him—he'd delight in you— you are just the sort of fellow he likes."

" There's nothing I should like better," answered I, " if I can get leave from headquarters ; but why did you want to know if I played at billiards ? "

" Oh, I have been playing a good deal lately with Cumberland, who seems very fond of the game, and I'm going to meet him at the rooms in F—— Street to-day ; so I thought, if you knew anything of the game, you might like to come with me."

" Cumberland is a first-rate player, isn't he ? " asked I.

" No, I do not think so ; we play very evenly, I should say ; but we are to have a regular match to-day, to decide which is the best player."

" Do you play for money ? "

" Just a trifle to give an interest to the game, nothing more," replied Oaklands ; " our match to-day is for a five-pound note."

I must confess that I could not help feeling extremely uneasy at the information Oaklands had just given me. The recollection of what Coleman had said concerning some gaming affair in which Cumberland was supposed to have behaved dishonourably, combined with a sort of general notion, which seemed to prevail, that he was not exactly a safe person to have much to do with, might in some degree account for this ; still, I always felt a kind of distinctive dislike and mistrust of Cumberland, which led me to avoid him as much as possible on my own account. In the present instance, when the danger seemed to threaten my friend, this feeling assumed a vague character of fear ; " and yet," reasoned I with myself, " what is there to dread ? Oaklands has plenty of money at his command ; besides, he says they play pretty evenly, so that he must win nearly as often as Cumberland ; then he is older than I am. and of course must be better able to judge what is right or wrong for him to do." However, remembering the old adage, that " lookers-on see most of the game," I determined, for once, to accompany him ; I therefore told him that, though I could not play myself, it would be an amuse- ment to me to watch them, and that, if he had no objection, I would go with him, to which proposition he willingly agreed. As we turned into F—— Street, we were joined by Cumberland, who, as I fancied, did not seem best pleased at seeing me, nor did the scowl which passed across his brow, on hearing I was to accompany them, tend to lessen this impression. He did not, however, attempt to make any opposition to the plan, merely remarking that, as I did not play myself, he thought I should find it rather dull. After proceeding about half-way down the street, Cumberland stopped in front of a small cigar shop, and, turning towards a private door, on which was a brass plate with the word "Billiards" engraved on it, knocked, and was admitted. Leading the way up a dark, narrow staircase, he opened a green baize door at the top, and ushered us into a tolerably large room, lighted by a skylight, immediately under which stood the billiard-table. On one side was placed a rack, containing a formidable arrangement of cues, maces, etc., while at the farther end two small dials, with a brass hand in the centre for the purpose of marking the scores of the different players, were fixed against the wall. As we entered, two persons who were apparently performing certain intricate manœuvres with the balls by way of practice, immediately left off playing and came towards us. One of these, a little man, with small keen gray eyes, and a quick, restless manner, which involuntarily reminded one of a hungry rat, rejoiced in the name of "Slipsey," and proved to be the billiard-marker; his companion was a tall stout personage, with a very red face, rather handsome features, large white teeth, and a profusion of bushy whiskers, moustaches, and imperial of a dark-brown colour. His dress consisted of a blue military frock-coat, which he wore open, to display a crimson plush waistcoat, and thick gold watch-chain, while his costume was completed by a pair of black and white plaid trousers, made in the extreme of the fashion, with a broad stripe down the outside of the leg. This personage swaggered up to Cumberland, and with a manner composed of impertinent familiarity and awkwardness, addressed him as follows,—

"How d'ye do, Mr. Cumberland? hope I see you well, sir. Terrible bad day, gentlemen, don't you think? dusty enough to pepper the devil, as we used to say in Spain, hey? Going to have a touch at the roly-polys, I suppose."

"We shall be disturbing you, Captain Spicer," said Cumberland, who, I thought, had tact enough to perceive that his friend's free and easy manner was the reverse of acceptable to Oaklands.

"Not at all, not at all," was the reply; "it was so terrible unpleasant out of doors, that, as I happened to be going by, I thought I'd look in to see if there was anything up; and as the table was lying idle, I got knocking the balls about with little Slipsey here, just to keep one's hand in, you know."

"Well, then, we had better begin at once," said Cumberland, to which Oaklands assented rather coldly.

As he was pulling off his great-coat, he whispered to me, "If that man stays here long, I shall never be able to stand it; his familiarity

is unbearable; there is nothing tires me so much as being obliged to
be civil to those kind of people."

"How is it to be?" said Cumberland, "whoever wins four games
out of seven is the conqueror, wasn't that it?"

"Yes, I believe so," was Oaklands' reply.

"A very sporting match,'pon my life," observed the Captain; "are
the stakes high?"

"Oh, no! a mere nothing; five or ten pounds, did we say?"
inquired Cumberland.

"Just as you like," replied Oaklands, carelessly.

"Ten pounds, by all means, I should say; five pounds is so shocking
small, don't you think? not worth playing for?" said the Captain.

"Ten let it be, then," said Cumberland; and after a few preliminaries they began playing.

I did not understand the game sufficiently to be able to give a
detailed account of the various chances of the match, nor would it
probably greatly interest the reader were I to do so. Suffice it, then,
to state that, as far as I could judge, Oaklands, disgusted by the
vulgar impertinence of the Captain (if Captain he was), thought the
whole thing a bore, and played carelessly. The consequence was that
Cumberland won the first two games. This put Oaklands upon his
mettle, and he won the third and fourth; the fifth was hardly
contested, Oaklands evidently playing as well as he was able, Cumberland also taking pains; but it struck me as singular that, in each
game, his play seemed to depend upon that of his adversary. When
Oaklands first began, Cumberland certainly beat him, but not by
many; and, as he became interested, and his play improved, so in the
same ratio did Cumberland's keep pace with it. Of course, there
might be nothing in this; the same causes that affected the one
might influence the other; but the idea having once occurred to me,
I determined to watch the proceedings still more closely, in order, if
possible, to make up my mind on the point. After a very close
contest Oaklands also won the fifth game; in the sixth he missed a
difficult stroke, after which he played carelessly, apparently intending
to reserve his strength for the final struggle, so that Cumberland won
it easily. Each had now won three games, and on the event of the
seventh depended the match. Again did Oaklands, who was evidently
deeply interested, use his utmost skill, and his play, which certainly
was very good, called forth frequent eulogiums from the Captain, who
offered to bet unheard-of sums on the certainty of his winning (which,
as there was no one in the room at all likely to accept his offer, was
a very safe and innocent amusement), and again, ' pari passu,' did
Cumberland's skill keep pace with his. After playing neck and neck,
till nearly the end of the game, Cumberland gained a slight advantage, which produced the following state of affairs :—It was Oaklands'
turn to play, and the balls were placed in such a position that by a
brilliant stroke he might win the game, but it required great skill to
do so. If he failed, the chances were so much in Cumberland's

favour as to render his success almost a certainty. It was an
anxious moment; for my own part I felt as if I scarcely dared
breathe, and could distinctly hear the throbbing of my own heart,
while the Captain, after having most liberally offered to bet five
hundred pounds to fivepence that he did it, remained silent and
motionless as a statue, watching the proceedings, with his eyeglass
screwed after some mysterious fashion into the corner of his eye.
And now, carefully and deliberately, Oaklands pointed his cue—his
elbow was drawn back for the stroke—for the last time his eye
appeared to measure and calculate the precise spot he must strike to
produce the desired effect—when suddenly, and at the exact moment
in which the cue struck the ball, a sonorous sneeze from the rat-like
billiard-marker resounded through the room; as a necessary consequence, Oaklands gave a slight start and missed his stroke. The
confusion that ensued can "better be imagined than described," as
the newspapers always say about the return from Epsom. With an
exclamation of anger and disappointment Oaklands turned away
from the table, while the Captain began storming at Slipsey, whom
he declared himself ready to kick till all was blue, for the trifling
remuneration of half a farthing. The marker himself apologized
with great contrition, for his delinquency, which he declared was
quite involuntary, at the same time asserting that, to the best of his
belief, the gentleman had made his stroke before he sneezed: this
Oaklands denied, and appealed to Cumberland for his opinion.
After trying in various ways to avoid giving a direct answer, and
appealing in his turn to Captain Spicer (who was so intensely
positive that the sneeze had preceded the stroke, that he was
willing to back his opinion to any amount), Cumberland very
unwillingly owned that, if he was forced to say what he thought, he
believed Oaklands had made his stroke before the sneeze caused him
to start, but that it was a near thing, and he might very possibly be
mistaken. This was quite enough for Oaklands, who declared that
he was perfectly satisfied, and begged Cumberland to play, which
with some apparent reluctance, he did, and, as was almost a matter
of certainty, proved the conqueror.

"'Pon my life, in all my experience, I never knew a gentleman lose
a match in such a tremendously unfortunate way," observed the
Captain. "I am certain that if you had not been flurried, Mr.
Oaklands, sir, you could have done the trick as clean as a whistle.
Allow me to place the balls as they were then—I know how they
stood to a nicety—there, that's it to a demi-semi fraction; oblige
me, sir, just as a personal favour, by trying the stroke once
more."

Thus invoked, Oaklands approached the table, and, without a
moment's deliberation, struck the ball, and succeeded in doing with
perfect ease the very thing which a minute before would have won
him ten pounds.

"There! I was super certain you could do it; the match was yours,.

sir, as safe as the bank, if that wretched little abortion there had'nt made that disgusting noise. Play him again, sir; play him again: Mr. Cumberland's a pretty player, a very pretty player; but you're too strong for him, Mr. Oaklands; it's my firm conviction you're too strong for him."

" What do you say to giving me my revenge, Cumberland ? " asked Oaklands.

" Oh ! I can have no possible objection," replied Cumberland, with the slightest imaginable assumption of superiority in his tone, which annoyed my ear, and which I felt sure would produce the same effect upon Oaklands. The next game Oaklands won; and they continued to play the rest of the afternoon with various success, and for what appeared to me very high stakes. I calculated that, by the time they left off, Oaklands must have lost more than thirty pounds; and yet, in spite of this, to a superficial observer he appeared to be the better player of the two: he certainly made the most brilliant strokes, but he also made blunders, and failed now and then; while Cumberland's score mounted up without one's exactly knowing how; he never seemed to be playing particularly well, and yet there was always something easy for him to do; while, when Oaklands had to play, the balls got into such awkward positions that it appeared as if they were leagued against him.

Besides this, many things concurred to strengthen me in my pre-conceived idea that Cumberland was accommodating his play to that of Oaklands, whom, I felt certain, he could have beaten easily, if he had been so inclined. If this were really the case, the only conclusion one could come to was, that the whole thing was a regularly arranged plot, the object of which was to win as much as he could of Oaklands' money. The marker's sneeze, too, occurring so very opportunely for Cumberland's interest; and the presence of the Captain, who, by his eulogiums on Oaklands' skill, had excited him to continue playing, while, by his observations and advice, he had endeavoured (whenever it was possible) to raise the amount of the stakes—all this favoured my view of the case. Still these were but suspicions; for I was utterly without proof: and could I on mere suspicion tell Oaklands that he was a dupe, and Cumberland a knave ? No, this would never do; so I determined, as people generally do when they are at their wits' end, and can hit on nothing better, to wait and see what time would bring forth, and act according to circumstances.

Should any of my readers think such penetration unnatural in a boy of my age, brought up in a quiet country parsonage, let them remember that, though utterly ignorant of the ways of the world, I was what is called a quick, sharp boy; that I had been informed Cumberland was not a person to be trusted, nay, that he was known to have cheated some young man before; and that, moreover, my very unworldliness and ignorance increased my suspicions, inasmuch, as it seemed to me, that playing billiards, at a public table, for what I considered large sums of money, was neither more nor less than gambling; and gambling I viewed in the light of a patent twenty-devil-power man-trap, fresh baited (in the present case with a billiard cue and balls) by the claws of the Evil One himself; consequently, I was prepared to view everything that passed with the greatest mistrust; and, in such a frame of mind, I must have been blind not to have perceived something of what was going on.

CHAPTER VIII.

GOOD RESOLUTIONS.

" Blest are those
Whose blood and judgment are so well commingled,
That they are not a pipe for Fortune's finger
To sound what stop she pleases."
Hamlet.

" There's a sweet little cherub that sits up aloft."
Naval Song.

As we were preparing to take our departure, I observed the Captain exchange glances with Cumberland, who turned to Oaklands saying,—

" Don't wait for me; I have one or two places to call at in my way back, and I shall only make you late;—when you get home, give Thomas a hint to keep back dinner five minutes or so—old Mildman won't say anything about it, if he fancies it's the servant's fault."

To this Oaklands replied " that it was rather a shame, but he'd see what he could do for once," and, with a very distant bow to the Captain, we left the room. As soon as we were in the street, Oaklands accosted me with,—

" Well, Frank, what do you think of billiards ? "

" Why," replied I, after a moment's thought, " as to the game itself, it's a very pretty game, and when you can play well, I have no doubt a very interesting one; too much so, perhaps."

" Too interesting! why, that's the beauty of it; almost every other game is a bore, and tires one, because one does not get sufficiently interested to forget the trouble of it; what can you mean by too interesting ? "

" You won't be angry at what I am going to say, will you ? " said I, looking up in his face.

" Angry with you, my dear boy! no fear of that; always say just what you think to me, and if it happens to be disagreeable, why, it can't be helped: I would rather hear a disagreeable truth from a friend any day, than have it left to some ill-natured person to bring out, when he wants to annoy me."

" All I meant to say was this," I replied; " it seems to me that you get so much excited by the game, that you go on playing longer, and for higher stakes than you intended to do when you began: surely," continued I, "it cannot be right to lose such sums of money merely for amusement; is it not gambling?"

"I believe you are right, Frank," replied Oaklands, after a short pause, during which he had apparently been revolving the matter in his mind; "when one comes to think seriously about it, it is a most unprofitable way of getting rid of one's money; you will scarcely credit it," continued he, half smiling, "but I declare to you I have been playing almost every day for the last two months."

"So long as that?" interrupted I, aghast.

"There or thereabouts," said Oaklands, laughing at the tone of horror in which I had spoken; "but I was going to say," he continued, "that till this moment—looking upon it merely as an amusement, something to keep one from going to sleep over a newspaper in that vile reading-room—I have never taken the trouble to consider whether there was any right or wrong in the matter. I am very much obliged to you for the hint, Frank; I'll think it over to-night, and see how much I owe Master Cumberland, and I'll tell you to-morrow what conclusion I have come to. I hate to do anything in a hurry—even to think; one must take time to do that well."

We had now reached home, and, mindful of his promise, Oaklands begged Thomas to use his interest with the cook for the purpose of postponing dinner for a few minutes, in order to give Cumberland a chance of being ready—to which Thomas replied,—

"Very well, sir, anything to oblige you, Mr. Oaklands," muttering to himself as he went off, "Wonder what that chap Cumberland is up to now; no good, I'll be bound."

In another minute we heard his voice in the lower regions, exclaiming,—

"I say, cook, musn't dish up for the next ten minutes; master ain't quite finished his next Sunday's sermon; he's got hitched just at thirdly and lastly, and musn't be disturbed; not on no account," which produced from that functionary the following pathetic rejoinder,—

"Then, it's hall hup with the pigeon pie, for it will be burnt as black as my blessed shoe by that time!"

As I was descending the stairs, ready to go out the next day, Oaklands called me into his room, and, closing the door, said,—

"Well, Fairlegh, I have thought over all you said yesterday—made up my mind, and acted upon it."

"Bravo!" replied I, "I am so glad, for whenever you will but rouse yourself, you are sure to act more rightly and sensibly than anybody else; but what have you done now? Let me hear all about it."

"Oh, nothing very wonderful," answered Oaklands; "when I came to look at my pocket-book, I found I had lost, from first to last, above £150."

"Good gracious!" cried I, aghast at the magnitude of the sum, "what will you do?"

Oaklands smiled at my look of horror, and continued,—

"About £100 of this I still owe Cumberland, for after my ready money was gone, I merely set down on paper all I won or lost, as he said I could pay him at any time, just as it suited me best; and I thought I would wait till I got my next quarter's allowance, pay him out of that, and be very economical ever after. Well, when I saw what the sums amounted to, I found this plan certainly would not answer, and that I was getting into a mess; so I made up my mind to put an end to the thing at once, and sat down to write to my father, telling him I had been playing billiards every day for some time past with a friend—of course I did not mention who—and that, without being at all aware of it, my losses had mounted up till I owed him £100. I mentioned at the same time that I had a pretty long bill at Smithson's: and then went on to say that I saw the folly, if not worse than folly, of what I had been doing; and that I applied to him, as the best friend I had in the world—and I am sure he is too, Frank—to save me from the consequences of my own imprudence."

"I am very glad you did that; it was much the wisest thing," interrupted I.

"As soon as I had written my letter," continued Oaklands, "I went to Cumberland, and told him that I found I had been going on over-fast,—that I owned he was too good a player for me,—and that I therefore did not mean to play any more, and would pay him as soon as I received my father's answer."

"And what did he say to that?" inquired I.

"Why, he seemed surprised and a little annoyed, I fancied. He denied being the best player, and begged I would not think of paying him yet, saying that I had been unlucky of late, but that if I would go on boldly, luck was sure to change, and that I should most likely win it all back again."

"And you?"

"Oh! I told him that was the true spirit of gambling: that I did not choose to owe so much to any man as I owed him, and that pay him I would. Well, then, he said that if I did not like to trouble my father about such a trifle, and yet was determined to pay him, it could be very easily managed. I asked how. He hummed and ha'd, and at last said that Smithson would advance me the money in a minute—that I should only have to sign a receipt for it, and need not pay him for years—not till I was of age, and not then if I did not like—that no one would be any the wiser—and he was going on with more in the same style, when I stopped him, by answering very abruptly that such an arrangement was not to my taste, and that I was not yet reduced to borrowing money of my tailor."

"Quite right, I am so glad you told him that," interposed I; "what did he say then?"

"Something about not intending to offend me, and its being a thing done every day."

"By him perhaps," said I, recollecting the scene I had witnessed soon after my arrival.

"Why! what do you mean?" said Oaklands.

"I'll tell you when you have done," replied I; "but I want to know how all this ended."

"There was not much more. He tried to persuade me to go again to-day, and play another match. I told him I was engaged to ride with you. Then he looked as if he was going to be angry. I waited to see, and he wasn't, and so we parted."

"And what think you of Cumberland now?" inquired I.

"I can't say I altogether like the way in which he has behaved about this," replied Oaklands; "it certainly looks as if he would have had no objection to win as much as he could from me, for he must have known all along that he was the best player. It strikes me that I am well out of the mess, and I have to thank you for being so too, old fellow."

"Nay, you have to thank your own energy and decision; I did nothing towards helping you out of your difficulties."

"Indeed! if a man is walking over a precipice with his eyes shut, is it nothing to cause him to open them, in order that he may see the dangers into which the path he is following will lead him?"

"Ah! Harry, if you would but exert yourself, so as to keep your own eyes open—"

"What a wide-awake fellow you would be!" interposed Coleman, who, after having tapped twice, without succeeding in making himself heard (so engrossed were we by the conversation in which we were engaged), had in despair opened the door in time to overhear my last remark. "I say, gents, as Thomas calls us," continued he, "what have you been doing to Cumberland, to put him into such a charming temper?"

"Is he out of humour then?" inquired Oaklands.

"I should say, rather," replied Coleman, winking ironically; "he came into our room just now, looking as black as thunder, and, as I know he hates to be spoken to when he is in the sulks, I asked him if you were going to play billiards with him to-day."

Harry and I exchanged glances, and Coleman continued,—

"He fixed his eyes upon me, and stared as if he would have felt greatly relieved by cutting my throat, and at last growled out, 'No; that you were going to ride with Fairlegh;' to which I replied that it was quite delightful to see what great friends you had become; whereupon he ground his teeth with rage, and told me 'to go to the devil for a prating fool:' so I answered that I was not in want of such an article just at present, and had not time to go so far to-day, and then I came here instead. Oh, he's in no end of a rage, I know."

"And your remarks would not tend to soothe him much either," said I. "Oaklands has just been telling him he does not mean to play billiards again."

"Phew!" whistled Coleman, "that was a lucky shot of mine; I

fancied it must have been something about Oaklands and billiards that had gone wrong, when I saw how savage it made him. I like to rile Cumberland sometimes, because he's always so soft and silky; he seems afraid of getting into a good honest rage, lest he should let out something he does not want one to know. I hate such extreme caution; it always makes me think there must be something very wrong to be concealed, when people are so mighty particular."

"You are not quite a fool, after all, Freddy," said Oaklands, encouragingly.

"Thank ye for nothing, Harry Longlegs," replied Coleman, skipping beyond the reach of Oaklands' arm.

A few mornings after this conversation took place, Oaklands, who was sitting in the recess of the window (from which he had ejected Lawless on the memorable evening of his arrival), called me to him, and asked in a low tone of voice, whether I should mind calling at the billiard-rooms when I went out, and paying a month's subscription which he owed there. He added that he did not like going himself, for fear of meeting Cumberland or the Captain, as if they pressed him to play, and he refused (which he certainly should do), something disagreeable might occur, which it was quite as well to avoid. In this I quite agreed, and willingly undertook the commission. While we were talking, Thomas came into the room with a couple of letters, one of which he gave to Oaklands, saying it had just come by the post, while he handed the other to Cumberland, informing him that the gentleman who brought it was waiting for an answer. I fancied that Cumberland changed colour slightly when his eye fell upon the writing. After rapidly perusing the note, he crushed it in his hand, and flung it into the fire, saying,—

" My compliments to the gentleman, and I'll be with him at the time he mentions."

" Well, this is kind of my father," exclaimed Oaklands, looking up with a face beaming with pleasure; "after writing me the warmest and most affectionate letter possible, he sends me an order for three hundred pounds upon his banker, telling me always to apply to him when I want money, or get into difficulties of any kind; and that if I will promise him that this shall be the case, I need never be afraid of asking for too much, as he should be really annoyed were I to stint myself."

"What a pattern for fathers!" exclaimed Coleman, rubbing his hands. "I only wish my old dad would test my obedience in that sort of way; I'd take care I would not annoy him by asking for too little; he need not fret himself on that account. Ugh!" continued he, with a look of intense disgust, "it's quite dreadful to think what perverted ideas he has on the subject; he actually fancies it his business to spend his money as well as to make it; and as for sons, the less they have the better, lest they should get into extravagant habits, forsooth! I declare it's quite aggravating to think of the

F

difference between people : a cheque for three hundred pounds from
a father, who'll be annoyed if one does not always apply to
him for money enough! Open the window there! I am getting
faint!"

" Don't you think there's a little difference between sons as well as
fathers, Master Fred, eh ?" inquired Lawless. "I should say some
sons might be safely trusted with three-hundred-pound cheques ;
while others are certain to waste two shillings, and misapply
sixpence, out of every half-crown they may get hold of."

" Sir, I scorn your insinuations ; sir, you're no gentleman," was the
reply, producing (as was probably intended) an attack from Lawless
which Coleman avoided for some time, by dodging round chairs and
under tables. After the chase had lasted for several minutes,
Coleman, when on the point of being captured, contrived, by a
master-stroke of policy, to substitute Mullins in his place, and the
affair ended by that worthy being knocked down by Lawless, "for
always choosing to interfere with everything," and being kicked up
again by Coleman "for having prevented him from properly
vindicating his wounded honour."

" Who's going near the post-office, and will put a letter in for
me ?" asked Oaklands.

"I am," replied Cumberland; "I've got one of my own to put in
also."

" Don't forget it or lose it, for it's rather important," added
Oaklands; "but I need not caution you, you are not one of the hare-
brained sort; if it had been my friend Freddy, now—"

" I'll tell you what it is, Mr. Oaklands," said Coleman, putting on
an air of offended dignity, in which, though very much exaggerated,
there was at the bottom the smallest possible spice of reality—a thing
by the way, one may often observe in people who have a very strong
appreciation of the ridiculous, and who, however fond they may be
of doing absurd things for the sake of being laughed at, do not
approve of their buffooneries being taken for granted—"I'll tell you
what it is, sir : you have formed a most mistaken estimate of my
character ; I beg to say that any affair I undertake is certain to be
conducted in a very sedate and business-like manner. My prudence
I consider unimpeachable; and as to steadiness, I flatter myself I go
considerably ahead of the Archbishop of Canterbury in that article.
If I hear you repeat such offensive remarks, I shall be under the
painful necessity of elongating your already sufficiently prolonged
proboscis."

" Come and try," said Oaklands, folding his arms with an air of
defiance. Coleman, reckoning on his adversary's dislike of exertion,
and trusting to his own extreme quickness and activity to effect his
escape scot-free, made a feint of turning away as if to avoid the
contest, and then, with a sudden spring, leaped upon Oaklands, and
succeeded in just touching his nose. The latter was, however, upon
his guard, and while, by seizing his outstretched arm with one hand,

he prevented him from attaining his object, he caught him by the coat-collar with the other, and detained him prisoner.

"I've got you this time, at all events, Master Freddy; now what shall I do with you, to pay you off for all your impertinence?" said Oaklands, looking round the room in search of something suitable to his purpose. "I have it," continued he, as his eyes encountered the bookcase, which was a large square-topped, old-fashioned affair, standing about eight feet high, and the upper part forming a sort of glass-fronted closet, in which the books were arranged on shelves. "Great men like you, who go a-head of archbishops and so on, should be seated in high places." So saying, he lifted Coleman in his arms with as much ease as if he had been a kitten; and stepping up on a chair which stood near, seated him on the top of the book-case, with his head touching the ceiling, and his feet dangling about six feet from the ground.

"What a horrid shame!" said Coleman; "come help me down again, Harry, there's a good fellow."

"I help you down!" rejoined Oaklands, "I've had trouble enough in putting you up, I think; I'm a great deal too much tired to help you down again."

"Well, if you won't, there's nobody else can," said Coleman, "unless they get a ladder, or a fire-escape—don't call me proud, gentlemen, if I look down upon you all, for I assure you it's quite involuntary on my part."

"A decided case of 'up aloft': he looks quite a cherub, does he not?" said Lawless.

"They are making game of you, Coleman," cried Mullins, grinning.

"I hope not," was the reply, "for in that case I should be much too high to be pleasant."

"They ought to keep you there for an hour longer for that vile pun," said Cumberland. "Is your letter ready, Oaklands, for I must be going?"

"It is upstairs; I'll fetch it," replied Oaklands, leaving the room.

"Well, as it seems I am here for life, I may as well make myself comfortable," said Coleman, and suiting the action to the word, he crossed his legs under him like a tailor, and, folding his arms, leaned his back against the wall, the picture of ease.

At this moment there was a gentle tap at the door; someone said, "Come in," and without a word of preparation Dr. Mildman entered the apartment. Our surprise and consternation at this apparition may easily be imagined. Cumberland and Lawless tried to carry it off by assuming an easy, unembarrassed air, as if nothing particular was going on; I felt strongly disposed to laugh, while Mullins looked much more inclined to cry; but the expression of Coleman's face, affording a regular series of "dissolving views" of varied emotions, was the "gem" of the whole affair. The unconscious

cause of all this excitement, whose back was turned towards
the bookcase, walked quietly up to his usual seat, saying as he
did so,—

" Don't let me disturb you—I only came to look for my eyeglass,
which I think I must have dropped."

" I see it, sir," said I, springing forward and picking it up; " how
lucky none of us happened to tread on it and break it ! "

" Thank you, Fairlegh, it is an old friend, and I should have been
sorry to have any harm happen to it," replied he, as he turned to
leave the room, without having once raised his eyes from the ground.
Coleman, who up to this moment had considered a discovery
inevitable, gave me a sign to open the door, and, believing the
danger over, was proceeding to relieve his feelings by making a
hideous face at his retiring tutor, when the bookcase, affected no
doubt by the additional weight placed upon it, suddenly gave a loud
crack.

" Bless my heart ! " said Dr. Mildman, looking up in alarm,
" what's that ?   Gracious me ! " continued he, starting back as his
eyes encountered Coleman, " there's something alive up there ! why
it's—eh ? " continued he, levelling his newly-restored eyeglass at the
object of his alarm; " yes, it certainly is Coleman; pray, sir, is it
usually your ' custom of an afternoon,' as Shakespeare has it, to sit
perched up there cross-legged, like a Chinese mandarin ?   It's a very
singular taste."

" Why, sir," replied Coleman, for once completely taken aback,
" you see I didn't—that is, I wasn't—I mean, if I hadn't—I
shouldn't."

" Hum," resumed Dr. Mildman with whom he was rather a
favourite, and who, now that he had satisfied himself it was not
some wild animal he had to deal with, was evidently amused by
Coleman's embarrassment, " that sentence of yours is not particularly clear or explanatory; but," continued he, as a new idea
occurred to him, " how in the world did you get up there ? you
must have flown."

" I didn't get up, I was—that is, he—" stammered Coleman,
remembering just in time that he could not explain without involving
Oaklands.

" And how are you ever to get down again ? " said Dr. Mildman.

" Has the pretty bird flown yet ? " cried Oaklands, hastily entering
the room; when, observing the addition the party had received
during his absence, he started back, murmuring in an undertone,
" The old gentleman, by Jove ! "   Quickly recovering himself, however, he sprang upon a chair, and seizing Coleman in his arms,
whisked him down with more haste than ceremony ; and going up to
Dr. Mildman, said respectfully, " That was a bit of folly of mine,
sir ; I put him up there; I merely did it for a joke, and I hadn't an
idea you would come in and find him."

" Never mind," replied Dr. Mildman, good-naturedly; " as you

have contrived to get him down again safely, there is no harm done,"
adding as he left the room, "That young man is as strong as
Hercules. I hope he'll never take it into his head to pop me up
anywhere, for I am sure he could do it if he chose."

CHAPTER IX.

A DENOUEMENT.

> " Play not for gain, but sport ; who plays for more
> Than he can lose with pleasure, stakes his heart."
> *Herbert.*

> " If you are so bold as to venture a blowing-up, look closely to it ! for the plot lies
> deadly deep . . . but of all things have a care of putting it in your pocket, . . . and if
> you can shun it, read it not ; . . . consider well what you do and look to yourself . . .
> for there is danger and jeopardy in it."—*Dr. Eachard.*

In the course of my walk that afternoon, I called at the billiard-
rooms in F—— Street, in order to pay Oaklands' subscription. On
inquiring for Mr. Johnson, the proprietor, I was told that he was
engaged at present, but that if I did not mind waiting for a few
minutes, he would be able to attend to me. To this I agreed, and
was shown into a small room downstairs, which, from its sanded
floor, and a strong odour of stale tobacco which pervaded it, was
apparently used as a smoking-room. It opened into what seemed
to be a rather spacious apartment from which it was divided
by a glass half-door, across the lower panes of which hung a green
blind : this door, on my entrance, was standing slightly ajar. The
day being cold, there was a bright fire burning on the hearth; near
this I seated myself, and, seduced by its drowsy influence, fell into a
kind of trance, in which, between sleeping and waking, my mind
wandered away to a far different scene, among well-known forms
and familiar faces, that had been strangers to me now for many a
long day. From this day-dream I was aroused by sounds which,
proceeding from the adjoining apartment, resolved themselves, as
I became more thoroughly awake, into the voices of two persons
apparently engaged in angry colloquy.

"I tell you," said a gruff voice, which somehow seemed familiar to
me—"I tell you it is the only chance for you; you must contrive to
bring him here again, and that without loss of time."

"Must I again repeat that the thing is impossible ? " was the reply,
in tones I knew but too well ; "utterly impossible: when once his
mind is made up, and he takes the trouble to exert himself, he is
immovable : nothing can shake his determination."

" And is this your boasted skill and management ? " rejoined the first speaker; " how comes it, pray, that this overgrown child, who seemed the other day to be held as nicely in leading-strings as need be—this raw boy, whose hot-headedness, simplicity, and indolence rendered him as easy a pigeon to pluck as one could desire; how comes it, I say, that he has taken alarm in this sudden manner, so as to refuse to come here any more? You've bungled this matter most shamefully, sir, and must take the consequences ! "

" That's just the point I cannot make out," replied the second speaker, who, as the reader has probably discovered, was none other than Cumberland; " it's easy enough for you to lay it all to my mismanagement, Captain Spicer, but I tell you it is no such thing: did I not accommodate my play to his, always appearing to win by some accident, so that the fool actually believed himself the better player, while he was losing from twenty to thirty pounds a day? Didn't I excite him, and lead him on by a mixture of flattery and defiance, so that he often fancied he was persuading me to play against my will, and was so ready to bet that I might have won three times what I have of him, if you had not advised me to go on quietly, and by degrees ? Did not you refuse when I wished you to take him in hand yourself, because you said I understood him best, and managed him admirably ? No, I believe that detestable young Fairlegh is at the bottom of it : I observed him watching me with that calm, steadfast glance of his, that I hated him for from the first moment I saw him ; I felt certain some mischief would arise from it.'

" Yes ! " replied Spicer, " that was your fault too: why did you let the other bring him ? Every fool knows that lookers-on see most of the game."

" I was afraid to say much against it, lest Oaklands should suspect anything," rejoined Cumberland; " but I wish to Heaven I had now ; I might have been sure no good would come from it—that boy is my evil genius."

" I have no time for talking about geniuses, and such confounded stuff," observed Spicer, angrily, " so now to business, Mr. Cumberland; you are aware you owe me two hundred pounds, I presume ? "

Cumberland grumbled out an unwilling assent, to which he appended a muttered remark not exactly calculated to enhance the Captain's future comfort.

" Like a good-natured fool," continued Spicer, " I agreed to wait for my money till you had done what you could with this Oaklands."

" For which forbearance you were to receive fifty pounds extra, besides anything you could make out of him by private bets," put in Cumberland.

" Of course I was not going to wait all that time for my money for nothing," was the reply ; " you have only as yet paid me fifty pounds, you tell me you can't persuade Oaklands to play again, so there's nothing more to be got from that quarter, consequently nothing more to wait for. I must trouble you, therefore, to pay me the two hundred pounds at once; for, to be plain with you, it won't do for me to remain here any longer—the air does not agree with my constitution."

"And where on earth am I to get two hundred pounds at a minute's notice?" said Cumberland; "you are as well aware the thing is impossible as I am."

"I am aware of this, sir," replied the Captain with an oath, "that I'll have my money; ay, and this very day too, or I'll expose you—curse me, if I don't! I know your uncle's address : yes! you may well turn pale and gnaw your lip—other people can plot and scheme as well as yourself; if I'm not paid before I leave this place, and that will be by to-night's mail, your uncle shall be told that his nephew is an insolvent gambler; and the old tutor, the Rev. Dr. Mildman, shall have a hint that his head pupil is little better than a blackleg."

"Now listen to me, Spicer," said Cumberland, quietly; "I know you might do what you have threatened, and that to me it would be neither more nor less than ruin ; but—and this is the real question —pray what possible advantage (save calling people's attention to the share, a pretty large one, you have had in making me what I am) would it be to you?"

"To me, sir? eh! why, what do you mean, sir? your uncle is a man of honour, and, of course, as such would pay his nephew's debts for him, more particularly when he knows that if he refuses to do so, that nephew will be sent to gaol ; yes, to gaol, sir."

"There! blustering is of no use with me, so you may save yourself that trouble, Captain," replied Cumberland; "as to sending me to gaol, that is absurd ; you can't arrest a minor for debt, and I shall not be of age these two years. My uncle is, as you say, what is called a man of honour, but he is not one of those over-scrupulous fools who will pay any demand, however dishonest and unreasonable, rather than tarnish the family honour forsooth! No! he will pay what the law compels him, and not a farthing more. I leave you to decide whether the law is likely to be of much use to you in the present case. Now, listen to me; though you cannot obtain the money by the means you proposed, you can, as I said before, do me serious injury ; therefore, if for no other reason but to stop your month, I would pay you the whole if I could, but I have not the power of doing so at present. What I propose, then, is this—Oaklands will pay me, in a day or two, one hundred pounds ; this I will hand over to you at once, and will give you a written promise to pay you the rest in the course of the next six months ; for before that time I must raise money somehow, even if I have to sell every farthing I expect to come into to the Jews, in order to do it."

"Won't do," was the reply; "the ready isn't enough ; I must leave this country in a day or two, and I must have money to' take with me ; come, one hundred and fifty pounds down, and I'll let you off the other fifty."

" It's impossible: I can get no other money yet excepting the sum Oaklands is to pay me."

" Yes! and how the devil am I to be sure he will pay you directly ? I'm pretty certain the fool's hard up himself ; he hasn't paid cash for a month past."

" If that's all you are afraid of, I can soon convince you to the contrary ; here's a letter to his father's banker, which I am going to put into the post directly, with a cheque for three hundred pounds in it ; there, hold it up to the light, and you can see the figures yourself."

" By Jove ! so it is," exclaimed Spicer; " I say, Cumberland," he continued, and then the voices almost sank into a whisper, so that I could not catch more than a word here and there, but by the tone I judged that the Captain was making some proposition, to which Cumberland refused to agree.

At length I heard the former say, " Fifty pounds down, and a receipt in full."

Cumberland's reply was inaudible, but when the Captain spoke again I caught the following words, " Not the slightest risk ; only you do as I say, and—"

At this moment the outer door of the room in which I was sitting opened, while the one communicating with the other apartment was violently slammed to from the farther side, and I heard no more.

The new-comer was a little slipshod girl in dirty curl-papers, who informed me that her master was sorry he could not see me that day, as he was particularly engaged, but if I would do him the favour of calling to-morrow, at the same hour, he should be at leisure, etc. To this I answered something, I scarcely knew what, and seizing my hat, rushed out at the front door, to the great astonishment of the curl-papered damsel, who cast an anxious glance at the pegs in the hall, ere she could convince herself that I had not departed with more hats and coats than legitimately belonged to me.

It was not until I had proceeded the length of two or three streets, that I could collect my ideas sufficiently to form anything like a just estimate of the extraordinary disclosures with which I had so unexpectedly become acquainted, and no sooner had I in some measure succeeded in so doing, than the puzzling question presented itself to me, what line of conduct it would be advisable to adopt, in consequence of what I had heard. I asked myself too, to begin with, what right I had to make any use of a private conversation, which accident alone had caused me to overhear. Would not people say I had behaved dishonourably in having listened to it at all ? But then, again, by preserving Cumberland's secret, and concealing his real character from Oaklands, should not I, as it were, become a party to any nefarious schemes he might contemplate for the future ? Having failed in one instance in his attempt on Oaklands' purse, would he not (having, as I was now fully aware, such a strong necessity for money) devise some fresh plan, which might succeed in its

object, were Oaklands still ignorant of the real character of the person
he had to deal with ? And in such case should not I be answerable
for any mischief which might ensue ? Nay, for aught I knew, some
fresh villainy might be afloat even now; what plan could Spicer have
been urging, which Cumberland seemed unwilling to adopt, if not
something of this nature, and which might be prevented were Oaklands made aware of all the circumstances ?

This last idea settled the business. I determined to reveal everything to Oaklands in confidence, and to be guided in my subsequent
conduct by his opinion. Having once arrived at this conclusion, the
next thing was to carry my intentions into effect with as little loss
of time as possible. I consequently started off at speed in a homeward direction, and succeeded in reaching my destination in rather
less than ten minutes, having, at various times in the course of
my route, run against and knocked over no less than six little
children, to the manifest discomposure and indignation of as many
nursery-maids, who evidently regarded me as a commissioned agent
of some modern Herod, performing my master's work zealously.

On arriving at home my impatience was doomed to be disappointed,
for Oaklands, who had gone out soon after I did, was not yet returned. This delay, in the feverish state of anxiety and excitement
in which I was, appeared to me intolerable ; and, unable to sit still, I
kept striding up and down the room, clenching my fists, and uttering
exclamations of impatience and vexation ; which unusual conduct on
my part so astonished and alarmed the worthy Thomas that, after
remaining in the room till he had exhausted every conceivable pretext for so doing, he boldly inquired whether " I did not feel myself
ill, no how ? " adding his hope that " I had not been a-exhaling
laughing gas, or any sich rum-bustical wegitable ? " after which he
favoured me with an anecdote of " a young man as he know'd, as had
done so, wot conducted hisself more like a hideotic fool than a
sanatory Christian, ever after." Perceiving at length that his
attentions were rapidly reducing me to the same state of mind as
that of his friend, he very considerately left me.

After half an hour of anxious expectation, in the course of which
I must have walked at least a mile or two over Dr. Mildman's parlour
carpet, Oaklands and Lawless returned together. I instantly called
the former aside, and told him I wished to speak to him alone, as I
had something of importance to communicate. To this he replied
that it was very near dinner-time ; but that if I would come up to his
room, I could talk to him while he dressed. As soon as we were
safely closeted together I began my relation, but scarcely had I got
beyond, " You asked me to go to the billiard-rooms, you know,"
when a hasty footstep was heard upon the stairs ; someone knocked
at the door, and immediately a voice, which I knew to be that of
Cumberland, asked to be let in, " as he had something particular to
say."

" The plot thickens," said Oaklands, as, without rising from his

seat, he stretched out an immense length of arm, and opened the
door.

" Hear what I have to say first," cried I; but it was too late, and
Cumberland entered breathless, and with his usually sallow complexion flushed with exercise and excitement.

" The most unfortunate thing !" he began ; and stopping to draw
breath, he added, " I have run all the way from the post-office as
hard as my legs would carry me—but I was going to tell you—as I
went down, I met Curtis of the —th, who told me their band was
going to play in Park Square, and asked me to go with him to hear
it ; and I'm afraid that, as I stood in the crowd, my pocket must have
been picked, for when I got to the post-office, I found that my letter,
my pocket handkerchief, and I am sorry to say your letter also, had
disappeared—so, remembering you had told me your letter was of
importance, I thought the best thing I could do was to come home
as fast as I could, and tell you."

" By Jove !" exclaimed Oaklands, " that's rather a bore, though ;
there was my father's cheque for three hundred pounds in it; I
suppose something ought to be done about it directly."

" Write a note to stop the payment; and—let me see—as it is too
late for the post now, if you will make a parcel of it, I'll run down
and give it to the guard of the mail, begging him to deliver it himself as soon as he gets to town—the cheque can't be presented till
to-morrow morning, so that it will be all right."

" What a head you have for business, to be sure !" said Oaklands;
" but why should you have the trouble of taking it ? I dare say
Thomas will go with it when we have done dinner, or I can take it
myself."

" Nay." replied Cumberland, " as I have contrived to lose your
letter, the least I can do is to take the parcel ; besides, I should like
to speak to the guard myself, so as to be sure there's no mistake."

While this was going on it may be imagined that my thoughts were
not idle. When Cumberland mentioned the loss of the letter, my
suspicions that some nefarious scheme might be on foot began for
the first time to resolve themselves into a tangible form ; but when
I perceived his anxiety to have the parcel entrusted to him, which
was to prevent the payment of the cheque, the whole scheme, or
something nearly approaching to it, flashed across me at once,
and without reflecting for a moment on what might be the consequences of doing so, I said,—

" If Oaklands will take my advice, he will not entrust you with
anything else, till you can prove that you have really lost the letter
as you say you have done."

Had a thunderbolt fallen in the midst of us, it could scarcely have
produced greater confusion than did this speech of mine. Oaklands
sprang upon his feet, regarding me with the greatest surprise as he
asked, " if I knew what I was saying ?" while Cumberland, in a voice
hoarse from passion, inquired, " What the devil I meant by my

insolence ? what did I dare to insinuate he had done with the letter,.
if he had not lost it ? "

" I insinuate nothing," was my reply; " but I tell you plainly that
I believe, and have good reason for believing, that you have not lost.
the letter, but given it to your gambling friend and accomplice,
Captain Spicer, who in return for it is to give you a receipt in full
for the two hundred pounds you owe him, and fifty pounds down."
On hearing this, Cumberland turned as pale as ashes, and leaned on
the back of a chair for support, while I continued, "You look
surprised, Oaklands, as well you may; but when you hear what I
have to tell, you will see that I do not make this accusation without
having good grounds to go upon."

"I shall not stay here," said Cumberland, making an effort to
recover himself, and turning towards the door, "I shall not remain
here, to be any further insulted ; I wish you good evening, Mr.
Oaklands."

" Not so fast," said Oaklands, springing to the door, and locking
it ; "if all this be true, and Fairlegh would not have said so much
unless he had strong facts to produce, you and I shall have an
account to settle together, Mr. Cumberland ; you will not leave this
room till I know the rights of the affair. Now, Frank, let us hear
how you learned all this."

"Strangely enough," replied I; and I then gave him an exact
account of all that had passed at the billiard-rooms, repeating the
conversation, word for word, as nearly as I could remember it,
leaving Oaklands to draw his own inferences therefrom. During
the whole of my recital, Cumberland sat with his elbows resting on
the table, and his face buried in his hands, without offering the
slightest interruption, scarcely, indeed, appearing aware of what was
going on, save once, when I mentioned the fact of the door between
the two rooms being slightly open, when he muttered something
about "what cursed folly!" When I had finished my account,
Oaklands turned towards Cumberland, and asked in a stern voice
" what he had to say to this statement ? " Receiving no answer, he
continued, " But it is useless, sir, to ask you: the truth of what
Fairlegh has said is self-evident—the next question is, what is to be
done about it ? " He paused for a moment as if in thought, and then
resumed : "In the position in which I now stand, forming one of
Dr. Mildman's household, and placed by my father under his control,
I scarcely consider myself a free agent. It seems to me, therefore,
that my course is clear ; it is evidently my duty to inform him of the
whole affair, and afterwards to act as he may advise. Do you agree
with me, Frank ? "

" It is exactly what I should have proposed, had you not mentioned
it first," was my answer.

" For God's sake, Oaklands, don't!" exclaimed Cumberland,.
raising himself suddenly; "he will write to my uncle—I shall be-
expelled—my character lost—it will be utter ruin ;—have pity upon

me—I will get you back your money, I will indeed: only don't tell Mildman."

" I have treated you up to the present time as a gentleman and a friend," replied Oaklands; "you have proved yourself unworthy of either title, and deserve nothing at my hands but the strictest justice; no one could blame me were I to allow the law to take its course with you, as with any other swindler, but this I shall be most unwilling to do; nothing short of Dr. Mildman's declaring it to be my positive duty will prevail upon me. But our tutor ought to be informed of it and shall: he is a good, kind-hearted man, and if his judgment should err at all, you may feel sure it will be on the side of mercy. Fairlegh, will you go down and ask Dr. Mildman if I can speak to him on a matter of importance, now, at once? You will find him in his study. Let me know when he is ready, and we will come down; for," added he, turning to Cumberland, "I do not lose sight of you till this business is settled one way or other."

When I had told my errand, Dr. Mildman, who looked a good deal surprised and a little frightened, desired me (on receiving my assurance that the business would not do as well after dinner) to tell Oaklands to come to him immediately. To this Oaklands replied by desiring me to hold myself in readiness for a summons, as he should want me presently. Then, linking his arm within that of Cumberland, he half led, half forced, him out of the room. In another minute I heard the study door close behind them.

" Now, Fairlegh," said Dr. Mildman, when, in about a quarter of an hour's time, I had been sent for. " I wish you to repeat to me the conversation you overheard at the billiard-room, as nearly word for word as you can remember it." This I hastened to do, the Doctor listening with the most profound attention, and asking one or two questions on any point which did not at first appear quite clear to him. When I had concluded, he resumed his inquiries by asking whether I had seen the parties who were speaking. To this I answered in the negative.

" But you imagined you recognized the voices? "

" Yes, sir."

" Whose did you take them to be? "

" One I believed to be Cumberland's, the other that of Captain Spicer, whom I had seen when I was there before."

" How often have you been there? "

" Twice, sir; once about a week ago, and again to-day."

" And have you the slightest moral doubt as to the fact of the persons you heard speaking being Cumberland and this Captain Spicer? "

" Not the slightest; I feel quite certain of it."

" That is all clear and straightforward enough," observed Dr. Mildman, turning to the culprit. " I am afraid the case is only too fully proved against you; have you anything to say which can at all establish your innocence? "

"It would be of no use if I were to do so," said Cumberland in a sullen manner; "it's all a matter of assertion; you choose to believe what they say, and if I were to deny it, you would not believe me without proof; and how can I prove a negative?"

"But do you deny it?" inquired Dr. Mildman, regarding him with a clear, scrutinizing look. Cumberland attempted to speak, but, meeting Dr. Mildman's eye, was unable to get out a word, and turned away, concealing his face in his handkerchief.

"This is a sad piece of business," said Dr. Mildman; "I suppose you mean to prosecute, Oaklands?"

"I shall be most unwilling to do so," was the reply; "nor will I, sir, unless you consider it my positive duty; I would rather lose the money ten times over than bring such a disgrace upon Cumberland."

"You are a kind-hearted fellow," replied the Doctor; "it really is a very difficult case in which to know how to act. As a general principle, I am most averse to anything like hushing up evil."

"For Heaven's sake have pity upon me, Dr. Mildman," cried Cumberland, throwing himself on his knees before him; "I confess it all. I did allow Spicer to keep the cheque; he threatened to expose me, and I did it to escape detection; but promise you will not prosecute me and I will tell you where he may be found, so that something may be done about it yet. I will pay anything you please. I shall come into money when I am of age, and I can make some arrangement. I don't care what I sacrifice, if I have to dig to earn my bread, only do not disgrace me publicly. Remember, I am very young, and, oh! if you knew what it is to be tempted as I have been! Oaklands, Fairlegh, intercede for me; think how you should feel, either of you, if you were placed in my situation!"

"Get up, Mr. Cumberland," observed Dr. Mildman, in a grave, impressive manner; "it is equally needless and unbecoming to kneel to man for forgiveness—learn to consider that position as a thing set apart and sacred to the service of One greater than the sons of men —One whom you have indeed grievously offended, and to whom, in the solitude of your chamber, you will do well to kneel, and pray that He who died to save sinners may, in the fulness of His mercy, pardon you also." He paused, and then resumed: "We must decide what steps had better be taken to recover your cheque, Oaklands; it is true we can send and stop the payment of it—but if you determine not to prosecute, for Cumberland's sake, you must let off this man Spicer also, in which case it would be advisable to prevent his presenting the cheque at all, as that might lead to inquiries which it would be difficult to evade. You said just now you knew where this bad man was to be found, Mr. Cumberland?"

"Yes, sir, if he is not at the billiard-rooms in F—— Street, his lodgings are at No. 14, Richmond Buildings," said Cumberland.

"Ay, exactly," replied Dr. Mildman; and resting his head upon his hand, he remained for some minutes buried in thought. Having at length apparently made up his mind, he turned to Cumberland

and said : " Considering all the circumstances of the case, Mr. Cumberland, although I most strongly reprobate your conduct, which has grieved and surprised me more than I can express, I am unwilling to urge Oaklands to put the law in force against you, for more reasons than one. In the first place I wish to spare your uncle the pain which such an exposure must occasion him ; and, secondly, I cannot but hope that at your age so severe a lesson as this may work a permanent change in you, and that at some future period you may regain that standing among honourable men, which you have now so justly forfeited, and I am anxious that this should not be prevented by the stigma which a public examination must attach to your name for ever. I will therefore go at once with you to the abode of this man Spicer, calling on my way at the house of a legal friend of mine, whom I shall try to get to accompany us. I presume we shall have no great difficulty in procuring restitution of the stolen letter, when the culprit perceives that his schemes are found out, and that it is consequently valueless to him. Having succeeded in this, we shall endeavour to come to some equitable arrangement in regard to his claims on you—do you agree to this ? " Cumberland bowed his head in token of assent, and Dr. Mildman continued,—

" And you, Oaklands, do you approve of this plan ? "

" It is like yourself, Doctor, the perfection of justice and kindness," replied Oaklands, warmly.

" That is well," resumed Dr. Mildman ; " I have one more painful duty to perform, which may as well be done at once—you are aware, Mr. Cumberland, that I must expel you ? "

" Will you not look over my fault this once ? " entreated Cumberland ; " believe me, I will never give you cause for complaint again."

" No, sir," was the reply ; " in justice to your companions I cannot longer allow you to remain under the same roof with them ; it is my duty to see that they associate only with persons fitted for the society of gentlemen, amongst whom, I am sorry to say, I can no longer class you. I shall myself accompany you to town to-morrow, and, if possible, see your uncle, to inform him of this unhappy affair. And now, sir, prepare to go with me to this Captain Spicer ;—on our return you will oblige me by remaining in your room during the evening. Oaklands, will you ask Lawless to take my place at the dinner-table, and inform your companions that Cumberland has been engaged in an affair, of which I so strongly disapprove, that I have determined on expelling him, but that you are not at liberty to disclose the particulars. I need scarcely repeat this caution to you, Fairlegh ; you have shown so much good sense and right feeling throughout the whole business that I am certain you will respect my wishes on this head."

I murmured some words in assent, and so ended one of the most painful and distressing scenes it has ever been my fate to witness.

CHAPTER X.

THE BOATING PARTY.

" Fair laughs the morn, and soft the zephyr blows,
As proudly riding o'er the azure realm
In gallant trim the gilded vessel goes ;
Youth on the prow, and Pleasure at the helm."
Gray's Bard.
" Shall I not take mine ease in mine inn ?"
Henry IV.

THE dinner passed off heavily ; every attempt to keep up a continued
conversation failed entirely ; and a general feeling of relief was
experienced when the time arrived for us to retire to the pupils' room.
Even here, however, the state of things was not much better. Lawless and the others, having in vain attempted to learn more of the
affair from Oaklands and myself than we felt at liberty to tell them,
lounged over a book, or dozed by the fire ; whilst we, unable to converse on the subject which alone engrossed our thoughts, and
disinclined to do so upon any other, were fain to follow their example.
About half-past eight Dr. Mildman and Cumberland returned, and
after dinner, which was served to them in the Doctor's study, Cumberland retired to his room, where he remained during the rest of the
evening. Oaklands then received a summons from the Doctor, and
on his return informed us that (as we had already heard) Cumberland
was to be expelled. He added that Dr. Mildman intended to take
him to town himself the next morning, as he was anxious to see
Cumberland's uncle, who was also his guardian : he would probably,
therefore, not return till the following day, in consequence of which
we should have a whole holiday, and he trusted to us to spend it in a
proper manner, which, as Coleman remarked, proved that he was of
a very confiding disposition indeed, and no mistake.

When we went up to bed Oaklands beckoned me into his room,
and, as soon as he had closed the door, gave me an account (having
obtained Dr. Mildman's permission to do so) of the interview with
Spicer. They found him, it seemed, at his lodgings, preparing for
his departure. At first he took a very high tone, denied the whole
thing, and was extremely blustering and impertinent ; but on being
confronted with Cumberland, and threatened by Dr. Mildman's legal
friend with the terrors of the law, he became thoroughly crestfallen,
restored the three-hundred-pound cheque, and consented, on the payment of fifty pounds, in addition to the fifty pounds he had already
received, to give up all claims on Cumberland, whereupon they paid
him the money down, made him sign a paper to the above effect, and
left him.

" And so, my dear Frank," said Oaklands, " there is an end of that

affair, and if it only produces as much effect upon Cumberland as it
has produced upon me, it will read him a lesson he will not forget
for many a long day. I blame myself excessively," he continued, "for
my own share in this matter; if it had not been for my easy, careless
way of going on, this scheme would never have been thought of—nay,
I might, perhaps, have been able to rescue Cumberland from the
hands of this sharper; but in this manner we neglect the opportunities
afforded us of doing good, and—Frank," he continued, with a sudden
burst of energy, "I will cure myself of this abominable indolence."
He paused for some minutes in thought, and then added, " Well, I
must not stand here raving at;you any longer : it is getting very
late; good-night, old fellow ! I shall be glad enough to tumble into
bed, for I'm as tired as a dog; it really is astonishing how easily I
am knocked up."

The absurdity of this remark, following upon the resolution he had
expressed with so much energy but a minute before, struck us both
at the same instant, and occasioned a fit of laughter, which we did
not check till we recollected with what dissonance any approach to
mirth must strike the ear of the prisoner (for such he was in fact, if
not in name) in the adjoining apartment.

" Now, sir; come, Mr. Fairlegh, you'll be late for breakfast," were
the first sounds that reached my understanding on the following
morning :—I say understanding, as I had heard, mixed up with my
dreams, sundry noises produced by unclosing shutters, arranging
water-jugs, etc., which appeared to my sleep-bewildered senses to
have been going on for at least half an hour. My faculties not being
sufficiently aroused to enable me to speak, Thomas continued,
" You'll be late, Mr. Fairlegh; " then came an aside, " My wig, how
he do sleep ! I hope he ain't been a-taking lauddelum, or morpheus,
or anything of a somnambulous natur. I wouldn't be master, always
to have six boys a-weighing on my mind, for all the wealth of the
Ingies—Mr. Fairlegh, I say !"

" There, don't make such a row," replied I, jumping out of bed and
making a dash at my clothes; " is it late ? "

" Jest nine o'clock, sir; master and Mr. Cumberland's been gone
these two hours. Shocking affair that, sir; it always gives me quite
a turn when any of our gents is expelled: it's like being thrown out
of place at a minute's warning, as I said to cook only this morning.
' Cook,' says I, ' life's a curious thing.' There's—"

" The breakfast bell ringing, by all that's unlucky ! " exclaimed I;
and downstairs I ran, with one arm in, and one out, of my jacket,
leaving Thomas to conclude his speculations on the mutability of
human affairs as he best might, solus.

" How are we going to kill time to-day ? " inquired Oaklands, as
soon as we had done breakfast.

" We mustn't do anything to outrage the proprieties," said Coleman; " remember we are on ' parole d'honneur.' "

" On a fiddlestick," interrupted Lawless; " let's all ride over to

the Duke of York, at Bradford, shoot some pigeons, have a champagne breakfast, and be home again in time for the old woman's
feed at five o'clock. I dare say I can pick up one or two fellows to
go with us."

"No," said Oaklands, "that sort of thing won't do to-day. I quite
agree with Freddy: we ought not to do anything to annoy the
Doctor upon this occasion; come, Lawless, I am sure you'll say so
too, if you give it a moment's thought."

"Well, he's a good old fellow in his way, I know; but what are we
to be at, then? something I must do, if it's only to keep me out of
mischief."

"It's a lovely day; let us hire a boat, and have a row," suggested
Coleman.

"That's not against the laws, is it?" asked Oaklands.

"Not a bit," replied Coleman; "we used to go pulling about like
bricks last summer, and Mildman rather approved of it than otherwise, and said it was a very healthy exercise."

"Yes, that will do," said Lawless; "I feel savage this morning,
and a good pull will take it out of me as well as anything. Now,
don't go wasting time; let's get ready, and be off;" and accordingly
in less than half an hour we were prepared, and on our way to the
beach.

"How are we going to do it?" inquired Lawless; "you'll take an
oar, Oaklands?"

Oaklands replied in the affirmative.

"Can you row, Fairlegh?"

I answered that I could a little.

"That will do famously, then," said Lawless; "we'll have a four-
oar; Wilson has a capital little boat that will be just the thing;
Freddy can steer, he's a very fair hand at it, and we four fellows will
pull, so that we need not be bothered with a boatman. I do
abominate those chaps, they are such a set of humbugs."

No objection was made to this plan. Lawless succeeded in getting
the boat he wished for: it was launched without any misadventure,
and we took our places, and began pulling away merrily, with the
wind (what little there was) and tide both in our favour.

The morning was beautiful: it was one of those enjoyable days,
which sometimes occur in early spring, in which Nature, seeming to
overleap at a bound the barrier between winter and summer, gives
us a delightful foretaste of the good things she has in store for us.
The clear bright sea, its surface just ruffled by a slight breeze from
the south-west, sparkled in the sunshine, and fell in diamond
showers from our oars as we raised them out of the water, while the
calm serenity of the deep blue sky above us appeared, indeed, a
fitting emblem of that heaven, in which "the wicked cease from
troubling, and the weary are at rest."

The peaceful beauty of the scene seemed to impress even the
restless spirits of which our little party was composed, and, by

G

common consent, we ceased rowing, and suffered the boat to drift
with the tide, merely pulling a stroke now and then to keep her head
in the right direction.   After drifting for some twenty minutes or so
in the manner I have described, Lawless, who could never remain
quiet long, dropped the blade of his oar into the water with a splash
that made us all start, exclaiming as he did so,—

"Well, this may be very sentimental and romantic, and all that
sort of thing, but it doesn't strike me as particularly entertaining.
Why, you fellows were all asleep I believe."

"Heigho!" exclaimed Oaklands, rousing himself, with a deep sigh.
"I was in such a delicious reverie; what a barbarian you are,
Lawless! you seem utterly ignorant of the pleasures of the 'dolce-
far-niente.'"

"Dolce-far-devilskin!" was the reply, in tones of the greatest
contempt.   "I would not be as lazy as you are, Oaklands. for any
money.   You are fitter to lounge about in some old woman's drawing-
room, than to handle an oar."

"Well, I don't know," answered Oaklands quietly, "but I think I
can pull as long as you can."

"You do, do you?" rejoined Lawless; "it will be odd to me, if
you can.   I don't think I was stroke oar in the crack boat at Eton
for a year, without knowing how to row a little; what do you say to
having a try at once?"

"With all my heart," replied Oaklands, divesting himself of his
waistcoat, braces, and neck-cloth, which latter article he braced
tightly round his waist—an example speedily followed by Lawless,
who exclaimed, as he completed his preparations,—

"Now, you young shavers, pull in your oars, and we'll give you a
ride, all free, gratis, for nothing."

Mullins and I hastened to comply with Lawless's directions, by
placing the oars and seating ourselves so as not to interfere with the
trim of the boat; while he and Oaklands, each taking a firm grasp
of his oar, commenced pulling away in real earnest.   They were
more evenly matched than may be at first imagined, for Lawless,
though much shorter than Oaklands, was very square built and
broad about the shoulders, and his arms, which were unusually long
in proportion to his height, presented a remarkable development of
muscle, while it was evident, from the manner in which he handled
his oar, that he was the more practised rower of the two.   The boat,
urged by their powerful strokes, appeared to fly through the water,
while cliff and headland (we were rowing along shore about half a
mile from the beach) came in view and disappeared again like scenes
in some moving panorama.   We must now have proceeded some
miles, yet still the rival champions continued their exertions with
unabated energy, and a degree of strength that seemed inexhaustible.
Greatly interested in the event, I had at first watched the contend-
ing parties with anxious attention, but, perceiving that the efforts
they were making did not produce any visible effects upon them, and

that the struggle was likely to be a protracted one, I took advantage of the opportunity to open a letter from my sister, which I had received just as I was leaving the house. I was sorry to find, on perusing it, that my father had been suffering from an inflammatory attack, brought on by a cold which he had caught in returning from a visit to a sick parishioner, through a pouring rain. A postscript from my mother, however, added that I need not make myself in the least uneasy, as the apothecary assured her that my father was going on as well as possible and would probably be quite restored in the course of a week or so. On observing the date of the letter, I found I ought to have received it the day before. Arguing from this (on the "no news being good news" system) that I should have heard again if anything had gone wrong, I dismissed the subject from my mind, and was reading Fanny's account of a juvenile party she had been at in the neighbourhood, when my attenton was roused by Coleman, who, laying his hand on my shou der, said,—

"Look out, Frank, it won't be long now before we shall see who's best man; the work's beginning to tell."

Thus invoked, I raised my eyes, and perceived that a change had come over the aspect of affairs while I had been engaged with my letter. Oaklands and Lawless were still rowing with the greatest energy, but it appeared to me that their strokes were drawn with less and less vigour each succeeding time, while their flushed faces and heavy breathing proved that the severe labour that they had undergone had not been without its effect. The only visible difference between them was, that Lawless, from his superior training, had not, as a jockey would say, "turned a hair," while the perspiration hung in big drops upon the brow of Oaklands, and the knotted, swollen veins of his hands stood out like tightly-strained cordage.

"Hold hard!" shouted Lawless. "I say, Harry," he continued, as soon as they left off rowing, "how are you getting on?"

"I have been cooler in my life," replied Oaklands, wiping his face with his handkerchief.

"Well, I think it's about a drawn battle," said Lawless, "though I am free to confess that, if you were in proper training, I should be no match for you, even with the oar."

"What made you stop just then?" inquired Oaklands; "I'm sure I could have kept on for a quarter of an hour longer, if not more."

"So could I," replied Lawless, "ay, or for half an hour, if I had been put to it; but I felt the work was beginning to tell, I saw you were getting used up, and I recollected that we should have to row back with the wind against us, which, as the breeze is freshening, will be no such easy matter; so I thought if we went on till we were both done up, we should be in a regular fix."

"It's lucky you remembered it," said Oaklands; "I was so excited, I should have gone on pulling as long as I could have held an oar we must be some distance from Helmstone by this time. Have you any idea whereabouts we are ? "

" Let's have a look," rejoined Lawless. " Yes, that tall cliff you see there is the Nag's Head, and in the little bay beyond stands the village of Fisherton. I vote we go ashore there, have some bread and cheese, and a draught of porter at the inn, and then we shall be able to pull back again twice as well."

This proposal seemed to afford general satisfaction ; Mullins and I resumed our oars, and in less than half an hour we were safely ensconced in the sanded parlour of the Dolphin, while the pretty barmaid, upon whom also devolved the duties of waitress, hastened to place before us a smoking dish of eggs and bacon, which we had chosen in preference to red herrings—the only other dainty the Dolphin had to offer us—Coleman observing that "a hard roe " was the only part of a herring worth eating, and we had that already, as we came along.

"I say, my dear, have you got any bottled porter?" inquired Lawless.

" Yes, sir, and very good it is," replied the smiling damsel.

" That's a blessing," observed Coleman piously.

" Bring us up a lot of it, my beauty," resumed Lawless, "and some pewter pots—porter's twice as good out of its own native pewter."

Thus exhorted, the blooming waitress tripped off, and soon returned with a basket containing six bottles of porter.

" That's the time of day," said Lawless ; " now for a corkscrew, pretty one ; here you are, Oaklands."

" I must own that is capital, after such hard work as we have been doing," observed Oaklands, as he emptied the pewter pot at a draught.

" I say, Mary," asked Coleman, " what's gone of that young man that used to keep company along with you—that nice young chap, that had such insinivatin' ways with him ? "

" I'm sure I don't know what you're taking about, sir; I've nothink to say to no young man whatsumever," replied the damsel addressed, shaking her curls coquettishly.

" Ah ! " sighed Coleman, " if I were but single now ! "

" Why, you never mean to say you've got a wife already, such a very young gentleman as you are ? "

" Not only that, but a small family with a large appetite," continued Coleman pathetically.

" Well, I never ! " exclaimed the barmaid, surprised for once out of her company manners ; then, observing a smile at her expense going the round of the party, she added, " I see how it is ; you are making fun of me, sir ; oh, fie ! you're a wicked young gentleman, I know you are."

" Never mind him, my dear," said Lawless, " but give me another bottle of porter."

In converse such as this, the meal and the half-dozen of porter were finished; in addition to which, Lawless chose to have a glass of brandy-and-water and a cigar. Having been rendered unusually hungry by the sea air and the unaccustomed exercise of rowing, I had both eaten and drunk more than I was in the habit of doing, to which cause may be attributed my falling into a doze—an example which, I have every reason to believe, was followed by most of the others. I know not how long my nap had lasted, when I was aroused by hearing Coleman exclaim,—

"Why, I think it rains! Lawless, wake up! I don't much like the look of the weather."

"What's the row?" inquired Lawless, leisurely removing his legs from the table on which they had been resting, and walking to the window—a feat, by the way, he did not perform quite as steadily as usual. "By Jove!" he continued, "the wind's blowing great guns! we must look sharp, and be off—we shall have the sea getting up!"

Accordingly, the bill was rung for and paid; Mary received half-a-crown and a kiss from Lawless, and down we ran to the beach, where difficulties we were little prepared for awaited us.

CHAPTER XI.

BREAKERS AHEAD!

"Now would I give a thousand furlongs of sea for an acre of barren ground. . . . The wills above be done, but I would fain die a dry death."
"I have great comfort from this fellow; methinks he hath no drowning mark upon him."—*Tempest.*

THE wind, which we had observed was rising when we landed, had increased during our stay at the inn, and was now blowing almost a gale from the south-west; whilst the sea, which we had left smooth as a lake, was rolling in and breaking on the beach in somewhat formidable waves.

"I tell you what," said Coleman, as soon as he had observed the state of affairs, "I won't attempt to steer in such a sea as that; it requires great skill and judgment, besides a stronger hand than mine, to keep the boat's head right; if I were to let her turn her broadside to one of those waves, it would be a case of 'Found drowned' with some of us, before long."

"What's to be done, then?" inquired Oaklands. "I am sure I can't do it; it's a thing I'm quite ignorant of; all my boating having been on the river."

"Let's hire one of those amphibious beggars out there to steer for us," proposed Lawless, pointing to a group of fishermen who were lounging round an old boat, not far from where we stood; "they're up to all the right dodges, you may depend. Here, my men! which of you will earn half-a-guinea, by steering our boat for us to Helmstone?"

"I wouldn't, master, for ten times the money," replied an old weather-beaten boatman, in a tarpaulin hat; "and if you'll take an old man's advice, gentlemen, you'll none of you venture out in that cockle-shell this afternoon; the wind's getting up every minute, and we shall have a rough night of it."

"Nonsense," replied Lawless; "I've often been out in worse weather than this. Are you, all of you, frightened by that old woman's croaking?" continued he, turning to the group of men.

"He's no old woman," replied a sturdy fellow, in a rough pea-jacket; "he's been a better sailor than ever you'll be, and he's right now too," he added. "It's as much as a man's life is worth to go to sea in that bit of a thing, with the waves running in as they do now —and with such a set of landlubbers as them for a crew," he muttered, turning away.

"Suppose we try and get something to take us home by land," suggested Oaklands, "and leave the boat for some of these good fellows to bring home as soon as the weather will allow."

"You'll have to walk, sir," replied one of them civilly; "I don't believe there's a cart or horse in the place; they all went inland this morning with fish, and won't return till to-morrow."

"There, you hear that," said Lawless, who had just drunk enough to render him captious and obstinate. "I'm not going to walk to please anybody's fancy; I see how it is,—I did not bid high enough. A couple of guineas for anyone who will come with us," added he.

"A couple of guineas is not to be got every day," observed a sullen, downcast-looking man, who had not yet spoken; "and it is not much odds to me whether I sink or swim now; those custom-house sharks," added he, with an oath, "look so close after one, that one can't do a stroke of work that will pay a fellow nowadays. Money down, and I'm your man, sir," he added, turning to Lawless.

"That's the ticket," said Lawless, handing him the money. "I'm glad to see one of you, at least, has got a little pluck about him. Come along."

I could see that Oaklands did not at all approve of the plan, evidently considering we were running a foolish risk; but, as nothing short of a direct quarrel with Lawless could have prevented it, his habitual indolence and easy temper prevailed, and he remained silent. I felt much inclined to object, in which case I had little doubt the majority of the party would have supported me; but a boyish dread, lest my refusal should be attributed to cowardice prevented my doing so. With the assistance of the bystanders we

contrived to launch our little bark without further misadventure
than a rather heavier sprinkling of salt water than was agreeable.
Rowing in such a sea, however, proved much harder work than I,
for one, had any idea of; we made scarcely any way against the
waves, and I soon felt sure that it would be utterly impossible for us
to reach Helmstone by any exertions we were capable of making.
The weather, too, was becoming worse every minute: it rained
heavily, and it was with the greatest difficulty we were able to
prevent the crests of some of the larger waves from dashing into
our boat; in fact, as it was, she was already half full of water, which
poured in faster than Coleman (who was the only person not
otherwise engaged) could bale it out.

"Upon my word, Lawless, it's madness to attempt to go on!"
exclaimed Oaklands; "we are throwing away our lives for nothing."

"It certainly looks rather queerish," replied Lawless. "What do
you say about it, my man?" he asked of the person whom he had
engaged to steer us.

"I say," replied the fellow in a surly tone, "that our only chance
is to make for the beach at once, and we shall have better luck than
we deserve if we reach it alive."

As he spoke, a larger wave than usual broke against the bow of the
boat, flinging in such a body of water that we felt her stagger under
it, and I believed, for a moment, that we were about to sink. This
decided the question; the boat's head was put about with some
difficulty, and we were soon straining every nerve to reach the shore.
As we neared the beach, we perceived that even during the short
time which had elapsed since we quitted it, the sea had become
considerably rougher, and the line of surf now presented anything
but an encouraging appearance. As we approached the breakers,
the steersman desired us to back with our oars till he saw a
favourable opportunity, and the moment he gave us the signal, to
pull in as hard as we were able. After a short pause the signal was
given, and we attempted to pull in as he had directed; but in doing
this we did not act exactly in concert—Lawless taking his stroke too
soon, while Mullins did not make his soon enough; consequently, we
missed the precise moment, the boat turned broadside to the beach,
a wave poured over us, and in another instant we were struggling in
the breakers. For my own part, I succeeded in gaining my legs, only
to be thrown off them again by the next wave, which hurried me
along with it, and flung me on the shingle, when one of the group of
fishermen who had witnessed the catastrophe ran in, and seizing me
by the arm, in time to prevent my being washed back again by the
under-tow, dragged me out of the reach of the waves.

On recovering my feet, my first impulse was to look round for my
companions. I at once perceived Lawless, Mullins, and Oaklands,
who were apparently uninjured, though the latter held his hand
pressed against his forehead, as if in pain; but Coleman was nowhere
to be seen. "Where is Coleman?" exclaimed I.

"There is someone clinging to the boat still," observed a bystander.

I looked anxiously in the direction indicated, and perceived the boat floating bottom upwards, just beyond the line of breakers while, clinging to the keel, was a figure which I instantly recognized to be that of Coleman. "Oh, save him, save him; he will be drowned!" cried I, in an agony of fear.

"Ten guineas for anyone who will get him out!" shouted Lawless; but nobody seemed inclined to stir.

"Give me a rope," cried I, seizing the end of a coil which one of the boatmen had over his shoulder, and tying it round my waist.

"What are you going to do?" asked Lawless.

While he spoke a large wave separated Coleman from the boat, and as it poured its huge volume upon the beach, bore him along with it. With the swiftness of thought I sprang forward, and succeeded in throwing my arms round him, ere the next advancing wave dashed over us. And now my foresight in fastening the rope around me proved, under Providence, the means of saving both our lives. Though thrown to the ground by the force of the water, I contrived to retain my grasp of Coleman, and we were hauled up and conveyed beyond the reach of the surf by the strong arms of those on shore ere another wave could approach to claim its victims.

On recovering my consciousness (I had been partially stunned by the violence of my last fall), I found myself lying on the beach, with my head resting on the breast of Oaklands.

"My dear, dear Frank, thank God that you are safe!" exclaimed he, pressing me more closely to him.

"What of Coleman?" asked I, endeavouring to raise myself.

"They are taking him to the inn," was the reply: "I will go and see if I can be of any use, now I know you are unhurt; but I could not leave you till I felt sure of that."

"I fancied you seemed in pain just now," said I.

"I struck my head against some part of the boat when she capsized," returned Oaklands, "and the blow stunned me for a minute or two, so that I knew nothing of what was going on till I saw you rush into the water to save Coleman; that roused me effectually, and I helped them to pull you both out. Frank, you have saved his life."

"If it is saved," rejoined I. "Let us go and see how he is getting on; I think I can walk now, if you will let me lean upon your arm."

With the assistance of Oaklands I contrived to reach the inn without much difficulty; indeed, by the time I got there (the walk having served in a great measure to restore my circulation) I scarcely felt any ill effects from my late exertions. The inn presented a rare scene of confusion: people were hurrying in and out, the messenger sent for the doctor had just returned, breathless, to say he was not to be found; the fat landlady, in a state of the greatest

excitement, was trotting about making impracticable suggestions
to which no one paid the slightest attention, while Coleman, still
insensible, lay wrapped in blankets before a blazing fire in the
parlour, with the pretty barmaid on her knees beside him sobbing
piteously, as she chafed his temples with some strong essence.

" That's the time of day!" exclaimed Lawless, as his eye fell upon
a printed card which the landlady had just thrust into his hand
headed, "The directions of the Humane Society for the restoration
of persons apparently drowned." " We shall have it now all right,"
added he, and then read as follows :—" The first observation we
must make, which is most important. is, that rolling the body on a
tub—"

" Bring a tub," cried the landlady eagerly, and off started several
of the bystanders to follow her injunctions—

" Is most injurious," continued Lawless ; " but holding up by the
legs with the head downwards "—a party of volunteers, commanded
by the landlady, rushed forward to obtain possession of Coleman's
legs—" is certain death," shouted Lawless, concluding the sentence.

While this was going on I had been rubbing Coleman's hands
between my own, in the hope of restoring circulation : and now, to
my extreme delight, I perceived a slight pulsation at the wrist; next
came a deep sigh, followed by a tremulous motion of the limbs ; and
before five minutes were over he was sufficiently restored to sit up,
and recognize those about him. After this, his recovery progressed
with such rapidity, that ere half an hour had elapsed he was able to
listen with interest to Oakland's account of the circumstances
attending his rescue, when Lawless, hastily entering the room,
exclaimed, " Here's a slice of good luck, at all events ; there's a
postchaise just stopped, returning to Helmstone, and the boy agrees
to take us all for a shilling a head, as soon as he has done watering
his horses. How is Freddy getting on ?—will he be able to go ? "

" All right, old fellow," replied Coleman. " Thanks to Fairlegh
in the first instance, and a stiff glass of brandy-and-water in the
second, ' Richard's himself again !' "

" Well, you've had a near shave for it this time, however," said
Lawless ; " there is more truth than I was aware of in the old
proverb, ' If you are born to be hanged you will never be drowned ; '
though, if it had not been for Frank Fairlegh, you would not have
lived to fulfil your destiny."

In another ten minutes we were all packed in and about the postchaise; Coleman, Oaklands, and myself occupying the interior, while
Lawless and Mullins rode outside. The promise of an extra half-
crown induced the driver to use his best speed. At a quarter before
five we were within a stone's throw of home; and if that day at
dinner Mrs. Mildman observed the pale looks and jaded appearance
of some of the party, I have every reason to believe she has
remained up to the present hour in total ignorance as to their cause.

CHAPTER XII.

DEATH AND CHANGE.

" The voice which I did more esteem
    Than Music on her sweetest key ;
Those eyes which unto me did seem
    More comfortable than the day—
Those now by me, as they have been,
Shall never more be heard or seen ;
But what I once enjoyed in them,
Shall seem hereafter as a dream.

" All earthly comforts vanish thus,
    So little hold of them have we,
That we from them, or they from us,
    May in a moment ravished be.
Yet we are neither just nor wise
If present mercies we despise,
Or mind not how these may be made
A thankful use of what we had."
                     Wither.

" Up springs at every stop to claim a tear,
Some youthful friendship form'd and cherish'd here."
                     Rogers.

"Time flies away fast !
    The while we never remember—
    How soon our life here
    Grows old with the year
That dies with the next December."
                     Herrick.

As I was undressing that night, Coleman came into my room, and grasping my hand with his own, shook it warmly, saying, " I could not go to sleep, Frank, without coming to thank you for the noble way in which you risked your own life to save mine to-day. I laughed it off before Lawless and the rest of the fellows, for when I feel deeply I hate to show it ; but, indeed " (and the tears stood in his eyes while he spoke), " indeed I am not ungrateful."

" My dear Freddy," returned I, "do not suppose I thought you so for a moment ; there, say no more about it ; you would have done the same thing for me that I did for you had our positions been reversed."

" I am not so sure of that," was his reply ; " I should have wished to do so ; but it is not everyone who can act with such promptitude and decision in moments of danger."

" There is one request I should like to make," said I.

" What is it ? " replied he quickly.

" Do not forget to thank Him whose instrument I was, for having so mercifully preserved your life."

A silent pressure of the hand was the only answer, and we parted for the night.

Owing, probably, to over-fatigue, it was some little time before I went to sleep. As I lay courting the fickle goddess (or god, as the case may be, for mythologically speaking, I believe Somnus was a he), I could not help contrasting my present feelings with those which I experienced on the first night of my arrival. Then, overcome by the novelty of my situation, filled with a lively dread of my tutor, bullied and despised by my companions, and separated for what I deemed an interminable period from all who were dear to me, my position was far from an enviable one. Now, how different was the aspect of affairs! With my tutor, who, from an object of dread, had become one of esteem and affection, I had every reason to believe myself a favourite; I was on terms of the closest friendship with those of my companions whose intimacy was best worth cultivating; while with the others I had gained a standing which would effectually prevent their ever venturing seriously to annoy me; and, above all, I had acquired that degree of self-confidence, without which one is alike impotent to choose the good or to refuse the evil. And it was with an honest pride that I reflected that this improvement in my position was mainly owing to a steady adherence to those principles which it had been the constant aim of ¡my dear parents to instil into me from my childhood. I fell asleep at last, endeavouring to picture to myself the delight of relating my adventures on my return home; how my mother and sister would shudder over the dangers I had escaped, while my father would applaud the spirit which had carried me through them. The vision was a bright and happy one: would it ever be realized?

To our surprise, we learned the next morning that Dr. Mildman had arrived by the last coach the previous evening, having fortunately met with Cumberland's uncle at his house of business in town, and delivered his nephew into his safe custody without further loss of time. The breakfast passed over without the Doctor making any inquiry how we had amused ourselves during his absence, nor, as may easily be believed, did we volunteer information on the subject. On returning to the pupils' room, I found a letter, in my sister's hand-writing, lying on the table. With a feeling of dread for which I could not account, I hastened to peruse it. Alas! the contents only served to realize my worst apprehensions. My father's illness had suddenly assumed a most alarming character, inflammation having attacked the lungs with such violence that the most active measures had failed to subdue it, and the physician whom my mother had summoned on the first appearance of danger, scarcely held out the slightest hope of his recovery. Under the circumstances, my mother wished me to return home without loss of time, as my father, before he became delirious, had desired that I might be sent for, expressing himself most anxious to see me; and the letter concluded with a line in my mother's handwriting, exhorting me to make every exertion to reach home without delay, if I wished to find him alive. For a minute or two, I sat with the letter still open in my hand, as if stunned by the intelligence I had received; then, recollecting that every instant was of importance. I sprang up, saying, "Where's Dr. Mildman? I must see him directly."

"My dear Frank, is anything the matter? you are not ill?" inquired Oaklands, anxiously.

"You have received some bad news, I am afraid," said Coleman.

"My father is very ill, dying perhaps," replied I, while the tears, which I in vain endeavoured to restrain, trickled down my cheeks. After giving way to my feelings for a minute or two, the necessity for action again flashed across me.

"What time is it now?" inquired I, drying my eyes.

"Just ten," replied Oaklands, looking at his watch.

"There is a coach which starts at the half-hour, is there not?"

"Yes, the Highflyer, the best drag on the road," returned Lawless; "takes you to town in five hours, and does the thing well too."

"I must go by that, then," replied I.

"What can I do to help you?" asked Coleman.

"If you would put a few things into my bag for me, while I speak to the Doctor," rejoined I.

"I will go and get a fly for you," said Lawless, "and then I can pick out a nag that will move his pins a bit; that will save you ten minutes, and you have no time to lose."

On acquainting Dr. Mildman with the sad intelligence I had received, and the necessity which existed for me to depart immediately, he at once gave me his permission to do so; and after speaking kindly to me, and showing the deepest sympathy for my distress, said he would not detain me longer, as I must have preparations to make, but should like to see me the last thing before I started, and wish me good-bye.

I found, on reaching my own room, my carpet-bag already packed, Coleman and Thomas (whose honest face wore an expression of genuine commiseration) having exerted themselves to save me all trouble on that head. Nothing, therefore, remained for me to do, but to take leave of my fellow-pupils and Dr. Mildman. After shaking hands with Lawless and Mullins (the former assuring me, as he did so, that I was certain not to be late, for he had succeeded in securing a trap, with a very spicy little nag in it, which would have me there in no time), I hastened to take leave of my tutor. The kind-hearted Doctor inquired whether I had sufficient money for my journey, and begging me to write him word how I got home, shook me warmly by the hand, saying, as he did so, "God bless you, my boy! I trust you may find your father better; but if this should not be the case, remember whose hand it is inflicts the blow, and strive to say, 'Thy will be done.' We shall have you among us again soon, I hope; but should anything prevent your return, I wish you to know that I am perfectly satisfied with the progress you have made in your studies; and, in other respects, you have never given me a moment's uneasiness since you first entered my house. Once more, good-bye; and remember, if ever you should want a friend, you will find one in Samuel Mildman."

The fly-horse proved itself deserving of Lawless's panegyric, and I arrived at the coach-office in time to secure a seat outside the High-flyer. After taking an affectionate leave of Oaklands and Coleman,

who had accompanied me, I ascended to my place; the coachman
mounted his box, exactly as the clock chimed the half-hour the horses
sprang forward with a bound, and ere ten minutes had elapsed, Helmstone lay at least a couple of miles behind us.

I accomplished my journey more quickly than I had deemed
possible, and had the melancholy satisfaction of reaching home in
time to receive my father's blessing. The powerful remedies to
which they had been obliged to have recourse, had produced their
effect, the inflammation was subdued; but the struggle had been protracted too long, and his constitution, already enfeebled by a life of
constant labour and self-denial, was unable to rally. Having given
me a solemn charge to cherish and protect my mother and sister, he
commended us all to the care of Him who is emphatically termed
"the God of the fatherless and widow;" and then, his only earthly
care being ended, he prepared to meet Death, as those alone can do
to whom "to die is gain." When the last beam of the setting sun
threw a golden tint around the spire of the little village church, those
lips which had so often breathed the words of prayer and praise
within its sacred walls were mute for ever, and the gentle spirit which
animated them had returned to God who gave it!

In regard to this portion of my career but little more remains to
be told. My father's income being chiefly derived from his church
preferment, and his charities having been conducted on too liberal a
scale to allow of his laying by money, the funds which remained at
my mother's disposal after winding up his affairs, though enough to
secure us from actual poverty, were not sufficient to allow of my continuing an inmate of an establishment so expensive as that of Dr.
Mildman. On being informed of this change of circumstances, the
Doctor wrote to my mother in the kindest manner, speaking of me in
terms of praise which I will not repeat, and inquiring what were her
future views in regard to me—expressing his earnest desire to assist
them to the utmost of his ability. At the same time I received letters
from Oaklands and Coleman, full of lamentations that I was not
likely to return; and promising, in the warmth of their hearts, that
their respective fathers should assist me in all ways, possible and impossible. Mr. Coleman, senior, in particular, was to do most unheard-
of things for me: indeed, Freddy more than hinted, that through his
agency I might consider myself secure of the Attorney-Generalship,
with a speedy prospect of becoming Lord Chancellor. I also found
enclosed a very characteristic note from Lawless; wherein he stated
that if I really was likely to be obliged to earn my own living, he could
put me up to a dodge by which all the disagreeables of having so to
do might be avoided. This infallible recipe proved to be a scheme
for my turning stage-coachman! After citing numerous examples
of gentlemen who had done so (amongst whom the name of a certain
baronet stood forth in high pre-eminence), he wound up by desiring me
to give the scheme my serious attention, and, if I agreed to it, to come
and spend a month with him when he returned home at Midsummer ;

by the end of which time he would engage to turn me out as finished
a " Waggoner" as ever handled the ribbons. To these letters I despatched suitable replies, thanking the writers for their kindness, but
refusing to avail myself of their offers, at all events for the present;
and I finished by expressing the hope that, be my fate in life what it
might, I should still preserve the regard and esteem of the friends
whose affection I prized so highly.

For some months after my father's death, I continued to live at the
rectory; Mr. Dalton, the new incumbent, who had been his curate,
and was unmarried, kindly allowing my mother to remain there till
her plans for the future should be so far arranged as to enable her to
determine in what part of the country it would be advisable for her to
reside. It had been my father's wish and intention, when I should
have attained a fit age, to send me to one of the Universities—a wish
my mother was most anxious to carry into effect. In order to accomplish this wish with her reduced means, it would have been
necessary for her, not only to have practised the strictest economy.
but also, in great measure, to have sacrificed my sister's education, as
she would have been utterly unable to afford the advantage of
masters. To this, of course, I would not consent; after much discussion, therefore, the idea of college was reluctantly given up, and,
as a last resource, my mother applied to an uncle of hers, engaged in
the West India trade, begging him to endeavour to procure for me a
clerkship in some mercantile establishment. She received a very
kind reply, saying that although he considered me too young at
present to be chained to a desk, he should advise me to apply myself
diligently to the study of French and book-keeping; and ending by
offering me a situation in his own counting-house, when I should
be eighteen. As my only alternative lay between accepting this
offer (however little suited to my taste) or remaining a burden
upon my mother, it may easily be imagined that I lost no
time in signifying my desire to avail myself of his kindness;
and ere a couple of months had elapsed I had plunged deeply
into the mysteries of book-keeping and could jabber French
with tolerable fluency. I was still working away at " Double Entry,"
and other horrors of a like nature, when one morning I received a
large business-like letter, in an unknown hand, the contents of which
astonished me not a little, as well they might; for they proved to be
of a nature once more entirely to change my prospects in life. The
epistle came from Messrs. Coutts, the bankers, and stated that they
were commissioned to pay me the sum of four hundred pounds per
annum, in quarterly payments, for the purpose of defraying my
expenses at college; the only stipulations being, that the money
should be used for the purpose specified, that I did not contract any
debts whatsoever, and that I made no inquiries, direct or indirect,
as to the source from which the sum proceeded. In the event of
my complying with these conditions, the same allowance was to be
continued to me till I should have taken my degree.

The immediate consequence of this most unexpected communication was, our devoting the greater part of a morning to vain speculations as to the possible source from which this liberal offer might have proceeded. After guessing everyone we could think of, likely or unlikely, we ended, as is usual in such cases, by becoming decidedly more puzzled than when we began. The only person with whom I was acquainted possessing both the will and the power to do such a thing was Sir John Oaklands; but he had already, in the kindest manner, tried to persuade my mother to allow me to accompany Harry to Trinity College, Cambridge, begging to be permitted to defray the expenses of my so doing himself; an offer which she (not choosing to place herself under so heavy an obligation to a comparative stranger) had, with many expressions of gratitude, declined. After consulting with our friend Mr. Dalton, it was decided that I should signify to Messrs. Coutts my readiness to comply with the required conditions, begging them to convey my best thanks to my mysterious benefactor, and to inform him that it was my intention (subject to his approval) to enter my name at Trinity without loss of time. In answer to this I received the following laconic epistle:—

" Messrs. Coutts beg to inform Mr. Frank Fairlegh that, in reply to his favour of the 21st ult., they are desired to state that the sum of four hundred pounds per annum will be placed at his disposal whenever he applies for it."

I now resumed my studies under the superintendence of Mr. Dalton, who had taken a good degree at Cambridge ; and alike delighted at my escape from the counting-house, and anxious to do credit to my benefactor's liberality, I determined to make the best use of my time, and worked " con amore." In this manner, the next year and a half passed away without anything worthy of remark occurring. I was happy to perceive a gradual improvement taking place in my mother's health and spirits, while Fanny was developing into a very pretty and agreeable girl.

Towards the expiration of this period, Mr. Dalton saw fit to take unto himself a wife, a circumstance which induced my mother to accept the offer of a cottage belonging to Sir John Oaklands, which was suited to her limited means. It was situated within the park gates, about a mile from Heathfield Hall, and, though small, appeared well-built, and exceedingly pretty.

This was an arrangement of which I highly approved, as it enabled me to renew my intercourse with Harry, who, having left Dr. Mildman's, was spending a few months at home with his father, previous to his matriculation at Trinity. I found him but little altered in any respect, save that he had become more manly-looking. For the rest, he was just as good-tempered, kind-hearted, and, alas ! indolent as ever. He informed me that Lawless also was going to Cambridge, and that Coleman, when he learned what a party of us there would be, had been most anxious to accompany us ; but his father, unfortunately, did not approve, and he was now articled to a solicitor, with a view to his succeeding eventually to his father's practice.

Time rolled on, and another three months beheld us duly installed in our rooms at Trinity, and dividing our time between reading (more or less, in accordance with our various idiosyncrasies), boating on the Cam, billiard-playing at Chesterton, " et hoc genus omne."

Of the details of my college life I shall say but little, a piece of forbearance for which I consider myself entitled to the everlasting gratitude of my readers, who, if they have not had their curiosity on that subject more than satisfied by the interminable narrations of " Peter Priggins," and his host of imitators, must indeed be insatiable. Suffice it, then, to say that, having from the first determined, if possible, to obtain a good degree, I made a resolute stand against the advances of Lawless (who, in consequence of his father's having for some reason best known to himself and the premier, received a peerage, had now become an " honourable ") and the " rowing set," amongst whom, by a sort of freemasonry of kindred souls, he had become enrolled immediately on his arrival. After several fruitless attempts to shake my determination, they pronounced me an incorrigible " sap," and, leaving me to my own devices, proceeded to try their powers upon Oaklands. They met with but little success in this quarter, however; not that with him they had any indomitable love of study to contend with, but that " all that sort of thing was too much trouble; he really didn't believe there was a single fellow among the whole lot who had the slightest appreciation of the ' dolce far niente.'" When, however, they found out that upon an emergency Harry could excel them all—whatever might be the nature of the feat to be performed—and that I could cross a country, pull an oar, or handle a bat with the best of them, they set us down as a pair of eccentric geniuses, and as such admitted us to a kind of honorary membership in their worshipful society; and thus, 'twixt work and play, the first two years of my residence at Cambridge passed happily enough.

CHAPTER XIII.

CATCHING A SHRIMP.

" Give me that boy."—*Shakespeare.*
" I was there
From college, visiting the son."
Princess.
" To bring in, Heaven shield us, a lion among ladies, is a most dreadful thing." ·
Shakespeare.

" A MIGHTY stupid chapter that last ! " " True for you, reader ; but how was it to be avoided ? It was necessary to give you that short summary of my proceedings, the better to enable you to understand all that is to follow, and so don't you see—" " Yes, that will do. Above all things, Master Frank, avoid being prosy ; it is the worst fault an author can fall into." " Reader, you're very cross ! "

It was towards the close of the long vacation that, one morning, as I was sitting at breakfast with my mother and sister, a note was brought to me. On opening it, it proved to be from Coleman, whose father had lately taken a country house near Hillingford, a small town about fifteen miles from Heathfield, where he was now about to give a grand ball to all the neighbourhood by way of house-warming. At this ball, Freddy (with whom I had kept up a constant correspondence, though we had never met since I left Dr. Mildman's) was most anxious I should be present, and his letter was really a masterpiece of persuasion: not only should I meet all the beauty and fashion of the county, but he had for some days past employed himself in paving the way for me with several of the most desirable young ladies of his acquaintance, who were now, as he assured me, actually pining to be introduced to me. Moreover, the Honourable George Lawless had promised to be there ; so we were safe for fun of some sort, Lawless's tastes and habits being about as congenial to the atmosphere of a ball-room as those of a bull to the interior of a china-shop.

These manifold temptations, together with the desire of again meeting Freddy himself, proved irresistible, and I decided to go. Oaklands, who had received a similar invitation, was unluckily not able to accept it, as his father had fixed a shooting-party for that day, at which, and at the dinner that was to follow, Harry's presence was indispensable.

It was in the afternoon of a glorious September day that I set off on horseback for Hillingford. I had accompanied the sportsmen in the morning, and had walked just enough to excite without fatiguing myself ; and now the elastic motion of the horse (a valuable hunter of Sir John's), the influence of the fair scene around me, as I cantered over the smooth turf of Heathfield Park, and

H

along the green lanes beyond it—the prospect of seeing again an old
companion of my boyhood's days—all contributed to produce in me
an exhilaration of spirits which seemed to raise me above the
" kleinigkeiten," the littlenesses (as the Germans so well express it)
of this world, and to exalt me to some higher and nobler sphere. Out of
this day-dream I was at length aroused by the clatter of horses' feet,
and the rattle of wheels in the lane behind me, while a man's voice
in tones not of the most gentle description, accosted me as follows :
" Now then, sir, if you've got a licence to take up the whole road, I'll
just trouble you to show it ! " With a touch of the spur I caused my
horse to bound on one side, and, as I did so, I turned to look at the
speaker. Perched high in mid-air, upon some mysterious species of
dog-cart bearing a striking resemblance to the box of a mail coach,
which had contrived, by some private theory of development of its
own, to dispense with its body, while it had enlarged its wheels to an
almost incredible circumference—perched on the top of this remarkable machine, and enveloped in a white great-coat undermined in
every direction by strange and unexpected pockets, was none other
than the Honourable George Lawless ! The turn-out was drawn by
a pair of thorough-breds, driven tandem, which were now (their iras-
cible tempers being disturbed by the delay which my usurpation
of the road had occasioned) relieving their feelings by executing a
kind of hornpipe upon their hind legs. The equipage was completed
by a tiger, so small that, beyond a vague sensation of top boots and
a livery hat, one's senses failed to realize him.

" Why, Lawless ! " exclaimed I, " you are determined to astonish
the natives, with a vengeance ; such a turn-out as that has never been
seen in these parts before, I'm certain."

" Frank Fairlegh, by Jove ! How are you, old fellow ! Is it my
trap you're talking about ? What do you think of it ? rather the
thing, isn't it, eh ? " I signified my approval, and Lawless continued,
" Yes, it's been very much admired, I assure you ;—quiet, mare !
quiet !—not a bad sort of dodge to knock about in, eh ?—What are
you at, fool !—Tumble out, Shrimp, and hit Spiteful a lick on the nose
—he's eating the mare's tail. Spicy tiger, Shrimp—did you ever hear
how I picked him up ? "

I replied in the negative, and Lawless resumed,—

" I was down at Broadstairs, the beginning of the long—wretched
place, but I went there for a boat-race with some more fellows ; well,
of course, because we wanted it to be fine, the weather turned sulky,
and the boat-race had to be put off ; so, to prevent ourselves from
going melancholy mad, we hired a drag and managed to get together
a team, such as it was. The first day we went out they elected me
waggoner, and a nice job I had of it ; three of the horses had never
been in harness before, and the fourth was a bolter. It was pretty
near half an hour before we could get them to start ; and, when they
were off, I had enough to do to keep their heads out of the shop
windows. However, as soon as they began to get warm to their

work, things improved and we rattled along merrily. We were
spinning away at about twelve miles an hour, when, just as we were
getting clear of the town, we came suddenly upon a covey of juvenile
blackguards, who were manufacturing dirt-pies right in the centre of
the road. As soon as I saw them, I sung out to them to clear the
course, but before they had time to cut away, we were slap into the
middle of them. Well, I thought it was to be a regular case of
Herod, and that there would be at least half-a-dozen of them spiffli-
cated; but they all managed to save their bacon, except Shrimp—
one of the wheels went over him and broke him somewhere. Where
was it, Shrimp?"

"Left arm, sir, if you please," replied Shrimp, in a shrill treble.

"Ay, so it was," continued Lawless. "As soon as I could contrive
to pull up, I sent the groom back, with orders to find a doctor, get
the boy repaired, and tell them to come to me at the hotel in the
morning, and I'd pay for all damages. Accordingly, while I was
eating my breakfast next morning, an amphibious old female in a
blue pea-jacket was shown in to me, who stated she was Shrimp's
mother. First, she was extremely lachrymose, and couldn't speak a
word; then she got the steam up, and began slanging me till all was
blue; I was 'an unchristian-like, hard-hearted, heathen Turk, so I
was, and I'd been and sp'lled her sweet boy completely, so I had;
such a boy as he was too, bless him; it was quite a sight to hear him
say his catechism; and as to reading his book, he'd beat the parson
himself into fits at it.' Fortunately for me, she was a little touched
in the wind, and when she pulled up to take breath for a fresh start,
I managed to cut in. 'I tell you what it is, old lady,' said I, 'there's
no need for you to put yourself into a fury about it; misfortunes will
happen in the best regulated families, and it seems to me a boy more
or less can make no great odds to anyone—no fear of the breed becoming extinct just at present if one may judge from appearances; however, as you seem to set a value upon this particular boy, I'll tell you
what I'll do: I'll buy him of you, and then, if anything should go wrong
with him, it will be my loss and not yours. I'll give you twenty
pounds for him, and that's more than he would be worth if he was
sound.' By Jove! the old girl brightened up in a moment, wiped
her eyes with the sleeve of her coat, and said: 'Five pounds more,
and it's a bargain.' And the end of it all was, the brat got well
before I left the place; I paid the old woman her money, and brought
Shrimp away with me, and it hasn't turned out such a bad spec
either, for he makes a capital tiger; and now I've broken him in, I
would not take twice the money for him. You'll be at old Coleman's
hop to-night, I suppose; so bye! bye! for the present."

Thus saying, he drew the whip lightly across the leader's back,
the horses sprang forward, and in another moment he was out of
sight.

Half an hour's ride brought me within view of Elm Lodge, the
house lately taken by Mr. Coleman, senior. As I rang at the bell a

figure leaped out of one of the front windows, and came bounding across the lawn to meet me, and in another minute my hand was seized and my arm nearly shaken off by Coleman.

"Freddy, old boy!" "Frank, my dear old fellow!" were our mutual exclamations, as we once more shook hands with an energy which must have highly edified a pompous footman whom my ring had summoned. After the first excitement of our meeting had a little subsided we found time to examine each other more minutely, and note the changes a couple of years had wrought in us. Coleman was the first to speak.

" Why, Frank, how you are altered!"

"If you were but decently civil, you would say 'improved' instead of 'altered,'" replied I; "but you'll never learn manners."

" Oh, if you want compliments I'll soon get up a few, but it strikes me they are not required. A man with such a face and figure as yours soon finds out that he is a deucedly good-looking fellow. Why, how high do you stand?"

"About six feet without my boots," replied I, laughing at Coleman, who kept turning me round, and examining me from top to toe, as if I had been some newly-discovered animal.

"Well, you are a screamer, and no mistake," exclaimed he at length. "Be merciful towards the young ladies to-night, or the floor will be so cumbered with the heaps of slain that we shall have no room to dance."

"Never fear," rejoined I, "the female breast is not so susceptible as you imagine; and I'll back your bright eyes and merry smile to do more execution than my long legs and broad shoulders any day."

"No soft sawder, Master Frank, if you please; it's an article for which I've a particular distaste: people never make pretty speeches to one's face without laughing at one behind one's back afterwards by way of compensation."

" Which rule of course applies to the remarks you have just been making about me," returned I.

" You've caught me there fairly," laughed Coleman; "but come along in, now, I want to introduce you to my mother and the governor; they are longing to see you after all I've told them about you, though I can't say you look much like the thin delicate youth I have described you."

Mr. Coleman, who was a short, stout, red-faced old gentleman, with a bald head and a somewhat pompous manner, came forward and welcomed me warmly, saying all sorts of complimentary things to me in extremely high-flown and grandiloquent language, and referring to my having saved his son's life, in doing which, however, he quite won my heart by the evident pride and affection with which he spoke of Freddy. The lady of the house was a little, round, merry-looking woman, chiefly remarkable (as I soon discovered) for a peculiar mental obliquity, leading her always to think of the wrong thing at the wrong time, whereby she was perpetually becoming involved in grievous colloquial entanglements, and meeting with innumerable small personal accidents, at which no one laughed so heartily as herself.

About half-past nine that evening some of the guests began to arrive, amongst the foremost of whom was Lawless, most expensively got up for the occasion in a stock and waistcoat, which, as Coleman observed, required to be seen ere they could be believed in. As the arrivals succeeded each other more rapidly, and the rooms began to fill, Lawless took me by the arm and led me to a corner, whence, unnoticed ourselves, we could observe the whole scene.

" This will be a very full meet, Fairlegh," he began ; " I'm getting confoundedly nervous, I can tell you ; I'm not used to this sort of affair, you know ; I used always to shirk everything of the kind, but my Mater has got it into her head, since she's become ' My Lady,' that she must flare up and give balls, because ' ladies of rank always do so,' forsooth ; and so she's taken me in hand, to try and polish me up into something like ' a man of fashion,' as she calls those confounded puppies one sees lounging about drawing-rooms. Well, as I didn't like to rile the old woman by refusing to do what she wanted, I went to a French mounseer, to teach me my paces ; I've been in training above a month, so I thought I'd come here just as a sort of trial to see how I could go the pace."

" This is your ' debut,' in fact," returned I.

" My how much ? " was the reply. " Oh, I see, starting for the maiden stakes, for untried horses only—that sort of thing—eh ? Yes, it's the first time I've been regularly entered ; I hope I shan't bolt off the course ; I feel uncommon shy at starting, I can assure you."

" Oh, you'll do very well when you're once off ; your partner will tell you if you are going to make any mistake," replied I.

" My partner, eh ? You mean one of those white-muslined young ladies, who is to run in double harness with me, I suppose ?—that's another sell ;—I shall be expected to talk to her, and I never know what to say to women ; if one don't pay 'em compliments, and do a bit of the sentimental, they set you down as a brute directly. What an ass I was to come here ! I wish it was bed-time ! "

" Nonsense, man ; never be afraid ! " exclaimed Freddy, who had just joined us ; " I'll pick you out a partner who's used to the thing, and will do all the talking herself, and be glad of the opportunity of giving her tongue a little exercise ; and here comes the very girl, of all others—Di Clapperton." Then, turning towards a tall. showy-looking girl, who had just arrived, he addressed her with—" Delighted to see you, Miss Clapperton ; a ball-room never appears to me properly arranged till it is graced by your presence : here's my friend, the Hon. George Lawless, dying to be introduced to you."

" Pleasure—ar—dancing—with you, eh ? " muttered the Hon.

George, giving a little quick nod between each word. and getting very red in the face.

The young lady smiled a gracious assent, and saying, " I think they are forming a quadrille—shall we take our places ?" marched him off in triumph.

"Frank, are you provided; or can I do anything for you?" inquired Coleman.

" Who is that interesting-looking girl, with dark hair?" asked I, in return.

" What, the she-male with the white camellia in her head, leaning on the arm of that old fellow with the cast-iron face?   What a splendid pair of eyes she has got!   I'll find out her name, and get you introduced," replied Coleman, disappearing in the crowd.   In a minute or two he returned, and informed me that the young lady's name was Saville.   " You've not made such a bad hit either," continued he; "they tell me she's to be a great heiress, and old Ironsides there is her guardian.   They say he keeps her shut up so close that nobody can see her; he would hardly let her come to-night, only he's under some business obligations to my governor, and he persuaded him to bring her, in order to give me a chance, I suppose."

" What an expression of sadness there is in those deep-blue eyes of hers!   I am afraid she is not happy, poor thing!" said I, half think-ing aloud.

" Why, you're getting quite romantic about it!" returned Coleman; "for my part, I think she looks rather jolly than otherwise;—see how she's laughing with my cousin, Lucy; by jove, how her face lights up when she smiles!—she's very decidedly pretty.   Well, will you be introduced?—they are going to waltz."

I signified my assent, and Coleman set off in search of his father to perform the ceremony, not having courage enough himself to face "old Stiff-back," as he irreverently termed the young lady's guardian.

" I am sorry to refuse your young friend, Mr. Coleman," was the reply to my introduction; " but Miss Saville never waltzes."

" Come, don't be crabbed, Vernor; young people ought to enjoy themselves; recollect we were young ourselves once!"

" If old Time had dealt as leniently by me as he seems to have done by you, Coleman, I should consider myself young yet," replied Mr. Vernor.   "I believe I have spoken my ward's wishes upon this point; but, if it would be more satisfactory to your friend to hear her decision from her own lips I can have no objection—Clara, my dear, this gentleman, Mr. Fairlegh, does you the honour of wishing to waltz with you."

Thus accosted, Miss Saville raised her eyes to my face for a moment, and instantly casting them down again, coloured slightly, as she replied—" If Mr. Fairlegh will excuse me, I had rather not waltz."

I could, of course, only bow in acquiescence, and was turning away when old Mr. Coleman stopped me with,—

"There, wait a minute, Mr. Fairlegh; my little niece, Lucy Markham, will be only too glad to console you for your disappointment; she's never so happy as when she's waltzing."

"If you are impertinent, uncle, I'll make you waltz with me till you're quite tired, by way of punishment!" replied his niece, as she accepted my proffered arm.

During a pause in the waltz I referred to the refusal just received, and asked my partner (a lively little brunette, with very white teeth, and a bewitching smile) whether her friend Miss Saville were not somewhat of a prude?

"Poor dear Clara—a prude?—oh no!" was the reply. "You mean because she would not waltz. I suppose?"

I bowed my head in assent, and she continued,—

"I gave you credit for more penetration, Mr. Fairlegh; did you not see it was all that horrible Mr. Vernor, her guardian?—he chose her not to waltz; and she is too much afraid of him to dare to do anything he does not approve;—he would hardly let her come here to-night, only Uncle Coleman worried him into it."

"She is exceedingly pretty," remarked I; "there is something peculiar in the expression of those beautiful blue eyes which particularly pleases me; an earnest, trustful look, which—you will laugh at what I am going to say—which I have never seen before, except in the eyes of a dog!"

"Oh! I know so well what you mean," replied my partner; "I have observed it often, but I never should have known how to express it. What a good idea!"

"May I ask whether you are very intimate with her? Is she an old friend of yours?"

"No, I never saw her till my uncle took this house; but Mr. Vernor sometimes brings her with him when he drives over on business, and she comes and sits with me while they are puzzling about their parchments. I like her so much; she seems as agreeable and good as she is pretty."

"How is it," asked I, "that my friend Freddy did not know her by sight even?—he had to inquire her name this evening."

"Why, Frederick is generally obliged to be in town, you know; and I have observed that when he is down here Mr. Vernor never brings her with him."

"He had better make a nun of her at once," said I.

"Perhaps she won't be a nun!" said, or rather sang, Lucy. And here we joined the waltzers again, and the conversation ended.

CHAPTER XIV.

THE BALL.

"I could be pleased with any one
Who entertained my sight with such gay shows
As men and women moving here and there;
That coursing one another in their steps,
Have made their feet a tune."—*Dryden.*

"And run through fire I will for thy sweet sake."

"Come now, what . . . shall we have,
To wear away this long ago of three hours,
Between our after-supper and bed-time?"
                              Midsummer Night's Dream.

"By Jove! this is hot work!" exclaimed Lawless, flinging himself
down on a sofa so violently as to make an old lady, who occupied the
farther end of it, jump to an extent which seriously disarranged an
Anglo-Asiatic nondescript, believed in by her as a turban, wherewith
she adorned her aged head. "If I have not been going the pace like
a brick for the last two hours, it's a pity; what a girl that Di
Clapperton is to step out!—splendid action she has, to be sure, and
giving tongue all the time too. She's in first-rate training, 'pon my
word: I thought she'd have sewn me up at one time—the pace was
terrific. I must walk into old Coleman's champagne before I make
a fresh start; when I've recovered my wind, and got a mouthful of
hay and water, I'll have at her again, and dance till all's blue before
I give in."

"My dear fellow," said I, "you must not dance all the evening
with the same young lady; you'll have her brother call upon you the
first thing to-morrow morning to know your intentions."

"He shall very soon learn them as far as he is concerned, then,"
replied Lawless, doubling his fist. "Let me have him to myself for
a quiet twenty minutes, and I'll send him home with such a face on
him that his nearest relations will be puzzled to recognize him for
the next month to come at least. But what do you really mean?"

"That it's not etiquette to go on dancing with one young lady the
whole evening; you must ask someone else."

"Have all the bother to go over again, eh? what a treat! Well,
we live and learn; it will require a few extra glasses of champagne
to get the steam up to the necessary height, that's all. And there
they are going down to supper; that's glorious!" and away he
bounded to secure Miss Clapperton's arm, while I offered mine to
the turbaned old lady, to compensate for her late alarm.

After supper the dancing was resumed with fresh energy, the
champagne having produced its usual exhilarating effects upon the
exhausted frames of the dancers. Notwithstanding my former
repulse, I made a successful attempt to gain Miss Saville's hand for

a quadrille, though I saw, or fancied I saw, the scowl on Mr. Vernor's. sour countenance grow deeper, as I led her away. My perseverance was not rewarded by any very interesting results, for my partner, who was either distressingly shy, or acting under constraint of some kind, made monosyllabic replies to every remark I addressed to her, and appeared relieved when the termination of the set enabled her to rejoin her grim protector.

" Of all the disagreeable faces I ever saw, Mr. Vernor's is the most repulsive," said I to Coleman ; " were I a believer in the power of the ' evil eye,' he is just the sort of looking person I should imagine would possess it. I am certain I have never met him before, and yet. strange to say, there is something which appears familiar to me in his expression, particularly when he frowns."

" He is a savage-looking old guy," replied Freddy, " and bullies that sweet girl shockingly, I can see. I should feel the greatest satisfaction in punching his head for him, but I suppose it would be hardly the correct thing on so short an acquaintance, and in my father's house too ; eh ? "

" Not exactly," replied I, turning away with a smile.

When Lawless made his appearance after supper, it was evident by his flushed face, and a slight unsteadiness in his manner of walking, that he had carried his intentions with regard to the champagne into effect ; and, heedless of my warning, he proceeded to lay violent siege to Miss Clapperton, to induce her to waltz with him. I was watching them with some little amusement, for the struggle in the young lady's mind between her sense of the proper, and her desire to waltz with an Honourable, was very apparent, when I was requested by Mrs. Coleman to go in search of a cloak appertaining to the turbaned old lady whom I had escorted down to supper, and who, being delicate in some way or other, required especial care in packing up. Owing to a trifling mistake of Mrs. Coleman's (who had described a red worsted shawl as a blue cloth cloak, which mistake I had to discover and rectify), my mission detained me some minutes. As I re-entered the ball-room, shawl in hand, I was startled by the crash of something heavy falling, followed by a shriek from several of the ladies at the upper end of the room ; and on hastening to the scene of action, I soon perceived the cause of their alarm.

During my absence, Lawless, having succeeded in overcoming Miss Clapperton's scruples, had recommenced waltzing with the greatest energy ; but unfortunately, after going round the room once or twice, " the pace," as he called it, becoming faster at every turn, the combined effects of the champagne and the unaccustomed exercise rendered him exceedingly giddy, and just before I entered the room, he had fallen against a small table supporting a handsome china candelabrum, containing several wax lights, the overthrow of which had occasioned the grand crash which I heard. The cause of the shriek, however, still remained to be discovered, and a' nearer approach instantly rendered it apparent. One of the wax candles, which had not been extinguished in its fall, had rolled against the ball dress of Miss Saville, who happened to be seated next the table, and set it on fire. After making an ineffectual attempt to put it out with her hands, she became alarmed, and as I approached, started wildly up, with the evident intention of rushing out of the room. Without a moment's hesitation I sprang forward, caught her in my arms, and flinging the worsted shawl over her dress, which was just beginning to blaze, enveloped her in it, and telling her if she only remained quiet she would be perfectly safe, laid her on the floor, while I continued to hold the thick shawl tightly down, till, to my very great delight, I succeeded in extinguishing the flames.

By this time several gentlemen had gathered round us, eager with their advice and offers of assistance. Having satisfied myself that the danger was entirely over, I raised Miss Saville from the ground, and making way through the crowd, half led, half carried her to the nearest sofa. After placing her carefully upon it, I left her to the care of Mrs. Coleman and Lucy Markham, while I sought out the turbaned old lady, whose shawl I had so unceremoniously made use of, and succeeded in making my peace with her, though I believe, in her own secret breast, she considered Miss Saville's safety dearly purchased at the expense of her favourite whittle. As I approached the sofa again, the following words, in the harsh tones of Mr. Vernor's voice, met my ear,—

" I have ascertained our carriage is here ; as soon, therefore, as you feel strong enough to walk, Clara, my dear, I should advise your accompanying me home ; quiet and rest are the best remedies after such an alarm as this."

" I am quite ready, sir," was the reply, in a faint tone of voice.

" Nay, wait a few minutes longer," said Lucy Markham, kindly ; " you are trembling from head to foot even yet."

" Indeed I am quite strong ; I have no doubt I can walk now," replied Miss Saville, attempting to rise, but sinking back again almost immediately from faintness.

" Can I be of any assistance ? " inquired I, coming forward.

" I am obliged to you for the trouble you have already taken, sir," answered Mr. Vernor, coldly, " but will not add to it. Miss Saville will be able to proceed with the assistance of my arm in a few minutes."

After a short pause, the young lady again announced her readiness to depart ; and, having shaken hands with Mrs. Coleman and Lucy Markham, turned to leave the room, leaning on Mr. Vernor's arm. As I was standing near the door, I stepped forward to hold it open for them, Mr. Vernor acknowledging my civility by the slightest imaginable motion of the head. Miss Saville, as she approached me, paused for a moment, as if about to speak, but apparently relinquishing her intention, merely bowed, and passed on.

" Well, if it's in that sort of way fashionable individuals demonstrate their gratitude for having their lives saved, I must say I don't

admire it," exclaimed Coleman, who had witnessed the cool behaviour
of Mr. Vernor and his ward; "it may be very genteel, but, were I in
your place I should consider it unsatisfactory in the extreme, and
allow the next inflammable young lady who might happen to attract
a spark in my presence, to consume as she pleased, without inter-
fering; and peace be to her ashes!"

"It was most fortunate that I happened to have that thick shawl
in my hand," said I; "in another minute her whole dress would have
been in a blaze, and it would have been next to impossible to save
her. What courage and self-command she showed! she never
attempted to move after I threw the shawl around her, till I told her
all danger was over."

"Very grand, all that sort of thing," returned Freddy; "but for
my own part I should like to see a little more feeling. I've no taste
for your 'marble maidens'; they always put me in mind of Lot's
wife."

"Eh! Mrs. Lot?" interrupted Lawless, coming up to us: "why
was she like me? do you give it up? Because she got into a pretty
pickle—there's a riddle for you. I say, I made a nice mess of it just
now, didn't I? that's what comes of going to these confounded balls.
The fact was," he continued, sinking his voice, "the filly bolted with
me; she took uncommon kindly to the champagne at supper; in
consequence, she was so fresh when we started that I couldn't hold
her; she kept pushing on faster and faster, till at last she was fairly
off with me; we did very well as long as we stuck to the open country,
but at last we contrived to get among some very awkward fences; the
first stiff bit of timber we came to she made a rush at, and down we
came, gate—I mean table, candlestick, and all, a regular smash; and
to make matters worse, one of the candles set the other young
woman's petticoat alight."

"In fact, after a very severe run, you were nearly being in at the
death," suggested Coleman.

"By Jove, it was nothing to laugh at, though!" remarked Lawless;
"she'd have been regularly cooked, if Frank Fairlegh hadn't put
her out when he did, and I should have been tried for 'Unjustifiable
Girl-icide,' or 'Maliciously setting fire to a marriageable female,' or
some such thing; and I dare say the young woman wasn't insured
anywhere: I should have got into a pretty mess; it would have been
a worse job than breaking Shrimp."

"Frederick, look here!" cried Lucy Markham, who was passing
the place where we stood; "see how Mr. Fairlegh's sleeve is scorched;
surely," she continued, turning to me, "your arm must be injured."

"It begins to feel rather painful," replied I; "but I daresay it's
nothing to signify."

"Come to my room," exclaimed Freddy, anxiously; "why did you
not mention it before?"

"Really I scarcely felt it in the excitement of the moment,"
returned I; "it can't be of any consequence."

On removing the coat-sleeve, however, a somewhat considerable
burn was apparent, extending about half-way from the wrist to the
elbow, and which, the moment it was exposed to the air, became
excessively painful.

Fortunately, among the guests who had not yet taken their
departure was the surgeon of the neighbourhood, who was speedily
summoned, and who, after having applied the proper remedies, recommended me to carry my arm in a sling for a few days, at the end of
which time, he assured me, it would cause me little inconvenience.

As it was, by great good luck, my left arm which was injured, I
submitted to this mandate with tolerable resignation, and returned
to the drawing-room to be pitied by the tongues of the old, and the
bright eyes of the young ladies, to an extent which (as at that time
of day I was somewhat addicted to the vice of shyness) was more
flattering than agreeable.

It was between two and three o'clock when Lawless and I prepared
to take our departure for the inn at which we were to sleep. Being
a lovely night, Coleman volunteered to accompany us for the sake of
the walk, telling the servants not to sit up for him, as he had a latch-
key in his pocket—an article regarding the possession of which a
constant civil war was carried on between his mother and himself,
wherein by dint of sundry well-contrived stratagems and deeply-laid
schemes, he invariably gained the victory.

" I tell you what," said Lawless, " the row and bother, and the whole
kick-up altogether, has made me alarmingly hungry ; the only decent
bit of chicken I managed to lay hands on at supper Di Clapperton
ate : precious twist that girl has, to be sure ; even after all the
ground she's been over to-night, going a topping pace the whole time
too, she wasn't a bit off her feed ; didn't she walk into the ham sand-
wiches—that's all ! I'd rather keep her for a week than a fortnight,
I can tell you ; she'd eat her head off in a month, and no mistake.
Here, waiter," he continued, " have you got anything to eat in
the house ? "

" Yes, sir, splendid barrel of oysters down by coach last night ;
capital brown stout, sir—real Guinness's ! "

" That's it, my man," was the rejoinder ; " trot 'em out by all
means. Freddy, old boy," he continued, " come along in with us,
and have some."

" Well, I don't mind astonishing the natives for once in a way,"
replied Freddy ; " but it's dreadfully debauched, eating oysters and
drinking porter at this time of day or night, whichever you are
pleased to call it ; you'll ruin my morals."

" The devil fly away with your morals, and he won't be over-loaded
either," was the polite rejoinder ; and in we all went together. The
oysters and porter soon made their appearance, and had ample justice
done them ; then, as a matter of course, spirits and water and cigars
were produced, " just to prevent the oysters from disagreeing with
us ; " and we sat talking over old times, and relating various adven-

tures which had occurred to us since, without troubling our heads
about the flight of minutes. At length Coleman, pulling out his
watch, exclaimed: "Past four o'clock, by the powers! I must be
getting to bed—I've got a lease to draw to-morrow, and my head
won't be over-clear as it is."

"Nonsense," replied Lawless; "bed's all a popular delusion; we
can't be better off than we are—sit still." But on Coleman's persist-
ing in his wish to depart, Lawless continued: "Well, take another
glass, and then Frank and I will walk home with you and see you
safe, for it's my belief that you're getting 'screwed,' or you'd never
think of going to bed." Freddy and I exchanged glances, for if any
of our party were in the condition expressed by the mysterious word
"screwed," it certainly was Lawless himself. After sitting some
little time longer, we once more sallied forth with the avowed intention of seeing Coleman home.

CHAPTER XV.

RINGING THE CURFEW.

"If the bell have any sides the clapper will find 'em."—*Ben Jonson.*

"—— ringing changes all our bells bath marr'd,
    Jangled they have and jarr'd
So long, they're out of tune, and out of frame;
    They seem not now the same.
Put them in frame anew, and once begin
To tune them so, that they chime all in."
                            Herbert.

"Great then are the mysteries of bell-ringing; and this may be said in its praise,
that of all devices which men have sought out for obtaining distinction by making a
noise in the world, it is the most harmless."—*The Doctor.*

As we proceeded through the town, Lawless, despite our endeavours
to restrain him, chose to vent his superabundant spirits by performing sundry feats at the expense of the public, which, had the police
regulations of the place been properly attended to, would have
assuredly gained us a sojourn in the watch-house. We had just
prevailed upon him to move on, after singing "We won't go home
till morning" under the windows of "the Misses Properprim's
Seminary for Young Ladies," when a little shrivelled old man, in a
sort of watchman's great-coat, bearing a horn lantern in his hand,
brushed past us, and preceded us down the street at a shuffling trot.

"Hulloa!" cried Lawless, "who's that old picture of ugliness?
Look what a pace the beggar's cutting along at! what on earth's he
up to?"

"That's the sexton and bell-ringer," returned Coleman; "they

keep up the old custom at Hillingford of ringing the curfew at daybreak, and he's going about it now, I suppose."

"What jolly fun!" said Lawless ; "come on, and let's see how the
old cock does it;" and suiting the action to the word, off he started
in pursuit.

"We'd better follow him," said I; "he'll be getting into some
mischief or other, depend upon it."

After running a short distance down the street, on turning a corner,
we found Lawless standing under a small arched doorway leading
into a curious old battlemented tower which did not form part of any
church or other building of the same date as itself, but stood alone,
showing, as it reared its time-worn head high above the more modern
dwellings of which the street was composed, like some giant relic
of the days of old. This tower contained a peal of bells, the fame of
which was great in that part of the country, and of which the townspeople were justly proud.

"All right!" cried Lawless; "the old scarecrow ran in here like a
lamp-lighter, as soon as he saw me bowling after him, and has left
the key in the lock; so I shall take the liberty of exploring a little;
I've a strong though undeveloped taste for architectural antiquities.
Twopence more, and up goes the donkey! come along!"

So saying he flung open the door, and disappeared up some
steps leading to the interior of the tower, and after a moment's hesitation Coleman and I followed him.

"Don't be alarmed, old boy!" observed Lawless, patting the sexton
(who looked frightened out of his wits at our intrusion) so forcibly
on the back as to set him coughing violently; "we're not come to
murder you for the sake of your lantern."

"This gentleman," said Coleman, who, by the cunning twinkle of
his eye, was evidently becoming possessed by the spirit of mischief,
"has been sent down by the Venerable Society of Antiquaries, to
ascertain whether the old custom of ringing the curfew is properly
performed here. He is, in fact, no other than the Noble President
of the Society himself. That gentleman" (pointing to me) "is the
Vice-President, and I, who have the honour of addressing you, am
the unworthy Secretary."

"That's it, daddy," resumed Lawless, coolly taking up the lantern
and lighting a cigar; "that's the precise state of the poll, I mean
case; so now go to work, and mind you do the trick properly."

Thus adjured, the old man, who appeared completely bewildered
by all that was going on, mechanically took hold of a rope, and began
slowly and at stated intervals tolling one of the bells.

"Where are your assistants, my good man?" inquired Coleman,
after a short pause. The only answer was a stare of vacant surprise,
and Coleman continued, "Why, you don't mean to say you only ring
one bell, to be sure? oh, this is all wrong:—what do you say, Mr.
President?"

"Wrong?" replied Lawless, removing the cigar from his mouth

and puffing a cloud of smoke into the sexton's face, "I should just think it was most particularly and confoundedly wrong. I'll tell you what it is, old death's-head and cross-bones: things can't be allowed to go on in this manner. Reform, sir, is wanting, 'the bill, the whole bill, and nothing but the bill.' I mean to get into Parliament some day. Fairlegh, when I am tired of knocking about, you know—but that wasn't exactly what I was going to say."

"Suppose we show him the proper way to do it, Mr. President!" suggested Freddy, catching hold of the rope of one of the bells.

"Off she goes," cried Lawless, seizing another.

"Gentlemen, good gentlemen, don't ring the bells, pray," implored the old man, "you'll raise the whole town: they are never rung in that way without there's a fire, or a flood, or the riot act read, or something of that dreadful nature the matter."

But his expostulations were vain. Lawless had already begun ringing his bell in a manner which threatened to stun us all; and Coleman, saying to me, "Come, Frank, we're regularly in for it, so you may as well take a rope and do the thing handsomely while we are about it; it would be horridly shabby of you to desert us now," I hastened to follow his example.

Now it must be known that when I arrived at the inn, before supper, owing probably to a combination of the fatigue of the day, the excitement of the evening, and the pain of my arm, I felt somewhat faint and exhausted, and should have greatly preferred going at once quietly to bed; but, as I was aware that by so doing I should break up the party, I resolved to keep up as well as I could, and say nothing about it. Finding myself refreshed by the bottled porter, I repeated the dose several times, and the remedy continuing to prove efficacious, without giving the thing a thought, I drank more deeply than was my wont, and was a good deal surprised, when I rose to accompany the others, to discover that my legs were slightly unsteady, and my head not so clear as usual. Still I had been far from approving the proceedings of my companions, and had any one told me, when I entered the tower, that I was going to ring all the good people of Hillingford out of their beds in a fright, I should indignantly have repelled the accusation. Now, however, owing to the way in which Coleman had requested my assistance, it appeared to my bewildered senses that I should be meanly deserting my friends the moment they had got into difficulties, if I were to refuse; but when he used the word "shabby," it settled the business, and seizing a rope with my uninjured hand, I began pulling away vigorously.

"Now, then, you wretched old beggar," shouted Lawless, "don't stand there winking and blinking like an owl; pull away like bricks, or I'll break your neck for you; go to work, I say!" and the miserable sexton, with a mute gesture of despair, resuming his occupation, a peal of four bells was soon ringing bravely out over hill and dale, and making "night horrible" to the startled inhabitants of Hillingford.

After the lapse of a few minutes a distant shout was heard; then a confused noise of people running and calling to each other in the streets reached our ears; and lastly the sound of several persons rapidly approaching the bell-tower became audible.

"We're in for a scrimmage now, I expect," said Lawless, leisurely turning up his sleeves.

"Not a bit of it," replied Freddy; "only leave it to me, and you'll see. All you fellows have got to do is to hold your tongues, and keep on ringing away till your arms ache; trust me to manage the thing all right. Lawless, keep your eye on ancient Methuselah there, and if he offers to say a word, just knock him head over heels by accident, will you?"

"Ay, ay, sir," replied Lawless, shaking his fist significantly at the sexton.

At this moment a short, fat man with a very red face (who we afterwards learned was no less a person than the mayor of Hilling-ford in his public, and a mighty tallow-chandler in his private, capacity) appeared, attired in a night-cap and great-coat, and bearing the rest of his wardrobe under his arm, followed by several of the townspeople, all in a similar state of undress, and with the liveliest alarm depicted on their countenances. The worthy mayor was so much out of breath by his unwonted exertions that some seconds elapsed before he could utter a word, and in the meantime we continued ringing as though our lives depended upon it. At length he contrived to gasp out a hurried inquiry (hardly audible amidst the clanging of the bells) as to what was the matter. To this Coleman replied by pointing with one hand to a kind of loophole, of which there were several for the purpose of supplying light and air to the interior of the tower, while with the other hand he continued ringing away more lustily than before.

"Bless my soul!" exclaimed the mayor, raising himself on tip-toe, and stretching his short neck in a vain endeavour to peep through the loophole, "it must be a fire in West Street!"

Two or three of the bystanders immediately rushed into the street, calling out, "A fire in West Street! send for the engines."

At this moment Freddy caught the eye of a tall, gaunt-looking man in a top-boot and plush breeches, but without coat or waistcoat, and wearing a gold-laced cocked hat on his head, hind part before, from beneath which peeped out a white cotton night-cap. Having succeeded in attracting the attention of this worthy, who in his proper person supported the dignity of parish beadle, Coleman repeated the same stratagem he had so successfully practised upon the mayor, save that in this instance he pointed to a loophole in a completely opposite direction to the one he had indicated previously. The beadle immediately ran out, muttering ere he did so, "I was certain sure as they was all wrong." In another minute we heard him shouting, "It's in Middle Street, I tell you, there's a fire in Middle Street!"

Coleman now turned to the mayor, who, having somewhat recovered his breath, was evidently preparing to question the sexton as to the particulars of the affair, and exclaimed in a tone of deep feeling, " I am surprised to see a person of your high station standing idle at a moment like this ! take a rope, sir, and lend a hand to assist us, if you be a man."

" To be sure, to be sure," was the reply, " anything for the good of he town," and, grasping an unoccupied rope, he began pulling away with all his might.

The hubbub and confusion now became something unparalleled—people without number kept running in and out of the tower, giving and receiving all kinds of contradictory orders; volunteers had been found to assist us, and the whole peal of eight bells was clashing and clanging away above the tumult, and spreading the alarm farther and wider; men on horseback were arriving from the country, eager to render assistance ; women were screaming, dogs barking, children crying ; and, to crown the whole, a violent and angry debate was being carried on by the more influential members of the crowd as to the quarter in which the supposed conflagration was raging—one party loudly declaring it was in Middle Street, while the other as vehemently protested it was in West Street.

The confusion had apparently attained its highest pitch, and the noise was perfectly deafening, when suddenly a shout was raised, " The engines! clear the way for the engines!" and in another moment the scampering of the crowd in all directions, the sound of horses' feet galloping, and the rattle of wheels, announced their approach. While all this was going on, Coleman had contrived silently and unperceived to substitute two of the bystanders in my place and his own, so that Lawless was the only one of our party actually engaged in ringing. Seizing the moment, therefore, when the shout of " The engines!" had attracted the attention of the loiterers, he touched him on the shoulder, saying, " Now's our time, come along," and joining a party who were going out, we reached the door of the bell-tower unobserved.

The scene which presented itself to our view as we gained the open street would require the pencil of a Wilkie, or the pen of a Dickens, to describe. The street widened in front of the bell-tower, so as to make a kind of square. In the centre of the space thus formed stood the fire-engine drawn by four post-horses, the post-boys sitting erect in their saddles, ready to dash forward the moment the firemen (who in their green coats faced with red, and shining leather helmets, imparted a somewhat military character to the scene) should succeed in ascertaining the place at which their assistance was required. The crowd, which had opened to admit the passage of the engine, immediately closed round it again in an apparently impenetrable phalanx, the individual members of which afforded as singular a variety of costume as can well be imagined, extending from the simple shirt of propriety to the decorated uniforms of the fire

I

brigade. As everyone who had an opinion to give was bawling it out
at the very top of his voice, whilst those who had none contented
themselves by shouting vague sentences devoid of particular meaning
of any kind, the noise and tumult were such as beggared description.
There was one short, stout, red-faced little fellow (for I succeeded in
catching sight of him at last) with a mouth of such fearful dimensions
that when it was open the upper half of his head appeared a mere lid,
whose intellects being partially under the dominion of sleep, evidently
imagined himself at the Election, which had taken place a short time
previously, and continued strenuously vociferating the name of his
favourite candidate, though the cry of "Judkins for ever!" did not
tend greatly to elucidate matters. Suddenly, and at the very height
of the confusion, the bells ceased ringing, and for a moment, as if
influenced by some supernatural power, the crowd to a man became
silent.

The transition from the Babel of sounds I have been describing to
such perfect tranquillity was most striking, and impressed one with
an involuntary feeling of awe. I was aroused by Coleman, who
whispered in an undertone, "The sexton has peached. depend upon
it, and the sooner we're off the better."

"Yes, and I'll go in style too; so good-bye, and take care of yourselves," exclaimed Lawless, and, springing forward, before anyone
was aware of his intention, he forced his way through the crowd,
overturning sundry members thereof in his progress, until he
reached the fire-engine, upon which he seated himself with a bound,
shouting as he did so—"Forward, forward! do you want the place
to be burnt to the ground? I'll show you the way; give 'em the
spur; faster, faster, straight on till I tell you to turn—faster, I
say!"

The appearance of authority, coupled with energy and decision,
will usually control a crowd. The firemen, completely taken in by
Lawless's manner, reiterated his orders; the post-boys applied both
whip and spur vigorously—the horses dashed forward, and, amidst
the enthusiastic cheering of the mob, the engine disappeared like a
flash of lightning.

"Well, I give the Honourable George credit for that!" exclaimed
Coleman, as soon as we had a little recovered from our surprise at
Lawless's elopement with the fire-engine; "it was a good idea, and he
worked it out most artistically; the air with which he waved his hat
to cheer them forward was quite melodramatic. I've seen the thing
not half so well done by several of the greatest generals who ever
lived—gallant commanders, whom their men would have followed
through any amount of the reddest possible fire during the whole of
Astley's campaigns, that is, if the commissariat department (consisting of the pot-boy stationed at the side-scenes with the porter) did
its duty efficiently."

"Freddy, they're beginning to come out of the bell-tower," interrupted I; "we shall be called upon to answer for our misdeeds if we

George Cruikshank

stay much longer: see, that long man in the cocked hat is coming towards us."

"So he is," returned Coleman; "it strikes me they've found us out; follow me, and try and look as if it wasn't you as much as possible, will you?" So saying, he began to make his way out of the crowd unperceived, an example I hastened to follow; but we were not destined to effect our purpose quite so easily. The point Coleman wished to gain was an arched gateway leading into a stable-yard, from which he hoped, by a footpath with which he was acquainted, across some fields, to reach without molestation the inn where I was to sleep. But, in order to effect this, we were obliged to pass the door of the bell-tower, from which several people, who appeared angry and excited, were now issuing. The foremost of these, the cocked-hatted official before mentioned, made his way up to us, exclaiming as he did so,—

"Here, you young gen'lmen, just you stop a bit, will yer? His wusshup the mayor seems to begin to think as somebody's been a-making a fool of him."

"A very natural idea," returned Coleman; "I only wonder it never occurred to him before; as far as my limited acquaintance with him will allow me to judge, the endeavour appears to have been perfectly successful. I wish you a very good-morning."

"That's all wery fine, but I must trouble yer to come along o' me; his wusshup wants to speak to yer," replied the beadle, seizing Coleman by the coat collar.

"That is a pleasure his 'wusshup' must contrive to postpone till he has caught me," answered Freddy, as with a sudden jerk he succeeded in freeing himself from his captor's grasp, while almost at the same moment he dealt him a cuff on the side of the head, which sent him reeling back to the door of the bell-tower, where, encountering the mayor, who had just made his appearance, he came headlong to the ground, dragging that illustrious functionary down with him in a frantic endeavour to save himself. Profiting by the confusion that ensued, Freddy and I sprang forward, darted through the archway, and, making the best use of our legs, soon found ourselves in the open fields, and quite beyond the reach of pursuit.

CHAPTER XVI.

THE ROMAN FATHER.

"If a dream should come in now to make you afear'd,
With a windmill on his head and bells at his beard ; .
Would you straight wear your spectacles here at your toes,
And your boots on your brows, and your spurs on your nose ?"
Ben Jonson.

" No —— he
With more than Roman fortitude is ever
First at the board in this unhappy process.
Against his last and only son."
The Two Foscari.

DREAMS, ye strange mysterious visions of the soul! Ye wild and
freakish gambollings of the spirit, freed from the incubus of matter,
and unfettered by the control of reason, of what fantastic caprices
are ye the originators—what caricatures of the various features of
our waking life do ye not exhibit to us, ludicrous and distorted
indeed, but still preserving through their most extravagant ex-
aggerations a wayward and grotesque likeness to the realities they
shadow forth ! And stranger even than your most strange vagaries,
is the cool, matter-of-fact way in which our sleeping senses calmly
accept and acquiesce in the medley of impossible absurdities you offer
to their notice. We conceive ourselves, for instance, proceeding
along a green lane on horseback ; the animal upon which we are
mounted becomes suddenly, we know and care not how, a copper
tea-kettle, and we ride quietly on without testifying, or even feeling,
the least symptom of surprise, as though the identity of hackneys and
tea-kettles was a fact generally recognized in natural history ; the
kettle perhaps addresses us, it converses with us on all the subjects
which interest us most deeply ; and we discuss our various hopes and
fears, joys and sorrows, loves and hates, with no other sentiment,
save a degree of pleasure at the very sensible and enlightened
views which the utensil takes of the matter. I might multiply
examples, 'ad infinitum,' to illustrate my meaning ; but to those
who are familiar with the phenomena alluded to, one instance will
suffice ; while those who have never experienced them will probably, at all events, take refuge in disbelief, and lament themselves with a self-satisfying sorrow over the fresh proof it adduces
of the truth of the Israelitish monarch's aphorism, that " all men are
liars."

Be this as it may, my sleep (when, at length, after the excitement
I had undergone, sleep condescended to visit me, which was not until,
contrary to all the rules of good breeding, Somnus had allowed me to
call upon him repeatedly in vain) was disturbed by all sorts and kinds
of visions. Lawlesses innumerable, attended by shoals of top-booted

shrimps—the visionary shrimp being a sort of compromise between the
boy so-called and the real article—drove impossible dog-carts drawn
by quadrupeds whose heads and necks bore a striking resemblance
to the waltz-loving Diana Clapperton, up and down ball-rooms, to the
unspeakable terror of squadrons of turbaned old ladies. Deafening
peals of bells, rung by troops of Freddy ColeMEN (which I take to be
the correct plural of Coleman), were rousing nightcapped nations
from their slumbers in alarm, to whom flocks of frightened mayors
were bleating forth bewildered orders, which resulted in perplexing
everybody ; and through it all, mixed up and combined with everything, the pale, interesting face of Clara'Saville, characterized by an
expression of the deepest sadness, gazed at me out of its large trustful
eyes, and rendered me intensely miserable. From dreams such as
these I was not sorry to be aroused by the sun shining brightly
through my window-shutter ; and on consulting my watch, I found,
somewhat to my surprise, that I had slept till nearly mid-day.

On reaching the breakfast-room my first inquiry was for Lawless,
in reply to which I was informed that he had returned (on the fire-
engine) about half an hour after I came in ; that immediately upon
his arrival he had called for unlimited supplies of rum, lemons, and
other suitable ingredients, wherewith he manufactured a monster
brewing of punch in a washing-tub for the benefit of the firemen,
with whom he had contrived to establish the most amicable relations ;
he then assisted in discussing the beverage he had prepared, which
appeared to produce no particular effects, until, wishing to rise to
return thanks when they drank his health, he suddenly lost his
balance, and being carried to bed by the waiter and boots, had not yet
reappeared. Not liking to disturb him, I breakfasted alone, and then
strolled out to look after Freddy. I found him sitting in the study,
busily engaged in drawing the lease he had mentioned to us the
night before. On seeing me, however, he sprang up, and shaking me
by the hand, inquired how I was after our adventures.

"That's all right, so far," was his reply to my assurance that my
injured arm was going on favourably, and that I felt no other ill
effects of any kind. "I tell you what," he continued, " my governor's
in no end of a rage about the bell-ringing affair ; that old fool of a
mayor recognized me, it seems, and vows vengeance, threatening to
do all sorts of things to me, and the governor swears he'll aid and
abet him in anything he chooses to do. They had better take care
what they are at, or they may find I'm not to be bullied with impunity;
but come along into the drawing-room ; I don't mind facing the elders
now I've got you to support me; and really, what between my father's
accusations and my mother's excuses, it's as good as a play."

"You're abominably undutiful, Master Fred," replied I, as I
turned to follow him.

On reaching the drawing-room we found Mr. Coleman standing
with his arms folded with an air of dignified severity, so exactly in
the centre of the hearth-rug, that he seemed to belong to the pattern.

Seated in a low arm-chair on the right-hand side of the fireplace was
Mrs. Coleman, apparently absorbed in the manufacture of some mysterious article of knitting, which constantly required propitiating by
the repetition of a short arithmetical puzzle, without which it would
by no means allow itself to be created. At her feet, engaged in the Sisy-
phian labour of remedying the effects of "a great fall" in worsteds,
scissors, and other "articles for the work-table," knelt Lucy Markham,
looking so piquante and pretty, that I could not help wondering how
my friend Freddy contrived to keep himself heart-whole, if, as I
imagined, he was thrown constantly into her society. The party
was completed by a large, sleek, scrupulously white cat, clearly a
privileged individual, who sat bolt upright in the chair, opposite Mrs.
Coleman, regarding the company with an air of intense self-satisfaction,
evidently considering the whole thing got up for her express delec-
tation. Mr. Coleman received me with pompous civility, hoping I
felt no ill effects from my exertions in the earlier part of the evening
—taking care to lay a marked emphasis on the word "earlier." Lucy
acknowledged my presence by a smile and a slight inclination of the
head, but without altering her position. Worthy Mrs. Coleman, however, jumped up and shook hands warmly with me, thereby providing
Lucy with full employment for the next ten minutes in picking up the
whole machinery of the knitting.

"Very glad indeed to see you, Mr. Lawless," commenced Mrs.
Coleman.

"It's Fairlegh, mother," interposed Freddy.

"Yes, my dear, yes, I knew it was Mr. Fairlegh, only I'm always
making a mistake about names; but I never forget a face I've once
seen; and I'm sure I'm not likely to forget Mr. Fairlegh's after
the noble way in which he behaved last night" (here Mr. Coleman
turned away with a kind of ironical growl, and began caressing the
cat). "I declare when I saw him setting Clara Saville's dress on fire,
so nicely made as it was too—"

"My dear aunt," remonstrated Lucy, "it was Mr. Lawless who
threw down the candelabrum, and set Clara's frock alight."

"Yes, my love, I know—I saw it all, my dear; and very kind it was
of him, I mean afterwards, in speaking to me of it; he said he was
so very sorry about it—and he called it something funny, poor young
man —' no end of a something or other '—"

"Sell," suggested Freddy.

"Oh yes, that was it, no end of a sell. What did he mean by that,
my dear?"

"I strongly disapprove," observed Mr. Coleman (who still continued stroking the cat as he spoke, which process he performed by
passing his hand deliberately from her head, along her back, to the
very tip of her tail, which he retained each time in his grasp for a
moment, ere he recommenced operations), "I highly disapprove of the
absurd practice, so common with young men of the present day, of
expressing their ideas in that low and incomprehensible dialect,

termed ' slang,' which, in my opinion, has neither wit nor refinement to redeem its vulgarity, and which effectually prevents their acquiring that easy yet dignified mode of expression, which should characterize the conversation of the true gentleman. In my younger days we took Burke for our model; the eloquence of Pitt and Fox gave the tone to society; and during our hours of relaxation, we emulated the polished wit of Sheridan: but it is a symptom of that fearful levelling system which is one of the most alarming features of the present age; instead of striving to raise and exalt—"

" Really, my dear Mr. Coleman, I beg your pardon for interrupting you," cried his wife, " but this is the second time you've lifted my poor little cat off her hind-legs by her tail; and though she's as good as gold, and let's you do just what you like to her, it can't be pleasant for her, I'm sure."

The only reply to this, if reply it can be called, was an angry " Psha!" and, turning on his heel, Mr. Coleman strode with great dignity towards the window, though the effect was considerably marred by his stumbling against an ottoman which stood in the way, and hurting his shin to an extent which entailed rubbing, albeit a sublunary and un-Spartan operation, as a necessary consequence. A pause ensued, which at length became so awkward, that I was about to hazard some wretched commonplace or other, for the sake of breaking the silence, when Mrs. Coleman addressed me with,—

" You'll take some luncheon, Mr. Lawless, I'm sure. Freddy, ring the bell!"

" He'll be ready enough to do that," growled Mr. Coleman; " you could not have asked a fitter person."

" Of course he will, a dear fellow," replied Mrs. Coleman; " he's always ready to oblige anybody."

" I disapprove greatly of such extreme facility of disposition," observed Mr. Coleman; " it lays a young man open to every temptation that comes in his way; and for want of a proper degree of firmness and self-respect, he gets led into all kinds of follies and excesses."

" Now, my dear Mr. Coleman," returned his wife, " I cannot bear to hear you talk in that way; you are too hard upon poor Freddy and his young friends; I'm certain they meant no harm;—if they did ring the bells by way of a joke, I daresay they had drunk rather more champagne than was prudent, and scarcely knew what they were about; and really all they seem to have done was to make people get up a little sooner than usual, and that is rather a good thing than otherwise, for I'm sure, if you did but know the trouble I have sometimes in getting the maids out of bed in the morning—and that lazy fine gentleman of a footman too, he's just as bad.—Why, what's the matter now ? "

" I really am astonished at you, Mrs. Coleman," exclaimed her husband, walking hurriedly across the room—although this time he took good care to avoid the ottoman, " encouraging that boy of yours

in such scandalous and ungentlemanly proceedings as those he was-
engaged in last night! No harm, indeed! I only hope (that is, I
don't hope it at all, for he deserves to be punished, and I wish he may)
that the laws of his country may think there's no harm in it. Mr.
Dullmug, the mayor, intends, very properly in my opinion, to appeal
to those laws; that is a thing, I am proud to say, no Englishman
ever does in vain. You may smile, sir," he continued, detecting
Freddy in the act of telegraphing to me his dissent from the last
doctrine propounded. "You may ridicule your old father's opinion,
but you'll find it no laughing matter to clear yourself, and justify
your conduct, in a court of justice. They may bring it in conspiracy,
for I daresay you plotted it all beforehand; they may bring it in riot
and illegal assembly, for there were three of you engaged in it; they
may bring it in treason, for you incited His Majesty's subjects to commit a breach of the peace, and interfered with the proper officers in
the discharge of their duty: 'pon my word, I don't know that they
may not bring it in murder, for the poor child that had the measles in
the town died between six and seven o'clock this morning, and no
doubt the confusion had something to do with accelerating its death.
So, sir, if you're not hanged, you're certain to be transported; and
don't ask me to assist you; I've lived by supporting the law for fifty
years, and I'm not going in my old age to lend my countenance to
those who break it, and set it at naught, though my own son be one of
them. I have spoken my mind plainly, Mr. Fairlegh, more so perhaps
than I should have done before a guest in my own house, but it is a
matter upon which I feel deeply. I wish you good-morning, sir." So
saying, he turned away, and stalked majestically out of the room,
closely followed, not to say imitated, by the cat, who held her tai
erect, so as to form a right angle with the line of her back, and
walked with a hypocritical air of meek dignity and chastened self-
approval.

"That's what I call pleasant and satisfactory," exclaimed Freddy,
after a pause, during which each member of the party exchanged
glances of consternation with somebody else. "Who would
ever have imagined the possibility of the governor's turning
cantankerous—assuming the character of the Roman father
upon the shortest possible notice, and thirsting to sacrifice
his son on the altar of the outraged laws of his country!
What an interesting victim I shall make, to be sure! Lucy
must lend me that wreath of roses she looked so pretty in last night,
to wear at the fatal ceremony. And my dear mother shall stand near,
tearing out those revered locks of hers by handfuls." (The reader
should perhaps be informed that Mrs. Coleman rejoiced in a false
front of so open and ingenuous a nature, that from its youth upwards
it never could have been guilty of deceiving anyone.) "May I ring
and tell John to have all the carving knives sharpened? it would be
more satisfactory to my feelings not to be slaughtered with a blunt
weapon."

"Don't talk in that way, Frederick," cried Mrs. Coleman. "I'm sure your father would never think of doing such dreadful things; but I believe you're only making fun of him, which isn't at all right of you. I'm not a bit surprised at his being angry with you, when you know how steady he always says he was as a young man (not that I ever quite believe it, though); he never went ringing bells, however late he might stay out at night, that I heard of (though I should never have known it if he had, very likely). I don't myself see any great harm in it, you know, Mr. Fairless, particularly after your saving poor Clara Saville, and Freddy from drowning, when you were all boys together—indeed, I shall always have the highest opinion of you for it, only I wish you had never done it at all, either of you, because of making your father so angry—you I mean, Frederick."

" Have you received any account of Miss Saville this morning ? " inquired I, anxious to change the conversation ; for I could see that Freddy, despite his assumed indifference, was a good deal annoyed at the serious light in which the old gentleman seemed to look upon our escapade. " I should be glad to know that she was none the worse for all the alarm she must have suffered."

" No, we have not heard anything of her," replied Lucy. " Should we not send to inquire after her, aunt ? "

" Certainly, my dear Lucy; I 'am glad you have reminded me; I always meant to send, only all this has put it out of my head."

"Now, Frank, there's a splendid chance for you," exclaimed Freddy; " nothing can be more correct than for you to call and make the proper inquiries in person; and then if old Stiffback should happen not to be at home, and you can contrive to get let in, and the young lady be not actually a stone—"

" Indeed, Frederick, she is nothing of the kind," interrupted Lucy warmly; "if you only knew her, you would be astonished to find what deep, warm feelings are concealed beneath that calm manner of hers; but she has wonderful self-control. I could see last night how much she was grieved at being obliged to go away without having thanked Mr. Fairlegh for saving her."

" Give her a chance to repair the error to-day, by all means, then," said Freddy; " and if you should succeed in gaining an interview, and she really is anxious to do a little bit of the grateful, and old Vernor does not kick you downstairs, I shall begin to regret that I didn't extinguish her myself."

"I really have a great mind to follow your advice," returned I ; " it is only proper to inquire after the young lady, and they need not let me in unless they like."

"If you should see her, Mr. Lawlegh," said Mrs. Coleman, "tell her from me, how very much vexed I was about the candelabrum being thrown down and setting fire to her dress; it was made of the very best Dresden china, and must have cost (only it was a present, which made it all the more valuable, you know) fifteen or sixteen

guineas; and, I'm sure I wonder, now I come to think of it, why it
did not flare up and burn her to death; but you were so quick and
clever, and entirely spoilt that beautiful whittle of old Mrs. Trottles,
with the greatest presence of mind; and I'm sure we ought all to be
thankful to you for it; and we shall be delighted to see her when she
has quite recovered it, tell her, particularly Lucy, who is nearest her
own age, you know."

"Let me see," said Freddy, musing; "Mrs. Trottles must be
seventy-two if she is a day; 'pon my word. Lucy, you're the youngest-
looking woman of your age I ever met with; if I had not heard my
mother say it myself, I'd never have believed it."

"Believed what, Freddy? What have I said?" asked Mrs.
Coleman.

"That Lucy was Mrs. Trottles' most intimate friend, because she
was nearest her own age," returned Freddy.

"No such thing, sir; I said, or I meant to say—only you are so
tiresome with your jokes, that you puzzle one—that Lucy being
her own age, I mean Clara's, Mr. Fairless was to tell her how very
glad she would be—and very natural it is for young people to like
young people—to see her; and I hope you'll remember to tell her
all I have said exactly, Mr. Fairless, for I'm always anxious to try
to please and amuse her, she's so very dull and stupid, poor
thing!"

To perform this utter impossibility I faithfully pledged myself;
and taking a hasty farewell of the ladies, hurried out of the room
to conceal a fit of laughter, which had been gradually becoming
irrepressible.

"Laugh away, old boy," cried Freddy, who had accompanied me
into the hall; "no wonder I'm an odd fellow, for, as Pat would say,
my mother was one before me, and no mistake. I wish you luck
with the fair Clara, not that you'll see her—old Vernor will take care
of that somehow or other; even if he's not at home, he'll have locked
her up safely before he went out, depend upon it."

"You do not mean that in sober earnest?" said I.

"Perhaps not actually in fact," replied Freddy, "but in effect I
believe he does. Clara tells Lucy she never sees anyone."

"She shall see me to-day, if I can possibly contrive it," said I.
"Oh for the good old days of chivalry, when knocking the guardian
on the head, and running away with the imprisoned damsel afterwards
would have been accounted a very moral and gentlemanlike way of
spending the morning!"

"Certainly they had a pleasant knack of simplifying matters,
those 'knights of old,'" replied Freddy; "but it's not a line of
business that would have suited me at all; in balancing their accounts
the kicks always appear to have obtained a very uncomfortable
preponderance over the half-pence; besides, the 'casus belli' was a
point on which their ideas were generally in a deplorable state of
confusion: when one kills a man, it's as well to have some slight

notion why one does it; and the case comes home to one still more closely, if it's somebody else who's going to kill you."

"You're about right there, Master Freddy," said I, smiling as I shook hands with him, and quitted the house.

CHAPTER XVII.

THE INVISIBLE GIRL.

" Aye, that's a dolt indeed, for he doth nothing but talk of his horse."—*Merchant of Venice.*

" Yond young fellow swears he will speak with you. What's to be said to him? He's fortified against any denial."—*Twelfth Night.*

" Be subject to no sight but mine; invisible
To every eyeball else."—*Tempest.*

ON arriving at the inn, to which I was forced to return to order my horse, I perceived Lawless's tandem waiting at the door, surrounded by a crowd of admiring rustics, with Shrimp, his arms folded with an air of nonchalant defiance, which seemed to say, "Oh! run over me by all means if you choose," stationed directly in front of the leader's head. On entering the parlour I found Lawless busily engaged in pulling on a pair of refractory boots, and looking very hot and red in the face from the exertion.

"How are you, Fairlegh? how are you? That stupid fool has made 'em too tight for anybody but Tom Thumb, and be hanged to him! Ever read fairy tales, Fairlegh? I did when I was a little shaver, and wore cock-tailed petticoats—all bare legs and bustle—' a Highland lad my love was born; ' that style of thing, rather, you know; never believed 'em, though : wasn't to be done even then; eh? Well, this is a puzzler; I can't get 'em on. Where's the fellow they call boots? Here, you sir, come and see if you can pull on these confounded namesakes of yours, and I'll tip you half-a-crown if you succeed; cheaper than breaking one's back, eh?"

"Where are you off to, supposing you should ever get those boots on?" asked I.

"Eh? I am going to call on the young woman I set alight at the hop last night, and tell her I'm quite down in the mouth about it; explain that I didn't go to do it; that it was quite a mistake, and all owing to the other young woman's being so fresh, in fact; and then offer to rig her out again, start her in new harness from bridle to crupper, all at my own expense, and that will be finishing off the affair handsomely, won't it?"

"I should advise your leaving out that last piece of munificence," replied I, "she might think it an insult."

"An insult, eh? Oh, if she's so proud as all that comes to, I'd better stay away altogether; I shall be safe to put my foot into it there, a good deal faster than I have into these villanous boots— that's it, Samson, another pull such as that and the deed's done," added Lawless, patting the human Boots on the back encouragingly.

" I was just going to ride over to inquire after Miss Saville myself," said I.

"That's the very thing, then," was the reply. " I'll drive you there instead; it will be better for your scorched fin" (pointing to my injured arm) " than jolting about outside a horse, and you shall tell me what to say as we go along; you seem to understand the sex, as they call the petticoats, better than I do, and can put a fellow up to a few of the right dodges. I only wish they were all horses, and then I flatter myself I should not require any man's advice how to harness, drive, train, or physic them."

" The ladies are infinitely indebted to you," replied I, as I ran upstairs to prepare for our expedition.

A drive of rather less than an hour and a half, during which the thorough-breds performed in a way to delight every lover of horse-flesh, brought us to the park gate of Barstone Priory, where Mr. Vernor resided. After winding in and out for some half-mile amongst groups of magnificent forest trees, their trunks partially concealed by plantations of rare and beautiful shrubs, a sudden turn of the road brought us in front of the Priory—an ancient, venerable-looking pile of building which had evidently, as its name implied, once belonged to some religious community. The alterations it had undergone, in order to adapt it to its present purpose, had been carried out with more taste and skill than are usually met with in such cases. The garden, with its straight terrace-walks and brilliant flower-beds, contrasted well with the gray stone of which the building was composed, while the smooth-shaven lawn, with an old, quaintly-carved sun-dial in the centre, and above all, the absence of any living creature whatsoever, imparted an air of severe formality to the scene, which, as the eye rested upon it, seemed to realize all one had read of monastic discipline and seclusion; and one half expected to see a train of dark-veiled nuns or sandalled friars winding slowly forth from the hall-door.

" What a singular old shop!" exclaimed my companion, regarding the structure with a look of displeased criticism; " wretched little windows as ever I saw; they must be all in the dark inside on a dull day, and every day would be dull if one lived there, I should think. It would puzzle a fellow to tell whether that building was clerical or lay, fish or flesh; a castle that had taken a serious turn, or a church out for the day in plain clothes; how people can like to live in such a mouldy, rusty, musty old barn, that looks as full of ghosts as a cheese is of mites, I can't conceive."

" There certainly is an appearance of gloom and loneliness about the place," replied I; "but I think it is chiefly owing to the absence of any living object—a herd of deer in the park, a group of children and dogs playing on the lawn—anything to give animation to the picture, would be the greatest improvement."

"I should just think it would," returned Lawless. "Fancy a pack of hounds under that jolly old oak yonder, the huntsman and whips in their bits of pink, and a field of about fifty of the right sort of fellows on thorough-breds, dawdling about, talking to one another, or taking a canter over the turf, just to settle themselves in the saddle; that would be a sight to make old Vernor look a little better pleased than he did last night, sing out for his boots and buckskins, and clap his leg over the first four-footed beast that came in his way, even if it should happen to be the old cow."

"I hope I may be there to see if he does," replied I, laughing.

On inquiring whether Mr. Vernor was at home, we were answered in the affirmative by a tall, gaunt-looking man-servant, with a stern, not to say surly, countenance, the expression of which was in some degree contradicted by a pair of quick, restless, little gray eyes, which in any other face one should have said twinkled merrily beneath the large grizzled eyebrows which o'ershadowed them.

Having, at Lawless's request, procured a nondescript hobbledehoy of indefinite character to stand at the horses' heads (we had left Shrimp behind, by common consent, that he might be no restraint on our conversation), he conducted us across the hall into a kind of morning-room, fitted up with oak panels, and with a very handsome old carved oak chimney-piece reaching half-way to the ceiling. He was leaving the room to inform his master of our arrival, when Lawless stopped him by saying,—

"Here, just wait a bit; tell the young woman—that is to say, don't tell her anything; but I mean, let Miss Saville be made aware (I see you're awake, for all your long face), put her up to our being here; don't you know, eh?"

"Tip him," whispered I.

"Eh, stop a bit; you're a very honest fellow, and it's right to reward faithful servants; and—you understand all about it, eh?"

One portion of this somewhat incoherent address he did understand, evidently, for without altering a muscle of his face he put out his hand, took the money, and left the room with the same unconscious air of imperturbability which he had maintained throughout the whole conference.

"Good move that, eh?" exclaimed Lawless, as soon as the door was closed; "that'll fetch her out of her hole, for a guinea. Mind, I shall do my best to cut you out, Master Frank. I don't see why I haven't a right to quite as large a share of her gratitude as you have, for if I hadn't set her on fire you'd never have put her out; so, in fact, she owes it all to me—don't you see?"

"I'm afraid there's a little sophistry in that argument," replied I; "but we had better wait till we find whether we shall have the opportunity afforded us of trying our powers of fascination before we quarrel about the effects to be produced by them. I cannot say I feel over-sanguine as to the success of your somewhat original negotiation with that raw-boned giant in the blue plush 'sine quâ nons,' as Coleman calls them."

"Time will show," rejoined Lawless, turning towards the door, which opened at this moment to admit Mr. Vernor; and, alas! him only.

His reception of us, though perfectly easy and well-bred, was anything but agreeable or encouraging. He answered our inquiries after Miss Saville's health by informing us, cursorily, that no ill effects had ensued from her alarm of the previous evening. He received Lawless's apologies with a calm half-ironical smile, and an assurance that they were not required; and he slightly thanked me for my obliging assistance in words perfectly unexceptionable in themselves, but which, from a peculiarity in the tone of voice more than anything else, impressed one with a sense of insult rather than of compliment. Still, in compliance with certain expressive looks from Lawless, who evidently was most unwilling to be convinced of the failure of his little bit of diplomacy, I used every means I could think of to prolong the visit. I first admired, then criticized, the carving of the chimney-piece; I dived into a book of prints which lay upon the table, and prosed about mezzotint and line engraving, and bored myself, and of course my hearers also, till our powers of endurance were taxed almost beyond their strength; and at last, having completely exhausted not only my small-talk, but my entire stock of conversation of all sorts and sizes, I was regularly beaten to a standstill, and obliged to take refuge in alternately teasing and caressing a beautiful black |and tan setter, which seemed the only member of the party thoroughly sociable and at his ease.

At length it became apparent even to Lawless himself that the visit could not be protracted longer, and we accordingly rose and took our leave, our host (I will not call him entertainer, for it would be a complete misnomer) preserving the same tone of cool and imperturbable politeness to the very last. On reaching the hall we encountered the surly old footman, whose features looked more than ever as if they had been carved out of some very hard species of wood.

"I say, old boy, where's the young lady, eh?" exclaimed Lawless, as soon as he caught sight of him; "she never showed so much as the tip of her nose in the room; how was that, eh?"

"If she com'd into the room when gentlemen was calling, master would eat her without salt," was the reply.

"Which fact you were perfectly aware of when you took my tip so quietly just now?"

"In course I was; why should I not be?"

"Done brown for once, by Jove!" muttered Lawless, as he left the hall; "a raw-boned old rogue, I'll be even with him some day, though—we shall see, eh?"

While Lawless was busily engaged in settling some of the harness which had become disarranged, the old footman came up to me and whispered, "Make use of your eyes as you drive through the park, and mayhap you'll spy some game worth looking after, young gentleman."

Surprised at this unexpected address, I turned to question him as to its meaning; but in vain; for no sooner had he finished speaking than he re-entered the hall and shut the door behind him.

What could he intend me to understand? thought I; he evidently wished to imply something beyond the simple meaning of the words "game worth looking after;" could he mean to——no! the thing is impossible—"absurd!" exclaimed I, as a wild idea shot through my brain and I felt myself colour like a girl, ·

" What's absurd ? " exclaimed Lawless, gathering up the reins as he spoke; " what are you talking about? why, you're ranting and staring about you like a play-actor; what's the matter with you, eh, Frank ? "

"Nothing," replied I, taking my seat; "don't drive too fast through the park, I want to look at the view as we go along."

In obedience to the gaunt domestic's mysterious injunction I made the best use of my eyes as we retraced our way through the park, and for my pains had the satisfaction of beholding a solitary rabbit, half hidden under a dock-leaf, and sundry carrion crows.

CHAPTER XVIII.

THE GAME IN BARSTONE PARK.

" The fringed curtains of thine eye advance, and say what thou see'st yond."
Tempest.
" Accost, Sir Andrew, accost."—*Twelfth Night.*
" Let us go thank him and encourage him :
My *Guardian's* rough and envious disposition
Strikes me at heart—Sir, you have well deserved."
As You Like It.

WE had arrived within a quarter of a mile of the gate, and I had just settled to my thorough dissatisfaction that the old footman must be a humourist, and had diverted himself by making a kind of April fool out of season of me, when, through the trees, which at that spot stretched their huge branches across the road so as to form a complete arch, I fancied I perceived the flutter of a woman's dress; and in another moment, a turn in the drive disclosed to my view a female form, which I instantly recognized as that of Clara Saville.

Without a minute's hesitation I sprang to the ground before Lawless had time to pull up, and, saying to him, "I shall be back again directly; wait for me, there's a good fellow," I hastily entered a winding path, which led through the trees to the spot where I had seen the young lady, leaving my companion mute from astonishment. Up to this moment, acting solely from a sort of instinctive impulse which made me wish to see and speak to Miss Saville, I had never considered the light in which my proceedings might appear to her. What right, I now asked myself, had I to intrude upon her privacy, and, as it were, force my company upon her, whether she wished it or not? Might she not look upon it as an impertinent intrusion? As these thoughts flitted through my brain, I slackened my pace; and had it not been for very shame, could have found in my heart to turn back again. This, however, I resolved not to do; having committed myself so far, I determined to give her an opportunity of seeing me, and if she should show any intention of avoiding me, it would then be time enough to retrace my steps and leave her unmolested. With this design I proceeded slowly up the path, stopping now and then as if to admire the view, until a turn of the walk brought me in sight of a rustic bench, on which was seated the young lady I had before observed. As soon as she perceived me, she rose and turned towards me, disclosing as she did so, the graceful form and lovely features of my partner of the preceding evening. The morning costume, including a most irresistible little cottage-bonnet lined with pink, was even more becoming to her than the ball-dress; and when, instead of the cold air of constraint which had characterized her manner of the previous evening, she advanced to meet me with a slight blush and the most bewitching smile of welcome that ever set man's heart beating, I thought I had never seen anything so perfectly beautiful before.

"I must ask your forgiveness for venturing thus to intrude upon you, Miss Saville," began I, after we had exchanged salutations; "but the temptation of learning from your own lips that you had sustained no injury was too strong to be resisted, more particularly after the disappointment of finding you were from home when I did myself the pleasure of calling on Mr. Vernor to inquire after you."

"Nay, there is nothing to forgive," replied Miss Saville; "on the contrary," she continued, blushing slightly, "I was anxious to see you, in order to thank you for the eminent service you rendered me yesterday evening."

" Really it is not worth mentioning," returned I; "it is only what any other gentleman in the room would have done had he been in my situation; it was good Mrs. Trottles' shawl saved you; I could have done nothing without that."

" You shall not cheat me out of my gratitude in that way," replied she, smiling: "the shawl would have been of little avail had it not been so promptly and energetically applied; and as for the other gentlemen, they certainly were very ready with their offers of assistance after the danger was over. I am afraid," she continued, looking down, "you must have repented the trouble you had taken when you found what a thankless person you had exerted yourself to save."

"Indeed, no such idea crossed my mind for an instant; the slight service I was able to render you was quite repaid by the pleasure of knowing that I had been fortunate enough to prevent you from sustaining injury," said I.

"You are very kind," was the reply; "but I can assure you I have been exceedingly annoyed by imagining how wholly destitute of gratitude you must have considered me?"

"Lucy Markham told me such would be the case," replied I, smiling.

"Did she?—a dear warm-hearted girl—she always does me justice!" exclaimed Miss Saville, as she raised her beautiful eyes, sparkling with animation, to my face. She then, for the first time, observed my injured arm, and added quickly, "But you wear your arm in a sling; I hope—that is—I am afraid—I trust it was not injured last night!"

"It is a mere trifle," replied I; "the wristband of my sleeve caught fire, and burnt my arm, but it is nothing of any consequence, I can assure you."

"I am sure you must have thought me sadly ungrateful," returned my companion; "you exerted yourself, and successfully, to save my life, receiving a painful injury in so doing, whilst I left the house without offering you the thanks due even to the commonest service imaginable."

"You were not then aware that I had burnt my arm, remember; and forgive me for adding," returned I (for I saw that she was really distressed at the idea of my considering her wanting in gratitude), "that it did not require any unusual degree of penetration to perceive that you were not altogether a free agent."

"No, indeed," replied she, eagerly catching at the idea; "Mr. Vernor, my guardian—he always means to be very kind, I am sure; but," she added, sinking her voice, "he is so very particular, and he speaks so sternly sometimes, that—I know it is very silly—but I cannot help feeling afraid of him. I mention this, sir, to prevent your judging me too harshly, and I trust to your generosity not to take any unfair advantage of my openness; and now," she added, fixing her large eyes upon me with an imploring look which would have melted the toughest old anchorite that ever chewed gray peas, "you will not think me so very ungrateful, will you?"

"My dear Miss Saville," replied I, "let me beg you to believe I never dreamt of blaming you for a moment; on the contrary, I pay you no compliment, but only mention the simple truth, when I tell you that I admired your behaviour throughout the whole affair exceedingly; your presence of mind and self-control were greater than, under the circumstances, I could have supposed possible." As she made no reply to this, but remained looking steadfastly on the

K

ground, with her head turned so as to conceal her face, I continued :
"I hope it is unnecessary for me to add that you need not entertain
the slightest fear of my making any indiscreet use of the frankness
with which you have done me the honour of speaking to me—but I
am forgetting half my business," added I, wishing to set her at ease
again : "I am charged with all sorts of kind messages to you from
good Mrs. Coleman and Miss Markham ; I presume you would wish
me to tell them I have had the pleasure of ascertaining that you
have sustained no ill effects from your alarm."

"Oh yes, by all means," replied Miss Saville, looking up with a
pleased expression, "give my kind love to them both, and tell dear
Lucy I shall come over to see her as soon as ever I can."

"I will not intrude upon you longer, then, having delivered my
message," said I ; "I have kept my companion, the gentleman who
was so unfortunate as to overturn the candelabrum, waiting an
unconscionable time already ; he is very penitent for his offence ;
may I venture to relieve his mind by telling him that you forgive
him ? "

"Pray do so," was the reply; "I never bear malice ; besides, it was
entirely an accident, you know. How thoroughly wretched he
seemed when he found what he had done ! frightened as I was. I
could scarcely help laughing when I caught a glimpse of his face, he
looked so delightfully miserable," added she, with a merry laugh.
After a moment's pause she continued : "I'm afraid Mr. Vernor will
think I am lost, if he should happen to inquire after me, and I'm
not forthcoming."

"Surely," said I, "he can never be so unreasonable as to blame you
for such a trifle as remaining five minutes too long ? Does he
expect you to be a nun because he lives in a priory ? "

"Almost, I really think," was the reply ; "and now good-bye, Mr.
Fairlegh," she continued—"I shall feel happier since I have been able
to explain to you that I am not quite a monster of ingratitude."

"If that is the case, I am bound to rejoice in it also," answered I,
"though I would fain convince you that the explanation was not
required."

Her only reply to this was an incredulous shake of the head ; and,
once more wishing me good morning, she tripped along the path ;
and when I turned to look again, her graceful figure had disappeared
among the trees.

With a flushed brow and beating heart (gentle reader, I was
barely twenty), I hastened to rejoin my companion, who, as might
be expected, was not in the most amiable humour imaginable,
having had to restrain the impatience of two fiery horses for a space
of time nearly approaching a quarter of an hour.

"Really, Lawless," I began, "I am quite ashamed."

"Oh, you are, are you ? " was the rejoinder. "I should rather
think you ought to be, too. But it's always the way with you fellows
who pretend to be steady and moral, and all that sort of thing :

when you do find a chance of getting into mischief, you're worse a
great deal than a man like myself, for instance, who, without being
bothered with any particular principles of any kind, has what I call
a general sense of fitness and propriety, and does his dissipation
sensibly and correctly. But to go tearing off like a lunatic after the
first petticoat you see fluttering among the bushes in a gentleman's
park, and leaving your friend to hold in two thoroughbred peppery
devils, that are enough to pull a man's arms off, for about a quarter
of a hour, it's too bad a great deal. Why, just before you came.
I fully expected when that mare was plunging about on her hind
legs—"

" How lovely she looked! " interrupted I, thinking aloud.

" You thought so, did you? " rejoined Lawless ; " I wish you'd just
had to hold her; her mouth's as hard—"

" Her mouth is perfect," replied I, emphatically; " quite perfect."

" Well, that's cool," muttered Lawless ; "he'll put me in a passion
directly ;—pray, sir, may I ask how on earth you come to know anything about her mouth? "

" How do I know anything about her mouth? " exclaimed I. " Did
I not watch with delight its ever-varying expressions—mark each
movement of those beautiful lips, and drink in every syllable that
fell from them ?—not observe her mouth ! Think you, when we have
been conversing together for the last quarter of an hour, that I
could fail to do so ? "

" Oh, he's gone stark staring mad! " exclaimed Lawless ; "strait-
waistcoats, Bedlam, and all that sort o' thing, you know ;—conversing
with my bay mare for the last quarter of an hour, and drinking in
every syllable that fell from her beautiful lips—oh, he's raving ! "

" What do you mean? " said I, at length awaking to some consciousness of sublunary affairs—" Your mare!—who ever thought
of your mare ? it's Miss Saville I'm talking about."

" Miss Saville! " repeated Lawless, giving vent to a long whistle,
expressive of incredulity ; " why, you don't mean to say you've been
talking to Miss Saville all this time, do you? "

" To be sure I have," replied I ; " and a very interesting and
agreeable conversation it was too."

" Well! " exclaimed Lawless, after a short pause ; " all the luck in
this matter seems to fall to your share; so the sooner I get out of it
the better. It won't break my heart, that's one comfort ;—if the
young woman has the bad taste to prefer you to me, why, it can't
be helped, you know ;—but what did she say for herself, eh ? "

" She sent you her forgiveness for one thing," replied I ; and I then
proceeded to relate such particulars of the interview as I considered
expedient; which recital, and our remarks thereupon, furnished
conversation during the remainder of our drive.

CHAPTER XIX.

TURNING THE TABLES.

"' You should also make no noise in the streets.'
"' You may stay him.'
"' Nay, by'r la'ly, that I think he cannot.'
"' Five shillings to one on't with any man that knows the statutes, he may stay him. His wits are not so blunt as, God help, I would desire they were. It is an offence to stay a man *against his will.* Dost thou not suspect my place? dost though not suspect my years? O that he were here to write me down an ass! but, masters, remember that I am an ass: though it be not written down, yet forget not that I am an ass.'"—*Much Ado About Nothing.*

ABOUT a week had elapsed after the events which I have just recorded, when one morning, shortly before my return to Cambridge, I received a letter from Coleman, detailing the finale of the bell-ringing affair. It ran as follows :—

"MY DEAR FRANK,—Doubtless you are, or ought to be, very anxious to hear how I contrived to get out of the scrape into which you and the Honourable George managed to inveigle me, having previously availed yourselves of my innocence, and succeeded through the seductive medium of oysters and porter, in corrupting my morals, and leaving me, poor victim! to bear the blame, and suffer the consequences, of our common misdemeanour. However, mine is no pitiful spirit to be quelled by misfortune, and, as dangers thickened around me, I bore up against them bravely, like—like—(was it Julius Cæsar or Coriolanus who did that sortlof thing?) but never mind—like a Roman brick, we'll say; the particular brick is quite immaterial. but I must beg you to believe the likeness was something striking. To descend to particulars: Hostilities were commenced by that old ass, Mayor Dullmug, who took out a summons against me for creating a riot and disturbance in the town, and the first day the bench sat, I was marched off by two policemen, and locked up in a little dirty room, to keep cool till their worships were ready to discuss me. Well, there I sat, kicking my heels, and chuckling over a heart-rending little scene I had just gone through with my mother, whose dread of the terrors of the law was greatly increased by the very vague ideas she possessed of the extent of its powers. The punishment she had settled in her own mind as likely to be awarded me was transportation, and her farewell address was as follows:—' If they should be cruel enough to order you to be transported for fourteen years, Freddy, my dear, I shall try to persuade your father (though he's just like a savage North American Indian about you) to get it changed ' for life ' instead, for they always die of the yellow fever for the sharks to eat them, when they've been over three or four years; and four years are better than fourteen, though bad's the best, and I'm a miserable woman. I read all about it last week in one of Captain Marryat's books, and very shocking I thought it.' Having ventured to hint that, if I was carried off by the yellow fever at the end of a year or two, the length of my sentence would not signify much to me when I was dead, I was rebuked with, 'Don't talk in that shocking way, Frederick, as if you were a heathen, in your situation, and I hearing you your collect every Sunday, besides Mrs. Hannah More, who might have been a saint if ever there was one, or anything else she liked, with her talents, only she was too good for this wicked world, and so she went to a better, and wrote that charming book, 'Coelebs in Search of a Wife.'' Oh, my poor dear mother's queer sentences! I was becoming shockingly tired of my own company, when it occurred to me that it would be the correct thing to carve my name on the Newgate stone a la Jack Shepherd; and I was just putting a few finishing strokes to the N of Coleman, wherewith, in characters at least six inches long, I had embellished a very conspicuous spot over the chimney-piece, when I was surprised, 'with my chisel so fine, tra la' (i.e. with a red-hot poker which I had been obliged to put up with instead, it being the only instrument attainable), by the officials, who came to summon me, and who did not appear in the slightest degree capable of appreciating the beauties of my performance. By them I was straightway conducted into the awful presence of sundry elderly gentlemen, rejoicing in all heads more or less bald, and faces expressing various degrees of solemn stupidity, who in their proper persons constituted 'the bench.' Before these grave and reverend signiors did Master Dullmug and his satellites

> 'Then and there,
> Rehearse and declare '

all my heinous crimes, offences, and misdemeanours; whereupon the aforesaid signiors did solemnly shake their bald heads, and appear exceedingly shocked and particularly puzzled. Well, at last I was called upon for my defence, and, having made up my mind for some time what line I would take, I cut the matter very short by owning to have assisted in ringing the bells, which I confessed was an act of folly, but nothing more, and that the idea of its constituting an offence punishable by law was absurd in the extreme. This sent them to book, and after turning over sundry ponderous tomes, and consulting various statutes of all sorts and sizes, besides whispering together, and shaking their heads once and again, till I began to fear that their necks would be dislocated, they arrived at the conclusion that I was right, or thereabouts. This fact the eldest, most bald, and most stupid of the party, chosen by common consent, doubtless in virtue of these attributes, as spokesman, proceeeded to communicate to me in a very prosy harangue, to which he appended a lecture —a sort of stock article, which he evidently kept constantly on hand with blanks which could be filled up to suit any class of offenders.

In this harangue he pointed out the danger of juvenile tricks, and the evils of dissipation, winding up with the assurance that, as I seemed deeply sensible of the error of my ways, they, the magistrates, would, on my making a suitable apology to that excellent public functionary, the Mayor of Hillingford, graciously deign to overlook my misconduct. During his long-winded address, a new idea struck me, and when he had concluded, I inquired, with all due respect, whether ' I was to understand that it was quite certain I had committed no offence punishable by law ?' To this he replied, 'that I might set my mind completely at ease upon that point; that though, morally speaking, I had been guilty of a very serious misdemeanour, in the eye of the law I was perfectly innocent.' 'In that case, gentlemen,' replied I, ' the liberty of the subject has been infringed; I have been kept in illegal confinement for some hours, and I believe I have my remedy in an action for false imprisonment against Mr. Dullmug. Does not the law bear me out in what I state ?' Again they had recourse to their books, and were unwillingly forced to confess that I was right. ' Then,' continued I, ' so far from making any apology to Mr. Dullmug, unless that gentleman consents to beg my pardon, and gives me a written apology for the unjust and illegal prosecution to which he has subjected me, I shall at once take the necessary steps to proceed against him.' Oh, Frank, I would have given something to have had you there, old boy! when I announced this determination: there was such a shindy as I never before witnessed : old Dullmug was furious, and vowed he'd never apologize: I declared if he didn't nothing should prevent me from bringing my action : the magistrates tried to persuade me, but I was inflexible; and (by Jove! I was very near forgetting the best part of it all) my governor, who was in court, the moment he saw the law was on my side, turned suddenly round, swore I had been shamefully used, and that if it cost him every farthing he possessed in the world, he would see justice done me. So the end of it was that old Dullmug was forced to write the apology; it now lies in my writing-desk, and I look upon it as one of the proudest trophies man ever possessed. So, Master Frank, considering all things, I think I may reckon I got pretty well out of that scrape.

"Ever your affectionate F. C.

" P.S.—What have you said or done to render old Vernor so bitter against you? Clara Saville tells Lucy that, when she informed him of her having met and conversed with you alone in the park that day, he flew into such a rage as she had never seen him in before, and abused you like a pickpocket; and she says she feels certain that, for some cause or other, he entertains a strong personal dislike to you. 'Entre nous,' I don't think the fair Clara seems exactly to sympathize with him in this feeling. Considering that you had somewhat less than half an hour to make play in, from Lucy's account you do not seem to have wasted much time. Ah ! Master Frank, you are a naughty boy ; I can't help sighing when I reflect how anxious your poor dear mother must feel about you, when she knows you're out."

"Still the same light-hearted merry fellow as ever," exclaimed I, as I closed the letter; "how long, I wonder, will those buoyant spirits of his resist the depressing effect which contact with the harsh realities of life appears always sooner or later to produce? Strange, what he says about that Mr. Vernor; I am not conscious that I ever met the man till the evening of the ball, and yet I fancied there was something which seemed not utterly unfamiliar to me in the expression of his face. Vernor! Vernor! I don't believe I ever heard the name before—it's very odd. Of course, what he says about Miss Saville is all nonsense; and yet there was something in her manner which made me fancy, if I had time and opportunity—pshaw! what absurdity—I shall have enough to do if I am to imagine myself in love with every nice girl who says, 'Thank you' prettily for any trifling service I may chance to render her. I am sure she is not happy, poor thing! Seriously, I wish I were sufficiently intimate with her to afford her the advice and assistance of a friend, should such be ever required by her. I should take the liberty of asking old Vernor what he meant by his extraordinary behaviour towards me, were I to see much more of him; there's nothing like a little plain speaking. But I need not trouble my brains about the matter; I shall probably never meet either of them again, so what does it signify? She certainly is the loveliest girl I ever saw, though! heigho!" and, with a sigh, for which I should have been somewhat puzzled rationally to account, I took up my gun and set off for a day's shooting with Harry Oaklands.

CHAPTER XX.

ALMA MATER.

"He's a good divine that follows his own instructions; I can easier teach twenty what were good to be done, than be one of the twenty to follow my own teaching. The brain may devise laws for the blood, but a hot temper leaps over a cold decree."—
Merchant of Venice.

TIME, that venerable and much-vituperated individual, who, if he has to answer for some acts savouring of a taste for wanton destruction—if he now and then lunches on some noble old abbey, which had remained a memorial of the deep piety and marvellous skill of our forefathers—if he crops, by way of salad, some wide-spreading beech or hoary patriarchal oak, which had flung its shade

over the tombs of countless generations, and, as it stood forming a
link between the present and the past, won men's reverence by force
of contrast with their own ephemeral existence—yet atones for his
delinquencies by softening the bitterness of grief, blunting the sharp
edge of pain, and affording to the broken-hearted the rest, and to the
slaves the freedom of the grave ;—old Time, I say, who should be
praised at all events for his perseverance and steadiness, swept
onward with his scythe, and cutting his way through the frost and
snow of winter, once more beheld the dust of that "brother of the
east wind," March, converted into mud by the showers of April, and
the summer was again approaching. It was on a fine morning in
May, that, as Oaklands and I were breakfasting together in my
rooms at Trinity, we heard a tap at the door, and the redoubtable
Shrimp made his appearance. This interesting youth had, under
Lawless's able tuition, arrived at such a pitch of knowingness, that it
was utterly impossible to make him credit anything; he had not the
smallest particle of confidence remaining in the integrity of man,
woman, or child; and, like many another of the would-be wise in
their generation, the only flaw in his scepticism was the bigoted
nature of his faith in the false and hateful doctrine of the universal
depravity of the human race. He was the bearer of a missive from
his master, inviting Oaklands and myself to a wine-party at his
rooms that evening.

"I suppose we may as well go," said Oaklands; "I like a positive
engagement somewhere—it saves one the trouble of thinking what
one shall do with one's self."

"You can accept it," replied I, "but it would be a waste of time
which I have no right to allow myself; not only does it make one
idle while it lasts, but the next day also, for I defy a man to read to
any purpose the morning after one of Lawless's symposia."

"Call it supper, my dear boy," returned Oaklands, stretching
himself; "why do you take the trouble to use a long word when a
short one would do just as well ?   If I could but get you to economize
your labour and take things a little more easily, it would be of the
greatest advantage to you;—that everlasting reading, too—I tell you
what, Frank, you are reading a great deal too hard; you look quite
pale and ill. I promised Mrs. Fairlegh I would not let you over-
work yourself, and you shall not either. Come, you must and shall
go to this party; you want relaxation and amusement, and those
fellows will contrive to rouse you up a bit, and do you good."

"To say the truth," I replied, "that is one of my chief objections
to going. Lawless I like, for the sake of old recollections, and
because he is at bottom a well-disposed, good-hearted fellow; but I
cannot approve of the set of men one meets there. It is not merely
their being what is termed 'fast' that I object to; for though I do
not set up for a sporting character myself, I am rather amused than
otherwise to mix occasionally with that style of men; but there is a
tone of recklessness in the conversation of the set we meet there, a

want of reverence for everything human and divine, which, I confess, disgusts me—they seem to consider no object too high or too low to make a jest of."

"I understand the kind of thing you refer to," answered Oaklands, "but I think it's only one or two of them who offend in that way; there's one man who is my particular aversion; I declare if I thought he'd be there to-night I would not go."

"I think I know who you mean," replied I; "Stephen Wilford, is it not? the man they call 'Butcher,' from some brutal thing he once did to a horse."

"You're right, Frank; I can scarcely sit quietly by and hear that man talk. I suppose he sees that I dislike him, for there is something in his manner to me which is almost offensive; really at times I fancy he wishes to pick a quarrel with me."

"Not unlikely," said I; "he has the reputation of being a dead shot with the pistol, and on the strength of it he presumes to bully every one."

"He had better not go too far with me," returned Oaklands, with flashing eyes; "men are not to be frightened like children; such a character as that is a public nuisance."

"He will not be there to-night, I am glad to say," replied I, "for I met him yesterday when I was walking with Lawless, and he said he was engaged with Wentworth this evening; but, my dear Harry, for Heaven's sake avoid any quarrel with this man; should you not do so, you will only be hazarding your life unnecessarily, and it can lead to no good result."

"My dear fellow, do I ever quarrel with anybody? there is nothing worth the trouble of quarrelling about in this world; besides, it would be an immense fatigue to be shot," observed Harry, smiling.

"I have no great faith in your pacific sensations, for they are nothing more," rejoined I; "your indolence always fails you where it might be of use in subduing (forgive me for using the term) your fiery temper; besides, in allowing a man of this kind to quarrel with you, you give him just the opportunity he wants; in fact, you are completely playing his game."

"Well, I can't see that exactly; suppose the worst comes to the worst, and you are obliged to fight him, he stands nearly as good a chance of being killed as you do."

"Excuse me, he does nothing of the kind; going out with a professed duellist is like playing cards with a skilful gambler; the chances are very greatly in his favour: in the first place, nine men out of ten would lose their nerve entirely when stationed opposite the pistol of a dead shot; then again, there are a thousand apparent trifles of which the initiated are aware, and which make the greatest difference, such as securing a proper position with regard to the sun, taking care that your figure is not in a direct line with any upright object, a tree or post, for instance, and lots of other things of a like nature which we know nothing about, all of which he is certain to

contrive to have arranged favourably for himself, and disadvan-
tageously for his opponent. Then, having, as it were, trained himself
for the occasion, he is perfectly cool and collected, and ready to avail
himself of every circumstance he might turn to his advantage—a
moment's hesitation in pulling the trigger when the signal is given,
and he fires first—many a man has received his death-wound before
now ere he had discharged his own pistol."

"My dear boy," said Harry, "you really are exciting and alarming
yourself very unnecessarily; I am not going to quarrel with Wilford
or anybody else; I detest active exertion of every kind, and consider
duelling as a fashionable compound of iniquity, containing equal
parts of murder and suicide—and we'll go to Lawless's this evening,
that I'm determined upon—and—let me see—I've got James's new
novel in my pocket. I shall not disturb you if I stay here, shall I?
I'm not going to talk."

Then, without waiting for an answer, he stretched himself at full
length on (and beyond) the sofa, and was soon buried in the pages of
that best of followers in the footsteps of the mighty Wizard of the
North—Walter Scott—leaving me to the somewhat less agreeable
task of reading mathematics.

CHAPTER XXI.

THE WINE-PARTY.

> "This night I hold an old-accustomed feast,
> Whereto I have invited many a guest,
> Such as I love."
> "A fair assembly, whither should they come?
> *Servant.*—Up——!
> *Romeo.*—Whither?
> *Servant.*—To supper."
> *Shakespeare.*
> "All is not false that seems at first a lie."
> *Southey.*
> "Do you bite your thumb at us, sir?
> I do bite my thumb, sir!
> Do you quarrel, sir?
> Quarrel, sir! No, sir!
> If you do, sir, I am for you."
> *Shakespeare.*

LET the reader imagine a long table covered with the remains of an
excellent dessert, interspersed with a multitude of bottles of all shapes
and sizes, containing every variety of wine that money could procure,
or palate desire; whilst in the centre stood a glorious old china bowl
of punch, which the guests were discussing in tumblers—wine-glasses

having been unanimously voted much too slow. Around this table let there be seated from fifteen to twenty men, whose ages might vary from nineteen to three or four and twenty; some smoking cigars, some talking vociferously, some laughing, some, though they were decidedly the minority, listening: but all showing signs of being more or less elated by the wine they had taken. Let the reader imagine all this, and he will have formed a pretty correct idea of the supper-party in Lawless's rooms, as it appeared about ten o'clock on the evening subsequent to the conversation I have just detailed.

"Didn't I see you riding a black horse with one white stocking yesterday, Oaklands?" inquired a young man with a round jovial countenance, which might have been reckoned handsome but for the extreme redness of the complexion and the loss of a front tooth, occasioned by a fall received in the hunting-field, whose name was Richard, or, as he was commonly termed, Dick Curtis.

"Yes," replied Oaklands, "I dare say you did; I was trying him."

"Ah! I fancied he was not one of your own."

"No; he belongs to Tom Barret, who wants me to buy him; but I don't think he's strong enough to carry my weight: there's not substance enough about him; I ride nearly eleven stone."

"Oh! he'll never do for you," exclaimed Lawless. "I know the horse well; they call him Blacksmith, because the man who bred him was named Smith; he lives down in Lincolnshire, and breeds lots of horses; but they are none of them, at least none that I have seen, what I call the right sort; don't you buy him, he's got too much daylight under him to suit you."

"Too long in the pasterns to carry weight," urged Curtis.

"Rather inclined to be cow-hocked," chimed in Lawless.

"Not ribbed home," remarked Curtis.

"Too narrow across the loins," observed Lawless.

"He'll never carry flesh," continued Curtis.

"It's useless to think of his jumping; he'll never make a hunter," said Lawless.

"Only hear them!" interrupted a tall, fashionable-looking young man, with a high forehead and a profusion of light, curling hair; "now those two fellows are once off, it's all up with anything like rational conversation for the rest of the evening."

"That's right, Archer, put the curb on 'em; we might as well be in Tattersall's yard at once," observed another of the company, addressing the last speaker.

"I fear it's beyond my power," replied Archer; "they've got such an incurable trick of talking equine scandal, and taking away the characters of their neighbours' horses, that nobody can stop them unless it is Stephen Wilford."

The mention of this name seemed to have the effect of rendering everyone grave, and a pause ensued, during which Oaklands and I exchanged glances. At length the silence was broken by Curtis, who said,—

"By the way, what's become of Wilford? I expected to meet him here to-night."

"He was engaged to dine with Wentworth," said Lawless; "but he promised to look in upon us in the course of the evening; I thought he would have been here before this."

As he spoke, a tap was heard at the room door.

"Well, that's odd," continued Lawless; "that's Wilford for a ducat; talk of the devil, eh, don't you know? Come in."

"You had better not repeat that in his hearing," observed Archer, "though I believe he'd take it as a compliment on the whole; it's my opinion he rather affects the satanic."

"Hush," said Curtis, pressing his arm, "here he is."

As he spoke, the door opened, and the subject of their remarks entered. He was rather above the middle height, of a slight but unusually elegant figure, with remarkably small hands and feet, the former of which were white and smooth as those of a woman. His features were delicately formed and regular, and the shape of his face a perfect oval; strongly marked eyebrows overshadowed a pair of piercing black eyes; his lips were thin and compressed, and his mouth finely cut; his hair, which was unusually glossy and luxuriant. was jet black, as were his whiskers, affording a marked contrast to the death-like pallor of his countenance. The only fault that could be found in the drawing of his face was that the eyes were placed too near together; but this imparted a character of intensity to his glance which added to, rather than detracted from, the general effect of his appearance. His features, when in repose, were usually marked by an expression of contemptuous indifference; he seldom laughed, but his smile conveyed an indication of such bitter sarcasm that I have seen men, whom he chose to make a butt for his ridicule, writhe under it as under the infliction of bodily torture. He was dressed, as was his wont, entirely in black; but his clothes, which were fashionably cut, fitted him without a wrinkle. He bowed slightly to the assembled company, and then seated himself in a chair which had been reserved for him at the upper end of the table, nearly opposite Oaklands and myself, saying as he did so: "I'm afraid I'm rather late, Lawless, but Wentworth and I had a little business to transact, and I could not get away sooner."

"What devil's deed have they been at now, I wonder?" whispered Oaklands to me.

"Manslaughter, most likely," replied Archer (who was seated next to me, and had overheard the remark). "Wilford appears so thoroughly satisfied with himself; that was just the way in which he looked the morning he winged Sherringham, for I saw him myself."

"Send me down the claret, will you, Curtis?" asked Wilford. "Punch is a beverage I don't patronize; it makes a man's hand shaky."

"If that is the case," said Archer, "you ought to make a point of drinking it for the good of society, my dear Wilford; let me help you to a glass."

"Nonsense, Archer, be quiet, man; here, taste this cool bottle, Wilford; claret's good for nothing if it's at all flat," exclaimed Lawless, drawing the cork of a fresh magnum as he spoke.

"I differ from you in that opinion, Archer," returned Wilford, fixing his keen black eyes upon the person he addressed with a piercing glance; "society is like the wine in this glass," and he filled a bumper to the brim as he spoke; "it requires a steady hand to keep it within its proper bounds, and to compel it to preserve an unruffled surface;" and so saying he raised the glass to his lips without spilling a drop, still keeping his eyes fixed upon Archer's face with the same withering glance.

"Well, I have often heard of looking daggers at a person," continued Archer, who had been drinking somewhat deeply during the evening, and now appeared possessed by a spirit of mischief leading him to tease and annoy Wilford in every way he could think of; "but Wilford does worse, he positively looks pistols—cocked and loaded pistols—at one. Fairlegh, I shall screen myself behind your broad shoulders: I never could stand fire." So saying, he seized me by the elbows, and, urging me forward, crouched down behind me, affecting the extremity of terror.

The scowl on Wilford's brow deepened as he spoke, but, after a moment's hesitation, apparently considering the affair too absurd to take notice of, he turned away with a contemptuous smile, saying, "You make your punch too strong, Lawless."

Archer instantly recovered his erect attitude, and with a flushed face seemed about to make some angry reply, when Lawless, who appeared nervously anxious that the evening should pass over harmoniously, interposed.

"Archer, you're absolutely incorrigible; keep him in order, Fairlegh, eh? give him some more punch, and fill your own glass—it has been empty I don't know how long. I'll find a toast that will make you drink—bumpers round, gentlemen, 'to the health of the prettiest girl in Hertfordshire.' Are you all charged? I beg to propose—"

"Excuse me interrupting you, Lawless," exclaimed I—for I felt certain who it was he was thinking of; and the idea of Miss Saville's name being mentioned and discussed with the tone of license common on such occasions, appeared to me such complete profanation, that I determined, be the consequences what they might, to prevent it; —"Excuse my interrupting you, but I should feel greatly obliged by your substituting some other toast for the one you are about to propose."

"Eh, what! not drink the young woman's health? why, I thought you admired her more than I do; not drink her health? how's that, eh?"

"I shall be most happy to explain to you the reasons for my request at some other time," replied I; "at present I can only add that I shall consider it as a personal favour if you will accede to it."

"It does not appear to me to require an Œdipus to discover Mr. Fairlegh's reasons for this request," observed Stephen Wilford; "he evidently does not consider the present company deserving of the high honour of drinking the health of a young lady whom he distinguishes by his admiration."

"Not over-flattering, I must say," muttered Lawless, looking annoyed.

"I suppose he's afraid of our hearing her name, lest some of us should go and cut him out." suggested Curtis in an undertone, which was, however, perfectly audible.

"In the meanwhile, Lawless, I hope you're not going to indulge your friend's caprice at the expense of the rest of the company," resumed Wilford; "having raised our expectations you are bound to gratify them."

Lawless, who evidently hesitated between his desire to assert his independence and his wish to oblige me, was beginning with his usual, "Eh? why, don't you see," when I interrupted him by saying. "Allow me to set this matter at rest in a very few words. Lawless. I hope, knows me well enough to feel sure that I could not intend any disrespect either to himself or to his guests—I believe it is not such an unheard-of thing for a gentleman to object to the name of any lady whom he respects being commented upon with the freedom incidental to a convivial meeting like the present—however that may be, I have asked Lawless as a favour not to drink a certain toast in my presence; should he be unwilling to comply with my request, as I would not wish to be the slightest restraint upon him at his own table, I shall request his permission to withdraw; on this point I await his decision. I have only one more observation to make," continued I, looking at Wilford, who was evidently preparing to speak, "which is, that if, after what I have just said, any gentleman should continue to urge Lawless to give the toast to which I object, I must perforce consider that he wishes to insult me."

As I concluded there was a murmur of applause, and Archer and one or two others turned to Lawless, declaring it was quite impossible to press the matter further after what I had said; when Wilford, in a cold sarcastic tone of voice, observed, "I am sorry Mr. Fairlegh's last argument should have failed in convincing me as easily as it seems to have done some others of the party; such, however, unfortunately being the case, I must repeat, even at the risk of incurring a thing so terrible as that gentleman's displeasure, my decided opinion that Lawless, having informed us that he was going to drink a particular toast, should not allow himself to be bullied out of it, in compliance with any man's humour."

This speech, as it might be expected, produced great excitement; I sprang to my feet (an example followed by several of the party), and was about to make an angry reply, when Oaklands, who, up to

this moment, had taken no part in the discussion, but sat sipping his wine with his usual air of listless contentment, apparently indifferent to, if not wholly unconscious of, all that was going on, now rose from his seat, and having obtained silence, said, " Really, gentlemen, all this confusion appears to me very unnecessary, when a word from our host will end it. Fairlegh has asked you not to propose a certain toast; it only remains for you, Lawless, to say whether you intend to do so or not."

Thus urged, Lawless replied, "Eh? no, certainly not; Frank Fairlegh's a trump, and I would not do anything to annoy him for more than I can tell : besides, when I come to think of it, I believe he was right, and I was wrong—but you see, women are a kind of cattle I don't clearly understand—if it was a horse now—"

A burst of laughter at this characteristic remark drowned the conclusion of the speech, but the announcement that the toast was given up appeared to produce general satisfaction; for, since I had spoken the popular opinion had been decidedly in my favour.

" The cause of this little interruption to the harmony of the evening being removed," resumed Oaklands, " suppose we see whether its effects may not as easily be got rid of. Every man, I take it, has a right to express his own opinion, and I think Fairlegh must allow that he was a little hasty in presupposing that by so doing an insult was intended. This being the case, he will, I am sure, agree with me that he ought not to take any notice of Mr. Wilford's remark."

" Yes, to be sure, that's it—all right, eh?" exclaimed Lawless " come, Fairlegh, as a favour to me, let the matter end here."

Thus urged, I could only reply that " I was quite willing to defer to their judgment, and do whatever they considered right "—and as Wilford (though I could see that he was annoyed beyond measure at having failed in persuading Lawless to give the toast) remained silent, merely curling his lip contemptuously when I spoke, here the affair ended.

As soon as the conversation became general, Oaklands turned to me with a mischievous smile, and asked, in an undertone, " Pray, Master Frank, what's become of all the wisdom and prudence recommended to me this morning? I am afraid you quite exhausted your stock, and have not reserved any for your own use. Who's the fire-eater now, I wonder? "

" Laugh away, Harry ; I may have acted foolishly, as is usually the case where one acts entirely from impulse ; but I could not have sat tamely by and heard Clara Saville's name polluted by [the remarks of such men as Curtis and Wilford—I should have got into a row with them sooner or later, and it was better to check the thing at once."

" My dear boy," returned Oaklands, " do not imagine for a moment that I am inclined to blame you; the only thing that I could not help feeling rather amused at was your throwing down the gauntlet to the gentleman opposite, when I recollected a certain lecture on prudence with which I was victimized this morning."

"As you are strong, be merciful," replied I; "and, whenever I do a foolish thing, may I always have such a friend at hand to save me from the consequences."

"That's a toast I will drink most willingly," said Oaklands, smiling; "the more so, as it reverses the position in which we generally stand with regard to each other, the alteration being decidedly in my favour: but—" he continued, interrupting himself, "what on earth are they laughing at, and making such a row about?"

"Oh, it's merely Curtis romancing with the most unmitigated effrontery about something that neither he, nor any one else, ever did out hunting," replied Arthur: "a tremendous leap, I fancy it was."

"Do not be too sure that it is impossible," replied I; "a horse once cleared the mouth of a chalk pit with me on its back, when I was a boy; Lawless remembers it."

"Eh! what? Mad Bess!" returned Lawless; "I should think I did too; I rode there afterwards and examined the place—a regular break-neck-looking hole as ever I saw in my life. Tell 'em about it, Frank."

Thus called upon, no choice was left me but to commence the recital, which, although there are few things to which I have a greater objection than being the hero of my own story, I accordingly did. Several remarks were made as I concluded, but, owing either to my well-known dislike of exaggeration, or to the air of truthfulness with which I had told the tale, nobody seemed inclined to doubt that the adventure had occurred in the manner I related, although it was of a more incredible nature than the feat Curtis had recounted. This fact had just excited my attention, when Wilford, turning to the man on his right hand, observed, "It's a great pity that some one hasn't taken notes of this evening's conversation; they would have afforded materials for a new volume of the adventures of Baron Munchausen."

My only answer to this remark, which was evidently intended for my hearing, was a slight smile, for I had determined I would not again be betrayed into any altercation with him, and, being now on my guard, I felt pretty sure of being able to maintain my resolution. To my annoyance, Oaklands replied, "If your remark is intended to throw any discredit upon the truth of the anecdote my friend has related, I must be excused for observing that Lawless and I, though not actually eye-witnesses of the leap, are yet perfectly aware that it took place."

"Was that observation addressed to me, Mr. Oaklands?" inquired Wilford, regarding Oaklands with an insolent stare.

"To you, sir, or to any other man who ventures to throw a doubt on what Fairlegh has just stated," replied Oaklands, his brow flushing with anger.

"Really," observed Wilford, with a contemptuous sneer, "Mr. Fairlegh is most fortunate in possessing such a steady and useful friend: first, when he dictates to Lawless what toasts he is to propose at his own table, and threatens the company generally with the weight of his displeasure should they venture to question the propriety of his so doing, Mr. Oaklands kindly saves him from the consequences of this warlike declaration, by advancing the somewhat novel doctrine that his friend, having spoken unadvisedly, ought not to act up to the tenor of his words. Again, Mr. Fairlegh relates a marvellous tale of his earlier days, and Mr. Oaklands is prepared to visit the most trifling indication of disbelief with the fire and fagots of his indignation. Gentlemen, I hope you are all good and true Fairleghites, or you will assuredly be burned at the stake, to satisfy the bigotry of Pope Oaklands the First."

During this speech, I could perceive by the veins on his forehead, swollen almost to bursting, his firmly-set teeth, and his hands clenched till the blood was forced back from the nails, that Oaklands was striving to master his passion; apparently he succeeded in a great measure, for, as Wilford concluded, he spoke calmly and deliberately: "The only reply, sir," he began, "that I shall deign to make to your elaborate insult is, that I consider it as such, and shall expect you to render me the satisfaction due to a gentleman."

"No, Harry," exclaimed I, "I cannot permit this: the quarrel, if it be a quarrel, is mine; on this point I cannot allow even you to interfere. Mr. Wilford shall hear from me."

"No, no!" exclaimed Lawless; "I'm sure you must see, Wilford, that this is not at all the sort of thing, eh? recollect Oaklands and Fairlegh are two of my oldest friends, and something is due to me at all events, eh?—Archer—Curtis—this cannot be allowed to go on."

By this time the party had with one accord risen from their seats, and divided into groups, some collecting round Wilford and Lawless others about Oaklands and myself, and the confusion of tongues was perfectly deafening. At length I heard Wilford's voice exclaim, "I consider it unfair in the extreme to lay all this quarrelling and disturbance to me, and, as it is not at all to my taste, I beg to wish you a very good-evening, Lawless."

"You will do no such thing," cried Oaklands, and, bursting through the cluster of men who surrounded him and endeavoured to detain him, he sprang to the door, double-locked it, and, placing his back against it, added, "no one leaves the room till this affair is settled one way or other." The action, the tone of voice, and the manner which accompanied them, reminded me so forcibly of a deed of a somewhat similar nature at Dr. Mildman's, when Oaklands first heard of the loss of his letter containing the cheque, and began to suspect foul play, that for a moment the lapse of years was forgotten, and it seemed as though we were boys together again.

Whenever Oaklands was excited by strong emotion of any kind, there was a proud consciousness of power in his every look and motion,

L

which possessed for me an irresistible attraction : and now, as he stood, his noble figure drawn up to its fullest height, his arms folded across his ample chest in an attitude of defiance a sculptor would have rejoiced to imitate ; his head thrown slightly back, and his handsome features marked by an expression of haughty indignation : when I reflected that it was a generous regard for my honour which excited that indignation, I felt that my affection for him was indeed " passing the love of women," and that he was a friend for whom a man might resolve to lay down his life willingly.

While these thoughts passed through my brain, Lawless and several of the more influential members of the party had been endeavouring to persuade Wilford to own that he was in the wrong, and ought to apologize, but in vain ; the utmost concession they could get him to make was, that " he was not aware that he had offered any particular insult to Mr. Oaklands, but if that gentleman chose to put such a construction upon his words, he could not help it, and should be ready to answer for them when and where he pleased."

They were then, as a last resource, about to appeal to Oaklands, when I interfered by saying " That the insult, if insult it was, had originated from the part I had taken in the proceedings of the evening, and was directed far more against me than Oaklands ; that under these circumstances it was impossible for me to allow him to involve himself further in the affair. If my veracity were impugned, I was the proper person to defend it ; there could be but one opinion on that subject."

To this they all agreed, and at length Oaklands himself was forced reluctantly to confess he supposed I was right.

" In this case, gentlemen," I continued, " my course is clear ; I leave my honour in your hands, certain that in so doing I am taking the wisest course; honourable men and men of spirit like yourselves will, I feel certain, never recommend anything incompatible with the strictest regard for my reputation as a gentleman ; neither will you needlessly hurry me into any act, the consequences of which might possibly embitter the whole of my after life. In order that personal feeling may not interfere any more with the matter, my friend and I will withdraw ; Lawless will kindly convey to me your decision, on which, be it what it may, I pledge myself to act; I wish you a very good-night."

Then telling Lawless I should sit up for him, and taking leave of two or three members of the party with whom I was most intimate, I drew Oaklands' arm within my own, and unlocking the door, left the room, Wilford's fierce black eyes glaring at us with a look of disappointed fury, such as I have witnessed in a caged tiger, being the last object I beheld.

CHAPTER XXII.

TAMING A SHREW.

"I remember a mass of things, but nothing distinctly.
A quarrel."
"I do repent, but Heaven hath pleased it so
To punish me with this."
"We will compound this quarrel."
"What's that?—"Why, a horse."
"Tell thou the tale,"
"Nay, I will win my wager better yet,
"And show more signs of her obedience."
"Now go thy ways, thou hast tamed a curst shrew."
Shakespeare.

"WHY did you prevent me from giving that insolent scoundrel the lesson he deserved?" was Oaklands' first observation as we left the quadrangle in which Lawless's rooms were situated; "I do not thank you for it, Frank."

"My dear Harry," replied I, "you are excited at present; when you are a little more cool you will see that I could not have acted otherwise than I did. Even supposing I could have borne such a thing myself, what would have been said of me if I had allowed you to fight in my quarrel? no honourable man would have permitted me to associate with him afterwards."

"But I don't see that the quarrel was yours at all," returned Oaklands; "your share of it was ended when the toast affair came to a conclusion; the rest of the matter was purely personal between him and myself."

"How can that be, when the origin of it was his doubting, or pretending to doubt, the truth of the anecdote which I related?" inquired I. "No; depend upon it, Harry, I have acted rightly, though I bitterly regret now having gone to the party, and so exposed myself to all this. I have always looked upon duelling with the greatest abhorrence. To run the risk of committing murder (for I can call it by no milder name), when at the very moment in which the crime is consummated you may fall yourself, and thus even the forlorn hope of living to repent be cut off from you, appears to me little short of madness. On one point I am resolved—if I do go out with him, nothing shall induce me to fire at him; I will not die a murderer, at all events."

"Should your life indeed be sacrificed," said Oaklands, and his deep voice trembled with emotion as he spoke, "I will follow this man as the avenger of blood, fix a mortal insult upon him wherever I meet him, and shoot him like a dog, convinced that I shall perform a righteous act in so doing by ridding the world of such a monster."

I saw by his manner that it would be useless to attempt to reason with him at that moment—his warm feelings, and the fiery though generous impulses of his impetuous nature, had so completely gained possession of him, that he was no longer a reasonable creature—we therefore walked in silence to my rooms, where we parted; I declining his offer to remain with me till I should learn the decision of Lawless and his friends, on the plea of wishing to be alone (which was, indeed, a true one), although my chief reason for so doing was to prevent the possibility of Oaklands saying anything in his present excited state of mind, which, if repeated, might in any way involve him with Wilford.

My first act, when I found myself once more alone, was to sit down, and endeavour calmly to review the situation in which I was placed. In the event of their deciding that the affair might be arranged amicably, my course was clear—I had only to avoid Wilford as much as possible during the time I should remain at Cambridge, and if ever I were obliged to be in his company, to treat him with a cool and studied civility, which would leave him no pretext for forcing a quarrel upon me. On the other hand, if they should think it imperative upon me to go out with him, then indeed was the prospect a gloomy one. Wilford, whose ruthless disposition was so well known as to have become, as it were, a by-word among the set he mixed with, was not a man to be offended with impunity, and as, moreover, I had made up my mind not to return his fire, the chances were strongly against my escaping with my life.

I am no coward; on the contrary, like most men whose physical energy is unimpaired, I am constitutionally fearless, and in moments of danger and excitement have never found myself wanting; still, it would be affectation to deny that the prospect of a sudden and violent death, thus unexpectedly forced upon me, impressed my mind with a vague sensation of terror, mingled with regret for the past, and sorrow for the future. To be thus cut off in the bright spring-time of vigorous manhood, when the warm blood of youth dances gladly through the veins, and every pulse throbs with the instinct of high and noble daring—to die with hopes unattained, wishes ungratified, duties unperformed—to leave those we love, without one parting look or word, to struggle on through this cold unsympathizing world alone and unprotected—and, above all, to lose one's life in an act the lawfulness of which was more than question-able—all these things contributed to form a picture, which it required either a very steadfast or an utterly callous heart to enable one to gaze upon without blanching. I thought of the misery I should entail upon my family; how, instead of fulfilling my father's dying injunctions to take his place, and devote myself to comfort and protect them, I should wound my mother's heart anew, and spread the dark mist of sorrow over the fair prospect of my sister's young existence; and I cursed my fastidious folly in objecting to the toast, to which, in my self-accusation, I traced all that had afterwards occurred. Then, with the inconsistency of human nature, I began to speculate upon what would be Clara Saville's feelings, were she to learn that it was to prevent the slightest breath of insult being coupled with her name that I was about to peril, not only my life, but, for aught I knew, my hopes of happiness here and hereafter. As the last awful possibility occurred to me, the burden of my misery became too great for me to bear, and, retiring to the privacy of my own chamber, I flung myself on my knees, and poured forth an earnest prayer for pardon for the past and deliverance for the future.

When I again returned to my sitting-room, my mind had nearly recovered its usual tone, and I felt prepared to meet and to go through whatever might be before me with calmness and determination. As I was uncertain how long it might be before Lawless would arrive, I resolved, in order to avoid the horrors of suspense, to employ myself, and taking up the mathematical treatise upon which I was engaged and by a vigorous effort of mind compelling my attention, I read steadily for about half an hour, at the end of which time the sound of hasty footsteps was heard ascending the stairs, and in another minute the door was flung open, and Lawless and Archer entered the apartment.

" Reading mathematics, as I'm a slightly inebriated Christian!" exclaimed Archer, taking the book out of my hands ; " well, if that isn't pretty cool for a man who may be going to be shot at six o'clock to-morrow morning, for anything he knows to the contrary, I'm no judge of temperature."

" Oh! bother mathematics," rejoined Lawless, flinging the book which Archer held out to him at a bust of Homer adorning the top of my bookshelves, which it fortunately missed—" Frank, old boy, it's all right—you're not to have a bullet through your lungs this time—shake hands, old fellow! I'm so glad about it that I've—"

" Drunk punch enough to floor any two men of ordinary capacity," interposed Archer.

" Of course I have," continued Lawless, "and I consider I've performed a very meritorious act in so doing ;—there was the punch, all the other fellows were gone away, somebody must have drunk it, or that young reprobate Shrimp would have got hold of it; and I promised the venerable fish-fag his mother to take especial care of his what do you call 'ums—morals, isn't it? and instil by precept, and—and—"

" Example," suggested Archer.

" Yes, all that sort of thing," continued Lawless, " a taste for, that is, an unbounded admiration of the sublime and beautiful, as exemplified under the form of—"

" Rum punch, and lashings of it," chimed in Archer; "but suppose you were to tell Fairlegh all that has passed since he came away, or let me do it for you, whichever you like best."

"Oh! you tell him by all means; I like to encourage ingenuous youth; fire away, Archer, my boy!"

Thus urged, Archer informed me that upon my departure there had been a somewhat stormy discussion, in which the events of the evening had been freely canvassed; and at last they came to the unanimous decision that any man was at liberty to withdraw, if a toast was proposed to which he objected, and that, if the toastmaster preferred giving it up rather than allow him to leave the party, he had a perfect right to do so. This being the case, they decided that Wilford, having been in the wrong, ought to confess he had spoken hastily, and that, if he would do so, and would add that he had meant nothing offensive either to me or Oaklands, there the matter might rest. This for a long time he positively refused to do; at length, finding he could get no one to support him, he said that, as I had owned I was wrong in attempting to prevent his expressing his opinion, he considered that, in all other respects, I had behaved in a gentlemanly way; therefore, if he had said anything which implied the contrary, he was willing to withdraw it. But, in regard to Mr. Oaklands, he considered he had interfered in a very uncalled-for manner; and he could only repeat, if that gentleman felt himself aggrieved by anything he had said, the remedy was in his own hands. As soon as he had spoken he withdrew.

The question was again debated, and at length they came to the conclusion that what Wilford had said amounted to an ample apology as far as I was concerned, which I was bound 'to accept; and that Oaklands, having agreed to consider the quarrel mine, could not take any further notice of it; therefore the affair was at an end.

"Well," said I, as he finished his recital, "I must ever feel grateful to you both for the trouble you have taken on my account, and the kind feeling you have shown towards me throughout. I will not pretend to deny that I am very glad the matter has been amicably arranged, for, circumstanced as I am, with everything depending upon my own exertions, a duel would have been ruin to me; but I must say I think the whole business thoroughly unsatisfactory, and it is only my conviction that a duel would make matters worse, instead of mending them, which leads me to agree to the arrangement. I sincerely hope Oaklands will not hear what Wilford said about him, for he is fearfully irritated against him already."

"I'll tell you what it is," interrupted Lawless; "it's my belief that Wilford's behaviour to you to-night was only assumed for the sake of provoking Oaklands. Master Stephen hates him as he does the very devil himself, and would like nothing better than to pick a quarrel with him, have him out, and, putting a brace of slugs into him, leave him—"

"Quivering on a daisy," said Archer, completing the sentence. "Really I think," he continued, "what Lawless says is very true; you see Oaklands' careless, nonchalant manner, which is always exactly the same whether he is talking to a beggar or a lord, gives

continual offence to Wilford, who has contrived somehow to exact a
sort of deference and respect from all the men with whom he associates till he actually seems to consider it his right. Then, Wilford's
overbearing manner irritates Oaklands; and so, whenever they have
met, the breach has gone on widening, till now they positively hate
one another."

"How is it you are so intimate with him?" asked I; "for nobody
seems really to like him."

" Well, hang me if I can tell," replied Lawless; "but you see he
has some good points about him, after all; for instance, I never saw
him out with the hounds yet that he didn't take a good place, aye,
and keep it too, however long the run and difficult the country. I
killed the best horse I had in my stables trying to follow him one
day in Leicestershire last season ; my horse fell with me going over
the last fence, and never rose again. Wilford, and one of the whips,
who was merely a feather-weight, were the only men in at the death.
I offered him three hundred guineas for the horse he rode, but he
only gave me one of his pleasant looks, and said it wasn't for
sale."

" You've seen that jet-black mare he rides now, haven't you,
Fairlegh?" asked Archer.

" Yes; what a magnificent creature it is!" was my reply.

" Did you ever hear how he came by it?"

On my answering in the negative, Archer continued—" Well, I
wonder at that, for it was in everybody's mouth at| one time : it's
worth hearing, if it were but to show the determined character of
the man. The mare belonged to Lord Foxington, Lord Sell-
borough's eldest son. I believe he gave five hundred guineas for her.
She was a splendid animal, high-couraged, but temperate. In fact,
when you were on her she hadn't a fault, but in the stable she was a
perfect devil; there was only one man who dared go near her, and he had
been with her from the time she was a filly: so that when Foxington
bought the mare he was forced to hire the groom too. The most
difficult thing of all was putting on the bridle; it was generally half
an hour's work before she would let even this groom do it. After
dinner one day Foxington began talking about this animal, saying
what a brute she was to handle, and adding what I have just told
you, as to the impossibility of putting on the bridle, when Wilford,
who was present, made some remark, which showed he did not
believe in the impossibility. Upon which Foxington inquired
whether he doubted the fact he had just heard? Wilford replied
that he was sure his lordship fully believed in the truth of what he
had just stated ; but, for his own part, he had so often found impossibilities of this nature yield to a little courage and determination,
that he confessed he was somewhat sceptical. Now, it so happened
that Foxington, soon after he bought the mare, had thought just as
Wilford did, and determined that he would put the bridle on.
Accordingly he attempted it, and the matter ended by his getting

regularly driven out of the stable by the animal, with a tolerably severe bite in the fleshy part of his shoulder. Wilford's remark, therefore, as may be imagined, rather nettled him; and he inquired, somewhat tartly, whether Wilford believed he could put the bridle on? and, if so, whether he were willing to try? Wilford replied, in his usual cool tone, that he had an idea he could do so, but that he had no particular inclination to try, as it would probably be some trouble, and the weather was too hot to render active exertion desirable. At this Foxington laughed derisively, saying that it sounded very like a put-off. 'Not at all,' returned Wilford; 'and to show you that I never say a thing without being ready to act up to it, I am willing to stake five hundred guineas against the mare herself that I go up to her and put the bridle on without any assistance, and without a stick or anything whatsoever in my hands.' Foxington accepted the bet gladly, reckoning himself safe to pocket the five hundred guineas. The affair was to come off the next morning at Foxington's stables at eleven o'clock. His lordship had invited all the men who had been present when the bet was made, to come and witness the event, expecting a complete triumph over Wilford. While they were standing about waiting, Foxington told them of his own attempt, and his conviction, from the experience he had then gained, that the thing could not be done; and the general opinion was that Wilford, under the influence of wine, had foolishly boasted of a thing which he would not be able to accomplish, and was certain to lose his money. As the time drew near, and he did not make his appearance, an idea began to gain ground that he meant to shirk the affair altogether; and Foxington was becoming exceedingly irate, when, just as the clock was on the stroke of eleven, the sound of a horse's feet was heard, and Wilford cantered quietly up, looking as if he felt no personal interest whatever in the event. On his arrival they proceeded at once to the stable in which the mare stood. She was kept in a loose box, with her clothes on, but her head entirely free."

"I ought, by-the-bye," said Archer, interrupting himself, "to have told you that I had the account from a man who was there at the time, and saw the whole thing."

"Well, as soon as they went into the stable, the mare left off feeding, and turning round so as to face them, stood with her ears pricked up, gazing wildly at them. Wilford just glanced at her and then leisurely divested himself of his coat, waistcoat and neckcloth, turned up the wristbands of his shirt, and taking the bridle from the groom, announced that he was ready. As soon as the door was open, Wilford fixed his eyes sternly on the mare, and walked towards her. To the surprise of everyone the animal allowed him to approach quietly and pat her, without showing any symptoms of vice. Men began to exchange inquiring glances with each other, and those who had betted heavily against him trembled for their money; but Foxington, who was better acquainted with the animal, exclaimed.

'Wait a minute; he has not tried to touch her head yet.' Wilford now moved his hand forward along the neck, patting her, and speaking soothingly to her as he advanced; but as he approached the head, she became impatient and fidgety, and when he attempted to take hold of the ear in order to put on the bridle, she flung up her head, reared, and ran back a few steps, where she stood, shaking her mane and pawing the ground. After remaining in this position a few seconds, she suddenly laid back her ears, and, showing the whites of her eyes, ran at Wilford with her mouth wide open, and as soon as she got within distance made a ferocious bite at him. By springing on one side with great agility he just contrived to avoid it; then, dropping the bridle, he threw himself into a sparring attitude (you know he's a capital boxer), and, as the mare again ran at him, hit out, and striking her just on a particular spot by the ear, brought her down like a bullock. As soon as she recovered her legs she renewed the attack, and Wilford received her as before, delivering his blow with the same coolness and precision. When the animal rose the second time she seemed partially stunned, and stood for a moment with her head hanging down and her ears drooping; but on Wilford's making a step towards her she again plunged forward, and attempted to seize him with her teeth. Once more did Wilford evade her bite by springing on one side, and seizing his opportunity, succeeded in planting his hit, and, for the third time, felled her to the ground. When she again rose, however, she showed no disposition to renew the attack, but stood trembling violently, with the perspiration running down her sides. She now allowed Wilford to approach her, to stroke her head, pull her ears, and finally to put the bridle on, and lead her out, completely conquered; and so my Lord Foxington lost the best horse in his stables, and Wilford gained his bet, and added to his character for invincibility, which, by the way, he cared about much the most."

"It was a bold deed," returned I, as Archer concluded his story, " but one does not like a man the better for having done it; there seems to me a degree of wanton cruelty in punishing an animal so severely, unless he had been actually forced to do it. Public executioners may be necessary for the prevention of crime; but that is no reason why one need volunteer as an amateur hangman."

"Everybody thought it an uncommonly plucky thing at the time, and there was an immense fuss made with him afterwards," replied Archer. "Why, Lawless, are you asleep? rouse up, man—to bed—to bed. Good-night, Fairlegh, you'll sleep all the better for knowing you are not to be shot at cock-crow."

So saying, he took Lawless by the arm and marched him off, though, it must be confessed, his gait, as he descended the stairs, was somewhat unsteady.

CHAPTER XXIII.

WHAT HARRY AND I FOUND WHEN WE LOST OUR WAY.

"It is too true an evil—gone she is.

"Unhappy girl! Ah! who would be a father?"
"Far in the lane a lonely hut he found,
No tenant ventured on th' unwholesome ground,
Here smokes his forge; he bares his sinewy arm,
And early strokes the sounding anvil warm;
Around his shop the steely sparkles flew,
As for the steed he shaped the bending shoe."
Gay's *Trivia*.

"He who thou wilt . . . thou art in no danger from me, so thou tell me the meaning of this practice, and why thou drivest thy trade in this mysterious fashion—"
"Your horse is shod, and your farrier paid—what need you cumber yourself further, than to mount and pursue your journey?"—*Kenilworth*.

ON the afternoon of the day after Lawless's wine party, Oaklands and I were walking down to the stables where his horses were kept (he having, in pursuance of his plan for preventing my over-reading myself, beguiled me into a promise to ride with him), when we encountered Archer.

"I suppose you have heard the news ' par excellence,' " said he, after we had shaken hands.

"No," replied I, " what may it happen to be? "

"Only that Lizzie Maurice, the pastrycook's daughter, disappeared last night, and old Maurice is going about like a distracted creature this morning, and can't learn any tidings of her."

"What, that pretty girl with long ringlets who used to stand behind the counter?" asked I. "What is supposed to have become of her? "

"Yes, that is the identical young lady," returned Archer. "All that seems to be known about her is, that she waited till her father went out to smoke his pipe, as he usually does for an hour or so every evening, and then got the urchin who runs of errands to carry a bundle for her, and set out without saying a word to anyone. After she had proceeded a little way, she was met by a man muffled up in a cloak, who took the bundle from the boy, threw him a shilling, and told him to go home directly. Instead of doing so, however, he let them proceed for a minute or two, and then followed them. They went at a quick pace along one or two streets, and at length turned down a lane, not far from the bottom of which a gig was waiting. Another man, also muffled up, was seated in the gig, into which the girl was handed by her companion, who said to the second man in a low tone, 'All has gone well, and without attracting notice.' He then added in a warning voice: 'Remember, honour bright, no nonsense, or—' and here he sunk his voice so that the boy could not catch what he said; but the other replied, 'On my word, on my honour!' They then shook hands; the second man gathered up the reins, drew the whip across the horse, which sprang forward at speed, and they were out of sight in a moment. The person who was left gazed after them for a minute or so, and then, turning briskly on his heel, walked away without perceiving the boy, who stood under the shadow of a doorway. On being questioned as to what the men were like, he said that the first kept his face entirely concealed, but he was rather tall, and had black hair; the second was a stout man, with light hair and a high colour—for a dark lantern which he had in the gig with him happened to throw its light on his face as he was lighting it."

" At what time in the evening did all this take place?" inquired Oaklands.

" Between nine and ten," replied Archer.

Oaklands and I exchanged glances; the same idea had evidently struck us both.

" Has anyone seen Wilford this morning?" asked Oaklands.

" Seen him!" returned Archer; " yes, to be sure, he and Wentworth have been parading about arm-in-arm all over the town : they were with me when I met poor old Maurice, and asked him all sorts of questions about the affair. Wilford seemed quite interested for him."

"Strange!" observed Oaklands, musing. "I don't make it out. I would not willingly wrong, even in thought, an innocent man. Archer," he continued, "you have a shrewd keen wit and sound judgment; tell me in confidence, man, who do you think has done this?"

" Nay, I am no diviner to guess other men's secrets," replied Archer; "and these are subjects about which it is not over-safe to hazard conjectures. I have told you all I can learn about it, and it is for you to draw your own conclusions. It is no use repeating things to you of which you are already aware; I might as well tell you dogs bark and cats mew—that Wilford has black hair, and Wentworth is a stout man with a high colour—or any other well-known truism. But I am detaining you—good-morning." So saying, he shook hands with us and left us.

After walking some distance in silence, Oaklands exclaimed abruptly, " It must be so! it is Wilford who has done this thing—you think as I do, do you not, Frank?"

" I am sure we have not evidence enough to prove it," replied I; " but I confess I am inclined, as a mere matter of opinion, to agree with you, though there are difficulties in the way for which it is not easy to account. For instance, why should Wilford have gone to that party last night and have incurred the risk of entrusting the execution of his schemes to another, instead of remaining to carry them out himself?"

" That is true," said Oaklands thoughtfully; "I do not pretend to understand it all clearly; but, somehow, I feel a conviction that Wilford is at the bottom of it."

" You should recollect, Harry, that you greatly dislike this man—

are, as I conceive, prejudiced against him—and are, therefore, of course, disposed to judge him harshly."

"Yes, I know all that; still, you'll see it will come out sooner or later, that Wilford is the man. Her poor old father! I have often observed how he appeared to dote upon that girl, and how proud he was of her; his pride will be converted into mourning now. It is fearful to think," continued Oaklands, "of what crimes men are guilty in their reckless selfishness! Here is the fair promise of an innocent girl's life blighted, and an old man's gray hairs brought down with sorrow to the grave, in order to gratify the passing fancy of a heartless libertine." He paused, and then continued, "I suppose one can do nothing in the matter, having no stronger grounds than mere suspicion to go upon ? "

"I should say nothing likely to be of the slightest benefit," replied I.

"Then the sooner we get to horse the better," returned Oaklands; "hearing of a thing of this kind always annoys me, and I feel disposed to hate my species : a good gallop may shake me into a better humour."

"And the 'dolce-far-niente' ? " I inquired.

"Oh! don't imagine me inconsistent," was the reply. "Only somehow just at present, in fact ever since the breeze last night, I've found it more trouble to remain quiet than to exert myself; so, if you would not tire me to death, walk a little faster, there's a good fellow."

After a brisk ride of nearly two hours along cross-roads, we came out upon a wild heath or common of considerable extent.

"Here's a famous place for a gallop!" exclaimed Oaklands; " I never can make up my mind which is the fastest of these two horses; let's have a race and try their speed. Do you see that tall poplar tree which seems poking its top into the sky on the other side the common ? that shall be the winning-post. Now, are you ready ? "

"All right, go ahead," replied I, bending forward and giving my horse the rein. Away we went merrily, the high-couraged animals bounding beneath us, and the fresh air whistling round our ears as we seemed to cut our way through it. For some time we kept side by side. The horse Oaklands rode was, if anything, a finer, certainly a more powerful animal than the one on which I was mounted; but this advantage was fully compensated by the fact of his riding nearly a stone heavier than I did. We were, therefore, on the whole, very fairly matched.

After riding at speed, as near as I could reckon, about two miles, Oaklands, to his great delight, had gained nearly a horse's length in advance of me—a space which it seemed beyond my powers of jockeyship to recover. Between us, however, and the tree he had fixed on as our goal, lay a small brook or watercourse, near the banks of which the ground became soft and marshy. In crossing this, the greater weight of man and horse told against Oaklands, and gradually I began to creep up to him. As we neared the brook, it struck me that his horse appeared to labour heavily through the stiff clay. Now or never, then, was my opportunity; and shouting gaily, "Over first, for a sovereign—good-bye, Harry," I gave my horse the spur, and putting him well at it, cleared the brook splendidly, and alighted safely on the farther bank.

Determined, if possible, not to be outdone, Harry selected a point, by crossing at which he could contrive to cut off a corner, and thus gain upon me considerably. In order to accomplish this, it was necessary for him to take his leap at a spot where the brook was some feet wider than ordinary. Relying, however, on the known good qualities of the animal he rode, he resolved to attempt it. Settling himself firmly in his saddle, he got his horse well together, and then throwing up his whip-hand, and (as Lawless would have termed it) "sticking in the persuaders," he charged the brook at speed.

It was a well-imagined and bold attempt, and had his horse been fresher, would have succeeded in winning the race; but we had kept up a fair pace during the whole of our ride, and now our gallop across the common, and more particularly the severe pace over the marshy ground, had tried his horse's wind considerably. Still, however, the noble animal strove to the utmost of its power, to answer the call made upon it, and by a vigorous effort succeeded in clearing the brook; but the ground on the other side was rugged and broken, and, apparently exhausted by the exertion he had made, he stumbled, and after a slight struggle to preserve his footing fell heavily forward, pitching Harry over his head as he did so.

Fortunately the ground was soft and clayey, and neither man nor horse seemed to have sustained any injury, for I had scarcely time to draw rein ere they were on their legs again, and as Harry's first act was to spring lightly into the saddle, I determined to secure the race at once; and cantering up to the poplar-tree, which was now within a hundred yards of me, I snapped off a bough in token of victory. As I turned back again I observed that Harry had dismounted and was examining his horse's foot.

"Nothing wrong, is there?" asked I, as I rejoined him.

"Yes, everything's wrong," was the reply; "you've been and gone and won the race, you villain, you—I've tumbled nose and knees into a mud-hole, and spoiled my white cord oh-no-we-never-mention-ums —and the 'Cid' has wrenched off one of his front shoes in the skrimmage."

"And that's the worst of all the misfortunes," said I, "for here we are some ten or twelve miles from Cambridge at least, in a region utterly unknown, and apparently devoid of inhabitants; so where we are to find a smith passes my poor skill to discover."

"You're wrong about the inhabitants, I flatter myself," replied Harry. "Do you see the faint white mist curling above those trees to the right? I take that to be smoke; where there's smoke there must be fire; fire must have been kindled by some human being or other—through that individual we will endeavour to obtain an introduction to some blacksmith, conjointly with sufficient topographical information to enable us to reach our destination in time for a certain meal called dinner, which has acquired an unusual degree of importance in my eyes within the last hour or so. I have spoken!"

"Like a book," replied I; "and the next thing is to bring your sapient deductions to the test of experiment. There is a cart track here which appears to lead towards the smoke you observed; let us try that." So saying, I also dismounted, and throwing my horse's bridle over my arm, we proceeded together on foot in the direction Oaklands had indicated.

Ten minutes' walking brought us into a rough country lane, widening picturesquely between high banks and green hedges, affording an agreeable contrast to the flat, unenclosed tracts of corn-land so general throughout Cambridgeshire. After following this lane about a quarter of a mile, we came upon a small, retired ale-house, surrounded by trees. As we approached the door, a stout, vulgar-looking woman, dressed in rather tawdry finery, ran out to meet us; on coming nearer, however, she stopped short as if surprised, and then re-entered the house as quickly as she had left it, calling to someone within as she did so. After waiting for a minute or two she came back, accompanied by a tall disagreeable-looking man in a velveteen shooting-jacket, with a remarkably dirty face, and hands to match.

"Is there a blacksmith living anywhere near here, my good man?" inquired Oaklands.

"Mayhap there is," was the reply in a surly tone.

"Can you direct us how to find him?" continued Oaklands.

"What might you want with him when you've found him?" was the rejoinder.

"My horse has cast a shoe, and I want one put on immediately," replied Oaklands, who was getting impatient at the man's unsatisfactory, not to say insolent manner.

"Mayhap you won't get it done in quite such a hurry as you seems to expect! There's a blacksmith lives at Stoney End, about five miles farther on. Go straight up the lane for about three miles, then turn to the right, then twice to the left, and then you'll see a finger-post that ain't got nothing on it—when you come to that—"

"Which I never shall do, depend upon it," replied Oaklands. "My good man, you don't imagine I'm going to fatigue myself and lame my horse by walking five miles up this unlucky lane, do you? If things really are as bad as you would make them out to be, I shall despatch a messenger to summon the smith, and employ myself in the meanwhile in tasting your ale, and consuming whatever you may happen to have in the house fit to eat."

I observed that the landlord and his wife, as I presumed her to be, exchanged very blank looks when Oaklands announced this determination. When he ceased speaking, she whispered a few words into the ear of the man, who gave a kind of surly grunt in reply, and then, turning to Harry, said, "Mayhap I'll shoe your horse for you myself if you'll make it worth while."

"You will? why, I thought you said there was not a smith within five miles?"

"No more there ain't, only me."

"And you've been worrying me, and tiring my patience all this time, merely to secure yourself a better bargain? Oh, the needless trouble people give themselves in this world! Shoe the horse, man, and make your own charge; be sure I'll not complain of it, only be quick," replied Oaklands.

"P'raps that worn't all," returned the fellow gruffly; "but if ye be in such a mighty hurry, bring 'un along here, and I'll clap a shoe on 'un for ye in a twinkling."

So saying, he led the way through an old gate, and down a stable-yard, behind the public-house, at the bottom of which, under a kind of half-barn, half-shed, was a blacksmith's shop, fitted up with a forge, and other appliances for shoeing. Our conductor (who having divested himself of the velveteen jacket, which he replaced with a leather apron, seemed now much more in his proper element) displayed greater quickness and skill in making and applying the shoe, than from his previous conduct I should have anticipated; and I began to flatter myself that our difficulties were in a fair way to be overcome.

I was drawing up the girths of my horse's saddle, which had become somewhat loosened from our gallop, when Oaklands, who had been sitting on a gate near, industriously flogging his boot with his riding-whip, jumped down, saying, "If you'll keep an eye to the horses. Frank, I'll go and see if I can get some of the worst of this mud brushed off."

"Better stay where you are! I shall a' done direc'ly," observed the smith; "you ain't wanted at ther house, I tell yer."

"You should stick to your original trade, for your manners as an innkeeper are certainly not calculated to fascinate customers, my friend," replied Oaklands, walking towards the house.

The man muttered an oath as he looked after him, and then applied himself to his work with redoubled energy. About ten minutes had elapsed, the shoe was made, fitted to the hoof, and the process of nailing on nearly concluded, but still Oaklands did not return. I was tying my horse's rein up to a hook in the wall, with the intention of seeking him, when I heard the noise of wheels in the lane, followed immediately by the clatter of a horse's feet, ridden at speed—both sounds at the moment ceased, as if the parties had stopped at the inn-door. The blacksmith also heard them, and appeared for a moment uncertain whether to continue his work or not; then, utter-ing an impatient exclamation, he began twisting off and clenching the points of the nails as though his life depended on his haste. Perceiving that Oaklands' horse would be ready for him to mount directly, I turned to unfasten my own, when the sound of men's voices raised high in angry debate became audible, then a confused noise as of blows and scuffling ensued, mingled with the screams of women; and immediately the blacksmith's wife ran out, calling to her husband to hasten in, for that " they had come back and quarrelled with the strange gentleman, and now they were fighting, and there would be murder done in the house."

Without waiting to hear more, I ran hastily up the yard, followed by the blacksmith and the woman. On reaching the front of the house, I perceived waiting at the door, a gig, in which was seated a man dressed in a suit of rusty black, while under the shade of the trees, a boy was leading up and down a magnificent black mare, which I instantly recognized as the identical animal Wilford had become possessed of in the manner Archer had related to me. The sounds of blows and struggling still continued, and proceeded, as I now ascertained, from the parlour of the ale-house. As the readiest method of reaching the scene of action, I flung open the window, which was not far from the ground, and without a moment's hesitation leaped into the room.

CHAPTER XXIV.

HOW OAKLANDS BROKE HIS HORSEWHIP.

" Away to heav'n, respective lenity,
And fire-eyed fury be my conduct now."
" Use every man after his desert, and who should 'scape whipping ? "
" He swore that he did hold me dear
As precious eyesight, and did value me
Above this world, adding thereto moreover
That he would wed me."
"Men's vows are women's traitors."
" To promise is most courtly and fashionable ; performance is a kind of will or testament which argues a great sickness in his judgment that makes it."—*Shakespeare.*

THE sight which met my eyes as I gazed around was one which time can never efface from my memory. In the centre of the room, his brow darkened by the flush of concentrated indignation, stood Oaklands, his left hand clenching tightly the coat-collar of a man, whom I at once perceived to be Wilford, while with his right hand he was administering such a horsewhipping as I hope never again to see a human being subjected to. Wilford, who actually writhed with mingled pain and fury, was making violent but ineffectual struggles to free himself. Near the door stood Wentworth, the blood dripping from his nose, and his clothes dusty and disorderly, as if from a fall. Crouching in a corner at the farther end of the room, the tears coursing down her fear-blanched cheeks, and her hands clasped in an agony of terror and despair, was a girl, about nineteen years of age, whom I had little difficulty in recognizing as Lizzie Maurice, the

daughter of the old confectioner, of whose elopement we had been that morning informed. On perceiving me she sprang forward. and clasping my knees, implored me to interfere and endeavour to separate them. I was not, however, called upon to do so, for, as she spoke, his riding whip broke short in Oaklands' hand, and dashing down the fragments with an exclamation of impatience, he flung Wilford from him with so much force that he staggered forward a few paces, and would have fallen, had not Wentworth caught him in his arms just in time to prevent it.

Oaklands then turned to the girl, whom I had raised from the ground and placed on a chair, and addressing her in a stern, impressive manner, said, " I will now resume what I was saying to you when yonder beaten hound dared to lay hands upon me. For the last time the choice is offered to you—either return home, and endeavour, by devoting yourself to your broken-hearted old father, to atone as best you may for the misery you have caused him; or, by remaining here, commence a life of infamy which will end sooner or later in a miserable death." He paused; then, as she made no reply, but sat with her face buried in her hands, sobbing as if her heart would break, he continued, " You tell me, the vile tempter who has lured you from your duty, promised to meet you here to-day, and, bringing a clergyman with him, to marry you privately; now if this is the truth—"

" It is! it is!" she faltered.

" If so," resumed Oaklands, " a knowledge of the real facts of the case may yet save you. This scoundrel who has proposed to marry you, and who belongs to a rank immeasurably above your own, is already notorious for what are termed, by such as himself, affairs of gallantry; while the wretched impostor whom he has brought with him to act the part of clergyman, is the marker at a low billiard-table, and no more a clergyman than I am."

" Is this really so?" exclaimed the girl, raising her eyes, which were swollen and red with weeping, to Wilford's face; " would you have deceived me thus, Stephen—you, whom I have trusted so implicitly?"

Wilford, who, since the severe discipline he had undergone, had remained seated, with his head resting on his hand, as if in pain, apparently unconscious of what was going on, glared at her ferociously with his flashing eyes, but made no reply. The girl waited for a minute; but, obtaining no answer, turned away with a half-shudder, murmuring, " Deceived, deceived!" then addressing Oaklands, she said, " I will go home to my father, sir; and if he will not forgive me, I can but lie down and die at his feet—better so than live on, to trust and be deceived again."

" You have decided rightly, and will not repent it," remarked Oaklands in a milder tone of voice; then, turning to the blacksmith (who had made his appearance, accompanied by his wife, the moment the affray had ended), he continued : " You must procure some conveyance immediately to take this young person back to Cambridge,

· M

and your wife must accompany her." Observing that the man hesitated, and cast an inquiring glance towards Wilford, he added sternly, "If you would not be compelled to answer for the share you have taken in this rascally business before the proper authorities, do as I have told you without loss of time."

The man having again failed in an attempt to attract Wilford's attention, asked in a surly tone if a spring-cart would do, and, being answered in the affirmative, left the room.

Lizzie Maurice withdrew to prepare for. her return home, the woman accompanied her; Oaklands strode to the window, and remained watching the operation of harnessing the horse to the tax-cart. Wilford still retained the same attitude, and neither spoke nor moved. Wentworth having glanced towards him once or twice, as if to divine his wishes, receiving no sign, lit a cigar, and leaning his back against the chimney-piece, began to smoke furiously, whilst I devoted myself to the pages of an old sporting magazine. Thus passed five minutes, which seeemed as if they would never come to an end, at the expiration of which time the tax-cart, driven by a stout country lad, drew up to the door, and the two women making their appearance at the same moment, Oaklands turned to leave the room. As he did so, Wilford, for the first time, raised his head, thereby disclosing a countenance which, pale as death, was charac-terized by an expression of such intense malignity, as one might conceive would be discernible in that of a corpse reanimated by some evil spirit. After regarding Oaklands fixedly for a moment, he said, in a low grating tone of voice, "You have foiled me once and again —when next we meet IT WILL BE MY TURN!" Oaklands merely smiled contemptuously, and quitted the house.

Having mounted our horses, we ordered the lad who drove the spring-cart to proceed at his fastest pace, while we followed at a sufficient distance to keep it in sight, so as to guard against any attempt which might be made by Wilford to repossess himself of his victim, without positively identifying ourselves with the party it contained. We rode in silence for the first two or three miles; at length I could refrain no longer, and, half uttering my thoughts aloud, half addressing my companion, I exclaimed, "Oh, Harry, Harry, what is all this that you have done?"

"Done!" replied Oaklands, with a heightened colour and flashing eyes: "rescued an innocent girl from a villain who would have betrayed her, and punished the scoundrel about half so severely as he deserved; but that was my misfortune, not my fault. Had not the whip broken—"

"You know that is not what I mean," returned I; "but this man will challenge you, will—you are aware of his accursed skill—will murder you. Oh! that fiendish look of his as you left the room—it will haunt me to my dying day."

"And would you have had me leave the poor girl to her fate from a coward fear of personal danger? You are strangely altered since you defied a room full of men last night rather than allow Clara Saville's name to be uttered by their profane lips; or, which is nearer the truth," he continued with a kind smile, "your affection for me blinds you."

"Not so, Harry," replied I; "but it is the recollection of my own feelings, when, while waiting for Lawless's report last night, I believed I should be forced to meet this Wilford—it is the misery, the self-reproach, the bitter penitence of that moment, when for the first time I was able to reflect on the fearful situation in which by my own rashness I had placed myself, a situation in which crime seemed forced upon me, and it appeared impossible to act rightly—it is the remembrance of all these things which causes me to lament that you, my more than brother, should have involved yourself in similar difficulties."

" But, Frank—" he began, then, interrupting himself, he seized my hand, and pressing it warmly between his own, exclaimed, " My dear old fellow, forgive me if I have spoken unkindly to you; but this man has maddened me, I believe." He paused, and then continued in a calmer voice, " Let me tell you how it occurred, and you will see I could scarcely have acted otherwise than I have done. You know I went into the public-house to brush off the mud after my tumble. The instant my step sounded in the passage, a girl tripped lightly down the stairs and ran towards me, exclaiming joyfully, ' You have come at last, then !' On finding that it was not the person she expected, she stopped in alarm, and I perceived to my astonishment that it was Lizzie Maurice. She recognized me at the same moment, and apparently a new idea struck her, for she again approached me, saying, ' Mr. Oaklands, tell me, sir, for heaven's sake, has anything happened to Wilford ?' Then, with woman's tact, perceiving her mistake, she blushed deeply, adding in a timid voice, ' I fancied you might have been riding with that gentleman; and seeing you alone, I was afraid some accident might have befallen your companion.' All this convinced me that my suspicions had not been misplaced ; and the thought occurred to me that possibly it might not yet be too late to endeavour to restore her to her father, while the recollec- tion of Archer's account of the old man's distress determined me to make the attempt.

" Taking her, therefore, by the hand, I led her into the parlour, and, begging her to listen to me for five minutes, told her I was aware of her elopement, and entreated her to return home again, adding that her father was broken-hearted at her loss. She shed tears when I mentioned the old man's grief, but positively refused to return home.

" Finding persuasion to be of no avail, I thought I would appeal to her fears : so I informed her that I was aware of the name of the villain who had enticed her away ; that I would seek him out and expose him, and that I should instantly acquaint her father with her place of refuge, and advise him to come provided with proper powers

to reclaim her. This produced more effect, and, after some hesitation, she told me proudly that I had done her foul wrong by my
doubts; that Mr. Wilford meant to make her his lawful wife; but
that, in order to prevent his great relations hearing of it till he could
break it to them cautiously, it was advisable to keep the affair quiet
—(the old story, in short, private marriage and all the rest of it)—a
friend of Wilford's, therefore, to avoid exciting suspicion, had kindly
driven her over there the night before, and she was now expecting
her lover to come, and bring a clergyman with him, who would marry
them by licence on the spot; when she heard my step she thought
they had arrived. The air of truth with which she told her tale
carried conviction with it.

"I was about to represent to her the improbability of Wilford's
intentions being as honourable as she fondly imagined them, when a
gig drove up to the door containing Wentworth and a fellow whom I
recognized as one of the billiard-markers in —— Street, dressed in a
seedy suit of black for the occasion; immediately afterwards Wilford
arrived on horseback. The whole thing was now perfectly clear.
Wilford, having made the girl believe he intended to marry her, persuaded Wentworth, who is completely his tool, to carry her off for
him; after which he went to Lawless's wine-party, in order to show
himself and thereby avert suspicion. He then bribed the billiard-
marker to play parson, got Wentworth to bring him, and going out
as if merely for a ride, had joined them here. I was considering
what would be the best course to pursue, and was just coming out to
consult you, when the door was flung open, and Wilford and Wentworth entered hastily. The moment Wilford's eyes fell upon me he
started as if a serpent had stung him, and his brow became black as
night.

"Advancing a step or two towards me, he inquired, in a voice
hoarse with rage, what I was doing there. I replied, 'Endeavouring
to prevent some of your evil designs from succeeding.' He tried to
answer me, but his utterance was literally choked by passion; and
turning away, he strode up and down the room, gnashing and grinding his teeth like a maniac. Having in some degree recovered his
self-control, he again approached me, drew himself up to his full
height, and, pointing to the door, desired me to leave the room.

"I replied I should not do so until I had given the young lady a
piece of information respecting the character of one of the party—
and I pointed to the billiard-marker, who had not yet alighted
—I should then, I added, learn from her own lips whether she still
wished to remain there, or would take my advice, and return to her
father.

"Again Wilford ground his teeth with rage, and desired me, in a
voice of thunder, to 'leave the room instantly'; to which I replied
flatly that I would not.

"He then made a sign to Wentworth, and they both approached
me, with the intention of forcing me out. Fearing that their com-

bined efforts might overpower me (for Wentworth, though short, is a broad-shouldered, strong man, and Wilford's muscles are like iron), I avoided their grasp by stepping backwards, and hitting out with my right hand as I did so, caught Wentworth full on the nose, tapping his claret for him as the pugilists call it, and sending him down like a shot. At the same moment Wilford sprang upon me with a bound like a tiger, and seizing me by the throat, a short but severe struggle took place between us. I was too strong for him, however; and finding this, he would gladly have ceased hostilities and quitted me, kindly postponing my annihilation till some future day, when it could be more conveniently accomplished by means of a pistol-bullet. But as you may imagine, my blood was pretty well up by this time, and I determined he should not get off quite so easily. Seizing, therefore, my whip in one hand, I detained him without much trouble with the other—his strength being thoroughly exhausted by his previous exertions—and administered such a thrashing as will keep him out of mischief for a week to come, at all events. It was while this was going on that you made your appearance, I think; so now you are 'au fait' to the whole affair—and, pray, what else could I possibly have done under the circumstances?"

"It is not easy to say," replied I. "I think the horse-whipping might have been omitted, though I suppose the result would have been the same at all events, and it certainly was a great temptation. The brightest side of the business is your having saved the poor girl, who I really believe is more to be pitied than blamed, having only followed the dictates of her woman's nature, by allowing her feelings to overrule her judgment."

"You have used exactly the right expression there," said Oaklands, "in such cases as the present, it is not that the woman is weak enough to be gulled by every plausible tale which may be told her, but that she has such entire confidence, such pure and child-like faith in the man she loves, that she will believe anything rather than admit the possibility of his deceiving her."

"The deeper villain he who can betray such simple trust," replied I.

"Villain, indeed!" returned Oaklands. "I would not have been in Wilford's place, to have witnessed that girl's look when the conviction of his baseness was forced upon her, for worlds; it was not a look of anger nor of sorrow, but it seemed as if the blow had literally crushed her heart within her—as if the brightness of her young spirit had fled for ever, and that to live would only be to prolong the duration of her misery. No; I would rather have faced death in its most horrible form than have met that look, knowing that my own treachery had called it forth."

We rode for some little distance in silence. At length I inquired how he meant to arrange for Lizzie Maurice's return to her home, as it would not do for us, unless he wished the part we had taken in the affair to be known all over Cambridge, to escort her to her father's door, in the order of procession in which we were then advancing.

"No, I was just thinking of that," replied Oaklands. "It appears to me that the quietest way of managing the affair will be, to pay the boy for the cart and horse at once, telling him to set Lizzie Maurice down within a short distance of her father's shop, and then to drive back with the woman. Lizzie can proceed on foot, and will probably at this time of the evening" (it was nearly seven o'clock) "be able to enter the house without attracting attention : we will, however, keep her in sight so as to be at hand to render her assistance, should she require it. I do not myself feel the slightest doubt but that her father will believe her tale, and treat her kindly. I shall, however, leave her my direction, and should she require my testimony in support of her veracity, or should the old man be unwilling to receive her, she must inform me of it, and I will call upon him, and try to bring him to reason."

"That will not be necessary, depend upon it," returned I; "he will only be too glad to recover her."

"So I think," replied Oaklands.

"What course shall you take with regard to Wilford?" inquired I.

"I shall never mention the affair to anyone, if he does not," answered Oaklands; "neither shall I take any step whatever in the matter. I am perfectly satisfied with the position in which I stand at present, and if he should not enjoy an equal share of contentment. it is for him to declare it—the next move must be his, and it will be time enough for me to decide how to act when we see what it may be. I shall now tell Lizzie Maurice of my plan for her, and inform her that as long as I hear she is living quietly at home, and leading a respectable life, my lips will be sealed with regard to the occurrences of to-day." So saying, he put his horse into a canter, and riding up to the side of the cart, conversed with the girl in a low tone of voice for several minutes ; then, drawing out his purse, handed some money to the driver, and rejoined me. "She is extremely grateful to me for my promise of silence," he commenced ; "seems very penitent for her fault, and declares that this is a lesson she shall never forget. She agrees to my plan of walking, and tells me there is a side-door to the house, by which she can enter unobserved. She promises to confess everything to her father, and hopes to obtain his forgiveness ; and appears altogether in 'a very proper frame of mind,' as the good books say."

"Long may she remain so!" returned I; "and now I am happy to say there are some of the towers of Cambridge visible, for, like you, I am becoming fearfully hungry."

"And for the first time during the last twenty-four hours I am actually beginning to feel as tired as a dog," rejoined Harry, shrugging his shoulders with an air of intense satisfaction.

CHAPTER XXV.

THE CHALLENGE.

"Patience perforce with wilful choler meeting,
Makes my flesh tremble in their different greeting.
I will withdraw ; but this intrusion shall,
Now seeming sweet, convert to bitter gall."
" More matter for a May morning."
" Here's the challenge, read it."
" If this letter move him not, his legs cannot."
" O ominous ! he comes to kill my heart."
                                        Shakespeare.

OLD MAURICE, the pastrycook, had welcomed his daughter gladly,
as one returned from the grave, and had learned from her own lips,
with mingled tears of joy and gratitude, how, thanks to noble Harry
Oaklands, she had escaped unscathed from the perils and temptations to which she had been exposed; many days had elapsed, the
Long Vacation had commenced, and the ancient town of Cambridge,
no longer animated by the countless throngs of gownsmen, frowned
in its unaccustomed solitude, like some City of the Dead, and still no
hostile message came from Wilford.   Various reports were circulated
concerning the reappearance of Lizzie Maurice: but none of them
bore the faintest resemblance to the truth, and to no one had the
possibility of Oaklands' interference in the matter occurred, save,
as it afterwards appeared, to Charles Archer.

For above a week Wilford was confined to his room, seeing only
Wentworth ; and it was given out that he had met with a severe fall
from his horse, and was ordered to keep perfectly quiet.   At the
expiration of that period he quitted Cambridge suddenly, leaving no
clue to his whereabouts.   This strange conduct scarcely excited any
surprise amongst the set he moved in, as it was usually his habit to
shroud all his proceedings under a veil of secrecy, assumed, as some
imagined, for the purpose of enhancing the mysterious and unaccountable influence he delighted to exercise over the minds of
men.

Oaklands remained a few days at Cambridge after Wilford's
departure, as he said, to pack up, but, as I felt certain, to prevent the
possibility of Wilford's imagining that he was anxious in any way to
avoid him.   Finding at length that his rooms were dismantled, and
that he would not in all probability return till the end of the Long
Vacation, Harry ceased to trouble his head any further about the
matter, and we set off for Heathfield, accompanied by Archer, whom
Harry had invited to pay him a visit.

We found all well at our respective homes ; my mother appeared
much stronger, and was actually growing quite stout, for her ; and

Fanny looked so pretty, that I was not surprised at the very particular attentions paid her from the first moment of his introduction by the volatile Archer (who, by the way, was a regular male flirt), attentions which I was pleased to perceive she appreciated exactly at their proper value. We soon fell into our old habits again, Oaklands and Archer setting out after breakfast for a stroll, or on a fishing expedition, which usually ended in Harry's coming to an anchor under some spreading oak or beech, where he remained, " doing a bit of the ¦dolce," as Archer called it, till luncheon-time; whilst I, who could not afford to be idle, read hard till about three o'clock and then joined in whatever amusement was the order of the day.

" Frank, may I come in ?" exclaimed Fanny's silvery voice outside my study door, one morning during my working hours, when I had been at home about a fortnight.

" To be sure you may, you little torment," replied I ; "are you coming to learn mathematics, or to teach me crochet ? for I see you are armed with that vicious little hook with which you delight to torture the wool of innocent lambs into strange shapes, for the purpose of providing your friends with innumerable small anomalous absurdities, which they had much rather be without."

" No such thing, Mr. Impudence; I never make any article which is not particularly useful as well as ornamental. But, Frank dear," she continued. " I should not have interrupted you, only I wanted to tell you something—it may be nothing to signify, and yet I cannot help feeling alarmed about it."

" What is it, darling?" said I, putting my arm round her taper little waist, and drawing her towards me.

" Why, Mr. Oaklands has been here this morning; he came to bring mamma a message from Sir John, inviting us all to dine with him to-morrow."

" Nothing very alarming so far," observed I ; "go on."

" Mamma said we should be extremely happy to do so, and quitted the room to find a receipt she had promised to the housekeeper at the Hall."

" And you were left alone with Harry—that was alarming certainly," said I.

" Nonsense." returned Fanny, while a very becoming blush glowed on her cheek; "how you do interrupt me! Mr. Oaklands had kindly offered to explain a difficult passage in Dante for me, and I was standing on a chair to get down the book—"

" Which he could have reached by merely stretching out his arm, I dare say, only he was too idle," interposed I.

" Indeed he could not," replied Fanny quickly, " for he was sitting in the low easy-chair, and trying to fasten mamma's spectacles on Donald's nose." (Donald being a favourite Scotch terrier belonging to Harry, and a great character in his way.) " Well, I had just found the book." she continued, " and we were going to begin, when a note was

given to Mr. Oaklands, which had been brought by a groom from the
Hall, with a message that the gentleman who had left it was waiting
at the inn in the village for an answer. Mr. Oaklands began to read
it in his usual quiet way, but no sooner had he thrown his eye over
the first few lines than his cheeks flushed, his brow grew dark, and
his face assumed that fearfully stern expression which I have heard
you describe, but had never before seen myself. As soon as he had
finished reading it he crushed the paper in his hand, and sprang up,
saying hurriedly, 'Is Frank—?' He then took two or three steps
towards the door, and I thought he was coming to consult you.
Suddenly, however, some new idea seemed to cross his mind, and
stopping abruptly, he strode towards the window, where he remained
for a few moments, apparently buried in thought. At length he
muttered, 'Yes, that will be better, better in all respects;' and
turning on his heel, he was about to quit the room, leaving his hat on
the table, when I ventured to hand it to him, saying. 'You are going
without your hat, Mr. Oaklands.' He started at the sound of my
voice, and seeming for the first time to recollect that I was in the
room, he took the hat from me, begging my pardon for his inattention, and adding, 'You must allow me to postpone our Italian lesson
till—till to-morrow, shall we say? I find there is a gentleman waiting
to see me.' He paused as if he wished to say more, but scarcely
knew how to express himself. 'You saw,' he continued, 'that is—
you may have observed that—that in fact there was something in
that note which annoyed me—you need not say anything about it to
Mrs. Fairlegh; she is rather given to alarming herself unnecessarily,
I fancy, he added with a faint smile; 'tell Frank I shall not be at
home till dinner-time, but that I shall see him in the evening.' He
then shook my hand warmly, and holding it for a moment in his own,
fixed his eyes on my face with a strange, half-melancholy expression
that frightened me, and once more saying 'good-bye,' he pressed his
hat over his brows, and bounding across the lawn, was out of sight
in an instant. His manner was so very odd, so unlike what it
generally is. Dear Frank, what is the meaning of all this? I am
sure there is something going to happen, something—"

"You silly child," replied I, affecting a careless composure I was
far from feeling, "how you frighten yourself about nothing! Harry
has probably received a threatening letter from a Cambridge dun,
and your lively imagination magnifies it into a "—" challenge," I was
going to add, but I substituted—" into something dreadful."

"Is that what you really think?" questioned Fanny, fixing her
large blue eyes upon my face inquiringly.

I am the worst hand in the world at playing the hypocrite, and
with ready tact she perceived at once that I was attempting to
deceive her.

"Frank," she resumed, "you have seen but little of me since we
were children together, and deem, possibly, that I am a weak, silly
girl, unfit to be trusted with evil tidings; but indeed, dear brother,

you do me injustice; the sorrows we have gone through," and her
eyes filled with tears as she spoke, "the necessity for exertion in
order to save mamma as much as possible, have given me more
strength of character and firmness of purpose than girls of my age in
general possess; tell me the truth, and fear not that power will be
given me to bear it, be it what it may; but, if I think you are trying
to hide it from me—and do not hope to deceive me; your face proves
that you are as much alarmed at what you have heard as I am myself, and probably with far better reason—I shall be unable to forget
it, and it will make me miserable."

"Well then," replied I, "thus far I will trust you. I do fear, from
what you have told me, that Oaklands has received some evil tidings
relative to a disagreeable affair in which he was engaged at
Cambridge, the results of which are not fully known at present, and
which, I am afraid, may yet occasion him much care and anxiety."

"And I had fancied him so light-hearted and happy." said Fanny
thoughtfully; "and is this all I'm to know about it, then?"

"All that I feel myself at liberty to tell at present." replied I;
"recollect, darling, it is my friend's secret, not my own, or you should
hear everything."

"Then you will tell me all your secrets if I ask you?" inquired
Fanny archly.

"Whom should I trust or confide in if not my own dear little
sister?" said I, stroking her golden locks caressingly. "And now,"
continued I, rising, "I will go and see whether I can do any good in
this affair; but when Master Harry is in one of his impetuous moods
he gets quite beyond my management."

"Oh! but you can influence him," exclaimed Fanny, her bright
eyes sparkling with animation; "you can calm his impetuosity with
your own quiet good sense and clear judgment—you can appeal to
his high and generous nature—you can tell him how dear he is to
you, how you love him with more than a brother's love: you can and
will do all this—will you not, dear Frank?"

"Of course, I shall do everything that I am able, my dear child,"
replied I, somewhat astonished at this sudden outburst; "and now
go, and be quiet, this business seems rather to have excited you. If
my mother asks for me, tell her I am gone up to the Hall."

"What warm-hearted creatures women are!" thought I, as I ran,
rather than walked through the park: "that little sister of mine,
now—no sooner does she hear that my friend has got into a scrape,
of the very nature of which she is ignorant (a pretty fuss she would
be in if she were aware that it was a duel, of which I am afraid),
than she becomes quite excited, and implores me, as if she were
pleading for her life, to use my influence with Harry to prevent his
doing—something, she has not the most remote notion what. I wish
she did not act quite so much from impulse. It's lucky she has got
a brother to take care of her; though it does not become me to find
fault with her, for it all proceeds from her affection for me; she

knows how wretched I should be if anything were to go wrong with Harry,"—and then I fell into a train of thought as to what it could be which had so suddenly excited him: something connected with Wilford, no doubt; but what?—my fears pointed to a challenge, and my blood ran cold at the thought. He must accept it; neither my influence, were it increased a hundredfold, nor that of anyone else, could make him apologize; besides, it is not very easy to imagine a satisfactory apology for horse-whipping a man till he cannot stand. And what course likely to be of any use could I take? On one point I was resolved—nothing should induce me to become his second. What would be my feelings in case of a fatal result were I to reflect that I had made all the arrangements for the murder of the friend I loved best in the world—that I had actually stationed him opposite the never-failing pistol of his most bitter enemy, and placed in his hand a deadly weapon wherewith to attempt the life of a fellow-creature, when the next moment he might be called upon to answer before the Judge of all mankind for the deeds which he had done in the flesh? No! I could not be his second. As my meditations reached this point, I overtook the groom who had brought the eventful note, and who was leisurely proceeding on foot towards the Hall, with that peculiar gait observable in men who spend much of their time on horseback, which consists of a compromise between walking and riding, and is strongly suggestive of their inability to realize the fact that they have not at all times and seasons a perpetual horse between their legs.

" Have you seen Mr. Oaklands, Harris?" inquired I, as the man touched his hat respectfully.

" Yes, sir, I may say I've seen him, and that's all." was the reply. "I brought him a note to the cottage, and was waiting for orders, when he came tearing out, ordered me to get off, sprang into my saddle, and without stopping for me to let down the stirrups, drove his heels into 'Tom-Trot'—that's the new grey horse, sir, if you please—and was out of sight like old boots."

Not having time to institute an inquiry into the amount of velocity with which the ancient articles referred to by Mr. Harris were accustomed to vanish, I asked if he knew who brought the note.

" A groom in a dark, claret-coloured livery, mounted on a splendid coal-black mare, nearly thorough-bred, but with more bone and substance about her than you generally see in them sort, and as clean on her pins as an unbroke colt. Sir John ain't got such a horse in his stables, nor Mr. Harry neither," was the reply.

This was conclusive evidence; the livery and the mare were alike Wilford's.

Leaving the groom to conjecture what he pleased, I hurried on, and reaching the Hall, inquired of the old butler whether Harry was at home.

" No, sir," was the reply, "they ain't any of them at home. Mr.

Harry came home a horseback about a quarter of an hour ago, and
called Mr. Archer into his own room, and they had a confab, and
then Mr. Archer went out a-riding on the same horse Mr. Harry
came back upon and would not take any o' the grooms with him—
and afore that Sir John had ordered the phaeton and Mr. Henry
being come home he asked him to go with him; so you see, Mr.
Fairlegh, they're none of 'em at home, sir."

"I'll go into the library and write a note. Edmonds," said I. as a
new idea entered my head, "you know Sir John is kind enough to
let me order a horse whenever I require one—will you tell Harris to
have one saddled for me in ten minutes' time?"

"Certainly, Mr. Fairlegh; we all of us have Sir John's orders to
attend to you, sir, the same as to Mr. Henry, and you're a young
gent as it's a pleasure to serve too, if you'll excuse me taking the
liberty of telling you so," replied the good old man, as he showed me
into the library.

The idea which had come into my head (and it was more for the
sake of doing something that I determined on it, than from any
great hope I entertained of its proving of much avail) was to ride
over to Hillingford, and consult Freddy Coleman on the subject.
Perhaps his clear head and quick wit might enable him to devise
some scheme by which, without betraying Harry's confidence, or
bringing the slightest imputation on his honour, this duel might be
prevented. What else could I do? It was quite clear to me, that
the note Harry had received was a challenge from Wilford, and that
the gentleman waiting at the inn was someone whom he had prevailed
upon to act as his second, probably Wentworth. Harry's first
impulse had evidently been to come to me, and ask me to be his
second; but, doubtless, guessing the distaste I should have to the
office, and reflecting on the difficulties in which, if anything serious
were to ensue, I might be involved, he had determined on asking
Archer instead. Archer, by instantly setting off on horseback alone,
had clearly agreed to his request, and was gone to make the necessary
arrangements; and Harry had gladly accompanied Sir John, in
order to be out of the way, and so avoid my questions and any
attempts I might have made to induce him to alter his purpose.
Were I to inform Sir John on his return, it would be an unpardonable breach of confidence towards Harry; were I to give notice to
the authorities, so as to enable them to take measures for preventing
the duel, it would always be said by Wilford that I did so with
Harry's connivance, because he was afraid to meet him: thus my
hands were tied in every way, and, as I said before, I could think of
nothing better than to ride over and consult Coleman, whose powers
of getting out of a scrape I had seen pretty well tested in the affair
of the bell-ringing. I therefore scrawled a hasty note to my mother,
telling her that I was going to take a long ride, and she had better
not wait dinner for me; and leaving a message for Oaklands with
the servant who announced the horse, that I should see him in the

evening, flung myself into the saddle, rode quietly till I was out of
sight of the house and then started at a gallop for Hillingford.
Unwilling to meet any of the Coleman family, I left my horse at
the inn, and pulling my hat over my brows, to avoid, if possible,
being recognized by their servant, rang the bell, and desired him to
tell Mr. Frederic that a gentleman wanted to speak with him on
particular business.

CHAPTER XXVI.

COMING EVENTS CAST THEIR SHADOWS BEFORE.

"If you think your mystery in stratagem can bring this instrument of honour again
into his native quarter, be magnanimous in the enterprise, and go on; I will grace the
attempt for a worthy exploit if you speed well in it."
"Now I see the bottom of your purpose."
"You see it lawful then."
"I love him, sir,
Dearer than eyesight, space, and liberty,
Beyond what can be valued rich or rare,
No less than life, with grace, health, beauty, honour;
A love that makes breath poor, and speech unable—"
"Adieu! these foolish drops do somewhat drown my manly spirit."
                                                        Shakespeare.

"FREDDY, can I have half an hour's private conversation with
you?" asked I, as soon as we had exchanged salutations.

"To be sure you can; but," he added, catching a glimpse of the
anxious expression of my face, "there is nothing wrong, is there?"

I made a gesture indicative of silence, and he opened a door into a
sort of lawyer's office, saying in a low voice,—

"Come in here, we shall not be interrupted; the governor's in
London, and the women are out walking."

"So much the better," replied I, "for the business I am come upon
is strictly private, and will not brook delay."

I then told him as concisely as possible the whole affair from
beginning to end; he listened attentively to my recital, merely
asking a question now and then to elucidate any particular point he
did not clearly understand. I fancy he made a gesture of surprise
when I first mentioned Wilford's name, and when I had concluded
he asked,—

"Wilford, you say, this man's name is? What is his Christian
name?"

"Stephen."

"And he's a young fellow?"

"About three or four and twenty."

"And you want to prevent his being able to shoot Harry Oaklands at five o'clock to-morrow morning ? "

"I do not know the hour, but I conclude the meeting will probably take place to-morrow morning. Wilford would not wish to remain in the neighbourhood longer than necessary, lest he should attract attention."

Coleman mused for some minutes, and then muttering as though he were thinking aloud,—

"It might be done, so ;˚yes, that would do. I suppose," he said, at length addressing me, "if Master Wilford were taken into custody on a magistrate's warrant at half-past four a.m., that would suit your ideas very nicely ? I can so arrange the matter that Wilford will never be able to trace the laying the information to our door."

"But how can you avoid that ? " inquired I.

"Why, if you must know," replied Freddy, "I am acquainted with a man who would give a hundred pounds any day to stop our friend Stephen from fighting a duel."

"What, do you know Wilford, then ? " asked I.

"Ray-ther," was the reply, accompanied by a very significant wink —"just a very few—I should say we were not entire strangers, though I have never enjoyed the honour of much personal inter-course with him ; but I do not so deeply regret that, as, from your account, it seems rather a dangerous privilege."

"How in the world do you know anything about him ? "

"Oh! it's a long story, but the chief points of it are these : The aforesaid Mr. Wilford, if he can continue to exist till he is five-and-twenty, comes into £5000 a year ; but if we don't interfere, and Harry Oaklands has the luck to send a bullet into him to-morrow morning, away it all goes to the next heir. Wilford is now three-and-twenty, and the trustees make him a liberal allowance of £800 per annum, on the strength of which he spends between £2000 and £3000 : of course, in order to do this, he has to raise money on his expectancies. About two months ago he wanted to sell the con-tingent reversion of a large estate in Yorkshire, from which the greater part of his future income is to be derived ; and a client of ours thought of buying it—ergo, we were set to work upon the matter : whilst we were investigating his right, title, and all that sort of thing, lo and behold! a heavy claim, amounting to some thousands, is made upon the property—by whom, do you think, of all people in the world ?—none other than our old acquaintance, Richard Cum-berland ! "

"Good heavens ! " exclaimed I, "how strange ! "

"Cumberland," continued Freddy, "has become somehow con-nected with a lot of bill-brokers—low stock-jobbers—in fact, a very shady set of people, with whom, however, in our profession, we cannot avoid being sometimes brought into contact ; he appears, indeed, himself to be a sort of cross between blackleg and money-lender, improved by a considerable dash of the gambler, and present-ing altogether a very choice specimen of the thorough and complete blackguard. Somehow or other he contrives to have cash at command, and, instead of being pigeoned, has now taken to pigeoning others; and, to give the devil his due, I fancy he does a very pretty stroke of business in that line. He is a good deal improved in manner and appearance since you remember him; and among people who don't know him very intimately, he affects the man about town: in short, he is quite at the top of his profession. Wilford became acquainted with him at one of the Newmarket meetings, lost money to him, and borrowed money of him, and giving him as security a contingent charge upon the estate of double the amount—ergo, don't you see, if Wilford should by any chance get his quietus from Harry's pistol, he won't live to come into his property, in which case Master Dicky Cumberland is minus some thousands. Now, if I contrive to give him a hint, depend upon it he stops the duel. I will caution him not to let my name appear—he will not hear yours; so in this way I think we may manage the affair, and defy the old gentleman himself, though he's a very cunning lawyer, to trace it to us."

" Well," said I, " as I see no other means of saving Oaklands' life—for this Wilford is a noted duellist, and no doubt thirsts to wash out the insult he has received in blood—I suppose we must do it; but it is an underhand proceeding which I do not at all like."

" There you go with your chivalric, high-flown, romantic notions; you would stand coolly by, and see the best friend you have in the world butchered before your eyes, rather than avail yourself of a splendid chance of saving him, which Fortune has thrown in your way, because, forsooth, it involves a little innocent manoeuvring!—for heaven's sake, my dear boy, get off your stilts, and give common sense fair play."

" I can only repeat what I have just said," replied I; " I will do it, because I believe it is the only thing to save Harry; but I do not like it, and never shall."

" I cry you mercy, Signor Francisco de Fairlegh, the veritable Don Quixote of the nineteenth century," laughed Freddy; " and now, most chivalrous sir, where do you imagine it probable that this evil ' faiteur,' this man of powder and pistols, hangs out?"

" He is most likely at the inn at Carsley, a village on the London road, about four miles from us," replied I; " I don't know of any other place in the neighbourhood where he could be lodged. But I'll tell you what I'll do—the name of the inn is the White Horse—if I should prove wrong in fancying he is there, I will send a message to that inn to say where he may be found."

" Exactly," returned Freddy, entering the White Horse, Carsley, in his tablets; " now I think I know all about it, and it shall not be my fault if this duel comes off to-morrow morning. Good-bye, old

fellow! I wish you did not look quite so grumpy about it, but it's all
those mediæval prejudices of yours. I dare say you'd think it a
much more manly way of stopping the business, to electrotype yourself in brass and steel, throw yourself across a cart-horse plated to
match, and shouting, 'Fairlegh to the rescue!' run a long pole.
pointed with iron, through Wilford's jugular. Now, I consider mine
much the most philosophical way of doing the trick; in fact, conducting a dodge of this kind always affords me intense satisfaction,
and puts me into the highest possible spirits. Have you ever seen
the war dance, in which the Hotto-potto-cum-from-the-wash-ki
Indians usually indulge before they set out on an expedition?—A
quarter to three," he continued, pulling out his watch, " the coach to
London passes in five minutes, I shan't have time to show it you—it
begins so." Thus saying, he flung himself into a perfectly indescribable attitude, and commenced a series of evolutions, more nearly
resembling the contortions of a dancing bear, than any other
Terpsichorean exhibition with which I was acquainted. Having
continued this until he had made himself very unnecessarily hot, he
wound up the performance by flinging a summerset, in doing which
he overturned himself and the coal-scuttle into a box of deeds;
whereby becoming embarrassed, he experienced much difficulty in
getting right end upwards again. "There," he exclaimed, throwing
himself into an arm-chair, commonly occupied by his father's portly
form—" There! talk of accomplishments—show me a fashionable
young lady who can do that, and I'll say she is accomplished. It's
rather warm work, though," he continued, wiping his brow, "unless
one wears the appropriate costume, which, I believe, consists of a
judicious mixture of red and yellow paint, three feathers, and the
scalp of your opposite neighbour. Pleasant that," he added, pointing
to the reversed coal-scuttle—"that's a new edition, not of 'Coke
upon Littleton,' but of Coal upon—what's the suit? aye, Buffer
versus Stoker. I shall have to make out a case of circumstantial
evidence against the cat, or I'm safe for a rowing from the governor.
Good-bye, old boy! don't fancy I'm mad; I'm not the fool I seem,
though I confess appearances are against me just at present. There's
the coach, by Jingo, three bays and a grey—no chance of the box—is
this a hat? off we go." So saying, he shook my hand warmly,
bounded down the steps, and the next moment was rattling away
towards London as fast as four horses could hurry him.

It was with a heavy heart, and a foreboding of coming evil, that I
mounted my horse, and slowly retraced my way towards Heathfield.
Coleman's exuberant spirits, which, I believe, were partly assumed,
with a view to cheer me by diverting my attention from the painful
subject which engrossed it, had produced an effect diametrically
opposite to that which he had intended, and I felt dissatisfied with
the step I had taken, doubtful of the success of his mission, anxious
to a degree, which was absolutely painful, about the fate of Harry,
and altogether thoroughly miserable. I reached home in time for

dinner, during which meal my abstracted manner and low spirits were so apparent, as to set my mother speculating on the chances of my having overheated myself and " got a chill," whilst Fanny's anxious questioning glances, to which I was well aware I could furnish no satisfactory reply, produced in me a degree of nervous excitement which was unbearable, and, the moment the cloth was withdrawn, I left the room, and rambled forth into the wildest parts of the park. The quiet peaceful beauty of the scene, and the refreshing coolness of the evening air, had, in a great measure, calmed the excitement under which I laboured, and I was turning my steps towards the Hall, when I met Oaklands and Archer, who, finding I was not at the cottage, had come in search of me. Half an hour's conversation served to render all my previous conjectures matters of certainty. The challenge had been given and accepted, Wentworth was to be Wilford's second, and he and his principal were staying at the inn at Carsley.

The spot chosen for the scene of action was a plot of grassland situated about half-way between Carsley and Heathfield, so as to be equally accessible to both parties; the time appointed was five o'clock the following morning. Archer was to act as Oaklands' second; everything had been managed with the greatest caution, and they did not believe a single creature, excepting themselves, had the slightest suspicion that such an event was likely to take place. They had resolved not to tell me till everything was settled, as they feared my opposition. Having thus taken me into their confidence, Archer left us, saying, that " probably Oaklands might like to have some private conversation with me, and he would join us again in half an hour." Rejoiced at this opportunity, I entered at once upon the subject which most interested me, and used every argument I could think of to induce Harry not to return Wilford's fire.

Oaklands heard me for some time in silence, and I began to fear my efforts would be fruitless, when suddenly he turned towards me, and said—his fine eyes beaming with an almost womanly expression of tenderness as he spoke—" Would this thing make you happier in case I fall?" A silent pressure of the hand was my only answer, and he added in a low voice, " then it shall be as you wish." A pause ensued : for my own part, the thought that this might be our last meeting, completely overpowered me; I did not know till that moment the strength and intensity of my affection for him. The silence was at length interrupted by Oaklands himself, and the low tones of his deep rich voice trembled with emotion, as they fell mournfully on the stillness of the evening air. " My father!" he said, " that kind old man, whose happiness is wrapped up in my welfare—it will break his heart, for he has only me to love. Frank, my brother!" he added, passing his arm round my neck, as he had used to do when we were boys together, " you are young; your mind is strong and vigorous, and will enable you to meet sorrow as a man should confront and overcome whatever is opposed to him in his

' N

path through life. I will not disguise from you that, looking
rationally and calmly at the matter, I have but little hope of quitting
the field to-morrow alive. My antagonist, naturally a man of
vindictive disposition, is incensed against me beyond all power of
forgiveness, and his skill is fully equal to his malice: should I fall, I
leave my father to your care; be a son to him in the place of the one
he will have lost. This is not a light thing which I ask of you,
Frank. I ask you to give up your independence, your high hopes of
gaining name and fortune by the exercise of your own talents and
industry, and to devote some of the best years of your life to the
weary task of complying with the caprices, and bearing the sorrows,
of a grief-stricken old man. Will you do this for me, Frank?"

"I will," replied I; "and may God help me, as I execute this trust
faithfully!"

"You have relieved my mind of half its burden," returned
Oaklands warmly. "I have only one thing more to mention: When
I came of age last year, my father's liberality made over to me an
ample income for a single man to live on: excepting a few legacies
to old servants, I have divided this between your good little sister
and yourself, which I thought you would prefer to my leaving it to
you alone."

"Harry! indeed, I cannot allow you to do this; others must surely
have claims upon you."

"There is not a being in the world who has a right to expect a
farthing at my death," answered he; "the next heir to the entailed
estates is a distant relation in Scotland, already wealthy. My father
has always been a careful man, and, should he lose me, will have a
larger income than he can possibly be able to spend; besides, as the
duties I have led you to undertake must necessarily prevent you
from engaging actively in any profession, I am bound in common
fairness to provide for you."

"Be it so, then," replied I, inwardly breathing a prayer that I
never might possess a sixpence of the promised fortune.

"One thing more," added Harry. "When you return to Trinity—
poor old Trinity, shall I ever visit you again?—find out how Lizzie
Maurice is going on, and if she should marry respectably in her own
rank, ask my father to give you £100 as a wedding present for her;
only hint that it was my wish, and he would give twenty times the
sum. And now good—pshaw!" he continued, drawing his hand
across his eyes, "I shall play the woman if I talk to you much more
—good-night, Frank—do you accompany us to the ground to-morrow
morning?"

"I will go with you," returned I, with difficulty overcoming a
choking sensation in my throat; "I may be able to be of some use."

"Here comes Archer," said Oaklands, "so once more good-night;
I must get home, or my father will wonder what is become of me."

My heart was too full to speak, and pressing his hand I turned
abruptly away, and walked quickly in the opposite direction.

CHAPTER XXVII.

THE DUEL.

"The sun begins to gild the western sky,
And now it is about the very hour.
  *   *   *   *They* will not fail,
Unless it be to come before their time ;
So much they spur their expedition."
                              Shakespeare.

"Now go thy way: faintness constraineth me
To measure out my length on this cold bed."
                              Shakespeare.

" And me they bear   .   .   .
To one deep chamber shut from sound, and due
To languid limbs and sickness."
                              Tennyson's " Princess."

I DID not return to the cottage until the usual hour for going to bed, as I did not dare subject myself to Fanny's penetrating glance in my present state of excitement. The moment family prayers were concluded, I took my candle, and, pleading fatigue, retired to my room. Knowing that sleep was out of the question in my then frame of mind, I merely substituted the clothes I intended to wear in the morning for those I had on, and wrapping my dressing-gown round me, flung myself on the bed. Here I lay, tossing about, and unable to compose myself for an hour or two, the one idea constantly recurring to me, " What if Coleman should fail ! "

At length, feverish and excited, I sprang up, and, throwing open the window which was near the ground, enjoyed the fresh breeze as it played around my heated temples. It was a lovely night; the stars, those calm eyes of Heaven, gazed down in their brightness on this world of sin and sorrow, seeming to reproach the stormy passions and restless strife of men by contrast with their own impassive grandeur. After remaining motionless for several minutes, I was about to close the window, when the sound of a footstep on the turf beneath caught my ear, and a form, which I recognized in the moon-light as that of Archer, approached.

" Up and dressed already, Fairlegh ? " he commenced in a low tone as he perceived me; " may I come in ? "

In silence I held out my hand to him, and assisted him to enter.

" Like me," he resumed. " I suppose you could not sleep ? "

" Utterly impossible," replied I; " but what brings you here—has anything occurred ? "

" Nothing," returned Archer ; " Oaklands retired early, as he said he wished to be alone, and I followed his example, but could not contrive to sleep. I don't know how it is, I was engaged in an affair of this nature once before, and never cared a pin about the matter ;

but somehow I have got what they call a presentiment that harm will come of to-morrow's business. I saw that man, Wilford, for a minute yesterday, and I know by the expression of his eye that he means mischief; there was such a look of fiendish triumph in his face when he found the challenge was accepted—if ever there was a devil incarnate, he is one."

A sigh was my only answer, for his words were but the echo of my forebodings.

" Now I will tell you what brought me here," he continued; " don't you think that we ought to have a surgeon on the ground, in case of anything going wrong ? "

" To be sure," replied I; " I must have been mad to have forgotten that it was necessary—what can be done ?—it is not every man that would choose to be mixed up with such an affair. Where is it that William Ellis's brother (Ellis of Trinity Hall, you know) has settled ?—he told me he had purchased a practice somewhere in our neighbourhood."

" The very man, if we could but get him," replied Archer; " the name of the village is Harley End; do you know such a place ? "

" Yes," returned I, " I know it well; it is a favourite meet of the hounds, about twelve miles hence. I'll find him, and bring him here —what time is it ? just two—if I could get a horse I would do it easily."

" My tilbury and horse are up at the village," said Archer; " now Harry's horses are at home, they could not take mine in at the Hall."

" The very thing," said I, " we shall not lose a moment in that case. Is your horse fast? I shall have to try his mettle."

" He'll not fail you," was the reply; " but don't spare him—I would rather you should ruin fifty horses than arrive too late."

On reaching the inn, we had to rouse a drowsy ostler in order to procure the key of the stables, and it was half-past two before I was able to start.

The road to Harley End was somewhat intricate, more than once I took a wrong turning, and was forced to retrace my steps; being aware also of the distance I had to perform, I did not care to hurry the horse too much, so that it only wanted a quarter to four when I reached my destination. Here, however, fortune favoured me, Mr. Ellis, it appeared, being an ardent disciple of Isaac Walton, had resolved to rise at daybreak in order to beguile sundry trout, and, at the entrance of the village, I met him strolling along, rod in hand. Two minutes sufficed to make him acquainted with the object of my mission, and in less than five minutes more (a space of time which I employed in washing out the horse's mouth at an opportune horse-trough, with which I took the liberty of making free) he had provided himself with a case of instruments, and other necessary horrors, all of which he described to me seriatim, as we returned, with an affectionate minuteness for which I could have strangled him.

We started at a rattling pace on our homeward drive, hedgerow and fence gliding by us like slides in a magic-lantern. Archer's horse did not belie the character he had given of him. With head erect, and expanded 'nostril, he threw his legs forward in a long slashing trot, whirled the light tilbury along at the rate of at least eleven miles an hour; and fortunate it was that he did not flinch from his work, for he had between thirteen and fourteen miles to perform in an hour and ten minutes, in order to reach the appointed spot by five o'clock. In our way we had to pass within a quarter of a mile of Heathfield Hall; all seemed quiet as we did so, and I heard the old clock over the stables strike a quarter to five.

" We shall be in capital time," said I, drawing a long breath, as I felt relieved from an anxious dread of being too late. " It was a near thing though, and if I had not met you as I did, we should scarcely have done it."

" Famous horse," replied Ellis; " but you've rather over-driven him the last two or three miles; if I were Archer, I should have a little blood taken from him—nothing like venesection; it's safe practice in such cases as the present. You've a remarkably clear head, Fairlegh, I know; now I'll just explain to you the common sense of the thing: the increased action of the heart forces the blood so rapidly through the lungs, that proper time is not allowed for oxygenization—"

" We shall be in sight of the place when we have advanced another hundred yards," interrupted I, as we turned down a green lane.

"Shall we ? " replied my companion, standing up in the gig, and shading his eyes with his hand. " Yes, I see them, they're on the ground already, and, by Jove. they are placing their men; they must have altered the time, for it wants full ten minutes of five now."

"If they have," replied I, lashing the horse into a gallop, as I remembered that this unhappy change would probably frustrate Coleman's scheme, "if they have all is lost."

My companion gazed upon me with a look of surprise, but had no time to ask for an explanation, for at that moment we reached the gate leading into the field, around which was collected a group, consisting of a gig and a dog-cart (which had conveyed the respective parties, and a servant attendant upon each, to the ground), and two or three labouring men, whom the unusual occurrence had caused to leave their work, and who were eagerly watching the proceedings— whilst, just inside the gate, a boy, whom I recognized as Wilford's tiger, was leading about a couple of saddle-horses, one of them being the magnificent black thorough-bred mare, of which mention has been already made.

Pulling up the horse with a jerk which threw him on his haunches, I sprang out, and, placing my hand on the top rail of the gate, leaped over it, gaining, as I did so, a full view of the antagonist parties, who were stationed at about two hundred yards from the spot where I alighted. Scarcely, however, had I taken a step or two towards the scene of action, when one of the seconds, Wentworth, I

believe, dropped a white handkerchief, and immediately the sharp
report of a pistol rang in my ear, followed instantaneously by a
second. From the first moment I caught sight of them my eyes had
become riveted by a species of fascination, which rendered it
impossible to withdraw them, upon Oaklands. As the handkerchief
dropped I beheld him raise his arm, and discharge his pistol in the
air, at the same moment he gave a violent start, pressed his hand to
his side, staggered blindly forward a pace or two, then fell heavily to
the ground (rolling partially over as he did so), where he lay perfectly
motionless, and to all appearance dead.

On finding all my worst forebodings thus apparently realized, I
stood for a moment horror-stricken by the fearful sight I had
witnessed. I was first roused to a sense of the necessity for action
by Ellis, the surgeon, who shouted as he ran past me,—

" Come on, for God's sake, though I believe he's a dead man !"

In another moment I was kneeling on the turf, assisting Archer
(who trembled so violently that he could scarcely retain his grasp) to
raise and support Oaklands' head.

"Leave him to me," said I; "I can hold him without assistance;
you will be of more use helping Ellis."

" Oh! he's dead—I tell you he is dead !" exclaimed Archer, in a
tone of the most bitter anguish.

"He is no such thing, sir," returned Ellis angrily; " hand me that
lint, and don't make such a fuss; you're as bad as a woman."

Though slightly reassured by Ellis's speech, I confess that, as I
looked upon the motionless form I was supporting, I felt half
inclined to fear Archer might be correct in his supposition. Oaklands' head, as it rested against me, seemed to lie a perfectly dead
weight upon my shoulder; the eyes were closed, the lips, partly
separated, were rapidly assuming a blue, livid tint, whilst from a
small circular orifice on the left side of the chest the life-blood was
gushing with fearful rapidity.

" Open that case of instruments, and take out the tenaculum. No,
no! not that; here, give them to me, sir; the man will bleed to death
while you are fumbling," continued Ellis, snatching his instruments
from the trembling hands of Archer. "You are only in the way
where you are," he added; "fetch some cold water, and sprinkle his
face; it will help to revive him."

At this moment Wilford joined the group which was beginning to
form round us. He was dressed as usual in a closely-fitting suit of
black, the single-breasted frock-coat buttoned up to the neck, so as
not to show a single speck of white which might serve to direct his
antagonist's aim. He approached with his wonted air of haughty indifference, coolly fastening the button of his glove. On perceiving
me, he slightly raised his hat, saying,—

"You are resolved to see this matter to its conclusion, then, Mr.
Fairlegh; no one can be better aware than you are how completely
your friend brought his fate upon himself."

He paused, as if for an answer; but, as I remained silent, not being able to trust myself to speak, he added, gazing sternly at the prostrate form before him—"Thus perish all who dare to cross my path!" Then casting a withering glance around, as he marked the indignant looks of the bystanders, he turned on his heel and stalked slowly away.

"He'd best quicken his pace," observed one of the countrymen who had joined the group, "for there's them a coming as may stop his getting away quite so easy."

As he spoke, the gate of the field was thrown open, and a couple of men on horseback rode hastily in. Wilford, however, as soon as he perceived their approach, made a sign to the boy to bring his horse, and, springing lightly into the saddle, waited quietly till they came near enough for him to recognize their faces, when, raising his voice, he said in a tone of the most cutting sarcasm,—

"As I expected, I perceive it is to Mr. Cumberland's disinterested attachment that I am indebted for this kind attempt to provide for my safety; it so happens you are a quarter of an hour too late, sir. I have the honour to wish you good-morning."

Thus saying, he turned his horse's head, and cantered across the field. The man he had addressed, and in whom, though he was considerably altered, I recognized the well-remembered features of Richard Cumberland, paused, as if in doubt what to do; not so his companion, however, who, shouting, "Come on, sir, we may nab him yet," drove the spurs into the stout roadster he bestrode and galloped furiously after him, an example which Cumberland, after a moment's hesitation, hastened to follow, though at a more moderate rate. Wilford suffered the foremost rider to come nearly up to him, and then, quickening his pace, led him round the two sides of the field; but perceiving the gate was closed, and that men had stationed themselves in front of it to prevent his egress, he doubled upon his pursuers, and putting the mare for the first time to her full speed, galloped towards the opposite side of the field, which was enclosed by a strong fence, consisting of a bank with oak palings on the top, and a wide ditch beyond. Slackening his pace as he approached this obstacle, he held his horse cleverly together, and, without a moment's hesitation, rode at it. The beautiful animal, gathering her legs well under her, faced it boldly, rose to the rail, and clearing it with the greatest ease, bounded lightly over the ditch, and continued her course on the further side with unabated speed. Apparently determined not to be outdone, his pursuer, whipping and spurring with all his might, charged the fence at the same spot where Wilford had cleared it; the consequence was his horse rushed against the rail, striking his chest with so much violence as to throw him-self down, pitching his rider over his head into the ditch beyond, whence he emerged, bespattered with mud, indeed, but other-wise uninjured. As he reappeared his companion rode up to him, and, after conversing with him earnestly for a minute or so, turned and left the field, without exchanging a word with any other person.

During this transaction, which did not occupy one-fourth of the time it has taken us to describe, Ellis had in a great measure succeeded in staunching the flow of blood, and a slight shade of colour became again visible in Oaklands' cheek.

" He will bear moving now," said Ellis quickly, " but you must find something to lay him upon ; take that gate off its hinges, some of you fellows—that will answer the purpose capitally. Come, bestir your-selves; every moment is of importance."

Thus urged, five or six sturdy labourers, who had been standing round, gazing with countenances of rude but sincere commiseration on the wounded man (for Harry's kindheartedness and liberality made him very popular amongst the tenantry), started off, and returned in an incredibly short space of time with the gate; upon this were spread our coats and waistcoats, so as to form a tolerably convenient couch, upon which, under Ellis's direction, we lifted with the greatest caution the still insensible form of Harry Oaklands.

" Now," exclaimed Ellis, " raise him very slowly on your shoulders, and take care to step together, so as not to jolt him ; if the bleeding should break out again, the whole College of Surgeons could not save him. Where's the nearest house he can be taken to ? He'll never last out till we reach the Hall."

" Take him to our cottage," said I eagerly; " it is more than half a mile nearer than the Hall."

" But your mother and sister ? " asked Archer.

" Of course it will be a great shock to them," replied I ; " but I know them both well enough to feel sure they would not hesitate a moment when Harry's life was in the balance. Do you want me for anything, or shall I go on and prepare them for your arrival ? "

" Do so, by all means," replied Ellis; " but stay—have you a bed-room on the ground-floor ? "

" Yes," returned I, " my own."

" Get the bed-clothes open," continued Ellis, " so that we can put him in at once ; it will save me half an hour's time afterwards, and is a thing which should always be thought of on these occasions."

" Anything else ? " inquired I.

" Yes, send somebody for the nearest surgeon ; two heads are better than one," said Ellis.

Remembering, as I approached the cottage, that the window of my room by which Archer and I had quitted it the previous night would be unfastened, I determined I would enter there, and, proceeding to my mother's door, call her up, and break the news as gently as the exigency of the case would permit, leaving her to act by Fanny as she should think best. Accordingly, I flung up the window, sprang in, and, throwing myself on the nearest chair, sat for a moment, panting from the speed at which I had come. As I did so, a timid knock was heard at the door. I instinctively cried, "Come in!" and Fanny entered.

"I have been so anxious all night about what you told me yesterday, that I could not sleep, so I thought I would come to see if you were up," she commenced; then, for the first time remarking my breathless condition and disordered dress, she exclaimed, "Good Heavens! are you ill? you pant for breath, and your hands and the sleeves of your coat are saturated with water—with—oh! it is blood; you are wounded!" she cried, sinking in a chair, and turning as pale as ashes.

"Indeed, darling, you are alarming yourself unnecessarily; I am perfectly uninjured," replied I, soothingly.

"Something dreadful has happened!" she continued, fixing her eye upon me; "I read it in your face."

"An accident has occurred," I began; "Oaklands—"

"Stop!" she exclaimed, interrupting me, "the two shots I heard but now—his agitation—his strange manner yesterday—oh! I see it all; he has been fighting a duel." She paused, pressed her hands upon her eyes, as if to shut out some dreadful vision, and then asked, in a low, broken voice, "Is he killed?"

"No," replied I, "on my word, on my honour, I assure you he is not; the bleeding had ceased when I left him, which is a very favourable symptom."

Fanny sighed heavily, as if relieved from some unbearable weight, and, after remaining silent for about a minute, she removed her hands from her face, and said, in a calm tone of voice,—

"And now, what is to be done? can I be of any use?"

Astonished at the rapidity with which she had regained her self-control and presence of mind after the violent emotion she had so recently displayed, I replied,—

"Yes, love, you can, the Hall is too far off, and they are bringing him here."

As I spoke these words, she shuddered slightly, but seeing I was doubtful whether to proceed, she said, "Go on, pray."

"Would you," I continued, "break this to my mother, and tell her I believe—that is, I trust—there is no great danger—and—and—do that first."

With a sad shake of the head, as if she mistrusted my attempt to reassure her, she quitted the room, whilst I obeyed Ellis's instructions by preparing the bed; after which I unclosed the hall-door, and despatching the gardener's boy to fetch the surgeon, stood anxiously awaiting the arrival of the party. I had not done so many minutes, when the measured tramp of feet gave notice of their approach, and in another instant they came in sight.

CHAPTER XXVIII.

THE SUBSTANCE OF THE SHADOW.

" Recovery, where art thou ?
Daughter of Heaven, where shall we seek thy help ? "

" Come thou and chase away
Sorrow and Pain, the persecuting Powers,
Who make the melancholy day so long,
So long the anxious night."

" I look for thy approach,
O, life-preserving power ! as one who strays
Alone in darkness o'er the pathless marsh,
Watches the dawn of day,"

Southey.

" ALL well so far," replied Ellis, in answer to my look of inquiry " the bleeding has ceased, and he is fast recovering consciousness. Where is the room ? We must get him into bed at once."

When we had placed him in the bed, Oaklands lay for a short space with his eyelids closed, uttering a low groan at intervals ; at length the quiet appeared in some measure to restore him, and, slowly opening his eyes, he gazed languidly around, asking in a low voice, " Where am I ? "

" Let me beg you not to speak, Mr. Oaklands," said Ellis ; " your safety depends upon your keeping silence ; you are at the cottage of your friend Fairlegh."

As he heard these words, Harry perceived me standing near the bed, and smiled faintly in token of recognition ; then, making a sign for me to stoop down to him, he whispered, " My father—you must break this to him—go, Frank."

" This instant," replied I, and I turned to leave the room, beckoning to Ellis, as I did so, to follow me. " Tell me the truth," exclaimed I, as he closed the door behind him, " will he live or die ? "

" It is too early in the business to pronounce a decided opinion," was the answer ; " nor can I venture as yet to do so ; everything depends upon the course the ball may have taken, and that, as soon as the other surgeon arrives, we must endeavour to ascertain ; all I can say at present is, that I have seen worse cases recover. There is one thing," he added, " which may be a satisfaction for you to know —if you had not brought me or someone in my profession, to the ground, he would have bled to death where he fell ; no one but a surgeon could have stopped that bleeding."

" If we had been too late I should never have forgiven myself, and we very nearly were so," returned I. " I cannot understand how it was."

" I can explain it," said Archer, who now joined us. " You left me

up at the village, you remember, Fairlegh, when you started to fetch
Mr. Ellis; well, just as I was leaving it to return to the Hall, a boy
ran past me at the top of his speed, and began knocking at one of the
cottage doors hard by; surprised to see any one about at so early an
hour in the morning, I inquired what was the matter. 'Master's just
had word brought him that some gem'men is a going to fight a jewel
at five o'clock, and I be come to call the constable, for master to give
him a warrant to take 'em hup.' 'And who is your master?' questioned I. 'Justice Bumbleby,' was the answer. This was enough for
me; I made the best of my way to the Hall, woke Oaklands, who was
sleeping as calmly as a child, poor fellow! and he immediately sent
his own groom, the lad who went with us to the field, to inform
Wilford and his second of what I had heard, and to propose that the
meeting should take place a quarter of an hour earlier than the time
originally agreed on, to which they willingly consented."

"This, then," thought I, "is the reason why Coleman's scheme
failed, and Cumberland arrived too late;—well, one good thing is, it
will clearly prove that neither Archer nor Oaklands connived at the
intended interruption."

The deep, the agonizing grief of Sir John Oaklands, on receiving
from my lips the account of his son's danger, was most painful to
witness, and I was obliged to yield to his desire to return with me to
the cottage, although Ellis had strictly forbidden his being allowed
to see Harry, lest the excitement should prove injurious to the
patient, in the precarious state in which he lay. On my return, I
found the surgeon of the neighbourhood, Mr. (or as he was more
commonly styled Dr.) Probehurt, had arrived, and that they were
endeavouring to extract the ball, which, after a long and painful
operation, they succeeded in doing. From the marks on the coat and
waistcoat, it appeared that Wilford had aimed straight for the heart;
but his deadly intentions had been providentially frustrated by the
accident of Oaklands having a half-crown piece in a small pocket in
his waistcoat, against which the ball struck, and glancing off, passed
between two of the ribs, finally lodging amongst the muscles immediately under the shoulder-blade. The great effusion of blood had
been occasioned by its having divided one of the smaller arteries,
which Ellis had succeeded in securing on the spot. The wound was,
therefore, a very severe one; but it was impossible to pronounce
upon the exact amount of danger at present, as the course which the
ball had taken trenched closely on so many important organs, that
time alone could show the extent of the injury sustained. With this
opinion, in which (strange to say) both doctors agreed, we were fain
to content ourselves, and we passed the rest of the day in alternately
watching by the wounded man, and attempting to comfort and
support Sir John, whom we had the greatest difficulty in keeping out
of Harry's room, till Ellis asked him abruptly, "whether he wanted
to murder his son?" after which nothing short of force could have
induced him to enter it. One of his first acts, having consulted with

Dr. Probehurt, who graciously approved of the measure, was to enter into an arrangement with Ellis, to induce him to remain constantly with Harry, till his health should be perfectly re-established, if, indeed, that happy event was ever destined to occur. As Sir John's liberality was unbounded, and Ellis's professional prospects rather hazy—his practice at Harley End being chiefly confined to the very poor, who went on the advice gratis system, and expected to have medicine given them into the bargain—the negotiation was soon concluded to the satisfaction of both parties.

Towards evening Harry became more restless; the pain of his wound increased, and feverish symptoms began to make their appearance. As the night advanced he grew delirious, and before morning was in a high state of fever. For many days his life was despaired of. Ellis never left his bedside, save to snatch an occasional hour's sleep on a sofa, when I took his place. Sir Benjamin Brodie was summoned from town, and held a consultation with Dr. Probehurt and Ellis.

Sir John's grief was something fearful to witness. Although naturally a strong-minded man, this unlooked-for blow and the subsequent anxiety had completely unnerved him. At times he would cry like a child; at others he would sit for hours without opening his lips, his head resting dejectedly on his hands, the image of despair: he could with difficulty be prevailed upon to take sufficient nourishment for his support, and appeared scarcely to notice anything that was going on. On these occasions Fanny was the only person whose influence was of the slightest avail; with her own hands she would prepare some delicacy of which she knew he was fond, and when with a melancholy shake of the head he rejected it, she would seat herself at his feet, and taking his hand within her own, whisper kind words of hope and consolation to him, till the old man's heart was softened, and he could refuse her nothing. Sometimes even this failed, and then she would begin singing in a low sweet voice some plaintive, simple air that he loved to hear, till the tears would steal down his grief-worn cheeks, and, laying his hand upon her fair young brow, he would bless her, and say that the God who was about to take his noble son from him had sent an angel to be a daughter to him in his stead. And so the weary days wore on—still vibrating between life and death, the strong man, his matchless powers now reduced to the weakness of infancy, lay stretched upon the couch of suffering, whence it appeared too probable that he might never be removed, save to the last sad resting-place of frail humanity—the grave.

About the eighth day the ligature with which Ellis had tied the artery came away, and the wound assumed a rather more favourable appearance, but the fever remained unsubdued, and the delirium continued. Each day which passed without improvement added to the length of Dr. Probehurt's solemn visage, and I could see that in his own mind he had little or no hope of the patient's recovery. Ellis was by far the most sanguine of the party, and, whenever we urged our gloomy forebodings upon him, invariably replied, "Yes, I know all that; it would have killed any other man, but it won't kill him. Wait a bit, and you'll see."

A fortnight had now elapsed, and the continued burden of his grief began to tell visibly upon Sir John. The ruddy hue of health faded from his cheeks; his eyes grew dim with weeping, his hands shook, and his firm, manly step became feeble and uncertain : it seemed as if in that short space of time he had grown ten years older. My mother also began to look ill and harassed, and Fanny, though she still kept up wonderfully, and was the life and soul of us all, waxed paler and thinner every day, while for my own part, I could neither eat, drink, nor sleep to any efficient purpose, and divided my time between watching in the sick-room, and pacing up and down the garden, beyond the precincts of which I never ventured, from a nervous dread lest anything might go wrong in my absence.

On one occasion Ellis, completely wearied out, had thrown himself on a sofa to snatch an hour's repose, while I took his place by Harry's bedside. It was between two and three o'clock in the morning, and the first rays of early dawn, stealing in through the partially closed shutters, and mingling with the faint glimmer of the night-lamp, threw a pale and ghastly light over the surrounding objects, when I fancied that I heard my name pronounced in a low, scarcely audible voice. I glanced at Ellis, but his hard and regular breathing proved him to be sound asleep. I next turned towards the bed where Harry lay, and carefully shading the lamp with my hand, advanced with noiseless step towards it. As I approached, I perceived the patient's eyes were open, and, oh, happiness ! once more animated with the mild light of reason.

" Harry," whispered I, " did you call ? Do you know me ? "

A faint smile passed across his pallid features as he replied in a voice so low and weak that I was obliged to stoop my head almost to a level with his lips, ere I could catch his words : " Know you, dear Frank ! why not ? "

" Thank heaven," murmured I, " he is no longer delirious ! "

As I again turned towards him, he endeavoured to stretch out his hand to me, but his strength was unequal even to that slight exertion, and his arm dropped heavily by his side ; as it did so he spoke again : " Frank, what is all this ? I cannot—I am very weak—very tired."

" Lie still, dear Harry, and do not try to talk—it may do you harm. You have been very ill, but God in His mercy will soon, I trust, restore you to health." I then crossed over to Ellis's sofa, and laid my hand lightly upon his shoulder. " Oaklands is no longer delirious," said I, as he started up ; " he knows me, and has spoken to me."

" Is he ?—does he ?—has he ? " exclaimed Ellis, in an eager whisper. " I told you it would never kill him. Why didn't you call me before ? but it's always the way : if I do by any chance fall asleep once in a week, there isn't another head properly so called in the whole house,

they might as well be chair nobs—yes, I know," he continued, as I
attempted to get in a word of explanation, "if you couldn't wake me
before it happened, that doesn't prevent your giving me the medicine-
chest now, does it ? "

I may as well take this opportunity of mentioning that Ellis, though
in the main one of the best-tempered fellows in the world, whenever
he was particularly interested or excited, became extremely cross and
snappish, and was certain at such times to scold everyone who fell in
his way, without the slightest regard to age, sex, or station. However, it was always over in two or three minutes, and I have seen him
laugh till the tears ran down his face, when the rude things he had
said were repeated to him afterwards. While he was staying with
his brother at Cambridge, it used to be a favourite amusement with
some of the men to start a subject which they knew would excite him.
for the sake of " getting a rise out of the doctor," as they termed it.
But I am digressing.

The medicine Ellis gave Harry threw him into a heavy sleep, from
which he did not awake until late in the morning, when he appeared
perfectly conscious. The fever had in great measure abated, and on
Dr. Probehurt's arrival he was fain to confess a surprising improvement had taken place, and that, if not positively out of danger,
the patient was in a fair way to become so. As for Ellis, he was
exactly like one beside himself. He ran all over the house—into bed-
rooms and all sorts of places where he had not the slightest business,
shaking hands with everyone, and repeating, " I knew it—I knew it
—I always told you so—it would have killed any other man, but it
couldn't kill him ! "

Let us pass in silence over the first interview between Sir John
Oaklands and his son. There are some of the deeper feelings of our
nature, planted in our bosoms by the hand of God Himself, which,
when called forth to their fullest extent by the chances of life, reveal
so clearly their Divine origin, that those who witness their display
stand reverently by and, with throbbing hearts and averted eyes, bow
the head as in presence of some holy thing ; and if such pure and
sacred influences shed their lustre over that meeting, and the old man
wept tears of deep and fervent thankfulness on the neck of the son
whom he had, as it were, received from the dead, far be it from us,
with sacrilegious hand, to remove the veil which shrouds the hallowed
mysteries of feeling.

From that day Oaklands began to amend slowly, and at the end of
another week even the cautious Dr. Probehurt declared all immediate
danger was over; for which admission, however, he took care fully to
indemnify himself, by detailing at length every possible evil which
might accrue for the future. The state of weakness to which Harry's
once herculean frame was reduced was melancholy to witness; for
many days he was unable to turn in his bed without assistance, and
even when he began to recover his strength, it was by very slow and
lingering degrees. Utterly unable to support himself, he was lifted

from his bed to a sofa, and wheeled into the drawing-room, where all our powers of entertainment were called into requisition to relieve the monotony of such a state of existence. In doing this, Fanny made herself pre-eminently useful; by a sort of intuition she appeared to divine everything he could possibly want before he asked for it, and contrived to have it waiting his pleasure as if by magic; and yet it was done so quietly, that I believe Harry had not a notion to whom he was indebted for the forestalment of his every wish. Did his lips appear parched and dry from the low fever which still hung about him—unobserved by anyone, Fanny would glide out of the room, and in another minute his servant would enter with a tray, containing jelly, lemonade, or some refreshment of a like nature; and Harry would say, with a languid smile, that the fairies must have been at work, for that Wilson had brought him the very thing he was wishing for. As he grew stronger, and required less attention, I yielded to his request, and once more resumed my studies, reading doubly hard in order to make up for lost time. The duel had taken place early in June, but it was not until the latter end of August that the surgeons could allow of their patient's removal to the Hall. Under Ellis's directions a kind of litter was prepared, drawn by a stout Shetland pony, and hung upon a complicated arrangement of springs, by which means all possibility of jolting was avoided. With the assistance of this vehicle, Harry was enabled to take short airings in the park, and when it was found that no ill effects ensued, a fine day was chosen, and Heathfield Hall flung wide its ample gates to receive once more within its walls the heir of that noble property. It was a glad day for everyone—the old servants shed mingled tears of joy and sorrow; of joy that their young master had been spared to come among them again, and of sorrow when they gazed on his pallid cheeks and long thin hands, and thought of the amount of suffering that manly frame must have undergone, ere it could have become such a wreck of its former self.

After his return home, Oaklands progressed very slowly; he so far recovered as to walk about the house and garden with the assistance of Ellis's arm; but the wound in his side still presented an unsatisfactory appearance, and obstinately refused to heal. Ellis's skill and attention were unparalleled; he took the greatest interest in the case, and though he pretended that his zeal was entirely professional, yet it was clear the fascination which Harry seemed unconsciously to exercise over everyone who became intimate with him, had subdued even the sturdy doctor, and that he had conceived the strongest affection for his patient.

The only one of the party on whom the fatigue and anxiety appeared to have produced any lasting effect was dear little Fanny, and she continued to look much more pale and thin than I liked to see her. Her spirits, also, seemed less gay and buoyant than usual, and when Sir John and Harry left us, and she had no longer any motive for exertion, a kind of languor came over her, producing a listless

distaste for all her former employments; and she would sit for hours
pouring over one of the Italian poets, without exchanging a word with
anyone. In order, if possible, to rouse her from this state of apathy,
I used every means in my power to interest and amuse her; but unfortunately, my time was now so fully occupied that I had little leisure
to bestow upon her. I was to take my degree at the commencement
of the new year; and as I had made up my mind to try for honours, I
had not a moment to lose, and read eight hours a day. The rest of
my time was devoted to Sir John and Harry (save an odd hour or two
for a constitutional scamper with my gun through the preserves to keep
down the rabbits, or a gallop across country, to prevent the hunters
from getting too fat), and our kind friends were never so pleased
as when they could persuade us all to come to them. My sister, however, seemed to prefer dreaming over her book to the exertion of
accompanying us to the Hall, and even when she did so, appeared
unequal to the labour of amusing Harry, and devoted herself to
the more easy task of pleasing Sir John, who, happy beyond
expression in the prospect of his son's recovery, was in the
highest good-humour with everybody and everything. Becoming
at length far from satisfied about Fanny, I mentioned my
uneasiness to my mother, who comforted me by the assurance
that she considered it merely the natural consequences of the
fatigue and anxiety she had undergone, a sort of reaction of the
spirits, for which time and rest would prove the most effectual
cure.

And once again the leaves upon the trees grew brown, presenting,
in their varied richness, those exquisite shades of colouring that
gladden a painter's eye—and the swallows, those summer parasites,
taking alarm at the first sharp blast from the north, had departed to
prosecute their annual pursuit of sunshine under difficulties, leaving
the honest robin redbreast to renew his friendship with the race of
men—when I, dissatisfied and anxious about those I was leaving
behind me, and nervous in the highest degree as to the result of the
struggle for distinction in which I was about to engage, once more
took up my abode at Trinity.

CHAPTER XXIX.

THE STRUGGLE IN CHESTERTON MEADOW.

"Men
Put forth their sons to seek preferment out.
Some to the studious universities,
For any or for all these exercises."
" Stand, sir, and throw us that you have about you ;
If not, we'll make you sit, and rifle you."
" A rescue ! a rescue ! Good people bring a rescue or two !"
" Construe me, art thou a gentleman ? What is thy name ? Discuss !"
Shakespeare.

HAVING now no one to interfere with me I determined to read as
hard as my powers, mental and bodily, would allow, so as to give my
talents, be they great or small, full scope, and endeavour to evince my
gratitude to my unknown benefactor in the only manner that lay
open to me, i.e. by proving to him that his liberality had not been
thrown away. As the men began to come up, I took care to let it be
generally known among my friends that I was reading steadily and
in earnest, with a view of going out in honours; and when they
became convinced that this was the case, and that whenever I " sported
oak " there was positively " no admittance," they left me to my fate,
as one who, in the words of Lawless, " having strayed from the paths
of virtue and—eh ! what do you call it ?—jollity—had fallen a victim
to the vice of mathematics : not a hope of recovery—a regular case
of hydrostatics on the brain—eh ! don't you see ? "

Besides the regular college tutor, I secured the assistance of what,
in the slang of the day, we irreverently termed " a coach," which
vehicle, for the conveyance of heavy learning (from himself to his
pupils), consisted of a gentleman, who but a few years older than those
whom he taught, possessed more practical knowledge, and a greater
aptitude for the highest scientific research, than it had ever before
been my fate to meet with combined in any one individual. Under
his able tuition I advanced rapidly, and reading men began to look
upon me as a somewhat formidable rival. Several of my opponents,
however, were men of first-rate talent, whose powers of mind, as I
could not for a moment disguise from myself, were infinitely superior
to my own, and with whom my only chance of competing successfully would be by the exercise of indefatigable perseverance and
industry. Daylight, therefore (which at this season did not make
its appearance over early), found me book in hand, and midnight
saw me still seated at my desk—sometimes with a wet towel bound
round my head to cool the throbbing of my heated brow ; at others,
with a teapot of strong green tea by my side, to arouse and stimulate

o

my wearied faculties; conventional specifics, of which, by the way, I very quickly discovered the fallacy.

A fear of completely knocking up, however, induced me to preserve some little method in my madness. I laid down a rule to walk for a couple of hours every day, and thus, although I grew pale and thin, no very dangerous effects appeared likely to ensue from my exertions.

One evening, about a week before the examinations were to begin, I was taking my usual constitutional after Hall; and, careless which way I turned my steps, crossed the river at Moore's, and followed the footpath which led over the fields to the village of Chesterton. There had been a cattle fair at some place in the neighbourhood, which had drawn together a number of disreputable characters, and in the course of my walk, I passed two or three parties of rather suspicious-looking men. Having nothing valuable about me, however, I continued my walk. I had advanced some half-mile or more when I was aroused from my meditations by a cry of "Thieves! thieves! help! hoy! thieves, I say!" accompanied by the noise of blows. When these sounds first reached me I was close to a hedge and stile, across which the footpath led, and from the farther side of which the cries proceeded. It was growing dark, but there still remained light enough to distinguish objects at a moderate distance. To bound over the stile and cast my eyes around was the work of a moment, nor was I much longer in taking part in an affray which was going on.

The person whose cries I had heard was a stout little man, respectably dressed, who was defending himself vigorously with what seemed in the twilight a club, but which turned out eventually to be an umbrella, against the attacks of a tall, strapping fellow, in a rough frieze coat, who was endeavouring to wrest his weapon from him. A still more formidable adversary was, however, approaching in the shape of a second ruffian, who had armed himself with a thick stake out of the hedge, and was creeping cautiously up behind the shorter man, with the evident intention of knocking him on the head. I instantly determined to frustrate his benevolent design, nor was there much time to lose, if I wished my assistance to prove of much avail. Shouting, therefore, as well to intimidate the scoundrels as to let the person attacked know that there was succour at hand, I sprang upon the man who held the cudgel, and seizing his uplifted arm, succeeded in averting the coming blow from the head of the intended victim, who, ignorant of the impending danger, was making most furious thrusts at his assailant with the point of his umbrella, a novel mode of attack, which seemed to perplex and annoy that individual in no small degree.

I had, however, but little time allowed me to make observations, as the fellow with whom I had interfered, as soon as he perceived that he had only an unarmed man to deal with, appeared determined not to give up his hopes of plunder without a struggle, and freeing his

wrist by a powerful jerk, he aimed a blow at me with the bludgeon. which, had it taken effect, would at once have ended all my anxieties. and brought this veracious history to an abrupt and untimely conclusion. Fortunately, however, for "my gentle public" and their humble servant, I was able, by dodging on one side, to avoid the stroke; and seeing that matters had now become serious, I closed with him, and, after a short but severe struggle, had the satisfaction of depositing him flat on his back on the greensward. As he fell he dropped his stick, of which I immediately possessed myself, and planting my foot upon his chest to prevent his rising. I turned to see how the other combatants were getting on. Dame Fortune had not. in this instance, acted up to her usual principle of favouring the brave, for the hero of the umbrella, having struggled gallantly for the preservation of his property and person, had apparently at length been overpowered, and, when I turned towards him, was lying on the ground, while his assailant was endeavouring to rifle his pockets, a matter which was rendered anything but easy of accomplishment by reason of the energetic kicks and struggles of the fallen warrior. It was clear that if I would not have the unfortunate little man robbed before my very eyes. I must go to his assistance. Giving, therefore, my prostrate foe a tap on the head with the stake, by way of a hint to lie still. I advanced to the rescue with uplifted weapon. No sooner did the rascal perceive my approach, than. quitting the fallen man, he sprang up and without waiting to be attacked. took to his heels and ran off as fast as his legs would carry him, an example which his companion, seeing the coast clear, hastened to emulate.

My first act, as soon as the thieves had departed, was to assist the old gentleman to rise. As soon as he was on his legs again he shook himself, as if to ascertain that he was uninjured, and exclaimed,—

"Umph! they're gone, are they? the scoundrels, high time they should, I think; where's my umbrella? umph! second I've lost this year—just like me."

The voice, the manner, but, above all, the emphatic grunts and the final self-accusing soliloquy, "just like me," could proceed but from one person, my old Helmstone acquaintance, Mr. Frampton; though by what strange chance he should be found wandering by owl-light in a meadow near Cambridge passed my comprehension to conceive. Feeling secure from the alteration which had taken place in me since I had last seen him—an alteration rendered still more complete by my academical costume—that he would be unable to recognize me, I determined to amuse myself a little at his expense before I made myself known to him. In pursuance of this plan I picked up his umbrella and handed it to him, saying in an assumed voice, as I did so, "Here is your umbrella, sir."

"Thank ye, young man, thank ye—cost five-and-twenty shillings last Friday week; umph! might have got a cotton one for less than one quarter of the money, that would have done just as well to thump thieves with—a fool and his money—just like me, umph!"

" I hope you are not injured by your fall, or by the rough treatment you have been subjected to ? " inquired I.

" Umph! injured ? " was the reply ; " I've got a great bump on the
back of my head, and burst all the buttons off my waistcoat—I don't
know whether you call that being injured ; but I can tell you I got
away from the Thugs at Strangleabad without any such injuries :
umph ! "

" It was fortunate that I happened to come up just when I did,"
observed I.

" Umph! glad you think so," was the answer ; " if that stick had
come down upon your skull, as the blackguard meant it to do, you
would not have found it quite so fortunate, I've a notion. Umph !
all the same, I'm much obliged to you ; I might have been robbed
and murdered too, if it had not been for you, young man, and if
you'll walk home with me to the Hoop—there's a name for an inn !—
I'll give you a couple of sovereigns, and that's more than you've
earned before to-day, I'll be bound—umph ! "

" I shall be delighted to see you safe home, sir, but you will excuse
my declining your pecuniary offer, though I must plead guilty to the
charge of not having earned as much—I believe I might say, in my
whole life before."

" Umph ! I see—a gentleman, eh ? and I to offer him money—just
like me—a lord or a duke, I shouldn't wonder—there are all sorts and
sizes of 'em here, they tell me—ask him to dinner. Umph ! perhaps
you'll do me the honour of dining with me, young man—my lord, I
mean,—mulligatawny—cat smothered in rice, which they call curry—
kibobs and kickshaws—the cook is not so bad for a white ; but you
should go to India if you care about eating—that's the place for
cookery, sir."

" I shall have much pleasure in accepting your invitation," replied
I, " if you will allow me to run away directly after dinner : I am
reading for my degree, and time is precious with me just now."

" Umph ! so it should be always. I see, now I come to look at you,
you are one of the cap and gown gentlemen." (Then came an aside :
" Cap, indeed ! it's a fool's cap would fit one half of 'em best !")
" Pray, may I ask what college you belong to, Mr. —— ? "

" Legh is my name, sir—Legh of Trinity."

" Umph! Trinity ; just the man I wanted to get hold of. My
name's Frampton, Mr. Lee : they know me well at the India House,
sir. When we've had a bit of dinner, and washed this horrid fog out
of our throats with a few glasses of wine, I shall be glad to ask you a
question or two. Umph ! "

" Any information it may be in my power to afford you—" I began.

" That'll do, sir, that'll do," was the reply. " Perhaps you won't be
quite so ready when you hear what it is I want." Then, in an undertone : "Tell me a parcel of lies, most likely ; I know how these
young scamps hang by one another, and think it high fun ' to do the
governor,' as they call it. Umph ! "

On our arrival at the Hoop, we were ushered into one of the best sitting-rooms the inn afforded, where a blazing fire soon effaced all traces of the wet-blanket-like fog in which we had been so lately enveloped. I was shown into a comfortable dressing-room to get ready for dinner, an opportunity of which I availed myself to render my appearance as unlike what it had been in former days as circumstances would allow, before again subjecting myself to Mr. Frampton's scrutiny. For this purpose, I combed my hair back from my face as far as possible, and brushed my whiskers—an acquisition of which I had only lately become possessed—as prominently forward as the growth of the crop permitted. I poked my shirt-collar entirely out of sight, and tied my black neckcloth stiffly up under my chin, and finally buttoned my coat, so as to show off the breadth of my chest and shoulders to the greatest advantage. Thus accoutred, and drawing myself up to my full height, I hastened to rejoin Mr. Frampton. My arrangements seemed thoroughly to have answered their purpose, for he gazed at me without evincing the slightest symptom of recognition. He shook me by the hand, however, and thanked me more cordially than he had yet done for the assistance rendered him, and then rang for dinner. The bill of fare embraced all the Asiatic luxuries he had enumerated, to which, on the strength of having invited a guest, sundry European dishes were added ; and with appetites sharpened by our recent adventures, we did full justice to the good cheer that was set before us.

CHAPTER XXX.

MR. FRAMPTON'S INTRODUCTION TO A TIGER.

"Had I been seized by a hungry *tiger*,
I should have been a breakfast to the beast."
Shakespeare.
" He started
Like one who sees a spectre, and exclaimed,
Blind that I was to know him not till now ! "
Southey.
" Go to, you are a counterfeit knave ! "—*Shakespeare.*

" I HOPE you feel no ill effects from your adventure, sir : you resisted the fellow's attack most spiritedly, and would have beaten him off, I believe, if you had possessed a more serviceable weapon than an umbrella," observed I to Mr. Frampton, as we drew our chairs to the fire after dinner.

" Umph ! all right, sir, all right : a little stiff or so across the back.

but not so bad as the tiger at Bundleapoor. I'm not as young as I
used to be, and there's a difference between young men and old ones.
Young men are all whalebone and whipcord, and it's nothing but
hopping, skipping, and jumping with them all day long; when you're
turned of sixty-five, sir, the whalebone gets stiff, the whipcord wears
out, the skip and jump take their departure, and the hop becomes
an involuntary accompaniment to the rheumatism—confound it!
Umph!"

"You have been in India, I presume; I think I heard you refer to
some adventure with a tiger," returned I.

"I've been everywhere, sir—north, south, east, and west. I ran
away from school at twelve years old, because the master chose to
believe one of the ushers rather than me, and flogged me for lying
when I had spoken the truth. I ran away, sir, and got aboard a ship
that was bound for the East Indies, and for five-and-forty years I
never saw the white cliffs of Old England; and when I did return,
I might as well have left it alone, for all who knew and cared for me
were dead and gone—all dead and gone—dead and gone!" he
repeated, in a tone of sorrowful earnestness. Then came an aside:
"Umph! wonder what I told him that for; something for him to go
and make fun of with other young scapegraces, instead of minding
their books: just like me!"

"You must have seen many strange things, and met with various
adventures worthy of note, in the course of your wanderings,"
remarked I.

"I must have been a fool if I hadn't," was the answer. "P'rhaps
you think I was—umph! Young folks always think old ones fools,
they say."

"Finish the adage, sir, that old folks know young ones to be so,
and then agree with me that it is a saying founded on prejudice, and
at variance with truth."

"Umph! strong words, young gentleman, strong words! I will
agree with you so far, that there are old fools as well as young ones
—old fools, who in their worldly wisdom stigmatize the generous
impulses and warm affections of youth as folly, who may yet live to
regret the feelings they have crushed, and the affections they have
alienated, and find out that the things which they deemed folly may
prove in the end the truest wisdom." Then came the soliloquy:
"There I go again—just like me! something else for him to laugh
at; don't think he will, though—seems a good lad—wish t'other boy
may be like him—umph!" He paused for a moment, and then
observed abruptly, "Umph! about that tiger at Bundleapoor.
You call to-night's an adventure, sir: wonder what you'd have said
if you'd been there!"

"As I was not, would it be asking too great a favour, if I request
you to relate the anecdote?"

"Ay, boy, ay, I see you know how to come round an old traveller:
set him gossiping about all the fine things he has seen and done in

his younger days, and you win his heart at once. Well, fill your glass, sir, and we'll see about it," was the reply.

I obeyed, Mr. Frampton followed my example, and after sipping his wine, and grunting several times to clear his throat, began the following recital :—

"Umph! ha! let me recollect. When I was a young shaver, having lived in the world some twenty years or so, I was engaged as a sort of supernumerary clerk in the house of Wilson and Brown at Calcutta; and, having no one else who could be so easily spared, they determined to despatch me on a business negotiation to one of the native princes, about eight hundred miles up the country. I travelled with a party of the —— Dragoons, commanded by a Captain Slingsby, a man about five years older than myself, and as good a fellow as ever lived. Well, somehow or other, he took a great fancy to me, and nothing would do but that I should accompany him in all his sporting expeditions—for I should tell you that he was a thorough sportsman, and, I believe, entertained some wild notion that he should be able to make one of me. One unfortunate morning he came into my tent, and woke me out of a sound sleep into which I had fallen, after being kept awake half the night by the most diabolical howls and screams that ever were heard out of Bedlam, expecting every minute to see some of the performers step in to sup, not with, but upon me.

"'Come, Frampton, wake up, man!' cried Slingsby; 'here's great and glorious news.'

"'What is it?' said I—'have they found another hamper of ale among the baggage?'

"'Ale! nonsense!' was the reply. 'A shikkaree (native hunter) has just come into camp to say that a young bullock was carried off yesterday, and is lying half eaten in the jungle about a mile from this place; so at last, my boy, I shall have the pleasure of introducing you to a real live tiger.'

"'Thank ye,' said I, 'you're very kind; but if it's at all inconvenient to you this morning you can put it off: another day will do quite as well for me—I'm not in the least hurry.'

"It was of no use, however; all I got for my pains was a poke in the ribs, and an injunction to lose no time in getting ready.

"Before we had done breakfast the great man of the neighbourhood, Rajah somebody or other, made his appearance on his elephant attended by a train of tawnies, who were to undertake the agreeable duty of beating. Not being considered fit to take care of myself—a melancholy fact of which I was only too conscious—it was decreed that Slingsby and I should occupy the same howdah. Accordingly, at the time appointed, we mounted our elephant; and having a formidable array of guns handed up to us, we started.

"As my companion, and, indeed, everyone else concerned in the matter, evidently considered it completely as a party of pleasure, and seemed prepared to enjoy themselves to the utmost, I endeavoured to persuade myself that I did so too; and, consoled by the reflection that if the tiger had positively eaten half a bullock yesterday afternoon, it never could be worth his while to scale our elephant, and run the risk of being shot, for the sake of devouring me, I felt rather bold than otherwise. After proceeding for some distance through the jungle, and rousing, as it seemed to me, every beast that had come out of Noah's Ark, except a tiger, our elephant, who had hitherto conducted himself in a very quiet and gentlemanly manner, suddenly raised his trunk, and trumpeted several times—a sure sign, as the mahout informed us, that a tiger was somewhere close at hand.

"'Now then, Frampton,' cried my companion, cocking his double-barrel, 'look out!'

"'For squalls,' returned I, finishing the sentence for him. 'Pray, is there any particular part they like to be shot in? whereabouts shall I aim?'

"'Wherever you can,' replied Slingsby; 'be ready—there he is, by Jupiter!' and, as he spoke, the long grass about a hundred yards in front of us was gently agitated, and I caught a glimpse of what appeared a yellow and black streak, moving swiftly away in an opposite direction. 'Tally-ho!' shouted Slingsby, saluting the tiger with both barrels. An angry roar proved that the shots had taken effect, and in another moment a large tiger, lashing his sides with his tail and his eyes glaring with rage, came bounding towards us.

"'Now what's to be done?' exclaimed I—'if you had but left him alone, he was going away as quietly as possible.'

"Slingsby's only reply was a smile, and seizing another gun, he fired again. On receiving this shot the tiger stopped for a moment, and then, with a tremendous bound, sprang towards us, alighting at the foot of a small tree, not a yard from the elephant's head.

"'That last shot crippled him,' said my companion, 'or we should have had the pleasure of his nearer acquaintance. Now for the "coup de grace"—fire away!' and as he spoke he leaned forward to take a deliberate aim, when suddenly the front of the howdah gave way, and to my horror Slingsby was precipitated over the elephant's head, into, as it seemed to me, the very jaws of the tiger. A fierce growl and a suppressed cry of agony proved that the monster had seized his prey; and I had completely given up my friend for lost, when the elephant, although greatly alarmed, being urged on by the mahout, took a step forward, and twisting his trunk round the top of the young tree, bent it down across the loins of the tiger, thus forcing the tortured animal to quit his hold, and affording Slingsby an opportunity of crawling beyond the reach of its teeth and claws. Forgetting my own fears in the imminence of my friend's danger, I only waited till I could get a shot at the tiger, without running the risk of hurting Slingsby, and then fired both barrels at its head, and was lucky enough to wound it mortally. The other sportsmen coming up at that moment, the brute received its quietus, but poor

Slingsby's arm was broken where the tiger had seized it with its teeth, and his shoulders and chest were severely lacerated by its claws, nor did he entirely recover the shock for many months.[1] And this was my first introduction to a royal tiger, sir. I saw many of 'em afterwards, during the time I spent in India, but I can't say I ever had much liking for their society—umph!"

This anecdote brought others in its train—minutes flew by apace, the wine grew low in the decanters, and it became apparent to me that if I would not lose the whole evening, and go home with my brains muddled beyond all possibility of reading, I must take my departure. Accordingly, pulling out my watch, I reminded Mr. Frampton of my previous stipulation to be allowed to run away as soon as dinner was concluded, adding that I had already stayed longer than was altogether prudent. The reply to this announcement was, "Umph! sit still, sir, sit still; I'm going to ring for another bottle of port."

Finding, however, that I was determined, he gave up the point, adding: "Umph! well, if you must go, you must, I suppose—though you might refuse a worse offer; but, if you really are anxious about your studies and wish to distinguish yourself, I won't be the man to hinder you—it's few enough of 'em are like you here, I expect;" then, sotto voce, "Wish t'other young monkey might be."

"You hinted before dinner at some information I might be able to give you?" said I, interrogatively.

"Umph! did I?—ay, so I did—you see. Mr. Lee, there's a young fellow at Trinity, about your age I should fancy, whom I used to know as a boy—and—he was a very good boy—and—and—his mother's a widow; poor thing—a very nice boy, I may say, he was— and as I feel a sort of interest about him I thought that you might, perhaps, give one an idea of how he's going on—just a notion—you understand—umph!"

"Exactly, sir," returned I. "and what may be the name of your friend?"

"Frank Fairlegh," was the answer.

"You could not have applied to a better person," replied I. "Frank Fairlegh!—why, he was one of my most intimate friends."

"Was—umph!"

"Why, yes, it's more was than is, certainly—for since I've been reading hard. it's a positive fact that I've scarcely seen his face."

"That looks as if he wasn't over-fond of reading, then, eh?— umph!"

"You may put that interpretation upon it, certainly," replied I, "but mind, I don't say it's the true one. I consider it would not be right in me to tell tales out of school; besides, there's nothing to tell —everybody knows Frank Fairlegh's a good fellow—ask Lawless— ask Curtis."

[1] The main facts of the foregoing anecdote are taken from Capt. Mundy's very interesting "Pen and Pencil Sketches."

"Umph! Lawless? what? that wild young scamp who goes tearing about the country in a tandem, as if a gig with one horse wasn't
dangerous enough, without putting on a second to make the thing
positively terrific? he must be badly off for something to do if he
can find no better amusement than trying how nearly he can break a
fool's neck, without doing it quite;—umph! Curtis, why, that's the
name of the young gentleman—very gentle—who, the landlord tells
me, has just been rusticated for insulting Dr. Doublechin. and
fastening a muzzle and chain on one of the men they call 'bull-dogs,'
saying, forsooth, that it wasn't safe to let such ferocious animals go
about loose—nice acquaintance Mr. Frank Fairlegh seems to choose,
and you know the quotation, 'Noscitur a sociis.'"

"Oh," replied I, "but he has others; I have seen him in company
with Mr. Wilford."

"Wilford? the noted duellist, that scoundrel who has lately shot
the son of Sir John Oaklands, as fine a young man as ever I set eyes
upon?—for I have often seen him when I was living at Helmstone;
if I thought, sir, that Fairlegh was a friend of that man—I'd—I'd—
well, sir," he exclaimed, seeing my eyes fixed upon him with a degree
of interest I could not conceal, "it's nothing to you, I suppose, what
I may intend to do by Mr. Frank Fairlegh! I may be his grand-
father for anything you can tell to the contrary; and I may choose to
cut him off with a shilling, I imagine, without its affecting you in any
way—umph!"

"Scarcely so, Mr. Frampton," replied I, turning away to hide an
irrepressible smile, "if it is in consequence of what I have told you
that you are angry with poor Frank."

"Angry, sir, angry"—was the answer—"I'm never angry—there's
nothing worth being angry about in this world. Do you take snuff,
sir? I've some that came from—umph! eh!" he continued, fumbling
in all his pockets—"hope I haven't lost my box—given me by the
Begum of Cuddleakee—splendid woman—only complexion too strong
of the tawny—umph! left it in the other room, I suppose—back in a
moment, sir—umph! umph!" and suiting the action to the word, he
went out, slamming the door behind him.

As the reader may suppose, I was equally surprised and pleased to
find that my old friend not only remembered our former intimacy,
but felt so warm an interest in my welfare as to have put himself
quite in a rage on hearing of my supposed delinquencies. Although
it had been the means of eliciting such strong indications of his continued regard for me, I felt half sorry for the deception I had
practised upon him—the only thing that could be done now, however,
was to make myself known to him without delay, and his absence
from the room enabled me to put in practice a plan for doing so
which I had had in my mind all along. Accordingly, going up to the
chimney-glass I shook my hair forward, so that it fell in waving curls
about my face and forehead—took the stiffener out of my neckcloth,
and, knotting the latter closely round my throat, turned down my

shirt-collar so as to resemble as nearly as possible the Byron-tie of my
boyhood—then unbuttoning and throwing open my coat I resumed
my seat, arranging the candles so as to throw the light full upon my
face as I did so. I had scarcely completed my arrangements when I
heard Mr. Frampton's footstep in the passage, and in another
moment he entered the room. "All right, Mr. Lee, all right, sir; I
found the box in my other coat-pocket; I was afraid the thieves
might have forestalled me; but—umph!—eh!—why?—who?"
Catching sight of me as he spoke, he stopped short, and shading his
eyes with his hand, gazed earnestly at me, with a look half
bewildered, half incredulous. Taking advantage of his silence I
inquired in my natural tone and manner whether he had seen Dr.
Mildman lately.

"Umph! eh! Dr. Mildman?" was the reply—"why, it can't be—
and yet it is—the boy Frank Fairlegh himself! Oh! you young
villain!" and completely overcome by the sudden and unexpected
nature of the surprise he sank back into a chair, looking the picture
of astonishment.

Springing to his side, and pressing his hand warmly between my
own, I exclaimed, "Forgive me for the trick I have played you, sir.
I knew you the moment I heard your voice, when I was helping you
up to-night, and, finding you did not recognize me, I could not resist
the temptation of preserving my incognito a little longer, and introducing myself as a stranger."

"Oh, you young scapegrace!" was the rejoinder, "if ever I forgive
you, I'll—umph!—that I will"—then changing his tone to one of
much feeling, he continued, "So you hadn't forgotten the old man,
then, Frank? good boy, good boy."

I had seated myself on a stool at his feet, and as he spoke he patted
my head with his hand, as if I had been a favourite dog.

"And all the things you said against yourself were so many lies,
I suppose? Umph! you are no friend to the homicide Wilford?"

"True to the ear, but false to the sense, sir," replied I. "Harry
Oaklands is the dearest friend I have on earth; we love each other
as brothers—between the man whose hand was so lately raised to
shed that brother's blood and myself, there can be little friendship—
if I do not positively hate him, it is only because I would not willingly
hate anyone. Lawless was an old fellow-pupil of mine, and, though
he has many follies about him, is at bottom more kind-hearted and
well-disposed than people give him credit for; we still continue
friends, therefore, but our habits and pursuits being essentially
different, I see very little of him—with Curtis I never exchanged half
a dozen words in my life."

"Umph! I understand, I understand; and how is Harry Oaklands?
better again, eh?"

The reply to this query led to my being obliged to give Mr. Frampton a succinct account of the duel, and it was not till I explained my intention of trying for honours, and made him comprehend the necessity

of my being fully prepared for the ensuing examination, that he would
hear of my departure; and when at last he did allow me to go, he insisted
on accompanying me to the gate of Trinity, and made me promise to
let him see me as often as I was able during his stay in Cambridge,
where, he informed me, he proposed remaining till after the degrees
were conferred.

CHAPTER XXXI.

HOW I RISE A DEGREE, AND MR. FRAMPTON GETS ELEVATED IN MORE WAYS THAN ONE.

> "This is as strange a thing as e'er I looked on."
>> *The Tempest.*
> "These news, my lords, may cheer our drooping spirits."
>> *Henry VI.*
> "And liquor, likewise, will I give to thee,
> And friendship shall combine, and brotherhood."
>> *Henry V.*

THE week passed away like a dream, and with a beating heart and
throbbing pulse I went through the various examinations, and
engaged with my competitors in the struggle for honours. Anxious
in the highest degree as to the result of my labours, I scarcely ate,
drank, or slept, and, had the necessity for exertion been protracted
much longer, my mind could not have borne the continued strain, and
I should probably have had a brain fever. It was the eventful Friday
morning on which the list was to come out, and in the course of an
hour or two my fate would be known. Utterly worn out by a night
which anxiety had rendered sleepless, I had hastily swallowed a cup
of tea, and, turning away from the untasted eatables, flung myself,
wrapped in a dressing-gown, on the sofa. I had not, however, lain
there above a quarter of an hour, when a tap was heard at the door,
and Mr. Frampton made his appearance, attired as usual in the well-
remembered blue coat with brass buttons, drab shorts, and gaiters,
with the broad-brimmed hat, lined with green, fixed sturdily on his
head, as if it was made to take off at any time.

"Umph! found my way up, you see! Fellow you call the gyp
wanted to make me believe you were out—thought I looked too like
a governor to be let in, I suppose; but it wouldn't do, sir: old birds
are not to be caught with chaff; and he spoke with an air of such
intense honesty that I felt sure he was lying, and told him so. Don't
get up, boy, don't get up; you look as jaded as a hunted antelope.

Why, you've never touched your breakfast; you'll kill yourself if you go on at this rate."

" It will not last much longer, sir," said I ; " in about another hour or so my fate will be known. The list comes out this morning. Some of my friends were to call for me, and we were to make a party to go down to the Senate House together, for there is sure to be a crowd ; but I shall let them go without me, for I'm in such a state of nervous anxiety that I feel fit for nothing."

" Umph ! I'll go with them if they've no objection," returned Mr. Frampton. " If I should happen to get knocked over in the scuffle, I shall want somebody to pick me up again. I shall like to see how near the tail of the list they stick your name, Frank—umph ! "

At this moment the door was flung open, and Lawless, Archer, and one or two more men of my acquaintance came tumbling over one another into the room, laughing vociferously at some unknown jest. Owing to the shape of the apartment, the place where Mr. Frampton had seated himself was not easily to be seen as you entered, consequently none of them observed him.

" Fairlegh, old boy—" began Archer.

" Eh ! here's such a tremendous go ! " broke in Lawless. " Where's the smelling-bottle ? Archer swears he has just seen the ghost of Noah's great-grandfather, as he appeared when dressed in his Sunday clothes ! "

" 'Pon my word, it's true, and what will you lay it's a lie ? " sang Archer. " Oh! if you had but seen him, Fairlegh ; he looked like— hang me if I know anything ugly enough to compare him to."

" Was he at all like me, sir ?—umph ! " inquired Mr. Frampton in his gruffest tone, putting on the broad-brimmed hat, rising slowly from his seat as he spoke.

" The very apparition itself, by Jingo ! " exclaimed Archer, starting back in alarm, half real, half affected, thereby nearly overturning Lawless, who was just behind him.

" Hold hard there, young fellow; where are you jibbing to? You'll smash my panels in a minute, if you don't look out—eh ?— why, surely it's the old boy from Helmstone," continued Lawless, aside ; " Mr. Frampton—sir, your most obedient."

" Same to you, sir," was the reply ; " glad to see your spirits don't seem likely to fail you, Mr. Lawless—laughing at me, all of 'em, impudent young dogs—what's t'other one's name, Frank, the one that took me for a ghost—umph ! "

" Allow me to introduce you—Mr. Frampton, Mr. Archer, Mr. Green, Mr. Lacy, Mr. Richards."

The individuals named delivered themselves of a series of nods and jerks as I pronounced their various patronymics, and Mr. Frampton took off his hat, and made a polite bow to each man separately ; then turning to Archer, he said,—

" Pray, sir, may I inquire when and how you became so intimate with Noah's great-grandfather as to mistake me for him—umph ! "

" Well, sir," said Archer, who was evidently taken somewhat aback
by this direct appeal, " it is an affair—that is, a circumstance—what
I mean to say is—the thing, as you must see, was completely—in fact,
it was quite by accident, and promiscuously, so to speak, that I mis-
took you for the respectable antediluvian—I should say, for his
ghost."

" Umph ! don't think I look much like a ghost, either. Not that
there are such things in reality ; all humbug, sir. A man goes and eats
beef and pudding enough for two, has the nightmare, fancies next
morning he has seen a ghost, and the first fool he tells it to believes
him. Well, Mr. Lawless, not made a ghost of yourself by breaking your neck out of that Infernal Machine of yours yet. Get
his ex-majesty Louis Philippe to go out for a ride with you in that,
and his life would be in greater danger than all the Fieschis in
France could ever put it in. Umph ! "

" The horses are in first-rate condition," returned Lawless,
" enough to pull a fellow's arms off till they've done about ten miles ;
that takes the steel out of them a bit, and then a child may guide
them. Happy to take you a drive, Mr. Frampton, any time that
suits you—eh ? "

" Thank ye, sir, when the time comes I'll let you know; but I hope
to live a few years longer yet, and therefore you'll excuse my not
accepting your kind offer. Besides, if Mr. Archer was to see the
ghost of Noah's great-grandfather in a tandem, he'd never get over
it." Then came the aside : " Umph ! had him there, the young
jackanapes."

" Well, Fairlegh, are you coming with us ? " asked Lacy ; " the
list must be out by this time."

" No ; 'pon my word I can't," replied I. " I'm good for nothing
this morning."

" Serve you right, too," said Lawless, " for refusing the second
bowl of punch last night. I told you no good would come of it,
eh ? "

" Positively we ought to be going," interposed Richards ; " we'll
bring you some news presently, Fairlegh, that will set you all right
again in no time."

" I only wish you may prove a true prophet," replied I.

" Umph ! if you'll allow me, I'll accompany you, gentlemen," said
Mr. Frampton : " make one of your party, umph ! "

Several of those thus appealed to exchanged glances of horror, and
at last Archer, who was rather an exclusive, and particularly sensitive
to ridicule, began,—

" Why, really, sir, you must excuse—"

" Umph ! excuse ? no excuses required, sir ; when you've lived as
long as I have, you'll learn not to care in what company you sail
so as it's honest company. Noah's great-grandfather found out
the truth of that, sir, when he had to be hail-fellow-well-met with
tiger-cats and hippopotamuses in the ark—hippopotami, I suppose

you classical men call it—though, now I come to think of it, he never was there at all. But you will let an old man go with you, there's good boys," continued Mr. Frampton in a tone of entreaty; "not one of you feels more interest in Frank Fairlegh's success than I do."

"Come along, governor," exclaimed Lawless, taking him by the arm, "you and I will go together, and if anybody gets in your way, down he goes, if he were as big as Goliath of Gath. You shall see the list as soon as anyone of them, for you're a trump—a regular brick!"

"With a very odd tile on the top of it," whispered Archer, pointing to the broad brim.

"Now, then," continued Lawless, "fall in there. Follow the governor. To the right about face! March!"

So saying, he flung open the door, and arm-in-arm with Mr. Frampton hurried down the stairs, followed by the others in double-quick time. When they were all gone, I made an effort to rouse myself from the state of lassitude and depression into which I had fallen, and succeeded so far as to recover sufficient energy to attempt the labour of dressing, though my hands trembled to such a degree that I could scarcely accomplish it, and was forced to postpone the operation of shaving to some more favourable opportunity.

Having made my outer man respectable, I re-entered the sitting-room, and waited with impatience for the return of my friends. Oh! the horrors of suspense! that toothache of the mind. in which each moment of anxiety, stretched on the rack of expectation, appears to the overwrought senses an eternity of gnawing anguish!—of all the mental tortures with which I am acquainted, defend me from suspense!

I had worked myself up into a thorough fever, and was becoming so excited that I was on the point of rushing out to learn the worst at once, when sundry shouts, mingled with peals of laughter, reached my ear—sounds which assured me that news was at hand. And now, with the inconsistency of human nature, I trembled at and would willingly have delayed my friends' arrival, lest it might bring me the certainty of failure, to which even the doubt and suspense I had been so lately chafing at appeared preferable. The sounds grew louder and louder—they were approaching. Oh! how my heart beat! in another moment they would be here. Sinking into a chair. for my knees trembled so that I could scarcely stand, I remained with my eyes fixed upon the door in a state of breathless anxiety. More shouting! surely that was a cheer—

"Hurrah! hurrah! out of the way there! room for the governor!" —a rush of many feet up the stairs—more cheering—the door is thrown open, and a party of from fifteen to twenty undergraduates come pouring in, with Mr. Frampton in the midst of them, carried in triumph on the shoulders of Lawless and another man, and waving a list in one hand, and the broad-brimmed hat in the other.

"Bravo, Fairlegh; all right, old fellow! never say die! hurrah!"

exclaimed half a score voices all at once, while both my hands were seized and nearly shaken off, and I was almost annihilated by congratulatory slaps on the back from my zealous and excited friends.

" Well," exclaimed I, as soon as I could make myself audible amidst the clamour, " I suppose by your congratulations I'm not plucked, but how high do I stand ? "

" Silence there ! " shouted Lawless. " Order ! order ! hear the governor ; he's got the list. Fire away, sir."

Thus appealed to, Mr. Frampton, who ,was still mounted on the shoulders of his supporters, having cleared his throat and grunted proudly, with an air of majesty read as follows :—

" Rushbrooke, Senior Wrangler—Crosby, second—Barham, third—Fairlegh, fourth ! "

" Nonsense," exclaimed I, springing up, " the thing's impossible ! "

" What an unbelieving Jew it is," said Archer; "hand him the list and let him read it himself. Seeing is believing, they say."

Yes, there it was, beyond the possibility of doubt; with my own eyes did I behold it. " Fairlegh, fourth Wrangler ! " Why, even in my wildest moments of hope my imagination had never taken so high a flight. Fourth Wrangler ! oh ! it was too delightful to be real. So overcome was I by this unexpected stroke of good fortune, that for a minute or two I was scarcely conscious of what was going on around me, and returned rambling and incoherent answers to the congratulations which were showered upon me. The first thing that roused my attention was a shout from Lawless, demanding a hearing, for that " the governor," as he persisted in calling Mr. Frampton, was going to make a speech. The cry was immediately taken up by the others, who for some moments defeated their own purpose by calling vociferously for " silence for the governor's speech ! " Having at length, from sheer want of breath, obtained the required boon, Mr. Frampton, waving his hand with a dignified gesture, began as follows :—

" Umph ! on this happy occasion, gentlemen—set of noisy young scamps !—on this happy occasion, 1 say,—(shouts of Encore ! Bravo ! &c.)—" what I was going to say was—umph ! " (a cry of " You have said it," from a man near the door, who thought he could not be seen, but was). " Much obliged to you, sir, for your observation," continued Mr. Frampton, fixing his glance unmistakably on the Detected One, " but I have not said it, nor does it seem very likely I ever shall say it, if you continue to interrupt me with your wretched attempts at wit." (Cries of " Hear, hear ! don't interrupt the governor ! Shame ! shame ! " and aside from Mr. Frampton, " Had him there, umph ! " during all of which the detected individual was striving to open the door which several men, who had perceived his design, held firmly against him.) " What I was going to say," resumed the speaker, " when that gentleman who is trying to leave the room interrupted me " (more cries of " Shame ! "), " was, that I beg, in the name of my friend, Frank Fairlegh, to invite you all to a champagne breakfast in his rooms to-morrow " (tremendous cheering, and a cry of " Bravo, governor ! you are a brick !" from Lawless), " and in my own name to thank you all, except the gentleman near the door, who has not yet, I see, had the grace to leave the room, for the patience with which you've listened to me " (laughter, and cries of· " It was a shame to interrupt him," at which the Detected One, with a frantic gesture, gives up the door, and turning very pale, glances insanely towards the window), " and for the very flattering attentions which you have all of you generally, and Mr. Archer in particular, done me the honour of paying me."

A perfect tornado of cheers and laughter followed Mr. Frampton's speech, after which I thanked them all for the kind interest they had expressed in my success, and begged to second Mr. Frampton's invitation, for the following day. This matter being satisfactorily arranged, certain of the party laid violent hands on the Detected One, who was a very shy freshman of the name of Pilkington, and, despite his struggles, made him go down on his knees and apologize in set phrase to Mr. Frampton for his late unjustifiable conduct; where· upon that gentleman, who enjoyed the joke and entered into it with as much zest as the veriest pickle among them, sternly, and with many grunts, rebuked and then pardoned him.

The champagne breakfast on the following morning who shall describe! What pen, albeit accustomed to the highest flights im· aginable, may venture to depict the humours of that memorable entertainment! How, when the company were assembled, it was discovered Mr. Pilkington was missing, and a party, headed by Lawless, proceeded to his rooms, which were on the same staircase, and brought him down, " vi et armis," in a state of mind bordering on distraction, picturesquely attired in a dressing-gown, slippers, and smoking-cap, of a decidedly Oriental character ; and how, when they had forced him into a seat of honour at Mr. Frampton's right hand, that gentleman discovered in him a striking likeness to his particular friend the Rajah of Bundleoragbag, which name being instantly adopted by the company, he was invariably addressed by ever after. How, as the champagne circulated, the various members of the party began to come out strong, according to their several idiosyncrasies, every man who had a peculiarity exhibiting it for the benefit of the others; while those who had not were even more amusing, either from their aping the manners of somebody else, or from the sheer absurdity of uttering insipid commonplaces in such an atmosphere of fun and frolic. How, later in the day, after healths had been drunk, and thanks returned, till every one, save Pilkington, was hoarse with shouting, that individual was partly coaxed, partly coerced into attempting to sing the only song he knew, which proved to be " We met; " in which performance, after making four false starts, and causing a great many more meetings to take place than the author of the song ever contemplated, he contrived, in a voice suggestive of a sudden attack of cholera, to get as far as the words

P

"For thou art the cause of this anguish, my mother," when he was interrupted by such a chorus of laughter as completely annihilated him for the rest of the day. How Mr. Frampton, without giving the slightest warning of his intention, or there being anything in the subject of the conversation generally to lead thereunto, began to relate his adventure with the tiger of Bundleapoor; while Lawless favoured the company with a full, true, and particular account of a surprising run with the royal stag hounds; and Archer, who had grown sentimental, with tears in his eyes, entered into a minute detail of certain passages in a romantic attachment he had conceived for a youthful female branch of the aristocracy, whom he designated as Lady Barbara B.; and how these three gentlemen continued their various recitals all at one and the same time, edifying the company by some such composite style of dialogue as the following:—

"So, sir, Slingsby roused me by a kick in the ribs, saying—umph!" —"Fairest, loveliest of thy sex,"—"Shove on your boots and buckskins, stick a cigar in your mouth, and clap your leg over,"—"An elephant half as high again as this room; take a couple of doublebarrelled rifles, and "—"Slap at everything that comes in your way; no craning, ram in the persuaders, and if you do get a purl "—"Look upon it as the purest, brightest gem of your noble father's coronet, for true affection "—"Flung him clean into the tiger's jaws, sir, and the beast "—"Drew her handkerchief across her eyes, and said, with a voice which quivered with emotion, 'Love between two young creatures, situated as we are, would be utter madness, Charles.' To which I replied, 'Barbara, my own sweet girl,'"—"Mind your eye, and look out for squalls, for that's a rasper, and no mistake."

How all this took place, together with much more notable merriment, not many degrees removed from "tipsy mirth and jollity," we will leave to the fertile imagination of the reader to depict. Suffice it to say that, ere we broke up, Mr. Frampton had distinctly pledged himself to ride one of Lawless's horses the next hunting-day, and to accompany Archer on a three weeks' visit to the country seat of Lady Barbara B.'s noble father, with some ulterior views on his own account in regard to a younger sister.

CHAPTER XXXII.

CATCHING SIGHT OF AN OLD FLAME.

" Give me thy hand . . . .
I'm glad to find thee here."
The Lover's Melancholy.

" Half light, half shade,
She stood a sight to make an old man young."
The Gardener's Daughter.

UTTERLY worn out, both in mind and body, by hard reading and confinement, I determined to return to Heathfield forthwith, with "all
my blushing honours thick upon me," and enjoy a few weeks' idleness
before again engaging in any active course of study which might be
necessary to fit me for my future profession. When the post came
in, however, I received a couple of letters which rather militated
against my intention of an immediate return home. A note from
Harry Oaklands informed me that having some weeks ago been
ordered to a milder air, he and Sir John had chosen Clifton, their
decision being influenced by the fact of an old and valued friend of
Sir John's residing there. He begged me to let him hear all the
Cambridge news, and hoped I should join him as soon as Mrs. Fairlegh and my sister would consent to part with me. For himself, he
said, he felt somewhat stronger, but still suffered much from the
wound in his side. The second letter was from my mother, saying
she had received an invitation from an old lady, a cousin of my
father's, who resided in London, and, as she thought change of scene
would do Fanny good, she had accepted it. She had been there
already one week, and proposed returning at the end of the next,
which she hoped would be soon enough to welcome me after the
conclusion of my labours at the University.

Unable to make up my mind whether to remain where I was for a
week longer, or to return and await my mother's arrival at the cottage,
I threw on my cap and gown and strolled out, the fresh air appearing
quite a luxury to me after having been shut up so long. As I passed
through the street where old Maurice the pastrycook lived, I thought
I would call and learn how Lizzie was going on, as I knew Harry
would be anxious for information on this point. On entering the
shop, I was most cordially received by the young lady herself, who
had by this time quite recovered her good looks, and on the present
occasion appeared unusually gay and animated, which was soon
accounted for when her father, drawing me aside, informed me that
she was going to be married to a highly respectable young baker, who
had long ago fallen a victim to her charms, and on whom she had
of late deigned to take pity; the severe lesson she had been taught

having induced her to overlook his intense respectability, high moral
excellence, and round good-natured face—three strong disqualifications, which had stood dreadfully in his way when striving to
render himself agreeable to the romantic Fornarina. I was answering their inquiries after Oaklands, of whom they spoke in terms of
the deepest gratitude, when a young fellow, wrapped up in a rough
pea-jacket, bustled into the shop, and, without perceiving me,
accosted Lizzie as follows :—

"Pray, young lady, can you inform me—what glorious buns !—
where Mr.—that is to say, which of these funny old edifices may
happen to be Trinity College ? "

On receiving the desired information, he continued, "Much obliged.
I really must trouble you for another bun. Made by your own fair
hands, I presume ? You see, I'm quite a stranger to this quaint old
town of yours, where half the houses look like churches, and all the
men like parsons and clerks belonging to them, taking a walk in their
canonicals, with four-cornered hats on their heads—abortive attempts
to square the circle, I conclude. Wonderful things, very. But when
I get to Trinity, how am I to find the man I want, one Mr. Frank
Fairlegh ? "

Here I took the liberty of interrupting the speaker, whom I had
long since recognized as Coleman—though what could have brought
him to Cambridge I was at a loss to conceive—by coming behind him,
and saying, in a gruff voice, " I am sorry you keep such low company,
young man."

"And pray who may you be that are so ready with your 'young
man,' I should like to know ? I shall have to teach you something
your tutors and dons seem to have forgotten, and that is, manners,
fellow ! " exclaimed Freddy, turning round with a face as red as a
turkey-cock, and not recognizing me at first in my cap and gown;
then looking at me steadily for a moment, he continued, " The very
man himself, by all that's comical ! This is the way you read for
your degree, is it ? " Then with a glance towards Lizzie Maurice, he
sang :—

> " ' My only books
> Were women's looks,
> And folly all they taught me."

It's a Master of He-arts you're striving to become, I suppose ? "

"Nonsense," replied I, quickly, for I saw poor Lizzie coloured and
looked uncomfortable ; " we don't allow bad puns to be made at
Cambridge."

"Then, faith ! unless the 'genius loci' inspires me with good ones,"
returned Freddy, as we left the shop together, " the sooner I'm out
of it the better."

Ten minutes' conversation served to inform me that Freddy, having
been down to Bury St. Edmunds on business, had stopped at Cambridge on his way back in order to find me out, and, if possible, induce
me to accompany him home to Hillingford, and spend a few days
there. This arrangement suited my case exactly, as it nearly filled

up the space of time which must elapse before my mother's return, and I gladly accepted his invitation. In turn, I pressed him to remain a day or two with me, and see the lions of Cambridge; but it appeared that the mission on which he had been despatched was an important one, and would not brook delay; he must therefore return at once to report progress. As he could not stay with me, the most advisable thing seemed to be that I should go back with him. Returning, therefore, to my rooms, I set Freddy to work on some bread and cheese and ale, whilst I hastened to cram a portmanteau and carpet-bag with various indispensables. I then ran to the Hoop, and took an affectionate farewell of Mr. Frampton, making him promise to pay me a visit to Heathfield Cottage; and, in less than two hours from the time Coleman had first made his appearance, we were seated together on the roof of a stage-coach, and bowling along merrily towards Hillingford.

During our drive, Coleman recounted to me his adventures in search of Cumberland, on the day preceding the duel, and gave me a more minute description than I had yet heard of the disreputable nature of that individual's pursuits. From what Coleman could learn, Cumberland, after having lost at the gaming-table large sums of money, of which he had by some means contrived to obtain possession, had become connected with a gambling-house not far from St. James's Street, and was supposed to be one of its proprietors. Just before Coleman left town, there had been an "exposé" of certain shameful proceedings which had taken place at this house—windows had been broken, and the police obliged to make a forcible entrance; but Cumberland had as yet contrived to keep his name from appearing, although it was known that he was concerned in the affair, and would be obliged to keep out of the way at present. " We shall take the old lady by surprise, I've a notion," said Freddy, as the coach set us down within ten minutes' walk of Elm Lodge. " I did not think I should have got the Bury St. Edmunds' job over till to-morrow, and wrote her word not to expect me till she saw me; but she'll be glad enough to have somebody to enliven her, for the governor's in town, and Lucy Markham is gone to stay with one of her married sisters."

" I hope I shall not cause any inconvenience, or annoy your mother."

" Annoy my grandmother! and she was dead before I was born!" exclaimed Freddy disdainfully. " Why, bless your sensitive heart, nothing that I can do annoys my mother: if I chose to bring home a mad bull in fits, or half-a-dozen young elephants with the hooping-cough she would not be annoyed." Thus assured, nothing remained for me but silent acquiescence, and in a few minutes we reached the house.

" Where's your mistress?" inquired Freddy of the manservant who showed us into the drawing-room.

" Upstairs, sir, I believe; I'll send to let her know that you are arrived."

" Do so," replied Coleman, making a vigorous attack upon the fire.

"Why, Freddy, I thought you said your cousin was away from home ? " inquired I.

"So she is; and what's more, she won't be back for a fortnight," was the answer.

"Here's a young lady's bonnet, however," said I.

"Nonsense," replied he; "it must be one of my mother's."

"Does Mrs. Coleman wear such spicy affairs as this ? " said I, holding up for his inspection a most piquant little velvet bonnet, lined with pink.

"By Jove, no ! " was the reply; "a mysterious young lady ! I say, Frank, this is interesting."

As he spoke, the door flew open, and Mrs. Coleman bustled in, in a great state of maternal affection, and fuss, and confusion, and agitation.

"Why, Freddy, my dear boy, I'm delighted to see you, only I wish you hadn't come just now;—and you too, Mr. Fairlegh—and such a small loin of mutton for dinner; but I'm so glad to see you—looking like a ghost, so pale and thin," she added, shaking me warmly by the hand; "but what am I to do about it, or to say to him when he comes back—only I'm not a prophet to guess things before they happen—and if I did I should always be wrong, so what use would that be, I should like to know ? "

"Why, what's the row, eh, mother; the cat hasn't kitten'd, has she ? " asked Freddy.

"No, my dear, no, it's not that; but your father being in town, it has all come upon me so unexpectedly; poor thing, and she looking so pretty, too; oh, dear ! when I said I was all alone, I never thought I shouldn't be; and so he left her here."

"And who may her be ? " inquired Freddy, setting grammar at defiance, "the cat or the governor ? "

"Why, my love, it's very unlucky, very awkward, indeed; but one comfort is we're told it's all for the best when everything goes wrong —a very great comfort that is if one could only believe it; but poor Mr. Vernor, you see he was quite unhappy, I'm sure, he looked so cross, and no wonder, having to go up to London all in a hurry, and such a cold day too."

At the mention of this name, my attention, which had been gradually dying a natural death, suddenly revived, and it was with a degree of impatience, which I could scarcely restrain, that I awaited the conclusion of Mrs. Coleman's rambling account. After a good deal of circumlocution of which I will mercifully spare the reader the infliction, the following facts were elicited : About an hour before our arrival, Mr. Vernor, accompanied by his ward, had called to see Mr. Coleman, and finding he was from home, had asked for a few minutes' conversation with the lady of the house. His reason for doing so soon appeared; he had received letters requiring his immediate presence in London on business, which might probably detain him a day or two: and not liking to leave Miss Saville quite alone,

he had called with the intention of begging Mrs. Coleman to allow her niece, Lucy Markham, to stay with her friend at Barstone Priory till his return, and to save her from the horrors of solitude. This plan being rendered impracticable by reason of Lucy's absence, Mrs. Coleman proposed that Miss Saville should remain with her till Mr. Vernor's return, which, she added, would be conferring a benefit on her, as her husband and son being both from home, she was sadly dull without a companion. This plan having removed all difficulties, Mr. Vernor proceeded on his journey without further delay. Good Mrs. Coleman's agitation on our arrival had been produced by the consciousness that Mr. Vernor would by no means approve of the addition of two dangerous young men to the party; however, Freddy consoled her by the ingenious sophism that it was much better for us to have arrived together than for him to have returned alone, as we should now neutralize each other's attractions; and, while the young lady's pleasure in our society would be doubled, she would be effectually guarded against falling in love with either of us, by reason of the impossibility of her overlooking the equal merits of what Mrs. Coleman would probably have termed "the survivor."

Having settled this knotty point to his own satisfaction, and perplexed his mother into the belief that our arrival was rather a fortunate circumstance than otherwise, Freddy despatched her to break the glorious tidings, as he called it, to the young lady, cautioning her to do so carefully, and by degrees, for that joy was very often as dangerous in its effects as sorrow.

Having closed the door behind her, he relieved his feelings by a slight extempore hornpipe, and then, slapping me on the back, exclaimed,—

"Here's a transcendent go; if this ain't taking the change out of old Vernor, I'm a Dutchman. Frank, you villain, you lucky dog, you've got it all your own way this time; not a chance for me; I may as well shut up shop at once, and buy myself a pair of pumps to dance in at your wedding."

"My dear fellow, how can you talk such utter nonsense?" returned I, trying to persuade myself that I was not pleased, but annoyed, at his insinuations.

"It's no nonsense, Master Frank, but, as I consider it, a very melancholy statement of facts. Why, even putting aside your 'antecedents,' as the French have it, the roasted wrist, the burnt ball-dress, and all the rest of it, look at your present advantages; here you are, just returned from the university covered with academical honours, your cheeks paled by deep and abstruse study over the midnight lamp; your eyes flashing with unnatural lustre; indicative of an overwrought mind; a graceful languor softening the nervous energy of your manner, and imparting additional tenderness to the fascination of your address; in fact, till you begin to get into condition again you are the very beau ideal of what the women consider interesting and romantic."

" Well done, Freddy," replied I, " we shall discover a hidden vein
of poetry in you some of these fine days; but talking of condition
leads me to ask what time your good mother intends us to dine ? "

" There, now you have spoilt it all," was the rejoinder; " however,
viewed abstractedly, and without reference to the romantic, it's not
such a bad notion either. I'll ring and inquire."

He accordingly did so, and, finding we had not above half an hour
to wait, he proposed that we should go to our dressing-rooms and
adorn before we attempted to face " the enemy," as he rudely
designated Miss Saville.

It was not without a feeling of trepidation, for which I should
have been at a loss to account, that I ventured to turn the handle of
the drawing-room door, where I expected to find the party assembled
before dinner. Miss Saville, who was seated on a low chair by Mrs.
Coleman's side, rose quietly on my entrance, and advanced a step or
two to meet me, holding out her hand with the unembarrassed
familiarity of an old acquaintance. The graceful ease of her
manner at once restored my self-possession, and, taking her
proffered hand, I expressed my pleasure at thus unexpectedly
meeting her again.

" You might have come here a hundred times without finding me,
although Mrs. Coleman is kind enough to invite me very often," she
replied. " But I seldom leave home ; Mr. Vernor always appears to
dislike parting with me."

" I can easily conceive that," returned I; " nay, although, in
common with your other friends, I am a sufferer by his monopoly, I
can almost pardon him for yielding to so strong a temptation."

" I wish I could flatter myself that the very complimentary construction you put upon it were the true one," replied Miss Saville,
blushing slightly ; " but I am afraid I should be deceiving myself if
I were to imagine my society were at all indispensable to my
guardian. I believe if you were to question him on the subject
you would learn that his system is based rather on the Turkish
notion, that in order to keep a woman out of mischief, you must shut
her up."

" Really, Miss Saville," exclaimed Coleman, who had entered the
room in time to overhear her speech, "I am shocked to find you
comparing your respectable and revered guardian to a heathen Turk,
and Frank Fairlegh, instead of reproving you for it, aiding, abetting,
encouraging, and to speak figuratively, patting you on the back."

" I'm sure, Freddy," interrupted Mrs. Coleman, who had been
aroused from one of her customary fits of absence by the last few
words, " Mr. Fairlegh was doing nothing of the sort; he knows
better than to think of such a thing. And if he didn't, do you
suppose I should sit here and allow him to take such liberties ? But
I believe it's all your nonsense—and where you got such strange
ideas I'm sure I can't tell; not out of Mrs. Trimmer's Sacred
History, I'm certain, though you used to read it with me every

Sunday afternoon when you were a good little boy, trying to look
out of the window all the time, instead of paying proper attention to
your books."

During the burst of laughter which followed this speech, and in
which Miss Saville, after an ineffectual struggle to repress the
inclination, out of respect to Mrs. Coleman, was fain to join, dinner
was announced, and Coleman pairing off with the young lady,
whilst I gave my arm to the old one, we proceeded to the dining-
room.

CHAPTER XXXIII.

WOMAN'S A RIDDLE.

"Let mirth and music sound the dirge of care,
But ask thou not if happiness be there."
The Lord of the Isles.

"And here she came . . . .
And sang to me the whole
Of those three stanzas."
The Talking Oak.

"Yet this is also true, that, long before,

My heart was like a prophet to my heart,
And told me I should love."
Tennyson.

"DON'T you consider Fairlegh to be looking very thin and pale,
Miss Saville?" inquired Coleman, when we joined the ladies after
dinner, speaking with an air of genuine solicitude, that any one not
intimately acquainted with him must have imagined him in earnest.
Miss Saville, who was completely taken in, answered innocently, "Indeed I have thought Mr. Fairlegh much altered since I had the
pleasure of meeting him before;" then glancing at my face with a
look of unfeigned interest, which sent the blood bounding rapidly
through my veins, she continued: "You have not been ill, I hope?"
I was hastening to reply in the negative, and to enlighten her as to
the real cause of my pale looks, when Coleman interrupted me by
exclaiming,—

"Ah! poor fellow, it is a melancholy affair. In those pale cheeks,
that wasted though still graceful form, and the weak, languid, and
unhappy, but deeply interesting 'tout ensemble,' you perceive the
sad results of—am I at liberty to mention it?—of an unfortunate
attachment."

"Upon my word, Freddy, you are too bad," exclaimed I, half

angrily, though I could scarcely refrain from ilaughing, for the
pathetic expression of his countenance was perfectly irresistible.
"Miss Saville, I can assure you—let me beg of you to believe that
there is not a word of truth in what he has stated."

"Wait a moment, you're so dreadfully fast, my dear fellow, you
won't allow a man time to finish what he is saying," remonstrated
my tormentor—"attachment to his studies, I was going to add, only
you interrupted me."

"I see I shall have to chastise you, before you learn to behave
yourself properly," replied I, shaking my fist at him playfully;
"remember you taught me how to use the gloves at Dr. Mildman's,
and I have not quite forgotten the science even yet."

"Hit a man your own size, you great big monster you," rejoined
Coleman, affecting extreme alarm. "Miss Saville, I look to you to
protect me from this tyranny; ladies always take the part of the weak
and oppressed."

"But they do not interfere to shield evil-doers from the punishment due to their misdemeanours," replied Miss Saville archly.

"There now," grumbled Freddy, "that's always the way; every
one turns against me. I'm a victim, though I've not formed an unfortunate attachment for—anything or anybody."

"I should like to see you thoroughly in love for once in your life,
Freddy," said I; "it would be as good as a comedy."

"Thank ye," was the rejoinder, "you'd be a pleasant sort of a
fellow to make a confidant of, I don't think. Here's a man now, who
calls himself one's friend, and fancies it would be 'as good as a
comedy' to witness the display of our noblest affections, and would
have all the tenderest emotions of our nature laid bare, for him to
poke fun at—the barbarian!"

"I did not understand Mr. Fairlegh's remark to apply to 'affaires
du cœur' in general, but simply to the effects likely to be produced
in your case by such an attack," observed Miss Saville, with a quiet
smile.

"A very proper distinction," returned I; "I see that I cannot do
better than leave my defence in your hands."

"It is quite clear that you have both entered into a plot against me,"
rejoined Freddy; "well, never mind, 'mea virtute me involvo': I
wrap myself in a proud consciousness of my own immeasurable
superiority, and despise your attacks."

"I have read that to begin by despising your enemy is one of the
surest methods of losing the battle," replied Miss Saville.

"Oh! if you are going to quote history against me, I yield at once
—there is nothing alarms me so much as the sight of a blue-stock-
ing," answered Freddy.

Miss Saville proceeded to defend herself with much vivacity
against this charge, and they continued to converse in the same
light strain for some time longer; Coleman, as usual, being
exceedingly droll and amusing, and the young lady displaying a

decided talent for delicate and playful badinage. In order to enter
" con spirito " into this style of conversation,¦we must either be in the
enjoyment of high health and spirits, when our light-heartedness
finds a natural vent in gay raillery and sparkling repartee, or we
must be suffering a sufficient degree of positive unhappiness to make
us feel that a strong effort is necessary to screen our sorrow from
the careless gaze of those around us. Now, though Coleman had
not been far wrong in describing me as "weak, languid, and
unhappy," mine was not a positive but a negative unhappiness, a
gentle sadness, which was rather agreeable than otherwise, and
towards which I was by no means disposed to use the slightest
violence. I was in the mood to have shed tears with the love-sick
Ophelia, or to moralize with the melancholy Jaques, but should
have considered Mercutio a man of no feeling, and the clown "a
very poor fool" indeed. In this frame of mind, the conversation
appeared to me to have assumed such an essentially frivolous turn,
that I soon ceased to take any share in it, and turning over the
leaves of a book of prints as an excuse for my silence, endeavoured
to abstract my thoughts altogether from the scene around me, and
employ them on some subject less dissonant to my present tone of
feeling. As is usually the result in such cases, the attempt proved a
dead failure, and I soon found myself speculating on the lightness
and frivolity of women in general, and of Clara Saville in particular.

" How thoroughly absurd and misplaced," thought I, as her
silvery laugh rang harshly on my distempered ear, " were all my
conjectures that she was unhappy, and that, in the trustful and
earnest expression of those deep blue eyes, I could read the evidence
of a secret grief, and a tacit appeal for sympathy to those whom her
instinct taught her were worthy of her trust and confidence ! Ah !
well, I was young and foolish then (it was not quite a year and a
half ago), and imagination found an easy dupe in me; one learns to
see things in their true light as one grows older, but it is sad how
the doing so robs life of all its brightest illusions."

It did not occur to me at that moment that there was a slight
injustice in accusing Truth of petty larceny in regard to a bright
illusion in the present instance, as the fact (if fact it were) of
proving that Miss Saville was happy instead of miserable could
scarcely be reckoned among that class of offences.

" Come, Freddy," exclaimed Mrs. Coleman, suddenly waking up to
a sense of duty out of a dangerous little nap in which she had been
indulging, and which occasioned me great uneasiness, by reason of
the opportunity it afforded her for the display of an alarming
suicidal propensity, which threatened to leave Mr. Coleman a disconsolate widower, and Freddy motherless.

As a warning to all somnolent old ladies, it may not be amiss to
enter a little more fully into detail. The attack commenced by her
sitting bolt upright in her chair, with her eyes so very particularly
open, that it seemed as if, in her case, Macbeth or some other wonder-

worker had effectually "murdered sleep." By slow degrees, however, her eyelids began to close; she grew less and less "wide
awake," and ere long was fast as a church; her next move was to
nod complacently to the company in general, as if to demand their
attention: she then oscillated gently to and fro for a few seconds
to get up the steam, and concluded the performance by suddenly
flinging her head back, with an insane jerk, over the rail of the chair,
at the imminent risk of breaking her neck, uttering a loud snort of
triumph as she did so.

Trusting the reader will pardon, and the humane society award
me a medal for this digression, I resume the thread of my
narrative.

"Freddy, my dear, can't you sing us that droll Italian song your
cousin Lucy taught you? I'm sure poor Miss Saville must feel quite
dull and melancholy."

"Would to Heaven she did!" murmured I to myself.

"Who is to play it for me?" asked Coleman.

"Well, my love, I'll do my best," replied his mother; "and, if I
should make a few mistakes, it will only sound all the funnier, you
know."

This being quite unanswerable, the piano was opened, and, after
Mrs. Coleman's spectacles had been hunted for in all probable
places, and discovered at last in the coal-scuttle, a phenomenon
which that good lady accounted for on the score of "John's having
flurried her so when he brought in tea;" and when, moreover, she
had been with difficulty prevailed on to allow the music-book to
remain the right way upwards, the song was commenced.

As Freddy had a good tenor voice, and sang Italian "buffa" songs
with much humour, the performance proved highly successful,
although Mrs. Coleman was as good as her word in introducing some
original and decidedly "funny" chords into the accompaniment,
which would have greatly discomposed the composer, if he had by
any chance overheard them.

"I did not know that you were such an accomplished performer,
Freddy," observed I; "you are quite an universal genius."

"Oh, the song was capital!" said Miss Saville, "and Mr. Coleman
sang it with so much spirit."

"Really," returned Freddy, with a low bow, "you do me proud, as
brother Jonathan says; I am actually—that is, positively—"

"My dear Freddy," interrupted Mrs. Coleman, "I wish you would
go and fetch Lucy's music; I'm sure Miss Saville can sing some of
her songs; it's—let me see—yes, it's either downstairs in the study,
or in the boudoir, or in the little room at the top of the house, or, if
it isn't, you had better ask Susan about it."

"Perhaps the shortest way will be to consult Susan at once,"
replied Coleman, as he turned to leave the room.

"I presume you prefer 'buffa' songs to music of a more pathetic
character?" inquired I, addressing Miss Saville.

" You judge from my having praised the one we have just heard,
I suppose ? "

" Yes, and from the lively style of your conversation; I have been
envying your high spirits all the evening."

" Indeed ! " was the reply; " and why should you envy them ? "

" Are they not an indication of happiness, and is not that an
enviable possession ? " returned I.

" Yes, indeed ! " she replied, in a low voice, but with such passionate
earnestness as quite to startle me. " Is laughing, then, such an
infallible indication of happiness ? " she continued.

" One usually supposes so," replied I.

To this she made no answer, unless a sigh can be called one, and,
turning away, began looking over the pages of a music-book.

" Is there nothing you can recollect to sing, my dear ? " asked Mrs.
Coleman.

She paused for a moment as if in thought ere she replied,—

" There is an old air, which I think I could remember; but I
do not know whether you will like it. The words," she added,
glancing towards me, " refer to the subject on which we have been
speaking."

She then seated herself at the instrument, and after striking a few
simple chords, sang, in a sweet, rich soprano, the following stanzas :—

I.

" Behold, how brightly seeming
 All nature shows :
 In golden sunlight gleaming,
 Blushes the rose.
How very happy things must be
That are so bright and fair to see
 Ah, no ! in that sweet flower,
 A worm there lies ;
 And lo ! within the hour,
 It fades—it dies.

II.

" Behold, young Beauty's glances
 Around she flings ;
 While as she lightly dances,
 Her soft laugh rings :
How very happy they must be,
Who are as young and gay as she !
 'Tis not when smiles are brightest,
 So old tales say,
 The bosom's lord sits lightest—
 Ah ! well-a-day !

III.

" Beneath the greenwood's cover
 The maiden steals,
 And as she meets her lover,
 Her blush reveals
How very happy all must be
Who love with trustful constancy.
 By cruel fortune parted,
 She learns too late,
 How some die broken-hearted—
 Ah ! hapless fate ! "

The air to which these words were set was a simple, plaintive, old
melody, well suited to their expression, and Miss Saville sang with
much taste and feeling. When she reached the last four lines of the
second verse, her eyes met mine for an instant, with a sad, reproach-

ful glance, as if upbraiding me for having misunderstood her; and there was a touching sweetness in her voice, as she almost whispered the refrain, "Ah! well-a-day!" which seemed to breathe the very soul of melancholy.

"Strange, incomprehensible girl!" thought I, as I gazed with a feeling of interest I could not restrain upon her beautiful features, which were now marked by an expression of the most touching sadness —"who could believe that she was the same person who, but five minutes since, seemed possessed by the spirit of frolic and merriment, and appeared to have eyes and ears for nothing beyond the jokes and drolleries of Freddy Coleman?"

"That's a very pretty song, my dear," said Mrs. Coleman; "and I'm very much obliged to you for singing it, only it has made me cry so, it has given me quite a cold in my head, I declare; and, suiting the action to the word, the tender-hearted old lady began to wipe her eyes, and execute sundry manœuvres incidental to the malady she had named. At this moment Freddy returned laden with music-books. Miss Saville immediately fixed upon a lively duet which would suit their voices, and song followed song, till Mrs. Coleman, waking suddenly in a fright, after a tremendous attempt to break her neck, which was very near proving successful, found out that it was past eleven o'clock, and consequently bed-time.

It can scarcely be doubted that my thoughts as I fell asleep (for, unromantic as it may appear, truth compels me to state that I never slept better in my life) turned upon my unexpected meeting with Clara Saville. The year and a half which had elapsed since the night of the ball had altered her from a beautiful girl into a lovely woman. Without in the slightest degree diminishing its grace and elegance, the outline of her figure had become more rounded, while her features had acquired a depth of expression which was not before observable, and which was the only thing wanting to render them (I had almost said) perfect. In her manner there was also a great alteration; the quiet reserve she had maintained when in the presence of Mr. Vernor, and the calm frankness displayed during our accidental meeting in Barstone Park, had alike given way to a strange excitability, which at times showed itself in the bursts of wild gaiety which had annoyed my fastidious sensitiveness in the earlier part of the evening, at others in the deep impassioned feeling she threw into her singing, though I observed that it was only in such songs as partook of a melancholy and even despairing character that she did so. The result of my meditations was, that the young lady was an interesting enigma, and that I could not employ the next two or three days to better advantage than in "doing a little bit of Œdipus," as Coleman would have termed it, or, in plain English, "finding her out"; and hereabouts I fell asleep.

CHAPTER XXXIV.

THE RIDDLE BAFFLES ME!

" Your riddle is hard to read."
Tennyson.

" Are you content?
    I am what you behold,
    And that's a mystery."
                        The Two Foscari.

THE post next morning brought a letter from Mr. Vernor to say that, as he found the business on which he was engaged must necessitate his crossing to Boulogne, he feared there was no chance of his being able to return under a week, but that, if it should be inconvenient for Mrs. Coleman to keep Miss Saville so long at Elm Lodge, he should wish her to go back to Barstone, where, if she was in any difficulty, she could easily apply to her late hostess for advice and assistance. On being brought clearly (though I fear the word is scarcely applicable to the good lady's state of mind at any time) to understand the position of affairs, Mrs. Coleman would by no means hear of Miss Saville's departure; but, on the contrary, made her promise to prolong her stay till her guardian should return, which, as Freddy observed, involved the remarkable coincidence that if Mr. Vernor should be drowned in crossing the British Channel, she (his mother) would have put her foot in it. The same post brought Freddy a summons from his father, desiring him the moment he returned from Bury with the papers, to proceed to town immediately. There was nothing left for him, therefore, but to deposit himself upon the roof of the next coach, blue bag in hand, which he accordingly did, after having spent the intervening time in reviling all lawyers, clients, deeds, settlements, in fact, every individual thing connected with the profession, excepting fees.

" Clara and I are going for a long walk, Mr. Fairlegh, and we shall be glad of your escort, if you have no objection to accompany us, and it is not too far for you," said Mrs. Coleman (who evidently considered me in the last stage of a decline), trotting into the breakfast-room where I was lounging, book in hand, over the fire, wondering what possible pretext I could invent for joining the ladies.

" I shall be only too happy," answered I, " and I think I can contrive to walk as far as you can, Mrs. Coleman."

" Oh! I don't know that," was the reply, " I am a capital walker, I assure you. I remember a young man, quite as young as you, and a good deal stouter, who could not walk nearly as far as I can; to be sure," she added as she left the room, " he had a wooden leg, poor fellow ! "

I soon received a summons to start with the ladies, whom I found awaiting my arrival on the terrace walk at the back of the house, comfortably wrapped up in shawls and furs, for, although a bright sun was shining, the day was cold and frosty.

"You must allow me to carry that for you," said I, laying violent hands on a large basket, between which and a muff, Mrs. Coleman was in vain attempting to effect an amicable arrangement.

"Oh, dear! I'm sure you'll never be able to carry it—it's so dreadfully heavy," was the reply.

"Nous verrons," answered I, swinging it on my forefinger, in order to demonstrate its lightness.

"Take care—you mustn't do so!" exclaimed Mrs. Coleman in a tone of extreme alarm; "you'll upset all my beautiful senna tea, and it will get amongst the slices of Christmas plum-pudding, and the flannel that I'm going to take for poor Mrs. Muddles' children to eat; do you know Mrs. Muddles, Clara, my dear?"

Miss Saville replied in the negative, and Mrs. Coleman continued,—

"Ah! poor thing! she's a very hard-working, respectable, excellent young woman; she has been married three years, and has got six children—no! let me see—it's six years, and three children—that's it—though I can never remember whether it's most pigs or children she has—four pigs, did I say?—but it doesn't much signify, for the youngest is a boy and will soon be fat enough to kill—the pig I mean; and they're all very dirty, and have never been taught to read, because she takes in washing, and has put a great deal too much starch in my nightcap this week—only her husband drinks—so I mustn't say much about it, poor thing, for we all have our failings, you know."

With such-like rambling discourse did worthy Mrs. Coleman beguile the way, until at length, after a walk of some two miles and a half, we arrived at the cottage of that much-enduring laundress, the highly respectable Mrs. Muddles, where in due form we were introduced to the mixed race of children and pigs, between which heads clearer than that of Mrs. Coleman might have been at a loss to distinguish; for if the pigs did not exactly resemble children, the children most assuredly looked like pigs. Here we seemed likely to remain for some time, as there was much business to be transacted by the two matrons. First, Mrs. Coleman's basket was unpacked, during which process that lady delivered a long harangue, setting forth the rival merits of plum-pudding and black draught, and ingeniously establishing a connection between them, which has rendered the former nearly as distasteful to me as the latter ever since. Thence glancing slightly at the over-starched nightcap, and delicately referring to the anti-teetotal propensities of the laundress's spouse, she contrived so thoroughly to confuse and interlace the various topics of her discourse, as to render it an open question whether the male Muddles had not got tipsy on black draught in consequence

of the plum-pudding having over-starched the nightcap; moreover, she distinctly called the latter article "poor fellow!" twice. In reply to this, Mrs. Muddles, the skin of whose hands was crimped up into patterns like seaweed, from the amphibious nature of her employment, and whose general appearance was, from the same cause, moist and spongy, expressed much gratitude for the contents of the basket, made a pathetic apology to the nightcap, tried to ignore the imbibing propensity of her better half; but, when pressed home upon the point, declared that when he was not engaged in the Circe-like operation of "making a beast of hisself," he was one of the most virtuousest of men; and finally wound up by a minute medical detail of Johnny's chilblain, accompanied by a slight retrospective sketch of Mary Anne's departed whooping-cough. How much longer the conversation might have continued, it is impossible to say, for it was evident that neither of the speakers had by any means exhausted her budget, had not Johnny, the unfortunate proprietor of the chilblain above alluded to, seen fit to precipitate himself, head-foremost, into a washing-tub of nearly scalding water, whence his mamma, with great presence of mind and much professional dexterity, extricated him, wrung him out, and set him on the mangle to dry, where he remained sobbing, from a vague sense of humid misery, until a more convenient season.

This little incident reminding Mrs. Coleman that the boiled beef preparing for our luncheon and the servants' dinner would inevitably be overdone, induced her to take a hurried farewell of Mrs. Muddles, though she paused at the threshold to offer a parting suggestion as to the advisability, moral and physical, of dividing the wretched Johnny's share of plum-pudding between his brothers and sisters, and administering a double portion of black draught by way of compensation, an arrangement which elicited from that much-wronged child a howl of mingled horror and defiance.

We had proceeded about a mile on our return when Mrs. Coleman, who was a step or two in advance, trod on a slide some boys had made, and would have fallen had I not thrown my arm round her just in time to prevent it.

"My dear madam," exclaimed I, "you were as nearly as possible down; I hope you have not hurt yourself."

"No, my dear—I mean—Mr. Fairlegh; no! I hope I have not, except my ankle. I gave that a twist somehow, and it hurts me dreadfully; but I dare say I shall be able to go on in a minute."

The good lady's hopes, however, were not destined in this instance to be fulfilled, for, on attempting to proceed, the pain increased to such an extent that she was forced, after limping a few steps, to seat herself on a stone by the wayside, and it became evident that she must have sprained her ankle severely, and would be utterly unable to walk home. In this dilemma it was not easy to discover what was the best thing to do—no vehicle could be procured nearer than Hillingford, from which place we were at least two miles distant, and I by no means approved of leaving my companions in their present helpless state, during the space of time which must necessarily elapse ere I could go and return. Mrs. Coleman, who, although suffering from considerable pain, bore it with the greatest equanimity and good nature, seeming to think much more of the inconvenience she was likely to occasion us than of her own discomforts, had just hit upon some brilliant but totally impracticable project when our ears were gladdened by the sound of wheels, and in another moment a little pony-chaise, drawn by a fat, comfortable-looking pony, came in sight, proceeding in the direction of Hillingford. As soon as the driver, a stout rosy-faced gentleman, who proved to be the family apothecary, perceived our party, he pulled up, and when he became aware of what had occurred, put an end to our difficulties by offering Mrs. Coleman the unoccupied seat in his chaise.

"Sorry I can't accommodate you also, Miss Saville," he continued, raising his hat; "but you see it's rather close packing as it is. If I were but a little more like the medical practitioner who administered a sleeping draught to Master Romeo, now, we might contrive to carry three."

"I really prefer walking such a cold day as this, thank you, Mr. Pillaway," answered Miss Saville.

"Mind you take proper care of poor Clara, Mr. Fairlegh," said Mrs. Coleman, "and don't let her sprain her ankle, or do anything foolish, and don't you stay out too long yourself and catch cold, or I don't know what Mrs. Fairlegh will say, and your pretty sister, too —what a fat pony, Mr. Pillaway! you don't give him much physic, I should think—good-bye, my dears, good-bye—remember the boiled beef."

As she spoke, the fat pony, admonished by the whip, described a circle with his tail, frisked with the agility of a playful elephant, and then set off at a better pace than from his adipose appearance I had deemed him capable of doing.

"With all her oddity, what an unselfish, kind-hearted, excellent little person Mrs. Coleman is!" observed I, as the pony-chaise disappeared at an angle of the road.

"Oh! I think her charming," replied my companion warmly, "she is so very good-natured."

"She is something beyond that," returned I; "mere good nature is a quality I rate very low: a person may be good-natured, yet thoroughly selfish, for nine times out of ten it is easier and more agreeable to say 'yes' than 'no;' but there is such an entire forgetfulness of self apparent in all Mrs. Coleman's attempts to make those around her happy and comfortable, that, despite her eccentricities, I am beginning to conceive quite a respect for the little woman."

"You are a close observer of character, it seems, Mr. Fairlegh," remarked my companion.

"I scarcely see how any thinking person can avoid being so," returned I; "there is no study that appears to me to possess a more deep and varied interest."

"You make mistakes, though, sometimes," replied Miss Saville, glancing quickly at me with her beautiful eyes.

"You refer to my hasty judgment of last night," said I, colouring slightly. "The mournful words of your song led me to conclude that, in one instance, high spirits might not be a sure indication of a light heart; and yet I would fain hope," added I, in a half-questioning tone, "that you merely sought to inculcate a general principle."

"Is not that a very unusual species of heath to find growing in this country?" was the rejoinder.

"Really, I am no botanist," returned I, rather crossly, for I felt that I had received a rebuff, and was not at all sure that I might not have deserved it.

"Nay, but I will have you attend; you did not even look towards the place where it is growing," replied Miss Saville, with a half-imperious, half-imploring glance, which it was impossible to resist.

"Is that the plant you mean?" asked I, pointing to a tuft of heath on the top of a steep bank by the roadside.

On receiving a reply in the affirmative, I continued: "Then I will render you all the assistance in my power, by enabling you to judge for yourself." So saying, I scrambled up the bank at the imminent risk of my neck; and after bursting the buttonholes of my straps, and tearing my coat in two places with a bramble, I succeeded in gathering the heath.

Elated by my success, and feeling every nerve braced and invigorated by the frosty air, I bounded down the slope with such velocity that, on reaching the bottom, I was unable to check my speed, and only avoided running against Miss Saville by nearly throwing myself down backwards.

"I beg your pardon!" exclaimed I; "I hope I have not alarmed you by my abominable awkwardness; but really the bank was so steep that it was impossible to stop sooner."

"Nay, it is I who ought to apologize for having led you to undertake such a dangerous expedition," replied she, taking the heath which I had gathered, with a smile which quite repaid me for my exertions.

"I do not know what could have possessed me to run down the bank in that insane manner," returned I; "I suppose it is this fine frosty morning which makes one feel so light and happy."

"Happy!" repeated my companion incredulously, and in a half-absent manner, as though she were rather thinking aloud than addressing me.

"Yes," replied I, surprised; "why should I not feel so?"

"Is anyone happy?" was the rejoinder.

"Very many people, I hope," said I; "you do not doubt it, surely."

"I well might," she answered with a sigh.

"On such a beautiful day as this, with the bright clear sky above us, and the hoar-frost sparkling like diamonds in the glorious sunshine, how can one avoid feeling happy?" asked I.

"It is very beautiful," she replied, after gazing around for a moment; "and yet can you not imagine a state of mind in which this fair scene, with all its varied charms, may impress one with a feeling of bitterness rather than of pleasure, by the contrast it affords to the darkness and weariness of soul within? Place some famine-stricken wretch beneath the roof of a gilded palace, think you the sight of its magnificence would give him any sensation of pleasure? Would it not rather, by increasing the sense of his own misery, add to his agony of spirit?"

"I can conceive such a case possible," replied I; "but you would make us out to be all famine-stricken wretches at this rate: you cannot surely imagine that everyone is unhappy?"

"There are, no doubt, different degrees of unhappiness," returned Miss Saville; "yet I can hardly conceive any position in life so free from cares as to be pronounced positively happy; but I know my ideas on this subject are peculiar, and I am by no means desirous of making a convert of you, Mr. Fairlegh; the world will do that soon enough, I fear," she added with a sigh.

"I cannot believe it," replied I warmly. "True, at times we must all feel sorrow; it is one of the conditions of our mortal lot, and we must bear it with what resignation we may, knowing that, if we but make a fitting use of it, it is certain to work for our highest good; but if you would have me look upon this world as a vale of tears, forgetting all its glorious opportunities for raising our fallen nature to something so bright and noble as to be even here but little lower than the angels, you must pardon me if I never can agree with you."

There was a moment's pause, when my companion resumed.

"You talk of opportunities of doing good, as being likely to increase our stock of happiness; and no doubt you are right; but imagine a situation in which you are unable to take advantage of these opportunities when they arise—in which you are not a free agent, your will fettered and controlled on every point, so that you are alike powerless to perform the good that you desire, and to avoid the evil you both hate and fear—could you be happy in such a situation, think you?"

"You describe a case which is, or ought to be, impossible," replied I; "when I say ought to be, I mean that in these days, I hope and believe, it is impossible for anyone to be forced to do wrong, unless, from a natural weakness and facility of disposition, and from a want of moral courage, their resistance is so feeble, that those who seek to compel them to evil are induced to redouble their efforts, when a little firmness and decision clearly shown, and steadily adhered to, would have produced a very different result."

"Oh that I could think so!" exclaimed Miss Saville ardently; she paused for a minute as if in thought, and then resumed in a low, mournful voice, "But you do not know—you cannot tell; besides, it is useless to struggle against destiny; there are people fated from childhood to grief and misfortune—alone in this cold world"—she paused, then continued abruptly, "you have a sister?"

"Yes," replied I; "I have as good a little sister as ever man was fortunate enough to possess—how glad I should be to introduce her to you!"

"And you love each other?"

"Indeed we do, truly and sincerely."

"And you are a man, one of the lords of the creation?" she continued, with a slight degree of sarcasm in her tone. "Well, Mr. Fairlegh, I can believe that you may be happy sometimes."

"And what am I to conjecture about you?" inquired I, fixing my eyes upon her expressive features.

"What you please," returned she, turning away with a very becoming blush—"or rather," she added, "do not waste your time in forming any conjectures whatever on such an uninteresting subject."

"I am more easily interested than you imagine," replied I, with a smile; "besides, you know I am fond of studying character."

"The riddle is not worth reading," answered Miss Saville.

"Nevertheless, I shall not be contented till I have found it out; I shall guess it before long, depend upon it," returned I.

An incredulous shake of the head was her only reply, and we continued conversing on indifferent subjects till we reached Elm Lodge.

CHAPTER XXXV.

A MYSTERIOUS LETTER.

"Good company's a chess-board—there are kings,
  Queens, bishops, knights, rooks, pawns. The world's a game."
                                                    Byron.
      "My soul hath felt a secret weight,
      A warning of approaching fate."
                                        Rokeby.
  "Oh! lady, weep no more; lest I give cause
  To be suspected of more *tenderness*
  Than doth become a man."
                                    Shakespeare.

THE next few days passed like a happy dream. Our little party
remained the same, no tidings being heard of any of the absentees,
save a note from Freddy, saying how much he was annoyed at being
detained in town, and begging me to wait his return at Elm Lodge,
or he would never forgive me. Mrs. Coleman's sprain, though not
very severe, was yet sufficient to confine her to her own room till
after breakfast, and to a sofa in the boudoir during the rest of the
day; and, as a necessary consequence, Miss Saville and I were chiefly
dependent on each other for society and amusement. We walked
together, read Italian (Petrarch, too, of all the authors we could have
chosen, to beguile us with his picturesque and glowing love conceits),
played chess, and, in short, tried in turn the usual expedients for
killing time in a country-house, and found them all very "pretty
pastimes" indeed. As the young lady's shyness wore off, and by
degrees she allowed the various excellent qualities of her head and
heart to appear, I recalled Lucy Markham's assertion, that "she was
as good and amiable as she was pretty," and acknowledged that she
had only done her justice. Still, although her manner was generally
lively and animated, and at times even gay, I could perceive that her
mind was not at ease; and whenever she was silent, and her features
were in repose, they were marked by an expression of hopeless
dejection which it grieved me to behold. If at such moments she
perceived anyone was observing her, she would rouse herself with a
sudden start, and join in the conversation with a degree of wild
vehemence and strange, unnatural gaiety, which to me had in it something shocking. Latterly, however, as we became better acquainted,
and felt more at ease in each other's society, these wild bursts of
spirits grew less frequent, or altogether disappeared, and she would
meet my glance with a calm melancholy smile, which seemed to say,
"I am not afraid to trust you with the knowledge that I am unhappy

—you will not betray me." Yet, though she seemed to find pleasure
in discussing subjects which afforded opportunity for expressing the
morbid and desponding views she held of life, she never allowed the
conversation to take a personal turn, always skilfully avoiding the
possibility of her words being applied to her own case : any attempt
to do so invariably rendering her silent, or eliciting from her some
gay, piquant remark, which served her purpose still better.

And how were my feelings getting on all this time ? Was I falling
in love with this wayward, incomprehensible, but deeply-interesting
girl, into whose constant society circumstances had, as it were, forced
me ? Reader, this was a question which I most carefully abstained
from asking myself. I knew that I was exceedingly happy ; and, as I
wished to continue so, I steadily forbore to analyze the ingredients
of this happiness too closely, perhaps from a secret consciousness that,
were I to do so, I might discover certain awkward truths, which
would prove it to be my duty to tear myself away from the scene of
fascination ere it was too late. So I told myself that I was bound by
my promise to Coleman to remain at Elm Lodge till my mother and
sister should return home, or, at all events, till he himself came back ;
this being the case, I was compelled by all the rules of good-breeding
to be civil and attentive to Miss Saville (yes, civil and attentive—I
repeated the words over two or three times ; they were nice, quiet,
cool sort of words, and suited the view I was anxious to take of the
case particularly well). Besides, I might be of some use to her, poor
girl ! by combating her strange, melancholy, half-fatalist opinions ; at
all events, it was my duty to try, decidedly my duty (I said that also
several times) ; and, as to my feeling such a deep interest about her,
and thinking of her continually, why, there was nothing else to think
about at Elm Lodge—so that was easily accounted for. All this, and
a good deal more of the same nature, did I tell myself ; and, if I did
not implicitly believe it, I was much too polite to think of giving
myself the lie, so I continued walking, talking, reading Petrarch, and
playing chess with Miss Saville all day, and dreaming of her all
night, and being very happy indeed.

Oh ! it's a dangerous game, by the way, that game of chess, with its
gallant young knights, clever fellows, up to all sorts of deep moves,
who are perpetually laying siege to queens, keeping them in check,
threatening them with the bishop, and, with his assistance, mating
at last ; and much too nearly does it resemble the game of life to be
played safely with a pair of bright eyes talking to you from the
other side of the board, and two coral lips—mute, indeed, but in their
very silence discoursing such " sweet music " to your heart, that the
silly thing, dancing with delight, seems as if it means to leap out of
your breast ; and it is not mere seeming either—for hearts have been
altogether lost in this way before now. Oh ! it's a dangerous game,
that game of chess. But to return to my tale.

About a week after the expedition to Mrs. Muddles's had taken
place, Freddy and his father returned just in time for dinner. As I

was dressing for that meal, Coleman came into my room, anxious to learn "how the young lady had conducted herself" during his absence : whether I had taken any unfair advantage, or acted honourably, and with a due regard to his interest, with sundry other jocose queries. all of which appeared to me exceedingly impertinent, and particularly disagreeable, and inspired me with a strong inclination to take him by the shoulders and march him out of the room ; instead, however, of doing so, I endeavoured to look amiable, and answer his inquiries in the same light tone in which they were made, and I so far succeeded as to render the amount of information he obtained exceedingly minute. The dinner passed off heavily ; Miss Saville was unusually silent, and all Freddy's sallies failed to draw her out. Mr. Coleman was very pompous, and so distressingly polite, that everything like sociability was out of the question. When the ladies left us matters did not improve ; Freddy, finding the atmosphere ungenial to jokes, devoted himself to cracking walnuts by original methods which invariably failed, and attempting to torture into impossible shapes oranges, which, when finished, were much too sour for anyone to eat ; while his father, after having solemnly, and at separate intervals, begged me to partake of every article of the dessert twice over, commenced an harangue, in which he set forth the extreme caution and reserve he considered it right and advisable for young gentlemen to exercise in their intercourse with young ladies. towards whom he declared they should maintain a staid deportment of dignified courtesy, tempered by distant but respectful attentions. This, repeated with variations, lasted us till the tea was announced, and we returned to the drawing-room. Here Freddy made a desperate and final struggle to remove the wet blanket which appeared to have extinguished the life and spirit of the party, but in vain ; it had evidently set in for a dull evening, and the clouds were not to be dispelled by any efforts of his ;—nothing, therefore, remained for him but to teaze the cat, and worry and confuse his mother, to which occupations he applied himself with a degree of diligence worthy a better object. During a fearful commotion consequent upon the discovery of the cat's nose in the cream-jug, into the commission of which delinquency Freddy had contrived to inveigle that amiable quadruped by a series of treacherous caresses, I could not help remarking to Miss Saville (next to whom I happened to be seated) the contrast between this evening and those which we had lately spent together.

"Ah! yes," she replied, in a half-absent manner, " I knew they were too happy to last; " then, seeing from the flush of joy which I felt rise to my brow, though I would have given worlds to repress it, that I had put a wrong construction on her words, or, as my heart would fain have me believe, that she had unconsciously admitted more than she intended, she added hastily, " What I mean to say is, that the perfect freedom from restraint, and the entire liberty to—to follow one's own pursuits, are pleasures to which I am so little accustomed, that I have enjoyed them more than I was perhaps aware of while they lasted."

" You are out of spirits this evening. I hope nothing has occurred to annoy you ? " inquired I.

" Do you believe in presentiments ? " was the rejoinder.

" I cannot say I do," returned I ; " I take them to be little else than the creations of our own morbid fancies, and attribute them in a great measure to physical causes."

" But why do they come true then ? " she inquired.

" I must answer your question by another," I replied, " and ask whether, except now and then by accident, they do come true ? "

" I think so," returned Miss Saville ; " at least, I can only judge as one usually does, more or less, in every case, by one's own experience —my presentiments always appear to come true ; would it were not so ! for they are generally of a gloomy nature."

" Even yet," replied I, " I doubt whether you do not unconsciously deceive yourself, and I think I can tell you the reason ; you remember the times when your presentiments have come to pass, because you considered such coincidences remarkable, and they made a strong impression on your mind, while you forget the innumerable gloomy forebodings which have never been fulfilled, the accomplishment being the thing which fixes itself on your memory—is not this the case ? "

" It may be so," she answered, " and yet I know not—even now there is a weight here ; " and she pressed her hand to her brow as she spoke, " a vague, dull feeling of dread, a sensation of coming evil which tells me that some misfortune is at hand, some crisis of my fate approaching. I daresay you consider all this very silly and romantic, Mr. Fairlegh ; but if you knew how everything I have most feared, most sought to avoid, has invariably been forced upon me, you would make allowance for me—you would pity me."

What answer I should have made to this appeal, had not Fate interposed in the person of old Mr. Coleman (who seated himself on the other side of Miss Saville, and began talking about the state of the roads), it is impossible to say. As it was, my only reply was by a glance, which, if it failed to convince her that I pitied her with a depth and intensity which approached alarmingly near the kindred emotion, love, must have been singularly inexpressive. And the evening came to an end, as all evenings, however long, are sure to do at last ; and in due course I went to bed, but not to sleep, for Clara Saville and her forebodings ran riot in my brain, and effectually banished the "soft restorer " till such time as that early egotist the cock began singing his own praises to his numerous wives, when I fell into a doze, with a strong idea that I had got a presentiment myself, though of what nature, or when the event (if event it was) was likely to "come off," I had not the most distant notion.

The post-bag arrived while we were at breakfast the next morning ; and it so happened that I was the only one of the party for whom it did not contain a letter. Having nothing, therefore, to occupy my attention, and being seated exactly opposite Clara Saville, I could scarcely fail to observe the effect produced by one which Mr. Coleman had handed to her. When her eye first fell on the writing she gave a slight start, and a flush (I could not decide whether of pleasure or anger) mounted to her brow. As she perused the contents she grew deadly pale, and I feared she was about to faint: recovering herself, however, by a strong effort, she read steadily to the end, quietly refolded the letter, and placing it in a pocket in her dress, apparently resumed her breakfast—I say apparently, for I noticed that, although she busied herself with what was on her plate, it remained untasted, and she took the earliest opportunity, as soon as the meal was concluded, of leaving the room.

"I'm afraid I must ask you to excuse me till after lunch, old fellow," said Coleman; "you see, we're so dreadfully busy just now with this confounded suit I went down to Bury about—'Bowler versus Stumps'; but if you can amuse yourself till two o'clock we'll go and have a jolly good walk to shake up an appetite for dinner."

" The very thing," replied I; "I have a letter to Harry Oaklands which has been on the stocks for the last four days, and which I particularly wish to finish, and then I'm your man, for a ten mile trot if you like it."

" So be it, then," said Freddy, leaving the room as he spoke.

As soon as he was gone, instead of fetching my half-written epistle I flung myself into an arm-chair, and devoted myself to the profitable employment of conjecturing the possible cause of Clara Saville's strange agitation on receiving that letter. Who could it be from ?—perhaps her guardian;—but if so, why should she have given a start of surprise ?—nothing could have been more natural or probable than that he should write and say when she might expect him home—she could not have felt surprise at the sight of his handwriting—but if not from him, from whom could it come ? She had told me that she had no near relations, no intimate friend. A lover, perchance—well, and if it were so, what was that to me ?—nothing—oh yes ! decidedly nothing—a favoured lover of course, else why the emotion ?—was this also nothing ?—yes, I said it was, and I tried to think so too: yet, viewing the matter so philosophically, it was rather inconsistent to spring from my seat as if an adder had stung me, and begin striding up and down the room as though I were walking for a wager. In the course of my rapid promenade, my coat-tail brushed against and nearly knocked down an inkstand, to which incident I was indebted for the recollection of my unfinished letter to Oaklands, and, my own thoughts being at that moment no over-pleasant companions, I was glad of any excuse to get rid of them. On looking about for my writing-case, however, I remembered that, when last I made use of it, we were sitting in the boudoir, and that there it had probably remained ever since; accordingly, without further waste of time, I ran upstairs to look for it.

As good Mrs. Coleman (although she most indignantly repelled

the accusation) was sometimes accustomed to indulge her propensity
for napping even in a morning, I opened the door of the boudoir, and
closed it again after me as noiselessly as possible. My precautions,
however, did not seem to have been necessary, for at first sight the
room appeared untenanted; but as I turned to look for my writing-
case a stifled sob met my ear, and a closer inspection enabled me to
perceive the form of Clara Saville, with her face buried in the
cushions, half sitting, half reclining on the sofa, while so silently had
I effected my entrance that as yet she was not aware of my approach.
My first impulse was to withdraw and leave her undisturbed, but
unluckily a slight noise which I made in endeavouring to do so
attracted her attention, and she started up in alarm, regarding me
with a wild, half-frightened gaze, as if she scarcely recognized me.

"I beg your pardon," I began hastily, "I am afraid I have disturbed you—I came to fetch—that is to look for—my—" and here
I stopped short, for to my surprise and consternation Miss Saville,
after making a strong but ineffectual effort to regain her composure,
sank back upon the sofa, and, covering her face with her hands,
burst into a violent flood of tears. I can scarcely conceive a situation more painful, or in which it would be more difficult to know how
to act, than the one in which I now found myself. The sight of a
woman's tears must always produce a powerful effect upon a man of
any feeling, leading him to wish to comfort and assist her to the
utmost of his ability; but if the fair weeper be one in whose welfare
you take the deepest interest, and yet with whom you are not on
terms of sufficient intimacy to entitle you to offer the consolation
your heart would dictate, the position becomes doubly embarrassing.
For my part, so overcome was I by a perfect chaos of emotions, that
I remained for some moments like one thunder-stricken, while she
continued to sob as though her heart were breaking. At length I
could stand it no longer, and scarcely knowing what I was going to
say or do, I placed myself on the sofa beside her, and taking one of her
hands, which now hung listlessly down, in my own, I exclaimed,—

"Miss Saville—Clara—dear Clara! I cannot bear to see you so
unhappy, it makes me miserable to look at you—tell me, what can I
do to help you—to comfort you—something must be possible—you
have no brother—let me be one to you—tell me why you are so
wretched—and oh! do not cry so bitterly!"

When I first addressed her she started slightly, and attempted to
withdraw her hand, but as I proceeded she allowed it to remain
quietly in mine, and though she still continued to weep, her tears fell
more softly, and she no longer sobbed in such a distressing manner.
Glad to find that I had in some measure succeeded in calming her, I
renewed my attempts at consolation, and again implored her to tell
me the cause of her unhappiness. Still for some moments she was
unable to speak, but at length making an effort to recover herself,
she withdrew her hand, and stroking back her glossy hair, which had
fallen over her forehead, said,—

"This is very weak—very foolish. I do not often give way in this manner, but it came upon me so suddenly—so unexpectedly; and now, Mr. Fairlegh, pray leave me; I shall ever feel grateful to you for your sympathy, for your offers of assistance, and for all the trouble you have kindly taken about such a strange, wayward girl, as I am sure you must consider me," she added with a faint smile.

"So you will not allow me to be of use to you?" returned I sorrowfully; "you do not think me worthy of your confidence."

"Indeed it is not so," she replied earnestly; "there is no one of whose judgment I think more highly; no one of whose assistance I would more gladly avail myself; on whose honour I would more willingly rely; but it is utterly impossible to help me. Indeed," she added, seeing me still look incredulous, "I am telling you what I believe to be the exact and simple truth."

"Will you promise me that, if at any time you should find that I could be of use to you, you will apply to me as you would to a brother, trusting me sufficiently to believe that I shall not act hastily, or in any way which could in the slightest degree compromise or annoy you? Will you promise me this?"

"I will," she replied, raising her eyes to my face for an instant with that sweet trustful expression which I had before noticed, "though I suppose such prudent people as Mr. Coleman," she added with a slight smile, "would consider me to blame for so doing; and were I like other girls—had I a mother's affection to watch over me—a father's care to shield me, they might be right; but situated as I am, having none to care for me—nothing to rely on save my own weak heart and unassisted judgment—while those who should guide and protect me appear only too ready to avail themselves of my helplessness and inexperience—I cannot afford to lose so true a friend, or believe it to be my duty to reject your disinterested kindness."

A pause ensued, during which I arrived at two conclusions—first, that my kindness was not so disinterested as she imagined; and secondly, that if I sat where I was much longer, and she continued to talk about there being nobody who cared for her, I should inevitably feel myself called upon to undeceive her, and, as a necessary consequence, implore her to accept my heart and share my patrimony—the latter, deducting my sister's allowance and my mother's jointure, amounting to the imposing sum of £90 14s. 6½d. per annum, which, although sufficient to furnish a bachelor with bread and cheese and broad-cloth, was not exactly calculated to afford an income for "persons about to marry." Accordingly, putting a strong force upon my inclinations, and by a desperate effort screwing my virtue to the sticking point, I made a pretty speech, clenching, and thanking her for, her promise of applying to me to help her out of the first hopelessly inextricable dilemma in which she might find herself involved, and rose with the full intention of leaving the room.

CHAPTER XXXVI.

THE RIDDLE SOLVED.

"Think'st thou there's virtue in constrainèd vows,
Half utter'd, soulless, falter'd forth in fear?
And if there is, then truth and grace are nought."
                                      Sheridan Knowles.

"For
The contract you pretend with that base wretch,
It is no contract—none."
                                      Shakespeare.

"Who hath not felt that breath in the air,
A perfume and freshness strange and rare,
A warmth in the light, and a bliss everywhere,
    When young hearts yearn together?
All sweets below, and all sunny above,
Oh! there's nothing in life like making love,
    Save making hay in fine weather!"
                                      Hood.

UPON what trifles do the most important events of our lives turn! Had I quitted the room according to my intention, I should not have had an opportunity of seeing Miss Saville alone again (as she returned to Barstone that afternoon), in which case she would probably have forgotten or felt afraid to avail herself of my promised assistance, all communication between us would have ceased, and the deep interest I felt in her, having nothing wherewith to sustain itself, would, as years passed by, have died a natural death.

Good resolutions are, however, proverbially fragile, and in nine cases out of ten appear made, like children's toys, only to be broken. Certain it is that in the present instance mine were rendered of none avail, and, for any good effect that they produced, might as well never have been formed.

As I got up to leave the room Miss Saville rose likewise, and in doing so accidentally dropped a, or rather the letter, which I picked up, and was about to return to her, when suddenly my eye fell upon the direction, and I started as I recognized the writing—a second glance served to convince me that I had not been mistaken, for the hand was a very peculiar one; and, turning to my astonished companion, I exclaimed, " Clara, as you would avoid a life of misery, tell me by what right this man dares to address you!"

" What! do you know him, then?" she inquired anxiously.

" If he be the man I mean," was my answer, " I know him but too well, and he is the only human being I both dislike and despise. Was not that letter written by Richard Cumberland?"

" Yes, that is his hateful name," she replied, shuddering while she spoke, as at the aspect of some loathsome thing; then, suddenly changing her tone to one of the most passionate entreaty, she clasped her hands, and advancing a step towards me, exclaimed,—

" Oh! Mr. Fairlegh, only save me from him, and I will bless you, will pray for you!" and completely overcome by her emotion, she sank backwards, and would have fallen had not I prevented it.

There is a peculiar state of feeling which a man sometimes experiences when he has bravely resisted some hydra-headed temptation to do anything " pleasant but wrong," yet which circumstances appear determined to force upon him: he struggles against it boldly at first; but, as each victory serves only to lessen his own strength, while that of the enemy continues unimpaired, he begins to tell himself that it is useless to contend longer—that the monster is too strong for him, and he yields at last, from a mixed feeling of fatalism and irritation—a sort of " have-it-your-own-way-then " frame of mind, which seeks to relieve itself from all responsibility by throwing the burden on things in general—the weakness of human nature—the force of circumstances—or any other indefinite and conventional scapegoat, which may serve his purpose of self-exculpation.

In much such a condition did I now find myself; I felt that I was regularly conquered—completely taken by storm—and that nothing was left for me but to yield to my destiny with the best grace I could. I therefore seated myself by Miss Saville on the sofa, and whispered, " You must promise me one thing more, Clara dearest—say that you will love me—give me but that right to watch over you—to protect you, and believe me, neither Cumberland nor any other villain shall dare for the future to molest you."

As she made no answer, but remained with her eyes fixed on the ground, while the tears stole slowly down her cheeks, I continued: " You own that you are unhappy—that you have none to love you—none on whom you can rely;—do not, then, reject the tender, the devoted affection of one who would live but to protect you from the slightest breath of sorrow—would gladly die if, by so doing, he could secure your happiness."

" Oh! hush, hush!" she replied, starting, as if for the first time aware of the tenor of my words; " you know not what you ask; or even you, kind, noble, generous as you are, would not seek to link your fate with one so utterly wretched, so marked out for misfortune as myself. Stay," she continued, seeing that I was about to speak, " hear me out. Richard Cumberland, the man whom you despise, and whom I hate only less than I fear, that man have I promised to marry, and ere this he is on his road hither to claim the fulfilment of the engagement."

" Promised to marry Cumberland!" repeated I mechanically, " a low, dissipated swindler—a common cheat, for I can call him nothing better; oh, it's impossible!—why, Mr. Vernor, your guardian, would never permit it."

" My guardian!" she replied, in a tone of the most cutting irony; " were it not for him, this engagement would never have been formed;

were it not for him, I should even now hope to find some means of prevailing upon this man to relinquish it and set me free. Richard Cumberland is Mr. Vernor's nephew, and the dearest wish of his heart is to see us united."

"He never shall see it while I live to prevent it!" replied I, springing to my feet, and pacing the room with angry strides. Oh, it was all plain to me now! when I had fancied her guardian's features were not unfamiliar to me, it was his likeness to Cumberland which had deceived me; his rudeness on the night of the ball; the strange dislike he appeared to feel towards me—all was now accounted for. His opinion of me, formed from Cumberland's report, was not likely to be a very favourable one; and this precious uncle and nephew were linked in a scheme to destroy the happiness of the sweetest girl living. the brightness of whose young spirit was already darkened by the shade of their vile machinations: but they had not as yet succeeded, and, if the most strenuous and unceasing exertions on my part could serve to prevent it, I inwardly vowed they never should. Let Master Richard Cumberland look to himself; I had foiled him once, and it would go hard with me, but I would do so again.

Having half thought, half uttered the foregoing resolutions, I once more turned towards Miss Saville, who sat watching me with looks of interest and surprise, and said,—

"This is a most strange and unexpected affair; but remember, dear Clara, you have appealed to me to save you from Cumberland. and to enable me to do so. you must tell me exactly how matters stand between you, and, above all. how and why you were induced to enter into this engagement, for I hope—I think—I am right in supposing—that affection for him had nothing to do with it."

"Affection!" she replied, in a tone of voice which, if any doubts still lingered in my mind. effectually dispelled them; "have I not already said that I hate this man, as, I fear, it is sinful to hate any human being; I disliked and dreaded him when we were boy and girl together, and these feelings have gone on increasing year by year, till my aversion to him has become one of the most deeply rooted instincts of my nature."

"And yet you allowed yourself to be engaged to him?" inquired I. "How could this have been brought about?"

"You may well ask," was the reply; "it was folly; it was weakness; but I was very young—a mere child, in fact; and they made me believe that it was my duty; then I hoped, I felt sure that I should die before the time arrived to fulfil the engagement; I fancied it was impossible to be so miserable, and yet to live: but Death is very cruel—he will not come to those who pine for him."

"Clara," interrupted I, "I cannot bear to hear you say such things; it is not right to give way to these feelings of despair."

"Is it wrong for the unhappy to wish to die?" she asked, with a calm. child-like simplicity which was most touching. "I suppose it is," she continued, "for I have prayed for death so often that God would have granted my prayer if it had been a right one. When I closed my eyes last night, oh! how I hoped—how I longed—never to open them again in this miserable world—for I felt that evil was at hand; you laughed at my presentiment: it has come true, you see."

"Believe me, you do wrong in giving way to these despairing thoughts—in encouraging these morbid fancies," returned I. "But time presses; will you not tell me the particulars of this unhappy engagement, that I may see how far you stand committed to this scoundrel Cumberland, and decide what is best to be done for the future?"

"It is a long story," she replied; "but I will tell it you as shortly as I can."

She then proceeded to inform me that her mother having died when she was an infant, she had become the idol of her surviving parent, who, inconsolable for the loss of his wife, lavished all his tenderness upon his little girl. She described her childhood as the happiest part of her life, although it must have been happiness of a tranquil nature, differing greatly from the boisterous merriment of children in general; its chief ingredient being the strong affection which existed between her father and herself. The only guest who ever appeared at the Priory (which I now for the first time learned had been the property of Sir Henry Saville) was his early friend, Mr. Vernor, who used periodically to visit them, an event to which she always looked forward with pleasure, not so much on account of the presents and caresses he bestowed on herself, as that his society appeared to amuse and interest her father. On one of these occasions, when she was about nine years of age, Mr. Vernor was accompanied by a lad some years older than herself, whom he introduced as his nephew. During his visit, the boy, who appeared gifted with tact and cunning beyond his years, contrived so much to ingratiate himself with Sir Henry Saville, that before he left the Priory, his host, who had himself served with distinction in the Peninsula, expressed his readiness to send him, on attaining a fit age, to one of the military colleges, promising to use his interest at the Horse Guards to procure a commission for him. These kind intentions, however, were fated not to be carried out. An old wound which Sir Henry had received at Vimiera broke out afresh, occasioning the rupture of a vessel on the lungs, and in the course of a few hours Clara was left fatherless. On examining the private papers of the deceased, it appeared that Mr. Vernor was constituted sole executor, trustee for the property, and guardian to the young lady. In these various capacities, he immediately took up his residence at Barstone, and assumed the direction of everything. And now for the first time did his true character appear—sullen and morose in temper, stern and inflexible in disposition, cold and reserved in manner, implacable when offended, requiring implicit obedience to his commands; he seemed calculated to inspire fear instead of love, aversion rather than esteem. The only sign of feeling he ever showed was in his

FRANK FAIRLEGH 241

behaviour towards Richard Cumberland. for whom he evidently entertained a strong affection. The idea of a military career having been abandoned at Sir Henry Saville's death, much of his time was now spent at the Priory. Although he was apparently fond of his little companion, and endeavoured on every occasion to render him-self agreeable to her, all his habitual cunning could not conceal from her his vile temper, or the unscrupulous means of which he was always willing to avail himself in order to attain his own ends. He had been away from the Priory on one occasion more than a year, when he suddenly returned with his uncle, who had been in town on business. He appeared sullen and uncomfortable, and she imagined that they must have had a quarrel. She was at that time nearly fifteen, and the marked devotion which Cumberland (who during his absence had greatly improved both in manner and appearance) now paid her, flattered and pleased her; and partly for this reason, partly because she had already learned to dread his outbreaks of temper, and was unwilling to do anything which might provoke one of them, she allowed him to continue his attentions unre-pulsed.

This went on for some weeks, and her old dislike was beginning to return as she saw more of her companion, when one morning Mr. Vernor called her into his study, and informed her that he considered she had arrived at an age when it was right that they should become aware of the arrangements he had made for her, in accordance with the wishes of her late father. He then showed her a letter in Sir Henry Saville's handwriting, dated only a few weeks before his death, part of which was to the following effect: "You urge the fact of your nephew's residing with you as an objection to my scheme for your living at Barstone, and assuming the guardianship of my daughter, in the event (which, if I may trust my own sensations, is not very far distant) of her being left an orphan. From what I have seen of the boy, as well as on the score of our old friendship, my dear Vernor, that which you view as an objection, I consider but an additional reason why the arrangement should take place. A marriage with your nephew would insure my child (who as my sole heiress will be possessed of considerable wealth) from that worst of all fates, falling a prey to some needy fortune-hunter; and should such a union ever be contemplated, let me beg of you to remember, and to impress upon Clara herself, that, had I lived, it would have met with my warmest approbation."

Having shown her this letter, Mr. Vernor went on to say that he had noticed with pleasure Richard's growing attachment, and the marked encouragement she had given him, and that, although they were too young to think of marrying for some years, and, as a general principle, he was averse to long engagements, yet under the peculiar circumstances in which they were placed, he had yielded to his nephew's importunity, and determined not only to lay his offer before her, but to allow her to accept it at once, if (as from her

R

manner he could scarcely be mistaken in supposing) her inclinations were in accordance with his.

Taken completely by surprise at this announcement, overpowered by the idea that by the encouragement she had given Cumberland the had irretrievably committed herself—strongly affected by her father's letter, having no one to advise her, what wonder that the persuasions of the nephew, backed by the authority of the uncle, prevailed over her youth and inexperience, and that the matter ended in her allowing herself to be formally engaged to Richard Cumberland.

Little more remained for her to tell; reckoning that he had gained his point, Cumberland became less careful in concealing his evil disposition, and her dislike to him and fear of him increased every day. At length this became evident to Mr. Vernor, but it appeared only to render him still more determined to bring about the match, and when once, nearly a twelvemonth before, she had implored him to allow her to break off the engagement, he had exhibited so much violence, declaring that he possessed the power of rendering her a beggar, and even threatening to turn her out of doors, that she had never dared to recur to the subject. For many months, however, she had seen nothing of her persecutor, and she had almost begun to hope that something had rendered him averse to the match, when all her fears were again aroused by a hint which Mr. Vernor had thrown out as he took leave of her at Mrs. Coleman's, desiring her to exercise great circumspection in her behaviour, and to recollect that she was under a solemn engagement, which she might before long be called upon to fulfil. The letter from Cumberland, she added, spoke of his immediate return to claim her hand, and a few lines from Mr. Vernor ordered her to await their arrival at Barstone.

"And now," she continued, looking up with that calm, hopeless smile which was so painful to behold, "have I not cause to be unhappy, and was I not right in telling you that no one could be of any assistance to me, or afford me help?"

"No!" replied I warmly; "I trust and believe that much may be done—nay, everything; but you are unequal to contend with these men alone; only allow me to hope that my affection is not utterly distasteful to you. Would you but give me that right to interfere in your behalf!"

"This is ungenerous—unlike yourself," she interrupted. "Have you already forgotten that I am the promised bride of Richard Cumberland? Were I free, indeed—"

"Oh! why do you pause?" exclaimed I passionately. "Clara, hear me—you deem it ungenerous in me to urge my suit upon you at this moment—perhaps think that I would take advantage of the difficulties which surround you, to induce you to promise me your hand as the price of my assistance. It is true that I love you deeply, devotedly, and the happiness of my whole life is centred in the hope of one day calling you my own; but I would use my utmost

endeavours to save you from Cumberland, even though I knew that
by so doing I forfeited all chance of ever seeing you again. Tell
me, would you wish this to be so—am I to believe that you dislike
me ? "

As she made no reply, merely blushing deeply, and casting down
her eyes, I ventured to continue, " Clara, dearest Clara, do you then
love me ? "

Well, reader, I think I've told you quite as much about it as you
have any business to know. Of course she did not say she loved me
—women never do upon such occasions; but I was just as well
contented as it was. Mendelssohn has composed songs without
words ("lieder ohne worte "), which tell their own tale very prettily,
and there have been many eloquent speeches made on a like silent
system. Suffice it to add that the next ten minutes formed such a
nice, bright, sunshiny little piece of existence as might deserve to be
cut out of the book of time, and framed, glazed, and hung up for the
inspection of all true lovers ; whilst no match-making mamma,
fortune-hunting younger brother, or girl of business on the look-out
for a good establishment, should be allowed a glimpse of it at any
price.

CHAPTER XXXVII.

THE FORLORN HOPE.

" ————Cumberland
. . . . . . Seeks thy hand ;
Itis shall it be—nay, no reply ;
Hence till those rebel eyes be dry."
The Lord of the Isles.

FREDDY COLEMAN was cheated of his walk that afternoon ; for an
old maiden lady in the neighbourhood, having read in a Sunday
paper that the plague was raging with great fury at Constantinople,
thought it as well to be prepared for the worst, and summoned Mr.
Coleman, to receive directions about making her will—and he being
particularly engaged, sent Freddy in his stead, who set out on the
mission in a state of comic ill-humour, which bid fair to render Mrs.
Aikinside's will a very original document indeed, and foreboded for
that good old lady herself an unprecedented and distracting afternoon.

I had assisted Mr. Coleman in conducting Clara Saville to the
carriage which arrived to convey her to Barstone, and had received

a kind glance and a slight pressure of the hand in return, which I
would not have exchanged for the smiles of an empress, when,
anxious to be alone with my own thoughts, I started off for a solitary
walk, nor did I relax my pace till I had left all traces of human
habitation far behind me, and green fields and leafless hedges were
my only companions. I then endeavoured in some measure to
collect my scattered thoughts, and to reflect calmly on the position
in which I had placed myself by the avowal the unexpected events
of the morning had hurried me into. But so much was I excited,
that calm reflection appeared next to impossible. Feeling—flushed
with the victory it had obtained over its old antagonist, Reason—
seemed, in every sense of the word, to have gained the day, and,
despite all the difficulties that lay before me—difficulties which I
knew must appear all but insurmountable whenever I should venture
to look them steadily in the face—the one idea that Clara Saville
loved me was ever present with me, and rendered me supremely
happy.

The condition of loving another better than one's self, conven-
tionally termed being " in love," is, to say the least, a very doubtful
kind of happiness; and poets have therefore, with great propriety,
described it as " pleasing pain," " delicious misery," and in many
other terms of a like contradictory character; nor is it possible that
this should be otherwise ; love is a passion, wayward and impetuous
in its very nature—agitating and disquieting in its effects, rendering
its votary the slave of circumstances—a mere shuttlecock alternating
between the extremes of hope and fear, joy and sorrow, confidence
and mistrust—a thing which a smile can exalt to the highest pinnacle
of delight, or a frown strike down to the depths of despair. But
in the consciousness that we are beloved, there is none of this
questionable excitement ; on the contrary, we experience a sensation
of deep, calm joy, as we reflect that in the true affection thus
bestowed on us we have gained a possession which the cares and
struggles of life are powerless to injure, and which death itself,
though it may interrupt for awhile, will fail to destroy.

These thoughts, or something like them, having entrenched themselves in the stronghold of my imagination, for some time held their
ground gallantly against the attacks of common-sense, but at length,
repulsed on every point, they deemed it advisable to capitulate, or
(to drop metaphor, a style of writing I particularly abominate,
perhaps because I never more than half understand what it means),
in plain English, I, with a sort of grimace, such as one makes before
swallowing a dose of physic, set myself seriously to work to reflect
upon my present position, and decide on the best line of conduct to
be pursued for the future.

Before our conference came to an end, I had made Clara
acquainted with my knowledge of Cumberland's former delinquencies,
as well as the reputation in which he was now held by such of his
associates as had any pretension to the title of gentlemen, and added

my conviction that, when once these facts were placed before Mr. Vernor, he must see that he could not, consistently with his duty as guardian, allow his ward to marry a man of such character. Cumberland had no doubt contrived to keep his uncle in ignorance of his mode of life, and it would only be necessary to enlighten him on that point, to insure his consent to her breaking off the engagement. Clara appeared less sanguine of success, even hinting at the possibility of Mr. Vernor's being as well informed in regard to his nephew's real character as we were; adding, that his mind was too firmly set on the match for him to give it up lightly. It was finally agreed between us, that she was to let me know how affairs went on after Mr. Vernor's return, and in the meantime I was to give the matter my serious consideration, and decide on the best course for us to follow. The only person in the establishment whom she could thoroughly trust was the extraordinary old footman (the subject of Lawless's little bit of diplomacy), who had served under her father in the Peninsula, and accompanied him home in the character of confidential servant. He had consequently known Clara from a child, and was strongly attached to her, so that she had learned to regard him more in the light of a friend than a servant. Through this somewhat original substitute for a confidant, we arranged to communicate with each other.

As to my own line of conduct, I very soon decided on that. I would only await a communication from Clara to assure me that Mr. Vernor's determination with regard to her remained unchanged, ere I would seek an interview with him, enlighten him as to Cumberland's true character, acquaint him with Clara's aversion to the match, and induce him to allow of its being broken off. I should then tell him of my own affection for her, and of my intention of coming forward to demand her hand, as soon as, by my professional exertions, I should have realized a sufficient independence to enable me to marry. As to Clara's fortune, if fortune she had, she might build a church, endow a hospital, or buy herself bonnet-ribbons with it, as she pleased, for not a farthing of it would I ever touch on any consideration. No one should be able to say that it was for the sake of her money I sought to win her.

Well, all this was very simple, straightforward work;—where, then, were the difficulties which had alarmed me so greatly? Let me see —Mr. Vernor might choose to fancy that it would take some years to add to the £90 14s. 6¾d. sufficiently to enable me to support a wife, and might disapprove of his ward's engaging herself to me on that account. What if he did? I wished for no engagement—let her remain free as air—her own true affection would stand my friend, and on that I could rely, content, if it failed me, to—to—well, it did not signify what I might do in an emergency which never could arise. No! only let him promise not to force her inclinations—to give up his monstrous project of wedding her to Cumberland—and to leave her free to bestow her hand on whom she would—and I should be perfectly satisfied. But suppose, as Clara seemed to fear, he should refuse to break off the engagement with his nephew—suppose he should forbid me the house, and, taking advantage of my absence, use his authority to force on this hateful marriage! All that would be extremely disagreeable, and I could not say I exactly saw, at the moment, what means I should be able to employ, effectually to prevent it. Still, it was only a remote contingency—an old man like him, with one foot, as you might say, in the grave (he could not have been above sixty, and his constitution, like everything else about him, appeared of cast-iron), must have some conscience, must pay some little regard to right and wrong : it would only be necessary to open his eyes to the enormity of wedding beauty and innocence such as Clara's to a scoundrel like Cumberland —a man destitute of every honourable feeling—oh ! he must see that the thing was impossible, and, as the thought passed through my mind, I longed for the moment when I should be confronted with him, and able to tell him so.

And Clara, too! sweet, bewitching, unhappy Clara ! what must not she have gone through, ere a mind, naturally buoyant and elastic as hers, could have been crushed into a state of such utter dejection, such calm, spiritless despair ! her only wish, to die—her only hope to find in the grave a place " where the wicked cease from troubling, and the weary are at rest !" But brighter days were in store for her —it should be my ambition to render her married life so happy that, if possible, the recollection of all she had suffered having passed away, her mind should recover its natural tone, and even her lightness of heart, which the chill atmosphere of unkindness for a time had blighted, should revive again in the warm sunshine of affection.

Thus meditating, I arrived at Elm Lodge in a state of feeling containing about equal parts of the intensely poetical and the very decidedly hungry.

On the second morning after the events I have described, a note was brought to me whilst I was dressing. With trembling fingers I tore open the envelope, and read as follows :—

"I promised to inform you of what occurred on my return here, and I must therefore do so, though what I have to communicate will only give you pain. All that my fears pointed at has come to pass, and my doom appears irrevocably sealed. Late on the evening of my return to Barstone, Mr. Vernor and his nephew arrived. I never shall forget the feeling of agony that shot through my brain, as Richard Cumberland's footstep sounded in the hall, knowing, as I too well did, the purpose with which he was come. I fancied grief had in great measure deadened my feelings, but that moment served to undeceive me—the mixture of horror, aversion, and fear, combined with a sense of utter helplessness and desolation, seemed, as it were, to paralyze me.

"But I know not why I am writing all this. The evening passed off without anything particular taking place. Mr. Cumberland's

manner towards me was regulated by the most consummate tact and
cunning, allowing the deep interest he pretends to feel in me to
appear in every look and action, yet never going far enough to afford
me an excuse for repulsing him. This morning, however, I have had
an interview with Mr. Vernor, in which I stated my repugnance to
the marriage as strongly as possible. He was fearfully irritated,
and at length, on my repeating my refusal, plainly told me that it
was useless for me to resist his will—that I was in his power, and, if
I continued obstinate, I must be made to feel it. Oh! that man's
anger is terrible to witness: it is not that he is so violent—he never
seems to lose his self-control—but says the most cutting things in a
tone of calm, sarcastic bitterness, which lends double force to all he
utters. I feel that it is useless for us to contend against fate: you
cannot help me, and would only embroil yourself with these men were
you to attempt to do so. I shall ever look back upon the few days
we spent together as a bright spot in the dark void of my life—that
life which you preserved at the risk of your own. Alas! you little
knew the cruel nature of the gift you were bestowing. And now
farewell for ever! That you may find all the happiness your kindness and generosity deserve is the earnest prayer of one whom, for
her sake as well as your own, you must strive to forget."

" If I do forget her," exclaimed I, as I pressed the note to my lips,
" may I— Well, never mind, I'll go over and have it out with that
old brute this very morning, and we'll see if he can frighten me."
And so saying, I set to work to finish dressing, in a great state of
virtuous indignation.

" Freddy," inquired I, when breakfast was at length concluded,
" where can I get a horse ? "

" Get a horse ?" was the reply. " Oh ! there are a great many
places—it depends upon what kind of a horse you want: for race-
horses, steeple-chasers, and hunters, I would recommend Tattersall's ;
for hacks or machiners, there's Aldridge's, in St. Martin's Lane ;
while Dixon's, in the Barbican, is the place to pick up a fine young
cart-horse—is it a young cart-horse you want ? "

" My dear fellow, don't worry me," returned I, feeling very cross
and trying to look amiable; "you know what I mean; is there anything rideable to be hired in Hillingford ? I have a call to make
which is beyond a walk."

" Let me see," replied Freddy, musing; "you wouldn't like a very
little pony, with only one eye and a rat-tail, I suppose—it might look
absurd with your long legs, I'm afraid—or else Mrs. Meek, the
undertaker's widow, has got a very quiet one that poor Meek used to
ride—a child could manage it. There's the butcher's fat mare, but
she won't stir a step without the basket on her back, and it would be
so troublesome for you to carry that all the way. Tomkins, the
sweep, has got a little horse he'd let you have, I dare say, but it
always comes off black on one's trousers; and the miller's cob is
just as bad the other way with the flour. I know a donkey—"

"So do I," was the answer, as, laughing in spite of myself, I turned to leave the room.

"Here, stop a minute!" cried Freddy, following me, "you are so dreadfully impetuous; there's nothing morally wrong in being acquainted with a donkey, is there? I assure you I did not mean anything personal; and now for a word of sense. Bumpus, at the Green Man, has got a tremendous horse, which nearly frightened me into fits the only time I ever mounted him, so that it will just suit you; nobody but a green man, or a knight-errant, which I consider much the same sort of thing, would patronize such an animal—still he's the only one I know of."

Coleman's tremendous horse, which proved to be a tall, pigheaded, hard-mouthed brute, with a very decided will of his own, condescended, after sundry skirmishes and one pitched battle, occasioned by his positive refusal to pass a windmill, to go the road I wished, and about an hour's ride brought me to the gate of Barstone Park.

So completely had I been hurried on by feeling in every stage of the affair, and so entirely had all minor considerations given way to the paramount object of securing Clara's happiness, with which, as I now felt, my own was indissolubly linked, that it was not until my eye rested on the cold gray stone of Barstone Priory, and wandered over the straight walks and formal lawns of the garden, that I became fully aware of the extremely awkward and embarrassing nature of the interview I was about to seek. To force myself into the presence of a man more than double my own age, and, from all I had seen or heard of him, one of the last people in the world to take a liberty with, for the purpose of informing him that his nephew, the only creature on earth that he was supposed to love, was a low swindler, the associate of gamblers and blacklegs, did not appear a line of conduct exactly calculated to induce him, at my request, to give up a scheme on which he had set his heart, or to look with a favourable eye on my pretensions to the hand of his ward. Still, there was no help for it: the happiness of her I loved was at stake, and had it been to face a fiend instead of a man, I should not have hesitated.

My meditations were here interrupted by a cock-pheasant, which, alarmed at my approach, rose immediately under my horse's nose; an unexpected incident, which caused that brute to shy violently, and turn short round, thereby nearly unseating me. Having by this manoeuvre got his head towards home, he not only refused to turn back again, but showed very unmistakable symptoms of a desire to run away. Fortunately, however, since the days of "Mad Bess," my arms had grown considerably stronger, and, by dint of pulling and sawing the creature's apology for a mouth with the bit, I was enabled to frustrate his benevolent intentions, and even succeeded in turning him round again; but here my power ceased—for in the direction of the Priory by no possibility could I induce him to move a step. I whipped and spurred, but in vain; the only result was a series of kicks and plunges, accompanied by a retrograde movement and a

shake of the head, as if he were saying, No! I next attempted the
soothing system, and lavished sundry caresses and endearing
expressions upon him, of which he was utterly undeserving; but my
attentions were quite thrown away, and might as well, for any good
they produced, have been bestowed upon a rocking-horse. At length,
after a final struggle, in which we were both within an ace of falling
into a water-course which crossed the park in that direction, I gave
the matter up as hopeless; and with a sigh (for I love not to be
foiled in anything I have attempted, and, moreover, I could not help
looking upon it as an unlucky omen) dismounted, and, leading my
rebellious steed by the rein, advanced on foot towards the house.
As I did so, a figure abruptly turned the corner of a shrubbery walk,
which ran at right angles to the road, and I found myself face to face
with Richard Cumberland!

For a moment he remained staring at me as if he scarcely
recognized me, or was unwilling to trust the evidence of his senses,
so confounded was he at my unexpected apparition; but as I met
his gaze with a cold, stern look, he seemed to doubt no longer, and
advancing a step towards me, said in a tone of ironical politeness,—

"Is it possible that I have the pleasure of seeing Mr. Fairlegh?"

"None other, Mr. Cumberland," returned I. "though I could
hardly have flattered myself that my appearance would have recalled
any very pleasurable associations, considering the last two occasions
on which we met."

"Ah! you refer to that unfortunate affair with Wilford," replied
Cumberland, purposely misunderstanding my allusion to Dr. Mildman's. "I had hoped to have been able to prevent the mischief which
occurred, but I was misinformed as to the time of the meeting—I
trust our friend Oaklands feels no ill effects from his wound."

"Mr. Oaklands, I am sorry to say, recovers but slowly; the wound
was a very severe one," returned I coldly.

"Well, I will not detain you any longer; it is a lovely morning for
a ride," resumed Cumberland; "can I be of any assistance in directing you? the lanes in this neighbourhood are somewhat intricate—
you are not perhaps aware that the road you are now following is a
private one?"

"Scarcely so private that those who have business with Mr.
Vernor may not make use of it, I presume," rejoined I.

"Oh, of course not," was the reply; "I did not know that you were
acquainted with my uncle; though, now I come to think of it, I do
recollect his saying that he had met you somewhere. He seldom
receives visitors in the morning—in fact, when I came out, I left
him particularly engaged. Perhaps I can save you the trouble of
going up to the house; is there any message I can deliver for
you?"

"I thank you," replied I, "but I do not think the business which
has brought me here could be well transacted through a third
person; at all events, I will take my chance of being admitted." I

paused, but could not refrain from adding, "Besides, if my memory fails not, you were a somewhat heedless messenger in days of yore."

This allusion to his embezzlement of Oaklands' letter stung him to the quick: he turned as white as ashes, and asked, in a voice that trembled with passion, "whether I meant to insult him!"

"I spoke heedlessly, and without deliberate intention," I replied; "but perhaps it is only fair to tell you that for the future there can be no friendly communication between us; we must either avoid each other altogether, which would be the most desirable arrangement, or meet as strangers. The disgraceful conduct of the boy I could have forgiven and forgotten, had not its memory been revived by the evil deeds of the man. Richard Cumberland, I KNOW you thoroughly; it is needless for me to add more."

As I spoke his cheek flushed, then grew pale again with shame and anger, while he bit his under lip so severely that a red line remained where his teeth had pressed it. When I concluded, he advanced towards me with a threatening gesture, but, unable to meet the steadfast look with which I confronted him, he turned abruptly on his heel, and muttering, "You shall repent this," disappeared among the shrubs.

CHAPTER XXXVIII.

FACING THE ENEMY.

"Sir," said the count, with brow exceeding grave,
  "Your unexpected presence here will make
It necessary for myself to crave
  Its import? But perhaps it's a mistake.
I hope it is so; and at once, to waive
  All compliment, I hope so for *your* sake.
You understand my meaning, or you *shall*."
    Beppo.

"Is your master—is Mr. Vernor at home?" inquired I of the grim-visaged old servant, who looked, if possible, taller and more wooden than when I had last seen him.

"Well, I suppose not, sir!" was the somewhat odd reply.

"You suppose!" repeated I; "if you have any doubt, had you not better go and see?"

"That won't be of no manner of use, sir," was the rejoinder; "I should not be none the wiser."

It was clear that the old man was a complete original; but his affection for Clara was a virtue which in my eyes would have atoned for any amount of eccentricity; and as I was anxious to stand well in his good graces. I determined to fall in with his humour; accordingly I replied with a smile, "How do you make out that—did you never hear that seeing is believing?"

"Not always, sir," he answered, "for if I'd a trusted to my eyesight—and it ain't so bad neither for a man that's no great way off sixty—I should have fancied Muster Wernor was a sitting in the liber-ary, but he told me he was not at home hisself, and he ought to know best."

"Tell him I won't detain him long," returned I, "but that I am come on business of importance."

"'Tain't of no manner of use, young gentleman," was the reply; "he told me he wasn't at home, and he said it uncommon cross, too, as if he meant it, and if I was to go to him twenty times he'd only say the same thing."

"What's your name, my good friend?" inquired I.

"Peter Barnett, at your service. sir," was the answer.

"Well. then, Peter, we must contrive to understand one another a little better. You have known your young mistress from a child, and have a sincere regard for her—is it not so?"

"What, Miss Clara, God bless her!—why, I love her as if she was my own flesh and blood; I should be a brute if I didn't, poor lamb!"

"Well, then, when I tell you that her happiness is very nearly connected with the object of my visit—when I say that it is to prevent her from being obliged to do something of which she has the greatest abhorrence that I am anxious to meet Mr. Vernor—I am sure you will contrive that I shall see him."

As I concluded, the old man, muttering to himself, "That's it, is it?" began to examine me from top to toe with a critical glance, as if I had been some animal he was about to purchase; and when he reached my face, gazed at me long and fixedly, as though striving to read my character. Apparently the result of his scrutiny was favourable, for after again saying in a low tone, "Well, I likes the looks of him," he added, "This way, young gentleman—you shall see him if that's what you want—it ain't a hanging matter, after all." As he spoke, he threw open the door of the library, saying, "Gentleman says his business is werry partiklar, so I thought you'd better see him yourself."

Mr. Vernor, who was seated at a table writing, rose on my entrance, bowed stiffly to me, and, casting a withering glance on Peter Barnett, signed to him to shut the door. As soon as that worthy had obeyed the command, he resumed his seat, and, addressing me with the same frigid politeness which he had shown on the occasion of my first visit to him, said, "I am somewhat occupied this morning, and must therefore be excused for inquiring at once what very particular business Mr. Fairlegh can have with me."

His tone and manner, as he spoke, were such as to render me

fully aware of the pleasant nature of the task before me; namely, to make the most disagreeable communication possible, to the most disagreeable person to whom such a communication could be made. Still, I was regularly in for it; there was nothing left for me but to "go ahead;" and as I thus thought of Clara and her sorrows, the task seemed to lose half its difficulty. However, it was not without some hesitation that I began,—

"When you learn the object of my visit, sir, you will perceive that I have not intruded upon you without reason." I paused; but, finding he remained silent, added: "As you are so much occupied this morning, I had better perhaps enter at once upon the business which has brought me here. You are probably aware that I have had the pleasure of spending the last few days in the same house with Miss Saville." As I mentioned Clara's name, his brow grew dark as night; but he still continued silent, and I proceeded: "It is, I should conceive, impossible for anyone to enjoy the privilege of that young lady's society, without experiencing the warmest feelings of admiration and interest. Towards the termination of her visit, accident led me to the knowledge of her acquaintance with Mr. Cumberland, who I then learned, for the first time, was your nephew. I would not willingly say anything which might distress or annoy you, Mr. Vernor," continued I, interrupting myself; "but I fear that, in order to make myself intelligible, I must advert to an affair which I would willingly have forgotten."

"Go on, sir," was the reply, in a cold sarcastic tone of voice— "pray finish your account without reference to my feelings; I am not likely to alarm your sensibility by any affecting display of them."

As the most sceptical could not have doubted for a moment the truth of this assertion, I resumed: "From my previous knowledge of Mr. Cumberland's character, I could not but consider him an unfit acquaintance for a young lady; and on hinting this, and endeavouring to ascertain the extent of Miss Saville's intimacy with him, I was equally shocked and surprised to learn that she was actually engaged to him, and that you not only sanctioned the engagement, but were even desirous that the match should take place. Feeling sure that this could only proceed from your being ignorant of the character of the class of persons with whom your nephew associates, and the more than questionable reputation he has thereby acquired, I considered it my duty to afford you such information as may enable you to ascertain for yourself the truth of the reports which have reached my ear."

"Exceedingly conscientious and praiseworthy: I ought to feel infinitely indebted to you, young gentleman," interrupted Mr. Vernor sarcastically; "of course you made the young lady acquainted with your disinterested and meritorious intentions?"

"I certainly thought it right to inform Miss Saville of the facts I have mentioned, and to obtain her permission, ere I ventured to interfere in her behalf."

As I spoke, the gloom on Mr. Vernor's brow grew darker, and I expected an outburst of rage, but his self-control was stronger than I had imagined, for it was in the same cold, ironical manner that he replied, "And may I ask, supposing this iniquitous engagement to have been broken off by your exertions, is Virtue to be its own reward? will you sit down content with having done your duty? or have you not some snug little scheme 'in petto,' to console the disconsolate damsel for her loss? If I am not mistaken, you were professing warm feelings of admiration for my ward a few minutes since."

"Had you waited till I had finished speaking, you would have perceived. sir, that your taunt was undeserved. I have no wish to conceal anything from you—on the contrary, one of my chief objects in seeking this interview was to inform you of the deep and sincere affection I entertain for Miss Saville, and of my intention of coming forward to seek her hand, as soon as my professional prospects shall enable me to support a wife."

" And have you succeeded in inducing the lady to promise that, in the event of my allowing her to break off her present engagement, she will wait for the somewhat remote and visionary contingency you have hinted at?"

" I have never made the attempt, sir," replied I, drawing myself up proudly, for I began to think that I was carrying forbearance too far, in submitting thus tamely to his repeated insults; "my only desire is to convince you of the necessity of breaking off this preposterous engagement. which is alike unsuitable in itself and distasteful to Miss Saville; for the rest, I must trust to time, and to the unshaken constancy of my own affection (with which it is only fair to tell you the young lady is acquainted), for the accomplishment of my hopes. Had I the power to fetter your ward by a promise which she might afterwards be led to repent, nothing should induce me to make use of it."

" Really, your moderation is quite unparalleled," exclaimed Mr. Vernor; "such generosity now might be almost calculated to induce a romantic girl to persuade her guardian to allow her to marry at once, and devote her fortune to the purpose of defraying the household expenses, till such a time as the professional expectations you mention should be realized; and Clara Saville is just the girl who might do it, for I am afraid I must distress your magnanimity by informing you of a circumstance of which, of course, you have not the slightest idea at present, namely, that if Miss Saville should marry with her guardian's consent, she will become the possessor of a very considerable fortune : what think you of such a plan?"

" Mr. Vernor," replied I, "I was aware that the communication I had to make to you was calculated to pain and annoy you, and that circumstances obliged me to urge my suit at a moment most disadvantageous to its success; I did not therefore imagine that our interview was likely to be a very agreeable one; but I own I did expect to have credit given me for honourable motives, and to be treated with the consideration due from one gentleman to another."

"It grieves me to have disappointed such moderate and reasonable expectations," was the reply ; "but, unfortunately, I have acquired a habit of judging men rather by their actions than their words, and forming my opinion accordingly; and by the opinion thus formed I regulate my conduct towards them."

"May I inquire what opinion you can possibly have formed of me, which would justify your treating me otherwise than as a gentleman ?" asked I, as calmly as I was able, for I was most anxious not to allow him to perceive the degree to which his taunts irritated me.

"Certainly; only remember, if it is not exactly what you approve, that I mention it in compliance with your own express request—but first, for I am unwilling to do you injustice, let me be sure that I understand you clearly :—you state that you are unable to marry till you shall have realized by your profession an income sufficient to support a wife; therefore I presume that your patrimony is somewhat limited."

"You are right, sir; my poor father was too liberal a man to die rich; my present income is somewhat less than £100 per annum."

"And your profession ?"

"It is my intention to begin reading for the bar almost immediately."

"A profession usually more honourable than lucrative for the first ten years or so. Well, young gentleman, the case seems to stand very much as I imagined, nor do I perceive any reason for altering my opinion of your conduct. Chance throws in your way a young lady, possessing great beauty, who is prospective heiress to a very valuable property, and it naturally enough occurs to you that making love is likely to be more agreeable, and in the present instance more profitable also, than reading law; accordingly you commence operations, and for some time all goes on swimmingly, Miss Saville, like any other girl in her situation, having no objection to vary the monotony of a long engagement by a little innocent flirtation—affairs of this kind, however, seldom run smoothly long together—and at some moment, when you were rather more pressing than usual, the young lady thinks it advisable to inform you that, in accordance with her father's dying wish, and of her own free will, she has engaged herself to the nephew of her guardian, who strangely enough happens to be an old schoolfellow of yours, against whom you have always nourished a strong and unaccountable feeling of dislike. Here, then, was a famous opportunity to display those talents for plotting and manœuvring which distinguished Mr. Fairlegh even in his boyish days; accordingly, a master-scheme is invented, whereby the guardian shall be cajoled and browbeaten into giving his consent, enmity satisfied by the rival's discomfiture and overthrow, and talent rewarded by obtaining possession of the young lady and her fortune. As a first step you take advantage of a lovers' quarrel to persuade

Miss Saville that she is averse to the projected alliance, and trump
up an old tale of some boyish scrape, to induce her to believe Cumberland unworthy of her preference, ending, doubtless, by modestly
proposing yourself as a substitute. Inexperience, and the natural
capriciousness of woman, stand your friend ; the young lady appears
for the moment gained over, and, flushed with success, the bold step
of this morning is resolved upon. Such, sir, is my opinion of your
conduct. It only remains for me to inform you that I have not the
slightest intention of breaking off the engagement in consequence
of your disinterested representations, nor, under any circumstances,
would I allow my ward to throw herself away upon a needy fortune-
hunter. There can be nothing more to say, I think; and as I have
some important papers to look over this morning, I dare say you
will excuse my ringing the bell."

"One moment, sir," replied I warmly : "although your age prevents my taking notice of the unprovoked insults you have seen fit
to heap upon me—"

" Really," interposed Mr. Vernor, in a deprecating tone, "you
must pardon me ; I have not time for all this sort of thing to-day."

"You SHALL hear me ! " exclaimed I passionately; "I have
listened in silence to accusations calculated to make the blood of
any man, worthy to be so called, boil in his veins—accusations
which, at the very moment you utter them, you know to be entirely
false : you know well Miss Saville's just and deeply-rooted aversion
to this match, and you know that it existed before she and I had
ever met ; you know the creditable nature of what you term the
'boyish scrape,' in which your nephew was engaged—a scrape which,
but for the generous forbearance of others, might have ended in his
transportation as a convicted felon; and this knowledge (even if you
are ignorant of the dishonourable and vicious course of life he now
leads) should be enough to prevent your sanctioning such a marriage.
I pass over your insinuations respecting myself in silence ; should I
again prefer my suit for Miss Saville's hand to you, it will be as no
needy fortune-hunter that I shall do so; but once more let me
implore you to pause—reconsider the matter—inquire for yourself
into your nephew's pursuits—ascertain the character of his associates,
and then judge whether he is a fit person to be entrusted with the
happiness of such a being as Clara Saville."

" Vastly well, sir ! exceedingly dramatic, indeed ! " observed Mr.
Vernor, with a sneer; " you really have quite a talent for—genteel
comedy, I think they call it; you would be perfect in the line of
character termed the 'walking gentlemen'—have you ever thought
of the stage ? "

" I perceive," replied I, "that by remaining here, I shall only
subject myself to additional insult: determined to carry out your
own bad purpose, you obstinately close your ears to the voice alike
of reason and of conscience ; and now," I added in a stern tone, "hear
my resolve : I have promised Miss Saville to save her from Richard

Cumberland : as the fairest and most honourable way of doing so, I
applied to you, her lawful guardian and protector ; I have failed, and
you have insulted and defied me. I now tell you that I will leave
NO MEANS untried to defeat your nefarious project, and, if evil or
disgrace should befall you or yours in consequence, upon your own
head be it. You may smile at my words, and disregard them as idle
threats which I am powerless to fulfil, but, remember, you have no
longer a helpless girl to deal with, but a determined man, who, with
right and justice on his side, may yet thwart your cunningly-devised
schemes; and so, having given you fair warning, I will leave you."

"Allow me to mention one fact, young sir," returned Mr. Vernor,
"which demands your serious attention, as it may prevent you from
committing a fatal error, and save you all further trouble. Should
Clara Saville marry without my consent, she does so penniless, and
the fortune devolves upon the next heir; ha!" he exclaimed, as I
was unable to repress an exclamation of pleasure, "have I touched
you there ? "

" You have indeed, sir," was my reply ; " for you have removed the
only scruple which stood in my way. No one can now accuse me of
interested motives ; ' needy fortune-hunters ' do not seek to ally
themselves to portionless damsels ; allow me to offer you my best
thanks for your information, and to wish you good-morning, sir."

So saying, I rose and quitted the room, leaving Mr. Vernor, in a
state of ill-suppressed rage, to the enjoyment of his own reflections.

On entering the hall, I found old Peter Barnett awaiting me. As
I appeared, his stiff features lighted up with a most sagacious grin
of intelligence, and approaching me, he whispered,—

" Did ye give it him strong ? " (indicating the person he referred
to by an expressive jerk of his thumb towards the library door). " I
heard ye blowing of him up—but did ye give it him reg'lar strong ? "

" I certainly told Mr. Vernor my opinion with tolerable plainness,"
replied I, smiling at the intense delight which was visible in every line
of the strange old face beside me.

"No! Did ye?—did ye ? That was right," was the rejoinder.
"Lor' ! how I wish I'd a been there to see ; but I heard ye, though—
I heard ye a-giving it to him ;" and again he relapsed into a
paroxysm of delight.

" Peter," said I, " I want to have a little private conversation with
you—how is that to be managed ? Is there any place near where
you could meet me ? "

" You come here from Hillingford, didn't ye, sir ? "

I nodded assent. He continued :—

" Did you notice a hand-post which stands where four roads meet,
about a mile and a half from here ? "

" I saw it," returned I, " and even tried to read what was painted
on it, but of course, after the manner of all country direction posts,
it was totally illegible."

" Well, when you get there, take the road to the left, and ride on till ye see an ale-house on the right-hand side, and stay there till I come to ye."

"I will," replied I, "but don't keep me waiting longer than you can help—there's a good man."

An understanding grin was his only answer; and mounting my unpleasant horse (who seemed much more willing to proceed quietly when his head was turned in a homeward direction), I rode slowly through the park, my state of mind affording a practical illustration that Quintus Horatius Flaccus was about right in his conjecture that Care sometimes indulged herself with a little equestrian exercise on a pillion.[1]

CHAPTER XXXIX.

THE COUNCIL OF WAR.

> "Oh! good old man: how well in thee appears
> The constant service of the antique world!"
> *As You Like It.*

> "Now will I deliver his letter; for the behaviour of the young gentleman gives him out to be of good capacity and breeding."—*Twelfth Night.*

> "Farewell! be trusty, and I'll quit thy pains.
> Farewell! commend me to thy mistress."
> *Romeo and Juliet.*

THE place of meeting appointed by Peter Barnett was easily discovered, and having tied up my horse under a shed, which served the double purpose of stable and coach-house, I took possession of a small room with a sanded floor, and throwing myself back in a most uneasy easy-chair, began to think over my late interview, and endeavour to devise some practicable plan for the future. The first thing was to establish some means of free communication with Clara, and this I hoped to accomplish by the assistance of Peter Barnett. I should thus learn Mr. Vernor's proceedings, and be able to regulate my conduct accordingly. If, as I dreaded, he should attempt to force on the marriage immediately, would Clara, alone and unassisted, have sufficient courage and strength of purpose to resist him? I feared not; and how was I effectually to aid her? The question was more easily asked than answered. It was clear that her fortune was the thing aimed at, for I could not believe either Mr. Vernor or his nephew likely to be actuated by disinterested motives;—and it was to their avarice, then, that Clara was to be sacrificed—had she been portionless she would have been free to marry whom she pleased. Of all sources of evil and misery, money appears to be the most prolific; in the present case its action was

1 "Post equitem sedet atra cura."

S

twofold—Clara was rendered wretched in consequence of possessing it, while the want of it incapacitated me from boldly claiming her hand at once, which appeared to be the only effectual method of assisting her.

My meditations were at this point interrupted by the arrival of my future privy councillor, Peter Barnett, who marched solemnly into the room, drew himself up to his full height, which very nearly equalled that of the ceiling, brought his hand to his forehead in a military salute, and then, closing the door cautiously, and with an air of mystery, stood at ease, evidently intending me to open the conversation.

" Well, Peter," began I, by way of something to say, for I felt the greatest difficulty in entering on the subject which then occupied my thoughts, before such an auditor. " Well, Peter, you have not kept me waiting long; I scarcely expected to see you so soon: do you imagine that Mr. Vernor will remark your absence ? "

"He knows it already," was the reply. " Why, bless ye, sir, he ordered me to go out hisself."

"Indeed ! how was that ? "

" Why, as soon as you was gone, sir, he pulled the bell like mad. 'Send Mr. Richard here,' says he. 'Yes, sir,' says I, 'certingly; only he's not at home, sir.' When he heard this he grumbled out an oath, or sumthin' of that nature, and I was going to take myself off, for I see he wasn't altogether safe, when he roars out, 'Stop!' ('You'd a-said "halt," if you'd a-been a officer or a gentleman, which you ain't neither,' thinks I.) 'What do you mean by letting people in when I have given orders to the contrairy ?' says he. 'Who was it as blowed me up for sending away a gent as said he wanted to see you on partiklar business, only yesterday ?' says I. That bothered him nicely, and he didn't know how to be down upon me ; but at last he thought he'd serve me one of his old tricks. So he says, 'Peter, what are you doing to-day ?' I see what he was at, and I thought I'd ketch him in his own trap, 'Very busy a-cleaning plate, sir,' says I. This was enough for him: if I was a-cleaning plate, in course I shouldn't like to be sent out; so says he, 'Go down to Barnsley, and see whether Mr. Cumberland is there.' 'But the plate, sir ?' 'Never mind the plate.' 'It won't never look as it ought to do, if I am sent about in this way,' says I. 'Do as you're ordered, and leave the room instantly,' says he, grinding his teeth reg'lar savage-like. So I took him at his word, and come away to see you as hard as I could pelt; but you've put him into a sweet temper, Mr. Fairlegh."

" Why, that, I'm afraid, was scarcely to be avoided," replied I, " as my business was to inform him that I considered his nephew an unfit person to marry his ward."

" Oh! did you tho' ?—did you tell him that ?" cried my companion, with a chuckle of delight; " that was right : I wonder how he liked that ? "

"As he did not exactly agree with me in this opinion, but, on the contrary, plainly declared his intention of proceeding with the match in spite of me, it is necessary for me to consider what means I can best use to prevent him from accomplishing his object; it is in this that I shall require your assistance."

"And what does Miss Clara say about it, young gentleman?" inquired the old man, fixing his eyes on me with a scrutinizing glance.

"Miss Saville dislikes Richard Cumberland, and dreads the idea of being forced to marry him above everything."

"Ah! I know she does, poor lamb! and well she may, for there ain't a more dissipateder young scoundrel to be found nowhere than Mr. Vernor's precious 'nephew,' as he calls him, tho' it's my belief he might call him 'son' without telling a lie."

"Indeed! I was not aware that Mr. Vernor had ever been married."

"No; I never heard that he was reg'lar downright married; but he may be his son, for all that. Howsumever, p'raps it is so, or p'raps it ain't; I'm only a-tellin' you what I fancies, sir," was the reply. "But what I wanted to know," he continued, again fixing his eyes on my face, "is, what does Miss Clara say to you? eh!"

"You put home questions, my friend," replied I, colouring slightly; "however, as Miss Saville tells me you are faithful and trustworthy, and as half-confidences are never of any use, I suppose you must hear all about it." I then told him as concisely as possible of my love for Clara, and my hopes of one day calling her my own; pointing out to him the difficulties that stood in the way, and explaining to him that the only one which appeared to me insurmountable was the probability of Mr. Vernor's attempting to force Clara into an immediate marriage with Cumberland. Having thus given him an insight into the true state of affairs, I showed him the necessity of establishing some means of communication between Clara and myself, as it was essential that I should receive the earliest possible information in regard to Mr. Vernor's proceedings.

"I understand, sir," interrupted Peter, "you want to be able to write to each other without the old 'un getting hold of your letters: well, that's very easily managed; only you direct to Mr. Barnett, to be left at the Pig and Pony, at Barstone; and anything you send for Miss Clara, I'll take care and give her when nobody won't be none the wiser for it; and any letters she writes I'll put into the post myself. I'd do anything rather than let that young villain Cumberland have her, and make her miserable, which his wife is safe to be, if ever he gets one; and if you likes her and she likes you, as seems werry probable, considering you saved her from being burnt to death, as they tell me, and is werry good-looking into the bargain— which goes a great way with young ladies, if you'll excuse the liberty I takes in mentioning of it—why, the best thing as you can do, is to get married as soon as you can."

"Very pleasant advice, friend Peter," returned I, "but not so easily acted upon; people cannot marry nowadays without something to live upon."

" Well, ain't Miss Clara got Barstone Priory, and plenty of money to keep it up with ?   Won't that do to live upon ? "

" And do you imagine I could ever feel content to be the creature of my wife's bounty ? prove myself a needy fortune-hunter, as that old man dared to term me ? " exclaimed I, forgetting the character of my auditor.

" Barstone Priory to live in, and more money than you know what to do with, ain't to be sneezed at neither," was the answer; " though I likes your independent spirit too, sir : but how do you mean to manage, then ? "

" Why, Mr. Vernor hinted that if his ward married without his consent her fortune was to be forfeited."

" Ah ! I believe there was something of that nature in the will : my poor master was so wrapped up in old Wernor that he wrote just what he told him ; if he'd only lived to see how he was going to use Miss Clara, he'd a-ordered me to kick him out of the house instead."

" Perhaps that pleasure may be yet in store for you, Peter," replied I, laughing at the zest with which he uttered the last few words, and an involuntary motion of the foot by which they were accompanied ; " but this power, which it seems Mr. Vernor really possesses, of depriving Miss Saville of her fortune, removes my greatest difficulty ; for in that case, if he should attempt to urge on this match, I can at least make her the offer of sharing my poverty ; there is my mother's roof to shelter her, and if her guardian refuses his consent to our marriage, why, we must contrive to do without it, that is all. So now, Peter, if you will wait a few minutes, I will give you a note for your young mistress, and then get to horse without further loss of time ; " and calling for pen, ink, and paper, I hastily scribbled a few lines to Clara, informing her of the events of the morning, and of my unalterable determination to save her from a union with Cumberland ; begging her, at the same time, to continue firm in her opposition, to acquaint me with everything that might occur, and to rely upon me for protection in the event of anything like force being resorted to. I then intrusted my note to old Peter, begged him to watch Master Richard Cumberland closely, told him that upon his care and vigilance depended in great measure the happiness of his young mistress's life; tipped him handsomely,. though I had some trouble in making him take the money ; and mounting my ill-disposed horse, rode back to Hillingford, on the whole tolerably well satisfied with my morning's work.

I found two letters awaiting my return : one from my mother, to say that she should be at Heathfield Cottage on the following day, and begging me to meet her; the other from Ellis, telling me that at length he hoped Oaklands was in a fair way to recover, it having been ascertained that a piece of the wadding of the pistol had remained behind when the ball was extracted ; this had now come away, and the wound was healing rapidly. As his strength returned, Harry was growing extremely impatient to get back to Heathfield; and Ellis concluded by saying that they might be expected any day, and begging me at the same time to remember that from the first he had always declared, in regard to his patient, that it would have killed any other man, but that it could not kill him.

Days glided by, the absentees returned, and matters fell so completely into their old train again that the occurrences of the last eight months seemed like the unreal creations of some fevered dream, and there were times when I could scarcely bring myself to believe them true.

Harry Oaklands had recovered sufficiently to resume his usual habits; and, except that he was strictly forbidden to over-exert or fatigue himself (an injunction he appeared only too willing to obey), he was nearly emancipated from medical control. Fanny had in great measure regained her good looks again; a slight delicacy of appearance, however, still remained, giving a tone of spirituality to the expression of her features, which was not before observable, and which to my mind rendered her prettier than ever: the listlessness of manner which had made me uneasy about her in the autumn had vanished, and her spirits seemed good; still, she was in a degree altered, and one felt in talking to her that she was a child no longer. Like Undine, that graceful creation of La Motte Fouqué's genius, she appeared to have changed from a " tricksy sprite " into a thinking and feeling woman.

One morning Oaklands and Ellis came to the cottage together, the latter in a great state of joy and excitement, produced by a most kind and judicious exercise of liberality on the part of Sir John. About a month before, the grave and pompous Dr. Probehurt had been seized with an illness, from which in all probability he would have recovered had he not steadily refused to allow a rival practitioner to be called in, in order that he might test a favourite theory of his own, embodying a totally novel mode of treatment for the complaint with which he was attacked. Unfortunately, the experiment failed, and the doctor died. Sir John, who had been long anxious to evince his gratitude to Ellis for the skill and attention he had bestowed upon his patient, the moment he heard of the event determined to purchase the business: he had that morning completed the negotiation, and offered the practice to Ellis, stating that he should consider his accepting it in the light of a personal favour, as in that case he would be always at hand should Harry feel any lasting ill effects from his wound. Ellis's joy was most amusing to witness.

" I tell you what, sir," he exclaimed, seizing me by a button of the coat, " I'm a made man, sir! there isn't a better practice in the county. Why, poor Probehurt told me himself old Mrs. Croaker Crawley alone was worth £100 per annum to him: four draughts and two

pills every day—prescription very simple—R. Pil. panis compos. ij.
nocte sum.; haust. aqua vitæ ℥, aqua pura ℥, saccar. viij. grs. pro re
nata. She's a strong old girl, and on brandy and water draughts and
French-roll pills may last for the next twenty years. Noble thing
of Sir John, very; 'pon my word, it has quite upset me—it's a fact,
sir, that when Mr. Oaklands told me of it I sat down and cried like
a child. I'm not over tender-hearted, either: when I was at Guy's I
amputated the left leg of a shocking accident, and dissected the
porter's mother-in law (whom he sold us cheap for old acquaintance'
sake) before breakfast one morning, without finding my appetite in
the slightest degree affected; but when I learned what Sir John
had done, I positively cried, sir."

"I say, Ellis," interrupted Harry, "I am telling Miss Fairlegh I
shall make you take her in hand; she has grown so pale and thin, I
am afraid she has never recovered all the trouble and inconvenience
we caused her."

"If Miss Fairlegh would allow me, I should recommend a little
more air and exercise," replied Ellis: "are you fond of riding on
horseback ? "

"Oh yes!" replied Fanny, smiling, and blushing slightly at thus
suddenly becoming the topic of conversation; "that is, I used to
delight in riding Frank's pony in days of yore; but he has not
kept a pony lately."

"That is easily remedied," returned Harry : "I am certain some
of our horses will carry a lady. I shall speak to Harris about it
directly, and we'll have some rides together, Fanny : it was only this
morning that I obtained my tyrant's permission to cross a horse
once more," he added, shaking his fist playfully at Ellis.

"The tyrant will agree to that more willingly than to your first
request. What do you think, Fairlegh," continued Ellis, appealing
to me, " of his positively wanting to go out hunting ? "

" And a very natural thing to wish too, I conceive," replied Harry ;
" but what do you think of his declaring that, if I did not faithfully
promise not to hunt this season, he would go into the stables and
divide, what he called in his doctor's lingo, the 'flexor metatarsi' of
every animal he found there, which, being interpreted, means neither
more nor less than hamstring all the hunters."

" Well, that would be better than allowing you to do anything
which might disturb the beautiful process of granulation going on
in your side. I remember, when I was a student at Guy's—"

" Come, doctor, we positively cannot stand any more of your
'Chronicles of the Charnel-house' this morning; you have horrified
Miss Fairlegh already to such a degree that she is going to run
away. If I should stroll down here again in the afternoon, Fanny,
will you take compassion on me so far as to indulge me with a game
of chess? I am going to send Frank on an expedition, and my
father and Ellis are off to settle preliminaries with poor Mrs. Probehurt, so that I shall positively not have a creature to speak to.

Reading excites me too much, and produces a state of——What is it you call it, doctor?"

"I told you yesterday I thought you were going into a state of coma, when you fell asleep over that interesting paper of mine in the 'Lancet,' 'Recollections of the Knife;' if that's what you call excitement," returned Ellis, laughing.

"Nonsense, Ellis, how absurd you are!" rejoined Oaklands, half amused and half annoyed at Ellis's remark; "but you have not granted my request yet, Fanny."

"I do not think we have any engagement—mamma will, I am sure, be very happy," began Fanny, with a degree of hesitation for which I could not account; but as I was afraid Oaklands might notice it, and attribute it to a want of cordiality, I hastened to interrupt her by exclaiming, "Mamma will be very happy—of course she will; and each and all of us are always only too happy to get you here, old fellow: it does one's heart good to see you beginning to look a little more like yourself again. If Fanny's too idle to play chess, I'll take compassion upon you, and give you a thorough beating myself."

"There are two good and sufficient reasons why you will not do anything of the kind," replied Oaklands: "in the first place, while you have been reading mathematics, I have been studying chess; and I think that I may, without conceit, venture to pronounce myself the better player of the two; and in the second place, as I told your sister just now, I am going to send you out on an expedition."

"To send me on an expedition!" repeated I; "may I be allowed to inquire its nature—where I am to go to—when I am to start—and all other equally essential particulars?"

"They are soon told," returned Oaklands. "I wrote a few days since to Lawless, asking him to come down for a week's hunting before the season should be over; and this morning I received the following characteristic answer:—'Dear Oaklands,—A man who refuses a good offer is an ass (unless he happens to have had a better one). Now, yours being the best offer down in my book at present, I say, "Done, along with you, old fellow," thereby clearly proving that I am no ass. Q.E.D.—eh? that's about the thing, isn't it? Now, look here. Jack Bassett has asked me down to Storley Wood for a day's pheasant-shooting on Tuesday; if you could contrive to send any kind of trap over about lunch-time on Wednesday, I could have a second pop at the long-tails, and be with you in time for a half-past six o'clock feed, as it is not more than ten miles from Storley to Heathfield. I wouldn't have troubled you to send for me, only the tandem's "hors de combat." I was fool enough to lend it to Muffington Spoffkins to go and see his aunt one fine day. The horses, finding a fresh hand on the reins, began pulling like steam-engines—Muffington could not hold them—consequently they bolted; and after running over two whole infant schools, and upsetting a retired grocer, they knocked the cart into " immortal smash " against a turnpike-gate, pitching Spoffkins into a horse-pond, with Shrimp atop of him. It was a regular sell for all parties : I got my cart broken to pieces. Shrimp was all but drowned, and Muffington's aunt cut him off with a shilling, because one extirpated squadron of juveniles turned out, unfortunately, to have been a picked detach-ment of infantry from her own village. If you could send to meet me at the Feathers public-house, which is just at the bottom of Storley great wood, it would be a mercy, for walking in cover doesn't suit my short legs, and I'm safe to be used up.—Remember us to Fairlegh and all inquiring friends, and believe me to remain, very heartily yours, George Lawless.' "

"I comprehend," said I, as Oaklands finished reading the note ; "you wish me to drive over this afternoon and fetch him : it will be a great deal better than merely sending a servant."

" Why, I had thought of going myself, but, 'pon my word, these sort of things are so much trouble—at least to me, I mean; and though Lawless is a capital, excellent fellow, and I like him extremely, yet I know he'll talk about nothing but horses all the way home ; and not being quite strong again yet, you've no notion how that kind of thing worries and tires me."

"Don't say another word about it, my dear Harry; I shall enjoy the drive uncommonly. What vehicle had I better take ?"

" The phaeton, I think," replied Oaklands, "and then you can bring his luggage, and Shrimp, or any of his people he may have with him."

"So be it," returned I ; "I'll walk back with you to the Hall, and then start as soon as you please."

CHAPTER XL.

LAWLESS'S MATINEE MUSICALE.

"I was deep in my tradesmen's books, I'm afraid,
    But not in my own, by-the-bye ;
And when rascally tailors came to be paid,
    There'll be time enough for that, said I."
                            Song—The Old Bachelor.

    " Here's a knocking, indeed ;
Knock, knock, knock. Who's there?
Faith, here's an English tailor come hither.
——Come in, tailor——
Knock, knock, Never at quiet !
What are you? I had thought to have let in
Some of all professions. Anon—anon."
                            Macbeth.

I SCARCELY know any excitement more agreeable than driving, on a fine frosty day, a pair of spirited horses, which demand the exercise of all one's coolness and skill to keep their fiery natures under proper control. Some accident had happened to one of Sir John's old

phaeton horses, and Harry, who fancied that, as he was not allowed
to use any violent exercise, driving would be an amusement to him,
had taken the opportunity of replacing them by a magnificent pair
of young, nearly thoroughbred chestnuts; and these were the steeds
now intrusted to my guidance. Not being anxious, however, to
emulate the fate of the unfortunate Muffington Spoffkins, I held
them well in hand for the first three or four miles, and as they
became used to their work, gradually allowed them to quicken their
pace, till we were bowling along merrily at the rate of ten miles an
hour.

A drive of about an hour and a quarter brought me within sight of
the little roadside public-house appointed for my rendezvous with
Lawless. As I drew sufficiently near to distinguish figures, I
perceived the gentleman in question scientifically and picturesquely
attired in what might with great propriety be termed no end of a
shooting jacket, inasmuch as its waist, being prolonged to a strange
and unaccountable extent, had, as a necessary consequence, invaded
the region of the skirt, to a degree which reduced that appendage
to the most absurd and infinitesimal proportions. This wonderful
garment was composed of a fabric which Freddy Coleman, when he
made its acquaintance some few days later, denominated the Mac
Omnibus plaid, a gaudy repertoire of colours, embracing all the tints
of the rainbow, and a few more besides, and was further embellished
by a plentiful supply of gent's sporting buttons, which latter articles
were not quite so large as cheese-plates, and represented in bas-relief
a series of moving incidents by flood and field. His nether man
exhibited a complicated arrangement of corduroys, leather gaiters,
and waterproof boots, which were, of course, wet through; while, to
crown the whole, his head was adorned with one of those round felt
hats, which exactly resemble a boiled apple-pudding, and are known
by the sobriquet of "widewakes," "cos they 'av'n't got no nap about
'em." A stout shooting pony was standing at the door of the ale-
house, with a pair of panniers, containing a portmanteau and a gun-
case, slung across its back, upon which was seated in triumph the
mighty Shrimp, who seemed to possess the singular property of
growing older, and nothing else; for, as well as one could judge by
appearances, he had not increased an inch in stature since the first
day of our acquaintance. His attitude, as I drove up, was one which
Hunt would have delighted to perpetuate. Perched on a kind of
pack-saddle, his legs stretched so widely apart, by reason of the
stout proportions of the pony, as to be nearly at right angles with
his upper man, he "held aloft" (not a "snowy scarf," but) a pewter-
pot, nearly as large as himself, the contents of which he was trans-
ferring to his own throat, with an air of relish and "savoir faire" which
would have done credit to a seven-feet-high coalheaver. The group
was completed by a gamekeeper, who, seated on a low wooden bench,
was dividing some bread and cheese with a magnificent black
retriever.

"By Jove! what splendid steppers!" was Lawless's exclamation as I drove up. "Now, that's what I call perfect action; high enough to look well, without battering the feet to pieces—the leg a little arched, and thrown out boldly—no fear of their putting down their pins in the same place they pick them up from. Ah!" he continued, for the first time observing me, "Fairlegh, how are you, old fellow? Slap-up cattle you've got there, and no mistake—belong to Sir John Oaklands, I suppose. Do you happen to know where he got hold of them?"

"Harry wanted a pair of phaeton horses, and the coachman recommended these," replied I; "but I've no idea where he heard of them."

"Rising five and six," continued Lawless, examining their mouths with deep interest; "no do there—the tush well up in one and nicely through in the other, and the mark in the nippers just as it should be to correspond: own brothers, I'll bet a hundred pounds—good full eyes; small heads, well set on; slanting shoulders; legs as clean as a colt's; hoofs a leetle small, but that's the breed. Whereabouts was the figure, did you hear?—five fifties never bought them, unless they were as cheap as dirt, eh?"

"That was about their price, if I remember correctly," replied I. "Harry thought it was too much to give; but Sir John, the moment he saw his son would like to have them, wrote the cheque, and paid for them on the spot."

"Well, I'll give him all the money any day, if he's tired of his bargain," rejoined Lawless; "but we won't keep them standing now they're warm. Here, Shrimp, my great-coat—get off that pony this instant, you luxurious young vagabond. Never saw such a boy in my life to ride as that is—if there is anything that can by possibility carry him, not a step will he stir on foot—doesn't believe legs were meant to walk with, it's my opinion. Why, this very morning, before they brought out the shooting pony, he got on the retriever; and he has such a seat too, that the dog could not throw him, till Bassett thought of sending him into the water: he slipped off in double quick time then, for he has had a regular hydrophobia upon him ever since his adventure in the horse-pond. What, not down yet? I shall take a horsewhip to you, sir, directly."

Thus admonished, Shrimp, who had taken advantage of his master's preoccupation to finish the contents of the pewter pot, tossed the utensil to the gamekeeper, having previously attracted that individual's attention by exclaiming, in a tone of easy familiarity—"Look out, Leggings!"—then, as the man, taken by surprise, and having some difficulty in saving himself from a blow on the nose, allowed the pot to slip through his hands, Shrimp continued, "Catch it, clumsy! well, I never—now mind, if you've gone and bumped it, it's your own doing, and you pays for dilapidations, as we calls 'em at Cambridge. Coming, sir—d'rec'ly, sir—yes, sir." So saying, he slipped down the pony's shoulder, shook himself to set his dress in

order as soon as he reached terra firma, and unbuckling Lawless's
driving coat, which was fastened round his waist by a broad strap,
jumped upon a horse-block, and held out the garment at arm's-length
for his master to put on. The gun-case and carpet-bag were then
transferred from the pony to the phaeton, and resigning the reins to
Lawless, who I knew would be miserable unless he were allowed to
drive, we started. Shrimp being installed in the hind seat, where,
folding his arms, he leaned back, favouring us with a glance which
seemed to say, " You may proceed; I am quite comfortable."

" It was about time for me to take an affectionate farewell of Alma
Mater," observed Lawless, after he had criticized and admired the
horses afresh, and at such length that I could not help smiling at
the fulfilment of Oaklands' prediction—" it was about time for me to
be off, for the duns were becoming rather too particular in their
attentions. I got a precious fright the other day, I can tell you. I
was fool enough to pay two or three bills, and that gave the rest of
the fellows a notion that I was about to bolt, I suppose, for one
morning I was regularly besieged by them. I taught them a trick or
two, though, before I had done with them: they won't forget me in a
hurry, I expect."

" Indeed! and how did you contrive to fix yourself so indelibly in
their recollections ?" asked I.

" Eh! ' though lost to sight, to memory dear '—rather that style of
thing, you know. So you want to hear all about it, eh ? Well, it
was a good lark, I must say; I was telling it to Bassett last night,
and it nearly killed him. I don't know whether you have seen him
lately, but he's grown horridly fat. He has taken to rearing prize
bullocks, and I think he has caught it of 'em; rides sixteen stone, if
he rides a pound. I tell him he'll break his neck some of these days
if he chooses to go on hunting—the horses can't stand it. However,
he went into such fits of laughter when I told him about it, that he
got quite black in the face, and I rang the bell, and swore he was in
an apoplexy; but the servant seemed used to the sort of thing, and
brought him a jug of beer, which resuscitated him. Well, to return
to my mutton, as the mounseers have it—the very day I intended to
leave Cambridge, Shrimp came in while I was breakfasting, with a
great coarse-looking letter in his hand.

" ' Please, sir, Mr. Pigskin has called with his little account, and
would be very glad if you could let him have the money.'

" ' Pleasant,' thinks I. 'Here, boy, let's have a look at this
precious little account—hum! ha! hunting-saddle, gag-bit for
Lamplighter, headpiece and reins to ditto, racing-saddle for chest-
nut-mare," etc., etc., etc.; a horrid affair as long as my arm—total
£96 18s. 2d.; and the blackguard had charged everything half as
much again as he had told me when I ordered it. Still, I thought
I'd pay the fellow, and have done with him, if I had got tin enough
left; so I told Shrimp to show him into the rooms of a man who
lived over me, but was away at the time, and there let him wait. Lo

and behold! when I came to look about the tin, I found that, instead of having ninety pounds at the banker's, I had overdrawn my account some hundred pounds or more; so that paying was quite out of the question, and I was just going to ring the bell, and beg Mr. Pigskin to call again in a day or two, by which time I should have been 'over the hills and far away,' when Shrimp made his appearance.

"'Please, sir, there's ever so many more 'gents called for their money. There's Mr. Flanker, the whip-maker, and Mr. Smokem, from the cigar-shop, and Trotter, the bootmaker, and—yes, sir, there's a young man from Mr. Tinsel, the jeweller: and, oh! a load more of 'em, if you please, sir.'

"This was agreeable, certainly; what to be at I didn't know, when suddenly a bright idea came across me.

"'What have you done with 'em?' asked I.

"'Put 'em all into Mr. Skulker's rooms, sir.'

"'That's the ticket,' said I. 'Now listen to me. Look out, and see if there are any more coming;—if there are, show 'em up to the others, take 'em a couple of bottles of wine and some glasses, and tell them I must beg them to wait a quarter of an hour or so, while I look over their bills; and as soon as the room is full, come and tell me.'

"In about ten minutes Shrimp reported that he could not see any more coming, and that he thought 'all the gents I dealt with was upstairs.'

"'That's the time of day!' exclaimed I, and taking out the key of the room, which Skulker had left with me, in case I might like to put a friend to sleep there, I slipped off my shoes, and creeping upstairs as softly as possible, I locked the door. 'Now then, Shrimp,' said I, 'run and fetch me some good stout screws, a gimlet, and a screw-driver.' He was not long getting them, and in less than five minutes I had them all screwed in as fast as if they had been in their coffins, for they were kicking up such a row over their wine that they never heard me at work. Well, as soon as I had bagged my game, Shrimp and I packed up the traps and sent them to the coach-office—found a coach about to start in half an hour, booked myself for the box, and then strolled back to see how the caged birds were getting on. By this time they had come to a sense of their 'sitivation,' and were hammering away, and swearing, and going on like troopers; but all to no purpose, for the door was a famous strong one, and they had no means of breaking it open. Well, after I had had a good laugh at the row they were making, I tapped at the door, and 'discoorsed' 'em, as Paddy calls it. I told them that I was so much shocked by the want of consideration, and proper feeling, and all that sort of thing, which they had shown, in coming and besieging me as they had done, that I felt it was a duty I owed to society at large, and to themselves in particular, to read them a severe lesson; therefore, on mature deliberation, I had sentenced them to imprisonment for the

term of one hour, and to wait for their money till such time as I
should further decree, which I begged to assure them would not be
until I might find it perfectly convenient to myself to pay them; and
I wound up by telling them to make themselves quite at home,
entreating them not to fatigue themselves by trying to get out, for
that they had not a chance of succeeding; inquiring whether they
had any commands for London, and wishing them a very affectionate
farewell for some time to come. And then down I ran, leaving them
roaring and bellowing like so many mad bulls—got to the office just
in time, and tipping the coachman, drove three parts of the way to
town, feeling as jolly as if I had won a thousand pounds on the
Derby."

"And what became of the locked-up tradesmen?" inquired I.

"Oh! why, they stayed there above two hours before anybody let
them out, amusing themselves by smashing the windows, breaking
the furniture to pieces (one of them was an upholsterer, and had an
eye to business, I dare say), and kicking all the paint off the door.
However, I have written to Skulker to get it all set to rights, and send
me the bill, so no harm's done—it will teach those fellows a lesson
they won't forget in a hurry, and the next time they wish to bully a
Cantab, they'll recollect my little 'matinee musicale,' as I call it. Oh!
they made a sweet row, I can assure you, sir."

The chestnuts trotted merrily on their homeward journey, and the
noble oaks of Heathfield Park, their leafless branches pointing like
giant arms to the cold blue sky above them, soon came in sight.

"You are a great deal too early for dinner, Lawless," said I, as we
drove up; "suppose you walk down to our cottage, and let me introduce you to my mother and sister: you'll find Oaklands there most
likely, for he talked of going to play chess."

"Eh! your mother and sister! by Jove, I never thought of them!
I declare I had forgotten there were any ladies in the case—I can't
go near them in this pickle. I'm all over mud and pheasant feathers;
they'll take me for a native of the Sandwich Islands, one of the boys
that cooked Captain Cook—precious tough work they must have had
to get their teeth through him, for he was no chicken; I wonder how
they trussed him, poor old beggar! No! I'll make myself a little
more like a Christian, and then I'll come down and be introduced to
them if it's necessary, but I shall not be able to say half a dozen
words to them: it's a fact, I never can talk to a woman, except that
girl at old Coleman's hop, Di Clapperton; she went the pace with
me, and no mistake. By the way, how's the other young woman,
Miss Clara Sav—"

"If you really want to dress before you come to the cottage,"
interrupted I hastily, "you have no time to lose."

"Haven't I? off we go, then," cried my companion. "Here, you
lazy young imp," he continued, seizing Shrimp by the collar of the
coat, and dropping him to the ground, as one would a kitten, "find
my room, and get out my things directly—brush along."

So saying, he sprang from the phaeton, and rushed into the hall, pushing Shrimp before him, to the utter consternation of the dignified old butler, who, accustomed to the graceful indolence which characterized his young master's every movement, was quite unprepared for such an energetic mode of proceeding.

Forgetting that politeness required me to wait for my companion, I threw the reins to a groom, and started off at a brisk walk in the direction of the cottage.

Lawless's concluding words had aroused a train of thought sufficiently interesting to banish every other recollection. Sweet Clara! it was quite a month since I had parted from her, but the soft tones of her silvery voice still lingered on my ear—the trustful expression of her bright eyes—the appealing sadness of that mournful smile, more touching in its quiet melancholy than many a deeper sign of woe, still presented themselves to my imagination with a vividness which was almost painful. I had received a note from her about a week before, in which she told me that Cumberland had been absent from the Priory for some days, and as long as this was the case, she was comparatively free from annoyance, but that Mr. Vernor's mind was evidently as much set upon the match as ever; nothing, however, she assured me, should induce her to consent, for much as she had always disliked the scheme, she now felt that death were far preferable to a union with a man she despised; and she ended by saying that whenever she felt inclined to give way to despair, the remembrance of my affection came across her like a sunbeam, and rendered her happy even in the midst of her distress. —Oh! what would I not have given to have possessed the dear privilege of consoling her, to have told her that she had nothing to fear, that my love should surround and protect her, and that, under the hallowing influence of sympathy, happiness for the future would be increased twofold, while sorrow shared between us would be deprived of half its bitterness!—in fact, long before I arrived at the cottage, I had worked myself up into a great state of excitement, and had originated more romantic nonsense than is promulgated in a ' seminary for young ladies,' in the interval between the time when the French teacher has put out the candle, and the fair pupils have talked themselves to sleep, which, if report does not belie them, is not until they have forfeited all chance of adding to their attractions by getting a little beauty-sleep before twelve o'clock.

" Ah, Frank! back already! what have you done with Lawless?" exclaimed Oaklands, raising his eyes from the chessboard as I entered our little drawing-room.

" He will be here shortly," replied I; " but he positively refused to face the ladies till he had changed his shooting costume, so I left him up at the Hall to adonize. But how goes the game? who is winning?"

" As was certain to be the case, I am losing," answered Fanny.

" Well, I won't disturb you," returned I, " and perhaps you will have finished before Lawless makes his appearance; where is my mother, by-the-bye?"

"She only left the room just as you returned," replied Fanny quickly; "she has been sitting here ever since Mr. Oaklands came."

"I do not wish to know where she has been, but where she is," rejoined I; "I want to tell her that Lawless is coming to be introduced to her: is she upstairs?"

"I believe she is," was the reply, "but you will only worry her if you disturb her; mamma particularly dislikes being hunted about, you know: you had better sit still, and she will be down again in a few minutes."

"There is no such thing as free-will in this world, I believe," exclaimed I, throwing myself back in an easy-chair; "however, as you do not very often play the tyrant, you shall have your own way this time. Harry, the chestnuts did their work to admiration; Lawless was delighted with them, and talked of nothing else half the way home."

"I don't doubt it—your queen's in danger, Fanny," was the answer.

Seeing that my companions appeared entirely engrossed by their game, I occupied myself with a book till I heard the ominous sounds, "Check! excuse me, the knight commands that square; you have but one move—checkmate!"

"Who has won? though I need not ask. How dare you beat my sister, Master Harry?"

"I had some trouble in doing it, I can tell you," replied Oaklands; then turning to Fanny, he continued, "Had you but moved differently when I castled my king to get out of your way, the game would have been entirely in your own hands, for I was so stupid, that up to that moment I never perceived the attack you were making upon me."

"Really I don't think I had a chance of beating you: Frank must take you in hand next; he is a much better player than I am."

"Indeed I am not going to be handed over to Frank, or anyone else, in that summary way, I can assure you; I intend to have another game of chess with you to-morrow, after we come in from our ride. I forgot to tell you that Harris says the little gray Arab carries a lady beautifully—however, I left orders for one of the boys to exercise her well this afternoon, with a side-saddle and a horse-cloth, to enact the part of a lady. At what hour shall we ride to-morrow? it is generally fine before luncheon at this time of year, I think."

"Oh you are very kind," replied Fanny hurriedly, "but I am afraid I cannot ride to-morrow."

"Why not? what are you going to do?" inquired Oaklands.

"I am not going to do anything particularly," returned Fanny, hesitating; "but I don't know whether my habit is in wearable order, and—well, I will talk to mamma about it. By-the-bye, I really must go and see what has become of her all this time," she continued, rising to leave the apartment.

"I thought there was nothing my mother disliked so much as being hunted about," rejoined I; "I wonder you can think of disturbing her."

A playful shake of the head was her only reply, and she quitted the room.

CHAPTER XLI.

HOW LAWLESS BECAME A LADY'S MAN.

"Doublet and hose should show itself courageous to petticoats. Therefore, courage!
—*As You Like It.*

"From the crown of his head to the sole of his foot he is all mirth.
He hath a heart as sound as a bell, and his tongue is the clapper, for what his heart thinks, his tongue speaks.

I hope he is in love."—*Much Ado About Nothing.*

"FRANK, I am not at all satisfied about your sister," began Oaklands, as the door closed after her. "She does not look well, and she seems entirely to have lost her spirits."

"I thought as you do before I went up for my degree," replied I; "but since my return I hoped she was all right again. What makes you imagine her out of spirits."

"Oh! several things; she never talks and laughs as she used to do. Why, all this afternoon I could scarcely get half a dozen words out of her; and she seems to have no energy to do anything. How unwilling she appeared to enter into my scheme about the riding! She evidently dislikes the idea of exertion of any kind: I know the feeling well; but it is not natural for her; she used to be surprisingly active, and was the life and soul of the party. But what, perhaps, has caused me to notice all this so particularly, and makes me exceedingly uncomfortable, is, that I am afraid it is all owing to me."

"Owing to you, my dear Harry! what can you mean?" inquired I.

"Why, I fear that business of the duel, and the great care she and your mother took of me (for which—believing as I do that, under Providence, it saved my life—I can never be sufficiently grateful), have been too much for her. Remember, she was quite a girl; and no doubt seeing an old friend brought to the house apparently dying, must have been a very severe shock to her, and, depend upon it, her nerves have never recovered their proper tone. However, I shall make it my business to endeavour to interest and amuse her, and you must do everything you can to assist me, Frank; we'll get all the new books down from London, and have some people to stay at the Hall. She has shut herself up too much; Ellis says she has; I shall make her ride on horseback every day."

" Horseback, eh!" exclaimed Lawless, who had entered the cottage without our perceiving him. " Ay, that's a prescription better than all your doctor's stuff; clap her on a side-saddle, and a brisk canter for a couple of hours every day across country will set the old lady up again in no time, if it's your mother that's out of condition, Frank. Why, Oaklands, man, you are looking as fresh as paint! getting sound again, wind and limb, eh ? "

" I hope so, at last," replied Harry, shaking Lawless warmly by the hand; "but I've had a narrow escape of losing my life, I can assure you."

" No; really I didn't know it had been as bad as that! By Jove! if he had killed you, I'd have shot that black-hearted villain, Wilford, myself, and chanced about his putting a bullet into me while I was doing it."

" My dear Lawless, I thank you for your kind feeling towards me; but I cannot bear to hear you speak in that light way of duelling," returned Oaklands gravely; "if men did but know the misery they were entailing on all those who cared for them by their rash acts, independently of all higher considerations, duelling, and its twin brother, suicide, would be less frequent than they are. When I have seen the tears stealing down my father's grief-worn cheeks, and witnessed the anxious, painful expression in the faces of the kind friends who were nursing me, and have reflected that it was by yielding to my own ungoverned passions that I had brought all this sorrow upon them, my remorse has often been far harder to bear than any pain my wound has caused me."

At this moment, my mother and Fanny making their appearance, I hastened to introduce Lawless, who, being greatly alarmed at the ceremony, grew very red in the face, shuffled my mother into a corner of the room, and upset a chair against her, stumbling over Harry's legs, and knocking down the chessboard in the excess of his penitence. Having, with my assistance, remedied these disasters, after stigmatizing himself as an awkward dog, and comparing himself to a bull in a china-shop, he turned to Fanny, exclaiming,—

" Delighted to have the pleasure of seeing you at last, Miss Fairlegh; it is several years since I first heard of you. Do you remember the writing-desk at old Mildman's, eh, Frank ? no end of a shame of me to spoil it; I have often thought so since; but boys will be boys, eh, Mrs. Fairlegh ? "

My mother acquiesced in this obstinate adherence to their primary formation on the part of the junior members of the nobler sex, with so much cordiality that Lawless was encouraged to proceed.

T

" Glad to find there's a chance of seeing you out with us some of
these days, ma'am ; shall we be able to persuade you to accompany
us to-morrow ? "

" Yes, I think it very likely that I may go," returned my mother,
who imagined he was referring to some proposed drive ; " in what
direction will it be, pray ? "

" Direction, eh ? Why, that of course depends very much on what
line he may happen to take when he breaks cover," returned Lawless.
My mother, who had been previously advised of Lawless's sporting
metaphors, concluding that he referred to Sir John Oaklands, calmly
replied,—

" Yes, certainly, I was mentioning the ruins of Saworth Abbey to
Sir John yesterday ; do you know them ? "

" I should think I did—rather," exclaimed Lawless, forgetting his
company manners in the interest of the subject. " Why, I have seen
more foxes run into the fields round Saworth than in any other
parish in the country. Whenever the meet is either at Grinder's
End or Chorley Bottom, the fox is safe to head for Saworth. Oh ! I
see you're up to the whole thing, Mrs. Fairlegh ; we shall have you
showing all of us the way across country in fine style to-morrow.
I expect there'll be some pretty stiff fencing, though, if he should
take the line you imagine ; but I suppose you don't mind anything
of that sort ; with a steady well-trained hunter (and a lady should
never ride one that is not), there's very little danger—take care to
keep out of the crowd when you're getting away ; don't check your
horse at his fences ; have a little mercy on his bellows over the heavy
ground ; and with a light weight like yours you may lead the field.
Why, Frank, you ought to be proud of Mrs. Fairlegh. I tell you
what—the first time the hounds meet near Leatherly, I'll have my
mother out, whether she likes it or not. I'll stand no nonsense
about it, you may depend ; she shall see a run for once in her life, at
all events. Mrs. Fairlegh, ma'am," he continued, rising and shaking
her warmly by the hand, " excuse my saying so, but you're a regular
brick—you are indeed ! "

The scene at this moment would not have made a bad study for a
painter. Oaklands, having struggled in vain to preserve his gravity,
was in fits of laughter. Fanny, who had from the first perceived
the equivoque, was very little better, while my mother, completely
mystified, sat staring at Lawless, whom she evidently considered a
little insane, with an expression of bewildered astonishment, not
unmixed with fear. As soon as I could contrive to speak (for Lawless's face, when he had discovered the effect he had produced,
completely finished me, and I laughed till the tears ran down my
cheeks), I explained to him that it was my sister, and not my
mother, who was thinking of riding, while the notion of hunting
originated wholly and solely in his own fertile imagination.

"Eh ? What ! she doesn't hunt?—ah ! I see, put my foot in it
pretty deep this time ; beg pardon, Mrs. Fairlegh—no offence meant,

I assure you. Well, I thought it was a very fast thing for an old——
I—that is, for a lady to do. I fancied you were so well up in the
whole affair, too: most absurd, really; I certainly am not fit for
female society. I think, when the hunting season's over, I shall put
myself to one of those tiptop boarding-schools, to learn manners for
a quarter; the sort of shop, you know, where they teach woman her
mission—how to get a rich husband, eh, Frank?—for £300 a year,
washing and church principles extra, and keep a 'Professor' to
instruct the young ladies in the art of getting out of a carriage on
scientific principles; that is, without showing their ankles. Didn't
succeed very well with my sister Julia, though; the girl happens to
be particularly clean about the pasterns, so she declared it was
infringing on the privileges of a free-born British subject, vowed her
ankles were her own property, and she had a right to do what she
liked with 'em, and carried out her principles by kicking the
Professor's shins for him. Plucky girl is Julia; she puts me very
much in mind of what I was when I was her age at Eton, and pinned
a detonating cracker to old Botherboy's coat-tail, so that, what
between the pin and the explosion, it's my belief he would have
found himself more comfortable in the battle of Waterloo, than he
felt the first time he sat down. Ah! those were happy days!"

Thus running on, Lawless kept us in a roar of laughter, till Oaklands, pulling out his watch, discovered it was time to return to the
Hall and prepare for dinner. It turned out, on examination, that
the habit did require altering, so the ride was put off till the
necessary repairs should be executed. As the next day proved too
frosty to hunt, Lawless and I, under the auspices of the head-keeper,
set to work to slaughter the supernumerary pheasants, Sir John and
Harry joining us for a couple of hours, though Ellis would not allow
the latter to carry a gun. We had a capital day's sport, and got
home just in time to dress, and Sir John having contrived in the
course of the afternoon to carry off my mother and Fanny, we were
a very comfortable little party. Sir John took my mother down to
dinner, and Lawless paired off with Fanny, an arrangement which,
as his eccentricities evidently afforded her great amusement, I was
not sorry for.

"Why, Fanny," whispered I, when we joined the ladies in the
drawing-room, "you are growing quite frisky: what a row you and
Lawless were making at dinner-time! I have not heard you talk and
laugh so much for many a day."

"Oh! your friend is famous fun," replied Fanny—"perfectly
irresistible; I assure you I am delighted with him—he is something
quite new to me."

"I am so glad you have asked Lawless here," observed I to Oaklands; "do you see how much pleased and amused Fanny is with
him?—he appears to have aroused her completely—the very thing
we were wishing for. He'll be of more use to her than all of us put
together."

"He seems to me to talk a vast deal of nonsense," replied Harry rather crossly, as I fancied.

"And yet I can't help being amused by it," replied I; "I'm like Fanny in that respect."

"I was not aware your sister had a taste for that style of conversation. I confess it's a sort of thing which very soon tires me."

"Splendid old fellow, Sir John," observed Lawless in an undertone, seating himself by Fanny; "I never look at him without thinking of one of those jolly old Israelites who used to keep knocking about the country with a plurality of wives and families, and an immense stud of camels and donkeys: they read 'em out to us at church, you know—what do you call 'em, eh?"

"One of the Patriarchs, I suppose you mean," replied Fanny, smiling.

"Eh—yes, that's the thing. Noah was rather in that line before he took to the water system, wasn't he? Well, now, if you can fancy one of these ancients, decently dressed in a blue coat with brass buttons, knee shorts, and silk stockings, like a Christian, it's my belief he'd be the very moral (as the old women call it) of Sir John; uncommonly handsome he must have been—even better looking than Harry, when he was his age."

"Mr. Oaklands is so pale and thin now," replied Fanny.

"Eh! isn't he just?" was the rejoinder. "Many a man has been booked for an inside place in a hearse for a less hurt than his! and I don't know that he is out of the wood even yet."

"Why, you don't think him worse?" exclaimed Fanny anxiously. "Nothing has gone wrong—you have not been told—are they keeping anything from me?"

"Eh! no! 'pon my word; Ellis, who is getting him into condition, says he's all right, and will be as fresh as a colt in a month or two. Why, you look quite frightened."

"You startled me for a moment," replied Fanny, colouring slightly; "any little relapse renders Sir John so uncomfortable that we are naturally anxious on his account."

"I am sure Lawless is boring your sister," observed Oaklands, who had been sitting quite at the farther end of the drawing-room, cutting open the leaves of a new book. "I know that worried look of hers so well—I shall go and interpose on her behalf. Lawless," he continued, crossing over to him, "the billiard-room is lighted up, if you like to challenge Fairlegh to a game."

"Billiards, eh?" returned Lawless; "why, really, if you had walked as many miles to-day as I have, I don't think you'd much fancy trotting round a billiard-table. Besides I am very well off where I am," he added, with what was intended for a gallant glance towards Fanny; "here's metal more attractive, as the fellow says in the play."

Oaklands' only reply was a slight curl of the lip, and, turning to Fanny, he said,—

"Are you at all inclined to take your revenge? We shall have time for a good game if we begin at once; will you come into the music-room, or shall I fetch the chess-men here?"

" Is it not rather late?" replied Fanny hesitatingly.

" Not if we begin now," returned Oaklands.

" Mr. Lawless was offering to show me some tricks with cards : as they will not take so long a time as a game of chess, perhaps that would be advisable this evening."

" Whichever you prefer; I will ring for cards," replied Oaklands coldly. He then waited until the servant had executed the order, and as soon as Lawless had attracted public attention to his performance, left the room unobserved.

Wonderful things did the cards effect under Lawless's able management—very wonderful indeed, until he showed you how they were done; and then the only wonder was that you had not found them out for yourself, and how you could have been stupid enough to be taken in by so simple a trick: and very great was Lawless on the occasion, and greater still was Ellis, who was utterly sceptical as to the possibility of performing any of the tricks beforehand. and quite certain, as soon as he had seen it, that he knew all about it, and could do it easily himself, and who, on trying, invariably failed; and yet, not profiting one bit by his experience, was just as sceptical and just as confident in regard to the next, which was of course attended by a like result. Very wonderful and very amusing was it all, and much laughter did it occasion; and the minutes flitted by on rapid wings, until my mother discovered that it was time for us to start on our walk to the cottage, a mode of progression of which Sir John by no means approved; he therefore rang the bell, and ordered the carriage. While they were getting it ready Harry's absence was for the first time observed, and commented on.

" Did anybody see when he left the room?" inquired Sir John.

" Yes," replied I; "he went away just as Lawless began his performances."

" Dear me! I hope he was not feeling ill," said my mother.

" Ill, ma'am!" exclaimed Ellis. "impossible; you don't know Mr. Oaklands' constitution as well as I do, or such an idea could never have occurred to you; besides, you can't for a moment suppose he would think of being taken suddenly ill without having consulted me on the subject. I must go and see after him, ma'am, directly, but it's quite impossible that he should be ill;" and as he spoke he left the room with hurried steps.

" My dear Fanny, how you made me jump! I hope you haven't done any mischief," exclaimed my mother, as Fanny, moving suddenly, knocked down the card-box, and scattered the contents on the carpet.

" I am sadly awkward," returned Fanny, stooping to pick up the box ; "I do not think it is injured."

" My dear child, it does not in the least signify," said Sir John,

taking her kindly by the hand. "Why, you have quite frightened
yourself, you silly little thing; you are actually trembling: sit down,
my dear, sit down—never mind the cards. Frank, if you'll ring the
bell, Edmunds will see to that."

"No, no! we'll pick 'em up," exclaimed Lawless, going down on all
fours; "don't send for the butler; he's such a pompous old boy; if I
were to see him stooping down here, I should be pushing him over,
or playing him some trick or other. I shouldn't be able to help it,
he's so jolly fat. What a glorious confusion! kings and queens and
little fishes all mixed up together!—here's the knave of clubs—hail-
fellow-well-met with a thing that looks like a salmon with a swelled
face! Well, you have been and gone and done it this time, Miss
Fairlegh—I could not have believed it of you, Miss Fairlegh, oh!"

"Mind you pick them up properly," retorted Fanny; "if you really
were such a conjurer as you pretended to be just now, you would
only have to say, 'hocus pocus,' and the cards would all jump into
the box again in proper order."

"Then I should lose the pleasure of going on my knees in your
service. There's a pretty speech for you, eh! I'll tell you what—
you'll make a lady's man of me now, before you've done with me.
I'm polishing rapidly—I know I am."

"It's all right!" exclaimed Ellis, entering. "I found Mr. Oaklands lying on the sofa in the library; he says he feels a little
knocked up by his walk this morning, and desired me to apologize
for his absence, and wish everybody good-night for him. I say,
Fairlegh," continued he, drawing me a little on one side, "has anything happened to annoy him?"

"Nothing particular, that I know of," replied I; "why do you
ask?"

"I thought he looked especially cross; and he called our friend
Lawless an intolerable puppy, and wondered how any woman of
common-sense could contrive to put up with him—that's all,"
rejoined Ellis.

"Fanny refused to play chess with him, because she thought it too
late in the evening;—that cannot have annoyed him?"

"Oh no!" was the reply. "I see exactly what it is now: since the
granulating process has been going on so beautifully in the side, his
appetite has returned, and as he must not take any very active exercise
just yet, the liver is getting torpid. I must throw in a little blue pill,
and he'll be as good-tempered as an angel again; for, naturally,
there is not a man breathing with a finer disposition, or a more
excellent constitution, than Mr. Oaklands. Why, sir, the other day,
when I had been relating a professional anecdote to him, he called
me a 'bloodthirsty butcher,' and I honoured him for it—no
hypocrisy there, sir."

At this moment the carriage was announced, and we proceeded to
take our departure, Lawless handing Fanny in, and then standing
chattering at the window, till I was obliged to give him a hint that

Sir John would not like to have the horses kept standing in the cold.

"You've made a conquest, Miss Fan," said I, as we drove off; "I never saw Lawless pay such attention to any woman before; even Di Clapperton did not produce nearly so strong an effect, I can assure you."

"I am quite innocent of any intention to captivate," replied Fanny. "Mr. Lawless amuses me, and I laugh sometimes at, and sometimes with him."

"Still, my dear, you should be careful," interposed my mother: "though it's play to you, it may be death to him, poor young man! I got into a terrible scrape once in that way myself, when I was a girl: laughing and joking with a young gentleman in our neighbourhood, till he made me an offer one morning, and I really believe I should have been persuaded into marrying him, though I did not care a bit about him, if I had not been attached to your poor dear father at the time: now you have nothing of that sort to save you; so, as I said before, my dear, mind what you are about."

"I don't think Mr. Lawless's heart will be broken while there is a pack of hounds within reach, mamma dear," replied Fanny, glancing archly at me as she spoke.

As we were about to proceed to our several rooms for the night, I contrived to delay my mother for a moment under the pretext of lighting a candle for her, and closing the door, I said:—

"My dear mother, if, by any odd chance, Fanny should be inclined to like Lawless, don't you say anything against it. Lawless is a good fellow; all his faults lie on the surface, and are none of them serious; he is completely his own master, and might marry any girl he pleased to-morrow, and I need not tell you would be a most excellent match for Fanny. He seems very much taken with her; and no wonder, for she is really excessively pretty; and when she is in spirits, as she was to-night, her manner is most piquante and fascinating."

"Well, my dear boy," was the reply, "you know your friend best, and if he and Fanny choose to take a fancy to each other, and you approve of it, I shall not say anything against it."

Whereupon I kissed her, called her a dear, good old mother, and carried up for her, in token of affection, her work-box, her reticule, her candle, and a basket containing a large bunch of keys, sundry halfpence, and three pairs of my own stockings which wanted mending, a process which invariably rendered them unwearable ever after.

CHAPTER XLII.

THE MEET AT EVERSLEY GORSE.

"We'll make you some sport with the fox
Ere we case him."
        All's Well that Ends Well.

"Oh for a fall, if fall she must,
On the gentle lap of Flora !
But still, thank Heaven, she clings to her seat."
        Hood.

.   .   . "She held his drooping head,
Till given to breathe the freer air,
Returning life repaid their care ;
He gazed on them with heavy sigh—
I could have wished e'en thus to die."
        Rokeby.

It had been arranged between my mother and Oaklands, in the earlier part of the evening on which the events described in the last chapter took place, that Fanny should have her first ride on the day but one following, by which time it was supposed that the habit would be fit for service, and the young lady's mind sufficiently familiarized with the idea, to overcome a rather (as I considered) unnecessary degree of alarm which I believe would have led her, had she been allowed to decide for herself, to relinquish it altogether· The only stipulation my mother insisted on was, that I should accompany my sister in the character of chaperon, an arrangement to which, as it was quite evident that Lawless intended to form one of the party, I made no objection. Accordingly, on the day appointed, Oaklands made his appearance about ten o'clock, mounted on his favourite horse, and attended by a groom, leading the grey Arab which was destined to carry Fanny, as well as a saddle-horse for me.

"Bravo, Harry! it does one good to see you and the 'Cid' together again," exclaimed I, patting the arched neck of the noble animal; "how well he is looking!"

"Is he not?" replied Oaklands warmly; "the good old horse knew me as well as possible, and gave a neigh of pleasure when first I spoke to him. Is Fanny nearly ready?"

"She will be here directly," replied I; and the words had scarcely escaped my lips when she made her appearance, looking so lovely in her hat and habit, that I felt sure it would be all over with Lawless as soon as he saw her.

"Why, Fanny," exclaimed Oaklands, dismounting slowly and with effort, for he was still lamentably weak, "I have not seen you in a habit so long, I declare I should scarcely have known you; the effect is quite magical."

A smile and a blush were her only reply; and Oaklands continued, "Will you not like to mount now? Lawless will join us; but he means to abandon us again when we get near Eversley Gorse, for the superior attractions of a run with the subscription pack."

" Oh, I hope the hounds will not come in our way!" exclaimed Fanny; " if you think there is any chance of their frightening my horse, I had better not ride to-day."

" I do not think you need feel the least alarm; though spirited, Rose Alba is perfectly quiet; besides, we are not bound to ride towards Eversley, unless you approve of doing so," replied Oaklands.

As he spoke, Lawless rode up just in time to catch the last few words. He was dressed in an appropriate hunting costume, and sat his horse (a splendid black hunter, whose fiery temper rendered all those in whom the bump of caution was properly developed remarkably shy of him) as easily as if he formed part of the animal. As he checked his impatient steed, and taking off his hat, bowed to Fanny, his eyes sparkling, and his whole countenance beaming with pleasure and excitement, he really looked quite handsome. The same idea seemed to strike Fanny, who whispered to me, "If ever your friend has his picture taken, it should be on horseback."

" Good-morning, Miss Fairlegh!" cried Lawless, as, flinging the rein to a groom, he sprang from the saddle, and bounded towards us ; " glad to see you in what I consider the most becoming dress a lady can wear—very becoming it is too," he added, with a slight bend of the head to mark the compliment. " What did I hear you say about not riding to Eversley ? You never can be so cruel as to deny me the pleasure of your company, and I must go there to join the meet. I would not have hunted to-day, though, if I had known you wished to ride in another direction."

" It was only that Fanny was afraid the hounds might frighten her horse." replied I.

" Oh, not the least danger; I'll take care of all that," returned Lawless ; " the little white mare is as gentle as a lamb: I cantered her across the park myself yesterday on purpose to try—the sweetest thing for a lady I ever set eyes on. You have got some good cattle in your stables, Harry, I must own that."

" Hadn't we better think of mounting ? Time will not stand still for us," observed I.

" Let me assist you, Fanny," said Oaklands, advancing towards her.

" Thank you," replied Fanny, drawing back ; "but I need not give you the trouble; Frank will help me."

" Here, get out of the way!" cried Lawless, as I hesitated, fancy-ing from the shade on Oaklands' brow that he might not like to be interfered with; "I see none of you know how to help a lady properly. Bring up that mare," he continued, "closer—that's it; stand before her head. Now, Miss Fairlegh, take a firm hold of the pummel; place your foot in my hand—are you ready?—spring! there we are—famously done! Oh, you know what you are about, I see. Let me give you the rein-- between the fingers; yes—the snaffle will manage her best; the curb may hang loose, and only use it if it is necessary; let the groom stand by her till I am mounted; the black horse is rather fidgety; soh! boy, soh! quiet!—stand, you brute!—there's a good boy; steady, steady—off we go!"

As Lawless pushed by me at the beginning of this speech, Oaklands advanced towards him, and his pale cheek flushed with anger. Apparently, however, changing his intention, he drew himself up haughtily, and, turning on his heel, walked slowly to his horse, mounted, and reining him back a few paces, sat motionless as an equestrian statue, gazing on the party with a gloomy brow until we had started, when, suddenly applying the spur, he joined us in a couple of bounds, and took his station at Fanny's left hand. Lawless, having appropriated the off side, devoted himself to the double task of managing the Arab and doing the agreeable to its fair rider, which latter design he endeavoured to accomplish by chattering incessantly.

After proceeding a mile or two, Lawless sustaining the whole burden of the conversation, while Oaklands never spoke a word, we came upon a piece of level greensward.

"Here's a famous place for a canter, Miss Fairlegh," exclaimed Lawless; "lean a little more towards me—that's right. Are you ready!—just tickle her neck with the whip—not too hard—jerk the rein slightly—gently, mare, gently—there's a good horse, that's it! Eh! don't you see she settles into her pace as quietly as a rocking-horse—oh! she's a sweet thing for a feather-weight;" and restraining the plunging of the fiery animal he rode, he leaned over, and patted the Arab's arched neck, as they went off at an easy canter.

I was about to follow their example, but observing that Oaklands delayed putting his horse in motion, it occurred to me that this being the first ride he had taken since his illness, the exertion might possibly be too much for his strength; I waited, therefore, till he joined me, when I inquired whether he felt any ill effects from the unwonted exertion?

"No," was the reply. "I feel an odd kind of fluttering in my side, but it is only weakness."

"Had you not better give it up for to-day, and let me ride back with you? I daresay Lawless would not care about hunting for once, and would see Fanny home."

"I will NOT go back," he replied sternly; then checking himself, he added in a milder tone, "I mean to say, it is not necessary—really I do not feel ill—besides, it was only a passing sensation, and is already nearly gone."

He paused for a moment, and then continued, "How very dictatorial and disagreeable Lawless has grown of late, and what absurd nonsense he does talk when he is in the society of ladies! I wonder your sister can tolerate it."

"She not only tolerates it," returned I, slightly piqued at the contemptuous tone in which he spoke of Lawless, "but is excessively amused by it; why, she said last night he was quite delightful."

"I gave her credit for better taste," was Oaklands' reply; and striking his horse impatiently with the spur, he dashed forward, and in a few moments we had rejoined the others.

" I hope illness has not soured Harry's temper, but he certainly appears more prone to take offence than in former days," was my inward comment, as I pondered over his last words. "I am afraid Fanny has annoyed him; I must speak to her, and give her a hint to be more careful for the future."

Half an hour's brisk riding brought us to the outskirts of a broad common, a great portion of which was covered by the gorse or furze from which it took its name. Around the sides of this were gathered from sixty to eighty well-mounted men, either collected in groups, to discuss the various topics of local interest which occupy the minds of country gentlemen, or riding up and down in parties of two and three together, impatient for the commencement of their morning's sport; while, in a small clear space, nearly in the centre of the furze-brake, were stationed the hounds, with the huntsman and whippers-in.

"There!" exclaimed Lawless, "look at that. Talk about operas and exhibitions! where will you find an exhibition as well worth seeing as that is? I call that a sight for an empress. Now are not you glad I made you come, Miss Fairlegh ?"

"The red coats look very gay and picturesque, certainly," replied Fanny; "and what loves of horses, with their satin skins glistening in the sunshine! But I wish Rose Alba would not prick up her ears in that way; I'm rather frightened."

While Lawless was endeavouring to convince her there was no danger, and that he was able and willing to frustrate any nefarious designs which might enter into the graceful little head of the white Arab, a young man rode up to Oaklands, and shaking him warmly by the hand, congratulated him on being once more on horseback.

" Ah, Whitcombe, it's a long time since you and I have met," returned Harry; " you have been abroad, I think ? "

" Yes," was the reply; " Charles and I have been doing the grand tour, as they call it."

"How is your brother ? "

" Oh, he's all right, only he has grown a great pair of moustaches, and won't cut them off; he has taken up a notion they make him look killing, I believe. He was here a minute ago—yes, there he is, talking to Randolph. Come and speak to him, he'll be delighted to see you."

" Keep your eye on Fanny's mare," said Oaklands, as he rode past me; " she seems fidgety, and that fellow Lawless is thinking more about the hounds than he is of her, though he does boast so much of the care he can take of her. I shall be with you again directly,"

" Do you see the gentleman on the bright bay, Miss Fairlegh ? " exclaimed Lawless; "there, he's speaking to Tom Field, the huntsman, now; he has got his watch in his hand; that's Mr. Rand, the master of the hounds; you'll see some fun directly. Ah! I thought so."

As he spoke, at a signal from the huntsman, the hounds dashed into cover, and were instantly lost to sight in a waving sea of gorse, save when a head or neck became visible for a moment, as some dog, more eager than the rest, sprang over a tangled brake, through which he was unable to force his way.

"Oh, you beauties!" resumed Lawless enthusiastically, "only watch them; they're drawing it in first-rate style, and there's rare lying in that cover. Now see how the furze shakes—look at their sterns flourishing; have at him there—have at him; that's right, Tom—cheer 'em on, boy—good huntsman is Tom Field—there again! —a fox, I'll bet £500 to a pony—hark! a whimper—now wait—a challenge!—another and another—listen to them—there's music— watch the right-hand corner—that's where he'll break cover for a thousand, and if he does, what a run we shall have! Look at those fools," he added, pointing to a couple of cockney-looking fellows who were cantering towards the very place he had pointed to; "they'll head him back, as sure as fate—hold hard there—why does not some-body stop them? By Jove, I'll give them a taste of the double thong when I get up with them, even if it's the Lord Mayor of London and his brother. Look to your sister, Frank; I'll be back directly."

"Wait one minute," shouted I, but in vain; for before the words were well out of my mouth, he had driven the spurs into his eager horse, and was galloping furiously in the direction of the unhappy delinquents who had excited his indignation. My reason for asking him to wait a minute was, that just as the hounds began drawing the cover, I had made the agreeable discovery that the strap to which one of my saddle girths was buckled had given way, and that there was nothing for it but to dismount and repair the evil; and I had scarcely concluded the best temporary arrangement I was able to effect, when Lawless started in pursuit of the cockneys. Almost at the same moment a countryman, stationed at the outside of the gorse, shouted "Tally-ho!" and the fox broke cover in gallant style, going away at a rattling pace, with four or five couple of hounds on his traces. In an instant all was confusion, cigars were thrown away, hats pressed firmly down upon the brow, and, with a rush like the outburst of some mighty torrent, the whole field, to a man, swept rapidly onward.

In the meanwhile Fanny's mare, which had for some minutes shown symptoms of excitement, pawing the ground with her fore-foot, pricking up her ears, and tossing her head impatiently, began, as Lawless rode off, to plunge in a manner which threatened at every moment to unseat her rider, and as several horsemen dashed by her, becoming utterly unmanageable, she set off at a wild gallop, drown-ing in the clatter of her hoofs Fanny's agonized cry for help. Driven nearly frantic by the peril in which my sister was placed, I was even yet prevented for a minute or more from hastening to her assistance,

as my own horse, frightened by the occurrences I have described,
struggled so violently to follow his companions as to render it very
difficult for me to hold, and quite impossible to remount him, so that
when at length I succeeded in springing on his back, the hounds
were already out of sight, and Fanny and her runaway steed so far
ahead of me, that it seemed inevitable some accident must occur
before I could overtake them, and it was with a sinking heart that I
gave my horse the rein, and dashed forward in pursuit.

The course which Lawless had taken when he started on his wild-
goose chase was down a ride cut through the furze, and it was along
this turfy track that Rose Alba was now hurrying in her wild career.
The horse on which I was mounted was a young thoroughbred,
standing nearly sixteen hands high, and I felt certain that in the
pursuit in which I was engaged, the length of his stride would tell,
and that eventually we must come up with the fugitives; but so fleet
was the little Arab, and so light the weight she had to carry, that I
was sorry to perceive I gained upon them but slowly. It was clear
that I should not overtake them before they reached the outskirts of
the common, and then who could say what course the mare might
take—what obstacles might not be in her way ?

On—on we go in our headlong course, the turf re-echoing to the
muffled strokes of the horse's feet, while the furze waving in the wind
seemed to glide by us in a rapid stream. Onward—still onward ; the
edge of the gorse appears a dark line in the distance—it is passed ;
we are crossing the belt of turf that surrounds it—and now, in what
direction will the mare proceed ? Will she take the broad road to
the left, which leads again to the open country by a gentle ascent,
where she can be easily overtaken and stopped ; or will she turn to
the right, and follow the lane, which leads across the terrace-field to
the brook, swollen by the late rains into a river ? See ! she slackens
her pace—she wavers, she doubts—she will choose the road ! No ; by
Heaven ! she turns ¹to the right, and dashing down the lane like a
flash of lightning, is for a moment hidden from view. But the space
of time, short as it was, when her speed slackened, has enabled me
to gain upon her considerably ; and when I again catch sight of her
she is not more than fifty yards ahead. Forward ! good horse—
forward ! Life or death hangs upon thy fleetness. Vain hope !
another turn brings us in sight of the brook, swollen by the breaking
up of the frost into a dark, turbulent stream. Fanny perceives it too,
and utters a cry of terror, which rings like a death-knell on my ear.
There seems no possibility of escape for her ; on the left hand an
impenetrable hedge ; on the right a steep bank, rising almost perpen-
dicularly to the height of a man's head ; in front the rushing water ;
while the mare, apparently irritated to frenzy by my pursuit, gallops
wildly forward. Ha ! what is that ? a shout ! and the figure of a
man on horseback appears on the high ground to the right, between
Fanny and the stream. He perceives the danger, and if he dare
attempt the leap from the bank, may yet save her. Oh that I were

in his place! Hark! he shouts again to warn us of his intention, and
putting spurs to his horse, faces him boldly at it.   The horse
perceives the danger, and will refuse the leap.   No! urged by his
rider, he will take it yet—now he springs it is certain destruction.
A crash! a fall; they are down! No: he has lifted his horse with the
rein—they are apparently uninjured. Rose Alba, startled by the
sudden apparition, slackens her pace; the stranger, taking advantage
of the delay, dashes forward, seizes the rein, and succeeds in stopping
her; as he does so, I approach near enough to recognize his
features.

Unlooked-for happiness! Fanny is saved, and Harry Oaklands is
her preserver!

My first act on joining them was to spring from my horse, and lift
Fanny out of the saddle. " Are you really unhurt, my own darling ? "
exclaimed I ; " can you stand without assistance ? "

" Oh, yes!" she replied, " it was only the fright—that dreadful
river—but—" and, raising her eyes timidly, she advanced a step
towards Oaklands.

" But you would fain thank Harry for saving you. My dear
Harry," continued I, taking his hand and pressing it warmly, " if
you only knew the agony of mind I have suffered on her account, you
would be able to form some slight idea of the amount of gratitude I
feel towards you for having rescued her. I shudder to think what
might have been the end had you not so providentially interposed ;
but you do not listen to me · you turn as pale as ashes—are you
ill ? "

" It is nothing—a little faint or so," was his reply, in a voice so
weak as to be scarcely audible ; and as he spoke, his head dropped
heavily on his shoulder, and he would have fallen from his horse had
not I caught him in my arms and supported him.

Giving the horses into the custody of a farming lad (who had seen
the leap, and run up, fearing some accident had occurred), I lifted
Oaklands from the saddle, and laying him on the turf by the roadside, supported his head against my knee, while I endeavoured
to loosen his neckcloth. Neither its removal, however, nor the un-
fastening his shirt-collar, appeared to revive him in the slightest
degree, and, being quite unaccustomed to seizures of this nature, I
began to feel a good deal frightened about him. I suppose my face
in some degree betrayed my thoughts, as Fanny, after glancing at me
for a moment, exclaimed, wringing her hands in the excess of her
grief and alarm, " Oh ! he is dead—he is dead ! and it is I who have
killed him !" Then, flinging herself on her knees by his side, and
taking his hand between both her own, she continued, " Oh, Harry,
look up—speak to me—only one word ;—he does not hear me—he will
never speak again ! Oh ! he is dead—he is dead ! and it is I who have
murdered him—I, who would gladly have died for him, as he has
died for me."

As she said this, her voice failed her, and, completely overcome by

the idea that she had been the cause of Harry's death, she buried her face in her hands and wept bitterly.

At this moment it occurred to me that water might possibly revive him, and rousing Fanny from the passion of grief into which she had fallen, I made her take my place in supporting Oaklands' head, and running to the stream, which was not above fifty yards from the spot, filled my hat with water, sprinkled his face and brow with it, and had the satisfaction of seeing him gradually revive under the application.

As consciousness returned, he gazed around with a bewildered look, and passing his hand across his forehead, inquired, "What is all this? where am I? Ah! Frank, have I been ill?"

"You fainted from over-exertion, Harry," replied I; "but all will be well now."

"From over-exertion?" he repeated slowly, as if striving to recall what had passed; "stay, yes, I remember, I took a foolish leap; why did I do it?"

"To stop Fanny's mare."

"Yes, to be sure, the water was out at the brook, and I thought the mare might attempt to cross it; but is Fanny safe? Where is she?"

"She is here," replied I, turning towards the place where she still knelt, her face hidden in her hands. "She is here to thank you for having saved her life."

"Why, Fanny, was it you who were supporting my head? how very kind of you! What, crying?" he continued, gently attempting to withdraw her hands; "nay, nay, we must not have you cry."

"She was naturally a good deal frightened by the mare's running away," replied I, as Fanny still appeared too much overcome to speak for herself; "and then she was silly enough to fancy, when you fainted, that you were actually dead, I believe; but I can assure you that she is not ungrateful."

"No, indeed," murmured Fanny, in a voice scarcely audible from emotion.

"Why, it was no very great feat, after all," rejoined Harry. "On such a jumper as the Cid, and coming down on soft marshy ground too, I would not mind the leap any day; besides, do you think I was going to remain quietly there, and see Fanny drowned before my eyes? if it had been a precipice, I would have gone over it." While he spoke Harry had regained his feet; and after walking up and down for a minute or so, and giving himself a shake, to see if he was all right, he declared that he felt quite strong again, and able to ride home. And so, having devised a leading-rein for Rose Alba, one end of which I kept in my own possession, we remounted our horses, and reached Heathfield without further misadventure.

CHAPTER XLIII.

A CHARADE—NOT ALL ACTING.

" And then, and much it helped his chance—
He could sing, and play first fiddle, and dance—
Perform charades, and proverbs of France."
                                        Hood.

"I have often heard this and that and t'other pain mentioned as the worst that
mortals can endure—such as the toothache, earache, cramp in the calf of the leg, a boil,
or a blister—now, I protest, though I have tried all these, nothing seems to me to come up
to a *pretty sharp fit of jealousy.*"—*Thinks I to Myself.*

LAWLESS'S penitence, when he learned the danger in which Fanny
had been placed by his thoughtlessness and impetuosity, was so deep
and sincere, that it was impossible to be angry with him; and even
Oaklands, who at first declared he considered his conduct unpardonable, was obliged to confess that, when a man had owned his fault
frankly, and told you he was really sorry for it, nothing remained but to
forgive and forget it. And so everything fell into its old train once
more, and the next few days passed smoothly and uneventfully. I
had again received a note from Clara, in answer to one I had written
to her. Its tenor was much the same as that of the last she had sent
me. Cumberland was still absent, and Mr. Vernor so constantly
occupied that she saw very little of him. She begged me not to attempt
to visit her at present; a request in the advisability of which reason
so fully acquiesced, that although feeling rebelled against it with the
greatest obstinacy, I felt bound to yield. Harry's strength seemed
now so thoroughly re-established, that Sir John, who was never so
happy as when he could exercise hospitality, had invited a party of
friends for the ensuing week, several of whom were to stay at the
Hall for a few days; amongst others Freddy Coleman, who was to
arrive beforehand, and assist in the preparations; for charades were
to be enacted, and he was reported skilful in the arrangement of these
saturnalia of civilized society, or, as he himself expressed it, he was
" up to all the dodges connected with the minor domestic enigmatical
melodrama." By Harry's recommendation I despatched a letter to
Mr. Frampton, claiming his promise of visiting me at Heathfield
Cottage, urging as a reason for his doing so immediately that he
would meet four of his old Helmstone acquaintance, viz., Oaklands,
Lawless, Coleman, and myself. The morning after Coleman's
arrival, the whole party formed themselves into a committee of taste,
to decide on the most appropriate words for the charades, select
dresses, and, in short, make all necessary arrangements for realizing
a few of the very strong and original, but somewhat vague ideas,
which everybody appeared to have conceived on the subject.

Now, ladies and gentlemen," began Freddy, who had been unanimously elected chairman, stage-manager, and commander-in-chief of
the whole affair, " in the first place, who is willing to take a part?
Let all those who wish for an engagement at the Theatre Royal,
Heathfield, hold up their hands."

Lawless, Coleman, and I were the first who made the required
signal, and next the little white palms of Fanny and Lucy Markham
(whom Mrs. Coleman had made over to my mother's custody for a few
days) were added to the number.

" Harry, you'll act, will you not?" asked I.

"Not if you can contrive to do without me," was the reply. "I did
it once, and never was so tired in my life before. I suppose you
mean to have speaking charades; and there is something in the feeling that one has so many words to recollect, which obliges one to keep
the memory always on the stretch, and the attention up to concert
pitch, in a way that is far too fatiguing to be agreeable."

" Well, as you please, most indolent of men, pray make yourself
quite at home—this is Liberty Hall, isn't it, Lawless?" returned
Coleman, with a glance at the person named, who, seated on the table,
with his legs twisted round the back of a chair, was sacrificing
etiquette to comfort with the most delightful unconsciousness.

" Eh! yes, to be sure, no end of liberty," rejoined Lawless ; " what
are you laughing at?—my legs? They are very comfortable, I can
tell you, if they're not over-ornamental ; never mind about attitude,
let us get on to business : I want to know what I'm to do?"

" The first thing is to find out a good word," returned Coleman.

" What do you say to Matchlock?" inquired I.

" You might as well have Blunderbuss while you are about it,"
was the reply. " No, both words are dreadfully hackneyed; let us try
and find out something original, if possible."

" Eh, yes, something original, by all means; what do you say to
Steeplechase?" suggested Lawless.

" Original, certainly," returned Freddy; " but there might be difficulties in the way. For instance, how would you set about acting a
steeple?"

" Eh! never thought of that," rejoined Lawless; " I really don't
know, unless Oaklands would stand with a fool's cap on his head to
look like one."

"Much obliged, Lawless; but I'd rather be excused," replied
Harry, smiling.

"I've got an idea!" exclaimed I.

" No, you don't say so? you are joking," remarked Freddy, in a
tone of affected surprise.

" Stay a minute," continued I, musing.

" Certainly, as long as you and Sir John like to keep me," rejoined
Coleman politely.

" Yes! that will do; come here, Freddy," added I, and, drawing him
on one side, I communicated to him my ideas on the subject, of which,

U

after suggesting one or two improvements on my original design, he was graciously pleased to approve. Of what this idea consisted, the reader will be apprised in due time. Suffice it at present to add that Fanny, having consented to perform the part of a barmaid, and it being necessary to provide her with a lover, Lawless volunteered for the character, and supported his claim with so much perseverance, not to say obstinacy, that Coleman, albeit he considered him utterly unsuited to the part, was fain to yield to his importunity.

For the next few days Heathfield Hall presented one continual scene of bustle and confusion. Carpenters were at work converting the library into an extempore theatre. Ladies and ladies'-maids were busily occupied in manufacturing dresses. Lawless spent whole hours in pacing up and down the billiard-room, reciting his part, which had been remodelled to suit him, and the acquisition of which appeared a labour analogous to that of Sisyphus, as, by the time he reached the end of his task, he had invariably forgotten the beginning. Everyone was in a state of the greatest eagerness and excitement about something—nobody exactly knew what; and the interest Ellis took in the whole affair was wonderful to behold. The unnecessary number of times people ran up and down 'stairs was inconceivable, and the pace at which they did so terrific. Sir John spent his time in walking about with a hammer and a bag of nails, one of which he was constantly driving in and clenching beyond all power of extraction, in some totally wrong place, a line of conduct which reduced the head-carpenter to the borders of insanity.

On the morning of the memorable day, when the event was to come off, Mr. Frampton made his appearance in a high state of preservation, shook my mother by both hands as warmly as if he had known her from childhood, and saluted the young ladies with a hearty kiss, to their extreme astonishment, which a paroxysm of grunting (wound up by the usual soliloquy, "Just like me!") did not tend to diminish. A large party was invited in the evening to witness our performance, and, as some of the guests began to arrive soon after nine, it was considered advisable that the actors and actresses should go and dress, so that they might be in readiness to appear when called upon.

The entertainments began with certain tableaux vivants, in which both Harry and I took a part; the former having been induced to do so by the assurance that nothing would be expected of him but to stand still and be looked at—an occupation which even he could not consider very hard work: and exceedingly well worth looking at he appeared when the curtain drew up, and discovered him as the Leicester in Scott's novel of "Kenilworth," the magnificent dress setting off his noble figure to the utmost advantage; while Fanny, as Amy Robsart, looked prettier and more interesting than I had ever seen her before. Various tableaux were in turn presented, and passed off with much "éclat," and then there was a pause, before the charade, the grand event of the evening, commenced. Oaklands and

I, having nothing to do in it (Fanny having coaxed Mr. Frampton into undertaking a short part which I was to have performed, but which she declared was so exactly suited to him that she would never forgive him if he refused to fill it), wished the actors success, and came in front to join the spectators.

After about ten minutes of breathless expectation, the curtain drew up and exhibited Scene I., the Bar of a Country Inn; and here I shall adopt the playwright's fashion, and leave the characters to tell their own tale :—

SCENE I.

Enter SUSAN COWSLIP, the Barmaid (FANNY), and JOHN SHORT-OATS, the Ostler (LAWLESS).

JOHN. Well, Susan, girl, what sort of a morning hast thee had of it ? how's master's gout to-day ?

SUSAN. Very bad, John, very bad indeed ; he has not got a leg to stand upon ; and as to his shoe, try everything we can think of, we can't get him to put his foot in it.

(Extempore soliloquy by Lawless, Precious odd if he doesn't, for he's not half up in his part, I know.)

JOHN. Can't thee, really ? well, if that be the case, I needn't ask how his temper is ?

SUSAN. Bad enough, I can tell you ; missus has plenty to bear, poor thing !

JOHN. Indeed she has, and she be too young and pretty to be used in that manner. Ah ! that comes of marrying an old man for his money ; she be uncommon pretty, to be sure ; I only knows one prettier face in the whole village.

SUSAN (with an air of forced unconcern). Ay, John, and whose may that be, pray ? Mary Bennett, perhaps, or Lucy Jones ?

JOHN. No, it ain't either of them.

SUSAN. Who is it, then ?

JOHN. Well, if thee must needs know, the party's name is Susan.

SUSAN (still with an air of unconsciousness). Let me see, where is there a Susan ; let me think a minute. Oh ! one of Darling the blacksmith's girls, I dare say ; it's Susan Darling !

JOHN (rubbing his nose, and looking cunning). Well, 'tis Susan, darling, certainly ; yes, thee be'st about right there—Susan, darling.

SUSAN (pouting). So you're in love with that girl, are you, Mr. John ? A foolish, flirting thing, that cares for nothing but dancing and finery ; a nice wife for a poor man she'll make, indeed—charming !

JOHN. Now, don't thee go and fluster thyself about nothing, it ain't that girl as I'm in love with ; I was only a-making fun of thee.

SUSAN (crossly). There, I wish you wouldn't keep teasing of me so ; I don't care anything about it—I dare say I've never seen her.

JOHN. Oh ! if that's all, I'll very soon show her to thee—come along. (Takes her hand, and leads her up to the looking-glass.) There's the Susan I'm in love with, and hope to marry some day. Hasn't she got a pretty face? and isn't she a DARLING? (Susan looks at him for a minute, and then bursts into tears, bell rings violently, and a gruff voice calls impatiently, Susan! Susan!)

SUSAN. Coming, sir, coming (Wipes her eyes with her apron.)

JOHN. Let the old curmudgeon wait! (Voice behind the scenes, John!—John Ostler, I say!) Coming, sir; yes, sir Sir, indeed—an old brute; but now, Susan, what dost thou say? wilt thou have me for a husband? (Takes her hand.)

(VOICE. John! John! I say. Susan! where are you? And enter Mr. Frampton, dressed as the Landlord, on crutches, and with his gouty foot in a sling.)

LANDLORD. John! you idle, good-for-nothing vagabond, why don't you come when you're called—eh?

SUSAN. Oh, sir! John was just coming, sir; and so was I, sir, if you please.

LANDLORD. You, indeed—ugh! you're just as bad as he is, making love in corners (aside. Wonder whether she does really) instead of attending to the customers, nice set of servants I have, to be sure! If this is all one gets by innkeeping, it's not worth having. I keep the inn, and I expect the inn to keep me (Aside. Horrid old joke, what made me put that in, I wonder? just like me —umph!) There's my wife, too—pretty hostess she makes.

JOHN. So she does, master, surely.

LANDLORD. Hold your tongue, fool what do you know about it? (Bell rings.) There, do you hear that? run and see who that is, or I shall loose a customer by your carelessness next. Oh! the bother of servants—oh! the trouble of keeping an inn! (Hobbles out, driving Susan and John before him. Curtain falls.)

As the first scene ended, the audience applauded loudly, and then began hazarding various conjectures as to the possible meaning of what they had witnessed. While the confusion of sounds was at the highest, Oaklands drew me on one side, and inquired, in an undertone, what I thought of Lawless's acting. "I was agreeably surprised," returned I, "I had no notion he would have entered into the part so thoroughly, or have acted with so much spirit."

"He did it 'con amore,' certainly," replied Oaklands with bitterness; "I considered his manner impertinent in the highest degree. I wonder you can allow him to act with your sister; that man is in love with her—I feel sure of it—he meant every word he said. I hate this kind of thing altogether—I never approved of it: no lady should be subjected to such annoyance."

"Supposing it really were as you fancy, Harry, how do you know it would be so great an annoyance? It is just possible Fanny may like him," rejoined I.

"Oh, certainly! pray let me know when I am to congratulate you,"

replied Oaklands, with a scornful laugh; and, turning away abruptly, he crossed the room, joined a party of young ladies, and began talking and laughing with a degree of recklessness and excitability quite unusual to him. While he was so doing, the curtain drew up, and discovered

SCENE II.—BEST ROOM IN THE INN.

Enter SUSAN, showing in HYACINTH ADONIS BROWN (COLEMAN), dressed as a caricature of the fashion, with lemon-coloured kid gloves, staring-patterned trousers, sporting-coat, etc.

SUSAN. This is the settin'-room, if you please, sir.

HYACINTH (fixing his glass in his eye, and scrutinizing the apartment). This is the settin'-woom, is it ? to set, to incubate as a hen—can't mean that, I imagine—pwovincial idiom, pwobably—aw —ya'as—I dare say I shall be able to exist in it as long as may be necessary—ar—let me have dinaar, young woman, as soon as it can be got weady.

SUSAN. Yes, sir. What would you please to like, sir ?

HYACINTH (looking at her with his glass still in his eye). Hem ! pwetty gal—ar—like, my dear, like ?—(Vewy pwetty gal !)

SUSAN. Beg pardon, sir, what did you say you would like ?

HYACINTH. Chickens tender here, my dear ?

SUSAN. Very tender, sir.

HYACINTH (approaching her). What's your name, my dear?

SUSAN. Susan, if you please, sir.

HYACINTH. Vewy pwetty name, indeed—(Aside, Gal's worth cultivating—I'll do a little bit of fascination.) Ahem ! Chickens, Susan, are not the only things that can be tendar. (Advances, and attempts to take her hand. Enter John hastily, and runs against Hyacinth, apparently by accident.)

HYACINTH (angrily). Now, fellar, where are you pushing to, eh ?

JOHN. Beg parding, sir, I was a-looking for you, sir. (Places himself between Susan and Hyacinth.)

HYACINTH. Looking for me, fellar ?

JOHN. I ha' rubbed down your horse, sir, and I was a wishin' to know when you would like him fed. (Makes signs to Susan to leave the room.)

HYACINTH. Fed ?—aw !—directly, to be su-ar. (To Susan, who is going out :) Ar—don't you go.

JOHN. No, sir, I ain't a-going. When shall I water him, sir ?

HYACINTH (aside, Fellar talks as if the animal were a pot of mignonette). Ar—you'll give him some wataar as soon as he's eaten his dinaar.

JOHN. Werry good, sir; and how about hay, sir ?

HYACINTH (aside, What a bo-ar the fellow is! I wish he'd take himself off). Weally, I must leave the hay to your discwession.

JOHN. Werry well, sir; couldn't do a better thing, sir. How

about his clothing! shall I keep a cloth on him, sir? (Winks at
Susan, who goes out laughing.)

HYACINTH. Yaas! You can keep a cloth on—ar—and—that
will do. (Waves his hand towards the door.)

JOHN. Do you like his feet stopped at night, sir?

HYACINTH. Ar—1 leave all these points to my gwoom—ar—
would you go?

JOHN. I suppose there will be no harm in water-brushing his
mane?

HYACINTH (angrily). Ar—weally I—ar—will you go?

JOHN. Becos some folks thinks it makes the hair come off.

HYACINTH (indignantly). Ar—leave the woom, fellar!

JOHN. Yes, sir; you may depend upon me takin' proper care on
him, sir; and if I should think o' anything else, I'll be sure to come
and ask you, sir. (Goes out grinning.)

HYACINTH. Howwid fellar—I thought I should never get wid of
him—it's evident he's jealous—ar, good idea—I'll give him something
to be jealous about. I'll wing the bell and finish captivating Susan.
(Rings. Re-enter John.)

JOHN. Want me, sir? Here I am, sir—fed the horse, sir.

HYACINTH (waving his hand angrily towards the door). Ar—go
away, fellar, and tell the young woman to answaar that bell. (John
leaves the room, muttering, If I do I'm blessed. HYACINTH struts
up to the glass, arranges his hair, pulls up his shirt-collar, and rings
again. Re-enter Susan.)

HYACINTH. Pway, Susan, are you going to be mawwied?

SUSAN (colouring). No, sir—a—yes, sir—I can't tell, sir.

HYACINTH. No, sir—yes, sir—ar—I see how it is—the idea has
occurred to you—it's that fellar John, I suppose?

SUSAN. Yes, sir—it's John, sir, if you please.

HYACINTH. Well—ar—perhaps I don't exactly please. Now,
listen to me, Susan. I'm an independent gentleman, vewy wich
(aside, Wish I was), lots of servants and cawwiages, and all that
sort of thing. I only want a wife, and—ahem—captivated by your
beauty, I'm wesolved to mawwy you. (Aside, That will do the
business.)

SUSAN. La! sir, you're joking.

HYACINTH. Ar—I never joke—ar—of course you consent!

SUSAN. To marry you, sir?

HYACINTH. Ar—yes—to mawwy me.

SUSAN. What! and give up John?

HYACINTH. I fear we cannot dispense with that sacwifice.

SUSAN. And you would have me prove false to my true love;
deceive a poor lad that cares for me; wring his honest heart, and
perhaps drive him to take to evil courses, for the sake of your fine
carriages and servants? No, sir, if you was a duke, I would not
give up John to marry you.

HYACINTH. Vewy fine, you did that little bit of constancy in very good style; but now, háving welieved your feelings, you may as well do a little bit of nature, and own that, womanlike, you have changed your mind.

SUSAN. When I do, sir, I'll be sure to let you know. (Aside, A dandified fop! why, John's worth twenty such as him.) I'll send John in with your dinner, sir. [Curtsies and exit, leaving Hyacinth transfixed with astonishment.]

SCENE III.—FRONT OF INN.

Enter SUSAN with black ribbons in her cap.

SUSAN. Heigho! so the gout's carried off poor old master at last. Ah! well, he was always a great plague to everybody, and it's one's duty to be resigned—he's been dead more than two months now, and it's above a month since mistress went to Broadstairs for a change, and left John and me to keep house—ah! it was very pleasant—we was so comfortable. Now, if in a year or two mistress was to sell the business, and John and me could save money enough to buy it, and was to be married, and live here; la! I should be as happy as the day's long. I've been dull enough the last week though —for last Monday—no, last Saturday—that is, the Saturday before last, John went for a holiday to see his friends in Yorkshire, and there's been nobody at home but me and the cat—I can't think what ailed him before he went away, he seemed to avoid me like; and when he bid me good-bye, he told me if I should happen to pick up a sweetheart while he was gone, he would not be jealous—what could he mean by that? I dare say he only said it to tease me. I ought to have a letter soon to say when mistress is coming back. (Enter boy with letter, which he gives to Susan, and exit.) Well, that is curious—it is from Broadstairs, I see by the postmark. Why, bless me, it's in John's handwriting—he can't be at Broad-stairs, surely—I feel all of a tremble. (Opens the letter and reads.) " My dear Seusan, Hafter i left yeu, I thort i should not ave time to go hall the way to York, so by way of a change i cum down here where I met poor Mrs., who seemed quite in the dumps and low like, about old master being dead, which is human natur cut down like grass, Seusan, and not having a creetur to speak to, naturally took to me, which was an old tho' humbel friend, Seusan—and—do not think me guilty of hinconstancy, which I never felt, but the long and short of it is that we was married " (the wretch!) " yesterday, and is comin' home to-morrow, where I hopes to remain very faithfully your affexionate Master and Mrs.

" JOHN AND BETSEY SHORTOATS."

(Susan tears the letter, bursts into tears, and sinks back into a chair fainting—curtain drops.)

CHAPTER XLIV.

CONFESSIONS.

". . . And sure the match
Were rich and honourable."
            Two Gentlemen of Verona.
" We that are true lovers run into strange capers."—*As You Like It.*
". . . . That which I would discover,
The law of friendship bids me to conceal."
            Two Gentlemen of Verona.
" Tarry I here, 1 but attend on death ;
But fly I hence, I fly away from life."

" DEAR me! what can it possibly mean ? how I wish I could guess it ! " said the youngest Miss Simper.

" Do you know what it is, Mr. Oaklands ? " asked the second Miss Simper.

" I am sure he does, he looks so delightfully wicked," added the eldest Miss Simper, shaking her ringlets in a fascinating manner, to evince her faith in the durability of their curl.

The eldest Miss Simper had been out four seasons, and spent the last winter at Nice, on the strength of which she talked to young men of themselves in the third person, to show her knowledge of the world, and embodied in her behaviour generally a complete system of " Matrimony-made-easy, or the whole Art of getting a good Establishment," proceeding from early lessons in converting acquaintance into flirts, up to the important final clause—how to lead young men of property to propose.

" Really," replied Oaklands, " my face must be far more expressive and less honest than I was aware of, for I can assure you they have studiously kept me in the dark as to the meaning."

" But you have made out some idea for yourself; it is impossible that it should be otherwise," observed the second Miss Simper, who had rubbed off some of her shyness upon a certain young Hebrew Professor at the last Cambridge Installation, and become rather blue from the contact.

" Have you ? " said the youngest Miss Simper, who, being as nearly a fool as it is possible to allow that a pretty girl of seventeen can be, rested her pretensions upon a plaintive voice and a pensive smile, which went just far enough to reveal an irreproachable set of teeth, and then faded away into an expression of gentle sorrow, the source of which, like that of the Niger, had as yet remained undiscovered.

" Oh, he has ! " exclaimed the eldest Miss Simper ; " that exquisitely sarcastic, yet tantalizing, curl of the upper-lip tells me that it is so."

" Since you press me," replied Oaklands, " I confess, I believe I have guessed it."

" I knew it—it could not have been otherwise," exclaimed the blue belle enthusiastically.

The youngest Miss Simper spoke not, but her appealing glance, and the slight exhibition of the pearl-like teeth, seemed to hint that some mysterious increase of her secret sorrow might be expected in the event of Oaklands refusing to communicate the results of his penetration.

" As I make it out," said Harry, " the first scene was Inn, the second Constancy, and the third Inconstancy."

" Ah ! that wretch John, he was the Inconstancy," observed the eldest Miss Simper, " marrying for money !—the creature !—such baseness ! but how delightfully that dear, clever Mr. Lawless acted; he made love with such naïve simplicity, too; he is quite irresistible."

" I shall take care to let him know your flattering opinion," returned Oaklands, with a faint attempt at a smile, while the gloom on his brow grew deeper, and the Misses Simper were in their turn deserted ; the eldest gaining this slight addition to her worldly knowledge, viz. that it is not always prudent to praise one friend to another, unless you happen to be a little more behind the scenes than had been the case in the present instance.

" Umph ! Frank Fairlegh, where are you ? come here, boy," said Mr. Frampton, seizing one of my buttons, and towing me thereby into a corner. " Pretty girl, your sister Fanny—nice girl, too—umph ! "

" I'm very glad she pleases you, sir," replied I; " as you become better acquainted with her, you will find that she is as good as she looks—if you like her now, you will soon grow very fond of her—everybody becomes fond of Fanny."

" Umph ! I can see one who is, at all events. Pray, sir, do you mean to let your sister marry that good-natured, well-disposed, harum-scarum young fool, Lawless ? "

" This is a matter I leave entirely to themselves ; if Lawless wishes to marry Fanny, and she likes him well enough to accept him, and his parents approve of the arrangements, I shall make no objection : it would be a very good match for her."

" Umph ! yes—she would make a very nice addition to his stud," returned Mr. Frampton, in a more sarcastic tone than I had ever heard him use before. " What do you suppose are the girl's own wishes ? is she willing to be Empress of the Stable ? "

" Really, sir, you ask me a question which I am quite unable to answer; young ladies are usually reserved upon such subjects, and Fanny is especially so; but from my own observations, I am inclined to think that she likes him."

" Umph ! dare say she does; women are always fools in these cases —men too, for that matter—or else they would take pattern by me, and continue in a state of single blessedness; " then came an aside, " Single wretchedness more likely, nobody to care about one—nothing to love—die in a ditch like a beggar's dog, without a pocket-hand-

kerchief wetted for one—there's single blessedness for you! ride
in a hearse, and have some fat fool chuckling in the sleeve of his
black coat over one's hard-earned money. Nobody shall do that with
mine, though; for I'll leave it all to build union workhouses and
encourage the slave-trade, by way of revenging myself on society at
large. Wonder why I said that, when I don't think it! just like me
—umph!"

"I am not at all sure but that this may prove a mere vision of our
own too lively imaginations, after all," replied I, "or that Lawless
looks upon Fanny in any other light than as the sister of his old
friend, and an agreeable girl to talk and laugh with; but if it should
turn out otherwise, I should be sorry to think that it is a match
which will not meet with your approval, sir."

"Oh! I shall approve—I always approve of everything—I dare say
he'll make a capital husband—he's very kind to his dogs and horses.
Umph! silly boy, silly girl—when she could easily do better, too.
Umph! just like me, bothering myself about other people, when I
might leave it alone—silly girl though, very!"

So saying, Mr. Frampton walked away, grunting like a whole drove
of pigs, as was his wont when annoyed.

The next morning I was aroused from an uneasy sleep by the sun
shining brightly through my shutters, and, springing out of bed, and
throwing open the window, I perceived that it was one of those
lovely winter-days which appear sent to assure us that fogs, frost,
and snow will not last for ever, but that Nature has brighter things
in store for us, if we will bide her time patiently. To think of lying
in bed on such a morning was out of the question, so, dressing
hastily, I threw on a shooting jacket, and sallied forth for a stroll.
As I wandered listlessly through the park, admiring the hoar-frost
which glittered like diamonds in the early sunshine, clothing the
brave old limbs of the time-honoured fathers of the forest with a
fabric of silver tissue, the conversation I had held with Mr. Frampton
about Fanny and Lawless recurred to my mind. Strange that
Harry Oaklands and Mr. Frampton—men so different, yet alike in
generous feeling and honourable principle—should both evidently
disapprove of such a union; was I myself, then, so blinded by ideas
of the worldly advantages it held forth, that I was unable to perceive
its unfitness? Would Lawless really prize her, as Tennyson has so
well expressed it in his finest poem, as

"Something better than his dog, a little dearer than his horse"?

and was I about to sacrifice my sister's happiness for rank and
fortune, those world-idols which, stripped of the supposititious
attributes bestowed upon them by the bigotry of their worshippers,
appear, in their true worthlessness, empty breath and perishable
dross? But most probably there was no cause for uneasiness; after
all, I was very likely worrying myself most unnecessarily: what
proof was there that Lawless really cared for Fanny? His attentions—oh! there was nothing in that—Lawless was shy and awkward

in female society, and Fanny had been kind to him, and had taken
the trouble to draw him out, therefore he liked her, and preferred
talking and laughing with her, rather than with any other girl with
whom he did not feel at his ease. However, even if there should be
anything more in it, it had not gone so far but that a little judicious
snubbing would easily put an end to it—I determined, therefore, to
talk to my mother about it after breakfast: she had now seen
enough of Lawless to form her own opinion of him: and if she
agreed with Oaklands and Mr. Frampton that his was not a style of
character calculated to secure Fanny's happiness, we must let her go
and stay with the Colemans, or find some other means of separating
them. I had just arrived at this conclusion, when, on passing round
the stem of an old tree which stood in the path, I encountered some
person who was advancing rapidly in an opposite direction, meeting
him so abruptly that we ran against each other with no small degree
of violence.

"Hold hard there! you're on your wrong side, young fellow, and
if you've done me the slightest damage, even scratched my varnish,
I'll pull you up."

"I wish you had pulled up a little quicker yourself, Lawless,"
replied I, for, as the reader has doubtless discovered from the style
of his address, it was none other than the subject of my late reverie
with whom I had come in collision. "I don't know whether I have
scratched your varnish, as you call it, but I have knocked the skin
off my own knuckles against the tree in the scrimmage."

"Never mind, man," returned Lawless, "there are worse misfortunes happen at sea; a little sticking-plaster will set all to rights
again. But look here, Fairlegh," he continued taking my arm, "I'm
glad I happened to meet you; I want to have five minutes' serious
conversation with you."

"Won't it do after breakfast?" interposed I, for my fears con-
strued this appeal into "confirmation strong as holy writ" of my
previous suspicions, and I wished to be fortified by my mother's
opinion before I in any degree committed myself. All my precautions were, however, in vain.

"Eh! I won't keep you five minutes, but you see this sort of thing
will never do at any price; I'm all wrong altogether—sometimes I
feel as if fire and water would not stop me, or cart-ropes hold me—
then again I grow as nervous as an old cat with the palsy, and sit
moping in a corner like an owl in fits. Last hunting-day I was just
as if I was mad—pressed upon the pack when they were getting
away—rode over two or three of the tail hounds, laid 'em sprawling
on their backs, like spread eagles, till the huntsman swore at me
loud enough to split a three-inch oak plank—went slap at everything
that came in my way—took rails, fences, and timber, all flying,
rough and smooth as nature made 'em—in short, showed the whole
field the way across country at a pace which rather astonished them,
I fancy; well, at last there was a check, and before the hounds

got on the scent again, something seemed to come over me
so that I could not ride a bit, and kept cranning at mole-hills and
shirking gutters, till I wound up by getting a tremendous spill from
checking my horse at a wretched little fence that he could have
stepped over, and actually I felt so faint-hearted that I gave it up as
a bad job, and rode home ready to eat my hat with vexation. But
I know what it is, I'm in love—that confounded charade put me up
to that dodge. I fancied at first that I had got an ague, one of those
off-and-on affairs that always come just when you don't want them,
and was going to ask Ellis to give me a ball, but I found it out just
in time, and precious glad I was too, for I never could bear taking
physic since I was the height of sixpenny-worth of halfpence."

"Really, Lawless, I must be getting home."

"Eh! wait a minute; you haven't an idea what a desperate state
I'm in ; I had a letter returned to me yesterday, with a line from the
post-office clerk, saying no such person could be found, and, when I
came to look at the address I wasn't surprised to hear it. I had
written to give some orders about a dog-cart that is building for me,
and directed my letter to Messrs. Lovely Fanny, Coachmakers, Long
Acre. Things can't go on in this way, you know—I must do something—come to the point, eh ?—What do you say ? "

"Upon my word," replied I, " this is a case in which I am the last
person to advise you."

"Eh ? no, it is not that—I'm far beyond the reach of advice ; but
what I mean is, your governor being dead—don't you see—I consider
you to stand 'in propria quæ maribus,' as we used to say at old
Mildman's."

"'In loco parentis ' is what you are aiming at, I imagine,"
returned I.

"Eh! psha, it's all the same!" continued Lawless impatiently;
" but what do you say about it ? Will you give your consent, and
back me up a bit in the business ?—for I'm precious nervous, I can
tell you."

"Am I to understand, then," said I, seeing an explanation was
inevitable, " that it is my sister who has inspired you with this very
alarming attachment ? "

" Eh ! yes, of course it is," was the reply ; " haven't I been talking
about her for the last ten minutes? You are growing stupid all
at once; did you think it was your mother I meant ? "

"Not exactly," replied I, smiling ; " but have you ever considered
what Lord Cashington would say to your marrying a poor clergyman's daughter ? "

" What! my governor ? oh ! he'd be so delighted to get me married
at any price, that he would not care who it was to, so that she was a
lady. He knows how I shirk female society in general, and he is
afraid I shall break my neck some of these fine days, and leave him
the honour of being the last Lord Cashington as well as the
first."

"And may I ask whether you imagine your suit likely to be favourably received by the young lady herself?"

" Eh! why, you see it's not so easy to tell; I'm not used to the ways of women, exactly. Now with horses I know every action, and can guess what they'd be up to in a minute; for instance, if they prick up their ears, one may expect a shy, when they lay them back you may look out for a bite or a kick; but, unluckily, women have not got movable ears."

" No," replied I, laughing at this singular regret; "they contrive to make their eyes answer nearly the same purpose, though. Well, Lawless, my answer is this—I cannot pretend to judge whether you and my sister are so constituted as to increase each other's happiness by becoming man and wife; that is a point I must leave to her to decide; she is no longer a child, and her destiny shall be placed in her own hands; but I think I may venture to say that if your parents are willing to receive her, and she is pleased to accept you, you need not fear any opposition on the part of my mother or myself."

"That's the time of day," exclaimed Lawless, rubbing his hands with glee, "this is something like doing business; oh! it's jolly fun to be in love, after all. Then everything depends upon Fanny now; but how am I to find out whether she will have me or not? eh! that's another sell."

" Ask her," replied I; and turning down a different path, I left him to deliberate upon this knotty point in solitude.

As I walked towards home my meditations assumed a somewhat gloomy colouring. The matter was no longer doubtful, Lawless was Fanny's declared suitor; this, as he had himself observed, was something like doing business. Instead of planning with my mother how we could prevent the affair from going any farther, I must now inform her of his offer, and find out whether she could give me any clue as to the state of Fanny's affections. And now that Lawless's intentions were certain, and that it appeared by no means improbable he might succeed in obtaining Fanny's hand, a feeling of repugnance came over me, and I began to think Mr. Frampton was right, and that my sister was formed for better things than to be the companion for life of such a man as Lawless. From a reverie which thoughts like these had engendered, I was aroused by Harry Oaklands' favourite Scotch terrier, which attracted my attention by jumping and fawning upon me, and on raising my eyes I perceived the figure of his master, leaning, with folded arms, against the trunk of an old tree. As we exchanged salutations I was struck by an unusual air of dejection both in his manner and appearance. " You are looking ill and miserable this morning, Harry; is your side painful?" inquired I anxiously.

" No," was the reply, " I believe it is doing well enough; Ellis says so;" he paused, and then resumed in a low hurried voice, "Frank, I am going abroad."

"Going abroad!" repeated I, in astonishment; "where are you going to? when are you going? this is a very sudden resolution, surely."

"I know it is, but I cannot stay here," he continued; "I must get away—I am wretched, perfectly miserable."

"My dear Harry," replied I, "what is the matter? come, tell me; as boys we had no concealments from each other, and this reserve which appears lately to have sprung up between us is not well: what has occurred to render you unhappy?"

A deep sigh was for some minutes his only answer; then, gazing steadily in my face, he said, "And have you really no idea?—But why should I be surprised at the blindness of others, when I myself have only become aware of the true nature of my own feelings when my peace of mind is destroyed, and all chance of happiness for me in this life has fled for ever!"

"What do you mean, my dear, Harry?" replied I; "what can you refer to?"

"Have you not thought me very much altered of late?" he continued.

"Since you ask me, I have fancied that illness was beginning to sour your temper." I replied.

"Illness of mind, not body," he resumed; "for now, when life has lost all charm for me, I am regaining health and strength apace. You must have observed with what a jaundiced eye I have regarded everything that Lawless has said or done; what was the feeling, think you, which has led me to do so? Jealousy!"

"Jealousy!" exclaimed I, as for the first time the true state of the case flashed across me. "Oh! Harry, why did you not speak of this sooner?"

"Why, indeed! because in my blindness I fancied the affection I entertained for your sister was merely a brother's love, and did not know, till the chance of losing her for ever opened my eyes effectually, that she had become so essential to my happiness that life without her would be a void. If you but knew the agony of mind I endured while they were acting that hateful charade last night! I quite shudder when I think how I felt towards Lawless; I could have slain him where he stood without a shadow of compunction. No, I must leave this place without delay; I would not go through what I suffered yesterday again for anything—I could not bear it."

"Oh! if we had but known this sooner," exclaimed I, "so much might have been done—I only parted from Lawless five minutes before I met you, telling him that if Fanny approved of his suit, neither my mother nor I would offer the slightest opposition. But is it really too late to do anything? shall I speak to Fanny?"

"Not for worlds!" exclaimed Oaklands impetuously; "do not attempt to influence her in the slightest degree. If, as my fears suggest, she really love Lawless, she must never learn that my affection for her has exceeded that of a brother—never know that from henceforth her image will stand between me and happiness, and cast its shadow over the whole future of my life."

He stood for a moment, his hands pressed upon his brow as if to shut out some object too painful to behold, and then continued abruptly, "Lawless has proposed, then?"

"He has asked my consent, and his next step will, of course, be to do so," replied I.

"Then my fate will soon be decided," returned Oaklands. "Now listen to me, Frank; let this matter take its course exactly as if this conversation had never passed between us. Should Fanny be doubtful, and consult you, do your duty as Lawless's friend and her brother—place the advantages and disadvantages fairly before her, and then let her decide for herself, without in the slightest degree attempting to bias her. Will you promise to do this, Frank?"

"Must it indeed be so? can nothing be done? no scheme hit upon?" returned I sorrowfully.

"Nothing of the kind must be attempted," replied Oaklands sternly: "could I obtain your sister's hand to-morrow by merely raising my finger, I would not do so while there remained a possibility of her preferring Lawless. Do you imagine that I could be content to be accepted out of compassion? No," he added, more calmly, "the die will soon be cast; till then I will remain; and if, as I fear is only too certain, Lawless's suit is favourably received, I shall leave this place instantly—put it on the score of health—make Ellis order me abroad—the German baths, Madeira, Italy, I care not: all places will be alike to me then."

"And how miserable Sir John will be at this sudden determination!" returned I; "and he is so happy now in seeing your health restored!"

"Ah! this world is truly termed a vale of tears," replied Harry mournfully, "and the trial hardest to bear is the sight of the unhappiness we cause those we love. Strange that my acts seem always fated to bring sorrow upon my father's gray head, when I would willingly lay down my life to shield him from suffering. But do not imagine that I will selfishly give way to grief—no; as soon as Lawless is married, I shall return to England and devote myself to my father; my duty to him, and your friendship, will be the only interests that bind me to life."

He paused, and then added, "Frank, you know me too well to fancy that I am exaggerating my feelings, or even deceiving myself as to the strength of them; this is no sudden passion, my love for Fanny has been the growth of years, and the gentle kindness with which she attended on me during my illness—the affectionate tact (for I believe she loves me as a brother, though I have almost doubted even that of late) with which she forestalled my every wish, proved to me how indispensable she has become to my happiness. But," he continued, seeing, I imagined, by the painful expression of my face, the effect his words were producing on me, "in my selfishness I am rendering you unhappy. We will speak no more of this matter till my fate is certain; should it be that which I expect, let us forget that this conversation ever passed; f, on the contrary, Lawless should meet with a refusal—but that is' an alternative I dare not contemplate.— And now, farewell."

So saying, he wrung my hand with a pressure that vouched for his returning strength, and left me. In spite of my walk, I had not much appetite for my breakfast that morning.

CHAPTER XLV.

HELPING A LAME DOG OVER A STILE.

"Marry, I cannot show it in rhyme; I have tried . . . No, I was not born under a rhyming planet; nor I cannot woo in festival terms."—*Much Ado About Nothing.*

"Now, let the verses be bad or good, it plainly amounts to a regular offer. I don't believe any of the lines are an inch too long or too short; but if they were it would be wicked to alter them, for they are really genuine."—*Thinks I to Myself.*

"We shall have a rare letter from him."—*Twelfth Night.*

IT was usually my custom of an afternoon to read law for a couple of hours, a course of training preparatory to committing myself to the tender mercies of a special pleader; and as Sir John's well-stored library afforded me every facility for so doing, that was the venue I generally selected for my interviews with Messrs. Blackstone, Coke upon Lyttelton, and other legal luminaries. Accordingly, on the day in question, after having nearly quarrelled with my mother for congratulating me warmly on the attainment of my wishes, when I mentioned to her Lawless's proposal, found fault with Fanny's Italian pronunciation so harshly as to bring tears into her eyes, and grievously offended our old female domestic by disdainfully rejecting some pet abomination upon which she had decreed that I should lunch, I sallied forth, and, not wishing to encounter any of the family, entered the hall by a side-door, and reached the library unobserved. To my surprise I discovered Lawless (whom I did not recollect ever to have seen there before, he being not much given to literary pursuits) seated pen in hand, at the table, apparently absorbed in the mysteries of composition.

"I shall not disturb you, Lawless," said I, taking down a book. "I am only going to read law for an hour or two."

"Eh! disturb me?" was the reply; "I'm uncommon glad to be disturbed, I can tell you, for hang me if I can make head or tail of it! Here have I been for the last three hours trying to write an offer to your sister, and actually have not contrived to make a fair start of it yet. I wish you would lend me a hand, there's a good fellow—I know you are up to all the right dodges—just give one a sort of notion, eh? don't you see?"

" What! write an offer to my own sister? Well, of all the quaint ideas I ever heard, that's the oddest—really you must excuse me."

" Very odd, is it?" inquired Coleman, opening the door in time to overhear the last sentence. " Pray let me hear about it, then, for I like to know of odd things particularly; but perhaps I'm intruding."

" Eh! no; come along here, Coleman," cried Lawless: "you are just the very boy I want—I am going to be married—that is, I want to be, don't you see, if she'll have me, but there's the rub; Frank Fairlegh is all right, and the old lady says she's agreeable, so every-thing depends on the young woman herself—if she will but say 'Yes,' we shall go ahead in style; but, unfortunately, before she is likely to say anything one way or the other, you understand, I've got to pop the question, as they call it. Now, I've about as much notion of making an offer as a cow has of dancing ¡a hornpipe—so I want you to help us a bit—eh?"

" Certainly," replied Freddy courteously; " I shall be only too happy, and as delays are dangerous, I had perhaps better be off at once—where is the young lady?"

" Eh! hold hard there! don't go quite so fast, young man," exclaimed Lawless, aghast; " if you bolt ¡away at that pace you'll never see the end of the run; why, you don't suppose I want you to go and talk to her—pop the question ' viva voce,' do you? You'll be advising me to be married by deputy, I suppose, next. No, no, I'm going to do the trick by letter—something like a valentine, only rather more so, eh! but I can't exactly manage to write it properly. If it was but a warranty for a horse, now, I'd knock it off in no time, but this is a sort of thing, you see, I'm not used to; one doesn't get married as easily as one sells a horse, nor as often, eh? and it's rather a nervous piece of business—a good deal depends upon the letter."

" You've been trying your hand at it already, I see," observed Coleman, seating himself at the table; " pretty consumption of paper! I wonder what my governor would say to me if I were to set about drawing a deed in this style; why, the stationer's bill would run away with all the profits."

" Never mind the profits, you avaricious Jew!" replied Lawless. " Yes, I've been trying effects, as the painters call it—putting down two or three beginnings to find out which looked the most like the time of day—you understand?"

" Two or three?" repeated Coleman, " six or seven rather, ' voyons.' ' Mr. Lawless presents his affections to Miss Fairlegh, and requests the hon—' Not a bad idea, an offer in the third person—the only case in which a third person would not be ' de trop ' in such an affair.'

" Eh! yes, I did the respectful when I first started, you know, but

x

I soon dropped that sort of thing when I got warm; you'll see, I stepped out no end afterwards."

"'Honoured Miss,'" continued Coleman, reading,—"'My sentiments, that is, your perfections, your splendid action, your high breeding, and the many slap-up points that may be discerned in you by any man that has an eye for a horse—'"

"Ah! that was where I spoiled it," sighed Lawless.

"Here's a very pretty one," resumed Freddy. "'Adorable and adored Miss Fanny Fairlegh,—Seeing you as I do with the eyes' (Why, she would not think you saw her with your nose, would she?) 'of fond affection, probably would induce me to overlook any unsoundness or disposition to vice—'"

"That one did not turn out civilly, you see," said Lawless, "or else it wasn't such a bad beginning."

"Here's a better," rejoined Coleman. "'Exquisitely beautiful Fanny, fairest of that lovely sex which, to distinguish it from us rough and ready fox-hunters, who, when once we get our heads at any of the fences of life, go at it, never mind how stiff it may be (matrimony has always appeared to me one of the stiffest), and generally contrive to find ourselves on the other side with our hind legs well under us;—a sex, I say, which, to distinguish it from our own, is called the fair sex, a stock of which I never used to think any great things, reckoning them only fit to canter round the parks with, until I saw you brought out, when I at once perceived that your condition—that is, my feelings—were so inexpressible, that—'"

"Ah!" interposed Lawless, "that's where I got bogged, sank in over the fetlocks, and had to give it up as a bad job."

"In fact, your feelings became too many for you," returned Coleman; "but what have we here?—verses, by all that's glorious!"

"No, no! I'm not going to let you read them," exclaimed Lawless, attempting to wrest the paper out of his hand.

"Be quiet, Lawless," rejoined Coleman, holding him off, "sit down directly, sir, or I won't write a word for you: I must see what all your ideas are in order to get some notion of what you want to say; besides, I've no doubt they'll be very original.

I.

"'Sweet Fanny, there are moments
When the heart is not one's own,
When we fain would clip its wild wing's tip,
But we find the bird has flown.

II.

"'Dear Fanny, there are moments
When a loss may be a gain,
And sorrow, joy—for the heart's a toy,
And loving's such sweet pain.

III.

"'Yes, Fanny, there are moments
When a smile is worth a throne,
When a frown can prove the power of love,
Must fade, and die alone.'

Why you never wrote those, Lawless?"

"Didn't I?" returned Lawless; "but I know I did, though—copied them out of an old book I found up there, and wrote some more to 'em, because I thought there wasn't enough for the money, besides putting in Fanny's name instead of—what do you think?—Phillis!—there's a name for you; the fellow must have been a fool. Why, I would not give a dog such an ill name, for fear somebody should hang him; but go on."

" Ah, now we come to the original matter," returned Coleman, " and very original it seems :

IV.

" ' Dear Fanny, there are moments
When love gets you in a fix,
Takes the bit in his jaws, and, without any pause,
Bolts away with you like bricks.

V.

" ' Yes, Fanny, there are moments
When affection knows no bounds,
When I'd rather be talking with you out a-walking,
Than rattling after the hounds.

VI.

" ' Dear Fanny, there are moments
When one feels that one's inspired,
And . . . . and . . . .'

It does not seem to have been one of those moments with you just then," continued Freddy, " for the poem comes to an abrupt and untimely conclusion, unless three blots. and something that looks like a horse's head, may be a hieroglyphic mode of recording your inspirations, which I'm not learned enough to decipher."

" Eh! no; I broke down there," replied Lawless; " the muse deserted me, and went off in a canter for—where was it those young women used to hang out?—the ' Gradus ad' place, you know?"

" The tuneful Nine, whom you barbarously designate young women." returned Coleman, " are popularly supposed to have resided on Mount Parnassus. which acclivity I have always imagined of a triangular or sugar-loaf form. with Apollo seated on the apex or extreme point. his attention divided between preserving his equilibrium and keeping up his playing, which latter necessity he provided for by executing difficult passages on a golden (or, more probably, silver-gilt) lyre."

" Eh! nonsense," rejoined Lawless; "now, do be serious for five minutes. and go ahead with this letter, there's a good fellow; for 'pon my word, I'm in a wretched state of mind—I am indeed. It's a fact. I'm nearly half a stone lighter than I was when I came here; I know I am, for there was an old fellow weighing a defunct pig down at the farm yesterday, and I made him let me get into the scales when he took piggy out. I tell you what, if I'm not married soon I shall make a job for the sexton; such incessant wear and tear of the sensibilities is enough to kill a prize-fighter in full training, let alone a man that has been leading such a molly-coddle life as I have of late, lounging about drawing-rooms like a lapdog."

"Well, then, let us begin at once," said Freddy, seizing a pen : "now, what am I to say ? "

" Eh ! why, you don't expect me to know, do you ? " exclaimed Lawless, aghast ; " I might just as well write it myself as have to tell you ; no, no, you must help me, or else I'd better give the whole thing up at once."

" I'll help you, man, never fear," rejoined Freddy, " but you must give me something to work upon : why, it's all plain sailing enough ; begin by describing your feelings."

"Feelings, eh ? " said Lawless, rubbing his ear violently. as if to arouse his dormant faculties, " that's easier said than done. Well, here goes for a start: ' My dear Miss Fairlegh.' "

" ' My dear Miss Fairlegh,' " repeated Coleman, writing rapidly, " yes."

" Have you written that ? " continued Lawless ; " ar—let me think —' I have felt for some time past very peculiar sensations, and have become, in many respects, quite an altered man.' "

" ' Altered man,' " murmured Freddy, still writing.

" ' I have given up hunting,' " resumed Lawless, " ' which no longer possesses any interest in my eyes, though I think you'd have said, if you had been with us the last time we were out, that you never saw a prettier run in your life ; the meet was at Chorley Bottom. and we got away in less than ten minutes after the hounds had been in cover, with as plucky a fox as ever puzzled a pack—' "

" Hold hard there ! " interrupted Coleman, " I can't put all that in ; nobody ever wrote an account of a fox-hunt in a love-letter—no ; you've given up hunting, which no longer possessed any interest in your eyes ; now go on."

" My ! yes," repeated Lawless reflectively ; " yes : ' I am become indifferent to everything ; I take no pleasure in the new dog-cart King in Long Acre is building for me, with cane sides, the wheels larger, and the seat, if possible, still higher than the last, and which, if I am not very much out in my reckoning, will follow so light—' "

" I can't write all that trash about a dog-cart," interrupted Freddy crossly ; " that's worse than t.e fox-hunting ; stick to your feelings. man. can't you ? "

" Ah ! you little know the effect such feelings produce," sighed Lawless.

" That's the style," resumed Coleman, with delight ; " that will come in beautifully—' such feelings produce ; ' now go on."

" ' At night my slumbers are rendered distracting, by visions of you—as—as—' "

" ' The bride of another,' " suggested Coleman.

" Exactly," resumed Lawless ; " or, ' sleep refusing to visit my—' "

" ' Aching eyeballs,' " put in Freddy.

" ' I lie tossing restlessly from side to side, as if bitten by—' "

" ' The gnawing tooth of Remorse ; ' that will do famously," added his scribe ; " now tell her that she is the cause of it."

" ' All these unpleasantnesses are owing to you,' " began Lawless.

" Oh! that won't do," said Coleman ; " no—' These tender griefs ' (that's the term, I think) ' are some of the effects, goods, and chattels '—psha! I was thinking of drawing a will—' the effects produced upon me by—' "

" ' The wonderful way in which you stuck to your saddle when the mare bolted with you,' " rejoined Lawless enthusiastically ; " what, won't that do either ? "

" No, be quiet; I've got it all beautifully now, if you don't interrupt me : ' Your many perfections of mind and person—perfections which have led me to centre my ideas of happiness solely in the fond hope of one day calling you my own.' "

" That's very pretty indeed," said Lawless ; " go on."

" ' Should I be fortunate enough,' " continued Coleman, " ' to succeed in winning your affection, it will be the study of my future life to prevent your every wish—' "

" Eh! what do you mean ? not let her have her own way ? Oh! that will never pay ; why, the little I know of women, I'm sure that, if you want to come over them, you must flatter 'em up with the idea that you mean to give 'em their heads on all occasions—let 'em do just what they like. Tell a woman she should not go up the chimney, it's my belief you'd see her nose peep out of the top before ten minutes were over, Oh! that'll never do! "

" Nonsense," interrupted Freddy ; " ' prevent ' means to forestall in that sense ; however, I'll put it ' forestall,' if you like it better."

" I think it will be the safest," replied Lawless, shaking his head solemnly.

" ' In everything your will shall be law,' " continued Coleman, writing.

" Oh! I say, that's coming it rather strong, though," interposed Lawless ; " query about that ? "

" All right," rejoined Coleman, " it's always customary to say so in these cases, but it means nothing ; as to the real question of mastery, that is a matter to be decided post-nuptially ; you'll be enlightened on the subject before long in a series of midnight discourses, commonly known under the title of curtain-lectures."

" Pleasant, eh ? " returned Lawless ; " well, I bet two to one on the grey mare, for I never could stand being preached to, and shall consent to anything for the sake of a quiet life—so move on."

" ' If this offer of my heart and hand should be favourably received by the loveliest of her sex,' " continued Coleman, " ' a line, a word, a smile, a—' "

" ' Wink,' " suggested Lawless.

" ' Will be sufficient to acquaint me with my happiness.' "

"Tell her to look sharp about sending an answer," exclaimed Lawless; "if she keeps me waiting long after that letter's sent, I shall go off pop, like a bottle of ginger-beer; I know I shall—string won't hold me, or wire either."

"'When once this letter is despatched, I shall enjoy no respite from the tortures of suspense till the answer arrives, which shall exalt to the highest pinnacle of happiness, or plunge into the lowest abysses of despair, one who lives but in the sunshine of your smile, and who now, with the liveliest affection, tempered by the most profound respect, ventures to sign himself. Your devotedly attached—'"

"'And love-lorn,'" interposed Lawless, in a sharp, quick tone.

"Love-lorn," repeated Coleman, looking up with an air of surprise; "sentimental and ridiculous in the extreme! I shall not write any such thing."

"I believe, Mr. Coleman, that letter is intended to express my feelings, and not yours?" questioned Lawless, in a tone of stern investigation.

"Yes, of course it is," began Coleman.

"Then write as I desire, sir," continued Lawless authoritatively; "I ought to know my own feelings best, I imagine; I feel love-lorn, and 'love-lorn' it shall be."

"Oh, certainly," replied Coleman, slightly offended, "anything you please. 'Your devotedly attached and love-lorn admirer;' here, sign it yourself, 'George Lawless.'"

"Bravo!" said Lawless, relapsing into his accustomed good humour the moment the knotty point of the insertion of "love-lorn" had been carried; "if that isn't first-rate, I'm a Dutchman; why, Freddy, boy, where did you learn it? how does it all come into your head?"

"Native talent," replied Coleman, "combined with a strong and lively appreciation of the sublime and beautiful, chiefly derived from my maternal grandmother, whose name was Burke."

"That wasn't the Burke who wrote a book about it, was it?" asked Lawless.

"Ah! no, not exactly," replied Coleman; "she would have been, I believe, had she been a man."

"Very likely," returned Lawless, whose attention was absorbed in folding, sealing, and directing the important letter, "'Miss Fairlegh.' Now, if she does but regard my suit favourably."

"You'll be suited with a wife," punned Coleman.

"But suppose she should say 'No,'" continued Lawless, musing.

"Why, then you'll be non-suited, that's all," returned the incorrigible Freddy; and making a face at me, which (as I was to all appearance immersed fathoms deep in Blackstone) he thought I should not observe, he sauntered out of the room humming the following scrap of some elegant ditty, with which he had become acquainted:

"'If ever I marry a wife,
   I'll marry a publican's daughter.
   I'll sit all day long in the bar,
   And drink nothing but brandy-and-water.'"

Lawless having completed his arrangements to his satisfaction, hastened to follow Coleman's example, nodding to me as he left the room, and adding, " Good-bye, Fairlegh ; read away, old boy, and when I see you again, I hope I shall have some good news for you."

Good news for me ! The news that my sister would be pledged to spend her life as the companion, or, more properly speaking, the plaything, of a man who had so little delicacy of mind, so little self-respect, as to have allowed his feelings (for that he was attached to Fanny, as far as he was capable of forming a real attachment, I could not for a moment doubt) to be laid bare to form a subject for Freddy Coleman to sharpen his wit upon; and to reflect that I had in any way assisted in bringing this result about, had thrown them constantly together—oh ! as I thought upon it, the inconceivable folly of which I had been guilty nearly maddened me. Somehow, I had never until this moment actually realized the idea of my sister's marrying him; even that night, when I had spoken to my mother on the subject, my motive had been more to prevent her from lecturing and worrying Fanny than anything else. But the real cause of my indifference was that during the whole progress of the affair my thoughts and feelings had been so completely engrossed by, and centred in, my own position in regard to Clara Saville, that although present in body my mind was in great measure absent. I had never given my attention to it; but had gone on in a dreamy kind of way, letting affairs take their own course, and saying and doing whatever appeared most consonant to the wishes of other people at the moment, until the discovery of Oaklands' unhappy attachment had fully aroused me, when, as it appeared, too late to remedy the misery which my carelessness and inattention had in a great measure contributed to bring about.

The only hope which now remained (and when I remembered the evident pleasure she took in his society, it appeared a very forlorn one) was that Fanny might of her own accord refuse Lawless.

By this time the precious document produced by the joint exertions of Lawless and Coleman must have reached its destination; and it was with an anxiety little inferior to that of the principals themselves that I looked forward to the result, and awaited with impatience the verdict which was to decide whether joy should brighten or sorrow shade the future years of Harry Oaklands.

CHAPTER XLVI.

TEARS AND SMILES.

> " Our doubts are traitors ;
> And make us lose the good we oft might win,
> By fearing to attempt."
> *Measure for Measure.*

> " ' Well, everyone can master grief but he that has it.
> " Yet say I he's in love."
> " The greatest note of it is his melancholy."
> " Nay, but I know who loves him.' "
> *Much Ado About Nothing.*

> " Joy, gentle friends! joy, and fresh days of love,
> Accompany your hearts."
> *Midsummer Night's Dream.*

READING law did not get on very well that day. De Lolme on the
Constitution might have been a medical treatise, for aught I knew to
the contrary—Blackstone a work on geology. After a prolonged
struggle to compel my attention, from which I did not desist until I
became suddenly aware that for the last half-hour I had been holding
one of the above-named ornaments to the profession the wrong way
upwards, I relinquished the matter as hopeless, and, pulling my hat
over my brows, sallied forth, and turned my moody steps in the
direction of the cottage. Feeling unwilling in my then humour to
encounter any of its inmates, I walked round to the back of the
house, and throwing open the window of a small room, which was
dignified by the name of the study, and dedicated to my sole use and
behoof, I leapt in, and closing the sash, flung myself into an easy-
chair, where, again involuntarily resuming the same train of
thought, I gave myself up a prey to unavailing regrets. On my way
I had encountered Freddy Coleman going to shoot wild-fowl, and he
had accosted me with the following agreeable remark: " Why,
Frank, old boy, you look as black as a crow at a funeral; I can't
think what ails you all to-day. I met Harry Oaklands just now,
seeming as much down in the mouth as if the bank had failed; so I
told him your sister was going to marry Lawless, just to cheer him
up a bit, and show him the world was all alive and merry, when off
he marched without saying a word, looking more grumpy than
ever."

" Why did you tell him what was not true ? " was my reply.

" Oh! for fun ; besides, you know, it may be true, for anything we
can tell," was the unsatisfactory rejoinder.

In order the better to enable the reader to understand what is to
follow, I must make him acquainted with the exact locale of the den
or study to which I have just introduced him. Let him imagine,

then, a small but very pretty little drawing-room, opening into a conservatory of such minute dimensions that it was, in point of fact, little more than a closet with glazed sides and a skylight: this, again, opened into the study, from which it was divided by a green baize curtain; consequently, it was very possible for anyone to over-hear in one room all that passed in the other, or even to hold a conversation with a person in the opposite apartment, Seeing, how-ever, was out of the question, as the end of a high stand of flowers intervened—purposely so placed, to enable me to lie " perdu " in the event of any visitors calling to whom I might be unwilling to reveal myself. On the present occasion, the possibility of anyone in the drawing-room seeing me was wholly precluded by reason of the curtain already mentioned being partially drawn.

I had not remained long in thought when my reverie was disturbed by someone entering the outer room and closing the door. The peculiar rustle of a lady's dress informed me that the intruder was of the gentler sex ; and the sound of the footstep, so light as to be scarcely audible, could proceed from no other inmate of the cottage but Fanny.

Even with the best intentions, one always feels a degree of shame in playing the eavesdropper; a natural sense of honour seems to forbid us, unnoticed ourselves, to remark the actions of others; yet so anxious was I, if possible, to gain some clue to the state of my sister's affections, that I could not resist the temptation of slightly changing my position, so that, concealed by a fold of the curtain, and peeping between two of the tallest camellias, I could command a view of the drawing-room. My ears had not deceived me ; on the sofa, up to which she had drawn a small writing-table, was seated Fanny ; her elbow was supported by the table before her, and her head rested on one of her little white hands, which was hidden amid the luxuriant tresses of her sunny hair. Her countenance, which was paler than usual, bore traces of tears. After remaining in this attitude for a few moments, motionless as a statue, she raised her head, and throwing back her curls from her face, opened the writing-case and wrote a hurried note ; but her powers of composition appearing to fail her before she reached the conclusion, she paused, and, with a deep sigh, drew from a fold in her dress a letter, which I instantly recognized as the remarkable document produced by the joint talents of Lawless and Coleman. As she perused this original manuscript, a smile, called forth by the singular nature of its con-tents, played for an instant over her expressive features, but was instantly succeeded by an expression of annoyance and regret.

At this moment a man's footstep sounded in the passage, and Fanny had scarcely time to conceal her letter ere the door was thrown open, and Harry Oaklands entered.

The change of light was so great on first coming into the room out of the open air, that, not until the servant had withdrawn, after say-ing, " You will find Mr. Fairlegh in the study, sir," was Harry able to perceive that, excepting himself, Fanny was the sole occupant of the apartment.

"I hope I am not disturbing you," he began, after an awkward pause, during which his cheek had flushed, and then again grown pale as marble. "The servant told me I should find Frank here alone, and that you and Mrs. Fairlegh were out walking."

"Mamma is gone to see the poor boy who broke his leg the other day; but I had a little headache, and she would not let me go with her."

"And Frank?"

"Frank went out soon after breakfast, and has not yet returned; I think he said he was going to the Hall—he wanted to find some book in the library, I fancy—I wonder you did not meet him."

"I have not been at home since the morning; my father carried me off to look at a farm he thinks of purchasing; but, as Frank is out, I will not interrupt you longer; I dare say I shall meet him in my way back. Good—good-morning!"

So saying, he took up his hat, and turned abruptly to leave the room. Apparently, however, ere he reached the door, some thought came across him which induced him to relinquish this design, for he stood irresolutely for a moment, with the handle in his hand, and then returned, saying in a low voice, "No, I cannot do it!—Fanny," he continued, speaking rapidly, as if mistrusting his self-control, "I am going abroad to-morrow; we may not meet again for years, perhaps (for life and death are strangely intermingled) we may meet in this world no more. Since you were a child we have lived together like brother and sister, and I cannot leave you without saying good-bye—without expressing a fervent wish that in the lot you have chosen for yourself you may meet with all the happiness you anticipate, and which you so well deserve."

"Going abroad?" repeated Fanny mechanically, as if stunned by this unexpected intelligence.

"Yes; I start for the Continent early to-morrow morning: you know I am always alarmingly hasty in my movements," he added, with a faint attempt at a smile.

"It must be on account of your health," exclaimed Fanny quickly. "Ah!" she continued, with a start, as a new and painful idea occurred to her, "the fearful leap you took to save me—the exertion was too much for you; I knew—I felt at the time it would be so; better, far better, had I perished in that dark river, than that you should have endangered your valuable life."

"Indeed, it is not so, Fanny," replied Oaklands kindly, and, taking her hand, he led her to the sofa, for she trembled so violently it was evident she could scarcely stand; "I am regaining strength daily, and Ellis will tell you that complete change of scene and air is the best thing for me."

"Is that really all?" inquired Fanny; "but why then go so suddenly? Think of your father; surely it will be a great shock to Sir John."

"I cannot stay here," replied Harry impetuously; "it would madden me." The look of surprise and alarm with which Fanny regarded him led him to perceive the error he had committed, and fearful of betraying himself, he added quickly, "You must make allowance for the morbid fancies of an invalid, proverbially the most capricious of all mortals. Six weeks ago I was in quite as great a hurry to reach this place as I now am to get away from it." He paused, sighed deeply, and then, with a degree of self-control for which I had scarcely given him credit, added, in a cheerful tone, "But I will not thrust my gloomy imaginings upon you; nothing dark or disagreeable should be permitted to cloud the fair prospect which to-day has opened before you. You must allow me," he continued, in a calm voice, though the effort it cost him to preserve composure must have been extreme—"you must allow me the privilege of an old friend, and let me be the first to tell you how sincerely I hope that the rank and station which will one day be yours—rank which you are so well fitted to adorn—may bring you all the happiness you imagine."

"Happiness, rank, and station! May I ask to what you refer, Mr. Oaklands?" replied Fanny, colouring crimson.

"I may have been premature in my congratulations," replied he; "I would not distress or annoy you for the world; but under the circumstances—this being probably the only opportunity I may have of expressing the deep interest I must always feel in everything that relates to your happiness—I may surely be excused; I felt I could not leave you without telling you this."

"You are labouring under some extraordinary delusion, Mr. Oaklands," rejoined Fanny, turning away her face, and speaking very quickly; "pray let this subject be dropped."

"You trifle with me," replied Oaklands sternly, his self-control rapidly deserting him, "and you know not the depth of the feelings you are sporting with. Is it a delusion to believe that you are the affianced bride of George Lawless?"

As he spoke, Fanny turned her soft blue eyes upon him with an expression which must have pierced him to the very soul—it was not an expression of anger—it was not exactly one of sorrow; but it was a look in which wounded pride at his having for a moment believed such a thing possible, was blended with tender reproach for thus misunderstanding her. The former feeling, however, was alone distinguishable, as, drawing herself up with an air of quiet dignity, which gave a character of severity to her pretty little features of which I could scarcely have believed them capable, she replied, "Since Mr. Lawless has not had sufficient delicacy to preserve his own secret, it is useless for me to attempt to do so; therefore, as you are aware that he has done me the honour of offering me his hand, in justice to myself I now inform you that it is an honour which I have declined, and, with it, all chance of attaining that 'rank and station' on which you imagined I had placed my hopes of happiness.

You will, perhaps, excuse me," she added, rising to leave the room;
" these events have annoyed and agitated me much."

" Stay !" exclaimed Oaklands, springing up impetuously, " Fanny,
for Heaven's sake, wait one moment. Am I dreaming? or did I hear
you say that you had refused Lawless ?"

" I have already told you that it is so," she replied; " pray let me
pass; you are presuming on your privileges as an old friend."

" Bear with me for one moment," pleaded Oaklands, in a voice
scarcely audible from emotion. " You have not refused him out of
any mistaken notions of generosity arising from difference of
station ? In a word—for I must speak plainly, though at the risk of
distressing you—do you love him ? "

" Really—" began Fanny, again attempting to quit the room, and
turning first red, then pale, as Oaklands still held his position
between her and the door.

" Oh! pardon me," he continued in the same broken voice, " deem
me presuming—mad—what you will ; but as you hope for happiness
here or hereafter, answer me this one question—Do you love him ? "

" No, I do not," replied Fanny, completely subdued by the violence
of his emotion.

" Thank God !" murmured Oaklands, and sinking into a chair, the
strong man, overcome by this sudden revulsion of feeling, buried his
face in his hands and wept like a child. There is no sight so affecting as that of manhood's tears. It seems natural for a woman's
feelings to find vent in weeping ; and though all our sympathies are
enlisted in her behalf, we deem it an April shower, which we hope to
see ere long give place to the sunshine of a smile; but tears are
foreign to the sterner nature of man, and any emotion powerful
enough to call them forth indicates a depth and intensity of feeling
which, like the sirocco of the desert, carries all before it in its resistless fury. Fanny must have been more than woman if she could
have remained an unmoved spectator of Harry Oaklands' agitation.

Apparently relinquishing her intention of quitting the room, she
stood with her hands clasped, regarding him with a look of mixed
interest and alarm ; but as his broad chest rose and fell, convulsed
by the sobs he in vain endeavoured to repress, she drew nearer to
him, exclaiming,—

" Mr. Oaklands, are you ill ? Shall I ring for a glass of water?"
Then, finding he was unable to answer her, completely overcome,
she continued, " Oh! what is all this ? what have I said ? what have
I done ? Harry, speak to me; tell me, are you angry with me?" and
laying her hand gently on his shoulder, she gazed up in his face with
a look of the most piteous entreaty.

Her light touch seemed to recall him to himself, and uncovering
his face, he made a strong effort to regain composure, which, after a
moment or two, appeared attended with success ; and taking her
hand between his own, he said, with a faint smile,—

" I have frightened you—have I not ? The last time I shed tears was at my mother's funeral, and I had never thought to weep again ; but what pain of body and anguish of mind were powerless to accomplish, joy has effected in an instant. This must all seem very strange to you, dear Fanny : even I myself am surprised at the depth and vehemence of my own feelings; but if you knew the agony of mind I have undergone since the night of that hateful charade— Fanny, did it never occur to you that I loved you with a love different to that of a brother ? "

As she made no reply, merely turning away her head, while a blush, faint as the earliest glance of young-eyed Morning, mantled on her cheek, he continued, " Yes, Fanny, I have known and loved you from childhood, and your affection has become, unconsciously as it were, one of the strongest ties that render life dear to me ; still, I frankly confess that till the idea of your loving another occurred to me, I was blind to the nature of my own affection. To be with you, to see and talk to you daily, to cultivate your talents, to lead you to admire the beauties that I admired, to take interest in the pursuits which interested me, was happiness enough—I wished for nothing more. Then came that business of the duel, and the affectionate kindness with which you forestalled my every wish ; the delicate tenderness and ready tact which enabled you to be more than a daughter—a guardian angel—to my father, in the days of his heavy sorrow— sorrow which my ungoverned passions had brought upon his gray head—all these things endeared you to me still more. Next followed a period of estrangement and separation, during which, as I now see, an undefined craving for your society preyed upon my spirits, and, as I verily believe, retarded my recovery. Hence, the moment I felt the slightest symptoms of returning health, my determination to revisit Heathfield. When we again met, I fancied you were ill and out of spirits."

"It was no fancy," murmured Fanny, in a low voice, as though thinking aloud.

"Indeed!" questioned Harry; "and will you not tell me the cause ? "

" Presently ; I did not mean to speak—to interrupt you."

" My sole wish and occupation," he continued, " was to endeavour to interest and amuse you, and to restore your cheerfulness, which I believe the anxiety and fatigue occasioned by my illness to have banished ; and I flattered myself I was in some degree succeeding, when Lawless's arrival, and his openly professed admiration of you, seemed to change the whole current of my thoughts—nay, my very nature itself. I became sullen and morose ; and the feeling of dislike with which I beheld Lawless's attentions to you gradually strengthened to a deep and settled hatred ; it was only by exercising the most unceasing watchfulness and self-control that I refrained from quarrelling with him ; but so engrossed was I by the painful interest I felt in all that was passing around me, that I never gave myself time to analyze my feelings; and it was not until the night of the charade that I became fully aware of their true character; it was not till then I learned that happiness could not exist for me unless you shared it. Conceive my wretchedness when, at the very moment in which this conviction first dawned upon me, I saw from Lawless's manner that in his attentions to you he was evidently in earnest, and that, as far as I could judge, you were disposed to receive those attentions favourably. My mind was instantly made up; I only waited till events should prove whether my suspicions were correct, and in case of their turning out so, feeling utterly unfit to endure the sight of Lawless's happiness, determined immediately to start for the Continent. Frank, who, taxing me with my wretched looks, elicited from me an avowal of the truth, told me Lawless was about to make you an offer; Coleman (probably in jest, but it chimed in too well with my own fears for me to dream of doubting him), that it had been accepted. The rest you know. And now, Fanny," he continued, his voice again trembling from the excess of his anxiety, " if you feel that you can never bring yourself to look upon me in any other light than as a brother, I will adhere to my determination of leaving England, and trust to time to reconcile me to my fate; but if, by waiting months, nay years, I may hope one day to call you my own, gladly will I do so—gladly will I submit to any conditions you may impose. My happiness is in your hands. Tell me, dear Fanny, must I go abroad to-morrow ? "

And what do you suppose she told him, reader ? That he must go ? Miss Martineau would have highly approved of her doing so; so would the late Poor-law Commissioners, and so would many a modern Draco, who, with the life-blood that should have gone to warm his own stony heart, scribbles a code to crush the kindly affections and genial home sympathies of his fellow-men. But Fanny was no female philosopher; she was only a pure, true-hearted, trustful, loving woman ; and so she gave him to understand that he need not set out on his travels, thereby losing a fine opportunity of " regenerating society," and vindicating the dignity of her sex. And this was not all she told him, either; for, having by his generous frankness won her confidence, he succeeded in gaining from her the secret of her heart—a secret which, an hour before, she would have braved death in its most horrible form rather than reveal. And then her happy lover learned how her affection for him, springing up in the pleasant days of childhood, had grown with her growth, and strengthened with her strength; until it became a deep and all-absorbing passion—the great reality of her spirit life ; for love such as hers, outstripping the bounds of time, links itself even with our hopes beyond the grave;—how, when he lay stretched upon the bed of suffering, oscillating between life and death, the bitter anguish that the thought of separation occasioned her, enlightened her as to the true nature of her feelings; how, as his recovery progressed, to watch over him, and minister to his comfort, was happiness beyond expression to her;—how, when he left the cottage, everything

seemed changed and dark, and a gulf appeared to have interposed
between them, which she deemed impassable ;—how, in the struggle
to conceal, and, if possible, conquer her attachment, she studiously
avoided all intercourse with him, and how the struggle ended in the
loss of health and spirits ;—how, during his absence, she felt it a
duty still to bear up against these feelings of despair, and to endure
her sad lot with patient resignation, and succeeded in some degree,
till his return once again rendered all her efforts fruitless ;—and how
she then avoided him more studiously than before, although she saw,
and sorrowed over, the evident pain her altered manner caused him ;
—how, always fearing lest he should question her as to her changed
behaviour, and by word or sign she should betray the deep interest
she felt in him, she had gladly availed herself of Lawless's attentions
as a means of avoiding Harry's kind attempts to amuse and occupy
her—attempts which, at the very moment she was wounding him by
rejecting them, only rendered him yet dearer to her ;—and how she
had gone on, thinking only of Harry and herself, until Lawless's offer
had brought her unhappiness to a climax, by adding self-reproach to
her other sources of unhappiness. All this, and much more, did she
relate ; for if her coral lips did not frame every syllable, her tell-tale
blushes filled up the gaps most eloquently.

And Harry Oaklands ?—Well, he did nothing desperate ; but after
his first transports had subsided into a more deep and tranquil joy,
he sat, with her little white hand clasped in his own, and looked into
her loving eyes, and for one bright half hour two of the wanderers
in this vale of tears were perfectly and entirely happy.

CHAPTER XLVII.

A CURE FOR THE HEARTACHE.

"Taste your legs, sir ; put them to motion."
"This is a practice as full of labour as a wise man's art."
Twelfth Night.
"Come, will you go with me ? "
"Whither ? "
"Even to the next willow—about your own business. What fashion will you wear the
garland of ? about your neck like a usurer's chain, or under your arm like a lieutenant's
scarf ? You must wear it some way ! "—*Much Ado About Nothing.*

YES ! they were very happy, Fanny and Oaklands, as they revelled in
the bright certainty of their mutual love, and entranced by the
absorbing contemplation of their new-found happiness, forgot in the
sunshine of each other's presence the flight of moments, whilst I,

involuntarily contrasting the fair prospects that lay open before them
with the dark cloudland of my own gloomy fortunes, had soon
traversed in thought the distance to Barstone Priory, and become
immersed in fruitless speculations as to what might eventually be
the result of Mr. Vernor's sordid and cruel policy. It was now longer
than usual since I had heard from Clara; suspense and impatience
were rapidly increasing into the most painful anxiety, and I had all
but determined, if the next day's post brought no relief, to disobey
her injunctions to the contrary, and once again make an attempt to
see her. Oh! it is hard to be banished from the presence of those
we love—with an air attuned to the gentle music of some well-
remembered voice, to be forced to listen to the cold, unmeaning
commonplaces of society—with the heart and mind engrossed by,
and centred on, one dear object, to live in a strange, unreal fellow-
ship with those around us, talking, moving, and acting mechanically
—feeling, as it were, but the outward form and shadow of one's self,
living two distinct and separate existences, present, indeed, in body,
but in the only true vitality—the life of the spirit—utterly and completely absent. From reflections such as these, I was aroused by
observing the deepening shades of evening, which were fast merging
into night; and collecting my ideas, I remembered that there were
many things which must be said and done in consequence of the
unexpected turn events had taken. No human being is so completely
isolated that his actions do not in some degree affect others, and in
the present instance this was peculiarly the case. Sir John and my
mother must be let into the secret, and poor Lawless must learn the
unsuccessful termination of his suit. But now, for the first time, the
somewhat equivocal situation in which chance had placed me, presented itself to my mind, and I felt a degree of embarrassment,
almost amounting to shame, at having to make my appearance, and
confess that I had been lying "perdu" during the whole of the preceding scene. Accident, however, stood my friend.

"I wonder where Frank is all this time!" exclaimed Harry, in
reply to a remark of Fanny's referring to the lateness of the hour;
"I want to see him, and tell him of my happiness; I made him
almost as miserable as myself this morning; he must be at the
Hall, I suppose, but I'm sure your servant told me he was at
home."

"She only spoke the truth if she did," said I, entering the drawing-
room as if nothing unusual had occurred.

Fanny started up with a slight shriek, and then, glancing at me
with a countenance in which smiles and tears were strangely commingled, ran out of the room to hide her confusion, while Harry
Oaklands—well, I hardly know what Harry did, but I have some
vague idea that he hugged me, for I recollect feeling a degree of
oppression on my breath, and an unpleasant sensation in my arms,
for the next five minutes.

"So you have heard it all, you villain, have you?" he exclaimed, as soon as his first transports had a little subsided. "Oh, Frank! my dear old fellow, I am so happy! But what a blind idiot I have been!"

"All's well that ends well," replied I, shaking him warmly by the hand; "they say lookers-on see most of the game, but in this case I was as blind as you were; it never for a moment occurred to me that Fanny cared for you otherwise than as a sister. Indeed, I have sometimes been annoyed that she did not, as I considered, properly appreciate you; but I understand it all now, and am only too glad that her pale looks and low spirits can be so satisfactorily accounted for."

"Frank," observed Oaklands gravely, "there is only one thing which casts the slightest shade over my happiness; how are we to break this to Lawless? I can afford to pity him now, poor fellow! I know by my own feelings the pang that hearing of a rival's success will cost him."

"I don't think his feelings are quite as deep and as intense as yours, Harry," replied I, smiling involuntarily at my reminiscences of the morning; "but I am afraid he will be terribly cut up about it; he was most unfortunately sanguine: I suppose I had better break it to him."

"Yes, and as soon as possible too," said Oaklands, "for I'm sure my manner will betray my happiness. I am the worst hand in the world at dissimulation. Walk back with me and tell him, and then stay and dine with us."

"Agreed," replied I; "only let me say half a dozen words to my mother;" and rushing upstairs, I dashed into her room, told her the whole matter on the spot, incoherently, and without the slightest preparation, whereby I set her crying violently, to make up for which I kissed her abruptly (getting very wet in so doing), pulled down the bell-rope in obedience to the dictates of a sudden inspiration that she would be the better for a maid-servant, and left her in one of the most fearful states of confusion on record, flurried into a condition of nerves which set camphor-julep completely at defiance, and rendered trust in sal volatile a very high act of faith indeed.

While Oaklands and I were walking up to the Hall, we overtook Coleman returning from shooting wild-fowl. As we came up with him, Oaklands seized him by the shoulder, exclaiming,—

"Well, Freddy, what sport, eh?"

"My dear Oaklands," returned he gravely, removing Harry's hand as he spoke, "that is a very bad habit of yours, and one which I advise you to get rid of as soon as possible; nobody who had ever endured one of your friendly grips could say with truth that you hadn't a vice about you."

"For which vile pun it would serve you right to repeat the dose," replied Oaklands, "only that I'm not in a vindictive mood at present."

"Then you must have passed the afternoon in some very mollify-ing atmosphere," returned Freddy, "for when I met you three hours

Y

ago, you seemed as if you could have cut anybody's throat with the greatest satisfaction."

The conscious half-cough, half-laugh, with which Oaklands acknowledged this sally, attracted Coleman's attention, and mimicking the sound, he continued, "A—ha—hem! and what may that mean? I say, there's some mystery going on here from which I'm excluded—that's not fair, though, you know. Come, be a little more transparent; give me a peep into the hidden recesses of your magnanimous mind; unclasp the richly-bound volume of your secret soul; elevate me to the altitude of the Indian herb, or, in plain slang—Young England's chosen dialect—'make me up to snuff.'"

"May I enlighten him?" asked I.

"Yes, to be sure," replied Oaklands; "I'll go on, for I am anxious to speak to my father. Freddy, old boy! shake hands; I'm the happiest fellow in existence!" so saying, he seized and wrung Coleman's hand with a heartiness which elicited sundry grotesque contortions, indicative of agony, from that individual, and, bounding forward, was soon lost to sight in the deepening twilight.

"And so, you see," continued I, after having imparted to Coleman as much as I considered necessary of the state of affairs, a confidence which he received with mingled exclamations of surprise and delight—"and so, you see, we've not only got to tell Lawless that he is refused, poor fellow! but that Fanny has accepted Oaklands; very awkward, isn't it?"

"It would be with anybody else," replied Coleman; "but I think there are ways and means of managing the thing which will prevent any very desperate consequences in the present instance; sundry ideas occur to me; would you mind my being in the room when you tell him?"

"As far as I am concerned, I should be only too glad to have you," returned I, "if you do not think it would annoy him."

"I'm not afraid of that," was the rejoinder; "as I wrote the offer for him, it strikes me I'm the very person he ought to select for his confidant."

"Do you think," he added, after a moment's thought, "Harry would sell those phaeton horses?"

"That's the line of argument you intend to bring forward by way of consolation, is it? Well, it is not such a bad notion," replied I; "but don't be too sure of success, 'Equo ne credite Teucri;' I doubt its being in the power of horse-flesh to carry such a weight of disappointment as I fear this news will occasion him."

"Well, I've other schemes to fall back upon if this should fail," returned Freddy; "and now let us get on, for the sooner we put him out of his misery the better."

"Where's the master?" inquired I, encountering Shrimp as we crossed the hall.

"He's upstairs, sir; in his own room, sir; a-going it like bricks, if you please, sir; you can hear him down here, gents."

"Stop a minute—listen!" said Coleman; "I can hear him now."

As he spoke, the sound of someone running quickly in the room overhead was distinctly audible; then came a scuffling noise, and then a heavyish fall.

" What's he doing ?" asked Coleman.

"He's a-trainin' of hisself for some match as must be a-coming off, sir; leastways, so I take it; he's been a-going on like that for the last hour and a quarter, and wery well he's lasted out, I say ; he'll be safe to win, don't you think, gents ? "

"Out of the way, you imp!" exclaimed Coleman, seizing Shrimp by the collar, and swinging him half across the hall, where, cat-like, he fell upon his legs, and walked off, looking deeply insulted.

"I can't make out what he can be doing," continued Freddy. "Come along!" So saying, he sprang up the staircase, two steps at a time, an example which I hastened to imitate.

"Come in!" cried the voice of Lawless, as Coleman rapped at the door ; and anxious to discover the occasion of the sounds which had reached our ears in the hall, we lost no time in obeying the summons. On entering the apartment, a somewhat singular spectacle greeted our sight. All the furniture of the room, which was a tolerably large one, was piled on two lines on either side, so as to leave a clear course along the middle ; in the centre of the space thus formed were placed two chairs about a yard apart, and across the backs of these was laid the joint of a fishing-rod.

As we entered, Lawless—who was without shoes, coat, or waistcoat —exclaiming, " Wait a minute, I've just done it "—started from one end of the room, and, running up to the chairs in the centre, leaped over the fishing-rod. " Ninety-nine!" he continued; then, proceeding to the other end, he again ran up to and sprang over the barrier, shouting as he did so, in a tone of triumph, " A hundred!" and dragging an easy-chair out of the chaotic heap of furniture, he flung himself into it to all appearance utterly exhausted.

" Why, Lawless, man!" cried Freddy, "what are you doing? Have you taken leave of your senses all of a sudden ? "

" Eh! I believe I should have, if I had not hit upon that dodge for keeping myself quiet."

" A somewhat Irish way of keeping quiet," returned Freddy; " why, the perspiration is pouring down your face—you look regularly used up."

" Well, I am pretty nearly done brown—rather baked than otherwise." replied Lawless; " let me tell you, it's no joke to jump five hundred times over a stick three feet high or more."

" And why, in the name of all that's absurd, have you been doing it, then ? "

" Eh! why, you see, after I had sent our letter, I got into such a dreadful state of impatience and worry, I didn't know what to do with myself; I could not sit still at any price, and, first of all, I thought I'd have a good gallop, but I declare to you I felt so reckless and desperate, that I fancied I should go and break my neck; well, then it occurred to me to jump over that stick till I had tired myself out —five hundred times have I done it, and a pretty stiff job it was, too. And now, what news have you got for me, Frank?"

"My dear Lawless," said I, laying my hand on his shoulder, "you must prepare for a disappointment."

"There, that will do," interrupted Lawless; "as to preparation, if my last hour's work is not preparation enough for anything, it's a pity. What! she'll have nothing to say to me at any price, eh?"

"Why, you see, we have all been labouring under a delusion," I began.

"I have, under a most precious one," continued Lawless—"regularly put my foot in it—made a complete ass of myself—eh! don't you see? Well, I'm not going to break my heart about it after all; it's only a woman, and it's my opinion people set a higher price upon those cattle than they are worth—they are a shying, skittish breed, the best of them."

"That's the light to take it in," exclaimed Coleman, coming forward; "if one woman says 'No,' there are a hundred others will say 'Yes'; and, after all, it's an open question whether a man's not better off without 'em."

"Eh! Freddy boy, our fine letter's been no go—turned out a regular sell, you see, eh?"

"Well, that only proves the young lady's want of taste," replied Coleman; "but we had not exactly a fair start. You have more to hear about it yet; the article you wished for was gone already—the damsel had not a heart to bestow. Tell him how it was, Frank."

Thus urged, I gave a hurried outline of the affair as it really stood, dwelling much on the fact that Oaklands and Fanny had become attached in bygone years, long ere she had ever seen Lawless—which I hoped might afford some slight consolation to his wounded self-love. As I concluded, he exclaimed: "So Fanny's going to marry Harry Oaklands—that's the long and short of it all. Well, I'm uncommonly glad to hear it—almost as glad as if I was going to marry her myself: there is not a better fellow in the world than Harry, though he has not regarded me with the most friendly looks of late. I was beginning not to like it, I can tell you, and meant to ask him why he did it; but I understand it all now. What a bore I must have been to them both! I declare I'm quite sorry; why, I would not have done it for any money, if I'd been up to the move sooner. Oh! I must tell Harry."

"You certainly are the most good-natured fellow breathing, Lawless," said I.

"Eh! yes, take me in the right way, I am quiet enough, a child may guide me with a snaffle; but stick a sharp bit in my mouth, and tickle my sides with the rowels, and I rear up before, and lash out behind, so that it would puzzle half the rough-riders in the country to back me. I always mean to go ahead straight enough if I can see my way clearly before me, but it's awkward driving when one gets among women, with their feelings, and sympathies, and all that style of article. I'm not used to it, you see, so no wonder if I run foul of their sensibilities and sentimentalities, and capsize a few of them. I've got pretty well knocked over myself, though, this time. Misfortunes never come alone too, they say; and I've just had a letter from Leatherly to tell me Spiteful got loose when the groom was leading him out to exercise, and trying to leap a fence, staked himself so severely that they were obliged to have him shot. I refused eighty guineas for him from Durham of the Guards only a month ago; I shall have my new tandem cart home, and no horses to run in it."

"How well those chestnuts would look tandem!" observed Coleman carelessly; "I wonder whether Harry would sell them?"

"By Jove; I shouldn't like to ask him," exclaimed Lawless quickly; "it is too much to expect of any man."

"Oh! as to that," replied Coleman, "I daresay I could contrive to to find it out, without exactly asking him to sell them."

"My dear fellow, if you would, I should be so much obliged to you," replied Lawless eagerly; "if I could but get those horses to start the new cart with, I should be as happy as a king—that is," he continued, checking himself, "I might become so; time, don't you see, resignation, and all that sort of thing—heigh-ho!—By the way, how far is it from dinner? for jumping over those confounded chairs has made me uncommonly peckish, I can tell you."

"He'll do," said Coleman, as we separated to prepare for dinner.

It was easy to see by Sir John's beaming face, and the hearty squeeze he gave my hand when I entered the drawing-room, that Harry would not have to fear much opposition to his wishes on the part of his father. The dinner passed off pleasantly enough, though even when the meal was concluded, and the servants had left the room, no allusion was made (out of delicacy to Lawless) to the subject which engrossed the thoughts of many of the party. As soon, however, as the wine had gone the round of the table, Lawless exclaimed: "Gentlemen! are you all charged?" and receiving affirmatory looks from the company in general, he continued, "Then I beg to propose a toast, which you must drink as such a toast ought to be drunk, 'con amore.' Gentlemen, I rise to propose the health of the happy couple that is to be."

"Umph! eh! what?—what are you talking about, sir—what are you talking about?" inquired Mr. Frampton, hastily setting down his wine untasted, and speaking quickly, and with much excitement.

"Do you see that?" whispered Lawless, nudging me, "he's off on a false scent; he never could bear the idea of my marrying Fanny, he as good as told me so one day; now be quiet, and I'll get a rise out of him." He then continued, addressing Mr. Frampton: "You're getting a little hard of hearing, I'm afraid, sir; I was proposing the health of a certain happy couple, or, rather. of two people who will, I hope, become so, in the common acceptation of the term, before very long."

" Umph ! I heard what you said, sir, plain enough (wish I hadn't), and I suppose I can guess what you mean. I'm a plain-spoken man, sir, and I tell you honestly I don't like the thing, and I don't approve of the thing—I never have, and so once for all—I—umph ! I won't drink your toast, sir, that's flat. Umph ! umph ! "

" Well," said Lawless, making a sign to Harry not to speak, "you are a privileged person, you know ; and if Sir John and my friend Harry here don't object to your refusing the toast, it's not for me to take any notice of it ; but I must say, considering the lady is the sister of your especial favourite, Frank Fairlegh, and the gentleman one whom you have known from boyhood, I take it as particularly unkind of you, Mr. Frampton, not even to wish them well."

" Eh ! umph ! it isn't that, boy—it isn't that," returned Mr. Frampton, evidently taken aback by this appeal to his kindly feeling. " But, you see," he added, turning to Sir John, " the thing is foolish altogether, they are not at all suited to each other ; and instead of being happy, as they fancy, they'll make each other miserable : the boy's a very good boy in his way, kind-hearted and all that, but truth is truth, and he's no more fit to marry Fanny Fairlegh than I am."

" Sorry I can't agree with you, Mr. Frampton," replied Sir John Oaklands, drawing himself up stiffly ; " I thank Mr. Lawless most heartily for his toast, and drink it without a moment's hesitation. Here's to the health of the young couple ! "

" Well, I see you are all against me," exclaimed Mr. Frampton, " and I don't like to seem unkind. They say marriages are made in heaven, so I suppose it must be all right. Here's the health of the happy couple, Mr. Lawless and Miss Fairlegh ! "

It was now Lawless's turn to look out of countenance, and for a moment he did appear thoroughly disconcerted, more especially as it was next to impossible to repress a smile, and Freddy Coleman grinned outright ; quickly recovering himself, however, he resumed, " Laugh away, Freddy, laugh away, it only serves me right for playing such a trick. I've been deceiving you, Mr. Frampton ; Miss Fairlegh is indeed going to be married, but she has had the good taste to choose a fitter bridegroom than she would have found in such a harum-scarum fellow as I am. So here's a long life, and a merry one, to Fanny Fairlegh and Harry Oaklands ; you won't refuse that toast, I dare say ? "

" Umph ! Harry Oaklands ! " exclaimed Mr. Frampton aghast ; " and I've been telling Sir John he wasn't good enough for Frank's sister—just like me, umph ! "

" My dear Lawless," said Harry, taking a seat next the person he addressed, which movement he accomplished during an immense row occasioned by Mr. Frampton, who was grunting forth a mixed monologue of explanations and apologies to Sir John, by whom they

were received with such a hearty fit of laughing that the tears ran
down his cheeks—"My dear Lawless, the kind and generous way in
which you take this matter makes me feel quite ashamed of my
behaviour to you lately, but I think, if you knew how miserable I
have been, you would forgive me."

"Forgive you! eh?" returned Lawless; "ay, a precious deal
sooner than I can forgive myself for coming here and making you
all uncomfortable. Nobody but such a thick-headed ass as I am
would have gone on all this time without seeing how the game stood.
I hate to spoil sport; if I had had the slightest idea of the truth, I'd
have been off out of your way long ago."

"You are a noble fellow!" exclaimed Harry, "and your friendship
is a thing to be proud of. If there is any way in which I can testify
my strong sense of gratitude, only name it."

"I'll tell you," said Coleman, who had caught the last few words—
"I'll tell you what to do to make him all right: sell him your
chestnuts."

"The phaeton horses?" replied Harry. "No, I won't sell them."

"Ah! I thought he would not," murmured Lawless; "it was too
much to expect of any man."

"But," continued Oaklands, "I am sure my father will join me in
saying that if Lawless will do us the favour of accepting them,
nothing would give us greater pleasure than to see them in the
possession of one who will appreciate their perfections as they
deserve."

"Nay, they are your property, Harry," returned Sir John; "I
shall be delighted if your friend will accept them, but the present is
all your own."

"Eh! give 'em me, all free gratis and for nothing!" exclaimed
Lawless, overpowered at the idea of such munificence. "Why,
you'll go and ruin yourself—Queen's Bench, whitewash, and all the
rest of it! Recollect, you'll have a wife to keep soon, and that isn't
done for nothing, they tell me—pin-money, ruination-shops,
diamonds, kid gloves, and bonnet-ribbons—that's the way to
circulate the tin; there are some losses that may be gains, eh?
When one comes to think of all these things, it strikes me I'm well
out of it, eh, Mr. Frampton?—Mind you, I don't think that really,"
he added aside to me, "only I want Harry to fancy I don't care two
straws about it; he's such a feeling fellow, is Harry, he would not be
properly jolly if he thought I took it to heart much."

"Umph! if those are your ideas about matrimony, sir," growled
Mr. Frampton, "I think you are quite right to leave it alone—puppy-
dogs have no business with wives."

"Now, don't be grumpy, governor," returned Lawless, "when
you've had your own way about the toast and all. Take another
glass of that old port, that's the stuff that makes your hair curl and
look so pretty" (Mr. Frampton's chevelure was to be likened only
to a gray scrubbing-brush); "we'll send for the new dog-cart

to-morrow, and you shall be the first man to ride behind the chestnuts."

" Thank ye kindly, I'll take your advice at all events," replied Mr. Frampton, helping himself to a glass of port ; "and as to your offer, why, I'll transfer that to him " (indicating Coleman), " ' funny boy,' as I used to call him, when he was a boy, and he doesn't seem much altered in that particular now. Umph ! "

This, as was intended, elicited a repartee from Coleman, and the evening passed away merrily, although I could perceive, in spite of his attempts to seem gay, that poor Lawless felt the destruction of his hopes deeply.

On my return to the cottage, the servant informed me that a man had been there who wished very particularly to see me ; that she had offered to send for me, but that he had professed himself unable to wait.

" What kind of looking person was he ? " inquired I.

" He was an oldish man, sir ; very tall and thin, with gray hair ; and he rode a little rough pony."

" Did he leave no note or message ? "

" He left this note, sir."

Hastily seizing it, I locked myself into my own room, and tearing open the paper, read as follows :—

" Honoured Sir,—In case I should not see you, has my time will be short, I takes the liberty of writin' a line, and ham appy to hinform you, as things seem to me awl a-goin' wrong, leastways I think you'll say so when you ears my tail. Muster Richard's been back above a week, and he and the Old Un is up to their same tricks again ; but that ain't awl—there's a black-haired pale chap cum with a heye like a nork, as seems to me the baddest of the lot, and that ain't sayin' a little. But there's worse news yet, for I'm afraid we ain't only got to contend hagainst the henemy, but there's a traytur in the camp. and that in a quarter where you cares most. Meet me to-morrow mornin' at the old place at seven o'clock, when you shall ear more from. Your umbel servant to comand,

" PETER BARNETT,

" late Sergeant in the —th Dragoons."

Reader, do you wish me a good-night ? Many thanks for your kindness, but if you have any hope that your wish will be realized. you must be of a very sanguine temperament, or you have never been in love.

CHAPTER XLVIII.

PAYING OFF OLD SCORES.

" Oh, most delicate fiend !
Who is't can read a woman ? Is there more?
More, sir, and worse."
Cymbeline.
' The Chamberlain was blunt and true, and sturdily said he :
' Abide, my lord, and rule your own, and take this rede from me,
That woman's faith's a brittle trust. Seven twelve-months didst thou say ?
I'll pledge me for no lady's truth beyond the seventh day.' "
Ballad of the Noble Moringer.

IT is a weary thing to lie tossing restlessly from side to side, sleepless, through the silent watches of the night, spirit and matter
warring against each other—the sword gnawing and corroding its
sheath. A weary and harassing thing it is even where the body is
the aggressor—when the fevered blood, darting like liquid fire
through the veins, mounts to the throbbing brow, and, pressing like
molten lead upon the brain, crushes out thought and feeling, leaving
but a dull consciousness of the racking agony which renders each
limb a separate instrument of torture. If, on the other hand, it be
the mind that is pestilence-stricken, the disease becomes well-nigh
unbearable as it is incurable ; and thus it was with me on the night
in question. The suspense and anxiety I had undergone during the
preceding day had indisposed me for sustaining any fresh annoyance
with equanimity, and now, in confirmation of my worst fear, that
hateful sentence in old Peter's note, warning me of treachery in the
quarter where I was most deeply interested, rose up before me like
some messenger of evil torturing me to the verge of distraction with
vague doubts and suspicious—fiends which the bright spirits of
Love and Faith were powerless to banish. The old man's meaning
was obvious; he imagined Clara inconstant, and was anxious to
warn me against some supposed rival ; this in itself was not agreeable ; but I should have reckoned at once that he must be labouring
under some delusion, and disregarded his suspicions as unworthy of
a moment's notice, had it not been for Clara's strange and unaccountable silence. I had written to her above a week before—in
fact, as soon as I became at all uneasy at not having heard from her,
urging her to relieve my anxiety, if but by half a dozen lines. Up to
this time I had accounted for not having received any answer, by the
supposition that Mr. Vernor had, by some accident, detected our
correspondence, and taken measures to interrupt it. But this
hypothesis was evidently untrue, or Peter Barnett would have
mentioned in his note such an easy solution of the difficulty. Yet,
to believe Clara false was treason against constancy. Oh! the thing
was impossible; to doubt her sincerity would be to lose my

confidence in the existence of goodness and truth on this side the
grave! The recollection of her simple, child-like confession of
affection—the happiness my love appeared to afford her—the tender
glance of those honest, trustful eyes—who could think of these
things and suspect her for one moment? But that old man's letter!
What did it—what could it mean? His allusion to some dark, hawk-
eyed stranger—ha!—and as a strange, improbable idea glanced like
lightning through my brain—like lightning, too, searing as it passed
—I half sprung from the bed, unable to endure the agony the
thought had cost me. Reason, however, telling me that the idea
was utterly fanciful and without foundation, restrained me from
doing—I scarcely know what—something desperately impracticable,
which should involve much violent bodily action, and result in
attaining some certain confirmation either of my hopes or fears,
being my nearest approach to any formed scheme. Oh! that night
—that weary, endless night! Would morning never, never come?

About five o'clock I arose, lighted a candle, dressed myself, and
then, sitting down, wrote a short note to my mother, telling her that
an engagement, formed the previous evening, to meet a friend,
would probably detain me the greater part of the day; and another
note to Oaklands, saying that I had taken the liberty of borrowing
a horse, begging him to speak of my absence as a thing of course,
and promising to tell him more when I returned. I then waited till
a faint gray tint in the eastern sky gave promise of the coming
dawn; when letting myself noiselessly out, I took my way towards
the Hall. It was beginning to get light as I reached the stables,
and arousing one of the drowsy helpers, I made him saddle a bay
mare, with whose high courage, speed, and powers of endurance I
was well acquainted, and started on my expedition.

As it was nearly eighteen miles to the place of meeting, I could
scarcely hope to reach it by seven o'clock, the time mentioned in old
Peter's note; but action was the only relief to my anxiety, and it
may easily be supposed I did not lose much time on the road, so that
it was but ten minutes after seven when I turned down the lane in
which the little alehouse appointed as our rendezvous was situated.
I found old Peter waiting to receive me, though the cloud upon his
brow, speaking volumes of dark mystery, did not tend to raise my
spirits.

"Late on parade, sir," was his greeting; "late on parade; we
should never have driven the Mounseers out of Spain if we'd been
ten minutes behind our time every morning."

"You forget, my friend, that I have had eighteen miles to ride,
and that your notice was too short to allow of my giving orders
about a horse over-night."

"You do not seem to have lost much time by the way," he added,
eyeing my reeking steed. "What a slap-up charger that mare would
make! Here, you boy, take her into the shed there, and throw a
sack or two over her, wash out her mouth, and give her a lock of hay

to nibble; but don't go to let her drink, unless you want my cane about your shoulders—do you hear? Now, sir, come in."

"What in the world did you mean by that note, Peter?" exclaimed I, as soon as we were alone; "it has nearly driven me distracted—I have never closed my eyes all night."

"Then it's done as I intended," was the satisfactory reply; "it's prepared you for the worst."

"Nice preparation!" muttered I, then added, "Worst! what do you refer to? Speak out, man—you are torturing me!"

"You'll hear it sooner than you like; try and take it easy, young gentleman. Do you feel yourself quite prepared?"

I am afraid my rejoinder was more energetic than correct; but it appeared to produce greater effect than my entreaties had done, for he continued,—

"Well, I see you will have it out, so you must, I suppose; only if you ain't prepared proper, don't blame me. As far as I can see and hear—and I keeps my eyes and ears open pretty wide, I can tell you —I feels convinced that Miss Clara's guv you the sack and gone and taken up with another young man." As he delivered himself of this pleasant opinion, old Peter slowly approached me, and ended by laying his hands solemnly on my shoulders, and, with an expression of fearful import stamped on his grotesque features, nodding thrice in my very face.

"Nonsense!" replied I, assuming an air of indifference I was far from feeling; "such a thing is utterly impossible—you have deceived yourself in some ridiculous manner."

"I only wish as I could think so, for all our sakes, Mr. Fairlegh; but facts is like jackasses, precious stubborn things. Why are they always a-walking together, and talking so loving like, that even the old 'un hisself looks quite savage about it? And why ain't she never wrote to you since he cum—though she's had all your letters —eh?"

"Then she has received my letters?"

"Oh yes! she's always had them the same as usual."

"And are you sure she has never written to me?"

"Not as I know on; I've never had one to send to you since she's took up with this other chap."

"And pray who or what is this other chap, as you call him, and how comes he to be staying at Barstone?"

"Well, sir, all as I can tell you about him is, that nigh upon a fort-night ago Muster Richard come home, looking precious ill and seedy; and the wery next morning he had a letter from this chap, as I take it. I brought it to him just as they rung for the breakfast things to be took away, so I had a chance of stopping in the room. Direc'ly he sot eyes on the handwriting, he looked as black as night, and seemed all of a tremble like as he hopened it. As he read he seemed to get less frightened and more cross; and when he'd finished it, he 'anded it to the old 'un, saying, 'It's all smooth, but he's taken it into his head to come down here. What's to be done, eh?' Mr. Vernor read it through, and then said in an undertone, 'Of course he must come if he chooses.' He then whispered something of which I only caught the words, 'Send her away;' to which Richard replied angrily. 'It shall not be; I'll shilly-shally no longer,—it must be done at once, I tell you, or I give the whole thing up altogether.' Then they went into the library, and I heard no more; but the wery next day come this here hidentical chap—he arrived in style, too—britska and post-horses. Oh! he's a reg'lar swell, you may depend; he looks something like a Spaniard, a foreigneering style of physiography, only he ain't so swarthy."

"Don't you know his name?" inquired I.

"They call him Mr. Fleming, but I don't believe that's his right name; leastways he had a letter come directed different, but I can't remember what it was; it was either—let me see—either a hess or a W; I think it was a hess, but I can't say for certain."

"But what has all this to do with Miss Saville?" asked I impatiently.

"Fair and easy, fair and easy; I'm a-coming to her direc'ly—the world was not made in a day; you'll know sooner than you likes, I expects, now, sir. Well, I didn't fancy him from the first; he looks more like Saytin himself than any Christian as ever I set eyes on, except Boneypart, which, being a Frenchman and a henemy, was not so much to be wondered at; however, he was wery quiet and civil and purlite to Miss Clara, and said wery little to her, while Muster Richard and the old 'un was by, and she seemed rather to choose to talk to him, as I thought, innocent-like, to avoid the t'other one; but afore long they got quite friends together, and I soon see that he meant business, and no mistake. He's as hartful and deep as Garrick; and there ain't no means of inweigling and coming over a woman as he don't try on her; ay, and he's a clever chap, too; he don't attempt to hurry the thing; he's wery respectful and attentive, and seems to want to show her the difference between his manners and Muster Richard's—not worriting her like; and he says sharp things to make Muster Richard look like a fool before her. I can't help larfing to myself sometimes to hear him,—Muster Dickey's met his match at last."

"And how does Cumberland brook such interference?"

"Why, that's what I can't make out; he don't like it, that's clear: for I've seen him turn pale with rage; but he seems afraid to quarrel with him, somehow. If ever he says a sharp word, Mr. Fleming gives him a scowling look with his wicked eyes, and Muster Richard shuts up direc'ly."

"And you fancy Miss Saville appears disposed to receive this man's advances favourably? Think well before you speak; do not accuse her lightly, for, by Heaven! if you have not good grounds for your insinuations, neither your age nor your long service shall avail to shield you from my anger! every word breathed against her is like a stab to me." As, in my grief and irritation, I threatened the old man, his brow reddened, and his eye flashed with all the fire of youth. After a moment's reflection, however, his mood changed, and, advancing towards me, he took my hand respectfully, and pressing it between his own, said,—

"Forgive me this liberty, sir, but I honours you, young gentleman, for your high spirit and generous feeling; your look and bearing, as you said them words, reminded me of my dear old master. It can't be no pleasure to me, sir, to blame his daughter, that I have loved for his sake, as if she had been a child of my own—but truth is truth;" and as he uttered these words, the big drops stood in his eyes, unfailing witnesses of his sincerity. There is something in the display of real deep feeling, which for the time appears to raise and ennoble those who are under its influence; and as the old man stood before me, I experienced towards him a mingled sentiment of admiration and respect, and I hastily endeavoured to atone for the injustice I had done him.

"Forgive me, Peter!" exclaimed I; "I did not mean what I said, —sorrow and annoyance made me unjust to you, but you will forgive it?"

"No need of that, sir," was the reply; "I respects you all the more for it. And now, in answer to your question, I will go on with the little that remains to tell, and you can judge for yourself. Miss Clara, then, avoids Mr. Richard more than hever, and talks kind and pleasant like with this Mr. Fleming—walks out with him, sometimes alone—rides with him—don't seem so dull and mopish like since he's been here, and has never hanswered your letters since she took up with him." As he concluded his catalogue of proofs, I threw myself into a chair, and sat with my hands pressed tightly on my brow for some minutes; my brain seemed on fire.

At length, starting up abruptly, I exclaimed: "This is utterly unbearable; I must have certainty, Peter: I must see her at once. How is that to be done?"

"You may well ask," was his reply; "better wait till I can find an opportunity, and let you know."

"Listen to me, old Peter," continued I, laying my hand on his shoulder; "there is that within me this day which can overcome all obstacles—I tell you I must see her, and I WILL!"

"Well, well, don't put yourself into a passion; the only chance as I knows of is to ketch Miss Clara out walking; and then ten to one Mr. Fleming will be with her."

"Let him!" exclaimed I; "why should I avoid him? I have not injured him, though he may have done me foul and bitter wrong; it is for him to shrink from the encounter."

"I know what the end of this will be," returned Peter Barnett; "you'll quarrel; and then, instead of off coats and having it out like Britons, there'll be a purlite hinvitation given, as kind and civil as if you was a-hasking him to dinner, to meet as soon as it's light to-morrow morning, and do you the favour of putting a brace of bullets into you."

"No, Peter, you do not understand my feeling on this subject; should you be right in your suspicions (and, although my faith in your young mistress is such that nothing but the evidence of my own senses can avail to shake it, I am fain to own circumstances appear fully to warrant them)—should these suspicions not prove unfounded, it is her falsehood alone that will darken the sunshine of my future life. Fleming, or any other coxcomb who had taken advantage of her fickleness, would be equally beneath my notice. But enough of this; where shall I be most likely to meet her?"

"You knows the seat in the shrubbery walk under the old beeches, where you saw Miss Clara the first time as ever you cum here?"

"Only too well," answered I, as the recollection of that morning contrasted painfully with my present feelings.

"Well, you be near there about eleven o'clock; and if Miss Clara don't walk that way, I'll send down a boy with hinformation as to the henemy's movements. Keep out of sight as much as you can."

"It shall be done," replied I.

Old Peter paused for a moment; then, raising his hand to his forehead with a military salute, turned away and left me.

Eight o'clock struck; a girl brought me in breakfast; nine and ten sounded from an old clock in the bar, but the viands remained untasted. At a quarter past ten I rang the bell, and asked for a glass of water, drained it, and pressing my hat over my brow, sallied forth. The morning had been misty when I first started, but during my sojourn at the inn the vapours had cleared away, and as, by the assistance of an old tree, I climbed over the paling of Barstone Park, the sun was shining brightly, wrapping dale and down in a mantle of golden light. Rabbits sprung up under my feet as I made my way through the fern and heather; and pheasants, their varied plumage glittering in the sunlight, ran along my path, seeking to hide their long necks under some sheltering furze brake, or rose heavily on the wing, scared at the unwonted intrusion. At any other time, the fair scene around me would have sufficed to make me light-hearted and happy, but in the state of suspense and mental torture in which I then was, the brightness of nature seemed only to contrast the more vividly with the darkness of soul within. And yet I could not believe her false. Oh no! I should see her, and all would be explained; and as this thought came across me, I bounded eagerly forward, and, anxious to accelerate the meeting, chafed at each trifling obstacle that opposed itself to my progress. Alas! one short hour from that time, I should have been glad had there been a lion in my path, so that I had failed to reach the fatal spot.

With my mind fixed on the one object of meeting Clara, I forgot the old man's recommendation to keep out of sight; and flinging myself at full length on the bench, I rested my head upon my hand and fell into a reverie, distorting facts and devising impossible contingencies to establish Clara's innocence. From this train of thought I was aroused by a muffled sound as of footsteps upon turf, and in another moment the following words, breathed in silvery accents, which caused my every pulse to throb with suppressed emotion, reached my ear:—

" It is indeed an engagement of which I now heartily repent, and from which I would willingly free myself; but—"

" But," replied a man's voice, in the cold sneering tone of which, though now softened by an expression of courtesy, I had almost said of tenderness, I instantly recognized that of Stephen Wilford—" but, having at one time encouraged the poor young man, your woman's heart will not allow you to say ' No' with sufficient firmness to show that he has nothing further to hope."

"Indeed it is not so," replied the former speaker, who, as the reader has doubtless concluded, was none other than Clara Saville; " you mistake me, Mr. Fleming; if a word could prove to him that his suit was hopeless, that word should soon be spoken."

" It is not needed!" exclaimed I, springing to my feet, and suddenly confronting them; " that of which the tongue of living man would have failed to convince me, my ears have heard and my eyes have seen! It is enough. Clara, from this moment you will be to me as if the grave had closed over you; yet not so, for then I could have loved your memory, and deemed that an angel had left this false and cruel world to seek one better fitted to her bright and sinless nature!—Farewell, Clara, may you be as happy as the recollection (which will haunt you at times, strive as you may to banish it) that by your falsehood you have embittered the life of one who loved you with a deep and true affection will permit!" and overcome by the agony of my feelings, I leaned against the bench for support, my knees trembling so that I could scarcely stand.

When I appeared before her so unexpectedly, Clara started back and uttered a slight scream; after which, apparently overwhelmed by my vehemence, she had remained perfectly silent; whilst her companion, who had at first favoured me with one of his withering glances, perceiving that I was so completely engrossed as to be scarcely conscious of his presence, resumed his usual manner of contemptuous indifference. He was, however, the first to speak.

" This gentleman, whom I believe I have the pleasure of recognizing," and here he slightly raised his hat, "appears, I can scarcely suppose a friend, but at all events, an intimate of yours, Miss Saville; if you wish me—that is, if I am at all ' de trop '"—and he stepped back a pace or two, as if only awaiting a hint from her to withdraw, while, with his snake-like glance riveted upon her features, he watched the effect of his words.

"No, pray do not leave me, Mr. Fleming," exclaimed Clara hurriedly; "Mr. Fairlegh must see the impossibility of remaining here. I am momentarily expecting Mr. Cumberland and my guardian to join us."

"I leave you," replied I, making an effort to recover myself; "I seek not to pain you by my presence, I would not add to your feelings of self-reproach by look or word of mine;" then, catching Wilford's glance fixed upon me with an expression of gratified malice, I continued, "For you, sir, I seek not to learn by what vile arts you have succeeded thus far in your iniquitous designs; it is enough for me that it should have been possible for you to succeed; my happiness you have destroyed; but I have yet duties to perform, and my life is in the hands of Him who gave it, nor will I risk it by a fruitless quarrel with a practised homicide."

The look of concentrated hatred with which he regarded me during this speech, changed again to scornful indifference, as he replied, with a contemptuous laugh, "Really, sir, you are labouring under some singular delusion; I have no intention of quarrelling; you appear to raise phantoms for the pleasure of combating them. However, as far as I can comprehend the affair, you are imputing to me an honour belonging rather to my friend Cumberland; and here, in good time, he comes to answer for himself. Cumberland, here's a gentleman mistaking me for you, I fancy, who seems labouring under some strange delusions about love and murder; you had better speak to him." As he concluded, Cumberland, attended by a gamekeeper leading a shooting pony, came up, looking flushed and angry.

"I should have been here sooner," he said, addressing Wilford, "but Browne told me he had traced poachers in the park; the foot-steps can be otherwise accounted for now, I perceive." He then made a sign for the keeper to approach, and turning towards me, added, "You are trespassing, sir."

His tone and manner were so insolent and overbearing, that my blood boiled in my veins. Unwilling, however, to bring on a quarrel in such a presence, I restrained my indignation, and replied, "I know not what devil sent you here at this moment, Richard Cumberland; I have been sorely tried, and I warn you not to provoke me further."

"I tell you, you are trespassing, fellow; this is the second time I have caught you lurking about; take yourself off instantly, or—" as he spoke he stepped towards me, raising his cane with a threatening gesture.

"Or what?" inquired I, at length thoroughly roused; and, drawing myself up to my full height, I folded my arms across my chest, and stood before him in an attitude of defiance.

As I did so, he turned deadly pale, and for a moment his resolution seemed to fail him; but catching the sound of Wilford's sneering laugh, and relying on the assistance of the gamekeeper, who, having tied the pony to a tree, was fast approaching the scene of action, he replied, "Or receive the chastisement due to such skulking vagabonds!" and springing upon me, he seized my collar with one hand, while with the other he drew the cane sharply across my shoulders.

To free myself from his grasp by a powerful effort was the work of a moment, while almost at the same time I struck him with my full force, and catching him on the upper part of the nose, dashed him to the ground, where he lay motionless, and apparently stunned, with the blood gushing from his mouth and nostrils.

CHAPTER XLIX.

MR. FRAMPTON MAKES A DISCOVERY.

"In a tandem I see nothing to induce the leader to keep his course straightforward, but an address on the part of the charioteer as nearly as can be supernatural. . . . And, for my own part, I think leaders of tandems are particularly apt to turn short round. And the impudence with which they do it, in some instances, is past all description, staring all the while full in the faces of those in the carriage, as much as to say, 'I must have a peep at the fools behind that are pretending to manage me.'"—*Thinks I to Myself.*

" But he grew rich, and with his riches grew so
Keen the desire to see his home again,
He thought himself in duty bound to do so.

. . . .
Lonely he felt at times as Robin Crusoe."
Beppo.

ALL that passed immediately after the events I have described left but a succession of vague and confused images on my memory. I have some dim recollection of seeing them raise Cumberland from the ground, and of his showing symptoms of returning animation; but I remember nothing distinctly till I again found myself a tenant of the little sanded parlour in the village inn. My first act was to ring for a basin of cold water and a towel, with which I well bathed my face and head ; in some degree refreshed by this process, I sat down and endeavoured to collect my scattered senses.

I had succeeded in my immediate object, and suspense was at an end. I had obtained certain proof of Clara's falsehood ; with her own lips I had heard her declare that she repented her engagement, and wished to be freed from it; and the person to whom she had confided this was a man whose attentions to her were so marked that even the very servants considered him an acknowledged suitor. What encouragement could be more direct than this ? Well, then, she was faithless, and the dream of my life had departed. But this was not all; my faith in human nature was shaken—nay, destroyed at a blow. If she could prove false, whom could I ever trust again ? Alas ! the grief—the bitter, crushing grief—when the consciousness is forced upon us that she with whom we have held sweet interchange of thought and feeling—with whom we have been linked by all the

z

sacred ties of mutual confidence—with whose sorrows we have
sympathized, and whose smiles we have hailed as the freed captive
hails the sunshine and the dews of heaven—that one whom for these
things we have loved with all the deepest instincts of an earnest and
impassioned nature, and for whose truth we would have answered as
for our own, is false and unworthy such true affection—oh! this is
bitter grief, indeed! Deep sorrow, absorbing all the faculties of the
soul, leaves no room for any other emotion; and the one idea, that
Clara Saville—the Clara Saville whom my imagination had depicted,
the simple, the loving, the true-hearted was lost to me for ever. I
forgot for some time the existence of Wilford or the fact that in my
anger I had stricken down and possibly seriously injured Cumberland. But as the first agony of my grief began to wear off, I became
anxious to learn the extent of the punishment I had inflicted on him,
and accordingly despatched a boy to Peter Barnett, requesting him
to send me word how matters stood.

During his absence it occurred to me that, as Wilford had been
introduced to her under a feigned name, Clara must be utterly
ignorant of the evil reputation attaching to him, and that—although
this did not in any way affect her heartless conduct towards me - it
was only right that she should be made aware of the true character
of the man with whom she had to deal; therefore, painful as it was
to hold any communication with her after what had passed, I felt
that the time might come when my neglect of this duty might afford
me cause for the most bitter self-reproach. Accordingly, asking for
pen, ink, and paper, I sat down and wrote the following note:—

"After the occurrences of this morning, I had thought never,
either by word or letter, to hold further communication with you; by
your own act you have separated us for ever; and I—yes, I can say
it with truth—am glad that it should be so—it prevents all conflict
between reason and feeling. But I have what I deem a duty to
perform towards you—a duty rendered all the more difficult, because
my motives are liable to cruel misconstruction; but it is a duty, and
therefore must be done. You are, probably, as little aware of the
true character of the man calling himself Fleming as of his real
name; of him may be said, as of the Italian of old, that 'his hate is
fatal to man, and his love to woman'; he is alike notorious as a
duellist and a libertine. My knowledge of him arises from his having
in a duel wounded almost unto death the dearest friend I have on
earth, who had saved an innocent girl from adding to his list of
victims. If you require proof of this beyond my word, ask Mr.
Stephen Wilford—for such is really his name—in your guardian's
presence, whether he remembers Lizzy Maurice and the smart of
Harry Oaklands' horsewhip. And now, having warned you, your
fate is under your own control. For what is past I do not reproach
you; you have been an instrument in the hands of Providence to
wean my affections from this world, and if it is His good pleasure that
instead of a field for high enterprise and honest exertion, I should

henceforth learn to regard it as a scene of broken faith and crushed hopes, it is not for me to rebel against His will. And so farewell for ever !—F. F."

I had not long finished writing the above when the boy returned, bringing the following missive from old Peter :—

"HONOURED SIR,

"The topper as you've give Muster Richard ain't done him no more harm, only lettin' hout a little of his mad blood, and teachin' 'im when he speaks to a gemman to baddress 'im as sich ; 'is face is swelled as big as too, and he'll 'ave a sweet pair of black hyes to-morrer, please goodness, which is a comfort to reflect on. Touchin' uther matturs, I've got scent of summut as may make things seeme not so black as we thort, but it's honly in the hegg at present, and may never come to a chickin, so don't go settin' too much on it ; but if you've nothin' better to do, ride over again the day arter to-morrer, by which time I may have more to communicate.

"Your humbel servant to command,
"PETER BARNETT."

I pondered for some minutes on what this enigmatical document might portend ; but a little reflection served to convince me that neither Peter nor anyone else could discover aught affecting the only feature of the whole affair which deeply interested me ; on that point I had obtained the information of my own senses, and there was nothing more to hope or fear. I had learned the worst ; the blow had fallen, and it only remained for me to bear it with what fortitude I might. Accordingly I enclosed my note to Clara in one to Peter Barnett, telling him I could see no reason for coming there again, and that in all probability I should not take the trouble of doing so, adding that if he had anything new to communicate he had better do so in writing, and then, ordering my horse, I rode slowly home, feeling more thoroughly miserable than I had ever done before in the whole course of my life.

The next morning was so fine that all kinds of pleasurable schemes were proposed and acceded to. Oaklands and Fanny rode out to-gether in all the unrestrained freedom of an engaged tete-a-tete. The new dog-cart had arrived, and the chestnuts were to make their debut ; consequently, Lawless spent the morning in the stable-yard, united by the closest bonds of sympathy with the head groom and an atten-dant harness maker, the latter being a young man whose distinguish-ing characteristics were a strong personal savour of new leather, hands gloved in cobbler's wax and harness-dye, and a general tendency to come off black upon everything he approached. Sir John and the rest of the party were to fill a britska, and the place of rendezvous was the ruins of an old abbey about eight miles distant.

Feeling quite unfit for society, I had excused myself on the plea (not altogether a false one) of a bad headache, and having witnessed

their departure from the library window, I drew an easy chair to the
fire, and prepared to enjoy the luxury (in my then state of feeling an
unspeakable one) of solitude. But I was not fated to avail myself of
even this small consolation, for scarcely ten minutes had elapsed
when the library door was opened, and Mr. Frampton made his
appearance.

" Umph! eh! umph!" he began ; " I've been seeing that young fool
Lawless start in his new tandem, as he calls it. A pretty start it was
too ; why, the thing's as high as a stage-coach—ought to have a
ladder to get up—almost as bad as mounting an elephant! And then
the horses, fiery devils! two men at each of their noses, and enough
to do to hold 'em even so! Well, out comes Master Lawless, in a
great-coat made like a coal-sack, with buttons as big as five-shilling
pieces, a whip as long as a fishing-rod in his hand, and a cigar in his
mouth. 'There's a picture!' says he. 'A picture of folly,' says I ;
'you're never going to be mad enough to trust yourself up there
behind those vicious brutes?' 'Come, governor, jump in, and let's
be off,' was all the answer I got. 'Thank ye,' says I; 'when you
see me jumping in that direction, pop me into a strait-waistcoat, and
toddle me off to Bedlam.' 'Eh, won't you go? Tumble in, then,
Shrimp!' 'Please, sir, it's so high I can't reach it.' 'We'll soon
see about that!' cries Lawless, flanking him with the long whip.
Well, the little wretch scrambled up somehow, like a monkey ; and as
soon as he was safely landed, what does he do but lean back, fold his
arms, winking at one of the helpers, squeak out, 'Oh, crickey! ain't
this spicy, just!' 'You're never going to take that poor child?'
says I; 'only think of his anxious mother!' Well, sir, if you'll
believe it, they every one of 'em burst out laughing—helpers, brat and
all—as if I'd said something very ridiculous. 'Never mind, governor,'
says Lawless; 'depend upon it, his mother knows he's out,' and
catching hold of the reins, he clambers up into his seat, shouting,
'Give 'em their heads! Stand clear! Chut! chut!' As soon as the
brutes found they were loose, instead of starting off at a jog-trot, as
reasonable, well-behaved horses ought to do, what do you suppose
they did? The beast they tied on in front turned short round, stared
Lawless in the face, and stood up on its hind-legs like a kangaroo,
while the other animal would not stir a peg, but, laying down his
ears, gave a sort of a screech, and kicked out behind. 'Pretty playful
things,' said Lawless, flipping the ashes off the end of his cigar. 'Put
his head straight, William. Chut! chut!' But the more he chutted
the more they wouldn't go, and began tearing and rampaging about
the yard till I thought they'd be over me, so I scrambled up a
little low wall to get out of their way, missed my footing and tumbled
over backwards on to a dung-heap, and before I got up again they
were off ; but if that young jackanapes don't break his neck some of
these days, I'm a Dutchman! Umph! umph!"

" Lawless is a capital whip," replied I, " and the chestnuts, though
fiery, are not really vicious. I don't think there is much danger."

"Ah! young men! young men! you're all foolish alike. I don't know how you'd get on if you hadn't a few old stagers like me to think for you and give you good advice. And that puts me in mind that I want to have half an hour's serious conversation with you, Frank. Can you listen to me now?"

"I am quite at your service, sir," replied I, resigning myself to my fate with the best grace I could command.

"Umph! Well, you see, Frank, I've no chick nor child of my own, and I've taken a kind of a fancy to you from a boy; you were always a good boy and a clever boy, and you've gone on well at college, and distinguished yourself, and have been a credit to the man that sent you there.—By-the-bye, didn't you ever want to know who it was sent you there?"

"Often and often," replied I, "have I longed to know to whose disinterested kindness and generosity I was indebted for so great an advantage."

"Umph! Well, you must be told some day, I suppose, so you may as well know now as at any other time. The man that sent you to college ain't very unlike me in the face. Umph!"

"My dear, kind friend," replied I seizing his hand and pressing it warmly, "and it is indeed you who have taken such interest in me? How can I ever thank you?"

"I want no thanks, boy; you did better than thank me when you came out fourth wrangler; why, I felt as proud that day when they were all praising you as if it had been my own son. Say no more about that; but now you've left college, what are your wishes—what do you think of doing? Umph!"

"I had thought of reading for the bar, deeming it a profession in which a man stands a fair chance of distinguishing himself by honourable exertion; I am aware it is somewhat uphill work at starting, but Mr. Coleman has promised to introduce me to several men in his branch of the profession, and to give me all the business he can himself, so I should not be quite a briefless barrister. But if there is anything else you wish to recommend, any other career you would advise me to pursue, I am very indifferent—that is, I am not at all bigoted to my own opinion."

"Umph! I never had any over-strong affection for lawyers—gentlemen that eat the oysters themselves and leave their clients the shells! However, I suppose there may be such things as honest lawyers to be met with, and it's better for every man to have a profession. Well, now, listen to me, Frank. I—umph!—your sister's going to be married, to be married to a young man for whom I've a very great respect and affection; Sir John Oaklands is a thorough specimen of a fine old English gentleman, and his son bids fair to become just such another, or even a yet higher character, for Harry's got the better head-piece of the two. However, I don't like your sister to marry into such a family without a little money of her own to buy a wedding bonnet; so you give her this letter, and tell her to mind and get a becoming one. We may trust a woman to take care of that. though, eh, Frank? Umph!"

"Really, sir, your kindness quite overpowers me; we have no possible claim upon your liberality."

"Yes, you have, boy—yes, you have," replied Mr. Frampton, "the strongest claim that can be; you have saved me from falling a victim to the worst disease a man can suffer under,—you have saved me from becoming a cold-hearted, soured misanthrope; you have given me something to love, some pure, unselfish interest in life. And now we are on the subject, I may as well tell you all my plans and wishes in regard to you: I have no soul belonging to me, not a relation in the wide world that I am aware of, and I determined, from the time when I first sent you to college, that if you conducted yourself well and honourably, I would make you my heir.—Don't interrupt me," he continued, seeing that I was about to speak, "let me finish what I have to say, and then you shall tell me whether you approve of it. You not only came up to, but far surpassed, my most sanguine expectations, and I saw therefore no reason to alter my original intentions. But it is stupid work for a man to wait till all the best days of his life are passed, without funds sufficient to render him independent, to feel all his energies cramped, his talents dwarfed, and his brightest aspirations checked, by a servile dependence on the will and caprice of another—waiting for dead men's shoes,—umph! and so Frank, as I feel pretty tough and hearty for sixty-five, and may live, if it please God, another ten or fifteen years to plague you, it's my wish to make you your own master at once, and I'll either assist you to enter any profession you please, or, if you like to settle down into a country gentleman, and can pick up a nice wife anywhere, I can allow you £1000 a year to begin with, and yet have more than I shall know how to spend during the rest of my days in the land of the living. For my own part, this last plan would give me the greatest satisfaction, for I should like to see you comfortably married and settled before I die. Now what do you say to it? Umph!"

What did I say?—what could I say? I got up, and having once again pressed his hands warmly between my own, began pacing the room, quite overcome by this unexpected liberality, and the conflicting nature of my own feelings. But two short days ago, and such an offer would have been—as I then fondly imagined—the only thing wanting to secure my happiness; possessed of such ample means of supporting her, I could at once have gone boldly to Mr. Vernor, and demanded Clara's hand—nor could he have found just cause for refusing my request; and now, when what once appeared the only insurmountable obstacle to our union was thus removed, the thought that, by her faithlessness and inconstancy, she had placed a barrier between us for ever, was indeed bitter. Surprised by the excess of my emotion, for which, of course, he was totally unable to account, Mr. Frampton sat gazing at me with looks of astonishment and dismay, till at length he broke out with the following interrogatory: "Umph! eh! why, Frank—

umph! anybody would think you had just heard you were going to be arrested for debt,;instead of having a fortune given you—umph!"

"My dear, kind friend," replied I, "forgive me. Your unparalleled liberality, and the generous interest you take in me, give you a father's right over me, and entitle you to my fullest confidence; such an offer as you have now made me would have rendered me, but one short week ago, the happiest of mortals; now, my only chance of regaining anything like tranquillity of mind lies in constant and active employment."

I then gave him, as briefly as I could, an outline of my singular acquaintance with Clara Saville, our engagement, and the events which had led to my breaking it off, to all of which he listened with the greatest interest and attention. In telling the tale I mentioned Wilford and Cumberland by name, as he knew the former by reputation, and had seen the latter when a boy at Dr. Mildman's; but I merely spoke of Clara as a young lady whom I had met at Mr. Coleman's, and of Mr. Vernor as her guardian. When I concluded, he remained for a moment buried in thought, and then said, "And you are quite sure she is false? Are you certain that what you heard her say (for that seems to me the strongest point) referred to you?"

"Would I could doubt it!" replied I, shaking my head mournfully.

"Umph!—Well, I dare say—she's only like all the rest of her sex: it's a pity the world can't go on without any women at all—what is her name?—a jilt!"

"Her name," replied I, shuddering as he applied the epithet of "jilt" to her—for, deserved as I could not but own it was, it yet appeared to me little short of profanation,—" her name is Clara Saville!"

"Umph! eh? Saville!" exclaimed Mr. Frampton. "What was her mother's name? Umph!"

"I never heard," replied I. "Her father, Colonel Saville, was knighted for his gallant conduct in the Peninsula. Her mother, who was an heiress, died abroad; her guardian, Mr. Vernor—"

"Umph! Vernor, eh! Vernor! Why, that's the fellow who wrote to me and told me—umph! wait a bit, I shall be back directly. I—eh!—umph! umph! umph!"

And so saying, Mr. Frampton rushed out of the room in a perfect paroxysm of grunting. It was now my turn to be astonished, and I was so most thoroughly. What could possibly have caused Mr. Frampton to be so strangely affected at the mention of Clara's name and that of her guardian? Had he known Mr. Vernor in former days? Had he been acquainted with Clara's father or mother? Could he have been attached to her as I had been to Clara, and like me, too, have become the dupe of a heartless jilt? A jilt—how I hated the word! how the blood boiled within me when that old man applied it to her! And yet it was the truth. But oh! the heart-spasm that darts through our breast when we hear some careless tongue proclaim, in plain intelligible language, the fault of one we love—a fault which, even at the moment when we may be suffering from it most deeply, we have striven sedulously to hide from others, and scarcely acknowledged definitely to ourselves. In vague musings, such as these, did I pass away the time till Mr. Frampton returned. As he approached, the traces of strong emotion were visible on his countenance; and when he spoke, his voice sounded hoarse and broken.

"The ways of God are indeed inscrutable," he said. "Information which for years I have vainly sought, and would gladly have given half my wealth to obtain, has come to me when I least expected it; and, in place of joy, has brought me deepest sorrow. Frank, my poor boy! she who has thus wrung thy true heart by her cruel falsehood is my niece, the orphan child of my sister!"

In reply to my exclamations of surprise, he proceeded to inform me that his father, a man of considerable property in one of the midland counties, had had three children : himself, an elder brother, and a sister some years his junior, whose birth deprived him of a mother's love. His brother tyrannized over him; and on the occasion of his father's second marriage he was sent to school, where he was again unfortunate enough to meet with harsh treatment, against which his high spirit rebelled; and having no better counsellors than his own inexperience and impetuosity, he determined to run away and go to sea. A succession of accidents conspired to prevent his return to his native country, until, being taken as clerk in a merchant's counting-house at Calcutta, he was eventually admitted into partnership, and acquired a large fortune. As he advanced beyond middle life, he felt a strong wish to return to England, seek out his family, and revisit the scenes of his boyhood; but on carrying his project into execution, he learned that his father and brother had both paid the debt of nature, while his sister, the only one of his relatives towards whom he had ever entertained much affection, had married a Colonel Saville; and having accompanied her husband to Spain, had died there without leaving any offspring. The last piece of information he had acquired from a Mr. Vernor, to whom he had been recommended to apply. His surprise, therefore, when he heard of the existence of Clara, may easily be imagined. A long conversation ensued between us, with the consequences of which the reader will be better acquainted when he shall have read the following chapter.

CHAPTER L.

A RAY OF SUNSHINE.

"When you shall please to play the thief for a wife
I'll watch as long for you."
Shakespeare.

"Hold! give me a pen and ink! Sirrah, can you with a grace deliver a supplication?"
Titus Andronicus.

THE result of my conversation with Mr. Frampton was that I agreed to ride over on the following day to the little inn at Barstone, see old Peter Barnett, hear his report, and learn from him further particulars concerning Clara Saville's parentage, in order to establish beyond the possibility of doubt the fact of her relationship to Mr. Frampton, who, in the event of his expectations proving well-founded, was determined to assert his claim, supersede Mr. Vernor in his office of guardian, and endeavour, by every means in his power, to prevent his niece's marriage either with Wilford or Cumberland. The only 'stipulation I made, was that when I had obtained the requisite information, he should take the affair entirely into his own hands, and, above all, promise me never to attempt, directly or indirectly, to bring about a reconciliation between Clara and myself. Not that I bore her any ill-will for the misery she had caused me. On the contrary, my feeling towards her had been from the very first one of grief rather than of anger. But a girl who could possibly have acted as Clara had done, was not one whom I ever should wish to make my wife. I could not marry a woman I despised.

After Mr. Frampton had left me, I sat pondering on the singular train of circumstances (chances as we unwisely, if not sinfully, term them) which occur in a man's life—how events which change the whole current of our existence appear to hang upon the merest trifles—the strange mysterious influence we exercise over the destinies of each other—how by a word, a look, we may heal an aching heart or—break it. It is, I think, in a poem of Faber's that the following lines occur (I quote from memory, and therefore, perhaps, incorrectly) :—

"Perchance our very souls
Are in each other's hands."

Life is, indeed, a fearful and wonderful thing—doubly fearful when we reflect, that every moment we expend for good or evil is a seed sown to blossom in eternity. As I thought on these things, something which Mr. Frampton had said, and which at the time I let pass without reflection, recurred to my mind. He had asked me whether I was

certain that the words I heard Clara address to Wilford referred to
me. Up to this moment I had felt perfectly sure they did; but,
after all, was it so certain ? might they not equally well apply to
Cumberland ? was there a chance, was it even possible, that I had
misunderstood her ? Oh, that I dare hope it ! gladly would I seek
her pardon for the injustice I had done her— gladly would I undergo
any probation she might appoint, to atone for my want of faith in
her constancy, even if it entailed years of banishment from her
presence, the most severe punishment my imagination could devise ;
but then the facts, the stubborn, immovable facts, my letters
received and unanswered—the confidential footing she was on with
Wilford—the—But why madden myself by recapitulating the hateful
catalogue ? I had learned the worst, and would not suffer myself to
be again beguiled by the mere phantom of a hope. And yet, so
thoroughly inconsistent are we, that my heart felt lightened of half
its burden ; and when the pleasure-seekers returned from their
expedition, I was congratulated by the whole party upon the
beneficial effects produced on my headache by perfect rest and quiet.
Lawless and Coleman made their appearance some half-hour after
the others, and just as Mr. Frampton had promulgated the cheering
opinion that they would be brought home on shutters, minus their
brains, if they ever possessed any. It seemed the chestnuts, having
at starting relieved their minds by the little " ballet d'action " which
had excited Mr. Frampton's terrors, did their work in so fascinating
a manner that Lawless, not being satisfied with Shrimp's declaration
that " they was the stunnin'est 'orses as hever he'd sot hyes on,"
determined (wishing to display their perfections to a higher audience)
that one of the party should accompany him on his return ; whereupon Freddy Coleman had been by common consent selected, much
against his will. However, " the victim," as he termed himself,
escaped without anything very tremendous happening to him, the
chestnuts (with the slight exception of running away across the
common, rushing through a flock of geese, thereby bringing a
premature Michaelmas on certain unfortunate individuals of the
party in a very reckless and unceremonious manner, and dashing
within a few inches of a gravel-pit, in a way which was more exciting
than agreeable) having conducted themselves (or more properly
speaking, allowed themselves to be conducted) as well-bred horses
ought to do.

When the party separated to prepare for dinner, I called Fanny
on one side, and gave her Mr. Frampton's letter : on opening it, a
banker's order for £3000 dropped out of it—a new instance of my
kind friend's liberality, which really distressed more than it gratified
me.

During the course of the evening Harry Oaklands expressed so
much anxiety about my ill looks, appearing almost hurt at my
reserve, that I could hold out no longer, but was forced to take him
into my confidence.

"My poor Frank!" exclaimed he, wringing my hand warmly, as I finished the recital, "to think that you should have been suffering all this sorrow and anxiety, while I, selfishly engrossed by my own feelings, had not an idea of it; but you ought to have told me sooner."

"Perhaps I should; but it has been, from the very beginning, such a strange, melancholy affair, so unlikely ever to turn out happily, that I have felt a strong repugnance to speak of it to any-one; and even now I must beg you not to mention it to Fanny—at all events, till my last act in the business is performed, and Mr. Frampton takes the matter into his own hands."

"After all," rejoined Oaklands, "I feel there must be some mistake; she never can be false to you—never love that villain Wilford. Oh, Frank! how can you bear to doubt her?"

"It is indeed misery to do so," replied I, sighing deeply; "and yet, when one's reason is convinced, it is weakness to give way to the suggestions of feeling."

"If Fanny were to prove false to me, I should lie down and die," exclaimed Oaklands vehemently.

"You might wish to do so," replied I; "but grief does not always kill; if it did, in many cases it would lose half its bitterness."

A look was his only answer, and we parted for the night.

Daylight the next morning found me again in the saddle, and I reached the little inn by eight o'clock. On my arrival, I despatched a messenger to old Peter Barnett, telling him I wished to see him, and then, determining that I would not allow myself to hope, only again to be disappointed, I rang for breakfast, and set resolutely to work to demolish it; in which I succeeded very respectably, merely stopping to walk round the room and look out of the window between every second mouthful. At length my envoy returned, with a message to the effect that Mr. Barnett would come down in the course of the morning, but that I was by no means to go away without seeing him, and that he hoped I would be careful not to show myself, as the enemy were out in great force, and all the sentries had been doubled.

"What does he mean by that?" inquired I of the boy who delivered the message—an intelligent little urchin, who was evidently well up in the whole affair, and appeared highly delighted at the trust reposed in him, to say nothing of the harvest of sixpences his various missions produced him.

"Vy, sir, he means that the gamekeeper has had two extra assistants allowed him since you vos there the other day, sir, and they has strict orders to take hup anybody as they finds in the park, sir."

"They need not alarm themselves," replied I; "I shall not intrude upon their domain again in a hurry. Now look out, and let me know when Peter Barnett is coming."

So saying, I gave him the wished-for sixpence, and with a grin of satisfaction he departed.

With leaden feet the hours crawled along, and still old Peter Barnett did not make his appearance; when, about twelve o'clock, a horseman passed by, followed by a groom. As he rode at a very quiet pace, his face was easily recognized, and I saw at a glance it was Mr. Vernor. Fortunately he never looked towards the window at which I was standing, or he must have seen me. Scarcely ten minutes had elapsed, when old Peter arrived, breathless from the speed at which he had come; his grotesque but expressive features gleaming with delight and sagacity, while his merry little eyes danced and twinkled as if they would jump out of their sockets. Reassured, in spite of myself, by his manner, I exclaimed, as I closed the parlour-door behind him, " Well, Peter; speak out, man—what is it ? "

" Oh ! my breath !" was the reply, " running don't suit old legs like it does young uns. I say, sir, did ye see him go by ? "

" I saw Mr. Vernor pass a few minutes since," replied I.

" Ah ! that's what I've been a-waiting for; we're safe from him for the next four hours : he didn't see you, did he ? "

" No," returned I ; " he was fortunately looking another way."

" Well, it's all right, then, everything's all right! oh! lor, I'm so happy."

" It's more than I am," replied I angrily ; for feeling convinced that nothing could have occurred materially to affect the position in which Clara and I stood towards each other, the old man's joy grated harshly on my gloomy state of mind, and I began to attribute his excessive hilarity to the influence of the ale-tap. " You will drive me frantic with your ridiculous and unseasonable mirth. If you have anything to communicate likely to relieve my sorrow and anxiety, in the name of common sense speak out, man."

" I beg your pardon, sir ; I was so happy myself, I was forgetting you ; I've got so much to tell you, I don't know where to begin rightly ; but, however, here goes—to the right about face ! March ! " He then proceeded to give me, with much circumlocution, which I will mercifully spare the reader, the following account : After he had left me at the conclusion of our last interview, feeling, as he said, " more wretcheder" than he had ever done before, in going through the park, he observed two persons, a man and a woman, in close conversation ; on his approach they separated, but not until he had been able to recognize Wilford, and one of the female servants, Clara's personal attendant. " This," as he continued, " set him a-thinking," and the result of his cogitations occasioned the mysterious hint thrown out to me in his note. On receiving my letter for Clara, he found an opportunity of delivering it in person, inquiring, when he did so, both when she had last heard from, and written to me ; at the same time informing her that he had a very particular reason for asking. He then learned what he had more than suspected from the interview he had witnessed in the park, namely, that since Wilford had been in the house, she had not only never received one of my letters, but had written to me more than once to ascertain the cause of such an unaccountable silence. These letters she had, as usual, given to her maid to convey to Peter Barnett; and the girl, cajoled and bribed by Wilford, had evidently given them to him instead. This induced Peter, as he expressed it, "to open his heart to his young mistress," and with deep contrition he confessed to her the suspicions he had entertained of her fickleness, how he had communicated them to me, and how circumstances had forced me to believe them. Clara, naturally much distressed and annoyed by this information, blamed him for not having spoken to her sooner, assuring him that he had wronged her deeply in imagining such things, and desired him somewhat haughtily to lose no time in un-deceiving Mr. Fairlegh. He then inquired whether she wished to send any answer to my note; on which she read it through with a quivering lip, and replied, " Yes, tell him, that as he finds it so easy to believe evil of me, I agree with him that it will be better our acquaintance should terminate." She then motioned to him to leave the room, and he was obliged to obey; but, glancing at her as he closed the door, he perceived that she had covered her face with her hands, and was weeping bitterly. He next set to work with the waiting-maid, and by dint of threats of taking her before Mr. Vernor, and promises, if she confessed all, that he would intercede with Clara for her forgiveness, he elicited from her the whole truth,— namely, that by the joint influence of bribes and soft speeches, Wil-ford had induced her to hand over to him her mistress's letters, and that he had detained every one either to or from me. "Well, sir," continued he, "that was not such a bad day's work altogether, but I ain't been idle since. Mr. Fleming, or Wilford, as you say he is, started off the first thing this morning for London, and ain't cumming back till the day after to-morrow; so, thinks I, we'll turn the tables upon you, my boy, for once—that 'ere letter dodge was very near a-ruining us, I wonder how it will hact t'other way: and a lucky thought it was too, Muster Fairlegh, for sich a scheme of willainy as I've descivered all dewised against poor dear Miss Clara—"

" A scheme against Miss Saville!" exclaimed I; "what do you mean ? "

" I'm a-going to tell you, sir, on'y you're in such a hurry, you puts me out. After the thought as I was a-mentioning cum into my head, off I walks to meet the postman—' Hany letters for us, Giles ? ' says I. ' Well, I don't rightly know,' says he, ' you've got some folks a-staying with you, ain't ye ? ' ' Let's look, my man,' says I, peeping over him as he sorted the letters. Presently he cum to one as seemed to puzzle him. ' W. I. L,' says he, ' W. I. L. F.—' ' Oh!' says I, ' that's the gent as is a-staying at our 'ouse; give us 'old on it.' ' And here's one for Mr. Wernor, and that's all,' says he, and he guv me the letter and walked off. ' That's right, Peter,' says I to myself, ' we shall know a little more of the henemy's movements, now

we've captivated some of their private despatches, by a " coo-dur-
mang," as the Mounseers call it;' so I locks myself into the pantry,
and sits down, and breaks the seal."

" You opened the letter ! " exclaimed I.

" In course I did; how was I to read it if I hadn't? all's fair in
love and war, you know—the blessed Duke of Wellington served
Bony so many a time, I'll be bound ; besides, hadn't he opened Miss
Clara's, the blackguard ? Well, sir, I read it, and it's lucky as I did ;
oh! he's a bad un ; he's a deal wickeder than Muster Richard hisself,
and that's saying sumthing—it's from a Captain—"

" Really, Peter, I cannot avail myself of information obtained in
such a manner," interrupted I.

" Ah! but you must, though," was the reply, " if you want to
prevent this black willain from carrying off Miss Clara, and marrying her, ' nolus bolus.' "

" Carrying off Miss Clara! what do you mean ? "

" I was a-going to tell you," returned old Peter, with a cunning
grin, producing a crumpled letter, " only you wouldn't listen to me."

As I (not being prepared with a satisfactory answer) remained
silent, he smoothed the letter with his hand, and read as follows :—

" MY DEAR SIR,—1 was unfortunately out of town when your
letter arrived, and it had to be sent after me ; but I hope you will
get this in time to prevent your having to come to London, which is
unnecessary, as I have been able to carry out all your arrangements
as you would wish. A carriage, with four horses, will be kept in
readiness, so that it can be brought to any point you may direct at
half an hour's notice. I presume you and I, with Wilson (that's his
valet) are sufficient to carry off the girl—young lady, I mean, even if
there be any papa or brother in the case, who would be the better
for a little knocking down; but if you like more assistance, I can lay
my hand on two or three sprightly lads, who would be very glad to
make themselves useful. You are flying at high game this time. Do
you really mean matrimony, or is it to be the old scheme, a mock
marriage ? I ask, because in the latter case I must look out for
somebody to play parson. Wishing you your usual luck,

" I remain, yours to command,
" FERDINAND SPICER,
" Captain in the Bilboa Fencibles."

" Spicer ! " I exclaimed, as he concluded; " I knew a Captain
Spicer once, who was a person likely enough to lend himself to a
scheme of this vile nature. Well, Peter, the information is most
important, however questionable the means by which it has been
acquired. The matter must be looked to; but first, I want to learn
a few particulars about Miss Saville's relations on the mother's side."
I then proceeded with a string of questions furnished me by Mr.
Frampton, by the answers to which I ascertained, beyond a doubt,

that Clara was indeed his niece, the orphan child of his favourite
sister. Having established this point to my own satisfaction, and
the unbounded delight of Peter Barnett, who at length began to
entertain a not unreasonable hope that his pet day-dream of kicking
Mr. Vernor out of Barstone Priory might, at some time or other, be
realized. I said, "Now, Peter, I must somehow contrive to see your
young mistress, and try to obtain her forgiveness; but as I cannot
say I managed the matter over-well the other day, I will put myself
into your hands, to be guided by you entirely."

"Ah! I thought what was a-coming; well, that is speaking
sensible-like for once; but do you think you could write anything as
would persuade her to meet you? She's precious angry, I'm afraid,
with us both, and small blame to her either; for bit ain't over-
pleasant to be suspected when one's innocent, and she has a high
spirit, bless her!—she wouldn't be her father's own daughter if she
hadn't."

" I can write a few lines to her, and try," replied I mournfully, for
the old man's words sounded like a death-knell to my hopes.

"Come, don't be out of spirits, and downcasted-like, sir," urged
Peter; "suppose she did make up her mind she'd give you the cold
shoulder, she'd be sure to change it again to-morrow, women is such
wersytile creeturs; besides, she couldn't do it if she wanted to; it
would break her heart, I know. I wonder where she'd find such
another sweetheart?" continued he, "sotto voce," as he turned to get
the writing materials; "good-looking, high-spirited, uncommon
pleasant to talk to, six foot one if he's an inch, and as upright as if
I'd had the drilling of him myself."

With an eager yet trembling hand (for I was in such a state of
agitation that I could scarcely write), I snatched a pen, and hastily
scrawled the following words :—

" Clara, will you—can you forgive me? It is of the utmost
importance that I should see you and speak to you without delay, if
but for five minutes; strange and unexpected things have come to
light, and it is necessary for your happiness, nay even for your very
safety, that you should be made acquainted with them. Clara,
dearest Clara, grant me this boon, if not for my sake, for your own;
if you knew the misery, the agony of mind I have endured for the
last two days, I think you would pity, would pardon me.

"F. F."

"There," said I, as I hastily sealed it, " I have done all I can, and
if she will not see me, I shall be ready to go and blow Wilford's
brains out first and my own afterwards. So, my good Peter, be off
at once, for every moment seems an hour till I learn her decision."

" Wait a bit, sir—wait a bit; you haven't heard my plan yet. You
can't set your foot in the park, for there's the keeper and two
assistants on the look-out; and if you could, you dare not show your
nose in the house, for there's Muster Richard with his lovely black
heyes a-setting in the liberary, and he's got ears like an 'are, besides

two or three of the servants as would tell him in a minute. No, this
is the way I means to manage—Miss Clara generally rides a-
horseback every day, and I rides behind her; and before I came out,
I ordered the horses as usual. So if she's willing to come, we'll go
out at the back gate by the great oak, a quarter of a mile farther
down this lane, and when we've got out of sight of the park paling
you've nothing to do but set spurs to your horse and join us;—
therefore, if you hears nothing to the contrairy, when I've been gone
half an hour, you mount your nag, ride quietly up the lane, and keep
your heyes open."

CHAPTER LI.

FREDDY COLEMAN FALLS INTO DIFFICULTIES.

I am he that am so love-shaked ; I pray you, tell me your remedy."
As You Like It.
" I am sprighted with a fool, frighted, and angered worse."
Cymbeline.

Oh ! that tedious half-hour ! I should like to know, merely as a
curious matter of calculation, how many minutes there were in that
half-hour—sixty-five at the very least ; the hands of my watch stuck
between the quarter and twenty minutes for full a quarter of an
hour, and as for the old Dutch clock in the bar, that was worn out,
completely good for nothing, I am certain, for I ordered my horse
round to the door above ten minutes too soon by that, and I'm sure
I didn't start before my time,—it would have been folly to do so, you
know, because it was possible old Peter might send at any moment
before the expiration of that half-hour. But at last even it came to
an end—and no message had arrived; so, burning with impatience, I
sprang into the saddle, and with difficulty restraining myself from
dashing off at a gallop, I reined in the mare, and proceeded at a
foot's pace up the lane.

After riding about a quarter of a mile, I perceived a small hand-
gate just under a magnificent oak, which I at once recognized as the
tree old Peter had described. Unwilling to attract the notice of the
gamekeeper and his myrmidons by loitering about in the lane, I
discovered a gap in a hedge on the other side the road, and, after
glancing round to see that I was unobserved, I rode at it, and leaped
into the opposite field, where, hidden behind a clump of alders, I could
perceive all that passed in the road. But for a long time nothing

did pass, save a picturesque donkey, whose fore-feet being fastened together by what are called "hobbles,"[1] advanced by a series of jumps—a mode of progression which greatly alarmed the sensitive nerves of my mare, causing her to plunge and pull in a way which gave me some trouble to hold her.

After I had succeeded in quieting her, I dismounted, and, tightening the saddle-girths, which had become loosened during her struggles, got on again; still no one came. At length, just as I was beginning to despair, I heard the sound of horses' feet, and old Peter, mounted on a stout cob, rode to the wicket-gate, and held it open, while Clara on a pretty chestnut pony cantered up, and passed through it.

Oh! how my heart beat, when, reining in her pony, she glanced round for a moment, as if in search of something, and then, with a slight gesture of disappointment, struck him lightly with her riding-whip, and bounded forward. Old Peter seemed still more puzzled, and looked up and down the road with an air of the most amusing perplexity, before he made up his mind to follow his mistress. About a hundred yards from this spot the lane turned abruptly to the left, skirting a second side of the square field in which I had taken up my position; by crossing this field, therefore, I conceived I should cut off a great angle, and regain the road before they came up.

Setting spurs to my horse then, I rode off at speed, trusting to find some gate or gap by which I might effect my exit. In this calculation, however, I was deceived; instead of anything of the sort, my eyes were greeted by a stiff ox-fence, with a rather unpleasantly high fall of ground into the lane beyond,—a sort of place well fitted to winnow a hunting field, and sift the gentlemen who come out merely to show their white gloves and buckskins, from the "real sort," who "mean going," and are resolved to see the end of the run. However, in the humour in which I then was, it would not have been easy to stop me, and holding the mare well together, I put her steadily at it. Fortunately, she was a first-rate fencer, and knew her work capitally, as she proved in the present instance, by rising to the leap, clearing the fence in beautiful style, and dropping lightly into the lane beyond, without so much as a stumble, just as Clara and her attendant turned the corner of the road and came in sight. My sudden appearance frightened Clara's pony to a degree which justified me in riding up and assisting her to reduce it to order. Having accomplished this not very difficult task, I waited for a moment, hoping she would be the first to speak, but finding she remained silent, I began, "Really, I am most unfortunate; I had no idea you were near enough for me to startle the pony—I hope I have not alarmed you."

"How can you risk your life so madly," she replied in a tone of reproach, "and for no reason, too?"

"Is my safety indeed an object of interest to you?" inquired I; then, unable to restrain myself any longer, I continued, "Clara,

[1] Query, whether so called because they oblige the wearer to hobble.

dearest Clara, have you forgiven me ? Indeed, I have been punished sufficiently; I have been so utterly, so intensely miserable."

"And have I been happy, do you think ? Frank, it was cruel of you to doubt me—you, to whom I have told everything you, who of all the world should have been the last to mistrust me ; I never could have doubted you."

" It was cruel ; it was ungenerous in the extreme. I own it and yet, believe me, dear Clara, I did not doubt you lightly ; proofs, that to my short-sightedness appeared incontrovertible, were brought against you ; the letters I wrote, entreating you if but by a line or message to relieve my anxiety, remaining unanswered letters which I was assured you had received—your sudden intimacy with that hateful Wilford—"

"Stay ! " she exclaimed, interrupting me, " let me explain that at once ; it is easy to show you how that is to be accounted for—"

" Indeed, Clara, it is unnecessary," I began.

" If not for your satisfaction, at least for my own, let me explain how this sudden good understanding with one so lately a stranger to me arose : " she continued. " Richard Cumberland, on his return, seemed resolved to throw off all disguise, and determined to make me feel that I was in his power ; his attentions became most intolerable, and all my endeavours to repulse him appeared but to increase the evil. This went on till I was obliged to remain in my own room the greater portion of every day, and actually dreaded the approach of dinner-time, when I knew I should be forced to endure his society. The arrival of Mr. Fleming, or Wilford, as you say his real name is, was therefore a great relief to me. Cumberland, for some reason or other, appears most anxious to keep on good terms with him—why, I cannot tell, for I am much mistaken if he does not both hate and fear him. Mr. Wilford, who, whatever his real character may be, possesses great tact and penetration, and can behave like a most refined and polished gentleman, appeared to discover by intuition that Cumberland's attentions were distasteful to me, and contrived in a thousand different ways to relieve me from them, always doing so with the most perfect ' sang-froid ' and apparent unconsciousness. Although, from the first moment I saw him, I felt an instinctive mistrust and fear of him, I could not but feel grateful for the delicate tact with which he came to my assistance ; and as the only effectual way to distance Richard Cumberland appeared to be conversing with Mr. Wilford, I can well understand even a more intelligent observer than my faithful old Peter fancying that I gave him encouragement. I was further induced to admit his society from the fact that he never attempted in the slightest degree to take unfair advantage of the unusual intimacy which circumstances had produced between us. He had never even alluded to Cumberland's attentions (though he must have been long aware of them, and of the annoyance they occasioned me) till that unfortunate morning when the encounter took place between you in the Park.

"At the breakfast-table that day, some scheme had been proposed which would have involved my riding alone with Mr. Cumberland; on my endeavouring to avoid doing so, provoked beyond endurance, he forgot his usual caution, and made some brutal allusion to the time when his will, and not my caprice, would be the law, doing so with such coarse violence that I left the room in tears. Mr. Vernor summoned me shortly afterwards to walk with him, in order, as I believe, to lecture me; but his purpose was frustrated by Mr. Wilford's joining us. Just before we met you, my guardian was accidentally called away, when Mr. Wilford expressed his indignation at the scene which had taken place at breakfast, and his surprise that I found it possible to endure such insolence, adding, that he had ventured to remonstrate with Mr. Cumberland on the subject, but had been angrily repulsed. I really felt obliged to him for what I deemed his disinterested kindness, and in the course of conversation allowed him to elicit from me an account of my early engagement to Richard Cumberland; and the words which you so strangely overheard referred, as you may easily believe, to that."

"Of course they did," exclaimed I. "What a self-tormenting idiot I have made of myself! However, I was only rightly served for ever having doubted your faith; but, dearest Clara, you must be subject no longer to the insolent attentions of Cumberland, or the sinister designs of Wilford; and it is at length my happiness to possess the power, as well as the will, to save you from further molestation; strange things have come to light."

I then informed her of the existence of Mr. Frampton, and his relationship to her; told her of his generous intentions in my behalf, and how, thanks to these circumstances, her consent was the only thing wanting to our immediate union. With mingled surprise and pleasure she listened to my recital; and with downcast eyes and most becoming blushes gave ear to my entreaties for pardon, and hopes that she would not throw any unnecessary delay in the way of our marriage. Before I left her, I had received full forgiveness for my unjust doubts and suspicions, and was allowed to indulge in a not unfounded hope that Mr. Frampton's recovery of his niece would only prove the precursor to my obtaining a wife. It was agreed that, on the following day but one, Mr. Frampton—who had to go to London to consult with his lawyer touching the legalities of the affair—should come to Barstone, and, bearding Mr. Vernor in his den, establish his claim. As Wilford was not to return till the same day, and as I proposed accompanying Mr. Frampton, I thought I should be alarming Clara unnecessarily if I were to inform her of Wilford's designs. I therefore merely cautioned her against him generally, begging her never to trust herself with him alone, and adding that I hoped she would see nothing more of him before she was placed under the protection of her uncle, of whom I drew—as he so well deserved at my hands—a most favourable picture, though I did not attempt to conceal his eccentricities either of manner or appearance, considering it better she should be prepared for them beforehand. So we rode on side by side, happy in each other's society, the bright sunshine, which threw its golden mantle over the gnarled limbs and wide-spreading branches of the old trees beneath which we passed, being scarcely brighter or more genial than the joy which shed its sunlight on our hearts, replacing the dreary shadows of the past with fair hopes and gladsome prospects for the future; and when we parted, which was not till we had ridden a circuit of some miles, and exercise had brought back the rose to Clara's pale cheeks, and joy the smile to her lip, we did so in the full assurance that after our next meeting, man's self-interest and injustice should be powerless to interfere further with our happiness. Were these bright hopes ever fated to be realized ?

After cautioning old Peter to watch over his young mistress as a mother over her child, telling him I should return in time to frustrate any plan Wilford might devise, and begging him, if anything unexpected should occur, instantly to despatch a messenger to me, I took leave of Clara with one of those lingering pressures of the hand which tell, better than words, of full hearts, to which it is indeed grief to separate; and setting spurs to my horse, I rode back to Heathfield as different a being from what I was when I left it, as though I had literally " changed my mind " for that of some other individual.

My first care on reaching the Hall was to relieve Mr. Frampton's anxiety, and when he learned that his niece was not the jilt he had deemed her, but QUITE PERFECTION (for that was what I stated, with the same quiet certainty of promulgating an incontrovertible fact, with which I should have declared twice two to be four), his delight knew no bounds, and the way in which he shook my hands, and slapped me on the back, and told me, with many grunts, that I should "marry the girl," even if he had to thrash old Vernor with his own hand in order to obtain possession of her for me, was enough to do anyone's heart good to witness. I had no lack of talking to get through myself, either; first Harry Oaklands had to be told the successful issue of the day's adventure, then Fanny was to be taken into our confidence; and next, the greatest caution was to be observed, and many deep and politic schemes concocted, in order to bring my mother to a proper comprehension of the whole matter without completely overwhelming her—all which cunning devices were frustrated by Mr. Frampton, who got at her surreptitiously and told her the entire affair in a short, sharp, and decisive language which completely upset her for the rest of the evening and left a permanent impression on her mind, that somehow or other I had behaved very ill.

Early on the following morning, Mr. Frampton went off to town to consult his lawyer, promising to return in time for dinner, if possible, but at all events so as to be ready to start on our Barstone campaign the first thing the next day, that no time might be lost in freeing Clara from the disagreeable, if not positive dangers, which surrounded her. As I was crossing the hall after seeing Mr. Frampton off, Lawless seized me by the arm, and drawing me on one side, began :—

" I say, Frank, I want a word with you; there's something gone wrong with Freddy Coleman. I never saw him so down in the mouth before; there's a screw loose somewhere, depend upon it."

" Something wrong with Freddy," repeated I, " impossible! why. I was laughing with him a quarter of an hour ago; he was making all sorts of quaint remarks on the chaise that came for Mr. Frampton, and poking fun at the post-boy. Where is he ? "

" Eh! wait a bit, I'll tell you directly; he had a letter brought him just as Governor Frampton started, and as he cast his eye over it, he first got as red as a carrot, then he turned as pale as a turnip, and bolted off into the library like a lamplighter, where he sits looking as if he had been to the wash, and come back again only half starched."

" That's better than if he were ' terribly mangled,' to carry on your simile," returned I; " but didn't you ask him what was the matter ? "

" Eh ? no, I've made such a mess of things lately, that I thought I'd better leave it alone, for that I was safe to put my foot in it one way or other, so I came and told you instead."

" Well, we'll see about it," replied I, turning towards the library; " perhaps he has received some bad news from home; his father or mother may be ill."

On entering the room we perceived Coleman seated in one of the windows, his head resting on his hand, looking certainly particularly miserable, and altogether unlike himself. So engrossed was he that he never heard our approach, and I had crossed the room, and was close to him, before he perceived me; consequently, the first word I uttered made him jump violently—an action which elicited from Lawless a " sotto voce " exclamation of. " Steady there, keep a tight hand on the near rein; well, that was a shy ! "

" Freddy," began I, " I did not mean to startle you so; but is any-thing the matter, old fellow ? "

" You've frightened me out of six months' growth," was the reply; " matter! what should make you think that ? "

" Well, if you must know," returned Lawless, " I told him I thought there was a screw loose with you, and I haven't changed my mind about it yet, either. Any unsoundness shown itself at home, eh? I thought your governor looked rather puffy about the pasterns the last time I saw him, besides being touched in the wind, and your mother has got a decided strain of the back sinews."

" No, they're well enough," replied Freddy, with a faint smile.

" Then you've entered your affections for some maiden stakes, and the favourite has bolted with a cornet of horse ? "

" That's more like it," returned Coleman, " though you've not quite

hit it yet—but I'll tell you, man, if it's any satisfaction to you to hear
that others are as unlucky as yourself, or worse, for what I know.
I'm not greatly given to the lachrymose and sentimental, in a
general way, but I must confess this morning to a little touch of
the heartache. You see, Frank," he continued, turning to me,
" there's my cousin, Lucy Markham, the little girl with the black
eyes—"

" You forget that she was staying with us last week," interrupted I.

" To be sure she was," resumed Freddy ; " this vile letter has put
everything out of my head—well, she and I—we've known each other
since we were children—in fact, for the last four or five years she has
nearly lived with us, and there's a great deal in habit, and propinquity,
and all that sort of thing. ' Man was not made to live alone,' and
I'm sure woman wasn't either, for they would have nobody to
exercise their tongues upon, and would die from repletion of small-
talk, or a pressure of gossip on the brain, or some such thing, and so
a complication of all these causes led us in our romantic moments to
indulge in visions of a snug little fireside, garnished with an intelligent
household cat, and a bright copper tea-kettle, with ourselves seated
one in each corner, regarding the scene with the complacent gaze of
proprietors ; and we were only waiting till my father should fulfil his
promise of taking me into partnership, to broach the said scheme to
the old people, and endeavour to get it realized. But lately there
has been a fat fool coming constantly to our house, who has chosen
to fancy Lucy would make him a good fooless ; and although the
dear girl has nearly teased, snubbed, and worried him to the borders
of insanity, he has gone on persevering with asinine obstinacy, till he
has actually dared to pop the question."

" Well, let her say ' no ' as if she meant it," said Lawless ; " women
can, if they like, eh ? and then it will all be as right as ninepence.
Eh ! don't you see ? "

" Easier said than done, Lawless, unfortunately," replied Coleman ;
" my fat rival is the son of an opulent drysalter, and last year he
contrived to get rid of his father."

" Dry-salted him, perhaps ? " suggested Lawless.

" The consequence is," continued Coleman, not heeding the interruption, " he is as rich as Crœsus ; now, Lucy hasn't a penny, and all
her family are as poor as rats, so what does he do but go to my
father, promises to settle no end of tin on her, and ends by asking
him to manage the matter for him. Whereupon the governor sends
for Lucy, spins her a long yarn about duty to her family, declares
she'll never get a better offer, and winds up by desiring her to accept
the dolt forthwith ; and Lucy writes to me, poor girl ! to say she's in
a regular fix, and thinks she'd better die of a broken heart on the
spot, unless I can propose any less distressing but equally efficient
alternative."

" What does your governor say ? that she'll never have a better
offer ? " asked Lawless.

" Yes," replied Freddy, "and in the common acceptation of the term, I'm afraid it's a melancholy truth."

" Hum ! yes, that'll do," continued Lawless meditatively. " Freddy, I've thought of a splendid dodge, by which we may obtain the following advantages. ' Imprimis,' selling the governor no end ; ' secundis,' insuring me a jolly lark—and 'pon my word I require a little innocent recreation to raise my spirits ; and, lastly, enabling you to marry your cousin, and thus end, as the pantomimes always do, with a grand triumph of virtue and true love over tyranny and oppression ! So now listen to me ! "

CHAPTER LII.

LAWLESS ASTONISHES MR. COLEMAN.

" Now, all your writers do consent that *ipse* is he ; now, you are not *ipse*, for I am he.
" Which he, sir ?
" He, sir, that must marry this woman. Therefore, you clown, abandon—which is, in the vulgar, leave—the society—which, in the boorish, is company—of this female—which, in the common, is woman—which together is, abandon the society of this female ; or clown . . . I will o'errun thee with policy ; therefore, tremble, and depart."
—*As You Like It.*

"As far as I understand the matter," said Lawless, nodding sapiently, "the great obstacle to your happiness is the drysalter, and the chief object you desire to attain is his total abolition, eh ? "

Coleman assenting to these premises, Lawless continued, " Supposing, by certain crafty dodges, this desirable consummation arrived at, if you could show your governor that you had four or five hundred pounds a year of your own to start with, one of his main objections to your union with this female—young woman would be knocked on the head ? "

" My good fellow," returned Freddy with a slight tone of annoyance, " I'm as fond of a joke as any man, but when I tell you that I am foolish enough to take this matter somewhat deeply to heart—that if Lucy is forced to marry the brute she'll be wretched for life, and I shall not be much otherwise—I think you'll choose some other subject for your mirth."

" Why, Freddy, old boy, you don't suppose I'm poking fun at you, do you ? Why, I would not do such a thing at any price—no ! 'pon my honour, I'm as serious as a judge, I am indeed ; but the best way will be to tell you my plan at once, and then you'll see the logic of the thing. In the first place, your governor says has Lucy is to marry the drysalter, because he's the best offer she's ever likely to have, doesn't he?"

" Yes, that's right enough, so far," replied Freddy.

" What's the drysalter worth? whereabouts is the figure?"

" Two thousand a year, they say," returned Freddy, with a sigh.

" And I shall come into nearer five, in a month's time," returned Lawless; " got the whip hand of him there, and no mistake!"

" You!" exclaimed Coleman, astonished.

" Eh, yes! I, my own self—the Honourable George Lawless, at your service, age five-and-twenty—height five feet nine—rides under ten stone—sound wind and limb—£5000 per annum, clear income, and a peerage in perspective—ain't that better than a drysalter, eh?"

" Why, Lawless, you are gone stark staring mad," interrupted I; " what on earth has all that got to do with Freddy and his cousin?"

" Don't stop him," cried Coleman, " I begin to see what he is aiming at."

" Eh! of course you do, Freddy, boy," continued Lawless; " and it's not such a bad dodge either, is it? Your governor lays down the broad principle that the highest bidder shall be the purchaser, and on this ground backs the drysalter; now, if I drive over this morning, propose in due form for your cousin's hand, and outbid the aforesaid drysalting individual, the governor must either sacrifice his consistency or accept my offer."

" Well, and suppose he does, what good have you done then?" asked I.

" Eh, good?" returned Lawless, " every good, to be sure; and first and foremost knocked over the drysalter—if I'm accepted, he must be rejected, that's a self-evident fact. Well, once get rid of him, and it's all plain sailing—I find a hundred reasons for delaying to fulfil my engagement; in a month's time I come into my property (the jolly old aunt who left it me tied it up till I was five-and-twenty— and the old girl showed her sense too, for ten to one I should have made ducks and drakes of it when I was young and foolish); very well—I appoint Freddy agent and receiver of the rents—(the fellow that has it now makes £500 a year of it, they tell me); and then suddenly change my mind, jilt Miss Markham, and if Governor Coleman chooses to cut up rough, he may bring an action of ' breach of promise,' lay the damages at £5000, and so get a nice little round sum to buy the young woman's wedding clothes when she marries Freddy. That's the way to do business, isn't it. eh?"

" 'Pon my word it's a grand idea," said Coleman: " how came you ever to think of it? But, my dear Lawless, are you really in earnest about the receivership?"

" In earnest? to be sure I am; I always intended it."

" I'm sure I'm very much obliged to you," replied Freddy, in a tone of grateful surprise; " it's the kindest thing in the world; but about the first part of your plan, I don't know what to say."

"You never can think of carrying out such a mad scheme," remonstrated I; "I thought, of course, you were only in jest."

"Can you propose anything better, eh?" asked Lawless.

"Why, I don't know," returned I, musing. "Suppose Freddy were to go and tell his father of his attachment, and say that the receivership, with a small share in the business, would enable him to support a wife comfortably—how would that do?"

"No use," said Freddy; "as long as that aggravating drysalter, with his £2000 per annum, is in the field, my father would consider it his duty to say 'No.'"

"Eh? yes, of course," rejoined Lawless, "fathers always do consider their duty to be intensely unpleasant on all such occasions, and it's a duty they never neglect, either—I will say that for them. No! depend upon it, mine is the only plan."

"Really, Frank, I don't see what else is to be done," urged Freddy; "the danger from the drysalter is great and imminent, remember."

"Well, you and Lawless can settle it between you: you are a pair of eccentric geniuses, and know how you like to manage your own affairs better than a sober-minded man such as I am."

"I tell you what, Mr. Sober-minded-man, I mean to take you with me on my expedition; I shall want somebody to pat me on the back—besides, your proper, well-behaved manner will give an air of respectability to the affair."

"Really you must—" began I.

"Really I won't," retorted Lawless, while Coleman, seizing me by the arm, drew me on one side.

"Frank, without any joke, I think this freak of Lawless's may enable me to get rid of my rival—this Mr. Lowe Brown—and I should take it as the greatest kindness if you would go with him, and keep him in order; of course I must not be seen at all in the matter myself."

"Well, if you are really in earnest, and want me to go, I'll do it," replied I; "though I don't see that I shall be of much use."

"Shall I write and put Lucy up to it, or not?" rejoined Coleman meditatively.

"If you take my advice, you will not," replied I; "in fact, the success of your scheme depends very much on keeping her in the dark as to Lawless's not being a 'bona-fide' offer. Either her simple woman's mind would dislike the trickery of the thing altogether, or she would excite suspicion by falling into the plot too readily. I would merely write her a cheering note, telling her that you were likely to get an appointment which would enable you to marry; urging her to be firm in her refusal of your abomination, Mr. Brown; hinting that a broken heart would be premature, if not altogether superfluous, and giving her a few general notions that the affair would end happily, without touching upon Lawless at all."

" Perhaps it would be as well," replied Freddy; " at all events, it
will add greatly to the fun of the thing."

" And let me tell you that's a consideration by no means to be lost
sight of," put in Lawless, who had overheard the last remark.
" Depend upon it, it's a man's duty—partly to himself, partly to his
neighbour—never to miss an opportunity of recruiting his exhausted
and careworn frame, and all that sort of thing, by enjoying a little
innocent recreation : ' nec semper '—what do ye call it ?—' tendit
Apollo,' eh ? "

" That's quite my view of the case," said Freddy, whose elastic
spirits were fast recovering their accustomed buoyancy. " I hate the
dolefuls—Care killed a cat."

" If that's the worst thing Care ever did, I'll forgive her, eh ? " said
Lawless, " for cats are horrid poaching varmints, and make awful
havoc among the young rabbits. Well, Fairlegh, have you made up
your mind ? "

" Yes," replied I, " I am at your service for this morning ; but,
understand, I merely go as a spectator of your prowess."

" As you like, man. I'll order the chestnuts—go and polish up a
little—and then for walking into Governor Coleman, and bowling out
the drysalter."

The chestnuts whirled us over to Hillingford in less than an hour.
Lawless, delighted at being allowed to put his project into execution,
was in wild spirits, and kept me in fits of laughter the whole way, by
his quaint remarks on men and things.

" Is the governor visible, John ? " was his address to the footman
who answered the door, and who, apparently not being favoured by
Nature with any superfluous acuteness of intellect or sweetness of
disposition, merely stared sulkily in reply.

" The fellow's a fool," muttered Lawless, " and can't understand
English. Hark ye, sirrah," he continued, " is your master at
home ? "

As the hero of the shoulder-knot vouchsafed an affirmative reply
to this somewhat more intelligible query, we alighted, and were
straightway ushered into the drawing-room, where we found Mr. and
Mrs. Coleman, and, as Lawless afterwards expressed it, " a party
unknown," who was immediately, with much pomp and ceremony,
introduced to us by the name of Mr. Lowe Brown, an announcement
which elicited from my companion the whispered remark, " The
drysalter himself, by Jingo ! this looks like business, old fellow ;
there's no time to be lost, depend upon it."

" Ah ! Mr. Lawlegh," exclaimed Mrs. Coleman, shaking hands
cordially with Lawless, " I thought we were never going to see you
again, and I'm sure I was quite delighted, though the servant kept
you so long waiting at the gate, till I got Mr. Brown to ring the
bell ; and Mr. Fairless too, so kind of him, with those beautiful
chestnut horses standing there catching cold, in that very high gig,
which must be so dangerous, if you were to fall out, both of you."

" No fear of that, ma'am," replied Lawless; "Fairlegh and I have known each other too long to think of falling out in a hurry—firm friends, ma'am, as your son Freddy would say."

" Poor Freddy," returned Mrs. Coleman affectionately, "did he send any message by you to say when he is coming home again? We shall have some good news for him, I hope—for he was always very fond of his cousin Lucy."

" Family affection is a fine thing, ma'am," said Lawless, winking at me, " and ought to be encouraged at any price, eh ? "

" Very true, Mr. Lawlegh, very true ; and I am glad to find you think so, instead of living at those nasty clubs all day, turning out wild, smoking cigars like a German student, and breaking your mother's heart with a latch-key, at one o'clock in the morning, after-wards, when you ought to have been in bed and asleep for the last three hours. Good-bye, and God bless you ! "

The six concluding words of Mrs. Coleman's not over-perspicuous speech were addressed to Mr. Lowe Brown, who rose to take leave. This gentleman (for such I presume one is bound to designate him, however little appearances might warrant such an appellation) was a short, stout, not to say fat personage, with an unmeaning pink and white face, and a smug self-satisfied manner and look, which involuntarily reminded one of a sleek and well-conditioned tom-cat. Old Mr. Coleman rose also, and shaking his hand with great " empressement," left the room with him in order to conduct him to the door with due honour.

" Look at the servile old rogue, worshipping that snob's £2000 per annum," whispered Lawless; "we'll alter his tune before long. Fascinating man, Mr. Brown, ma'am ? " he continued, addressing Mrs. Coleman.

" Yes, I'm glad you like him ; he's a very good, quiet young man, and constantly reminds me of my poor dear aunt Martha, who is a peaceful saint in Brixton churchyard, after this vale of tears, where we must all go, only she hadn't £2000 a year, though she was so lucky at short whist, always turning up honours when she liked."

" Trump of a partner she must have been, and no mistake ! " said Lawless enthusiastically. "I suppose she didn't leave the recipe behind her, ma'am ? "

" No, Mr. Fairless, no ! at least, I never heard she did, though I've got a recipe of hers for cherry-brandy, which she was so fond of, and a very good one it is, poor thing ! But Mr. Brown, you see, with his fortune, might look so much higher, that, as Mr. Coleman says, it's a chance she may never have again, and it would be madness to throw it away, in her circumstances, too."

" Did Mr. Brown think of marrying your aunt, then, ma'am ? " asked Lawless, with an air of would-be innocence.

" No, my dear—I mean, Mr. Lawlegh, no—she died, and he went to Merchant Taylor's School together, that is in the same year; we were making it out last night—no, it's Lucy, poor dear ! and a famous thing it is for her, only I'm afraid she can't bear the sight of him."

At this moment Mr. Coleman returned, and Lawless, giving me a sly glance, accosted him with a face of the most perfect gravity, begging the favour of a few minutes' private conversation with him, a request which that gentleman, with a slight appearance of surprise, immediately granted, and they left the room together.

During their absence, good Mrs. Coleman confided to me, with much circumlocution, her own private opinion, that Lucy and Mr. Brown were by no means suited to each other, "because, you see, Mr. Fairless, my dear, Lucy's clever, and says sharp funny things that make one laugh, what they call 'piquante,' you know, and poor Mr. Brown, he's very quiet and good-natured, but he's not used to that sort of thing; and she, what you call, laughs at him;" ending with a confession that she thought Freddy and Lucy were made for each other, and that she had always hoped some day to see them married.

Dear, kind-hearted, puzzle-headed little woman! how I longed to comfort her, by giving her a glimpse behind the scenes! but it would have entailed certain ruin; she would have made confusion worse confounded of the best-laid scheme that Machiavelli ever concocted.

When Lawless and Mr. Coleman returned from their "tete-a-tete," it was easy to see, by the flattered but perplexed expression discernible in the countenance of the elder, and a grin of mischievous delight in that of the younger gentleman, that the stratagem had succeeded so far, and that a cloud had already shaded the fair hopes of the unconscious Mr. Lowe Brown.

"Ah—a—hem! my dear Mrs. Coleman," began her spouse, his usually 'pompous manner having gained an accession of dignity, which to those who guessed the cause of it was irresistibly absurd.

"A-hem—as I am, I believe, right in supposing Mr. Fairlegh is acquainted with the object of his friend's visit—"

"All right, sir!" put in Lawless; "go ahead."

"And as I am particularly requested to inform you of the honour" (with a marked stress on the word) "done to a member of my family, I conceive that I am guilty of no breach of confidence in mentioning that Mr. Lawless has proposed to me, in due form, for the hand of my niece, Lucy Markham, offering to make most liberal settlements; indeed, considering that the fortune Lucy is justified in expecting at her father's death is very inconsiderable—an income of £400 a year divided amongst thirteen children, deducting a jointure for the widow, should my sister survive Mr. Markham—"

"Never mind the tin, Mr. Coleman," interrupted Lawless, "you don't catch me buying a mare for the sake of her trappings. In the first place, second-hand harness is never worth fetching home; and in the next, let me tell you, sir, it's your niece's good points I admire: small head well set on—nice light neck—good slanting shoulder—pretty fore-arm—clean about the pasterns—fast springy action—

good-tempered, a little playful, but no vice about her; and altogether as sweet a thing as a man need wish to possess. Depend upon it, Mr. Coleman," continued Lawless, who, having fallen into his usual style of speech, was fairly off, "depend upon it, you'd be very wrong to let her get into a dealer's hands—you would indeed, sir; and if Mr. Brown isn't in that line it's odd to me. I've seen him down at Tattersall's in very shady company, if I'm not much mistaken; he's the cut of a leg, every inch of him."

Want of breath fortunately obliging him to stop, Lawless's chief auditors, who had gleaned about as much idea of his meaning as if he had been haranguing them in Sanscrit, now interposed; Mrs. Coleman to invite us to stay to luncheon, and her husband to beg that his niece Lucy might be summoned to attend him in his study, as he should consider it his duty to lay before her Mr. Lawless's very handsome and flattering proposal.

"And suppose Lucy should take it into her head, by any chance, to say 'Yes'" ("Never thought of that, by Jove!—That would be a sell!" muttered Lawless, aside)—"what's to become of poor dear Mr. Lowe Brown?" inquired Mrs. Coleman anxiously.

"In such a case," replied her lord and master, with a dignified wave of the hand, pausing as he left the room, and speaking with great solemnity,—"in such a case, Mr. Lowe Brown will perceive that it is his duty, his direct and evident duty, to submit to his fate with the calm and placid resignation becoming the son of so every way respectable and eminent a man as his late lamented father, my friend, the drysalter."

CHAPTER LIII.

A COMEDY OF ERRORS.

"Content you, gentlemen, I'll compound this strife
. . . He of both
That can assure *my niece's* greatest dower,
Shall have her love."

"I must confess your offer is the best,
And let your father make her the assurance,
She is your own."

Taming of the Shrew.

POOR pretty little Lucy Markham! what business had tears to come and profane, with their tell-tale traces, that bright, merry face of thine—fitting index to thy warm heart and sunny disposition! And yet, in the quenched light of that dark eye, in the heavy swollen lid, and in the paled roses of thy dimpled cheek, might be read the tokens of a concealed grief, that, like "a worm i' the bud," had already begun to mar thy sparkling beauty. Heed it not, pretty Lucy—sorrow such as thine is light and transient, and succour, albeit in a disguise thou canst not penetrate, is even now at hand. As the young lady in question entered the luncheon-room, returning Lawless's salutation with a most becoming blush, the thought crossed my mind that in his position I should be almost tempted to regret I was destined to perform the lover's part "on that occasion only." Such, however, were not the ideas of my companion, for he whispered to me : " I say, Frank, she looks uncommon friendly, eh ? —I don't know hardly what to make of it, I can tell you ; this is getting serious."

" You must endeavour by your manner to neutralize your many fascinations," replied I, striving to hide a smile, for he was evidently in earnest.

"Neutralize my grandmother!" was the rejoinder ; "I can't go and be rude to the young woman. How d'ye do, miss?" he continued gruffly ; "how d'ye do ? You see, we left Fred—" (here I nudged him, to warn him to avoid that subject)—"that is, we left Heathfield,—I mean started early—Let me help you, Mrs. Coleman ; precious tough customer that chicken seems to be—elderly bird, ma'am, and no mistake—who'll have a wing?"

" Really, Mr. Lawless, you are very rude to my poor chicken ; it's out of our own farmyard. I assure you ; and the turkeycock, his sister, that's Lucy's mother, sent him here ; she has thirteen children you know, poor thing ! and lives at Dorking ; they are famous for all having five toes, you know, and growing so very large, and this must be one of them, I think."

" They were Dorking fowls mamma sent you, aunt ; you don't keep turkeys," interposed Lucy, as Lawless fairly burst out laughing— an example which it was all I could do to avoid imitating.

" Yes, to be sure, my dear, I said so, didn't I ? I remember very well they came in a three-dozen hamper, poor things ! and were put in the back kitchen because it was too late to turn them out ; and as soon as it was light they began to crow, and to make that noise about laying eggs, you know, so that I never got a wink of sleep after, thinking of your poor mother, and all her troubles—thirteen of them, dear me ! till Mr. Coleman got up and turned them out, with a bad cold, in his dressing-gown and slippers."

" Freddy begged me to tell you that he would write to you to-morrow," observed I, aside to Lucy ; adding the enigmatical message, that " he had some good news to communicate, and that matters were not so bad as you imagined."

" Ah ! but doesn't—he can't know—Mr. Fairlegh," she added, looking at me with an earnest, inquiring glance ; "you are his most intimate friend ; has he told you the cause of his annoyance ?"

" Allow me to congratulate you, Mr. Fairlegh, on the very

excellent match your sister is about to make—the Oaklands family is one of the oldest in the county," said Mr. Coleman with an air of solemn politeness.

"Oh yes, we are all so glad to hear of it, your sister is so pretty, and we had been told there was some young scamp or other dangling after her."

"Um! eh? oh! that's rather too much, though," said Lawless, turning very red, and fidgeting on his chair; "pray may I ask, Mrs. Coleman, whether it was a man you happened to hear that from? because he must be—ar—funny—fellow—ar—worth knowing—ar—I should like to make his acquaintance."

"Why, really I—let me see—was it Jones the grocer, or Mrs. Muddles when she brought home the clean linen? I think it was Jones, but I know it came with the clean clothes, and they had heard it from some of the servants," returned Mrs. Coleman.

"I'll boil Shrimp alive when I get back," muttered Lawless, "and have him sent up in the fish sauce."

"Yes," replied I to Lucy, as soon as the conversation again became general, "Freddy gave me an outline of the cause of his disquietude; but from a hint Lawless dropped in our way here to-day, Mr. Lowe Brown is likely to have a somewhat powerful rival, is he not?"

"Oh! then you know all, Mr. Fairlegh," she replied; "what am I to do? I am so unhappy—so bewildered!"

"If you will allow me to advise you," returned I, "you will not positively refuse Lawless; on the contrary, I should encourage him so far as to insure the dismissal of Mr. Brown, at all events."

"But would that be right? besides, I should be forced to marry Mr. Lawless, if I once said Yes."

"I should not exactly say Yes," replied I, smiling at the naive simplicity of her answer; "I would tell my uncle that, as he was aware, I had always disliked the attentions of Mr. Brown, and that I begged he might be definitely informed that it would be useless for him to attempt to prosecute his suit any farther. I would then add that it was impossible for me to agree to accept at once a man of whom I knew so little as of Lawless, but that I had no objection to his visiting here, with a view to becoming better acquainted with him. By this means you will secure the positive advantage of getting rid of the drysalter, as Freddy calls him, and you must leave the rest to time. Lawless is a good-natured, generous-spirited fellow, and if he were made aware of the true state of the case, I do not think he would wish to interfere with Freddy's happiness, or annoy you by addresses which he must feel were unacceptable to you."

"But what will Freddy say if I appear to encourage Mr. Lawless? you don't know how particular he is."

"If you will permit me, I will tell him exactly what has passed between us to-day, and explain to him your reasons for what you are about to do."

" Will you really be so kind ? " she answered, with a grateful smile; " then I shall do exactly as you have told me. How shall I ever thank you for your kindness ? "

" By making my friend Freddy a good wife, and being married on the same day that I am."

" That you are! are you joking ? "

" Never was more serious in my life, I can assure you."

" Are you really going to be married ? oh, I am so glad! Is the lady a nice person ? do I know her ? "

" The most charming person in the world," replied I, " and you know her intimately."

" Why, you can't mean Cla—"

" Hush!" exclaimed I, as a sudden silence rendered our conversation no longer private.

" Lucy, my dear, may I request your company for a few minutes in my study ? " said Mr. Coleman, holding the door open with an air of dignified courtesy for his niece to pass out. She had acquired double importance in his eyes, since the eldest son of a real live peer of the realm had declared himself her suitor.

" Allow me, Governor—ar—Mr. Coleman, I mean," said Lawless, springing forward, " it's for us young fellows to hold doors open, you know—not old reprobates like you," he added in an undertone, making a grimace for my especial benefit at the retreating figure of the aforesaid irreverently apostrophized legal luminary.

" Ah!" said Mrs. Coleman, by whom this by-play had been unobserved, " I wish all young men were like you, Mr. Lawless : we see very little respect to gray hairs nowadays."

" Very little indeed, ma'am," returned Lawless, winking furiously at me; " but from a boy I've always been that way inclined : I dare say that you observed that I addressed Mr. Coleman as ' Governor ' just now ? "

" Oh yes, I think I did," replied Mrs. Coleman innocently.

" Well, ma'am, that's a habit I've fallen into from unconsciously giving utterance to my feelings of veneration. To govern is a venerable attribute—governor signifies one who governs—hence my inadvertent application of the term to your revered husband, eh ? "

" Ah!" returned poor Mrs. Coleman, thoroughly mystified, " it's very kind of you to say so, I'm sure. I wonder whether I left my knitting upstairs, or whether it went down in the luncheon-tray."

In order to solve this important problem, the good lady trotted off, leaving Lawless and myself " tete-a-tete."

" I say, Frank," he began, as the door closed after her, " did you put the young woman up to the trap at all! I saw you were ' discoorsing ' her, as Paddy says, while we were at luncheon, eh ? "

" No," replied I, " it was agreed that she was not to be let into the scheme, you know."

" By Jove! then all those kind looks she threw at me were really in earnest! I tell you what, I don't half like it, I can assure you, sir! I shall put my foot in it here too, if I don't mind what I'm at. Suppose, instead of marrying Freddy, she were to take it into her head she would like to be a peeress some day, what would become of me, eh?"

At this moment Mr. Coleman returned, his face beaming with dignity and self-satisfaction. Approaching Lawless, he motioned him to a chair, and then, seating himself exactly opposite, gave one or two deep hems to clear his throat, and then began,—

"I am empowered by my niece, standing as I may say 'in loco parentis'—(for though her parents are not positively defunct, still they have so completely delegated to me all control and authority over their daughter, that they may morally be considered dead)—I am empowered, then, by my niece to inform you, in answer to your very flattering proposal of marriage, that although she has not had sufficient opportunity of becoming acquainted with your character and general disposition, to justify her in at once ratifying the contract, she agrees to sanction your visits here in the character of her suitor." (Lawless's face on receiving this announcement was as good as a play to behold.) "In fact, my dear sir," continued Mr. Coleman, warming with the subject, "as my niece at the same time has signified to me her express desire that I should definitely and finally reject the suit of a highly amiable young man of fortune, who has for some time past paid his addresses to her, I think that we may consider ourselves fully justified in attributing the slightly equivocal nature of her answer to a pardonable girlish modesty and coyness, and that I shall not be premature in offering you my hearty congratulations on the successful issue of your suit—ahem!" And so saying, Mr. Coleman rose from his seat, and taking Lawless's unwilling hand in his own, shook it with the greatest "empressement."

"Thank ye, Gov—that is, Mr. Coleman—Uncle, I suppose I shall soon have to call you," said Lawless, with a wretched attempt at hilarity; "it's very flattering, you know, and of course I feel excessively, eh! uncommon, don't you see?—Get me away, can't you?" he added in an angry whisper, turning to me; "I shall go mad, or be ill, or something, in a minute."

"I think the tandem has been here some time," interposed I, coming to his assistance; "the horses will get chilled standing."

"Eh! yes! very true, we must be cutting away; make ourselves scarce, don't you see?" rejoined Lawless, brightening up at the prospect of escape.

"Let me ring for the ladies," said Mr. Coleman, moving towards the bell.

"Eh! not for the world, my dear sir, not for the world," exclaimed Lawless, interposing to prevent him. "Really, my feelings—your feelings, in fact all our feelings, have been sufficiently excited—steam got up—high pressure, eh?—some other day—pleasure. Good morning. Don't come out, pray."

And so saying, he fairly bolted out of the room, an example

B b

which I was about to follow, when Mr. Coleman, seizing me by the button, began,—

"I can see, Mr. Fairlegh, that Mr. Lawless is naturally uneasy and annoyed at Mr. Brown's attentions; but he need not be—pray assure him of this - Mr. Brown is a highly estimable young man, but his family are very much beneath ours in point of rank. I shall write to him this afternoon, and inform him that, on mature deliberation, I find it impossible to allow my niece to contract a matrimonial alliance with anyone in trade—that will set the matter definitely at rest. Perhaps you will kindly mention this to your friend?"

"I shall be most happy to do so," replied I, "nor have I the slightest doubt that my friend will consider the information perfectly satisfactory." And with many assurances of mutual consideration and esteem we parted.

Oh! the masks and dominoes of the mind! what mountebank ever wore so many disguises as the heart of man? If some potent spirit of evil had suddenly converted Elm Lodge into the palace of Truth, the light of its master's countenance would have grown dark as he read the thoughts that were passing in my breast; and instead of bestowing upon me the attentions due to the chosen friend of the wealthy suitor to his portionless niece, he would have done his best to kick me down the steps as an impostor plotting to marry his son to a beggar. When will men learn to value money at its real worth, and find out that warm loving hearts and true affections are priceless gems that wealth cannot purchase?

We drove for some time in silence, which was at length broken by Lawless, who in a tone of the deepest dejection began,—

"The first tolerably deep gravel-pit we come to, I must trouble you to get out, if you please."

"Get out at a gravel-pit! for goodness' sake why?" inquired I.

"Because I intend to back the tandem into it and break my neck," was the unexpected answer.

"Break your neck! nonsense, man. Why, what's the matter now? Hasn't your mad scheme succeeded beyond all expectation?"

"Ah! you may well say that!" was the rejoinder. "Beyond all expectation, indeed! yes, I should think so, rather. If I'd expected anything of the kind, it's thirty miles off I'd have been at the very least by this time—more, if the horses would have done it, which I think they would with steady driving, good luck, and a feed of beans."

"Why, what is it you fancy you've done, then?"

"Fancy I've done, eh? Well, if that isn't enough to make a fellow punch his own father's head with vexation. What have I done, indeed! why, I'll tell you what I've done, Mr. Frank Fairlegh, since you are so obtuse as not to have found it out by your own powers of observation. I've won the heart of an innocent and unsuspecting young female— I've destroyed the dearest hopes of my particular friend—and I've saddled myself with a superfluous wife, when my affections are reposing in the cold—ar—what do you call it, tomb, eh? of the future Lady Oaklands—if that isn't a pretty fair morning's work, it's a pity, eh ? "

" My dear Lawless," replied I, with difficulty repressing a laugh, " you don't really suppose Lucy Markham means to accept you ? "

" Eh! why not ? Of course I do; didn't Governor Coleman tell me so? an old reptile!"

" Set your mind at ease," replied I ; and I then detailed to him my conversation with Lucy Markham, and convinced him that her partial acceptance of his proposal, which had been made the most of by Mr. Coleman, was merely done at my suggestion, to insure the dismissal of Mr. Lowe Brown. As I concluded, he broke forth,—

" Ah ! I see, sold again ! It's an easy thing to make a fool of me where women are concerned ; they're a kind of cattle I never shall understand, if I were to live as long as Saint Methuselah, and take Old Parr's life pills twice a day into the bargain. Anything about a horse, now—"

" Then you'll postpone the gravel-pit performance ' ad infinitum ' ? " interrupted I.

" Eh ! yes ! it would be a pity to go and sacrifice the new tandem if it is not absolutely necessary to one's peace of mind, so I shall think better of it this time," was the rejoinder.

" By the way," resumed Lawless, as we drove through Heathfield Park, " I must not forget that I've got to immolate Shrimp on the altar of my aspersed reputation—call his master ꝑ ' scamp,' the amphibious little reprobate ? a brat that's neither fish, flesh, nor fowl, nor good red-herring—that spent his pitiful existence in making mud-pies in a gutter, till I was kind enough to—"

" Run over him, and break his arm," added I.

" Exactly," continued Lawless, " and a famous thing it was for him, too. Just see the advantages to which it has led ; look at the education I have given him ; he can ride to hounds better than many grooms twice his age, and bring you a second horse, in a long run, just at the nick of time when you want it, as fresh, with that feather-weight on its back, as if it had only just come out of the stable ; he can drive any animal that don't pull too strong for him, as well as I can myself ; he can brew milk-punch better than a College Don, and drink it like an undergraduate ; he can use his fists as handily as Ben Caunt, or the Master of T——y, and polish off a boy a head taller than himself, in ten minutes, so that his nearest relations would not recognize him ; and he won five pounds last year in a Derby sweepstakes, besides taking the long odds with a pork butcher, and walking into the piggycide to the tune of thirty shillings. No," continued Lawless, who had quite worked himself into a state of excitement, "whatever follies I may have been guilty of, nobody can accuse me of having neglected my duty in regard to that brat's education ; and now, after all my solicitude, the young viper goes and spreads reports that a ' scamp,' meaning me, is about to marry your sister ! I'll flay him alive, and put him in salt afterwards ! "

"But, my dear Lawless, out of the host of servants at Heathfield, how do you know it was Shrimp who did it?"

"Oh, there's no mischief going on that he's not at the bottom of; besides, a boy is never the worse for a flogging, for if he has not done anything wrong beforehand, he's sure to make up for it afterwards; so it comes right in the end, you see."

Thus saying, he roused the leader by a scientific application of the thong, dashed round the gravel-sweep, and brought his horses up to the hall-door in a neat and artist-like manner.

CHAPTER LIV.

MR. VERNOR MEETS HIS MATCH.

"If thou dost find him tractable to us,
Encourage him, and tell him all our reasons.
If he be leaden, icy, cold, unwilling,
Be thou so too."
Richard III.

" For the intent and purpose of the law
Hath full relation to the penalty,
Which here appeareth due,"
",Tarry a little, there is something else."
Merchant of Venice.

" Your looks are pale and wild, and do import some misadventure."
Romeo and Juliet.

ANY tender-hearted reader who may feel anxious concerning the fate of the unjustly-suspected Shrimp, will be glad to learn that this hopeful candidate for the treadmill (not to mention a more airy and exalted destiny) escaped his promised castigation, for, the moment we alighted, Freddy Coleman dragged us into the library, and Lawless, in the excitement of relating the morning's adventure, entirely forgot his threatened vengeance. Lawless's account of the affair was, as may well be imagined, rich in the extreme, worth walking barefoot twenty miles to hear, Freddy Coleman declared afterwards; and an equally laborious pilgrimage would have been quite repaid by witnessing the contortions of delight with which the aforesaid Freddy listened to him.

"So you have positively settled the drysalter, and stand pledged to marry my cousin Lucy, if she approves of you on further acquaintance? What will you give me to hand her over to you?"

"Give you, eh? the soundest thrashing you ever had in your life—one that will find you something to think about for the next fortnight, and no mistake. The idea of,putting the young woman's affections up to auction! why, you're worse than your old governor: he only wants to sell her to the highest;bidder."

" Well, he's been sold himself this time, pretty handsomely," replied Freddy; "I only hope it will be a lesson to him for the future."

" It strikes me he'd be all the better for a few more lessons of the sort, eh ? go through a regular 'educational course,' as they call it. Governors nowadays get so dreadfully conceited and dictatorial—they know best—and they will have this—and they won't have that. It's no joke to be a son, I can tell you.—' Latchkey, sir! only let me hear of your caring to introduce that profligate modern invention into my house, and I'll cut you off with a shilling.' "

" The most unkindest cut of all," quoted Freddy.

" Worse than 'cut behind' for the small boys, who indulge their locomotive propensities by sitting on the spikes at the backs of carriages, eh ? " said Lawless.

" Sharp set they must be, very ! " put in Freddy.

" Well, of all the vile puns I ever heard, that, which I believe to be an old Joe Miller, is the worst ! " exclaimed I. " Not to subject myself any longer to such wretched attempts, I shall go and dress for dinner."

" By way of obtaining re-dress ! Well, I hope we shall be better suited when we meet again," rejoined Freddy, fairly punning me out of the room.

Mr. Frampton returned from town late that evening, but in high health and spirits, having been closeted for some hours with his legal adviser, who had given him clear instructions as to the course he was to pursue to obtain possession of his niece on the following day.

When I retired to my room that night, I was too much excited to sleep, but it was excitement of a pleasurable nature. I lay picturing to myself the next day's scene—the surprise and anger of Mr. Vernor—the impotent fury of Cumberland's disappointed avarice—the grotesque joy of old Peter Barnett—and, above all, the unspeakable delight of rescuing my sweet Clara from a home so unfitted to her gentle nature, and removing her to an atmosphere of kindness and affection ; and with such pleasant thoughts wandering through my brain, towards morning I fell into a sound sleep. The sun was shining brightly when I again unclosed my eyes, and, hastily dressing, I hurried down to the breakfast-room, where I found Mr. Frampton already engaged in discussing a very substantial meal.

" Umph ! I didn't expect you would have turned lie-a-bed this morning, of all the days in the year, Master Frank," was his salutation on my entrance."

" I really am ashamed of myself," replied I, sitting down to the breakfast-table; "but my thoughts were so busy, and my mind so filled with anticipations of coming happiness, that I did not contrive to get to sleep till quite morning."

" Umph ! serve you right—you never should anticipate anything ; depend upon it, it's the surest way to prevent what you wish for coming to pass. When I was in the Mahratta country, I anticipated

I was going to marry the Begum of Tincummupeo—splendid woman! kept forty-two elephants for her own special riding, and wore a necklace of pearls as big as hazel nuts. What was the consequence? Instead of fulfilling my expectations, one fine morning she changed her mind, took up with a tawny, and ordered me to be strangled, only I got timely notice of her benevolent intentions, and lost no time in putting myself under the protection of my old crony, Blessimaboo, the Rajah of Coddleafellah. Umph!"

"Let me give you another cup of coffee, since the lady with the unpronounceable name did not succeed in her amiable design of destroying your swallowing powers for ever," returned I.

"Umph! I won't say no—there's nothing like serving out good rations to your men before they go into action; I've seen campaigning enough to know that."

"On the strength of which argument I shall cut you another slice of ham," replied I, suiting the action to the word. At length even Mr. Frampton's excellent appetite appeared exhausted, and he declared himself ready to face old Vernor if he should prove as cantankerous as a rhinoceros in hysterics; after which statement we proposed to start on our expedition. During his visit to town on the previous day, Mr. Frampton had purchased a very handsome light travelling carriage, which, with post-horses, was now in waiting to convey us to Barstone.

On our way thither, my companion informed me of the particulars of his interview with his legal adviser, and the powers with which he was invested, and which were to be brought to bear upon Mr. Vernor, if, as was to be expected, he should attempt to resist the claim. As the effect of the information thus acquired will appear in the course of this veritable history, I need say no more concerning the matter at present. We then proceeded to lay down the plan of operations, which embraced an innocent little stratagem for more effectually taking " the change " out of Mr. Vernor, as Lawless would have termed it. It was agreed, in pursuance of this scheme, that I should open the conversation, by informing Clara's guardian that, owing to an unexpected change in my fortunes, I was now in possession of means amply sufficient to maintain a wife, and had therefore come to renew my suit for the hand of his fair ward, merely introducing Mr. Frampton as a friend of mine who was prepared to furnish proof of the truth of my statement, if Mr. Vernor were not satisfied with my bare assertion. According to the way in which he should behave when this communication was made to him, were we to regulate our after-conduct. I now learned for the first time that Frampton was not my benefactor's real name, but one which he had adopted when he commenced his wanderings, and which he determined to retain on learning, as he imagined he had done indisputably, that his family was extinct. This accounted for the otherwise strange fact that Mr. Vernor should have remained in ignorance, up to the present period, of the existence of his ward's uncle. Lady Saville's maiden name, as I had been previously told, was Elliot, and my companion's real title, therefore, was Ralph Elliot. So occupied were we in discussing these interesting topics, that we had reached the gates of Barstone Park before our conversation began to flag; but the sight of the old quaintly-built lodge, realizing as it did, the object of our visit, raised a host of varying thoughts and feelings too powerful for utterance; and by mutual consent we finished our drive in silence.

A servant whose face was unknown to me answered the door; and replying in the affirmative to my inquiry whether Mr. Vernor was at home, led the way to the library.

"What name shall I say, sir?"

"Merely say two gentlemen wish to see Mr. Vernor upon business," was my reply; and in another moment I was once again face to face with Clara's guardian. He looked older and thinner than when I had seen him before, and care and anxiety had left their traces even on his iron frame: he was less erect than formerly, and I observed that, when his eyes fell upon me, his lip quivered, and his hand shook with suppressed irritation. Still his face wore the same cold, immovable, relentless expression as ever; and when he spoke, it was .with his usual sarcastic bitterness.

"I cannot imagine under what possible pretext Mr. Fairlegh can expect to be regarded in this house in any other light than as an unwelcome intruder, after his late outrageous conduct," was the speech with which he received me.

"If you refer, sir, to the well-merited chastisement I inflicted on your nephew, I can only say that Mr. Cumberland alike provoked the quarrel and commenced the attack; if you have received a true account of the matter, you must be aware it was not until your nephew had struck me more than once with his cane, that I returned the blow."

" Well, sir, we will not discuss the affair any further, as I presume it was scarcely for the purpose of justifying yourself that you have come hither to-day."

"You are right, sir," returned I; "and not to prolong a conversation which appears disagreeable to you, I will proceed at once to the purport of my visit. You have not, I imagine, forgotten the occasion of my former intrusion, as you termed it?"

"No, sir," he replied angrily, "I have not forgotten the presumptuous hopes you entertained, nor the cool effrontery with which you, a needy man—not to use any stronger term—preferred your suit for the hand and fortune," he added, laying a strong emphasis upon the last word, " of my ward, Miss Saville."

"That suit, sir, I am now about to renew," replied I, " but no longer as the needy fortune-hunter you were pleased to designate me. My friend here is prepared to show you documents to prove, if you require it, that I am, at this moment, in possession of an income amply sufficient to support a wife, and that, should my proposal find

favour with your ward, I am in a position to offer her an establishment embracing not only the comforts, but the refinements of life,
and am prepared to make as liberal settlements as can reasonably be
required of me: her own fortune I wish to have placed entirely under
her own control."

As I spoke his brow grew dark as night, and rising from his chair
he exclaimed, "I'll not believe it, sir! This is some new trick I
know your scheming talents of old; but, however," he continued,
seeing, no doubt, from my manner, that I was in a position to prove
the truth of my assertions, "rich or poor, it makes no difference in
my decision; I have but one answer to give I have other prospects
in view, other intentions in regard to the disposal of my ward's
hand, and, once for all, I finally and unhesitatingly reject your
offer."

"I believe, sir," replied I, restraining by an appealing glance Mr.
Frampton, whose zeal in my cause was becoming almost ungovernable, and who was evidently burning to be at him, as he afterwards
expressed it—"I believe, sir, I am right in imagining Miss Saville is
of age, in which case I must insist upon your laying my proposal
before her, and on receiving her decision from her own lips."

"She is of age, but her late father, knowing how liable girls
are, from their warm feelings, and ignorance of the ways of the
world, to become the prey of designing persons, wisely inserted a
clause in his will, by which it is provided that, in case of her marrying without my consent, her fortune shall pass into my hands, to be
disposed of as I may consider advisable. I need scarcely add that,
in the event of her marrying Mr. Fairlegh, she will do so without a
farthing."

"Umph! eh? perhaps not, sir—perhaps not; you seem to me to
look upon this matter in a false light, Mr. Vernor—umph! a very
false light; and not to treat my young friend with the degree of
courtesy which he and every other honourable man has a right to
expect from any one calling himself a gentleman. Umph! umph!"

"Really I cannot be expected to discuss the matter further,"
replied Mr. Vernor, with greater irritation of manner than he had
yet suffered to appear. "I have not formed my opinion of Mr.
Fairlegh hastily, nor on insufficient grounds, and it is not very
probable that I shall alter it on the representations of a nameless
individual, brought here for the evident purpose of chorusing Mr.
Fairlegh's assertions, and assisting to browbeat those who may be
so unfortunate as to differ from him. You must find such a friend
invaluable, I should imagine," he added, turning towards me with a
supercilious smile.

"Umph! nameless individual, sir—nameless individual, indeed!
Do you know who you are talking to?" Then came the aside, "Of
course he does not, how should he? Umph!"

"I think you must by this time see the folly of attempting to
prolong this absurd scene, Mr. Fairlegh," said Mr. Vernor, addressing

me without noticing Mr. Frampton's observation otherwise than by
a contemptuous glance; "I presume we have come to the last act of
this revival of the old comedy, ' A Bold Stroke for a Wife,' and I
think you are pretty well aware of my opinion of the performance."

"Umph! eh!—I fancy you'll find there's another act before the play
is ended yet, sir," returned Mr. Frampton, who was now thoroughly
roused; "an act that, with all your cunning, you are not prepared
for, and that even your unparalleled effrontery will be insufficient to
carry you through unmoved. You say, sir, that by the will of the
late Sir Henry Saville, his daughter's inheritance descends to you in
the event of her marrying without your consent. May I ask whether
there is not a certain contingency provided for, which might divert
the property into another channel? Umph!"

"Really, sir, it is long since I looked at the will," exclaimed Mr.
Vernor, for the first time dropping his usual tone of contemptuous
indifference, and speaking quickly and with excitement: "May I
inquire to what you refer?"

"Was there not a clause to this effect, sir?" continued Mr.
Frampton sternly; and, producing a slip of paper, he read as
follows:—

"But whereas it was the firm belief and conviction of the aforesaid
Clara Rose Elliot, afterwards Lady Saville, my late lamented wife,
that her brother Ralph Elliot, supposed to have perished at sea, had
not so perished, but was living in one of our colonies, I hereby will
and direct, that in the event of the said Ralph Elliot returning to
England, and clearly proving and establishing his identity, £300 per
annum shall be allowed him out of my funded property, for his
maintenance during the term of his natural life; and I further will
and direct that, in the event of my daughter, Clara Saville, by dis-
obedience to the commands of her guardian, Richard Vernor,
forfeiting her inheritance as, by way of penalty, I have above
directed, then I devise and bequeath the before-mentioned funded
property, together with Barstone Priory and the lands and rents
appertaining thereunto, to the aforesaid Ralph Elliot, for his absolute
use and behoof."

As he listened to the reading of this portion of the will, Mr.
Vernor's usually immovable features assumed an expression of
uneasiness which increased into an appearance of vague and undefined alarm; and when Mr. Frampton concluded, he exclaimed
hurriedly, "Well, sir, what of that? The man has been drowned
these forty years."

"Umph! I rather think not," was the reply; "I don't look much
like a drowned man, do I? Umph!"

So saying, he strode up to Mr. Vernor, and, regarding him with a
stern expression of countenance, added: "You were pleased in your
insolence, just now, to term me a 'nameless individual'; these
papers," he continued, producing a bundle, "will prove to you that
Ralph Elliot was not drowned at sea, as you imagine, but that the

nameless individual whom in my person you have treated with un-
merited insult, is none other than he."

"It is false!" exclaimed Mr. Vernor, turning pale with rage.
"This is all a vile plot, got up in order to extort my consent to this
marriage. But I'll expose you—I'll—"

At this moment the library door was thrown violently open, and
old Peter Barnett, his face bleeding and discoloured, as if from
fighting, and his clothes torn and muddy, rushed into the centre of
the apartment.

CHAPTER LV.

THE PURSUIT.

"Let not search and inquisition fail to bring again those . . . runaways."
As You Like It.

"Fetch me that handkerchief,
My mind misgives."
Othello.

"Sharp goads the spur, and heavy falls the stroke,
Rattle the wheels, the reeking horses smoke."
The Elopement.

ON the sudden appearance of old Peter in the deplorable condition
described in the last chapter, we all sprang to our feet, eager to learn
the cause of what we beheld. We were not long kept in suspense,
for as soon as he could recover breath enough to speak, he turned to
Mr. Vernor, saying, in a voice hoarse with sorrow and indignation,—

"If you knows anything of this here wickedness, as I half suspects
you do, servant as I am, I tells you to your face you're a willain, and
I could find in my heart to serve you as your precious nephew (as
you calls him) and his hired bullies have served me."

"How dare you use such language to me?" was the angry reply.
"You have been drinking, sirrah; leave the room instantly."

"Tell me, Peter," exclaimed I, unable to restrain myself, "what
has happened? Your mistress—Clara—is she safe?"

"That's more than I knows," was the reply; "if she is now, she
won't be soon, without we moves pretty sharp; for she's in precious
unsafe company. While we was a-looking after one thief, we've been
robbed by t'other; we was watching Master Wilford, and that young
scoundrel Cumberland has cut in, and bolted with Miss Clara!"

"Distraction!" exclaimed I, nearly maddened by the intelligence;
"which road have they taken? how long have they been gone?"

"Not ten minutes," was the reply; "for as soon as ever they had

knocked me down, they forced her into the carriage, and was off like
lightning; and I jumped up, and ran here as hard as legs would
carry me."

" Then they may yet be overtaken," cried I, seizing my hat; " but
are you sure Wilford has nothing to do with it ? "

" Quite certain," was the answer; " for I met him a-going a-shooting
as I cum in, and he stopped me to know what was the matter; and
when I told him, he seemed quite flustered like, and swore he'd make
Cumberland repent it."

" Mad, infatuated boy!" exclaimed Mr. Vernor; "bent on his
own ruin." And burying his face in his hands, he sank into a chair,
apparently insensible to everything that was passing.

" Now, Peter," I continued, "every moment is of importance; tell
me which road to take, and then get me the best horse in the
stable, without a moment's delay. I will bear you harmless."

" I've thought of all that, sir," rejoined Peter Barnett. "It's no
use your going alone; there's three of them besides the post-boys.
No! you must take me with you; and they've knocked me about so,.
that I don't think I could sit a horse, leastways not to go along
as we must go, if we mean to catch 'em. No! I've ordered fresh
horses to your carriage, it's lighter than the one they have got, and
that will tell in a long chase ; you must take me to show you the way,.
Muster Fairlegh."

" Well, come along, then. Mr. Frampton, I'll bring you your niece
in safety, or this is the last time we shall meet, for I never will return
without her."

" Umph ! eh ? I'll go with you, Frank, I'll go with you."

" I would advise you not, sir," replied I ; " it will be a fatiguing, if
not a dangerous expedition."

" Ain't I her uncle, sir? umph !" was the reply. "I tell you I will
go. Danger, indeed ! why, boy, I've travelled more miles in my life
than you have inches."

" As you please, sir," replied I ; " only let us lose no time." And
taking his arm, I hurried him away.

Glancing at Mr. Vernor as we left the library, I perceived that he
still remained motionless in the same attitude. As we reached the
hall door, I was glad to find that Peter's exertions had procured four
stout horses, and that the finishing stroke was being put to their
harness as we came up.

" Who is that ? " inquired I, as my eye caught the figure of a horseman, followed by a second, apparently a groom, riding rapidly across
the park.

" That's Mr. Fleming, sir," replied one of the helpers ; " he came
down to the stable, and ordered out his saddle-horses in a great
hurry ; I think he's gone after Mr. Cumberland."

" What are we waiting for ? " exclaimed I, in an agony of impatience. " Peter !—Where's Peter Barnett ? "

" Here, sir," he exclaimed, making his appearance a moment after

I had first observed his absence. "It ain't no use to start on a march without arms and baggage," he added, flinging a wrapping great-coat (out of the pocket of which the butts of a large pair of cavalry pistols protruded) into the rumble, and climbing up after it.

"Now, sir," exclaimed I; and half lifting, half pushing Mr. Frampton into the carriage, I bounded in after him: the door was slammed to, and, with a sudden jerk, which must have tried the strength of the traces pretty thoroughly, the horses dashed forward, old Peter directing the post-boys which road they were to follow. The rocking motion of the carriage (as, owing to the rapid pace at which we proceeded, it swung violently from side to side) prevented anything like conversation, while for some time a burning desire to get on seemed to paralyze my every faculty, and to render thought impossible. Trees, fields, and hedges flew past in one interminable, bewildering, ever-moving panorama, while to my excited imagination we appeared to be standing still, although the horses had never slackened speed from the moment we started, occasionally breaking into a gallop wherever the road would permit. After proceeding at this rate, as nearly as I could reckon, about ten miles, old Peter's voice was heard shouting to the post-boys, and we came to a sudden stop.

"What is it?" inquired I eagerly; but Peter, without vouchsafing any answer, swung himself down from his seat, and ran a short distance up a narrow lane, which turned off from the high-road, stopped to pick up something, examined the ground narrowly, and then returned to the carriage, holding up in triumph the object he had found, which, as he came nearer, I recognized to be a silk handkerchief I had seen Clara wear.

"I didn't think my old eyes could have seen so quickly," was his observation as he approached; "we was almost overrunning the scent, Muster Fairlegh, and then we should 'a been ruined—horse, fut, and artillery. Do you know what this is?"

"Clara's handkerchief! It was round her neck when I met her two days ago."

"Ay! bless her!" was the old man's reply. "And she's been clever enough to drop it where they turned off here, to let us know which way they have taken her. Lucky none of 'em didn't see her a-doin' it."

"How fortunate you observed it! And now where does this lane lead to?"

"Well, that's what puzzles me," returned Peter, rubbing his nose with an air of perplexity. "It don't lead to anything except old Joe Hardman's mill. But they're gone down here, that's certain sure, for there was that handkerchief, and there's the mark of wheels and 'osses' feet."

"Well, if it is certain they have gone that way," continued I, "let us lose no time in following them. How far off is this mill?"

"About a couple of miles out of the road, sir," replied one of the post-boys.

"Get on then," said I; "but mind you do not lose the track of their wheels. It's plain enough on the gravel of the lane."

"All right, sir," was the reply; and we again dashed forward.

As we got farther from the high-road, the ruts became so deep that we were obliged to proceed at a more moderate pace. After skirting a thick wood for some distance, we came suddenly upon a small bleak, desolate-looking common, near the centre of which stood the mill, which appeared in a somewhat dilapidated condition. A little half-ruinous cottage, probably the habitation of the miller, lay to the right of the larger building; but no signs of carriage or horses were to be perceived, nor, indeed, anything which might indicate that the place was inhabited.

As we drew up at a gate of a farmyard, which formed the approach both to the mill and the house, Peter Barnett again got down, and having carefully examined the traces of the wheel-marks, observed,—

"They've been here, that I'll take 'my Bible oath on. The wheel-tracks go straight into the yard. But there's some fresh marks here I can't rightly make out. It looks as if a horse had galloped up to the gate and leaped hover it."

"Wilford!" exclaimed I, as a sudden idea came into my head. "We have not got to the truth of this matter yet, depend upon it. There is some collusion between Wilford and Cumberland."

"Umph! rascals!" ejaculated Mr. Frampton. "But they shall both hang for it, if it costs me every farthing I possess in the world."

"It's Mr. Fleming's black mare as has been hover 'ere," said one of the post-boys, who, I afterwards learned, was a stable-helper at Barstone, and had volunteered to drive in the sudden emergency. "I knows her marks from any hother 'orse's. She's got a bar-shoe on the near forefoot."

"Is there nobody here to direct us?" asked I. "Let me out. Who is this miller, Peter?" I continued, as I sprang to the ground.

"Well, he's a queer one," was the reply. "Nobody rightly knows what to make of him. He's no great good, I expects; but good or bad, we'll have him out."

So saying he opened the gate, and going to the cottage door, which was closed and fastened, commenced a vigorous assault upon it. For some time his exertions appeared productive of no result, and I began to imagine the cottage was untenanted.

"We are only wasting our time to no purpose," said I. "Let us endeavour to trace the wheel-marks, and continue our pursuit."

"I'm certain sure there's someone in the house," rejoined old Peter, after applying his ear to the keyhole; "I can hear 'em moving about."

"We'll soon see," replied I, looking round for some implement fitted for my purpose.

In one corner lay a heap of wood, apparently part of an old paling.

Selecting a stout post which had formed one of the uprights, I dashed it against the fastenings of the door with a degree of force which made lock and hinges rattle again. I was about to repeat the attack when a gruff voice from within the house shouted,—

" Hold hard there, I'm a-coming ! " and in another minute the bolts were withdrawn, and the door opened.

" What do you mean by destroying a man's property in this manner ? " was the salutation with which we were accosted.

The speaker was a short, thickset man, with brawny arms, and a head unnaturally large, embellished by a profusion of red hair, and a beard of at least a week's growth. The expression of his face, surly in the extreme, would have been decidedly bad, had it not been for a look of kindness in the eye, which in some degree redeemed it.

" What do you mean by allowing people to stand knocking at your door for five minutes, my friend, without taking any notice of them ? You obliged us to use summary measures," replied I.

" Well, I wor a-laying on the bed when you cum. I slipped down with a sack of flour this morning, and hit my head, so I thought I'd turn in and take a snooze, do you see ? " and as he spoke he pointed to his face, one side of which I now perceived was black and swollen as if from a blow.

" That's a lie, Joe! and you [knows it," said Peter Barnett abruptly.

" You speaks pretty plainly, at all events, Master Barnett," was the reply, but in a less surly tone than he had hitherto used.

The man was clearly an original ; and it was equally evident that Peter knew how to deal with him, and that I did not. I therefore called the former on one side, and desired him, if bribing was of any use, to offer the miller £50, if through his information we were enabled to overtake the fugitives. Upon this a conversation ensued between the pair, which appeared as if it would never come to a termination ; but just as my patience was exhausted, and I was about to break in upon them, Peter informed me that if I would engage to pay Hardman £50, and to protect him from Wilford's anger, he would tell me everything he knew, and put me on the right track. To this I agreed, and he proceeded to give me the following account :—

In the course of the previous day, a vagabond of his acquaintance who called himself a rat-catcher, but was a professional poacher and an amateur pugilist, came to him, and told him that a gentleman who had a little job in hand wanted the use of the cottage, as it was a nice out-of-the-way place, and that, if he would agree, the gent would call and give him his instructions. He inquired of what the job consisted ; and on being told that a girl was going to run away from home with her sweetheart—that being, as he observed, merely an event in the course of nature—he agreed. In the evening he was visited by Wilford, and a man who was addressed as Captain. They directed him to have a room in the cottage ready by the next morning for the reception of a lady ; and at the same time a sealed paper

was handed to him, which he was directed to lock up in some safe
place, and in the event of the lady and her maid-servant being given
into his custody unharmed, he was to deliver up the paper to a
gentleman who should produce a signet ring then shown him.
This being successfully accomplished, he and his friend the poacher
were alike to prevent the lady's escape, and protect her against all
intrusion, till such time as Wilford should arrive to claim her; for
which services the worthy pair were to receive conjointly the sum
of £20.

In pursuance of these instructions, he had locked up the paper,
and prepared for locking up the lady. About half an hour before
we made our appearance, a carriage had arrived with four smoking
posters; it contained two females inside; the Captain and a gentleman (whom the miller recognized as Mr. Cumberland of Barstone
Priory) were seated in the rumble, while his friend the poacher was
located on a portmanteau in front.

Cumberland and his companion alighted, and the former immediately asked for the paper, producing the ring, and saying that the
plan had been changed, and that the lady was to go on another stage.
Joe Hardman, however, was not, as he expressed it, "to be done so
easy," and positively refused to give up the paper till the lady was
consigned to his custody. A whispered consultation took place
between Cumberland and the Captain, the carriage door was opened,
and the lady and her maid requested to alight. Joe then ushered
them into the room prepared for them, the windows of which had
been effectually secured, locked them in, and leaving the poacher on
guard, hastened to get the paper, which, on receiving the ring, he
delivered up to Cumberland. No sooner, however, had Cumberland
secured the document, than he made a signal to the Captain; they
both threw themselves upon Hardman, and endeavoured to overpower him. He resisted vigorously, shouting loudly to the poacher
for assistance, an appeal to which that treacherous ally responded
by bestowing upon him a blow which stretched him on his back,
and damaged his physiognomy in the manner already described.
Having put him "hors de combat," they took the key from him,
released the lady, forced her and her maid to re-enter the carriage, and
drove off, leaving him to explain her absence as best he might.

They had not been gone more than ten minutes when Wilford and
his groom rode up at speed, and on learning the trick which had
been played upon him, swore a fearful oath to be avenged on
Cumberland, and after ascertaining which direction they had taken,
followed eagerly in pursuit.

He added that his chief inducement for making this confession
was his conviction that something dreadful would occur unless
timely measures were taken to prevent it. He declared Cumberland's manner to have been that of a man driven to desperation;
and he had noticed that he had pistols with him. Wilford's ungovernable fury, on being informed how he had been deceived, was

described by Hardman as enough to make a man's blood run cold to witness. Having, in addition, ascertained the route they had taken, and the means by which we should be likely to trace them, we returned to the carriage—my heart heavy with the most dire forebodings—and inciting the drivers, by promises of liberal payment, to use their utmost speed, we once again started in pursuit.

CHAPTER LIV.

RETRIBUTION.

" Fell retribution, like a sleuth-hound, still
    The footsteps of the wicked sternly tracks,
    And in his mad career o'ertaking him,
    Brings, when he least expects it, swift destruction,
    And with a bitter, mocking justice, marks
    Each sin that did most easily beset him.
    The eye that spared not woman in its lust,
    Glaring with maniac terror, sinks in death.
    The homicidal hand, whose fiendish skill
    Made man its victim, crushed and bleeding lies.
    The crafty tongue, a ready instrument
    Of that most subtle wickedness, his brain,
    Babbles in fatuous imbecility."
                    Holofernes, a Mystery.

" We meet to part no more." —*Amatory Sentiment.*

AFTER proceeding about a mile, at a pace which consorted ill with the fever of impatience that tormented me, we came once again upon the high-road; and having got clear of ruts and mud-holes, were enabled to resume our speed. Half an hour's gallop advanced us above six miles on our route, and brought us to the little town of M——. Here we were compelled to stop to change our smoking horses, and had the satisfaction of learning that a carriage answering to old Peter's description of the one we were in pursuit of, had changed horses there about twenty minutes before our arrival, and that a gentleman and his groom had since been observed to ride at speed through the town, and to follow the course taken by the carriage without drawing.bridle. Whilst making these inquiries four stout posters had been attached to our vehicle, and we again dashed forward. Another half-hour of maddening suspense followed, although the post-boys, stimulated by the promise of reward, exerted themselves to the utmost, till the carriage swung from side to side with a degree of violence which rendered an overturn by no means an improbable contingency. No signs of the fugitives were to be discerned, and I was beginning to speculate on the possibility of their having again attempted to deceive us by turning off from the high-road, when an exclamation from Peter Barnett (who, from his exalted station, was able to command a more extended view than ourselves) attracted my attention. We were at the moment descending a hill, which from its steepness obliged the postilions to proceed at a more moderate pace. Thrusting my head and shoulders out of one of the front windows, and raising myself by my hands I contrived to obtain a view of the scene which had called forth Peter's ejaculation. Rather beyond the foot of the hill, where the ground again began to ascend, a group of persons, apparently farming labourers, were gathered round some object by the way-side, while almost in the centre of the road lay a large dark mass, which, as I came nearer, I perceived to be the dead carcase of a horse; another horse. snorting with terror at the sight of its fallen companion, was with difficulty prevented from breaking away by a groom, who, from his dark and well-appointed livery, I immediately recognized as a servant of Wilford's.

With a sensation of horror, such as I do not remember ever before to have experienced, I shouted to the post-boys to stop, and spring-ing out, hastened to join the crowd collected by the roadside. They made way for me as I approached, thereby enabling me to perceive the object of their solicitude. Stretched at full length upon the grass, and perfectly motionless, lay the form of Wilford; his usually pale features wore the livid hue of death, and his long black hair was soaked and matted with blood, which trickled slowly from a fearful contused wound towards the back of the head. His right shoulder, which was crushed out of all shape, appeared a confused mass of mud and gore, while his right—his pistol arm—lay bent in an un-natural direction, which showed that it was broken in more places than one. He was perfectly insensible, but that he was still alive was proved, as well by his hard and painful breathing, as by a low moan of agony to which he occasionally gave utterance. " How has this happened ? " inquired I, turning away with a thrill of horror.

" Well, as I make out, the mare crushed him when she fell upon him; but he knows best, for he saw it all," replied one of the country-men, pointing to the groom, who now came forward.

On questioning the servant, I learned that Wilford, before he went out shooting that morning, had ordered his saddle-horses to be ready for him at a certain hour, adding that the black mare, of which mention has been so often before made in this history, was to be saddled for his own riding. Immediately after Peter Barnett had returned with the news of Miss Saville's abduction, Wilford had called for his horses in great haste, told the servant to follow him, and ridden off at speed, through fields and along by-lanes, till he arrived at Hardman's mill. There he was made acquainted (as I knew from the miller's confession) with the decep-tion which had been practised upon him, and, muttering impreca-tions against Cumberland, he started in pursuit, riding at such a pace that the groom, although well mounted, had the greatest

c c

difficulty in keeping up with him. At length they caught sight of a carriage with four horses descending the steep hill already mentioned, and proceeding at a rate which proved that time was a more important consideration than safety to those it contained. Regardless of the dangerous nature of the ground Wilford continued his headlong course, and overtook the fugitives just at the bottom of the hill. Riding furiously up to the side of the vehicle, he shouted to the drivers to stop, in a voice hoarse with passion. Intimidated by his furious gestures, and uncertain whether to obey or not, the post-boys, in their irresolution, slackened their speed, when Cumberland, urged apparently to desperation, leaned out of the window with a cocked pistol in his hand, ordered the drivers to proceed, and turning to Wilford, desired him to give up the pursuit, or, levelling the pistol at him as he spoke, he would blow his brains out. Wilford, taking no notice of the threat, again shouted to the postilions to stop, and was about to ride forward to compel their obedience, when Cumberland, after hesitating for a moment, suddenly changed the direction of the pistol, and aiming at the horse instead of the rider, fired.

Simultaneously with the report, the mare plunged madly forward, reared up till she stood almost erect, pawed the air wildly with her forefeet, and then dropped heavily backwards, bearing her rider with her, and crushing him as she fell. The ball had entered behind the ear, and passing in an oblique direction through the brain, had produced instant death. Without waiting to ascertain the effect of his shot, Cumberland again compelled the post-boys to proceed, and by the time the groom reached the scene of action the carriage was rapidly getting out of sight. The servant, being unable to extricate his master from the fallen horse, was about to ride off for assistance, when some labourers, attracted by the report of the pistol, had come up, and by their united efforts had succeeded in freeing the sufferer, but only, as it seemed, to die from the serious nature of the injuries he had sustained.

"Umph! eh!—the man's a dead man, or next door to it," exclaimed Mr. Frampton, who had joined me while the groom was giving the above recital. "Nevertheless, we must do what we can for him, scoundrel as he is. How's a doctor to be obtained? Umph!"

"Where does the nearest surgeon live?" asked I.

"There ain't none nearer than M—— " was the reply, naming the town through which we had passed.

"I must leave you to settle this matter," continued I; "too much time has already been lost for me to attempt to overtake Cumberland with the carriage; I must follow them on horseback. Take off the leaders and shift the saddle on to the led horse; he seems the freshest."

"Umph! go and get shot, like the wretched man here," put in Mr. Frampton. "You shan't do it, Frank."

"With his fate before me, I will be careful, sir," replied I; "but think of Clara in the power of that villain! Your niece must be rescued at all hazards; still, even for her sake, I will be cautious—Is that horse ready?"

"If you please, sir," said one of the postilions, a quick, intelligent lad, who, while we were speaking, had removed the saddle from the dead mare to the back of the off leader, "If you will take me with you, I can show you how to stop them." He then explained that about five miles further on there was a turnpike at the top of a long hill which a heavy carriage must ascend slowly, and that he knew a short cut across some fields, by means of which, if we made the best of our way, we might reach the turnpike in time to close the gate before those of whom we were in pursuit should arrive. This plan appeared so sensible and comparatively easy of execution, that even Mr. Frampton could offer no objection to it, and mounting our horses, we again resumed the chase.

And now, for the first time since I had heard of Clara's abduction, did I at all recover my self-command, or venture to hope the affair would be brought to a favourable issue. But the change from in-action to vigorous exertion, and the refreshing sensation of the cool air as it whistled round my throbbing temples, tended to restore the elasticity of my spirits, and I felt equal to any emergency that might arise. After following the highroad for about a mile, we turned down a lane on the right, and leaving this when we had proceeded about half a mile farther, we entered a large grass field, which we dashed over in gallant style, and making our way across sundry other fields, and over, through, and into (for the post horses, though not by any means despicable cattle in their degree, were scarcely calculated for such a sudden burst across country as that to which we were treating them) the respective hedges and ditches by which they were divided, we regained the highroad, after a rattling twenty minutes' gallop. The point at which we emerged was just at the top of a very steep hill, up which the road wound in a serpentine direction.

"Are we before them, do you think?" inquired I of my companion, as we reined in our panting steeds.

"I'm sure as we must be, sir, by the pace we've come. I didn't think the old 'osses had it in 'em; but you does ride slap hup, sir, and no mistake—pity as you ain't on the road, your honour."

"If I pass behind those larch trees," asked I, smiling at the post-boy's compliment, "I can see down the hill without being seen, can I not?"

His reply being in the affirmative, I advanced to the spot I had indicated, and to my delight, perceived a carriage and four making its way up the hill with as great rapidity as the nature of the ground rendered possible. Turning my horse's head, I rejoined my com-panion, and we rode on to the turnpike.

Half a dozen words served to convey my wishes to the turnpike-

man, as many shillings rendered him my firm friend, and half the
number of minutes sufficed to close and effectually bolt and bar the
gate.

The post-boy having by my orders tied up the horses to a rail on
the other side of the gate, we all three entered the turnpike house,
where with breathless impatience I awaited the arrival of the
carriage. In less time than even I had imagined possible, the
sound of horses' feet, combined with the rattle of wheels, and the
shouting of the drivers, when they perceived the gate was shut, gave
notice of their approach.

"Wait," exclaimed I, laying my hand on the boy's arm to restrain
his impetuosity, "wait till they pull up, and then follow me, both of
you ; but do not interfere unless you see me attacked, and likely to
be overpowered."

As I spoke, the horses were checked so suddenly as to throw them
on their haunches, and, amidst a volley of oaths at the supposed
inattention of the turnpike-man, one of the party (in whose coarse
bloated features and corpulent figure I at once recognized my ci-
devant acquaintance of the billiard-room, Captain Spicer) jumped
down to open the gate. This was the moment I had waited for, and
bounded forward, followed by my satellites, I sprang to the side of
the carriage. A cry of joy from Clara announced that I was recognized, and with an eager hand she endeavoured to let down the glass,
but was prevented by Cumberland, who was seated on the side
nearest the spot where I was standing. In an instant my resolution
was taken ; wrenching open the carriage door, and flinging down the
steps, I sprang upon him, and seizing him by the coat-collar before
he had time to draw a pistol, I dragged him out head foremost, and,
giving way to an ungovernable impulse of rage, shook him till I
could hear all the teeth rattle in his head, and threw him from me
with such violence that he staggered and fell. In another moment
Clara was in my arms.

"Clara, dearest! my own love!" whispered I, as, shedding tears of
joy, she rested her head upon my shoulder, "what happiness to have
saved you!"

There are moments when feeling renders us eloquent, when the
full heart pours forth its riches in eager and impassioned words ; but
there are other times, and this was one of them, when language is
powerless to express the deep emotion of the soul, and our only
refuge is in silence. Clara was the first to speak.

"Frank—tell me—what has become of Mr. Fleming—the pistol
shot—that maddened plunging horse—I am sure something dreadful
has happened."

"He is indeed severely injured by the fall," replied I, wishing the
truth to break upon her by degrees; "but I was unable to remain to
learn a surgeon's opinion—and this reminds me that I have still
a duty to perform ; Cumberland must be detained to answer
for his share in this transaction ;" and leading Clara to a bench

outside the turnpike house, I proceeded to put my intentions into practice.

But whilst I had been thus engrossed, affairs had assumed a somewhat different aspect. The turnpike-man was actively engaged in a pugilistic contest with Captain Spicer, who, on his attempting to lay hands on him, had shown fight, and was punishing his adversary pretty severely. Cumberland's quick eye had perceived the horses the moment he had regained his feet, and when he saw that I was fully occupied, he had determined to seize the opportunity for effecting his escape. Springing over the gate, he untied one of the horses, and striking down the boy who attempted to prevent him, rode away at a gallop, at the moment I reappeared upon the scene; while the second horse, after struggling violently to free itself, had snapped the bridle and dashed off in pursuit of its retreating companion. This being the case, it was useless to attempt to follow him; and not altogether sorry that circumstances had rendered it impossible for me to be his captor, I turned to assist my ally, the turnpike-man, who, to use the language of the "Chicken," immortalized by Dickens, appeared in the act of being "gone into and finished" by the redoubtable Captain Spicer. Not wishing to have my facial development disfigured by the addition of a black eye, however, I watched my opportunity, and springing aside to avoid the blow with which he greeted me, succeeding in inserting my fingers within the folds of his neckcloth, after which I had little difficulty in choking him into a state of incapacity, when he submitted to the indignity of having his hands tied behind him, and was induced to resume his seat in the rumble as a prisoner, till such time as I should learn Mr. Frampton's opinion as to the fittest manner of disposing of him. I then replaced Clara in the carriage, which by my orders had turned round, rewarded the turnpike-man, as well as the boy to whose forethought and able guidance I was mainly indebted for my success, and taking my seat beside my prisoner, we started on our return.

One naturally feels a certain degree of awkwardness in attempting to make conversation to a man whom only five minutes before one has nearly succeeded in strangling, however thoroughly the discipline may have been deserved—and yet silence is worse; at least, I found it so; and after clearing my throat once or twice, as if I had been the person half throttled rather than the throttler, I began :—

"It is some years since we have met, Captain Spicer."

The individual thus addressed turned round quickly as I spoke, and favoured we with a scrutinizing glance—it was evident he did not recognize me.

"Have you forgotten the billiard-room in F—— Street, and the way in which your pupil and associate, Mr. Cumberland, cheated my friend Oaklands?"

The Captain, on having this somewhat unpleasant reminiscence of bygone hours forced upon him, turned—I was going to say pale, but that was an impossibility—rather less red than usual ere he replied :—

"I beg pardon, Mr. Fairlegh, but I'd forgotten you, sir; 'pon my conscience I had. Ah, that was a foolish piece of business, sir; but Mr. Cumberland, he always was a bad 'un."

"The man who encouraged and assisted him, not to mention working on his fears, and goading him to desperation, is scarcely the person to blame him," replied I sternly.

"Ah! you don't know all, sir; he was a precious sight worse than you're awake to yet, Mr. Fairlegh. I could tell you things that would surprise you; and if I thought that you would save yourself the trouble of taking me any further than M——, which is, I believe, the nearest place where I can pick up a coach to London, I don't know that I should mind explaining matters a bit. What do you say, sir? you are lawyer enough to know that you can't do anything to me for this morning's work, I dare say."

"I am not so certain of that," replied I; "abduction and manslaughter are legal offences, I believe."

"I had nothing to do with the last job," was the reply; "I could not have prevented Cumberland's shooting the mare if my own brother had been riding her."

This I believed to be true, and I was far from certain that, although morally guilty, Captain Spicer had committed any offence for which he could be punished by law; moreover, as he had been a good deal knocked about in his conflict with the turnpike-man, and I had more than half strangled him with my own hands, I felt leniently disposed towards him. I therefore replied :—

"Tell me, truly and honestly, supposing you can for once contrive to do so, all you know about this business; and if, as I imagine, you have only been the tool of others in the affair, it is possible my friend, Mr. Frampton, may be induced to let you off."

Upon this hint, the Captain having prevailed upon me to remove his extempore handcuffs, and passed his word not to attempt to escape, proceeded to give me the following particulars :—

About a year or so before he had acted in some mysterious capacity at a gambling house, of which Cumberland was part proprietor, and which was one of Wilford's favourite resorts. The debts which, as a boy, Cumberland had begun to contract, had increased till he became deeply involved; and after availing himself of every kind of subterfuge to postpone the evil day, he was on the point of being arrested by his principal creditor, a money-lender, to whom he owed £750. Shortly before the day on which he had promised to meet the demand, Spicer, getting a cheque cashed at a banker's in the city, was present when an agent of Wilford's paid in to his account £2000, which circumstance he mentioned to Cumberland. That evening Cumberland induced Wilford to play piquet; they played high, but fortune varied, and at the end of the game Cumberland rose a winner of eighty pounds, for which Wilford wrote him a cheque. On exam-

ining his banker's book shortly afterwards, Wilford discovered that
a cheque for £800 had been presented and duly honoured, which
proved, on minute inspection, to be the cheque written for Cumberland, and of course a forgery. For reasons of his own, one of which no
doubt was to obtain absolute power over Cumberland, Wilford refused
to prosecute. When, some months after this transaction, Spicer
was summoned to assist in carrying off Clara, Cumberland sought him
out, told him that he had a scheme to frustrate Wilford and gain
possession of Clara, and proved to him that he had by some means
obtained £5000 in specie, of which he offered him £1000 if he would
assist him, his object being to escape to America, and live there upon
Clara's fortune. Captain Spicer, tempted by the magnitude of the
sum mentioned, aware that his character was too well known in
London to render that city a desirable place of residence, and having
a strong idea that he could turn his talents to account among the
Yankees, stipulated that in addition to the sum proposed, Cumberland should pay his passage out, and agreed to the plan. The further
details of the plot have been already partially explained. Aware of
Wilford's predilection for keeping up appearances, and conducting
his intrigues with so much cunning as in many instances to divert
suspicion into some other channel, Cumberland sought him out, and
telling him that he had observed his passion for Clara, professed that
her money was his only object, spoke of his desire to reside in
America, and wound up by offering, if Wilford would give up the
forged paper, and agree to allow him a certain sum quarterly out of
Clara's fortune, to run off with her, and hand her over to him. To
this Wilford, relying on Spicer and determining to retain the forged
cheque as a guarantee for Cumberland's fidelity until Clara was
placed in the hands of Hardman, agreed. With the results of this
arrangement the reader is already acquainted.

As my disreputable companion came to the end of his recital,
we drove up to the door of the principal inn of the little town of
M——.

CHAPTER THE LAST.

WOO'D AND MARRIED AND A'.

" 'Tis a strange compact, still I see no better,
  So by your leave we'll sit and write this letter."
    Ye Merrie Bacheloure.

" The ancient saying is no heresy,
  Hanging and wiving goes by destiny."
    Merchant of Venice.

THE heart of the wandering Swiss bounds within him at the sound
of the " Ranz des Vaches," dear to the German exile are the soul-
stirring melodies of his fatherland ; but never did the ear of German
or of Swiss drink in with greater delight the music that his spirit loved

than did mine the transport of grunting by which Mr. Frampton welcomed his niece, the daughter of his childhood's friend, his fondly remembered sister.

" Umph ! eh ! so you've let that rascal Cumberland slip through your fingers, Master Frank ? Umph ! stupid boy, stupid. I wanted to have him hanged."

" I am afraid, sir, the law would scarcely have sanctioned such a proceeding."

" Umph ! why not, why not ? He richly deserved it, the scoundrel —daring to run off with my niece. Dear child ! she's as like her poor —umph—umph ! the Elliots were always reckoned a handsome race. What are you laughing at, you conceited puppy ? It's my belief that when I was your age I was a great deal better looking a fellow than you are. Some people admire a snub nose ; there was the Begum of Cuddleakee, splendid woman—Well, what do you want, sir, eh ? "

The last words were addressed to Captain Spicer, to whom (as since our late truce he had become all amiability) I had entrusted the commission of ascertaining Wilford's state, and who now appeared at the door, and beckoned me out of the room.

"I shall be with you again immediately," said I, rising ; and, replying to Clara's anxious glance by a smile and a pressure of the hand, I hastened to obey the summons.

" Wilford is in a sad state, Mr. Fairlegh," he began, as I closed the door behind me ; " dreadful, 'pon my life, sir ; but here's the surgeon —you'd better speak to him yourself."

In a little ante-room adjoining the chamber to which Wilford had been conveyed, I found the surgeon, who seemed an intelligent and gentlemanly person. He informed me that his patient had not many hours to live ; the wound in the head was not mortal, but the spine had received severe injuries, and his lower extremities were already paralyzed ; he inquired whether I was acquainted with any of his relations, adding that they ought to be sent for without a minute's delay.

" Really I am not," replied I ; " I never was at all intimate with him ; but I have heard that, even with those whom he admitted to his friendship, he was strangely reserved on such subjects."

" Better question the servant," suggested the surgeon ; " the patient himself is quite incapable of giving us any information ; the concussion has affected the brain, and he is now delirious."

The only information to be gained by this means was, that the servant believed his master had no relations in England ; he had heard that he had been brought up in Italy, and therefore imagined that his family resided there : he was able, however, to tell the name of his man of business in London, and a messenger was immediately despatched to summon him. Having done this, at the surgeon's request I accompanied him to the chamber of the sufferer.

As we entered, Wilford was lying in bed, supported by pillows, with his eyes half shut, apparently in a state of stupor ; but the sound of our footsteps aroused him, and opening his eyes, he raised his head and stared wildly about him. His appearance, as he did so, was ghastly in the extreme. His beautiful black hair had been shorn away at the temples to permit his wound to be dressed, and his head was enveloped in bandages, stained in many places with blood; his face was pale as death, save a bright hectic spot in the centre of each cheek, fatal evidence of the inward fever which was consuming him. His classical features, already pinched and shrunken, their paleness enhanced by contrast with his black whiskers, were fixed and rigid as those of a corpse; while his eyes, which burned with an unnatural brilliancy, glared on us with an expression of mingled hate and terror. He seemed partially to recognize me, for, after watching me for a moment, his lips working convulsively, as if striving to form articulate sounds, he exclaimed in a low, hoarse voice :—

" Ha! on the scent already! The staid sober lover—let him take care the pretty Clara does not jilt him. I know where she is ?—not I—that's a question you must demand of Mr. Cumberland, sir. I beg your pardon, did you say you doubted my word ?—I have the honour to wish you good-morning—my friend will call upon you. What!—Lizzy Maurice! who dares to say I wronged her ?—'tis false. Take that old man away, with his grey hair—why does he torment me ?—I tell you the girl's safe, thanks to—to—my head's confused— the 'long man,' as Curtis calls him, Harry Oaklands, handsome Harry Oaklands. What did I hear you mutter ? that he horse-whipped me ?—and if he did, there was a day of retribution—ha !— ha !—Sir, I shot him for it; shot him like a dog—I hated him, and he perished—the strong man died—died! and what then ?—what becomes of dead men ? A long-faced fool said I was dying, just now —he thought I didn't hear him—I not hear an insult! and I consider that one—I'll have him out for it—I'll—" and he endeavoured to raise himself, but was scarcely able to lift his head from the pillow, and sank back with a groan of anguish. After a moment he spoke again, in a low, plaintive voice, " I am very ill, very weak—send for her—she will come—oh yes, she will come, for she loves me; she knows my fiery nature—knows my vices, as men call them, and yet she loves me—the only one who ever did—send for her—she will come, it is her son who wishes for her." Then, in a tone of the fondest endearment he continued, " Lucia, bella madre, il tuo figlio tia chiama."

" He has been speaking Italian for some time," observed the surgeon in a whisper.

" That man Spicer told me he thought he was of Italian extraction," replied I.

Low as were our voices, the quick ear of the sufferer caught the name I had mentioned.

"Spicer," he exclaimed eagerly; "has he returned ? Well, man, speak! is she safely lodged ? Cumberland has done his part admirably, then. Oh, it was a grand scheme !—Ha! played me false—I'll

not believe it—he dares not—he knows me—knows I should dog him
like his shadow till we met face to face, and I had torn his false
heart out of his dastardly breast. I say he dares not do it!" and
yelling out a fearful oath, he fell back in a fainting fit.

Let us draw a veil over the remainder of the scene. The death-bed
of the wicked is a horrible lesson, stamped indelibly on the memory
of all who have witnessed it. Happy are they whose pure hearts
need not such fearful training; and far be it from me to dim the
brightness of their guileless spirits by acquainting them with its
harrowing details.

Shortly after the scene I have described, internal hemorrhage
commenced; ere another hour had elapsed the struggle was over, and
a crushed and lifeless corpse, watched by hirelings, wept over by
none, was all that remained on earth of the man whom society
courted while it feared, and bowed to while it despised—the successful libertine, the dreaded duellist, Wilford! I learned some time
afterwards that his father had been an English nobleman, his mother
an Italian lady of good family. Their marriage had been private,
and performed only according to the rites of the Romish Church,
although the earl was a Protestant. Availing himself of this
omission, on his return to England he pretended to doubt the
validity of the contract, and having the proofs in his own possession,
contrived to set the marriage aside, and wedded a lady of rank in
this country. Lucia Savelli, the victim of his perfidy, remained in
Italy, devoting herself to the education of her son, whom she
destined for the Romish priesthood. Her plans were, however,
frustrated by the information that the earl had died suddenly, leaving
a large fortune to the boy, on condition that he never attempted to
urge his claim to the title, and finished his education in England.
With his subsequent career the reader is sufficiently acquainted. On
hearing of her son's melancholy fate, Lucia Savelli, to whom the
whole of his fortune was bequeathed, retired to a convent, which she
endowed with her wealth.

As Barstone was out of our way from M—— to Heathfield, and as
Clara was too much overcome by all she had gone through to bear
any further agitation, we determined to proceed at once to my
mother's cottage, and despatched Peter Barnett to inform Mr.
Vernor of the events of the day and communicate to him Mr.
Frampton's resolution to leave him in undisturbed possession of
Barstone, for a period sufficiently long to enable him to wind up all
his affairs and seek another residence.

The return to Heathfield Cottage I shall not attempt to describe.
Clara's tears, smiles, and blushes—Fanny's tender and affectionate
solicitude—my mother's delighted, but somewhat fussy, hospitality—
and my own sensations, which were an agreeable compound of those
of everyone else—each and all were perfect in their respective ways.
But the "creme de la creme," the essence of the whole affair, that on
which the tongue of the poet and the pen of the romance-writer must

alike rejoice to expatiate, was the conduct of Mr. Frampton; how he
was seized, at one and the same moment, with two separate irresistible, and apparently incompatible manias, one for kissing everybody, and the other for lifting and transporting (under the idea that
he was thereby facilitating the family arrangements) bulky and
inappropriate articles which no one required, all of which he
deposited, with an air composed of equal parts of cheerful alacrity
and indomitable perseverance, in the drawing-room, grunting the
whole time as man never grunted before; a wild and unlooked-for
course of proceeding which reduced my mother to the borders of
insanity. Finding that argument was not of the least avail in
checking his rash career, I seized him by the arm, just as he was
about to establish on my sister's work-table a large carpet bag and
an umbrella, which had accompanied him through the adventures of
the day, and, dragging him off to his own room, forced him to begin
to prepare for dinner, while I turned a deaf ear to his remonstrance,
that "it was quite absurd to umph! umph! prevent him from
making himself useful, when there was so much to be done in the
house. Umph!" Having promulgated this opinion, he shook
me by the hand till my arm ached, and, declaring that he was
the happiest old man in the world, sat down and cried like a
child.

Worn out by the fatigues and anxieties of the day, we gladly
followed my mother's suggestion of going to bed in good time,
although I did not retire for the night till I had seen Harry
Oaklands, and given him an account of our adventures. Wilford's
fate affected him strongly, and, shading his brow with his hand, he
sat for some moments wrapped in meditation. At length he said in
a deep low tone, "These things force thought upon one, Frank.
How nearly was this man's fate my own! How nearly was I being
hurried into eternity with a weight of passions unrestrained, of sins
unrepented of, clinging to my guilty soul! God has been very
merciful to me." He paused, then, pressing my hand warmly, he
added, "And now good-night, Frank; to-morrow I shall be more fit
to rejoice with you in your prospects of coming happiness; to-night
I would fain be alone—you understand me." My only reply was by
wringing his hand in return, and we parted.

Reader, such thoughts as these working in a mind like that of
Harry Oaklands, could not be without their effect; and when in
after years, having by constant and unceasing watchfulness conquered
his constitutional indolence, his voice has been raised in the senate
of his country to defend the rights and privileges of our pure and
holy faith—when men's hearts, spell-bound by his eloquence, have
been turned from evil to follow after the thing that is good, memory
has brought before me that conversation in the library at Heathfield;
and, as I reflected on the effect produced on the character of Oaklands
by the fearful death of the homicide, Wilford, I have acknowledged
that the ways of Providence are indeed inscrutable.

I was roused from a deep sleep at an uncomfortably early hour on the following morning, by a sound much resembling a " view, halloo," coupled with my own name, shouted in the hearty tones of Lawless, and, flinging open the window, I perceived that indefatigable young gentleman employed in performing some incomprehensible ma- nœuvres with two sticks and a large flint stone, occasionally varying his diversion by renewing the rough music which had broken my slumbers.

" Why, Lawless, what do you mean by rousing me at this un- reasonable hour ? it's not six o'clock yet. And what in the world are you doing with those sticks ? "

" Unreasonable, eh ? well, that's rather good, now ! Just tell me which is the most unreasonable, to lie snoring in bed like a fat pig or a fatter alderman, such a beautiful morning as this is, or to be out enjoying it, eh ? "

" You have reason on your side, so far, I must confess."

" Eh ! yes, and so I always have, to be sure. What am I doing with the sticks, did you say ? can't you see ? "

" I can see you are fixing one in the ground, taking extreme pains to balance the stone on the top of it, and instantly endeavouring to knock it off again with the other ; in which endeavour you appear generally to fail."

" Fail, eh ? It strikes me that you are not half awake yet, or else your eyesight is getting out of condition. Six times running, except twice, when the wind or something got in the way, did I knock that blessed stone off, while I was trying to wake you. Epsom's coming round soon, don't you see, so I'm just getting my hand in for a slap at the snuff-boxes. But jump into your togs as fast as you can and come out, for I've got such a lark to tell you."

A few minutes sufficed to enable me to follow Lawless's recommen- dation, and long before he had attained the proficiency he desired in his " snuff-box practice," I had joined him.

" There ! " he exclaimed, as he made a most spiteful shot at the stone ; " that's safe to do the business. By Jove, it has done it, too, and no mistake," he continued, as the stick, glancing against the branch of a tree, turned aside, and ruining a very promising bed of hyacinths, finally alighted on a bell-glass placed over some pet flower of Fanny's, both of which it utterly destroyed.

" Pleasant that, eh ? ah, well, we must lay it to the cats—though if the cats in this part of the country are not unusually robust and vicious, there's not a chance of our being believed."

" Never mind," remarked I, " better luck next time. But now that you have succeeded in dragging me out of bed, what is it that you want with me ? "

" Want with you, eh ? " returned Lawless, mimicking the half- drowsy, half-cross tone in which I had spoken ; " you're a nice young man to talk to, I don't think. Never be grumpy, man, when I've got the most glorious bit of fun in the world to tell you, too. I had my

adventures yesterday as well as you. Who do you think called upon
me after you set out? You'll never guess, so I may as well tell you
at once; it was—but you shall hear how it happened. I was just
pulling my boots on to try a young bay thoroughbred, that Reynolds
thinks might make a steeple-chaser—he's got some rare bones about
him, I must say. Well, I was just in the very act of pulling on my
boots, when Shrimp makes his appearance, and squeaking out,
'Here's a gent as vonts to see you, sir, partic'lar,' ushers in no less
a personage than Lucy Markham's devoted admirer, the drysalter."

"What! the gentleman whose business we settled so nicely the
day before yesterday? Freddy Coleman's dreaded rival?"

" Eh! yes, the very identical, and an uncommon good little fellow
he is too, as men go, I can tell you. Well, you may suppose I was
puzzled enough to find out what he could want with me, and was
casting about for something to say to him, when he makes a sort of
a bow, and begins,—

"'The Honourable George Lawless, I believe?'

"'The same, sir, at your service,' replies I, giving a stamp with my
foot to get my boot on.

"'May I beg the favour of five minutes' private conversation with
you?'

"'Eh? oh yes, certainly,' says I. 'Get out of this, you inquisi-
tive little imp of darkness, and tell Reynolds to tie the colt up to the
pillar-reins, and let him champ the bit till I come down; that's the
way to bring him to a mouth;' and, hastening Shrimp's departure
by throwing the slippers at his head, I continued, 'Now, sir, I'm
your man; what's the row, eh?'

"'A.-hem! yes, sir, really it is somewhat a peculiar—that is, a
disagreeable business. I had thought of getting a friend to call upon
you.'

"'A friend, eh? oh! I see the move now—pistols for two, and
coffee for four; invite a couple of friends to make arrangements for
getting a bullet put into you in the most gentlemanly way possible,
and call it receiving satisfaction—very satisfactory, certainly. Well,
sir, you shall soon have my answer: no man can call George Lawless
a coward!; if he did, he'd soon find his eyesight obscured, and a
marked alteration in the general outline of his features; but I never
have fought a duel, and I never mean to fight one. If I've smashed
your panels, or done you any injury, I'm willing to pay for repairs,
and make as much apology as one man has any right to expect from
another; or if it will be a greater ease to your mind, we'll off coats,
ring for Shrimp and Harry Oaklands's boy to see fair play, and have
it out on the spot, all snug and comfortable; but no pistolling work,
thank ye.'

" Well, the little chap didn't seem to take at all kindly to the
notion, though, as I fancied he wasn't much of a bruiser, I offered to
tie my right hand behind me, and fight him with my left, but it was
clearly no go; so I thought I'd better hold my tongue, and leave him

to explain himself. After dodging about the bush for some time, he began to get the steam up a little, and when he did break cover, went away at a rattling pace—let out at me in style, I can tell you. His affections had been set on Lucy Markham ever since he had any, and I had been and destroyed the happiness of his whole life, and rendered him a miserable individual—a mark for the finger of scorn to poke fun at. Shocking bad names he did call himself, to be sure poor little beggar! till, 'pon my word, I began to get quite sorry for him. At last it came out that the thing which chiefly aggravated him was, that Lucy should have given him up for the sake of marrying a man of rank. If it had been anyone she was deeply attached to, he would not have so much minded; but it was nothing but a paltry ambition to be a peeress : she was mercenary, he knew it, and it was that which stung him to the quick.

" Well, as he said this, a bright idea flashed across me, that I could satisfy the little ' victim,' as he called himself, and get my own neck out of the collar, at one and the same time ; so I went up to him, and giving him a slap on the back that set him coughing like a broken-winded hunter after a sharp burst, I said. " Mr. Brown, I what the females call sympathize with you ;—your thing-em-bobs—sentiments, eh ? are perfectly correct, and do you credit. Now listen to me, young feller ;—I'm willing to do my best to accommodate you in this matter, and, if you're agreeable, this is the way we'll settle it. You don't choose Lucy should marry me, and I don't choose she should marry you ;—now, if you'll promise to give her up, I'll do the same. That's fair, ain't it !' ' Do you mean it, really ? ' says he. ' Really and truly,' says I. ' Will you swear ? ' says he. ' Like a trooper, if that will please you.' says I. ' Sir, you're a gentleman—a generous soul,' says he, quite overcome ; and grasping my hands, sobs out, ' I'll promise.' ' Done, along with you, drysalter,' says I, ' you're a trump ; ' and we shook hands till he got so red in the face, I began to be afraid of spontaneous combustion. ' There's nothing like striking when the iron's hot,' thinks I : so I made him sit down there and then, and we wrote a letter together to old Coleman, telling him the resolution we had come to, and saying, if he chose to bring an action for breach of promise of marriage against us, we would defend it conjointly, and pay the costs between us. What do you think of that, Master Frank ? Eh ? "

" That you certainly have a more wonderful knack of getting into scrapes, and out of them again, than any man I ever met with," replied I, laughing.

Before we had finished breakfast, Peter Barnett made his appearance. On his return to Barstone, he was informed that Mr. Vernor had been seized with an apoplectic fit, probably the result of the agitation of the morning. He was still in a state of stupor when Peter started to acquaint us with the fact, and the medical man who had been sent for considered him in a very precarious condition. Under these circumstances, Mr. Frampton immediately set out for Barstone, where he remained till the following morning, when he rejoined us. A slight improvement had taken place in the patient's health : he had recovered his consciousness, and requested to see Mr. Frampton. During the interview which ensued, he acknowledged Mr. Frampton's rights, and withdrew all further opposition to his wishes.

After the lapse of a few days, Mr. Vernor recovered sufficiently to remove from Barstone to a small farm which he possessed in the north, where he lingered for some months, shattered alike in health and spirits. He steadily refused to see either Clara or myself, or to accept the slightest kindness at our hands; but we have since had reason to believe that in this he was actuated by a feeling of compunction, rather than of animosity. Nothing is so galling to a proud spirit, as to receive favours from those it has injured. In less than a year from the time he quitted Barstone Priory, a second attack terminated his existence. On examining his papers after his decease, Peter Barnett's suspicion that Richard Cumberland was Mr. Vernor's natural son was verified, and this discovery tended to account for a considerable deficiency in Clara's fortune, the unhappy father having been tempted to appropriate large sums of money to relieve his spendthrift son's embarrassments. This also served to explain his inflexible determination that Clara should marry Cumberland, such being the only arrangement by which he could hope to prevent the detection of his dishonesty.

Reader, the interest of my story, always supposing it to have possessed any in your eyes, is now over.

Since the occurrence of the events I have just related the course of my life has been a smooth and, though not exempt from some share in the "ills that flesh is heir to," an unusually happy one.

In an address, whether from the pulpit, or the rostrum, half the battle is to know when you have said enough—the same rule applies with equal force to the tale-writer. There are two errors into which he may fall—he may say too little or he may say too much. The first is a venial sin, and easily forgiven—the second nearly unpardonable. Such, at all events, being my ideas on the subject, I shall merely proceed to give a brief outline of the fate of the principal personages who have figured in these pages ere I bring this veritable story to a close.

Cumberland, after his flight from the scene at the turnpike house, made his way to Liverpool, and, his money being secreted about his person, hastened to put his original plan into execution. A vessel was about to start for America, by which he obtained a passage to New York. In the United States he continued the same vicious course of life which had exiled him from England, and, as a natural consequence, sank lower and lower in the scale of humanity. The last account heard of him stated that, having added drinking to the catalogue of his vices, his constitution, unable to bear up against the inroads made by dissipation, was rapidly failing, while he was described to be in the most abject poverty. The captain of an American vessel with whom I am slightly acquainted promised me that he would gain more particulars concerning him, and, if he were in actual want, leave money with some responsible person for his use, so as to insure him against starvation. The result of his inquiries I have yet to learn.

Old Mr. Coleman was, as may be imagined, dreadfully irate on the receipt of the singular epistle bearing the joint signatures of Lawless and Mr. Lowe Brown, and was only restrained from bringing an action for breach of promise by having it strongly represented to him that the effect of so doing would be to make himself and his niece ridiculous. Freddy and Lucy Markham had the good sense to wait till Mr. Coleman had taken the former into partnership, which he fortunately inclined to do almost immediately; being then, with the aid of Lawless's receivership, in possession of a very comfortable income, the only serious objection to the marriage was removed; and the father, partly to escape Mrs. Coleman's very singular and not over-perspicuous arguments, partly because he loved his son better than he was himself aware, gave his consent.

George Lawless is still a bachelor. If questioned on the subject his invariable reply is, "Eh, married? Not I! Women are a kind of cattle, don't you see, that I never did understand. If it was anything about a horse, now—" There are some, however, who attribute his celibacy to another cause, and deem that he has never yet seen anyone calculated to efface the memory of his sincere though eccentric attachment to my sister Fanny.

It was on a bright summer morning that the bells of the little church of Heathfield pealed merrily to celebrate a triple wedding; and fairer brides than Fanny, Clara, and Lucy Markham, or happier bridegrooms than Harry Oaklands, Freddy Coleman, and myself, never pronounced the irrevocable "I will." There were smiles on all faces; and if there were a few tears also, they were such as angels might not grudge to weep—tears of pure, unalloyed happiness.

Years have passed away since that day—years of mingled light and shade; but never, as I believe, have either of the couples then linked together shown by thought, word, or deed that they have failed in gratitude to the Giver of all good things, who in His mercy had granted them the rare and inestimable blessing of sharing the joys and sorrows of this world of trial with a loving and beloved companion.

Clara and I reside at Barstone Priory, which is also Mr. Frampton's home, when he is at home; but his wandering habits lead him to spend much of his time in a round of visits to his friends; and Heathfield Hall and Cottage, Leatherly and Elm Grove, are in turn gladdened by the sound of his kindly laugh and sonorous grunts.

THE END.

GILBERT AND RIVINGTON, LIMITED, ST. JOHN'S HOUSE, CLERKENWELL, LONDON, E.C.